The Scarlet Pimpernel

Baroness Orczy (1865–1947)—whose full name was Emmuska Magdalena Rosalia Marie Josepha Barbara, Baroness Orczy—was born in Hungary, and was educated in Brussels, Paris, and London. Her father, Baron Felix Orczy, once managed the family estates in Hungary, but gave up after his attempt to introduce his peasants to modern farming techniques and equipment ended in revolt and the destruction of his crops. He was a well-known composer and conductor, and introduced young Emma to famous composers such as Wagner and Liszt.

When Emma was fifteen years old, the family settled in London, where she attended art school and met the illustrator Montagu Barstow. They were married in 1894.

Emma began writing for magazines in the 1890s. She also wrote several children's books before turning to historical fiction in 1899 with *The Emperor's Candlesticks*. Though she did not speak English before moving to London, she wrote all of her books in that language. Her great fame rests on *The Scarlet Pimpernel*. Its protagonist, Sir Percy Blakeney, is one of the most famous characters in English popular fiction. Indeed, years later, the baroness's son wrote under the pseudonym of John Blakeney.

The Scarlet Pimpernel did not, however, have an easy passage to publication: It was rejected by every publisher who saw it. The baroness and her husband then turned it into a play, and its success on stage captured the publishers' attention. The story finally appeared in book form in 1905, several years after Orczy had written it.

A number of sequels followed, and the baroness continued to turn out historical novels at the rate of one or two a year. During her lifetime, her style of melodramatic romantic fiction was very popular, but among her many titles only *The Scarlet Pimpernel* has securely stood the test of time.

Some other Puffin classics to enjoy

PRIDE AND PREJUDICE
Jane Austen

JANE EYRE
Charlotte Brontë

WUTHERING HEIGHTS
Emily Brontë

ROBINSON CRUSOE
Daniel Defoe

KING ARTHUR AND HIS KNIGHTS OF THE ROUND TABLE
TALES OF THE GREEK HEROES
Roger Lancelyn Green

THE PHANTOM OF THE OPERA
Gaston Leroux

TREASURE ISLAND
Robert Louis Stevenson

BARONESS ORCZY

The Scarlet Pimpernel

PUFFIN BOOKS

To
Julia Neilson and Fred Terry
whose genius created the rôles of Sir Percy
and Lady Blakeney on the stage,
this book
is affectionately dedicated

PUFFIN BOOKS
Published by the Penguin Group
Penguin Putnam Inc., 345 Hudson Street, New York, New York 10014, U.S.A.
Penguin Books Ltd, 27 Wrights Lane, London W8 5TZ, England
Penguin Books Australia Ltd, Ringwood, Victoria, Australia
Penguin Books Canada Ltd, 10 Alcorn Avenue, Toronto, Ontario, Canada M4V 3B2
Penguin Books (N.Z.) Ltd, 182–190 Wairau Road, Auckland 10, New Zealand

Penguin Books Ltd, Registered Offices: Harmondsworth, Middlesex, England

First published in 1905
Published in Puffin Books, 1989
Reissued in Puffin Books, 1997
3 5 7 9 10 8 6 4 2

The Library of Congress has cataloged the earlier Puffin edition under
catalog card number 89-61293
This edition ISBN: 0-14-037454-X

Printed in the United States of America
by Arcata Graphics, Kingsport, Tennessee

Contents

1

Paris: September, 1792

A surging, seething, murmuring crowd of beings that
are human only in name, for to the eye and ear they
seem naught but savage creatures, animated by vile
passions and by the lust of vengeance and of hate. The
hour, some little time before sunset, and the place, the
West Barricade, at the very spot where, a decade later,
a proud tyrant raised an undying monument to the nation's glory and his own vanity.

During the greater part of the day the guillotine had
been kept busy at its ghastly work: all that France had
boasted of in the past centuries, of ancient names, and
blue blood, had paid toll to her desire for liberty and for
fraternity. The carnage had only ceased at this late hour
of the day because there were other more interesting
sights for the people to witness, a little while before the
final closing of the barricades for the night.

And so the crowd rushed away from the Place de la
Grève and made for the various barricades in order to
watch this interesting and amusing sight.

It was to be seen every day, for those aristos were
such fools! They were traitors to the people of course,
all of them, men, women, and children, who happened
to be descendants of the great men who since the Cru-
sades had made the glory of France: her old *noblesse*.
Their ancestors had oppressed the people, had crushed
them under the scarlet heels of their dainty buckled
shoes, and now the people had become the rulers of

France and crushed their former masters—not beneath their heel, for they went shoeless mostly in these days—but beneath a more effectual weight, the knife of the guillotine.

And daily, hourly, the hideous instrument of torture claimed its many victims—old men, young women, tiny children, even until the day when it would finally demand the head of a King and of a beautiful young Queen.

But this was as it should be: were not the people now the rulers of France? Every aristocrat was a traitor, as his ancestors had been before him: for two hundred years now the people had sweated, and toiled, and starved, to keep a lustful court in lavish extravagance; now the descendants of those who had helped to make those courts brilliant had to hide for their lives—to fly, if they wished to avoid the tardy vengeance of the people.

And they did try to hide, and tried to fly: that was just the fun of the whole thing. Every afternoon before the gates closed and the market carts went out in procession by the various barricades, some fool of an aristo endeavoured to evade the clutches of the Committee of Public Safety. In various disguises, under various pretexts, they tried to slip through the barriers which were so well guarded by citizen soldiers of the Republic. Men in women's clothes, women in male attire, children disguised in beggars' rags: there were some of all sorts: ci-devant counts, marquises, even dukes, who wanted to fly from France, reach England or some other equally accursed country, and there try to rouse foreign feeling against the glorious Revolution, or to raise an army in order to liberate the wretched prisoners in the Temple, who had once called themselves sovereigns of France.

But they were nearly always caught at the barricades. Sergeant Bibot especially at the West Gate had a wonderful nose for scenting an aristo in the most perfect disguise. Then, of course, the fun began. Bibot would look at his prey as a cat looks upon the mouse, play with him, sometimes for quite a quarter of an hour, pretend to be hoodwinked by the disguise, by the wigs and other bits of theatrical make-up which hid the identity of a *ci-devant* noble marquise or count.

Oh! Bibot had a keen sense of humour, and it was well worth hanging round that West Barricade, in order to see him catch an aristo in the very act of trying to flee from the vengeance of the people.

Sometimes Bibot would let his prey actually out by the gates, allowing him to think for the space of two minutes at least that he really had escaped out of Paris, and might even manage to reach the coast of England in safety, but Bibot would let the unfortunate wretch walk about ten mètres towards the open country, then he would send two men after him and bring him back, stripped of his disguise.

Oh! that was extremely funny, for as often as not the fugitive would prove to be a woman, some proud marchioness, who looked terribly comical when she found herself in Bibot's clutches after all, and knew that a summary trial would await her the next day and after that, the fond embrace of Madame la Guillotine.

No wonder that on this fine afternoon in September the crowd round Bibot's gate was eager and excited. The lust of blood grows with its satisfaction, there is no satiety: the crowd had seen a hundred noble heads fall beneath the guillotine to-day, it wanted to make sure that it would see another hundred fall on the morrow.

Bibot was sitting on an overturned and empty cask close by the gate of the barricade; a small detachment of citoyen soldiers was under his command. The work had been very hot lately. Those cursed aristos were becoming terrified and tried their hardest to slip out of Paris: men, women and children, whose ancestors, even in remote ages, had served those traitorous Bourbons, were all traitors themselves and right food for the guillotine. Every day Bibot had had the satisfaction of unmasking some fugitive royalists and sending them back to be tried by the Committee of Public Safety, presided over by that good patriot, Citoyen Foucquier-Tinville.

Robespierre and Danton both had commended Bibot for his zeal and Bibot was proud of the fact that he on his own initiative had sent at least fifty aristos to the guillotine.

But to-day all the sergeants in command at the various barricades had had special orders. Recently a very great number of aristos had succeeded in escaping out of France and in reaching England safely. There were curious rumours about these escapes; they had become very frequent and singularly daring; the people's minds were becoming strangely excited about it all. Sergeant Grospierre had been sent to the guillotine for allowing a whole family of aristos to slip out of the North Gate under his very nose.

It was asserted that these escapes were organised by a band of Englishmen, whose daring seemed to be unparalleled, and who, from sheer desire to meddle in what did not concern them, spent their spare time in snatching away lawful victims destined for Madame la Guillotine. These rumours soon grew in extravagance; there was no doubt that this band of meddlesome Englishmen did exist; moreover, they seemed to be under the leadership of a man whose pluck and audacity were almost fabulous. Strange stories were afloat of how he and those aristos whom he rescued became suddenly invisible as they reached the barricades and escaped out of the gates by sheer supernatural agency.

No one had seen these mysterious Englishmen; as for their leader, he was never spoken of, save with a superstitious shudder. Citoyen Foucquier-Tinville would in the course of the day receive a scrap of paper from some mysterious source; sometimes he would find it in the pocket of his coat, at others it would be handed to him by someone in the crowd, whilst he was on his way to the sitting of the Committee of Public Safety. The paper always contained a brief notice that the band of meddlesome Englishmen were at work, and it was always signed with a device drawn in red—a little star-shaped flower, which we in England call the Scarlet Pimpernel. Within a few hours of the receipt of this impudent notice, the citoyens of the Committee of Public Safety would hear that so many royalists and aristocrats had succeeded in reaching the coast, and were on their way to England and safety.

The guards at the gates had been doubled, the sergeants in command had been threatened with death, whilst liberal rewards were offered for the capture of these daring and impudent Englishmen. There was a sum of five thousand francs promised to the man who laid hands on the mysterious and elusive Scarlet Pimpernel.

Everyone felt that Bibot would be that man, and Bibot allowed that belief to take firm root in everybody's mind; and so, day after day, people came to watch him at the West Gate, so as to be present when he laid hands on any fugitive aristo who perhaps might be accompanied by that mysterious Englishman.

"Bah!" he said to his trusted corporal, "Citoyen Grospierre was a fool! Had it been me now, at that North Gate last week . . ."

Citoyen Bibot spat on the ground to express his contempt for his comrade's stupidity.

"How did it happen, citoyen?" asked the corporal.

"Grospierre was at the gate, keeping good watch," began Bibot, pompously, as the crowd closed in round him, listening eagerly to his narrative. "We've all heard of this meddlesome Englishman, this accursed Scarlet Pimpernel. He won't get through *my* gate, *morbleu!* unless he be the devil himself. But Grospierre was a fool. The market carts were going through the gates; there was one laden with casks, and driven by an old man, with a boy beside him. Grospierre was a bit drunk, but he thought himself very clever; he looked into the casks—most of them, at least—and saw they were empty, and let the cart go through."

A murmur of wrath and contempt went round the group of ill-clad wretches, who crowded round Citoyen Bibot.

"Half an hour later," continued the sergeant, "up comes a captain of the guard with a squad of some dozen soldiers with him. 'Has a car gone through?' he asks of Grospierre, breathlessly. 'Yes,' says Grospierre, 'not half an hour ago.' 'And you have let them escape,' shouts the captain furiously. 'You'll go to the guillotine for this, citoyen sergeant! that cart held concealed the *ci-devant* Duc de Chalis and all his family!' 'What!' thunders Grospierre, aghast. 'Aye! and the driver was none other than that cursed Englishman, the Scarlet Pimpernel.' "

A howl of execration greeted this tale. Citoyen Grospierre had paid for his blunder on the guillotine, but what a fool! oh! what a fool!

Bibot was laughing so much at his own tale that it was some time before he could continue.

" 'After them, my men,' shouts the captain," he said after a while, " 'remember the reward; after them, they cannot have gone far!' And with that he rushes through the gate followed by his dozen soldiers."

"But it was too late!" shouted the crowd, excitedly.

"They never got them!"

"Curse that Grospierre for his folly!"

"He deserved his fate!"

"Fancy not examining those casks properly!"

But these sallies seemed to amuse Citoyen Bibot exceedingly; he laughed until his sides ached, and the tears streamed down his cheeks.

"Nay, nay!" he said at last, "those aristos weren't in the cart; the driver was not the Scarlet Pimpernel!"

"What?"

"No! The captain of the guard was that damned Englishman in disguise, and everyone of his soldiers aristos!"

The crowd this time said nothing: the story certainly savoured of the supernatural, and though the Republic had abolished God, it had not quite succeeded in killing the fear of the supernatural in the hearts of the people. Truly that Englishman must be the devil himself.

The sun was sinking low down in the west. Bibot prepared himself to close the gates.

"*En avant* the carts," he said.

Some dozen covered carts were drawn up in a row, ready to leave town, in order to fetch the produce from the country close by, for market the next morning. They were mostly well known to Bibot, as they went through his gate twice every day on their way to and from the town. He spoke to one or two of their drivers—mostly women—and was at great pains to examine the inside of the carts.

"You never know," he would say, "and I'm not going to be caught like that fool Grospierre."

The women who drove the carts usually spent their day on the Place de la Grève, beneath the platform of the guillotine, knitting and gossiping, whilst they watched the rows of tumbrils arriving with the victims the Reign of Terror claimed every day. It was great fun to see the aristos arriving for the reception of Madame la Guillotine, and the places close by the platform were very much sought after. Bibot, during the day, had been on duty on the Place. He recognized most of the old hats, "tricotteuses," as they were called, who sat there and knitted, whilst head after head fell beneath the knife, and they themselves got quite bespattered with the blood of those cursed aristos.

"Hé! la mère!" said Bibot to one of these horrible hags, "what have you got there?"

He had seen her earlier in the day, with her knitting and the whip of her cart close beside her. Now she had fastened a row of curly locks to the whip handle, all colours, from gold to silver, fair to dark, and she stroked them with her huge, bony fingers as she laughed at Bibot.

"I made friends with Madame Guillotine's lover," she said with a coarse laugh, "he cut these off for me from the heads as they rolled down. He has promised me some more to-morrow, but I don't know if I shall be at my usual place."

"Ah! how is that, la mère?" asked Bibot, who, hardened soldier though he was, could not help shuddering at the awful loathsomeness of this semblance of a woman, with her ghastly trophy on the handle of her whip.

"My grandson has got the small-pox," she said with a jerk of her thumb towards the inside of her cart, "some say it's the plague! If it is, I sha'n't be allowed to come into Paris to-morrow."

At the first mention of the word small-pox, Bibot had stepped hastily backwards, and when the old hag spoke of the plague, he retreated from her as fast as he could.

"Curse you!" he muttered, whilst the whole crowd hastily avoided the cart, leaving it standing all alone in the midst of the place.

The old hag laughed.

"Curse you, citoyen, for being a coward," she said. "Bah! what a man to be afraid of sickness."

"*Morbleu!* the plague!"

Everyone was awe-struck and silent, filled with horror for the loathsome malady, the one thing which still had the power to arouse terror and disgust in these savage, brutalised creatures.

"Get out with you and with your plague-stricken brood!" shouted Bibot, hoarsely.

And with another rough laugh and coarse jest, the old hag whipped up her lean nag and drove her cart out of the gate.

This incident had spoilt the afternoon. The people were terrified of these two horrible curses, the two maladies which nothing could cure, and which were the precursors of an awful and lonely death. They hung about the barricades, silent and sullen for a while, eyeing one another suspiciously, avoiding each other as if by instinct, lest the plague lurked already in their midst. Presently, as in the case of Grospierre, a captain of the guard appeared suddenly. But he was known to Bibot, and there was no fear of his turning out to be a sly Englishman in disguise.

"A cart, . . ." he shouted breathlessly, even before he had reached the gates.

"What cart?" asked Bibot, roughly.

"Driven by an old hag. . . . A covered cart . . ."

"There were a dozen . . ."

"An old hag who said her son had the plague?"

"Yes . . ."

"You have not let them go?"

"Morbleu!" said Bibot, whose purple cheeks had suddenly become white with fear.

"The cart contained the *ci-devant* Comtesse de Tournay and her two children, all of them traitors and condemned to death."

"And their driver?" muttered Bibot, as a superstitious shudder ran down his spine.

"Sacré tonnerre," said the captain, "but it is feared that it was that accursed Englishman himself—the Scarlet Pimpernel."

2

Dover: "The Fisherman's Rest"

In the kitchen Sally was extremely busy—saucepans and frying-pans were standing in rows on the gigantic hearth, the huge stock-pot stood in a corner, and the jack turned with slow deliberation, and presented alternately to the glow every side of a noble sirloin of beef. The two little kitchen-maids bustled around, eager to help, hot and panting, with cotton sleeves well tucked up above the dimpled elbows, and giggling over some private jokes of their own, whenever Miss Sally's back was turned for a moment. And old Jemima, stolid in temper and solid in bulk, kept up a long and subdued grumble, while she stirred the stock-pot methodically over the fire.

"What ho! Sally!" came in cheerful if none too melodious accents from the coffee-room close by.

"Lud bless my soul!" exclaimed Sally, with a good-humoured laugh, "what be they all wanting now, I wonder!"

"Beer, of course," grumbled Jemima, "you don't 'xpect Jimmy Pitkin to 'ave done with one tankard, do ye?"

"Mr. 'Arry, 'e looked uncommon thirsty too," simpered Martha, one of the little kitchen-maids; and her beady black eyes twinkled as they met those of her companion, whereupon both started on a round of short and suppressed giggles.

Sally looked cross for a moment, and thoughtfully

rubbed her hands against her shapely hips; her palms were itching, evidently, to come in contact with Martha's rosy cheeks—but inherent good-humour prevailed, and with a pout and a shrug of the shoulders, she turned her attention to the fried potatoes.

"What ho, Sally! hey, Sally!"

And a chorus of pewter mugs, tapped with impatient hands against the oak tables of the coffee-room, accompanied the shouts for mine host's buxom daughter.

"Sally!" shouted a more persistent voice, "are ye goin' to be all night with that there beer?"

"I do think father might get the beer for them," muttered Sally, as Jemima, stolidly and without further comment, took a couple of foam-crowned jugs from the shelf, and began filling a number of pewter tankards with some of that home-brewed ale for which "The Fisherman's Rest" had been famous since the days of King Charles. " 'E knows 'ow busy we are in 'ere."

"Your father is too busy discussing politics with Mr. 'Empseed to worry 'isself about you and the kitchen," grumbled Jemima under her breath.

Sally had gone to the small mirror which hung in a corner of the kitchen, and was hastily smoothing her hair and setting her frilled cap at its most becoming angle over her dark curls; then she took up the tankards by their handles, three in each strong, brown hand, and laughing, grumbling, blushing, carried them through into the coffee-room.

There, there was certainly no sign of that bustle and activity which kept four women busy and hot in the glowing kitchen beyond.

The coffee-room of "The Fisherman's Rest" is a show place now at the beginning of the twentieth century. At the end of the eighteenth, in the year of grace 1792, it had not yet gained that notoriety and importance which a hundred additional years and the craze of the age have since bestowed upon it. Yet it was an old place, even then, for the oak rafters and beams were already black with age—as were the panelled seats, with their tall backs, and the long polished tables between, on which innumerable pewter tankards had left fantastic patterns of many-sized rings. In the leaded window, high up, a row of pots of scarlet geraniums and blue larkspur gave the bright note of colour against the dull background of the oak.

That Mr. Jellyband, landlord of "The Fisherman's Rest" at Dover, was a prosperous man, was of course clear to the most casual observer. The pewter on the fine old dressers, the brass above the gigantic hearth, shone like silver and gold—the red-tiled floor was as brilliant as the scarlet geranium on the window sill—this meant that his servants were good and plentiful, that the custom was constant, and of that order which necessitated the keeping up of the coffee-room to a high standard of elegance and order.

As Sally came in, laughing through her frowns, and displaying a row of dazzling white teeth, she was greeted with shouts and chorus of applause.

"Why, here's Sally! What ho, Sally! Hurrah for pretty Sally!"

"I thought you'd grown deaf in that kitchen of yours," muttered Jimmy Pitkin, as he passed the back of his hand across his very dry lips.

"All ri'! all ri'!" laughed Sally, as she deposited the freshly-filled tankards upon the tables, "why, what a 'urry, to be sure! And is your gran'mother a-dyin' an' you wantin' to see the pore soul afore she'm gone! I never see'd such a mighty rushin'!"

A chorus of good-humoured laughter greeted this witticism, which gave the company there present food for many jokes, for some considerable time. Sally now seemed in less of a hurry to get back to her pots and pans. A young man with fair curly hair, and eager, bright blue eyes, was engaging most of her attention and the whole of her time, whilst broad witticisms anent Jimmy Pitkin's fictitious grandmother flew from mouth to mouth, mixed with heavy puffs of pungent tobacco smoke.

Facing the hearth, his legs wide apart, a long clay pipe in his mouth, stood mine host himself, worthy Mr. Jellyband, landlord of "The Fisherman's Rest," as his father had been before him, aye, and his grandfather and great-grandfather too, for that matter. Portly in build, jovial in countenance and somewhat bald of pate, Mr. Jellyband was indeed a typical rural John Bull of those days—the days when our prejudiced insularity was at its height, when to an Englishman, be he lord, yeoman, or peasant, the whole of the continent of Europe was a den of immorality, and the rest of the world an unexploited land of savages and cannibals.

There he stood, mine worthy host, firm and well set up on his limbs, smoking his long churchwarden and caring nothing for nobody at home, and despising everybody abroad. He wore the typical scarlet waistcoat, with shiny brass buttons, the corduroy breeches, the grey worsted stockings and smart buckled shoes, that characterised every self-respecting innkeeper in Great Britain in these days—and while pretty, motherless Sally had need of four pairs of brown hands to do all the work that fell on her shapely shoulders, worthy Jellyband discussed the affairs of nations with his most privileged guests.

The coffee-room indeed, lighted by two well-polished lamps, which hung from the raftered ceiling, looked cheerful and cosy in the extreme. Through the dense clouds of tobacco smoke that hung about in every corner, the faces of Mr. Jellyband's customers appeared red and pleasant to look at, and on good terms with themselves, their host and all the world; from every side of the room loud guffaws accompanied pleasant, if not highly intellectual, conversation—while Sally's repeated giggles testified to the good use Mr. Harry Waite was making of the short time she seemed inclined to spare him.

They were mostly fisher-folk who patronised Mr. Jellyband's coffee-room, but fishermen are known to be very thirsty people; the salt which they breathe in, when they are on the sea, accounts for their parched throats when on shore. But "The Fisherman's Rest" was something more than a rendezvous for these humble folk. The London and Dover coach started from the hostel daily, and passengers who had come across the Channel, and those who started for the "grand tour," all became acquainted with Mr. Jellyband, his French wines and his home-brewed ales.

It was towards the close of September, 1792, and the weather which had been brilliant and hot throughout the month had suddenly broken up; for two days torrents of rain had deluged the south of England, doing its level best to ruin what chances the apples and pears and late plums had of becoming really fine, self-respecting fruit. Even now it was beating against the leaded windows, and tumbling down the chimney, making the cheerful wood fire sizzle in the hearth.

"Lud! did you ever see such a wet September, Mr. Jellyband?" asked Mr. Hempseed.

He sat in one of the seats inside the hearth, did Mr. Hempseed, for he was an authority and an important personage not only at "The Fisherman's Rest," where Mr. Jellyband always made a special selection of him as a foil for political arguments, but throughout the neighbourhood, where his learning and notably his knowledge of the Scriptures was held in the most profound awe and respect. With one hand buried in the capacious pockets of his corduroys underneath his elaborately-worked, well-worn smock, the other holding his long clay pipe, Mr. Hempseed sat there looking dejectedly across the room at the rivulets of moisture which trickled down the window panes.

"No," replied Mr. Jellyband, sententiously, "I dunno, Mr. 'Empseed, as I ever did. An' I've been in these parts nigh on sixty years."

"Aye! you wouldn't rec'llect the first three years of them sixty, Mr. Jellyband," quietly interposed Mr. Hempseed. "I dunno as I ever see'd an infant take much note of the weather, leastways not in these parts, an' *I*'ve lived 'ere nigh on seventy-five years, Mr. Jellyband."

The superiority of this wisdom was so incontestable that for the moment Mr. Jellyband was not ready with his usual flow of argument.

"It do seem more like April than September, don't it?" continued Mr. Hempseed, dolefully, as a shower of raindrops fell with a sizzle upon the fire.

"Aye! that it do," assented the worthy host, "but then what can you 'xpect, Mr. 'Empseed, I says, with sich a government as we've got?"

Mr. Hempseed shook his head with an infinity of wisdom, tempered by deeply-rooted mistrust of the British climate and the British Government.

"I don't 'xpect nothing, Mr. Jellyband," he said. "Pore folks like us is of no account up there in Lunnon, I knows that, and it's not often as I do complain. But when it comes to sich wet weather in September, and all me fruit a-rottin' and a-dyin' like the 'Guptian mother's first born, and doin' no more good than they did, pore dears, save to a lot of Jews, pedlars and sich, with their oranges and sich like foreign ungodly fruit, which nobody'd buy if English apples and pears was nicely swelled. As the Scriptures say—"

"That's quite right, Mr. 'Empseed," retorted Jellyband, "and as I says, what can you 'xpect? There's all them Frenchy devils over the Channel yonder a-murderin' their king and nobility, and Mr. Pitt and Mr. Fox and Mr. Burke a-fightin' and a-wranglin' between them, if we Englishmen should 'low them to go on in their ungodly way. 'Let 'em murder!' says Mr. Pitt. 'Stop 'em!' says Mr. Burke."

"And let 'em murder, says I, and be demmed to 'em," said Mr. Hempseed, emphatically, for he had but little liking for his friend Jellyband's political arguments, wherein he always got out of his depth, and had but little chance for displaying those pearls of wisdom which had earned for him so high a reputation in the neighbourhood and so many free tankards of ale at "The Fisherman's Rest."

"Let 'em murder," he repeated again, "but don't let's 'ave sich rain in September, for that is agin the law and the Scriptures which says—"

"Lud! Mr. 'Arry, 'ow you made me jump!"

It was unfortunate for Sally and her flirtation that this remark of hers should have occurred at the precise moment when Mr. Hempseed was collecting his breath, in order to deliver himself of one of those Scriptural utterances which had made him famous, for it brought down upon her pretty head the full flood of her father's wrath.

"Now then, Sally, me girl, now then!" he said, trying to force a frown upon his good-humoured face, "stop that fooling with them young jackanapes and get on with the work."

"The work's gettin' on all ri', father."

But Mr. Jellyband was peremptory. He had other views for his buxom daughter, his only child, who would in God's good time become the owner of "The Fisherman's Rest," than to see her married to one of these young fellows who earned but a precarious livelihood with their net.

"Did ye hear me speak, me girl?" he said in that quiet tone, which no one inside the inn dared to disobey. "Get on with my Lord Tony's supper, for, if it ain't the best we can do, and 'e not satisfied, see what you'll get, that's all."

Reluctantly Sally obeyed.

"Is you 'xpecting special guests then to-night, Mr. Jellyband?" asked Jimmy Pitkin, in a loyal attempt to divert his host's attention from the circumstances connected with Sally's exit from the room.

"Aye! that I be," replied Jellyband, "friends of my Lord Tony hisself. Dukes and duchesses from over the water yonder, whom the young lord and his friend, Sir Andrew Ffoulkes, and other young noblemen have helped out of the clutches of them murderin' devils."

But this was too much for Mr. Hempseed's querulous philosophy.

"Lud!" he said, "what they do that for, I wonder? I don't 'old not with interferin' in other folks' ways. As the Scriptures say—"

"Maybe, Mr. 'Empseed," interrupted Jellyband, with biting sarcasm, "as you're a personal friend of Mr. Pitt, and as you says along with Mr. Fox: 'Let 'em murder!' says you."

"Pardon me, Mr. Jellyband," feebly protested Mr. Hempseed, "I dunno as I ever did."

But Mr. Jellyband had at last succeeded in getting upon his favourite hobby-horse, and had no intention of dismounting in any hurry.

"Or maybe you've made friends with some of them French chaps 'oo they do say have come over here o' purpose to make us Englishmen agree with their murderin' ways."

"I dunno what you mean, Mr. Jellyband," suggested Mr. Hempseed, "all I know is—"

"All *I* know is," loudly asserted mine host, "that there was my friend Peppercorn, 'oo owns the 'Blue-Faced Boar,' an' as true and loyal an Englishman as you'd see in the land. And now look at 'im!—'E made friends with some o' them frog-eaters, 'obnobbed with them just as if they was Englishmen, and not just a lot of immoral, God-forsaking furrin' spies. Well! and what happened? Peppercorn 'e now ups and talks of revolutions, and liberty, and down with the aristocrats, just like Mr. 'Empseed over 'ere!"

"Pardon me, Mr. Jellyband," again interposed Mr. Hempseed feebly, "I dunno as I ever did—"

Mr. Jellyband had appealed to the company in general, who were listening awe-struck and open-mouthed at the recital of Mr. Peppercorn's defalcations. At one table two customers—gentlemen apparently by their clothes—had pushed aside their half-finished game of dominoes, and had been listening for some time, and evidently with much amusement at Mr. Jellyband's international opinions. One of them now, with a quiet, sarcastic smile still lurking round the corners of his mobile mouth, turned towards the centre of the room where Mr. Jellyband was standing.

"You seem to think, mine honest friend," he said quietly, "that these Frenchmen,—spies I think you called them—are mighty clever fellows to have made mincemeat so to speak of your friend Mr. Peppercorn's opinions. How did they accomplish that now, think you?"

"Lud! sir, I suppose they talked 'im over. Those Frenchies, I've 'eard it said, 'ave got the gift of gab— and Mr. 'Empseed 'ere will tell you 'ow it is that they just twist some people round their little finger like."

"Indeed, and is that so, Mr. Hempseed?" inquired the stranger politely.

"Nay, sir!" replied Mr. Hempseed, much irritated, "I dunno as I can give you the information you require."

"Faith, then," said the stranger, "let us hope, my worthy host, that these clever spies will not succeed in upsetting your extremely loyal opinions."

But this was too much for Mr. Jellyband's pleasant equanimity. He burst into an uproarious fit of laughter, which was soon echoed by those who happened to be in his debt.

"Hahaha! hohoho! hehehe!" He laughed in every key, did my worthy host, and laughed until his sides ached, and his eyes streamed. "At me! hark at that! Did ye 'ear 'im say that they'd be upsettin' my opinions?— Eh?—Lud love you, sir, but you do say some queer things."

"Well, Mr. Jellyband," said Mr. Hempseed, sentenstiously, "you know what the Scriptures say: 'Let 'im 'oo stands take 'eed lest 'e fall.' "

"But then hark'ee, Mr. 'Empseed," retorted Jellyband, still holding his sides with laughter, "the Scriptures didn't know me. Why, I wouldn't so much as drink a glass of ale with one o' them murderin' Frenchmen, and nothin' 'd make me change my opinions. Why! I've 'eard it said that them frog-eaters can't even speak the King's English, so, of course, if any of 'em tried to speak their God-forsaken lingo to me, why, I should spot them directly, see!—and forewarned is forearmed, as the saying goes."

"Aye! my honest friend," assented the stranger cheerfully, "I see that you are much too sharp, and a match for any twenty Frenchmen, and here's to your very good health, my worthy host, if you'll do me the honour to finish this bottle of mine with me."

"I am sure you're very polite, sir," said Mr. Jellyband, wiping his eyes which were still streaming with the abundance of his laughter, "and I don't mind if I do."

The stranger poured out a couple of tankards full of

wine, and having offered one to mine host, he took the other himself.

"Loyal Englishmen as we all are," he said, whilst the same humorous smile played round the corners of his thin lips—"loyal as we are, we must admit that this at least is one good thing which comes to us from France."

"Aye! we'll none of us deny that, sir," assented mine host.

"And here's to the best landlord in England, our worthy host, Mr. Jellyband," said the stranger in a loud tone of voice.

"Hi, hip, hurrah!" retorted the whole company present. Then there was loud clapping of hands, and mugs and tankards made a rattling music upon the tables to the accompaniment of loud laughter at nothing in particular, and of Mr. Jellyband's muttered exclamations:

"Just fancy *me* bein' talked over by any God-forsaken furriner!—What?—Lud love you, sir, but you do say some queer things."

To which obvious fact the stranger heartily assented. It was certainly a preposterous suggestion that anyone could ever upset Mr. Jellyband's firmly-rooted opinions anent the utter worthlessness of the inhabitants of the whole continent of Europe.

3

THE REFUGEES

Feeling in every part of England certainly ran very high at this time against the French and their doings. Smugglers and legitimate traders between the French and English coasts brought snatches of news from over the water, which made every honest Englishman's blood boil, and made him long to have "a good go" at those murderers, who had imprisoned their king and all his family, subjected the queen and the royal children to every species of indignity, and were even now loudly demanding the blood of the whole Bourbon family and of every one of its adherents.

The execution of the Princesse de Lamballe, Marie Antoinette's young and charming friend, had filled every one in England with unspeakable horror, the daily execution of scores of royalists of good family, whose only sin was their aristocratic name, seemed to cry for vengeance to the whole of civilised Europe.

Yet, with all that, no one dared to interfere. Burke had exhausted all his eloquence in trying to induce the British Government to fight the revolutionary government of France, but Mr. Pitt, with characteristic prudence, did not feel that this country was fit yet to embark on another arduous and costly war. It was for Austria to take the initiative; Austria, whose fairest daughter was even now a dethroned queen, imprisoned and insulted by a howling mob; and surely 'twas not—so argued Mr. Fox—for the whole of England to take up arms, because one set of Frenchmen chose to murder another.

As for Mr. Jellyband and his fellow John Bulls, though they looked upon all foreigners with withering contempt, they were royalist and anti-revolutionists to a man, and at this present moment were furious with Pitt for his caution and moderation, although they naturally understood nothing of the diplomatic reasons which guided that great man's policy.

But now Sally came running back, very excited and very eager. The joyous company in the coffee-room had heard nothing of the noise outside, but she had spied a dripping horse and rider who had stopped at the door of "The Fisherman's Rest," and while the stable boy ran forward to take charge of the horse, pretty Miss Sally went to the front door to greet the welcome visitor.

"I think I see'd my Lord Antony's horse out in the yard, father," she said, as she ran across the coffee-room.

But already the door had been thrown open from outside, and the next moment an arm, covered in drab cloth and dripping with the heavy rain, was round pretty Sally's waist, while a hearty voice echoed along the polished rafters of the coffee-room.

"Aye, and bless your brown eyes for being so sharp, my pretty Sally," said the man who had just entered, whilst worthy Mr. Jellyband came bustling forward, eager, alert and fussy, as became the advent of one of the most favoured guests of his hostel.

"Lud, I protest, Sally," added Lord Antony, as he deposited a kiss on Miss Sally's blooming cheeks, "but you are growing prettier and prettier every time I see you—and my honest friend, Jellyband here, must have hard work to keep the fellows off that slim waist of yours. What say you, Mr. Waite?"

Mr. Waite—torn between his respect for my lord and his dislike of that particular type of joke—only replied with a doubtful grunt.

Lord Antony Dewhurst, one of the sons of the Duke of Exeter, was in those days a very perfect type of a young English gentleman—tall, well set-up, broad of shoulders and merry of face, his laughter rang loudly wherever he went. A good sportsman, a lively companion, a courteous, well-bred man of the world, with not too much brains to spoil his temper, he was a universal favourite in London drawing-rooms or in the coffee-rooms of village inns. At "The Fisherman's Rest" everyone knew him—for he was fond of a trip across to France, and always spent a night under worthy Mr. Jellyband's roof on his way there or back.

He nodded to Waite, Pitkin and the others as he at last released Sally's waist, and crossed over to the hearth to warm and dry himself: as he did so, he cast a quick, somewhat suspicious glance at the two strangers, who had quietly resumed their game of dominoes, and for a moment a look of deep earnestness, even of anxiety, clouded his jovial young face.

But only for a moment; the next he had turned to Mr. Hempseed, who was respectfully touching his forelock.

"Well, Mr. Hempseed, and how is the fruit?"

"Badly, my lord, badly," replied Mr. Hempseed, dolefully, "but what can you 'xpect with this 'ere government favourin' them rascals over in France, who would murder their king and all their nobility."

"Odd's life!" retorted Lord Antony; "so they would, honest Hempseed,—at least those they can get hold of, worse luck! But we have got some friends coming here to-night, who at any rate have evaded their clutches."

It almost seemed, when the young man said these words, as if he threw a defiant look towards the quiet strangers in the corner.

"Thanks to you, my lord, and to your friends, so I've heard it said," said Mr. Jellyband.

But in a moment Lord Antony's hand fell warningly on mine host's arm.

"Hush!" he said peremptorily, and instinctively once again looked towards the strangers.

"Oh! Lud love you, they are all right, my lord," retorted Jellyband; "don't you be afraid. I wouldn't have spoken, only I knew we were among friends. That gentleman over there is as true and loyal a subject of King George as you are yourself, my lord, saving your presence. He is but lately arrived in Dover, and is settling down in business in these parts."

"In business? Faith, then, it must be as an undertaker, for I vow I never beheld a more rueful countenance."

"Nay, my lord, I believe that the gentleman is a widower, which no doubt would account for the melancholy of his bearing—but he is a friend, nevertheless, I'll vouch for that—and you will own, my lord, that who should judge of a face better than the landlord of a popular inn—"

"Oh, that's all right, then, if we are among friends," said Lord Antony, who evidently did not care to discuss the subject with his host. "But, tell me, you have no one else staying here, have you?"

"No one, my lord, and no one coming, either, least-ways—"

"Leastways?"

"No one your lordship would object to, I know."

"Who is it?"

"Well, my lord, Sir Percy Blakeney and his lady will be here presently, but they ain't a-goin' to stay—"

"Lady Blakeney?" queried Lord Antony, in some astonishment.

"Aye, my lord. Sir Percy's skipper was here just now. He says that my lady's brother is crossing over to France to-day in the *Day Dream*, which is Sir Percy's yacht, and Sir Percy and my lady will come with him as far as here to see the last of him. It don't put you out, do it, my lord?"

"No, no, it doesn't put me out, friend; nothing will put me out, unless that supper is not the very best which Miss Sally can cook, and which has ever been served in 'The Fisherman's Rest.' "

"You need have no fear of that, my lord," said Sally, who all this while had been busy setting the table for supper. And very gay and inviting it looked, with a large bunch of brilliantly coloured dahlias in the centre, and the bright pewter goblets and blue china about.

"How many shall I lay for, my lord?"

"Five places, pretty Sally, but let the supper be enough for ten at least—our friends will be tired, and, I hope, hungry. As for me, I vow I could demolish a baron of beef to-night."

"Here they are, I do believe," said Sally, excitedly, as a distant clatter of horses and wheels could now be distinctly heard, drawing rapidly nearer.

There was general commotion in the coffee-room.

Everyone was curious to see my Lord Antony's swell friends from over the water. Miss Sally cast one or two quick glances at the little bit of mirror which hung on the wall, and worthy Mr. Jellyband bustled out in order to give the first welcome himself to his distinguished guests. Only the two strangers in the corner did not participate in the general excitement. They were calmly finishing their game of dominoes, and did not even look once towards the door.

"Straight ahead, Comtesse, the door on your right," said a pleasant voice outside.

"Aye! there they are, all right enough," said Lord Antony, joyfully; "off with you, my pretty Sally, and see how quick you can dish up the soup."

The door was thrown wide open, and, preceded by Mr. Jellyband, who was profuse in his bows and welcomes, a party of four—two ladies and two gentlemen—entered the coffee-room.

"Welcome! Welcome to old England!" said Lord Antony, effusively, as he came eagerly forward with both hands outstretched towards the newcomers.

"Ah, you are Lord Antony Dewhurst, I think," said one of the ladies, speaking with a strong foreign accent.

"At your service, Madame," he replied, as he ceremoniously kissed the hands of both the ladies, then turned to the men and shook them both warmly by the hand.

Sally was already helping the ladies to take off their traveling cloaks, and both turned, with a shiver, towards the brightly-blazing hearth.

There was a general movement among the company in the coffee-room. Sally had bustled off to her kitchen, whilst Jellyband, still profuse with his respectful saluta-

tions, arranged one or two chairs around the fire. Mr.
Hempseed, touching his forelock, was quietly vacating
the seat in the hearth. Everyone was staring curiously,
yet deferentially, at the foreigners.

"Ah, Messieurs! what can I say?" said the elder of the
two ladies, as she stretched a pair of fine, aristocratic
hands to the warmth of the blaze, and looked with unspeakable gratitude first at Lord Antony, then at one of
the young men who had accompanied her party, and
who was busy divesting himself of his heavy, caped
coat.

"Only that you are glad to be in England,
Comtesse," replied Lord Antony, "and that you have
not suffered too much from your trying voyage."

"Indeed, indeed, we are glad to be in England," she
said, while her eyes filled with tears, "and we have already forgotten all that we have suffered."

Her voice was musical and low, and there was a great
deal of calm dignity and of many sufferings nobly endured marked in the handsome, aristocratic face, with
its wealth of snow-white hair dressed high above the
forehead, after the fashion of the times.

"I hope my friend, Sir Andrew Ffoulkes, proved an
entertaining travelling companion, madame?"

"Ah, indeed, Sir Andrew was kindness itself. How
could my children and I ever show enough gratitude to
you all, Messieurs?"

Her companion, a dainty, girlish figure, childlike and
pathetic in its look of fatigue and of sorrow, had said
nothing as yet, but her eyes, large, brown, and full of
tears, looked up from the fire and sought those of Sir
Andrew Ffoulkes, who had drawn near to the hearth
and to her; then, as they met his, which were fixed with

unconcealed admiration upon the sweet face before him, a thought of warmer colour rushed up to her pale cheeks.

"So this is England," she said, as she looked round with childlike curiosity at the great open hearth, the oak rafters, and the yokels with their elaborate smocks and jovial, rubicund, British countenances.

"A bit of it, Mademoiselle," replied Sir Andrew, smiling, "but all of it, at your service."

The young girl blushed again, but this time a bright smile, fleet and sweet, illumined her dainty face. She said nothing, and Sir Andrew too was silent, yet those two young people understood one another, as young people have a way of doing all the world over, and have done since the world began.

"But, I say, supper!" here broke in Lord Antony's jovial voice, "supper, honest Jellyband. Where is that pretty wench of yours and the dish of soup? Zooks, man, while you stand there gaping at the ladies, they will faint with hunger."

"One moment! one moment, my lord," said Jellyband, as he threw open the door that led to the kitchen and shouted lustily: "Sally! Hey, Sally there, are ye ready, my girl?"

Sally was ready, and the next moment she appeared in the doorway carrying a gigantic tureen, from which rose a cloud of steam and an abundance of savoury odour.

"Odd's my life, supper at last!" ejaculated Lord Antony, merrily, as he gallantly offered his arm to the Comtesse.

"May I have the honour?" he added ceremoniously, as he led her towards the supper table.

There was general bustle in the coffee-room: Mr. Hempseed and most of the yokels and fisher-folk had gone to make way for "the quality," and to finish smoking their pipes elsewhere. Only the two strangers stayed on, quietly and unconcernedly playing their game of dominoes and sipping their wine; whilst at another table Harry Waite, who was fast losing his temper, watched pretty Sally bustling round the table.

She looked a very dainty picture of English rural life, and no wonder that the susceptible young Frenchman could scarce take his eyes off her pretty face. The Vicomte de Tournay was scarce nineteen, a beardless boy, on whom the terrible tragedies which were being enacted in his own country had made but little impression. He was elegantly and even foppishly dressed, and once safely landed in England he was evidently ready to forget the horrors of the Revolution in the delights of English life.

"Pardi, if zis is England," he said as he continued to ogle Sally with marked satisfaction, "I am of it satisfied."

It would be impossible at this point to record the exact exclamation which escaped through Mr. Harry Waite's clenched teeth. Only respect for "the quality," and notably for my Lord Antony, kept his marked disapproval of the young foreigner in check.

"Nay, but this *is* England, you abandoned young reprobate," interposed Lord Antony with a laugh, "and do not, I pray, bring your loose foreign ways into this most moral country."

Lord Antony had already sat down at the head of the table with the Comtesse on his right. Jellyband was bustling round, filling glasses and putting chairs

straight. Sally waited, ready to hand round the soup.
Mr. Harry Waite's friends had at last succeeded in taking him out of the room, for his temper was growing
more and more violent under the Vicomte's obvious
admiration for Sally.

"Suzanne," came in stern, commanding accents
from the rigid Comtesse.

Suzanne blushed again; she had lost count of time
and of place whilst she had stood beside the fire, allowing the handsome young Englishman's eyes to dwell
upon her sweet face, and his hand, as if unconsciously,
to rest upon hers. Her mother's voice brought her back
to reality once more, and with a submissive "Yes,
Mama," she too took her place at the supper table.

They all looked a merry, even a happy party, as they sat round the table; Sir Andrew Ffoulkes and Lord Antony Dewhurst, two typical good-looking, well-born and well-bred Englishmen of that year of grace 1792, and the aristocratic French comtesse with her two children, who had just escaped from such dire perils, and found a safe retreat at last on the shores of protecting England.

In the corner the two strangers had apparently finished their game; one of them arose, and standing with his back to the merry company at the table, he adjusted with much deliberation his large triple caped coat. As he did so, he gave one quick glance all around him. Everyone was busy laughing and chatting, and he murmured the words "All safe!": his companion then, with the alertness borne of long practice, slipped on to his knees in a moment, and the next had crept noiselessly under the oak bench. The stranger then, with a loud "Good-night," quietly walked out of the coffee-room.

Not one of those at the supper table had noticed this curious and silent manoeuvre, but when the stranger finally closed the door of the coffee-room behind him, they all instinctively sighed a sigh of relief.

"Alone, at last!" said Lord Antony, jovially.

Then the young Vicomte de Tournay rose, glass in hand, and with the graceful affectation peculiar to the times, he raised it aloft, and said in broken English,—

"To His Majesty George Three of England. God bless him for his hospitality to us all, poor exiles from France."

"His Majesty the King!" echoed Lord Antony and Sir Andrew as they drank loyally to the toast.

"To His Majesty King Louis of France," added Sir Andrew, with solemnity. "May God protect him, and give him victory over his enemies."

Everyone rose and drank this toast in silence. The fate of the unfortunate King of France, then a prisoner of his own people, seemed to cast a gloom even over Mr. Jellyband's pleasant countenance.

"And to M. le Comte de Tournay de Basserive," said Lord Antony, merrily. "May we welcome him in England before many days are over."

"Ah, Monsieur," said the Comtesse, as with a slightly trembling hand she conveyed her glass to her lips, "I scarcely dare to hope."

But already Lord Antony had served out the soup, and for the next few moments all conversation ceased, while Jellyband and Sally handed round the plates and everyone began to eat.

"Faith, Madame!" said Lord Antony, after a while, "mine was no idle toast; seeing yourself, Mademoiselle Suzanne and my friend the Vicomte safely in England now, surely you must feel reasured as to the fate of Monsieur le Comte."

"Ah, Monsieur," replied the Comtesse, with a heavy sigh, "I trust in God—I can but pray—and hope . . ."

"Aye, Madame!" here interposed Sir Andrew Ffoulkes, "trust in God by all means, but believe also a little in your English friends, who have sworn to bring the Count safely across the Channel, even as they have brought you to-day."

"Indeed, indeed, Monsieur," she replied, "I have the fullest confidence in you and your friends. Your fame, I assure you, has spread throughout the whole of France. The way some of my own friends have escaped from the clutches of that awful revolutionary tribunal was nothing short of a miracle— —and all done by you and your friends—"

"We were but the hands, Madame la Comtesse . . ."

"But my husband, Monsieur," said the Comtesse, whilst unshed tears seemed to veil her voice, "he is in such deadly peril—I would never have left him, only . . . there were my children . . . I was torn between my duty to him, and to them. They refused to go without me . . . and you and your friends assured me so solemnly that my husband would be safe. But, oh! now that I am here—amongst you all—in this beautiful, free England—I think of him, flying for his life, hunted like a poor beast . . . in such peril . . . Ah! I should not have left him . . . I should not have left him! . . ."

The poor woman had completely broken down; fatigue, sorrow and emotion had overmastered her rigid, aristocratic bearing. She was crying gently to herself, whilst Suzanne ran up to her and tried to kiss away her tears.

Lord Antony and Sir Andrew had said nothing to interrupt the Comtesse whilst she was speaking. There was no doubt that they felt deeply for her; their very silence testified to that—but in every century, and ever since England has been what it is, an Englishman has always felt somewhat ashamed of his own emotion and of his own sympathy. And so the two young men said nothing, and busied themselves in trying to hide their feelings, only succeeding in looking immeasurably sheepish.

"As for me, Monsieur," said Suzanne, suddenly, as she looked through a wealth of brown curls across at Sir Andrew, "I trust you absolutely, and I *know* that you will bring my dear father safely to England, just as you brought us to-day."

This was said with so much confidence, such unuttered hope and belief, that it seemed as if by magic to dry the mother's eyes, and to bring a smile upon everybody's lips.

"Nay! You shame me, Mademoiselle," replied Sir Andrew; "though my life is at your service, I have been but a humble tool in the hands of our great leader, who organised and effected your escape."

He had spoken with so much warmth and vehemence that Suzanne's eyes fastened upon him in undisguised wonder.

"Your leader, Monsieur?" said the Comtesse, eagerly. "Ah! of course, you must have a leader. And I did not think of that before! But tell me where is he? I must go to him at once, and I and my children must throw ourselves at his feet, and thank him for all that he has done for us."

"Alas, Madame!" said Lord Antony, "that is impossible."

"Impossible?—Why?"

"Because the Scarlet Pimpernel works in the dark, and his identity is only known under the solemn oath of secrecy to his immediate followers."

"The Scarlet Pimpernel?" said Suzanne, with a

merry laugh. "Why! what a droll name! What is the Scarlet Pimpernel, Monsieur?"

She looked at Sir Andrew with eager curiosity. The young man's face had become almost transfigured. His eyes shone with enthusiasm; hero-worship, love, admiration for his leader seemed literally to glow upon his face. "The Scarlet Pimpernel, Mademoiselle," he said at last "is the name of a humble English wayside flower; but it is also the name chosen to hide the identity of the best and bravest man in all the world, so that he may better succeed in accomplishing the noble task he has set himself to do."

"Ah, yes," here interposed the young Vicomte, "I have heard speak of this Scarlet Pimpernel. A little flower—red?—yes! They say in Paris that every time a royalist escapes to England that devil, Foucquier-Tinville, the Public Prosecutor, receives a paper with that little flower dessinated in red upon it. . . . Yes?"

"Yes, that is so," assented Lord Antony.

"Then he will have received one such paper to-day?"

"Undoubtedly."

"Oh! I wonder what he will say!" said Suzanne, merrily. "I have heard that the picture of that little red flower is the only thing that frightens him."

"Faith, then," said Sir Andrew, "he will have many more opportunities of studying the shape of that small scarlet flower."

"Ah! monsieur," sighed the Comtesse, "it all sounds like a romance, and I cannot understand it all."

"Why should you try, Madame?"

"But, tell me, why should your leader—why should you all—spend your money and risk your lives—for it is your lives you risk, Messieurs, when you set foot in

France—and all for us French men and women, who are nothing to you?"

"Sport, Madame la Comtesse, sport," asserted Lord Antony, with his jovial, loud and pleasant voice; "we are a nation of sportsmen, you know, and just now it is the fashion to pull the hare from between the teeth of the hound."

"Ah, no, no, not sport only, Monsieur . . . you have a more noble motive, I am sure, for the good work you do."

"Faith, Madame, I would like you to find it then . . . as for me, I vow, I love the game, for this is the finest sport I have yet encountered.—Hair-breadth escapes . . . the devil's own risks!—Tally ho!—and away we go!"

But the Comtesse shook her head, still incredulously. To her it seemed preposterous that these young men and their great leader, all of them rich, probably well-born, and young, should for no other motive than sport, run the terrible risks, which she knew they were constantly doing. Their nationality, once they had set foot in France, would be no safeguard to them. Anyone found harbouring or assisting suspected royalists would be ruthlessly condemned and summarily executed, whatever his nationality might be. And this band of young Englishmen had, to her own knowledge, bearded the implacable and bloodthirsty tribunal of the Revolution, within the very walls of Paris itself, and had snatched away condemned victims, almost from the very foot of the guillotine. With a shudder, she recalled the events of the last few days, her escape from Paris with her two children, all three of them hidden beneath the hood of a rickety cart, and lying amidst a heap of turnips and cabbages, not daring to breathe, whilst the mob howled, "A la lanterne les aristos!" at the awful West Barricade.

It had all occurred in such a miraculous way; she and her husband had understood that they had been placed on the list of "suspected persons," which meant that their trial and death were but a matter of days—of hours, perhaps.

Then came the hope of salvation; the mysterious epistle, signed with the enigmatical scarlet device; the clear, peremptory directions; the parting from the Comte de Tournay, which had torn the poor wife's heart in two; the hope of reunion; the flight with her two children; the covered cart; that awful hag driving it, who looked like some horrible evil demon, with the ghastly trophy on her whip handle!

The Comtesse looked round at the quaint, old-fashioned English inn, the peace of this land of civil and religious liberty, and she closed her eyes to shut out the haunting vision of that West Barricade, and of the mob retreating panic-stricken when the old hag spoke of the plague.

Every moment under that cart she expected recognition, arrest, herself and her children tried and condemned, and these young Englishmen, under the guidance of their brave and mysterious leader, had risked their lives to save them all, as they had already saved scores of other innocent people.

And all only for sport? Impossible! Suzanne's eyes as she sought those of Sir Andrew plainly told him that she thought that *he* at any rate rescued his fellowmen from terrible and unmerited death, through a higher and nobler motive than his friend would have her believe.

"How many are there in your brave league, Monsieur?" she asked timidly.

"Twenty all told, Mademoiselle," he replied, "one to command, and nineteen to obey. All of us Englishmen, and all pledged to the same cause—to obey our leader and to rescue the innocent."

"May God protect you all, Messieurs," said the Comtesse, fervently.

"He has done that so far, Madame."

"It is wonderful to me, wonderful!—That you should all be so brave, so devoted to your fellowmen—yet you are English!—and in France treachery is rife—all in the name of liberty and fraternity."

"The women even, in France, have been more bitter against us aristocrats than the men," said the Vicomte, with a sigh.

"Ah, yes," added the Comtesse, while a look of haughty disdain and intense bitterness shot through her melancholy eyes. "There was that woman, Marguerite St. Just for instance. She denounced the Marquis de St. Cyr and all his family to the awful tribunal of the Terror."

"Marguerite St. Just?" said Lord Antony, as he shot a quick and apprehensive glance across at Sir Andrew.

"Marguerite St. Just?—Surely . . ."

"Yes!" replied the Comtesse, "surely you know her. She was a leading actress of the Comèdie Française, and she married an Englishman lately. You must know her—"

"Know her?" said Lord Antony. "Know Lady Blakeney—the most fashionable woman in London—the wife of the richest man in England? Of course, we all know Lady Blakeney."

"She was a school-fellow of mine at the convent in Paris," interposed Suzanne, "and we came over to England together to learn your language. I was very fond of Marguerite, and I cannot believe that she ever did anything so wicked."

"It certainly seems incredible," said Sir Andrew. "You say that she actually denounced the Marquis de St. Cyr? Why should she have done such a thing? Surely there must be some mistake—"

"No mistake is possible, Monsieur," rejoined the Comtesse, coldly. "Marguerite St. Just's brother is a noted republican. There was some talk of a family feud between him and my cousin, the Marquis de St. Cyr. The St. Justs are quite plebeian, and the republican government employs many spies. I assure you there is no mistake. . . . You had not heard this story?"

"Faith, Madame, I did hear some vague rumours of it, but in England no one would credit it. . . . Sir Percy Blakeney, her husband, is a very wealthy man, of high social position, the intimate friend of the Prince of Wales . . . and Lady Blakeney leads both fashion and society in London."

"That may be, Monsieur, and we shall, of course, lead a very quiet life in England, but I pray God that while I remain in this beautiful country, I may never meet Marguerite St. Just."

The proverbial wet-blanket seemed to have fallen over the merry little company gathered round the table. Suzanne looked sad and silent; Sir Andrew fidgeted uneasily with his fork, whilst the Comtesse, encased in the plate-armour of her aristocratic prejudices, sat, rigid and unbending, in her straight-backed chair. As for Lord Antony, he looked extremely uncomfortable, and glanced once or twice apprehensively towards Jellyband, who looked just as uncomfortable as himself.

"At what time do you expect Sir Percy and Lady Blakeney?" he contrived to whisper unobserved, to mine host.

"Any moment, my lord," whispered Jellyband in reply.

Even as he spoke, a distant clatter was heard of an approaching coach; louder and louder it grew, one or two shouts became distinguishable, then the rattle of horses' hoofs on the uneven cobble stones, and the next moment a stable boy had thrown open the coffee-room door and rushed in excitedly.

"Sir Percy Blakeney and my lady," he shouted at the top of his voice, "they're just arriving."

And with more shouting, jingling of harness, and iron hoofs upon the stones, a magnificent coach, drawn by four superb bays, had halted outside the porch of "The Fisherman's Rest."

5

Marguerite

In a moment the pleasant oak-raftered coffee-room of the inn became the scene of hopeless confusion and discomfort. At the first announcement made by the stable boy, Lord Antony, with a fashionable oath, had jumped up from his seat and was now giving many and confused directions to poor bewildered Jellyband, who seemed at his wits' end what to do.

"For goodness' sake, man," admonished his lordship, "try to keep Lady Blakeney talking outside for a moment while the ladies withdraw. Zounds!" he added, with another more emphatic oath, "this is most unfortunate."

"Quick, Sally! the candles!" shouted Jellyband, as hopping about from one leg to another, he ran hither and thither, adding to the general discomfort of everybody.

The Comtesse, too, had risen to her feet: rigid and erect, trying to hide her excitement beneath more becoming *sang-froid,* she repeated mechanically,—

"I will not see her!—I will not see her!"

Outside, the excitement attendant upon the arrival of very important guests grew apace.

"Good-day, Sir Percy!—Good-day to your ladyship! Your servant, Sir Percy!"—was heard in one long, continued chorus, with alternate more feeble tones of—"Remember the poor blind man! of your charity, lady and gentleman!"

Then suddenly a singularly sweet voice was heard through all the din.

"Let the poor man be—and give him some supper at my expense."

The voice was low and musical, with a slight sing-song in it, and a faint *soupçon* of foreign intonation in the pronunciation of the consonants.

Everyone in the coffee-room heard it and paused instinctively, listening to it for a moment. Sally was holding the candles by the opposite door, which led to the bedrooms upstairs, and the Comtesse was in the act of beating a hasty retreat before that enemy who owned such a sweet musical voice; Suzanne reluctantly was preparing to follow her mother, while casting regretful glances towards the door, where she hoped still to see her dearly-beloved, erstwhile school-fellow.

Then Jellyband threw open the door, still stupidly and blindly hoping to avert the catastrophe, which he felt was in the air, and the same low, musical voice said, with a merry laugh and mock consternation,—

"B-r-r-r-r! I am as wet as a herring! *Dieu!* has anyone ever seen such a contemptible climate?"

"Suzanne, come with me at once—I wish it," said the Comtesse, peremptorily.

"Oh! Mama!" pleaded Suzanne.

"My lady . . . er . . . h'm! . . . my lady! . . ." came in feeble accents from Jellyband, who stood clumsily trying to bar the way.

"*Pardieu,* my good man," said Lady Blakeney, with some impatience, "what are you standing in my way for, dancing about like a turkey with a sore foot? Let me get to the fire, I am perished with the cold."

And the next moment Lady Blakeney, gently pushing mine host on one side, had swept into the coffee-room.

There are many portraits and miniatures extant of Marguerite St. Just—Lady Blakeney as she was then—but it is doubtful if any of these really do her singular beauty justice. Tall, above the average, with magnificent presence and regal figure, it is small wonder that even the Comtesse paused for a moment in involuntary admiration before turning her back on so fascinating an apparition.

Marguerite Blakeney was then scarcely five-and-twenty, and her beauty was at its most dazzling stage. The large hat, with its undulating and waving plumes, threw a soft shadow across the classic brow with the aureole of auburn hair—free at the moment from any powder; the sweet, almost childlike mouth, the straight chiselled nose, round chin, and delicate throat, all seemed set off by the picturesque costume of the period. The rich blue velvet robe moulded in its every line the graceful contour of the figure, whilst one tiny hand held, with a dignity all its own, the tall stick adorned with a large bunch of ribbons which fashionable ladies of the period had taken to carrying recently.

With a quick glance all around the room, Marguerite Blakeney had taken stock of every one there. She nodded pleasantly to Sir Andrew Ffoulkes, whilst extending a hand to Lord Antony.

"Hello! my Lord Tony, why—what are *you* doing here in Dover?" she said merrily.

Then, without waiting for a reply, she turned and faced the Comtesse and Suzanne. Her whole face lighted up with additional brightness, as she stretched out both arms towards the young girl.

"Why! if that isn't my little Suzanne over there. *Pardieu*, little citizeness, how came you to be in England? And Madame too?"

She went up effusively to them both, with not a single touch of embarrassment in her manner or in her smile. Lord Tony and Sir Andrew watched the little scene with eager apprehension. English though they were, they had often been in France, and had mixed sufficiently with the French to realise the unbending hauteur, the bitter hatred with which the old *noblesse* of France viewed all those who had helped to contribute to their downfall. Armand St. Just, the brother of beautiful Lady Blakeney—though known to hold moderate and conciliatory views—was an ardent republican; his feud with the ancient family of St. Cyr—the rights and wrongs of which no outsider ever knew—had culminated in the downfall, the almost total extinction, of the latter. In France, St. Just and his party had triumphed, and here in England, face to face with these three refugees driven from their country, flying for their lives, bereft of all which centuries of luxury had given them, there stood a fair scion of those same republican families which had hurled down a throne, and uprooted an aristocracy whose origin was lost in the dim and distant vista of bygone centuries.

She stood there before them, in all the unconscious insolence of beauty, and stretched out her dainty hand to them, as if she would, by that one act, bridge over the conflict and bloodshed of the past decade.

"Suzanne, I forbid you to speak to that woman," said

the Comtesse, sternly, as she placed a restraining hand upon her daughter's arm.

She had spoken in English, so that all might hear and understand; the two young English gentlemen as well as the common innkeeper and his daughter. The latter literally gasped with horror at this foreign insolence, this impudence before her ladyship--who was English, now that she was Sir Percy's wife, and a friend of the Princess of Wales to boot.

As for Lord Antony and Sir Andrew Ffoulkes, their very hearts seemed to stand still with horror at this gratuitous insult. One of them uttered an exclamation of appeal, the other one of warning, and instinctively both glanced hurriedly towards the door, whence a slow, drawly, not unpleasant voice had already been heard.

Alone among those present Marguerite Blakeney and the Comtesse de Tournay had remained seemingly unmoved. The latter, rigid, erect and defiant, with one hand still upon her daughter's arm, seemed the very personification of unbending pride. For the moment Marguerite's sweet face had become as white as the soft fichu which swathed her throat, and a very keen observer might have noted that the hand which held the tall, beribboned stick was clenched, and trembled somewhat.

But this was only momentary; the next instant the delicate eyebrows were raised slightly, the lips curved sarcastically upwards, the clear blue eyes looked straight at the rigid Comtesse, and with a slight shrug of the shoulders—

"Hoity-toity, citizeness," she said gaily, "what fly stings you, pray?"

"We are in England now, Madame," rejoined the Comtesse, coldly, "and I am at liberty to forbid my daughter to touch your hand in friendship. Come, Suzanne."

She beckoned to her daughter, and without another look at Marguerite Blakeney, but with a deep, old-fashioned curtsey to the two young men, she sailed majestically out of the room.

There was silence in the old inn parlour for a moment, as the rustle of the Comtesse's skirts died away down the passage. Marguerite, rigid as a statue followed with hard, set eyes the upright figure, as it disappeared through the doorway—but as little Suzanne, humble and obedient, was about to follow her mother, the hard, set expression suddenly vanished, and a wistful, almost pathetic and childlike look stole into Lady Blakeney's eyes.

Little Suzanne caught that look; the child's sweet nature went out to the beautiful woman, scarce older than herself; filial obedience vanished before girlish sympathy; at the door she turned, ran back to Marguerite, and putting her arms round her, kissed her effusively; then only did she follow her mother, Sally bringing up the rear, with a pleasant smile on her dimpled face, and with a final curtsey to my lady.

Suzanne's sweet and dainty impulse had relieved the unpleasant tension. Sir Andrew's eyes followed the pretty little figure, until it had quite disappeared, then they met Lady Blakeney's with unassumed merriment.

Marguerite, with dainty affectation, had kissed her hand to the ladies, as they disappeared through the door, then a humorous smile began hovering round the corners of her mouth.

"So that's it, is it?" she said gaily. "La! Sir Andrew, did you ever see such an unpleasant person? I hope when I grow old I sha'n't look like that."

She gathered up her skirts, and assuming a majestic gait, stalked towards the fireplace.

"Suzanne," she said, mimicking the Comtesse's voice, "I forbid you to speak to that woman!"

The laugh which accompanied this sally sounded perhaps a trifled forced and hard, but neither Sir Andrew nor Lord Tony were very keen observers. The mimicry was so perfect, the tone of the voice so accurately reproduced, that both the young men joined in a hearty cheerful "Bravo!"

"Ah! Lady Blakeney!" added Lord Tony, "how they must miss you at the Comèdie Française, and how the Parisians must hate Sir Percy for having taken you away."

"Lud, man," rejoined Marguerite, with a shrug of her graceful shoulders, " 'tis impossible to hate Sir Percy for anything; his witty sallies would disarm even Madame la Comtesse herself."

The young Vicomte, who had not elected to follow his mother in her dignified exit, now made a step forward, ready to champion the Comtesse should Lady Blakeney aim any further shafts at her. But before he could utter a preliminary word of protest, a pleasant, though distinctly inane laugh, was heard from outside, and the next moment an unusually tall and very richly dressed figure appeared in the doorway.

6

An Exquisite of '92

Sir Percy Blakeney, as the chronicles of the time inform us, was in this year of grace 1792, still a year or two on the right side of thirty. Tall, above the average, even for an Englishman, broad-shouldered and massively built, he would have been called unusually good-looking, but for a certain lazy expression in his deep-set blue eyes, and that perpetual inane laugh which seemed to disfigure his strong, clearly-cut mouth.

It was nearly a year ago now that Sir Percy Blakeney, Bart. one of the richest men in England, leader of all the fashions, and intimate friend of the Prince of Wales, had astonished fashionable society in London and Bath by bringing home, from one of his journeys abroad, a beautiful, fascinating, clever, French wife. He, the sleepiest, dullest, most British Britisher that had ever set a pretty woman yawning, had secured a brilliant matrimonial prize for which, as all chroniclers aver, there had been many competitors.

Marguerite St. Just had first made her *début* in artistic Parisian circles, at the very moment when the greatest social upheaval the world has ever known was taking place within its very walls. Scarcely eighteen, lavishly gifted with beauty and talent, chaperoned only by a young and devoted brother, she had soon gathered round her, in her charming apartment in the Rue Richelieu, a coterie which was as brilliant as it was exclusive—exclusive, that is to say, only from one point of

view. Marguerite St. Just was from principle and by
conviction a republican—equality of birth was her
motto—inequality of fortune was in her eyes a mere
untoward accident, but the only inequality she admitted was that of talent. "Money and titles may be hered-
itary," she would say, "but brains are not," and thus
her charming salon was reserved for originality and intellect, for brilliance and wit, for clever men and talented women, and the entrance into it was soon looked
upon in the world of intellect—which even in those
days and in those troublous times found its pivot in
Paris—as the seal to an artistic career.

Clever men, distinguished men, and even men of exalted station formed a perpetual and brilliant court
round the fascinating young actress of the Comédie
Française, and she glided through republican, revolutionary, bloodthirsty Paris like a shining comet with a
trail behind her of all that was most distinguished, most
interesting, in intellectual Europe.

Then the climax came. Some smiled indulgently and
called it an artistic eccentricity, others looked upon it as
a wise provision, in view of the many events which were
crowding thick and fast in Paris just then, but to all, the
real motive of that climax remained a puzzle and a mystery. Anyway, Marguerite St. Just married Sir Percy
Blakeney one fine day, just like that, without any warning to her friends, without a *soirée de contrat* or *dîner de
fiançailles* or other appurtenances of a fashionable
French wedding.

How that stupid, dull Englishman ever came to be
admitted within the intellectual circle which revolved
round "the cleverest woman in Europe," as her friends
unanimously called her, no one ventured to guess—

golden key is said to open every door, asserted the more malignantly inclined.

Enough, she married him, and "the cleverest woman in Europe" had linked her fate to that "demmed idiot" Blakeney, and not even her most intimate friends could assign to this strange step any other motive than that of supreme eccentricity. Those friends who knew, laughed to scorn the idea that Marguerite St. Just had married a fool for the sake of the worldly advantages with which he might endow her. They knew, as a matter of fact, that Marguerite St. Just cared nothing about money, and still less about a title; moreover, there were at least half a dozen other men in the cosmopolitan world equally well-born, if not so wealthy as Blakeney, who would have been only too happy to give Marguerite St. Just any position she might choose to covet.

As for Sir Percy himself, he was universally voted to be totally unqualified for the onerous post he had taken upon himself. His chief qualifications for it seemed to consist in his blind adoration for her, his great wealth and the high favour in which he stood at the English court; but London society thought that, taking into consideration his own intellectual limitations, it would have been wiser on his part had he bestowed those worldly advantages upon a less brilliant and witty wife.

Although lately he had been so prominent a figure in fashionable English society, he had spent most of his early life abroad. His father, the late Sir Algernon Blakeney, had had the terrible misfortune of seeing an idolized young wife become hopelessly insane after two years of happy married life. Percy had just been born when the late Lady Blakeney fell a prey to the terrible malady which in those days was looked upon as hopelessly incurable and nothing short of a curse of God upon the entire family. Sir Algernon took his afflicted young wife abroad, and there presumably Percy was educated, and grew up between an imbecile mother and a distracted father, until he attained his majority. The death of his parents following close upon one another left him a free man, and as Sir Algernon had led a forcibly simple and retired life, the large Blakeney fortune had increased tenfold.

Sir Percy Blakeney had travelled a great deal abroad, before he brought home his beautiful, young, French wife. The fashionable circles of the time were ready to receive them both with open arms; Sir Percy was rich, his wife was accomplished, the Prince of Wales took a very great liking to them both. Within six months they were the acknowledged leaders of fashion and of style. Sir Percy's coats were the talk of the town, his inanities were quoted, his foolish laugh copied by the gilded youth at Almack's or the Mall. Everyone knew that he was hopelessly stupid, but then that was scarcely to be wondered at, seeing that all the Blakeneys for generations had been notoriously dull, and that his mother had died an imbecile.

Thus society accepted him, petted him, made much of him, since his horses were the finest in the country, his *fêtes* and wines the most sought after. As for his marriage with "the cleverest woman in Europe," well! the inevitable came with sure and rapid footsteps. No one pitied him, since his fate was of his own making. There were plenty of young ladies in England, of high birth and good looks, who would have been quite willing to help him to spend the Blakeney fortune, whilst smiling indulgently at his inanities and his good-humoured foolishness. Moreover, Sir Percy got no pity, because he seemed to require none—he seemed very proud of his clever wife, and to care little that she took no pains to disguise that good-natured contempt which she evidently felt for him, and that she even amused herself by sharpening her ready wits at his expense.

But then Blakeney was really too stupid to notice the ridicule with which his clever wife covered him, and if his matrimonial relations with the fascinating Parisienne had not turned out all that his hopes and his dog-like devotion for her had pictured, society could never do more than vaguely guess at it.

In his beautiful house at Richmond he played second fiddle to his clever wife with imperturbable *bonhomie;* he lavished jewels and luxuries of all kinds upon her, which she took with inimitable grace, dispensing the hospitality of his superb mansion with the same graciousness with which she had welcomed the intellectual coterie of Paris.

Physically, Sir Percy Blakeney was undeniably handsome—always excepting the lazy, bored look which was habitual to him. He was always irreproachably dressed, and wore the exaggerated "Incroyable" fashions, which had just crept across from Paris to England, with the perfect good taste innate in an English gentleman. On this special afternoon in September, in spite of the long journey by coach, in spite of rain and mud, his coat set irreproachably across his fine shoulders, his hands looked almost femininely white, as they emerged through billowy frills of finest Mechlin lace: the extravagantly short-waisted satin coat, wide-lapelled waistcoat, and tight-fitting striped breeches, set off his massive figure to perfection, and in repose one might have admired so fine a specimen of English manhood, until the foppish ways, the affected movements, the perpetual inane laugh, brought one's admiration of Sir Percy Blakeney to an abrupt close.

He had lolled into the old-fashioned inn parlour, shaking the wet off his fine overcoat; then putting up a gold-rimmed eye-glass to his lazy blue eye, he surveyed the company, upon whom an embarrassed silence had suddenly fallen.

"How do, Tony? How do, Ffoulkes?" he said, recognizing the two young men and shaking them by the hand. "Zounds, my dear fellow," he added, smothering a slight yawn, "did you ever see such a beastly day? Demmed climate this."

With a quaint little laugh, half of embarrassment and half of sarcasm, Marguerite had turned towards her husband, and was surveying him from head to foot, with an amused little twinkle in her merry blue eyes.

"La!" said Sir Percy, after a moment or two's silence, as no one offered any comment, "how sheepish you all look. . . . What's up?"

"Oh, nothing, Sir Percy," replied Marguerite, with a certain amount of gaiety, which, however, sounded somewhat forced, "nothing to disturb your equanimity—only an insult to your wife."

The laugh which accompanied this remark was evidently intended to reassure Sir Percy as to the gravity of the incident. It apparently succeeded in that, for, echoing the laugh, he rejoined placidly—

"La, m'dear! you don't say so. Begad! who was the bold man who dared to tackle you—eh?"

Lord Tony tried to interpose, but had no time to do so, for the young Vicomte had already quickly stepped forward.

"Monsieur," he said, prefixing his little speech with an elaborate bow, and speaking in broken English, "my mother, the Comtesse de Tournay de Basserive, has offenced Madame, who, I see, is your wife. I cannot ask your pardon for my mother; what she does is right in my eyes. But I am ready to offer you the usual reparation between men of honour."

The young man drew up his slim stature to its full height and looked very enthusiastic, very proud, and very hot as he gazed at six foot odd of gorgeousness, as represented by Sir Percy Blakeney, Bart.

"Lud, Sir Andrew," said Marguerite, with one of her merry infectious laughs, "look on that pretty picture— the English turkey and the French bantam."

The simile was quite perfect, and the English turkey looked down with complete bewilderment upon the dainty little French bantam, which hovered quite threateningly around him.

"La! sir," said Sir Percy at last, putting up his eye glass and surveying the young Frenchman with undisguised wonderment, "where, in the cuckoo's name, did you learn to speak English?"

"Monsieur!" protested the Vicomte, somewhat abashed at the way his warlike attitude had been taken by the ponderous-looking Englishman.

"I protest 'tis marvellous!" continued Sir Percy, imperturbably, "demmed marvellous! Don't you think so, Tony—eh? I vow I can't speak the French lingo like that. What?"

"Nay, I'll vouch for that!" rejoined Marguerite. "Sir Percy has a British accent you could cut with a knife."

"Monsieur," interposed the Vicomte earnestly, and in still more broken English, "I fear you have not understand. I offer you the only posseeble reparation among gentlemen."

"What the devil is that?" asked Sir Percy, blandly.

"My sword, Monsieur," replied the Vicomte, who, though still bewildered, was beginning to lose his temper.

"You are a sportsman, Lord Tony," said Marguerite, merrily; "ten to one on the little bantam."

But Sir Percy was staring sleepily at the Vicomte for a moment or two, through his partly closed heavy lids, then he smothered another yawn, stretched his long limbs, and turned leisurely away.

"Lud love you, sir," he muttered good-humouredly. "demmit, young man, what's the good of your sword to me?"

What the Vicomte thought and felt at that moment, when that long-limbed Englishman treated him with such marked insolence, might fill volumes of sound reflections. . . . What he said resolved itself into a single articulate word, for all the others were choked in his throat by his surging wrath—

"A duel, Monsieur," he stammered.

Once more Blakeney turned, and from his high altitude looked down on the choleric little man before him; but not even for a second did he seem to lose his own imperturbable good-humour. He laughed his own pleasant and inane laugh, and burying his slender, long hands into the capacious pockets of his overcoat, he said leisurely—

"A duel? La, is that what he meant? Odd's fish! you
are a bloodthirsty young ruffian. Do you want to make
a hole in a law-abiding man? . . . As for me, sir, I never
fight duels," he added, as he placidly sat down and
stretched his long, lazy legs out before him. "Demmed
uncomfortable things, duels, ain't they, Tony?"

Now the Vicomte had no doubt vaguely heard that in
England the fashion of duelling amongst gentlemen
had been surpressed by the law with a very stern hand;
still to him, a Frenchman, whose notions of bravery
and honour were based upon a code that had centuries
of tradition to back it, the spectacle of a gentleman actually refusing to fight a duel was a little short of an
enormity. In his mind he vaguely pondered whether he
should strike that long-legged Englishman in the face
and call him a coward, or whether such conduct in a
lady's presence might be deemed ungentlemanly, when
Marguerite happily interposed.

"I pray you, Lord Tony," she said in that gentle,
sweet, musical voice of hers, "I pray you play the
peacemaker. The child is bursting with rage, and,"
she added with a *soupçon* of dry sarcasm, "might do
Sir Percy an injury." She laughed a mocking little
laugh, which, however, did not in the least disturb her
husband's placid equanimity. "The British turkey has
had the day," she said. "Sir Percy would provoke all
the saints in the calendar and keep his temper the
while."

But already Blakeney, good-humoured as ever, had
joined in the laugh against himself.

"Demmed smart that now, wasn't it?" he said, turning pleasantly to the Vicomte. "Clever woman my wife,

sir. . . . You will find *that* out if you live long enough in England."

"Sir Percy is in the right, Vicomte," here interposed Lord Antony, laying a friendly hand on the young Frenchman's shoulder. "It would hardly be fitting that you should commence your career in England by provoking him to a duel."

For a moment longer the Vicomte hesitated, then with a slight shrug of the shoulders directed against the extraordinary code of honour prevailing in this fog-ridden island, he said with becoming dignity,—

"Ah, well! if Monsieur is satisfied, I have no griefs. You, mi'lor', are our protector. If I have done wrong, I withdraw myself."

"Aye, do!" rejoined Blakeney, with a long sigh of satisfaction, "withdraw yourself over there. Demmed excitable little puppy," he added under his breath. "Faith, Ffoulkes, if that's a specimen of the goods you and your friends bring over from France, my advice to you is, drop 'em 'mid Channel, my friend, or I shall have to see old Pitt about it, get him to clap on a prohibitive tariff, and put you in the stocks an you smuggle."

"La, Sir Percy, your chivalry misguides you," said Marguerite, coquettishly, "you forget that you yourself have imported one bundle of goods from France."

Blakeney slowly rose to his feet, and, making a deep and elaborate bow before his wife, he said with consummate gallantry,—

"I had the pick of the market, Madame, and my taste is unerring."

"More so than your chivalry, I fear," she retorted sarcastically.

"Odd's life, m'dear! be reasonable! Do you think I am going to allow my body to be made a pincushion of, by every little frog-eater who don't like the shape of your nose?"

"Lud, Sir Percy!" laughed Lady Blakeney as she bobbed him a quaint and pretty curtsey, "you need not be afraid! 'Tis not the *men* who dislike the shape of my nose."

"Afraid be demmed! Do you impugn my bravery, Madame? I don't patronise the ring for nothing, do I, Tony? I've put up the fists with Red Sam before now, and—and he didn't get it all his own way either—"

"S'faith, Sir Percy," said Marguerite, with a long and merry laugh, that went echoing along the old oak rafters of the parlour, "I would I had seen you then . . . ha! ha! ha! ha!—you must have looked a pretty picture. . . . and . . . and to be afraid of a little French boy . . . ha! ha! . . . ha! ha!"

"Ha! ha! ha! he! he! he!" echoed Sir Percy, good-humouredly. "La, Madame, you honour me! Zooks! Ffoulkes, mark ye that! I have made my wife laugh!— The cleverest woman in Europe! . . . Odd's fish, we must have a bowl on that!" and he tapped vigorously on the table near him. "Hey! Jelly! Quick, man! Here, Jelly!"

Harmony was once more restored. Mr. Jellyband, with a mighty effort, recovered himself from the many emotions he had experienced within the last half hour. "A bowl of punch, Jelly, hot and strong, eh?" said Sir Percy. "The wits that have just made a clever woman laugh must be whetted! Ha! ha! ha! Hasten, my good Jelly!"

"Nay, there is no time, Sir Percy," interposed Marguerite. "The skipper will be here directly and my brother must get on board, or the *Day Dream* will miss the tide."

"Time, m'dear? There is plenty of time for any gentleman to get drunk and get on board before the turn of the tide."

"I think, your ladyship," said Jellyband, respectfully, "that the young gentleman is coming along now with Sir Percy's skipper."

"That's right," said Blakeney, "then Armand can join us in the merry bowl. Think you, Tony," he added, turning towards the Vicomte, "that that jackanapes of yours will join us in a glass? Tell him that we drink in token of reconciliation."

"In fact you are all such merry company," said Marguerite, "that I trust you will forgive me if I bid my brother good-bye in another room."

It would have been bad form to protest. Both Lord Antony and Sir Andrew felt that Lady Blakeney could not altogether be in tune with them at that moment. Her love for her brother, Armand St. Just, was deep and touching in the extreme. He had just spent a few weeks with her in her English home, and was going back to serve his country, at a moment when death was the usual reward for the most enduring devotion.

Sir Percy also made no attempt to detain his wife. With that perfect, somewhat affected gallantry which characterised his every movement, he opened the coffee-room door for her, and made her the most approved and elaborate bow, which the fashion of the time dictated, as she sailed out of the room without bestowing on him more than a passing, slightly contemptuous glance. Only Sir Andrew Ffoulkes, whose every thought since he had met Suzanne de Tournay seemed keener, more gentle, more innately sympathetic, noted the curious look of intense longing, of deep and hopeless passion, with which the inane and flippant Sir Percy followed the retreating figure of his brilliant wife.

7

THE SECRET ORCHARD

Once outside the noisy coffee-room, alone in the dimly-lighted passage, Marguerite Blakeney seemed to breathe more freely. She heaved a deep sigh, like one who had long been oppressed with the heavy weight of constant self-control, and she allowed a few tears to fall unheeded down her cheeks.

Outside the rain had ceased, and through the swiftly passing clouds, the pale rays of an after-storm sun shone upon the beautiful white coast of Kent and the quaint, irregular houses that clustered round the Admiralty Pier. Marguerite Blakeney stepped on to the porch and looked out to sea. Silhouetted against the ever-changing sky, a graceful schooner, with white sails set, was gently dancing in the breeze. The *Day Dream* it was, Sir Percy Blakeney's yacht, which was ready to take Armand St. Just back to France into the very midst of that seething, bloody Revolution which was over-throwing a monarchy, attacking a religion, destroying a society, in order to try and rebuild upon the ashes of tradition a new Utopia, of which a few men dreamed, but which none had the power to establish.

In the distance two figures were approaching "The Fisherman's Rest": one, an oldish man, with a curious fringe of grey hairs round a rotund and massive chin, and who walked with that peculiar rolling gait which invariably betrays the seafaring man: the other, a young, slight figure, neatly and becomingly dressed in a dark, many caped overcoat; he was clean-shaved, and his dark hair was taken well back over a clear and noble forehead.

"Armand!" said Marguerite Blakeney, as soon as she saw him approaching from the distance, and a happy smile shone on her sweet face, even through the tears.

A minute or two later brother and sister were locked in each other's arms, while the old skipper stood respectfully on one side.

"How much time have we got, Briggs?" asked Lady Blakeney, "before M. St. Just need go on board?"

"We ought to weigh anchor before half an hour, your ladyship," replied the old man, pulling at his grey forelock.

Linking her arm in his, Marguerite led her brother towards the cliffs.

"Half an hour," she said, looking wistfully out to sea, "half an hour more and you'll be far from me, Armand! Oh! I can't believe that you are going, dear! These last few days—whilst Percy has been away, and I've had you all to myself, have slipped by like a dream."

"I am not going far, sweet one," said the young man gently, "a narrow channel to cross—a few miles of road—I can soon come back."

"Nay, 'tis not the distance, Armand—but that awful Paris . . . just now . . ."

They had reached the edge of the cliff. The gentle sea-breeze blew Marguerite's hair about her face, and sent the ends of her soft lace fichu waving round her, like a white and supple snake. She tried to pierce the distance far away, beyond which lay the shores of France: that relentless and stern France which was exacting her pound of flesh, the blood-tax from the noblest of her sons.

"Our own beautiful country, Marguerite," said Armand, who seemed to have divined her thoughts.

"They are going too far, Armand," she said vehemently. "You are a republican, so am I . . . we have the same thoughts, the same enthusiasm for liberty and equality . . . but even *you* must think that they are going too far . . ."

"Hush!—" said Armand, instinctively, as he threw a quick, apprehensive glance around him.

"Ah! you see: you don't think yourself that it is safe even to speak of these things—here in England!" She clung to him suddenly with strong, almost motherly, passion: "Don't go, Armand!" she begged; "don't go back! What should I do if . . . if . . . if . . ."

Her voice was choked in sobs, her eyes, tender, blue and loving, gazed appealingly at the young man, who in his turn looked steadfastly into hers.

"You would in any case be my own brave sister," he said gently, "who would remember that, when France is in peril, it is not for her sons to turn their backs on her."

Even as he spoke, that sweet, childlike smile crept back into her face, pathetic in the extreme, for it seemed drowned in tears.

"Oh! Armand!" she said quaintly, "I sometimes wish you had not so many lofty virtues. . . . I assure you little sins are far less dangerous and uncomfortable. But you *will* be prudent?" she added earnestly.

"As far as possible . . . I promise you."

"Remember, dear, I have only you . . . to . . . to care for me. . . ."

"Nay, sweet one, you have other interests now. Percy cares for you. . . ."

A look of strange wistfulness crept into her eyes as she murmured,—

"He did . . . once . . ."

"But surely . . ."

"There, there, dear, don't distress yourself on my account. Percy is very good . . ."

"Nay!" he interrupted energetically, "I will distress myself on your account, my Margot. Listen, dear, I have not spoken of these things to you before; something always seemed to stop me when I wished to question you. But, somehow, I feel as if I could not go away and leave you now without asking you one question. . . . You need not answer it if you do not wish," he added, as he noted a sudden hard look, almost of apprehension, darting through her eyes.

"What is it?" she asked simply.

"Does Sir Percy Blakeney know that . . . I mean, does he know the part you played in the arrest of the Marquis de St. Cyr?"

She laughed—a mirthless, bitter, contemptuous laugh, which was like a jarring chord in the music of her voice.

"That I denounced the Marquis de St. Cyr, you mean, to the tribunal that ultimately sent him and all his family to the guillotine? Yes, he does know. . . . I told him after I married him. . . ."

"You told him all the circumstances—which so completely exonerated you from any blame?"

"It was too late to talk of 'circumstances'; he heard the story from other sources; my confession came too tardily, it seems. I could no longer plead extenuating circumstances: I could not bemean myself by trying to explain—"

"And?"

"And now I have the satisfaction, Armand, of knowing that the biggest fool in England has the most complete contempt for his wife."

She spoke with vehement bitterness this time, and Armand St. Just, who loved her so dearly, felt that he had placed a somewhat clumsy finger upon an aching wound.

"But Sir Percy loved you, Margot," he repeated gently.

"Loved me?—Well, Armand, I thought at one time that he did, or I should not have married him. I daresay," she added, speaking very rapidly, as if she were about to lay down a heavy burden, which had oppressed her for months, "I daresay that even you thought—as everybody else did—that I married Sir Percy because of his wealth—but I assure you, dear, that it was not so. He seemed to worship me with a curious intensity of concentrated passion, which went straight to my heart. I had never loved any one before, as you know, and I was four-and-twenty then—so I naturally thought that it was not in my nature to love. But it has always seemed to me that it *must* be *heavenly* to be loved blindly, passionately, wholly . . . worshipped, in fact—and the very fact that Percy was slow and stupid was an attraction for me, as I thought he would love me all the more. A clever man would naturally have other interests, an ambitious man other hopes. . . . I thought that a fool would worship, and think of nothing else. And I was ready to respond, Armand; I would have allowed myself to be worshipped, and given infinite tenderness in return. . . ."

She sighed—and there was a world of disillusionment in that sigh. Armand St. Just had allowed her to speak on without interruption: he listened to her, whilst allowing his own thoughts to run riot. It was terrible to see a young and beautiful woman—a girl in all but name—still standing almost at the threshold of her life, yet bereft of hope, bereft of illusions, bereft of those golden and fantastic dreams, which should have made her youth one long, perpetual holiday.

Yet perhaps—though he loved his sister dearly—perhaps he understood: he had studied men in many countries, men of all ages, men of every grade of social and intellectual status, and inwardly he understood what Marguerite had left unsaid. Granted that Percy Blakeney was dull-witted, but in his slow-going mind, there would still be room for that ineradicable pride of a descendant of a long line of English gentlemen. A Blakeney had died on Bosworth Field, another had sacrificed life and fortune for the sake of a treacherous Stuart: and that same pride—foolish and prejudiced as the republican Armand would call it—must have been stung to the quick on hearing of the sin which lay at Lady Blakeney's door. She had been young, misguided, ill-advised perhaps. Armand knew that: and those who took advantage of Marguerite's youth, her impulses and imprudence, knew it still better; but Blakeney was slow-witted, he would not listen to "circumstances," he only clung to facts, and these had shown him Lady Blakeney denouncing a fellow man to a tribunal that knew no pardon: and the contempt he would feel for the deed she had done, however unwittingly, would kill that same love in him, in which sympathy and intellectuality could never have had a part.

Yet even now, his own sister puzzled him. Life and love have such strange vagaries. Could it be that with the waning of her husband's love, Marguerite's heart had awakened with love for him? Strange extremes meet in love's pathway: this woman, who had had half intellectual Europe at her feet, might perhaps have set her affections on a fool. Marguerite was gazing out towards the sunset. Armand could not see her face, but presently it seemed to him that something which glittered for a moment in the golden evening light, fell from her eyes onto her dainty fichu of lace.

But he could not broach that subject with her. He knew her strange, passionate nature so well, and knew that reserve which lurked behind her frank, open ways.

They had always been together, these two, for their parents had died when Armand was still a youth, and Marguerite but a child. He, some eight years her senior, had watched over her until her marriage; had chaperoned her during those brilliant years spent in the flat of the Rue de Richelieu, and had seen her enter upon this new life of hers, here in England, with much sorrow and some foreboding.

This was his first visit to England since her marriage, and the few months of separation had already seemed to have built up a slight, thin partition between brother and sister; the same deep, intense love was still there, on both sides, but each now seemed to have a secret orchard, into which the other dared not penetrate.

There was much Armand St. Just could not tell his sister; the political aspect of the revolution in France

was changing almost every day; she might not understand how his own views and sympathies might become
modified, even as the excesses, committed by those
who had been his friends, grew in horror and in intensity. And Marguerite could not speak to her brother
about the secrets of her heart; she hardly understood
them herself, she only knew that, in the midst of luxury,
she felt lonely and unhappy.

And now Armand was going away; she feared for his
safety, she longed for his presence. She would not spoil
these last few sadly-sweet moments by speaking about
herself. She led him gently along the cliffs, then down
to the beach; their arms linked in one another's, they
had still so much to say that lay just outside that secret
orchard of theirs.

8

THE ACCREDITED AGENT

The afternoon was rapidly drawing to a close; and a long, chilly English summer's evening was throwing a misty pall over the green Kentish landscape.

The *Day Dream* had set sail, and Marguerite Blakeney stood alone on the edge of the cliff for over an hour, watching those white sails, which bore so swiftly away from her the only being who really cared for her, whom she dared to love, whom she knew she could trust.

Some little distance away to her left the lights from the coffee-room of "The Fisherman's Rest" glittered yellow in the gathering mist; from time to time it seemed to her aching nerves as if she could catch from thence the sound of merry-making and of jovial talk, or even that perpetual, senseless laugh of her husband's, which grated continually upon her sensitive ears.

Sir Percy had had the delicacy to leave her severely alone. She supposed that, in his own stupid, good-natured way, he may have understood that she would wish to remain alone, while those white sails disappeared into the vague horizon, so many miles away. He, whose notions of propriety and decorum were supersensitive, had not suggested even that an attendant should remain within call. Marguerite was grateful to her husband for all this; she always tried to be grateful to him for his thoughtfulness, which was constant, and for his generosity, which really was boundless. She tried even at times to curb the sarcastic, bitter thoughts of him, which made her—in spite of herself—say cruel, insulting things, which she vaguely hoped would wound him.

Yes! she often wished to wound him, to make him feel that she too held him in contempt, that she too had forgotten that once she had almost loved him. Loved that inane fop! whose thoughts seemed unable to soar beyond the tying of a cravat or the new cut of a coat. Bah! And yet! . . . vague memories, that were sweet and ardent and attuned to this calm summer's evening, came wafted back to her memory, on the invisible wings of the light sea-breeze: the time when first he worshipped her; he seemed so devoted—a very slave— and there was a certain latent intensity in that love which had fascinated her.

Then suddenly that love, that devotion, which throughout his courtship she had looked upon as the slavish fidelity of a dog, seemed to vanish completely. Twenty-four hours after the simple little ceremony at old St. Roch, she had told him the story of how, inadvertently, she had spoken of certain matters connected with the Marquis de St. Cyr before some men—her friends—who had used this information against the unfortunate Marquis, and sent him and his family to the guillotine.

She hated the Marquis. Years ago, Armand, her dear brother, had loved Angèle de St. Cyr, but St. Just was a plebeian, and the Marquis full of the pride and arrogant prejudices of his caste. One day Armand, the respectful, timid lover, ventured on sending a small poem—enthusiastic, ardent, passionate—to the idol of his dreams. The next night he was waylaid just outside

Paris by the valets of the Marquis de St. Cyr, and igno-
miniously thrashed—thrashed like a dog within an inch
of his life—becuase he had dared to raise his eyes to the
daughter of the aristocrat. The incident was one which,
in those days, some two years before the great Revolution, was of almost daily occurrence in France; inci-
dents of that type, in fact, led to the bloody reprisals,
which a few years later sent most of those haughty
heads to the guillotine.

Marguerite remembered it all: what her brother must
have suffered in his manhood and his pride must have
been appalling; what she suffered through him and with
him she never attempted even to analyse.

Then the day of retribution came. St. Cyr and his
kind had found their masters, in those same plebeians
whom they had despised. Armand and Marguerite,
both intellectual, thinking beings, adopted with the enthusiasm of their years the Utopian doctrines of the
Revolution, while the Marquis de St. Cyr and his family fought inch by inch for the retention of those privi-
leges which had placed them socially above their
fellow-men. Marguerite, impulsive, thoughtless, not
calculating the purport of her words, still smarting
under the terrible insult her brother had suffered at the
Marquis' hands, happened to hear—amongst her own
coterie—that the St. Cyrs were in treasonable corre-
spondence with Austria, hoping to obtain the Emperor's support to quell the growing revolution in their
own country.

In those days one denunciation was sufficient: Marguerite's few thoughtless words anent the Marquis de
St. Cyr bore fruit within twenty-four hours. He was arrested. His papers were searched: letters from the Aus-

trian Emperor, promising to send troops against the
Paris populace, were found in his desk. He was ar-
raigned for treason against the nation, and sent to the
guillotine, whilst his family, his wife and his sons,
shared this awful fate.

Marguerite, horrified at the terrible consequences of
her own thoughtlessness, was powerless to save the
Marquis: her own coterie, the leaders of the revolutionary movement, all proclaimed her as a heroine: and
when she married Sir Percy Blakeney, she did not perhaps altogether realise how severely he would look
upon the sin, which she had so inadvertently committed, and which still lay heavily upon her soul. She made
full confession of it to her husband, trusting to his blind
love for her, her boundless power over him, to soon
make him forget what might have sounded unpleasant
to an English ear.

Certainly at the moment he seemed to take it very
quietly; hardly, in fact, did he appear to understand the
meaning of all she said; but what was more certain still,
was that never after that could she detect the slightest
sign of that love, which she once believed had been
wholly hers. Now they had drifted quite apart, and Sir
Percy seemed to have laid aside his love for her, as he
would an ill-fitting glove. She tried to rouse him by
sharpening her ready wit against his dull intellect; endeavoured to excite his jealousy, if she could not rouse
his love; tried to goad him to self-assertion, but all in
vain. He remained the same, always passive, drawling,
sleepy, always courteous, invariably a gentleman: she
had all that the world and a wealthy husband can give
to a pretty woman, yet on this beautiful summer's
evening, with the white sails of the *Day Dream* finally

hidden by the evening shadows, she felt more lonely than that poor tramp who plodded his way wearily along the rugged cliffs.

With another heavy sigh, Marguerite Blakeney turned her back upon the sea and cliffs, and walked slowly back towards "The Fisherman's Rest." As she drew near, the sound of revelry, of gay, jovial laughter, grew louder and more distinct. She could distinguish Sir Andrew Ffoulkes' pleasant voice, Lord Tony's boisterous guffaws, her husband's occasional, drawly, sleepy comments; then realising the loneliness of the road and the fast gathering gloom round her, she quickened her steps . . . the next moment she perceived a stranger coming rapidly towards her. Marguerite did not look up: she was not the least nervous, and "The Fisherman's Rest" was now well within call.

The stranger paused when he saw Marguerite coming quickly towards him, and just as she was about to slip past him, he said very quietly:

"Citoyenne St. Just."

Marguerite uttered a little cry of astonishment, at thus hearing her own familiar maiden name uttered so close to her. She looked up at the stranger, and this time, with a cry of unfeigned pleasure, she put out both her hands effusively towards him.

"Chauvelin!" she exclaimed.

"Himself, citoyenne, at your service," said the stranger, gallantly kissing the tips of her fingers.

Marguerite said nothing for a moment or two, as she surveyed with obvious delight the not very prepossessing little figure before her. Chauvelin was then nearer forty than thirty—a clever, shrewd-looking personality, with a curious fox-like expression in the deep, sunken

eyes. He was the same stranger who an hour or two
previously had joined Mr. Jellyband in a friendly glass
of wine.

"Chauvelin . . . my friend . . ." said Marguerite, with
a pretty little sigh of satisfaction. "I am mightily pleased
to see you."

No doubt poor Marguerite St. Just, lonely in the
midst of her grandeur, and of her starchy friends, was
happy to see a face that brought back memories of that
happy time in Paris, when she reigned—a queen—over
the intellectual coterie of the Rue de Richelieu. She did
not notice the sarcastic little smile, however, that hovered round the thin lips of Chauvelin.

"But tell me," she added merrily, "what in the world,
or whom in the world, are you doing here in England?"

She had resumed her walk towards the inn, and
Chauvelin turned and walked beside her.

"I might return the subtle compliment, fair lady," he
said. "What of yourself?"

"Oh, I?" she said, with a shrug of the shoulders. "Je
m'ennuie, mon ami, that is all."

They had reached the porch of "The Fisherman's
Rest," but Marguerite seemed loth to go within. The
evening air was lovely after the storm, and she had
found a friend who exhaled the breath of Paris, who
knew Armand well, who could talk of all the merry,
brilliant friends whom she had left behind. So she
lingered on under the pretty porch, while through
the gaily-lighted dormer-window of the coffee-room
sounds of laughter, of calls for "Sally" and for beer, of
tapping of mugs, and clinking of dice, mingled with Sir
Percy Blakeney's inane and mirthless laugh. Chauvelin

stood beside her, his shrewd, pale, yellow eyes fixed on the pretty face, which looked so sweet and childlike in this soft English summer twilight.

"You surprise me, citoyenne," he said quietly, as he took a pinch of snuff.

"Do I now?" she retorted gaily. "Faith, my little Chauvelin, I should have thought that, with your penetration, you would have guessed that an atmosphere composed of fogs and virtues would never suit Marguerite St. Just."

"Dear me! is it as bad as that?" he asked, in mock consternation.

"Quite," she retorted, "and worse."

"Strange! Now, I thought that a pretty woman would have found English country life peculiarly attractive."

"Yes! so did I," she said with a sigh. "Pretty women," she added meditatively, "ought to have a good time in England, since all the pleasant things are forbidden them—the very things they do every day."

"Quite so!"

"You'll hardly believe it, my little Chauvelin," she said earnestly, "but I often pass a whole day—a whole day—without encountering a single temptation."

"No wonder," retorted Chauvelin, gallantly, "that the cleverest woman in Europe is troubled with *ennui.*"

She laughed one of her melodious, rippling, childlike laughs.

"It must be pretty bad, mustn't it?" she said archly, "or I should not have been so pleased to see you."

"And this within a year of a romantic love match! . . ."

"Yes! . . . a year of a romantic love match . . . that's just the difficulty . . ."

"Ah! . . . that idyllic folly," said Chauvelin, with quiet sarcasm, "did not then survive the lapse of . . . weeks?"

"Idyllic follies never last, my little Chauvelin . . . They come upon us like the measles . . . and are as easily cured."

Chauvelin took another pinch of snuff: he seemed very much addicted to that pernicious habit, so prevalent in those days; perhaps, too, he found the taking of snuff a convenient veil for disguising the quick, shrewd glances with which he strove to read the very souls of those with whom he came in contact.

"No wonder," he repeated, with the same gallantry, "that the most active brain in Europe is troubled with *ennui.*"

"I was in hopes that you had a prescription against the malady, my little Chauvelin."

"How can I hope to succeed in that which Sir Percy Blakeney has failed to accomplish?"

"Shall we leave Sir Percy out of the question for the present, my dear friend?" she said drily.

"Ah! my dear lady, pardon me, but that is just what we cannot very well do," said Chauvelin, whilst once again his eyes, keen as those of a fox on the alert, darted a quick glance at Marguerite. "I have a most perfect prescription against the worst form of *ennui,* which I would have been happy to submit to you, but—"

"But what?"

"There *is* Sir Percy."

"What has he to do with it?"

"Quite a good deal, I am afraid. The prescription I would offer, fair lady, is called by a very plebeian name: Work!"

"Work?"

Chauvelin looked at Marguerite long and scrutinis-
ingly. It seemed as if those keen, pale eyes of his were
reading every one of her thoughts. They were alone together; the evening air was quite still, and their soft
whispers were drowned in the noise which came from
the coffee-room. Still, Chauvelin took a step or two
from under the porch, looked quickly and keenly all
round him, then, seeing that indeed no one was within
earshot, he once more came back close to Marguerite.

"Will you render France a small service, citoyenne?"
he asked, with a sudden change of manner, which lent
his thin, fox-like face singular earnestness.

"La, man!" she replied flippantly, "how serious you
look all of a sudden. . . . Indeed I do not know if I *would*
render France a small service—at any rate, it depends
upon the kind of service she—or you—want."

"Have you ever heard of the Scarlet Pimpernel,
Citoyenne St. Just?" asked Chauvelin, abruptly.

"Heard of the Scarlet Pimpernel?" she retorted with
a long and merry laugh, "Faith, man! we talk of nothing else. . . . We have hats 'à la Scarlet Pimpernel'; our
horses are called 'Scarlet Pimpernel'; at the Prince of
Wales' supper party the other night we had a 'soufflé à
la Scarlet Pimpernel.' . . . Lud!" she added gaily, "the
other day I ordered at my milliner's a blue dress
trimmed with green, and bless me, if she did not call
that 'à la Scarlet Pimpernel.' "

Chauvelin had not moved while she prattled merrily
along; he did not even attempt to stop her when her
musical voice and her childlike laugh went echoing
through the still evening air. But he remained serious
and earnest whilst she laughed, and his voice, clear, in-

cisive, and hard, was not raised above his breath as he said,—

"Then, as you have heard of that enigmatical personage, citoyenne, you must also have guessed, and known, that the man who hides his identity under that strange pseudonym, is the most bitter enemy of our republic, of France . . . of men like Armand St. Just."

"La! . . ." she said, with a quaint little sigh, "I dare swear he is. . . . France has many bitter enemies these days."

"But you, citoyenne, are a daughter of France, and should be ready to help her in a moment of deadly peril."

"My brother Armand devotes his life to France," she retorted proudly; "as for me, I can do nothing . . . here in England. . . ."

"Yes, you . . ." he urged still more earnestly, whilst his thin fox-like face seemed suddenly to have grown impressive and full of dignity, "here, in England, citoyenne . . . you alone can help us. . . . Listen!—I have been sent over here by the Republican Government as its representative: I present my credentials to Mr. Pitt in London to-morrow. One of my duties here is to find out all about this League of the Scarlet Pimpernel, which has become a standing menace to France, since it is pledged to help our cursed aristocrats—traitors to their country, and enemies of the people—to escape from the just punishment which they deserve. You know as well as I do, citoyenne, that once they are over here, those French *émigrés* try to rouse public feeling against the Republic . . . They are ready to join issue with any enemy bold enough to attack France . . . Now, within the last month scores of these

émigrés, some only suspected of treason, others actually
condemned by the Tribunal of Public Safety, have succeeded in crossing the Channel. Their escape in each
instance was planned, organized and effected by this
society of young English jackanapes, headed by a man
whose brain seems as resourceful as his identity is mysterious. All the most strenuous efforts on the part of my
spies have failed to discover who he is; whilst the others
are the hands, he is the head, who beneath this strange
anonymity calmly works at the destruction of France. I
mean to strike at that head, and for this I want your
help—through him afterwards I can reach the rest of
the gang: he is a young buck in English society, of that
I feel sure. Find that man for me, citoyenne!" he urged,
"find him for France!"

Marguerite had listened to Chauvelin's impassioned
speech without uttering a word, scarce making a movement, hardly daring to breathe. She had told him before that this mysterious hero of romance was the talk
of the smart set to which she belonged; already, before
this, her heart and her imagination had been stirred by
the thought of the brave man, who, unknown to fame,
had rescued hundreds of lives from a terrible, often an
unmerciful fate. She had but little real sympathy with
those haughty French aristocrats, insolent in their pride
of caste, of whom the Comtesse de Tournay de
Basserive was so typical an example; but, republican
and liberal-minded though she was from principle, she
hated and loathed the methods which the young Republic had chosen for establishing itself. She had not
been in Paris for some months; the horrors and bloodshed of the Reign of Terror, culminating in the September massacres, had only come across the Channel

to her as a faint echo. Robespierre, Danton, Marat, she had not known in their new guise of bloody justiciaries, merciless wielders of the guillotine. Her very soul recoiled in horror from these excesses, to which she feared her brother Armand—moderate republican as he was—might become one day the holocaust.

Then, when first she heard of this band of young English enthusiasts, who, for sheer love of their fellow-men, dragged women and children, old and young men, from a horrible death, her heart had glowed with pride for them, and now, as Chauvelin spoke, her very soul went out to the gallant and mysterious leader of the reckless little band, who risked his life daily, who gave it freely and without ostentation, for the sake of humanity.

Her eyes were moist when Chauvelin had finished speaking, the lace at her bosom rose and fell with her quick, excited breathing; she no longer heard the noise of drinking from the inn, she did not heed her husband's voice or his inane laugh, her thoughts had gone wandering in search of the mysterious hero! Ah! There was a man she might have loved, had he come her way: everything in him appealed to her romantic imagination; his personality, his strength, his bravery, the loyalty of those who served under him in the same noble cause, and, above all, that anonymity which crowned him, as if with a halo of romantic glory.

"Find him for France, citoyenne!"

Chauvelin's voice close to her ear roused her from her dreams. The mysterious hero had vanished, and, not twenty yards away from her, a man was drinking and laughing, to whom she had sworn faith and loyalty.

"La! man," she said with a return of her assumed

flippancy, "you are astonishing. Where in the world am I to look for him?"

"You go everywhere, citoyenne," whispered Chauvelin, insinuatingly, "Lady Blakeney is the pivot of social London, so I am told . . . you see everything, you *hear* everything."

"Easy, my friend," retorted Marguerite, drawing herself up to her full height and looking down, with a slight thought of contempt on the small, thin figure before her. "Easy! you seem to forget that there are six feet of Sir Percy Blakeney, and a long line of ancestors to stand between Lady Blakeney and such a thing as you propose."

"For the sake of France, citoyenne!" reiterated Chauvelin, earnestly.

"Tush, man, you talk nonsense anyway; for even if you did know who this Scarlet Pimpernel is, you could do nothing to him—an Englishman!"

"I'd take my chance of that," said Chauvelin, with a dry, rasping little laugh. "At any rate we could send him to the guillotine first to cool his ardour, then, when there is a diplomatic fuss about it, we can apologise— humbly—to the British Government, and, if necessary, pay compensation to the bereaved family."

"What you propose is horrible, Chauvelin," she said, drawing away from him as from some noisome insect. "Whoever the man may be, he is brave and noble, and never—do you hear me?—never would I lend a hand to such villainy."

"You prefer to be insulted by every French aristocrat who comes to this country?"

Chauvelin had taken sure aim when he shot this tiny shaft. Marguerite's fresh young cheeks became a thought more pale and she bit her under lip, for she would not let him see that the shaft had struck home.

"That is beside the question," she said at last with indifference. "I can defend myself, but I refuse to do any dirty work for you—or for France. You have other means at your disposal; you must use them, my friend."

And without another look at Chauvelin, Marguerite Blakeney turned her back on him and walked straight into the inn.

"That is not your last word, citoyenne," said Chauvelin, as a flood of light from the passage illumined her elegant, richly-clad figure, "we meet in London, I hope!"

"We meet in London," she said, speaking over her shoulder at him, "but that is my last word."

She threw open the coffee-room door and disappeared from his view, but he remained under the porch for a moment or two, taking a pinch of snuff. He had received a rebuke and a snub, but his shrewd, fox-like face looked neither abashed nor disappointed; on the contrary, a curious smile, half sarcastic and wholly satisfied, played around the corners of his thin lips.

9

The Outrage

A beautiful starlit night had followed on the day of incessant rain: a cool, balmy, late summer's night, essentially English in its suggestion of moisture and scent of wet earth and dripping leaves.

The magnificent coach, drawn by four of the finest thoroughbreds in England, had driven off along the London road, with Sir Percy Blakeney on the box, holding the reins in his slender feminine hands, and beside him Lady Blakeney wrapped in costly furs. A fifty-mile drive on a starlit summer's night! Marguerite had hailed the notion of it with delight. . . . Sir Percy was an enthusiastic whip; his four thoroughbreds, which had been sent down to Dover a couple of days before, were just sufficiently fresh and restive to add zest to the expedition, and Marguerite revelled in anticipation of the few hours of solitude, with the soft night breeze fanning her cheeks, her thoughts wandering, whither away? She knew from old experience that Sir Percy would speak little, if at all: he had often driven her on his beautiful coach for hours at night, from point to point, without making more than one or two casual remarks upon the weather or the state of the roads. He was very fond of driving by night, and she had very quickly adopted his fancy: as she sat next to him hour after hour, admiring the dexterous, certain way in which he handled the reins, she often wondered what went on in that slow-going head of his. He never told her, and she had never cared to ask.

At "The Fisherman's Rest" Mr. Jellyband was going the round, putting out the lights. His bar customers had all gone, but upstairs in the snug little bedrooms, Mr. Jellyband had quite a few important guests: the Comtesse de Tournay, with Suzanne, and the Vicomte, and there were two more bedrooms ready for Sir Andrew Ffoulkes and Lord Antony Dewhurst, if the two young men should elect to honour the ancient hostelry and stay the night.

For the moment these two young gallants were comfortably installed in the coffee-room, before the huge logfire, which, in spite of the mildness of the evening, had been allowed to burn merrily.

"I say, Jelly, has everyone gone?" asked Lord Tony, as the worthy landlord still busied himself clearing away glasses and mugs.

"Everyone, as you see, my lord."

"And all your servants gone to bed?"

"All except the boy on duty in the bar, and," added Mr. Jellyband with a laugh, "I expect he'll be asleep afore long, the rascal."

"Then we can talk here undisturbed for half an hour?"

"At your service, my lord . . . I'll leave your candles on the dresser . . . and your rooms are quite ready . . . I sleep at the top of the house myself, but if your lordship'll only call loudly enough, I daresay I shall hear."

"All right, Jelly . . . and . . . I say, put the lamp out— the fire'll give us all the light we need—and we don't want to attract the passer-by."

"All ri', my lord."

Mr. Jellyband did as he was bid—he turned out the quaint old lamp that hung from the raftered ceiling and blew out all the candles.

"Let's have a bottle of wine, Jelly," suggested Sir Andrew.

"All ri', sir!"

Jellyband went off to fetch the wine. The room now was quite dark, save for the circle of ruddy and fitful light formed by the brightly blazing logs in the hearth.

"Is that all, gentlemen?" asked Jellyband, as he returned with a bottle of wine and a couple of glasses, which he placed on the table.

"That'll do nicely, thanks, Jelly!" said Lord Tony.

"Good-night, my lord! Good-night, sir!"

"Good-night, Jelly!"

The two young men listened, whilst the heavy tread of Mr. Jellyband was heard echoing along the passage and staircase. Presently even that sound died out, and the whole of "The Fisherman's Rest" seemed wrapt in sleep, save the two young men drinking in silence beside the hearth.

For a while no sound was heard, even in the coffee-room, save the ticking of the old grandfather's clock and the crackling of the burning wood.

"All right again this time, Ffoulkes?" asked Lord Antony at last.

Sir Andrew had been dreaming evidently, gazing into the fire, and seeing therein, no doubt, a pretty, piquant face, with large brown eyes and a wealth of dark curls round a childish forehead.

"Yes!" he said, still musing, "all right!"

"No hitch?"

"None."

Lord Antony laughed pleasantly as he poured himself out another glass of wine.

"I need not ask, I suppose, whether you found the journey pleasant this time?"

"No, friend, you need not ask," replied Sir Andrew, gaily. "It was all right."

"Then here's to her very good health," said jovial Lord Tony. "She's a bonnie lass, though she *is* a French one. And here's to your courtship—may it flourish and prosper exceedingly."

He drained his glass to the last drop, then joined his friend beside the hearth.

"Well! you'll be doing the journey next, Tony, I expect," said Sir Andrew, rousing himself from his meditations, "you and Hastings, certainly; and I hope you may have as pleasant a task as I had, and as charming a travelling companion. You have no idea, Tony. . . ."

"No! I haven't," interrupted his friend pleasantly, "but I'll take your word for it. And now," he added, whilst a sudden earnestness crept over his jovial young face, "how about business?"

The two young men drew their chairs closer together, and instinctively, though they were alone, their voices sank to a whisper.

"I saw the Scarlet Pimpernel alone, for a few moments in Calais," said Sir Andrew, "a day or two ago. He crossed over to England two days before we did. He had escorted the party all the way from Paris, dressed—you'll never credit it!—as an old market woman, and driving—until they were safely out of the city—the covered cart, under which the Comtesse de Tournay, Mlle. Suzanne, and the Vicomte lay concealed among the turnips and cabbages. They, themselves, of course, never suspected who their driver was. He drove them right through a line of soldiery and a yelling mob, who were screaming, 'À bas les aristos!' But the market cart got through along with some others, and the Scarlet Pimpernel, in shawl, petticoat and hood, yelled 'À bas les aristos!' louder than anybody. Faith!" added the young man, as his eyes glowed with enthusiasm for the beloved leader, "that man's a marvel! His cheek is preposterous, I vow!—and that's what carries him through."

Lord Antony, whose vocabulary was more limited than that of his friend, could only find an oath or two with which to show his admiration for his leader.

"He wants you and Hastings to meet him at Calais," said Sir Andrew, more quietly, "on the 2nd of next month. Let me see! that will be next Wednesday."

"Yes."

"It is, of course, the case of the Comte de Tournay, this time; a dangerous task, for the Comte, whose escape from his château, after he had been declared a 'suspect' by the Committee of Public Safety, was a masterpiece of the Scarlet Pimpernel's ingenuity, is now under sentence of death. It will be rare sport to get *him* out of France, and you will have a narrow escape, if you get through at all. St. Just has actually gone to meet him—of course, no one suspects St. Just as yet; but after that . . . to get them both out of the country! I'faith, 'twill be a tough job, and tax even the ingenuity of our chief. I hope I may yet, have orders to be of the party."

"Have you any special instructions for me?"

"Yes! rather more precise ones than usual. It appears that the Republican Government have sent an accredited agent over to England, a man named Chauvelin, who is said to be terribly bitter against our league, and determined to discover the identity of our leader, so that he may have him kidnapped, the next time he attempts to set foot in France. This Chauvelin has brought a whole army of spies with him, and until the chief has sampled the lot, he thinks we should meet as seldom as possible on the business of the league, and on no account should talk to each other in public places for a time. When he wants to speak to us, he will contrive to let us know."

The two young men were both bending over the fire, for the blaze had died down, and only a red glow from the dying embers cast a lurid light on a narrow semi-circle in front of the hearth. The rest of the room lay buried in complete gloom; Sir Andrew had taken a pocketbook from his pocket, and drawn therefrom a paper, which he unfolded, and together they tried to read it by the dim red firelight. So intent were they upon this, so wrapt up in the cause, the business they had so much at heart, so precious was this document which came from the very hand of their adored leader, that they had eyes and ears only for that. They lost count of the sounds around them, of the dropping of the crisp ash from the grate, of the monotonous ticking of the clock, of the soft, almost imperceptible rustle of something on the floor close beside them. A figure had emerged from under one of the benches; with snake-like, noiseless movements it crept closer and closer to the two young men, not breathing, only gliding along the floor, in the inky blackness of the room.

"You are to read these instructions and commit them to memory," said Sir Andrew, "then destroy them."

He was about to replace the letter-case into his pocket, when a tiny slip of paper fluttered from it and fell on to the floor. Lord Antony stooped and picked it up.

"What's that?" he asked.

"I don't know," replied Sir Andrew.

"It dropped out of your pocket just now. It certainly did not seem to be with the other paper."

"Strange!—I wonder when it got there? It is from the chief," he added, glancing at the paper.

Both stooped to try and decipher this last tiny scrap of paper on which a few words had been hastily scrawled, when suddenly a slight noise atrracted their attention, which seemed to come from the passage beyond.

"What's that?" said both instinctively. Lord Antony crossed the room towards the door, which he threw open quickly and suddenly; at that very moment he received a stunning blow between the eyes, which threw him back violently into the room. Simultaneously the crouching, snake-like figure in the gloom had jumped up and hurled itself from behind upon the unsuspecting Sir Andrew, felling him to the ground.

All this occurred within the short space of two or three seconds, and before either Lord Antony or Sir Andrew had time or chance to utter a cry or to make the faintest struggle. They were each seized by two men, a muffler was quickly tied round the mouth of each, and they were pinioned to one another back to back, their arms, hands, and legs securely fastened.

One man had in the meanwhile quietly shut the door; he wore a mask and now stood motionless while the others completed their work.

"All safe, citoyen!" said one of the men, as he took a final survey of the bonds which secured the two young men.

"Good!" replied the man at the door; "now search their pockets and give me all the papers you find."

This was promptly and quietly done. The masked man having taken possession of all the papers, listened for a moment or two if there were any sound within "The Fisherman's Rest." Evidently satisfied that this dastardly outrage had remained unheard, he once more opened the door and pointed peremptorily down the passage. The four men lifted Sir Andrew and Lord Antony from the ground, and as quietly, as noiselessly as they had come, they bore the two pinioned young gallants out of the inn and along the Dover Road into the gloom beyond.

In the coffee-room the masked leader of this daring attempt was quickly glancing through the stolen papers.

"Not a bad day's work on the whole," he muttered, as he quietly took off his mask, and his pale, fox-like eyes glittered in the red glow of the fire. "Not a bad day's work."

He opened one or two more letters from Sir Andrew Ffoulkes' pocket-book, noted the tiny scrap of paper which the two young men had only just had time to read; but one letter specially, signed Armand St. Just, seemed to give him strange satisfaction.

"Armand St. Just a traitor after all," he murmured. "Now, fair Marguerite Blakeney," he added viciously between his clenched teeth, "I think that you will help me to find the Scarlet Pimpernel."

10

In the Opera Box

It was one of the gala nights at Covent Garden Theatre, the first of the autumn season in this memorable year of grace 1792.

The house was packed, both in the smart orchestra boxes and the pit, as well as in the more plebeian balconies and galleries above. Glück's *Orpheus* made a strong appeal to the more intellectual portions of the house, whilst the fashionable women, the gaily-dressed and brilliant throng, spoke to the eye of those who cared but little for this "latest importation from Germany."

Selina Storace had been duly applauded after her grand *aria* by her numerous admirers; Benjamin Incledon, the acknowledged favourite of the ladies, had received special gracious recognition from the royal box; and now the curtain came down after the glorious finale to the second act, and the audience, which had hung spell-bound on the magic strains of the great maestro, seemed collectively to breathe a long sigh of satisfaction, previous to letting loose its hundreds of waggish and frivolous tongues.

In the smart orchestra boxes many well-known faces were to be seen. Mr. Pitt, overweighted with cares of state, was finding brief relaxation in to-night's musical treat; the Prince of Wales, jovial, rotund, somewhat coarse and commonplace in appearance, moved about from box to box, spending brief quarters of an hour with those of his more intimate friends.

In Lord Grenville's box, too, a curious, interesting personality attracted everyone's attention; a thin, small figure with shrewd, sarcastic face and deep-set eyes, attentive to the music, keenly critical of the audience, dressed in immaculate black, with dark hair free from any powder. Lord Grenville—Foreign Secretary of State—paid him marked, though frigid deference.

Here and there, dotted about among distinctly English types of beauty, one or two foreign faces stood out in marked contrast: the haughty aristocratic cast of countenance of the many French royalist *émigrés* who, persecuted by the relentless, revolutionary faction of their country, had found a peaceful refuge in England. On these faces sorrow and care were deeply writ; the women especially paid but little heed, either to the music or to the brilliant audience; no doubt their thoughts were far away with husband, brother, son maybe, still in peril, or lately succumbed to a cruel fate.

Among these the Comtesse de Tournay de Basserive, but lately arrived from France, was a most conspicuous figure: dressed in deep, heavy black silk, with only a white lace kerchief to relieve the aspect of mourning about her person, she sat beside Lady Portarles, who was vainly trying by witty sallies and somewhat broad jokes, to bring a smile to the Comtesse's sad mouth. Behind her sat little Suzanne and the Vicomte, both silent and somewhat shy among so many strangers. Suzanne's eyes seemed wistful; when she first entered the crowded house, she had looked eagerly all around, scanned every face, scrutinised every box. Evidently the one face she wished to see was not there, for she settled herself down quietly behind her mother, listened apathetically to the music, and took no further interest in the audience itself.

"Ah, Lord Grenville," said Lady Portarles, as following a discreet knock, the clever, interesting head of the Secretary of State appeared in the doorway of the box, "you could not arrive more *à propos*. Here is Madame la Comtesse de Tournay positively dying to hear the latest news from France."

The distinguished diplomatist had come forward and was shaking hands with the ladies.

"Alas!" he said sadly, "it is of the very worst. The massacres continue; Paris literally reeks with blood; and the guillotine claims a hundred victims a day."

Pale and tearful, the Comtesse was leaning back in her chair, listening horror-struck to this brief and graphic account of what went on in her own misguided country.

"Ah, monsieur!" she said in broken English, "it is dreadful to hear all that—and my poor husband still in that awful country. It is terrible for me to be sitting here, in a theatre, all safe and in peace, whilst he is in such peril."

"Lud, Madame!" said honest, bluff Lady Portarles, "your sitting in a convent won't make your husband safe, and you have your children to consider: they are too young to be dosed with anxiety and premature mourning."

The Comtesse smiled through her tears at the vehemence of her friend. Lady Portarles, whose voice and manner would not have misfitted a jockey, had a heart of gold, and hid the most genuine sympathy and most gentle kindliness, beneath the somewhat coarse manners affected by some ladies at that time.

"Besides which, Madame," added Lord Grenville, "did you not tell me yesterday that the League of the Scarlet Pimpernel had pledged their honour to bring M. le Comte safely across the Channel?"

"Ah, yes!" replied the Comtesse, "and that is my only hope. I saw Lord Hastings yesterday . . . he reassured me again."

"Then I am sure you need have no fear. What the league have sworn, that they surely will accomplish. Ah!" added the old diplomatist with a sigh, "if I were but a few years younger . . ."

"La, man!" interrupted honest Lady Portarles, "you are still young enough to turn your back on that French scarecrow that sits enthroned in your box to-night."

"I wish I could . . . but your ladyship must remember that in serving our country we must put prejudices aside. M. Chauvelin is the accredited agent of his Government . . ."

"Odd's fish, man!" she retorted, "you don't call those bloodthirsty ruffians over there a government, do you?"

"It has not been thought advisable as yet," said the Minister, guardedly, "for England to break off diplomatic relations with France, and we cannot therefore refuse to receive with courtesy the agent she wishes to send to us."

"Diplomatic relations be demmed, my lord! That sly little fox over there is nothing but a spy, I'll warrant, and you'll find—an I'm much mistaken, that he'll concern himself little with diplomacy, beyond trying to do mischief to royalist refugees—to our heroic Scarlet Pimpernel and to the members of that brave little league."

"I am sure," said the Comtesse, pursing up her thin lips, "that if this Chauvelin wishes to do us mischief, he will find a faithful ally in Lady Blakeney."

"Bless the woman!" ejaculated Lady Portarles, "did ever anyone see such perversity? My Lord Grenville, you have the gift of the gab, will you please explain to Madame la Comtesse that she is acting like a fool. In your position here in England, Madame," she added, turning a wrathful and resolute face towards the Comtesse, "you cannot afford to put on the hoity-toity airs you French aistocrats are so fond of. Lady Blakeney may or may not be in sympathy with those Ruffi-ans in France; she may or may not have had anything to do with the arrest and condemnation of St. Cyr, or whatever the man's name is, but she is the leader of fashion in this country; Sir Percy Blakeney has more money than any half-dozen other men put together, he is hand and glove with royalty, and your trying to snub Lady Blakeney will not harm her, but will make you look a fool. Isn't that so, my Lord?"

But what Lord Grenville thought of this matter, or to what reflections this homely tirade of Lady Portarles led the Comtesse de Tournay, remained unspoken, for the curtain had just risen on the third act of *Orpheus,* and admonishments to silence came from every part of the house.

Lord Grenville took a hasty farewell of the ladies and slipped back into his box, where M. Chauvelin had sat all through this *entr'acte,* with his eternal snuff-box in his hand, and with his keen pale eyes intently fixed upon a box opposite to him, where, with much frou-frou of silken skirts, much laughter and general stir of curiosity amongst the audience, Marguerite Blakeney had just entered, accompanied by her husband, and looking divinely pretty beneath the wealth of her golden, reddish curls, slightly besprinkled with powder, and tied back at the nape of her graceful neck with a gigantic black bow. Always dressed in the very latest vagary of fashion, Marguerite alone among the ladies that night had discarded the crossover fichu and broad-lapelled over-dress, which had been in fashion for the last two or three years. She wore the short-waisted classical-shaped gown, which so soon was to become the approved mode in every country in Europe. It suited her graceful, regal figure to perfection, composed as it was of shimmering stuff which seemed a mass of rich gold embroidery.

As she entered, she leant for a moment out of the box, taking stock of all those present whom she knew. Many bowed to her as she did so, and from the royal box there came also a quick and gracious salute.

Chauvelin watched her intently all through the commencement of the third act, as she sat enthralled with the music, her exquisite little hand toying with a small jewelled fan, her regal head, her throat, arms and neck covered with magnificent diamonds and rare gems, the gift of the adoring husband who sprawled leisurely by her side.

Marguerite was passionately fond of music. *Orpheus* charmed her to-night. The very joy of living was writ plainly upon the sweet young face, it sparkled out of the merry blue eyes and lit up the smile that lurked around the lips. She was after all but five-and-twenty, in the hey day of youth, the darling of a brilliant throng, adored, *fêted*, petted, cherished. Two days ago the *Day*

Dream had returned from Calais, bringing her news that her idolised brother had safely landed, that he thought of her, and would be prudent for her sake.

What wonder for the moment, and listening to Glück's impassioned strains, that she forgot her disillusionments, forgot her vanished love-dreams, forgot even the lazy, good-humoured nonentity who had made up for his lack of spiritual attainments by lavishing worldly advantages upon her.

He had stayed beside her in the box just as long as convention demanded, making way for His Royal Highness, and for the host of admirers who in a continued procession came to pay homage to the queen of fashion. Sir Percy had strolled away, to talk to more congenial friends probably. Marguerite did not even wonder whither he had gone—she cared so little; she had had a little court round her, composed of the *jeunesse dorée* of London, and had just dismissed them all, wishing to be alone with Glück for a brief while.

A discreet knock at the door roused her from her enjoyment.

"Come in," she said with some impatience, without turning to look at the intruder.

Chauvelin, waiting for his opportunity, noted that she was alone, and now, without pausing for that impatient "Come in," he quietly slipped into the box, and the next moment was standing behind Marguerite's chair.

"A word with you, citoyenne," he said quietly.

Marguerite turned quickly, in alarm, which was not altogether feigned.

"Lud, man! you frightened me," she said with a

forced little laugh, "your presence is entirely inopportune. I want to listen to Glück, and have no mind for talking."

"But this is my only opportunity," he said, as quietly, and without waiting for permission, he drew a chair close behind her—so close that he could whisper in her ear, without disturbing the audience, and without being seen, in the dark background of the box. "This is my only opportunity," he repeated, as she vouchsafed him no reply, "Lady Blakeney is always so surrounded, so *fêted* by her court, that a mere old friend has but very little chance."

"Faith, man!" she said impatiently, "you must seek for another opportunity then. I am going to Lord Grenville's ball to-night after the opera. So are you, probably. I'll give you five minutes then. . . ."

"Three minutes in the privacy of this box are quite sufficient for me," he rejoined placidly, "and I think that you will be wise to listen to me, Citoyenne St. Just."

Marguerite instinctively shivered. Chauvelin had not raised his voice above a whisper; he was now quietly taking a pinch of snuff, yet there was something in his attitude, something in those pale, foxy eyes, which seemed to freeze the blood in her veins, as would the sight of some deadly hitherto unguessed peril.

"Is that a threat, citoyen?" she asked at last.

"Nay, fair lady," he said gallantly, "only an arrow shot into the air."

He paused a moment, like a cat which sees a mouse running heedlessly by, ready to spring, yet waiting with that feline sense of enjoyment of mischief about to be done. Then he said quietly—

"Your brother, St. Just, is in peril."

Not a muscle moved in the beautiful face before him. He could only see it in profile, for Marguerite seemed to be watching the stage intently, but Chauvelin was a keen observer; he noticed the sudden rigidity of the eyes, the hardening of the mouth, the sharp, almost paralysed tension of the beautiful, graceful figure.

"Lud, then," she said, with affected merriment, "since 'tis one of your imaginary plots, you'd best go back to your own seat and leave me enjoy the music."

And with her hand she began to beat time nervously against the cushion of the box. Selina Storace was singing the "Che faro" to an audience that hung spellbound upon the prima donna's lips. Chauvelin did not move from his seat; he quietly watched that tiny nervous hand, the only indication that his shaft had indeed struck home.

"Well?" she said suddenly and irrelevantly, and with the same feigned unconcern.

"Well, citoyenne?" he rejoined placidly.

"About my brother?"

"I have news of him for you which, I think, will interest you, but first let me explain. . . . May I?"

The question was unnecessary. He felt, though Marguerite still held her head steadily averted from him, that her every nerve was strained to hear what he had to say.

"The other day, citoyenne," he said, "I asked for your help. . . . France needed it, and I thought I could rely on you, but you gave me your answer. . . . Since then the exigencies of my own affairs and your own social duties have kept us apart . . . although many things have happened. . . ."

"To the point, I pray you, citoyen," she said lightly; "the music is entrancing, and the audience will get impatient of your talk."

"One moment, citoyenne. The day on which I had the honour of meeting you at Dover, and less than an hour after I had your final answer, I obtained possession of some papers, which revealed another of those subtle schemes for the escape of a batch of French aristocrats—that traitor de Tournay amongst others—all organized by that arch-meddler, the Scarlet Pimpernel. Some of the threads, too, of this mysterious organization have come into my hands, but not all, and I want you—nay! you *must* help me to gather them together."

Marguerite seemed to have listened to him with marked impatience; she now shrugged her shoulders and said gaily—

"Bah! man. Have I not already told you that I care nought about your schemes or about the Scarlet Pimpernel. And had you not spoken about my brother . . ."

"A little patience, I entreat, citoyenne," he continued imperturbably. "Two gentlemen, Lord Antony Dewhurst and Sir Andrew Ffoulkes were at 'The Fisherman's Rest' at Dover that same night."

"I know. I saw them there."

"They were already known to my spies as members of that accursed league. It was Sir Andrew Ffoulkes who escorted the Comtesse de Tournay and her children across the Channel. When the two young men were alone, my spies forced their way into the coffee-room of the inn, gagged and pinioned the two gallants, seized their papers, and brought them to me."

In a moment she had guessed the danger. Papers?

. . . Had Armand been imprudent? . . . The very thought struck her with nameless terror. Still she would not let this man see that she feared; she laughed gaily and lightly.

"Faith! and your impudence passes belief," she said merrily. "Robbery and violence!—in England!—in a crowded inn! Your men might have been caught in the act!"

"What if they had? They are children of France, and have been trained by your humble servant. Had they been caught they would have gone to jail, or even to the gallows, without a word of protest or indiscretion; at any rate it was well worth the risk. A crowded inn is safer for these little operations than you think, and my men have experience."

"Well? And those papers?" she asked carelessly.

"Unfortunately, though they have given me cognisance of certain names . . . certain movements . . . enough, I think, to thwart their projected *coup* for the moment, it would only be for the moment, and still leaves me in ignorance of the identity of the Scarlet Pimpernel."

"La! my friend," she said, with the same assumed flippancy of manner, "then you are where you were before, aren't you? and you can let me enjoy the last strophe of the *aria*. Faith!" she added, ostentatiously smothering an imaginary yawn, "had you not spoken about my brother . . ."

"I am coming to him now, citoyenne. Among the papers there was a letter to Sir Andrew Ffoulkes, written by your brother, St. Just."

"Well? And?"

"That letter shows him to be not only in sympathy with the enemies of France, but actually a helper, if not a member, of the League of the Scarlet Pimpernel."

The blow had been struck at last. All along, Marguerite had been expecting it; she would not show fear, she was determined to seem unconcerned, flippant even. She wished, when the shock came, to be prepared for it, to have all her wits about her—those wits which had been nicknamed the keenest in Europe. Even now she did not flinch. She knew that Chauvelin had spoken the truth; the man was too earnest, too blindly devoted to the misguided cause he had at heart, too proud of his countrymen, of those makers of revolutions, to stoop to low, purposeless falsehoods.

That letter of Armand's—foolish, imprudent Armand—was in Chauvelin's hands. Marguerite knew that as if she had seen the letter with her own eyes; and Chauvelin would hold that letter for purposes of his own, until it suited him to destroy it or to make use of it against Armand. All that she knew, and yet she continued to laugh more gaily, more loudly than she had done before.

"La, man!" she said, speaking over her shoulder and looking him full and squarely in the face, "did I not say it was some imaginary plot. . . . Armand in league with that enigmatic Scarlet Pimpernel! . . . Armand busy helping those French aristocrats whom he despises! . . . Faith, the tale does infinite credit to your imagination!"

"Let me make my point clear, citoyenne," said Chauvelin, with the same unruffled calm, "I must assure you that St. Just is compromised beyond the slightest hope of pardon."

Inside the orchestra box all was silent for a moment

or two. Marguerite sat, straight upright, rigid and inert, trying to think, trying to face the situation, to realise what had best be done.

In the house Storace had finished the *aria,* and was even now bowing in her classic garb, but in approved eighteenth-century fashion, to the enthusiastic audience, who cheered her to the echo.

"Chauvelin," said Marguerite Blakeney at last, quietly, and without that touch of bravado which had characterised her attitude all along, "Chauvelin, my friend, shall we try to understand one another. It seems that my wits have become rusty by contact with this damp climate. Now, tell me, you are very anxious to discover the identity of the Scarlet Pimpernel, isn't that so?"

"France's most bitter enemy, citoyenne . . . all the more dangerous, as he works in the dark."

"All the more noble, you mean. . . . Well!—and you would now force me to do some spying work for you in exchange for my brother Armand's safety?—Is that it?"

"Fie! two very ugly words, fair lady," protested Chauvelin, urbanely. "There can be no question of force, and the service which I would ask of you, in the name of France, could never be called by the shocking name of spying."

"At any rate, that is what it is called over here," she said drily. "That is your intention, is it not?"

"My intention is, that you yourself win a free pardon for Armand St. Just by doing me a small service."

"What is it?"

"Only watch for me to-night, Citoyenne St. Just," he said eagerly. "Listen: among the papers which were found about the person of Sir Andrew Ffoulkes there was a tiny note. See!" he added, taking a tiny scrap of paper from his pocket-book and handing it to her.

It was the same scrap of paper which, four days ago, the two young men had been in the act of reading, at the very moment when they were attacked by Chauvelin's minions. Marguerite took it mechanically and stooped to read it. There were only two lines, written in a distorted, evidently disguised, handwriting; she read them half aloud—

" 'Remember we must not meet more often than is strictly necessary. You have all instructions for the 2nd. If you wish to speak to me again, I shall be at G.'s ball.' "

"What does it mean?" she asked.

"Look again, citoyenne, and you will understand."

"There is a device here in the corner, a small red flower . . ."

"Yes."

"The Scarlet Pimpernel," she said eagerly, "and G.'s ball means Grenville's ball. . . . He will be at my Lord Grenville's ball to-night."

"That is how I interpret the note, citoyenne," concluded Chauvelin, blandly. "Lord Antony Dewhurst and Sir Andrew Ffoulkes, after they were pinioned and searched by my spies, were carried by my orders to a lonely house on the Dover Road, which I had rented for the purpose: there they remained close prisoners until this morning. But having found this tiny scrap of paper, my intention was that they should be in London, in time to attend my Lord Grenville's ball. You see, do you not? that they must have a great deal to say to their chief . . . and thus they will have an opportunity of speaking to him to-night, just as he directed them to do. Therefore, this morning, those two young gallants found every bar and bolt open in that lonely house on the Dover Road, their jailers disappeared, and two good horses standing ready saddled and tethered in the yard. I have not seen them yet, but I think we may safely conclude that they did not draw rein until they reached London. Now you see how simple it all is, citoyenne!"

"It does seem simple, doesn't it?" she said, with a final bitter attempt at flippancy, "when you want to kill a chicken . . . you take hold of it . . . then you wring its neck . . . it's only the chicken who does not find it quite so simple. Now you hold a knife at my throat, and a hostage for my obedience. . . . You find it simple. . . . I don't."

"Nay, citoyenne, I offer you a chance of saving the brother you love from the consequences of his own folly."

Marguerite's face softened, her eyes at last grew moist, as she murmured, half to herself:

"The only being in the world who has loved me truly and constantly. . . . But what do you want me to do, Chauvelin?" she said, with a world of despair in her tear-choked voice. "In my present position, it is well-nigh impossible!"

"Nay, citoyenne," he said drily and relentlessly, not heeding that despairing, childlike appeal, which might have melted a heart of stone, "as Lady Blakeney, no one suspects you, and with your help to-night I may—who knows?—succeed in finally establishing the identity of the Scarlet Pimpernel. . . . You are going to the ball anon. . . . Watch for me there, citoyenne, watch and listen. . . . You can tell me if you hear a chance

word or whisper. . . . You can note everyone to whom
Sir Andrew Ffoulkes or Lord Antony Dewhurst will
speak. You are absolutely beyond suspicion now. The
Scarlet Pimpernel will be at Lord Grenville's ball to-
night. Find out who he is, and I will pledge the word of
France that your brother shall be safe."

Chauvelin was putting the knife to her throat. Marguerite felt herself entangled in one of those webs, from
which she could hope for no escape. A precious hostage
was being held for her obedience: for she knew that this
man would never make an empty threat. No doubt Armand was already signalled to the Committee of Public
Safety as one of the "suspect"; he would not be allowed
to leave France again, and would be ruthlessly struck, if
she refused to obey Chauvelin. For a moment—wom-
anlike—she still hoped to temporise. She held out her
hand to this man, whom she now feared and hated.

"If I promise to help you in this matter, Chauvelin,"
she said pleasantly, "will you give me that letter of St.
Just's?"

"If you render me useful assistance to-night,
citoyenne," he replied with a sarcastic smile, "I will give
you that letter . . . to-morrow."

"You do not trust me?"

"I trust you absolutely, dear lady, but St. Just's life is
forfeit to his country . . . it rests with you to redeem it."

"I may be powerless to help you," she pleaded, "were
I ever so willing."

"That would be terrible indeed," he said quietly, "for
you . . . and for St. Just."

Marguerite shuddered. She felt that from this man
she could expect no mercy. All-powerful, he held the
beloved life in the hollow of his hand. She knew him

too well not to know that, if he failed in gaining his own ends, he would be pitiless.

She felt cold in spite of the oppressive air of the operahouse. The heart-appealing strains of the music seemed to reach her, as from a distant land. She drew her costly lace scarf up around her shoulders, and sat silently watching the brilliant scene, as if in a dream.

For a moment her thoughts wandered away from the loved one who was in danger, to that other man who also had a claim on her confidence and her affection. She felt lonely, frightened for Armand's sake; she longed to seek comfort and advice from someone who would know how to help and console. Sir Percy Blakeney had loved her once; he was her husband; why should she stand alone through this terrible ordeal? He had very little brains, it is true, but he had plenty of muscle: surely, if she provided the thought, and he the manly energy and pluck, together they could outwit the astute diplomatist, and save the hostage from his vengeful hands, without imperilling the life of the noble leader of that gallant little band of heroes. Sir Percy knew St. Just well—he seemed attached to him—she was sure that he could help.

Chauvelin was taking no further heed of her. He had said his cruel "Either—or—" and left her to decide. He, in his turn now, appeared to be absorbed in the soul-stirring melodies of *Orpheus,* and was beating time to the music with his sharp, ferret-like head.

A discreet rap at the door roused Marguerite from her thoughts. It was Sir Percy Blakeney, tall, sleepy, good-humoured, and wearing that half-shy, half-inane smile, which just now seemed to irritate her every nerve.

"Er . . . your chair is outside . . . m'dear," he said, with his most exasperating drawl, "I suppose you will want to go to that demmed ball. . . . Excuse me—er—Monsieur Chauvelin—I had not observed you. . . ."

He extended two slender, white fingers toward Chauvelin, who had risen when Sir Percy entered the box.

"Are you coming, m'dear?"

"Hush! Sh! Sh!" came in angry remonstrance from different parts of the house.

"Demmed impudence," commented Sir Percy with a good-natured smile.

Marguerite sighed impatiently. Her last hope seemed suddenly to have vanished away. She wrapped her cloak round her and without looking at her husband:

"I am ready to go," she said, taking his arm. At the door of the box she turned and looked straight at Chauvelin, who, with his *chapeau-bras* under his arm, and a curious smile round his thin lips, was preparing to follow the strangely ill-assorted couple.

"It is only *au revoir,* Chauvelin," she said pleasantly, "we shall meet at my Lord Grenville's ball, anon."

And in her eyes the astute Frenchman, read, no doubt, something which caused him profound satisfaction, for, with a sarcastic smile, he took a delicate pinch of snuff, then, having dusted his dainty lace jabot, he rubbed his thin, bony hands contentedly together.

11

Lord Grenville's Ball

The historic ball given by the then Secretary of State for Foreign Affairs—Lord Grenville—was the most brilliant function of the year. Though the autumn season had only just begun, everybody who was anybody had contrived to be in London in time to be present there, and to shine at this ball, to the best of his or her respective ability.

His Royal Highness the Prince of Wales had promised to be present. He was coming on presently from the opera. Lord Grenville himself had listened to the two first acts of *Orpheus*, before preparing to receive his guests. At ten o'clock—an unusually late hour in those days—the grand rooms of the Foreign Office, exquisitely decorated with exotic palms and flowers, were filled to overflowing. One room had been set apart for dancing, and the dainty strains of the minuet made a soft accompaniment to the gay chatter, the merry laughter of the numerous and brilliant company.

In a smaller chamber, facing the top of the fine stairway, the distinguished host stood ready to receive his guests. Distinguished men, beautiful women, notabilities from every European country had already filed past him, had exchanged the elaborate bows and curtsies with him, which the extravagant fashion of the time demanded, and then, laughing and talking, had dispersed in the ball, reception, and card rooms beyond.

Not far from Lord Grenville's elbow, leaning against

one of the console tables, Chauvelin, in his irreproachable black costume, was taking a quiet survey of the
brilliant throng. He noted that Sir Percy and Lady
Blakeney had not yet arrived, and his keen, pale eyes
glanced quickly towards the door every time a newcomer appeared.

He stood somewhat isolated: the envoy of the Revolutionary Government of France was not likely to be
very popular in England, at a time when the news of the
awful September massacres, and of the Reign of Terror
and Anarchy, had just begun to filtrate across the
Channel.

In his official capacity he had been received courte-
ously by his English colleagues: Mr. Pitt had shaken
him by the hand; Lord Grenville had entertained him
more than once; but the more intimate circles of London society ignored him altogether; the women openly
turned their backs upon him; the men who held no official position refused to shake his hand.

But Chauvelin was not the man to trouble himself
about these social amenities, which he called mere inci-
dents in his diplomatic career. He was blindly enthusiastic for the revolutionary cause, he despised all social
inequalities, and he had a burning love for his own
country: these three sentiments made him supremely
indifferent to the snubs he received in this fog-ridden,
loyalist, old-fashioned England.

But, above all, Chauvelin had a purpose at heart. He
firmly believed that the French aristocrat was the most
bitter enemy of France; he would have wished to see
every one of them annihilated: he was one of those
who, during this awful Reign of Terror, had been the
first to utter the historic and ferocious desire "that aris-

tocrats might have but one head between them, so that it might be cut off with a single stroke of the guillotine." And thus he looked upon every French aristocrat, who had succeeded in escaping from France, as so much prey of which the guillotine had been unwarrantably cheated. There is no doubt that those royalist *émigrés,* once they had managed to cross the frontier, did their very best to stir up foreign indignation against France. Plots without end were hatched in England, in Belgium, in Holland, to try and induce some great power to send troops into revolutionary Paris, to free King Louis, and to summarily hang the bloodthirsty leaders of that monster republic.

Small wonder, therefore, that the romantic and mysterious personality of the Scarlet Pimpernel was a source of bitter hatred to Chauvelin. He and the few young jackanapes under his command, well furnished with money, armed with boundless daring, and acute cunning, had succeeded in rescuing hundreds of aristocrats from France. Nine-tenths of the *émigrés,* who were *fêted* at the English court, owed their safety to that man and to his league.

Chauvelin had sworn to his colleagues in Paris that he would discover the identity of that meddlesome Englishman, entice him over to France, and then . . . Chauvelin drew a deep breath of satisfaction at the very thought of seeing that enigmatic head falling under the knife of the guillotine, as easily as that of any other man.

Suddenly there was a great stir on the handsome staircase, all conversation stopped for a moment as the major-domo's voice outside announced,—

"His Royal Highness the Prince of Wales and suite, Sir Percy Blakeney, Lady Blakeney."

Lord Grenville went quickly to the door to receive his exalted guest.

The Prince of Wales, dressed in a magnificent court suit of salmon-coloured velvet richly embroidered with gold, entered with Marguerite Blakeney on his arm; and on his left Sir Percy, in gorgeous shimmering cream satin, cut in the extravagant "Incroyable" style, his fair hair free from powder, priceless lace at his neck and wrists, and the flat *chapeau-bras* under his arm.

After the few conventional words of deferential greeting, Lord Grenville said to his royal guest,—

"Will your Highness permit me to introduce M. Chauvelin, the accredited agent of the French Government?"

Chauvelin, immediately the Prince entered, had stepped forward, expecting this introduction. He bowed very low, whilst the Prince returned his salute with a curt nod of the head.

"Monsieur," said His Royal Highness coldly, "we will try to forget the government that sent you, and look upon you merely as our guest—a private gentleman from France. As such you are welcome, Monsieur."

"Monseigneur," rejoined Chauvelin, bowing once again. "Madame," he added, bowing ceremoniously before Marguerite.

"Ah! my little Chauvelin!" she said with unconcerned gaiety, and extending her tiny hand to him. "Monsieur and I are old friends, your Royal Highness."

"Ah, then," said the Prince, this time very graciously, "you are doubly welcome, Monsieur."

"There is someone else I would crave permission to

present to your Royal Highness," here interposed Lord Grenville.

"Ah! who is it?" asked the Prince.

"Madame la Comtesse de Tournay de Basserive and her family, who have but recently come from France."

"By all means!—They are among the lucky ones then!"

Lord Grenville turned in search of the Comtesse, who sat at the further end of the room.

"Lud love me!" whispered his Royal Highness to Marguerite, as soon as he had caught sight of the rigid figure of the old lady; "Lud love me! she looks very virtuous and very melancholy."

"Faith, your Royal Highness," she rejoined with a smile, "virtue is like precious odours, most fragrant when it is crushed."

"Virtue, alas!" sighed the Prince, "is mostly unbecoming to your charming sex, Madame."

"Madame la Comtesse de Tournay de Basserive," said Lord Grenville, introducing the lady.

"This is a pleasure, Madame; my royal father, as you know, is ever glad to welcome those of your compatriots whom France has driven from her shores."

"Your Royal Highness is ever gracious," replied the Comtesse with becoming dignity. Then, indicating her daughter, who stood timidly by her side: "My daughter Suzanne, Monseigneur," she said.

"Ah! charming!—charming!" said the Prince, "and now allow me, Comtesse, to introduce to you, Lady Blakeney, who honours us with her friendship. You and she will have much to say to one another, I vow. Every compatriot of Lady Blakeney's is doubly welcome for her sake . . . her friends are our friends . . . her enemies, the enemies of England."

Marguerite's blue eyes had twinkled with merriment at this gracious speech from her exalted friend. The Comtesse de Tournay, who lately had so flagrantly insulted her, was here receiving a public lesson, at which Marguerite could not help but rejoice. But the Comtesse, for whom respect of royalty amounted almost to a religion, was too well-schooled in courtly etiquette to show the slightest sign of embarrassment, as the two ladies curtsied ceremoniously to one another.

"His Royal Highness is ever gracious, Madame," said Marguerite, demurely, and with a wealth of mischief in her twinkling blue eyes, "but here there is no need for his kind mediation. . . . Your amiable reception of me at our last meeting still dwells pleasantly in my memory."

"We poor exiles, Madame," rejoined the Comtesse, frigidly, "show our gratitude to England by devotion to the wishes of Monseigneur."

"Madame!" said Marguerite, with another ceremonious curtsey.

"Madame," responded the Comtesse with equal dignity.

The Prince in the meanwhile was saying a few gracious words to the young Vicomte.

"I am happy to know you, Monsieur le Vicomte," he said. "I knew your father well when he was ambassador in London."

"Ah, Monseigneur!" replied the Vicomte, "I was a leetle boy then . . . and now I owe the honour of this meeting to our protector, the Scarlet Pimpernel."

"Hush!" said the Prince, earnestly and quickly, as he

indicated Chauvelin, who had stood a little on one side throughout the whole of this little scene, watching Marguerite and the Comtesse with an amused, sarcastic little smile around his thin lips.

"Nay, Monseigneur," he said now, as if in direct response to the Prince's challenge, "pray do not check this gentleman's display of gratitude; the name of that interesting red flower is well known to me—and to France."

The Prince looked at him keenly for a moment or two.

"Faith, then, Monsieur," he said, "perhaps you know more about our national hero than we do ourselves . . . perchance you know who he is. . . . See!" he added, turning to the groups round the room, "the ladies hang upon your lips . . . you would render yourself popular among the fair sex if you were to gratify their curiosity."

"Ah, Monseigneur," said Chauvelin, significantly, "rumour has it in France that your Highness could—an you would—give the truest account of that enigmatical wayside flower."

He looked quickly and keenly at Marguerite as he spoke; but she betrayed no emotion, and her eyes met his quite fearlessly.

"Nay, man," replied the Prince, "my lips are sealed! and the members of the league jealously guard the secret of their chief . . . so his fair adorers have to be content with worshipping a shadow. Here in England, Monsieur," he added, with wonderful charm and dignity, "we but name the Scarlet Pimpernel, and every fair cheek is suffused with a blush of enthusiasm. None have seen him save his faithful lieutenants. We know not if he be tall or short, fair or dark, handsome or ill-formed; but we know that he is the bravest gentleman in all the world, and we all feel a little proud, Monsieur, when we remember that he is an Englishman."

"Ah, Monsieur Chauvelin," added Marguerite, looking almost with defiance across at the placid, sphinx-like face of the Frenchman, "His Royal Highness should add that we ladies think of him as of a hero of old . . . we worship him . . . we wear his badge . . . we tremble for him when he is in danger, and exult with him in the hour of his victory."

Chauvelin did no more than bow placidly both to the Prince and to Marguerite; he felt that both speeches were intended—each in their way—to convey contempt or defiance. The pleasure-loving, idle Prince he despised: the beautiful woman, who in her golden hair wore a spray of small red flowers composed of rubies and diamonds—her he held in the hollow of his hand: he could afford to remain silent and to wait events.

A long, jovial, inane laugh broke the sudden silence which had fallen over everyone.

"And we poor husbands," came in slow, affected accents from gorgeous Sir Percy, "we have to stand by . . . while they worship a demmed shadow."

Everyone laughed—the Prince more loudly than anyone. The tension of subdued excitement was relieved, and the next moment everyone was laughing and chatting merrily as the gay crowd broke up and dispersed in the adjoining rooms.

12

The Scrap of Paper

Marguerite suffered intensely. Though she laughed and chatted, though she was more admired, more surrounded, more *fêted* than any woman there, she felt like one condemned to death, living her last day upon this earth.

Her nerves were in a state of painful tension, which had increased a hundredfold during that brief hour which she had spent in her husband's company, between the opera and the ball. The short ray of hope—that she might find in this good-natured, lazy individual a valuable friend and adviser—had vanished as quickly as it had come, the moment she found herself alone with him. The same feeling of good-humoured contempt which one feels for an animal or a faithful servant, made her turn away with a smile from the man who should have been her moral support in this heart-rending crisis through which she was passing: who should have been her cool-headed adviser, when feminine sympathy and sentiment tossed her hither and thither, between her love for her brother, who was far away and in mortal peril, and horror of the awful service which Chauvelin had exacted from her, in exchange for Armand's safety.

There he stood, the moral support, the cool-headed adviser, surrounded by a crowd of brainless, empty-headed young fops, who were even now repeating from mouth to mouth, and with every sign of the keenest enjoyment, a doggerel quatrain which he had just given forth.

Everywhere the absurd, silly words met her: people seemed to have little else to speak about, even the Prince had asked her, with a laugh, whether she appreciated her husband's latest poetic efforts.

"All done in the tying of a cravat," Sir Percy had declared to his clique of admirers.

> "We seek him here, we seek him there,
> Those Frenchies seek him everywhere.
> Is he in heaven?—Is he in hell?
> That demmed, elusive Pimpernel?"

Sir Percy's *bon mot* had gone the round of the brilliant reception-rooms. The Prince was enchanted. He vowed that life without Blakeney would be but a dreary desert. Then, taking him by the arm, had led him to the card-room, and engaged him in a long game of hazard.

Sir Percy, whose chief interest in most social gatherings seemed to centre round the card-table, usually allowed his wife to flirt, dance, to amuse or bore herself as much as she liked. And to-night, having delivered himself of his *bon mot,* he had left Marguerite surrounded by a crowd of admirers of all ages, all anxious and willing to help her to forget that somewhere in the spacious reception rooms, there was a long, lazy being who had been fool enough to suppose that the cleverest woman in Europe would settle down to the prosaic bonds of English matrimony.

Her still overwrought nerves, her excitement and agitation, lent beautiful Marguerite Blakeney much additional charm: escorted by a veritable bevy of men of all ages and of most nationalities, she called forth many exclamations of admiration from everyone as she passed.

She would not allow herself any more time to think. Her early, somewhat Bohemian training had made her something of a fatalist. She felt that events would shape themselves, that the directing of them was not in her hands. From Chauvelin she knew that she could expect no mercy. He had set a price upon Armand's head, and left it to her to pay or not, as she chose.

Later on in the evening she caught sight of Sir Andrew Ffoulkes and Lord Antony Dewhurst, who seemingly had just arrived. She noticed at once that Sir Andrew immediately made for little Suzanne de Tournay, and that the two young people soon managed to isolate themselves in one of the deep embrasures of the mullioned windows, there to carry on a long conversation, which seemed very earnest and very pleasant on both sides.

Both the young men looked a little haggard and anxious, but otherwise they were irreproachably dressed, and there was not the slightest sign, about their courtly demeanour, of the terrible catastrophe, which they must have felt hovering round them and round their chief.

That the League of the Scarlet Pimpernel had no intention of abandoning its cause, she had gathered through little Suzanne herself, who spoke openly of the assurance she and her mother had had that the Comte de Tournay would be rescued from France by the league, within the next few days. Vaguely she began to wonder, as she looked at the brilliant and fashionable crowd in the gaily-lighted ball-room, which of these worldly men round her was the mysterious "Scarlet Pimpernel," who held the threads of such daring plots, and the fate of valuable lives in his hands.

A burning curiosity seized her to know him: although for months she had heard of him and had accepted his anonymity, as everyone else in society had done; but now she longed to know—quite impersonally, quite apart from Armand, and oh! quite apart from Chauvelin—only for her own sake, for the sake of the enthusiastic admiration she had always bestowed on his bravery and cunning.

He was at the ball, of course, somewhere, since Sir Andrew Ffoulkes and Lord Antony Dewhurst were here, evidently expecting to meet their chief—and perhaps to get a fresh *mot d'ordre* from him.

Marguerite looked round at everyone, at the aristocratic high-typed Norman faces, the squarely-built, fair-haired Saxon, the more gentle, humorous caste of the Celt, wondering which of these betrayed the power, the energy, the cunning which had imposed its will and its leadership upon a number of high-born English gentlemen, among whom rumour asserted was His Royal Highness himself.

Sir Andrew Ffoulkes? Surely not, with his gentle blue eyes, which were looking so tenderly and longingly after little Suzanne, who was being led away from the pleasant *tête-à-tête* by her stern mother. Marguerite watched him across the room, as he finally turned away with a sigh, and seemed to stand, aimless and lonely, now that Suzanne's dainty little figure had disappeared in the crowd.

She watched him as he strolled towards the doorway, which led to a small boudoir beyond, then paused and leaned against the framework of it, looking still anxiously all round him.

Marguerite contrived for the moment to evade her present attentive cavalier, and she skirted the fashionable crowd, drawing nearer to the doorway, against which Sir Andrew was leaning. Why she wished to get closer to him, she could not have said: perhaps she was impelled by an all-powerful fatality, which so often seems to rule the destinies of men.

Suddenly she stopped: her very heart seemed to stand still, her eyes, large and excited, flashed for a moment towards that doorway, then as quickly were turned away again. Sir Andrew Ffoulkes was still in the same listless position by the door, but Marguerite had distinctly seen that Lord Hastings—a young buck, a friend of her husband's and one of the Prince's set— had, as he quickly brushed past him, slipped something into his hand.

For one moment longer—oh! it was the merest flash—Marguerite paused: the next she had, with admirably played unconcern, resumed her walk across the room—but this time more quickly towards that doorway whence Sir Andrew had now disappeared.

All this, from the moment that Marguerite had caught sight of Sir Andrew leaning against the doorway, until she followed him into the little boudoir beyond, had occurred in less than a minute. Fate is usually swift when she deals a blow.

Now Lady Blakeney had suddenly ceased to exist. It was Marguerite St. Just who was there only: Marguerite St. Just who had passed her childhood, her early youth, in the protecting arms of her brother Armand. She had forgotten everything else—her rank, her dignity, her secret enthusiasms—everything save that Armand stood in peril of his life, and that there, not twenty feet away from her, in the small boudoir which was quite deserted, in the very hands of Sir Andrew Ffoulkes, might be the talisman which would save her brother's life.

Barely another thirty seconds had elapsed between the moment when Lord Hastings slipped the mysterious "something" into Sir Andrew's hand, and the one when she, in her turn, reached the deserted boudoir. Sir Andrew was standing with his back to her and close to a table upon which stood a massive silver candelabra. A slip of paper was in his hand, and he was in the very act of perusing its contents.

Unperceived, her soft clinging robe making not the slightest sound upon the heavy carpet, not daring to breathe until she had accomplished her purpose, Marguerite slipped close behind him. . . . At that moment he looked round and saw her; she uttered a groan, passed her hand across her forehead, and murmured faintly:

"The heat in the room was terrible . . . I felt so faint . . . Ah! . . ."

She tottered almost as if she would fall, and Sir Andrew, quickly recovering himself, and crumpling in his hand the tiny note he had been reading, was only, apparently, just in time to support her.

"You are ill, Lady Blakeney?" he asked with much concern. "Let me . . ."

"No, no, nothing—" she interrupted quickly. "A chair—quick."

She sank into a chair close to the table, and throwing back her head, closed her eyes.

"There!" she murmured, still faintly; "the giddiness

is passing off. . . . Do not heed me, Sir Andrew; I assure you I already feel better."

At moments like these there is no doubt—and psychologists actually assert it—that there is in us a sense which has absolutely nothing to do with the other five: it is not that we see, it is not that we hear or touch, yet we seem to do all three at once. Marguerite sat there with her eyes apparently closed. Sir Andrew was immediately behind her, and on her right was the table with the five-armed candelabra upon it. Before her mental vision there was absolutely nothing but Armand's face. Armand, whose life was in the most imminent danger, and who seemed to be looking at her from a background upon which were dimly painted the seething crowd of Paris, the bare walls of the Tribunal of Public Safety, with Foucquier-Tinville, the Public Prosecutor, demanding Armand's life in the name of the people of France, and the lurid guillotine with its stained knife waiting for another victim . . . Armand! . . .

For one moment there was dead silence in the little boudoir. Beyond, from the brilliant ball-room, the sweet notes of the gavotte, the frou-frou of rich dresses, the talk and laughter of a large and merry crowd, came as a strange, weird accompaniment to the drama which was being enacted here.

Sir Andrew had not uttered another word. Then it was that that extra sense became potent in Marguerite Blakeney. She could not see, for her eyes were closed, she could not hear, for the noise from the ball-room drowned the soft rustle of that momentous scrap of paper; nevertheless she knew—as if she had both seen and heard—that Sir Andrew was even now holding the paper to the flame of one of the candles.

At the exact moment that it began to catch fire, she opened her eyes, raised her hand and, with two dainty fingers, had taken the burning scrap of paper from the young man's hand. Then she blew out the flame, and held the paper to her nostril with perfect unconcern.

"How thoughtful of you, Sir Andrew," she said gaily, "surely 'twas your grandmother who taught you that the smell of burnt paper was a sovereign remedy against giddiness."

She sighed with satisfaction, holding the paper tightly between her jewelled fingers; that talisman which perhaps would save her brother Armand's life. Sir Andrew was staring at her, too dazed for the moment to realize what had actually happened; he had been taken so completely by surprise, that he seemed quite unable to grasp the fact that the slip of paper, which she held in her dainty hand, was one perhaps on which the life of his comrade might depend.

Marguerite burst into a long, merry peal of laughter.

"Why do you stare at me like that?" she said playfully. "I assure you I feel much better; your remedy has proved most effectual. This room is most delightfully cool," she added, with the same perfect composure, "and the sound of the gavotte from the ball-room is fascinating and soothing."

She was prattling on in the most unconcerned and pleasant way, whilst Sir Andrew, in an agony of mind, was racking his brains as to the quickest method he could employ to get that bit of paper out of that beautiful woman's hand. Instinctively, vague and tumultuous thoughts rushed through his mind: he suddenly remembered her nationality, and worst of all, recollected that horrible tale anent the Marquis de St. Cyr, which in England no one had credited, for the sake of Sir Percy, as well as for her own.

"What? Still dreaming and staring?" she said, with a merry laugh, "you are most ungallant, Sir Andrew; and now I come to think of it, you seemed more startled than pleased when you saw me just now. I do believe, after all, that it was not concern for my health, nor yet a remedy taught you by your grandmother that caused you to burn this tiny scrap of paper. . . . I vow it must have been your lady love's last cruel epistle you were trying to destroy. Now confess!" she added, playfully holding up the scrap of paper, "does this contain her final *congé*, or a last appeal to kiss and make friends?"

"Whichever it is, Lady Blakeney," said Sir Andrew, who was gradually recovering his self-possession, "this little note is undoubtedly mine, and . . ."

Not caring whether his action was one that would be styled ill-bred towards a lady, the young man had made a bold dash for the note; but Marguerite's thoughts flew quicker than his own; her actions, under pressure of this intense excitement, were swifter and more sure. She was tall and strong; she took a quick step backwards and knocked over the small Sheraton table which was already top-heavy, and which fell down with a crash, together with the massive candelabra upon it.

She gave a quick cry of alarm:

"The candles, Sir Andrew—quick!"

There was not much damage done; one or two of the candles had blown out as the candelabra fell; others had merely sent some grease upon the valuable carpet; one had ignited the paper shade over it. Sir Andrew quickly and dexterously put out the flames and replaced the candelabra upon the table; but this had taken him a few seconds to do, and those seconds had been all that Marguerite needed to cast a quick glance at the paper, and to note its contents—a dozen words in the same distorted handwriting she had seen before, and bearing the same device—a star-shaped flower drawn in red ink.

When Sir Andrew once more looked at her, he only saw on her face alarm at the untoward accident and relief at its happy issue; whilst the tiny and momentous note had apparently fluttered to the ground. Eagerly the young man picked it up, and his face looked much relieved, as his fingers closed tightly over it.

"For shame, Sir Andrew," she said, shaking her head with a playful sigh, "making havoc in the heart of some impressionable duchess, whilst conquering the affections of my sweet little Suzanne. Well, well! I do believe it was Cupid himself who stood by you, and threatened the entire Foreign Office with destruction by fire, just on purpose to make me drop love's message, before it had been polluted by my indiscreet eyes. To think that, a moment longer, and I might have known the secrets of an erring duchess."

"You will forgive me, Lady Blakeney," said Sir Andrew, now as calm as she was herself, "if I resume the interesting occupation which you have interrupted?"

"By all means, Sir Andrew! How should I venture to thwart the love-god again? Perhaps he would mete out some terrible chastisement against my presumption. Burn your love-token, by all means!"

Sir Andrew had already twisted the paper into a long spill, and was once again holding it to the flame of the candle, which had remained alight. He did not notice the strange smile on the face of his fair *vis-à-vis*, so intent was he on the work of destruction; perhaps, had he done so, the look of relief would have faded from his face. He watched the fateful note, as it curled under the flame. Soon the last fragment fell on the floor, and he placed his heel upon the ashes.

"And now, Sir Andrew," said Marguerite Blakeney, with the pretty nonchalance peculiar to herself, and with the most winning of smiles, "will you venture to excite the jealousy of your fair lady by asking me to dance the minuet?"

13

Either—Or?

The few words which Marguerite Blakeney had managed to read on the half scorched piece of paper, seemed literally to be the words of Fate. "Start myself tomorrow. . . ." This she had read quite distinctly; then came a blur caused by the smoke of the candle, which obliterated the next few words; but, right at the bottom, there was another sentence, which was now standing clearly and distinctly, like letters of fire, before her mental vision. "If you wish to speak to me again I shall be in the supper-room at one o'clock precisely." The whole was signed with the hastily-scrawled little device—a tiny star-shaped flower, which had become so familiar to her.

One o'clock precisely! It was now close upon eleven, the last minuet was being danced, with Sir Andrew Ffoulkes and beautiful Lady Blakeney leading the couples, through its delicate and intricate figures.

Close upon eleven! the hands of the handsome Louis XV. clock upon its ormolu bracket seemed to move along with maddening rapidity. Two hours more, and her fate and that of Armand would be sealed. In two hours she must make up her mind whether she will keep the knowledge so cunningly gained to herself, and leave her brother to his fate, or whether she will wilfully betray a brave man, whose life was devoted to his fellow-men, who was noble, generous, and above all, unsuspecting. It seemed a horrible thing to do. But then, there was Armand! Armand, too, was noble and brave, Armand, too, was unsuspecting. And Armand loved her, would have willingly trusted his life in her hands, and now, when she could save him from death, she hesitated. Oh! it was monstrous; her brother's kind, gentle face, so full of love for her, seemed to be looking reproachfully at her. "You might have saved me, Margot!" he seemed to say to her, "and you chose the life of a stranger, a man you do not know, whom you have never seen, and preferred that he should be safe, whilst you sent me to the guillotine!"

All these conflicting thoughts raged through Marguerite's brain, while, with a smile upon her lips, she glided through the graceful mazes of the minuet. She noted—with that acute sense of hers—that she had succeeded in completely allaying Sir Andrew's fears. Her self-control had been absolutely perfect—she was a finer actress at this moment, and throughout the whole of this minuet, than she had ever been upon the boards of the Comédie Française; but then, a beloved brother's life had not depended upon her histrionic powers.

She was too clever to overdo her part, and made no further allusions to the supposed *billet doux,* which had caused Sir Andrew Ffoulkes such an agonising five minutes. She watched his anxiety melting away under her sunny smile, and soon perceived that, whatever doubt may have crossed his mind at the moment, she had, by the time the last bars of the minuet had been played, succeeded in completely dispelling it; he never realised in what a fever of excitement she was, what effort it cost her to keep up a constant ripple of *banal* conversation.

When the minuet was over, she asked Sir Andrew to take her into the next room.

"I have promised to go down to supper with His Royal Highness," she said, "but before we part, tell me . . . am I forgiven?"

"Forgiven?"

"Yes! Confess, I gave you a fright just now. . . . But, remember, I am not an English woman, and I do not look upon the exchanging of *billet doux* as a crime, and I vow I'll not tell my little Suzanne. But now, tell me, shall I welcome you at my water-party on Wednesday?"

"I am not sure, Lady Blakeney," he replied evasively. "I may have to leave London to-morrow."

"I would not do that, if I were you," she said earnestly; then seeing the anxious look once more reappearing in his eyes, she added gaily; "No one can throw a ball better than you can, Sir Andrew, we should so miss you on the bowling-green."

He had led her across the room, to one beyond, where already his Royal Highness was waiting for the beautiful Lady Blakeney.

"Madame, supper awaits us," said the Prince, offering his arm to Marguerite, "and I am full of hope. The goddess Fortune has frowned so persistently on me at hazard, that I look with confidence for the smiles of the goddess of Beauty."

"Your Highness has been unfortunate at the card tables?" asked Marguerite, as she took the Prince's arm.

"Aye! most unfortunate. Blakeney, not content with being the richest among my father's subjects, has also the most outrageous luck. By the way, where is that inimitable wit? I vow, Madam, that this life would be but a dreary desert without your smiles and his sallies."

14

One O'Clock Precisely!

Supper had been extremely gay. All those present declared that never had Lady Blakeney been more adorable, nor that "demmed idiot" Sir Percy more amusing.

His Royal Highness had laughed until the tears streamed down his cheeks at Blakeney's foolish yet funny repartees. His doggerel verse, "We seek him here, we seek him there," etc., was sung to the tune of "Ho! Merry Britons!" and to the accompaniment of glasses knocked loudly against the table. Lord Grenville, moreover, had a most perfect cook—some wags asserted that he was a scion of the old French *noblesse*, who having lost his fortune, had come to seek it in the *cuisine* of the Foreign Office.

Marguerite Blakeney was in her most brilliant mood, and surely not a soul in that crowded supper-room had even an inkling of the terrible struggle which was raging within her heart.

The clock was ticking so mercilessly on. It was long past midnight, and even the Prince of Wales was thinking of leaving the supper-table. Within the next half-hour the destinies of two brave men would be pitted against one another—the dearly-beloved brother and he, the unknown hero.

Marguerite had not tried to see Chauvelin during this last hour; she knew that his keen, fox-like eyes would terrify her at once, and incline the balance of her decision towards Armand. Whilst she did not see him, there still lingered in her heart of hearts a vague, undefined hope that "something" would occur, something big, enormous, epoch-making, which would shift from her young, weak shoulders this terrible burden of responsibility, of having to choose between two such cruel alternatives.

But the minutes ticked on with that dull monotony which they invariably seem to assume when our very nerves ache with their incessant ticking.

After supper, dancing was resumed. His Royal Highness had left, and there was general talk of departing among the older guests; the young ones were indefatigable and had started on a new gavotte, which would fill the next quarter of an hour.

Marguerite did not feel equal to another dance; there is a limit to the most enduring self-control. Escorted by a Cabinet Minister, she had once more found her way to the tiny boudoir, still the most deserted among all the rooms. She knew that Chauvelin must be lying in wait for her somewhere, ready to seize the first possible opportunity for a *tête-à-tête*. His eyes had met hers for a moment after the 'fore-supper minuet, and she knew that the keen diplomatist, with those searching pale eyes of his, had divined that her work was accomplished.

Fate had willed it so. Marguerite, torn by the most terrible conflict heart of woman can ever know, had resigned herself to its decrees. But Armand must be saved at any cost; he, first of all, for he was her brother, had been mother, father, friend to her ever since she, a tiny babe, had lost both her parents. To think of Armand dying a traitor's death on the guillotine was too horrible even to dwell upon—impossible, in fact. That could never be, never. . . . As for the stranger, the hero . . . well! there, let Fate decide. Marguerite would redeem her brother's life at the hands of the relentless enemy, then let that cunning Scarlet Pimpernel extricate himself after that.

Perhaps—vaguely—Marguerite hoped that the daring plotter, who for so many months had baffled an army of spies, would still manage to evade Chauvelin and remain immune to the end.

She thought of all this, as she sat listening to the witty discourse of the Cabinet Minister, who, no doubt, felt that he had found in Lady Blakeney a most perfect listener. Suddenly she saw the keen, fox-like face of Chauvelin peeping through the curtained doorway.

"Lord Fancourt," she said to the Minister, "will you do me a service?"

"I am entirely at your ladyship's service," he replied gallantly.

"Will you see if my husband is still in the card-room? And if he is, will you tell him that I am very tired, and would be glad to go home soon."

The commands of a beautiful woman are binding on all mankind, even on Cabinet Ministers. Lord Fancourt prepared to obey instantly.

"I do not like to leave your ladyship alone," he said.

"Never fear. I shall be quite safe here—and, I think, undisturbed . . . but I am really tired. You know Sir Percy will drive back to Richmond. It is a long way, and we shall not—an we do not hurry—get home before daybreak."

Lord Fancourt had perforce to go.

The moment he had disappeared, Chauvelin slipped

into the room, and the next instant stood calm and impassive by her side.

"You have news for me?" he said.

An icy mantle seemed to have suddenly settled round Marguerite's shoulders; though her cheeks glowed with fire, she felt chilled and numbed. Oh, Armand! will you ever know the terrible sacrifice of pride, of dignity, of womanliness a devoted sister is making for your sake?

"Nothing of importance," she said, staring mechanically before her, "but it might prove a clue. I contrived—no matter how—to detect Sir Andrew Ffoulkes in the very act of burning a paper at one of these candles, in this very room. That paper I succeeded in holding between my fingers for the space of two minutes, and to cast my eye on it for that of ten seconds."

"Time enough to learn its contents?" asked Chauvelin, quietly.

She nodded. Then she continued in the same even, mechanical tone of voice—

"In the corner of the paper there was the usual rough device of a small star-shaped flower. Above it I read two lines, everything else was scorched and blackened by the flame."

"And what were these two lines?"

Her throat seemed suddenly to have contracted. For an instant she felt that she could not speak the words, which might send a brave man to his death.

"It is lucky that the whole paper was not burned," added Chauvelin, with dry sarcasm, "for it might have fared ill with Armand St. Just. What were the two lines, citoyenne?"

"One was, 'I start myself to-morrow,' " she said qui-

etly; "the other—'If you wish to speak to me, I shall be
in the supper-room at one o'clock precisely.' "

Chauvelin looked up at the clock just above the man-
tel-piece.

"Then I have plenty of time," he said placidly.

"What are you going to do?" she asked.

She was pale as a statue, her hands were icy cold, her
head and heart throbbed with the awful strain upon her
nerves. Oh, this was cruel! cruel! What had she done to
have deserved all this? Her choice was made: had she
done a vile action or one that was sublime? The recording angel, who writes in the book of gold, alone could
give an answer.

"What are you going to do?" she repeated mechanically.

"Oh, nothing for the present. After that it will
depend."

"On what?"

"On whom I shall see in the supper-room at one
o'clock precisely."

"You will see the Scarlet Pimpernel, of course. But
you do not know him."

"No. But I shall presently."

"Sir Andrew will have warned him."

"I think not. When you parted from him after the
minuet he stood and watched you, for a moment or
two, with a look which gave me to understand that
something had happened between you. It was only natural, was it not? that I should make a shrewd guess as
to the nature of that 'something.' I thereupon engaged
the young gallant in a long and animated conversation—we discussed Herr Glück's singular success in
London—until a lady claimed his arm for supper."

"Since then?"

"I did not lose sight of him through supper. When we all came upstairs again, Lady Portarles buttonholed him and started on the subject of pretty Mlle. Suzanne de Tournay. I knew he would not move until Lady Portarles had exhausted the subject, which will not be for another quarter of an hour at least, and it is five minutes to one now."

He was preparing to go, and went up to the doorway, where, drawing aside the curtain, he stood for a moment pointing out to Marguerite the distant figure of Sir Andrew Ffoulkes in close conversation with Lady Portarles.

"I think," he said, with a triumphant smile, "that I may safely expect to find the person I seek in the dining-room, fair lady."

"There may be more than one."

"Whoever is there, as the clock strikes one, will be shadowed by one of my men; of these, one, or perhaps two, or even three, will leave for France to-morrow. *One* of these will be the 'Scarlet Pimpernel.' "

"Yes?—And?"

"I also, fair lady, will leave for France to-morrow. The papers found at Dover upon the person of Sir Andrew Ffoulkes speak of the neighborhood of Calais, of an inn which I know well, called 'Le Chat Gris,' of a lonely place somewhere on the coast—the Père Blanchard's hut—which I must endeavour to find. All these places are given as the point where this meddlesome Englishman has bidden the traitor de Tournay and others to meet his emissaries. But it seems that he has decided not to send his emissaries, that 'he will start himself to-morrow.' Now, one of those persons whom

I shall see anon in the supper-room, will be journeying to Calais, and I shall follow that person, until I have tracked him to where those fugitive aristocrats await him; for that person, fair lady, will be the man whom I have sought for, for nearly a year, the man whose energy has outdone me, whose ingenuity has baffled me, whose audacity has set me wondering—yes! me!—who have seen a trick or two in my time—the mysterious and elusive Scarlet Pimpernel."

"And Armand?" she pleaded.

"Have I ever broken my word? I promise you that the day the Scarlet Pimpernel and I start for France, I will send you that imprudent letter of his by special courier. More than that, I will pledge you the word of France, that the day I lay hands on that meddlesome Englishman, St. Just will be here in England, safe in the arms of his charming sister."

And with a deep and elaborate bow and another look at the clock, Chauvelin glided out of the room.

It seemed to Marguerite that through all the noise, all the din of music, dancing, and laughter, she could hear his cat-like tread, gliding through the vast reception-rooms; that she could hear him go down the massive staircase, reach the dining-room and open the door. Fate *had* decided, had made her speak, had made her do a vile and abominable thing, for the sake of the brother she loved. She lay back in her chair, passive and still, seeing the figure of her relentless enemy ever present before her aching eyes.

When Chauvelin reached the supper-room it was quite deserted. It had that woebegone, forsaken, tawdry appearance, which reminds one so much of a ball-dress, the morning after.

Half-empty glasses littered the table, unfolded nap-
kins lay about, the chairs—turned towards one another
in groups of twos and threes—seemed like the seats of
ghosts, in close conversation with one another. There
were sets of two chairs—very close to one another—in
the far corners of the room, which spoke of recent whispered flirtations, over cold game-pie and champagne;
there were sets of three and four chairs, that recalled
pleasant, animated discussions over the latest scandal;
there were chairs straight up in a row that still looked
starchy, critical, acid, like antiquated dowagers; there
were a few isolated, single chairs, close to the table, that
spoke of gourmands intent on the most *recherché* dishes,
and others overturned on the floor, that spoke volumes
on the subject of my Lord Grenville's cellars.

It was a ghostlike replica, in fact, of that fashionable
gathering upstairs; a ghost that haunts every house
where balls and good suppers are given; a picture
drawn with white chalk on grey cardboard, dull and
colourless, now that the bright silk dresses and gor-
geously embroidered coats were no longer there to fill
in the foreground, and now that the candles flickered
sleepily in their sockets.

Chauvelin smiled benignly, and rubbing his long,
thin hands together, he looked round the deserted supper-room, whence even the last flunkey had retired in
order to join his friends in the hall below. All was silence in the dimly-lighted room, whilst the sound of the
gavotte, the hum of distant talk and laughter, and the
rumble of an occasional coach outside, only seemed to
reach this palace of the Sleeping Beauty as the murmur
of some flitting spooks far away.

It all looked so peaceful, so luxurious, and so still,

that the keenest observer—a veritable prophet—could never have guessed that, at this present moment, that deserted supper-room was nothing but a trap laid for the capture of the most cunning and audacious plotter those stirring times had ever seen.

Chauvelin pondered and tried to peer into the immediate future. What would this man be like, whom he and the leaders of a whole revolution had sworn to bring to his death? Everything about him was weird and mysterious; his personality, which he had so cunningly concealed, the power he wielded over nineteen English gentlemen who seemed to obey his every command blindly and enthusiastically, the passionate love and submission he had roused in his little trained band, and, above all, his marvellous audacity, the boundless impudence which had caused him to beard his most implacable enemies, within the very walls of Paris.

No wonder that in France the *sobriquet* of the mysterious Englishman roused in the people a superstitious shudder. Chauvelin himself as he gazed round the deserted room, where presently the weird hero would appear, felt a strange feeling of awe creeping all down his spine.

But his plans were well laid. He felt sure that the Scarlet Pimpernel had not been warned, and felt equally sure that Marguerite Blakeney had not played him false. If she had . . . a cruel look, that would have made her shudder, gleamed in Chauvelin's keen, pale eyes. If she had played him a trick, Armand St. Just would suffer the extreme penalty.

But no, no! of course she had not played him false!

Fortunately the supper-room was deserted: this would make Chauvelin's task all the easier, when presently that unsuspecting enigma would enter it alone. No one was here now save Chauvelin himself.

Stay! as he surveyed with a satisfied smile the solitude of the room, the cunning agent of the French Government became aware of the peaceful, monotonous breathing of some one of my Lord Grenville's guests, who, no doubt, had supped both wisely and well, and was enjoying a quiet sleep, away from the din of the dancing above.

Chauvelin looked round once more, and there in the corner of a sofa, in the dark angle of the room, his mouth open, his eyes shut, the sweet sounds of peaceful slumbers proceeding from his nostrils, reclined the gorgeously-apparelled, long-limbed husband of the cleverest woman in Europe.

Chauvelin looked at him as he lay there, placid, unconscious, at peace with all the world and himself, after the best of suppers, and a smile, that was almost one of pity, softened for a moment the hard lines of the Frenchman's face and the sarcastic twinkle of his pale eyes.

Evidently the slumberer, deep in dreamless sleep, would not interfere with Chauvelin's trap for catching that cunning Scarlet Pimpernel. Again he rubbed his hands together, and, following the example of Sir Percy Blakeney, he too, stretched himself out in the corner of another sofa, shut his eyes, opened his mouth, gave forth sounds of peaceful breathing, and . . . waited!

15

Doubt

Marguerite Blakeney had watched the slight sable-clad figure of Chauvelin, as he worked his way through the ball-room. Then perforce she had had to wait, while her nerves tingled with excitement.

Listlessly she sat in the small, still deserted boudoir, looking out through the curtained doorway on the dancing couples beyond: looking at them, yet seeing nothing, hearing the music, yet conscious of naught save a feeling of expectancy, of anxious, weary waiting.

Her mind conjured up before her the vision of what was, perhaps at this very moment, passing downstairs. The half-deserted dining-room, the fateful hour— Chauvelin on the watch!—then, precise to the moment, the entrance of a man, he, the Scarlet Pimpernel, the mysterious leader, who to Marguerite had become almost unreal, so strange, so weird was this hidden identity.

She wished she were in the supper-room, too, at this moment, watching him as he entered; she knew that her woman's penetration would at once recognise in the stranger's face—whoever he might be—that strong individuality which belongs to a leader of men—to a hero: to the mighty, high-soaring eagle, whose daring wings were becoming entangled in the ferret's trap.

Woman-like, she thought of him with unmixed sadness; the irony of that fate seemed so cruel which allowed the fearless lion to succumb to the gnawing of a rat! Ah! had Armand's life not been at stake! . . .

"Faith! your ladyship must have thought me very re-miss," said a voice suddenly, close to her elbow. "I had a deal of difficulty in delivering your message, for I could not find Blakeney anywhere at first . . ."

Marguerite had forgotten all about her husband and her message to him; his very name, as spoken by Lord Fancourt, sounded strange and unfamiliar to her, so completely had she in the last five minutes lived her old life in the Rue de Richelieu again, with Armand always near her to love and protect her, to guard her from the many subtle intrigues which were forever raging in Paris in those days.

"I did find him at last," continued Lord Fancourt, "and gave him your message. He said that he would give orders at once for the horses to be put to."

"Ah!" she said, still very absently, "you found my husband, and gave him my message?"

"Yes; he was in the dining-room fast asleep. I could not manage to wake him up at first."

"Thank you very much," she said mechanically, trying to collect her thoughts.

"Will your ladyship honour me with the *contredanse* until your coach is ready?" asked Lord Fancourt.

"No, I thank you, my lord, but—and you will forgive me—I really am too tired, and the heat in the ball-room has become oppressive."

"The conservatory is deliciously cool; let me take you there, and then get you something. You seem ailing, Lady Blakeney."

"I am only very tired," she repeated wearily, as she allowed Lord Fancourt to lead her, where subdued lights and green plants lent coolness to the air. He got her a chair, into which she sank. This long interval of waiting was intolerable. Why did not Chauvelin come and tell her the result of his watch?

Lord Fancourt was very attentive. She scarcely heard what he said, and suddenly startled him by asking abruptly,—

"Lord Fancourt, did you perceive who was in the dining-room just now besides Sir Percy Blakeney?"

"Only the agent of the French Government, M. Chauvelin, equally fast asleep in another corner," he said. "Why does your ladyship ask?"

"I know not . . . I . . . Did you notice the time when you were there?"

"It must have been about five or ten minutes past one. . . . I wonder what your ladyship is thinking about," he added, for evidently the fair lady's thoughts were very far away, and she had not been listening to his intellectual conversation.

But indeed her thoughts were not very far away: only one storey below, in this same house, in the dining-room where sat Chauvelin still on the watch. Had he failed? For one instant that possibility rose before her as a hope—the hope that the Scarlet Pimpernel had been warned by Sir Andrew, and that Chauvelin's trap had failed to catch his bird; but that hope soon gave way to fear. Had he failed? But then—Armand!

Lord Fancourt had given up talking since he found that he had no listener. He wanted an opportunity for slipping away; for sitting opposite to a lady, however fair, who is evidently not heeding the most vigorous efforts made for her entertainment, is not exhilarating, even to a Cabinet Minister.

"Shall I find out if your ladyship's coach is ready," he said at last, tentatively.

"Oh, thank you . . . thank you . . . if you would be so kind . . . I fear I am but sorry company . . . but I am really tired . . . and, perhaps, would be best alone."

She had been longing to be rid of him, for she hoped that, like the fox he so resembled, Chauvelin would be prowling round, thinking to find her alone.

But Lord Fancourt went, and still Chauvelin did not come. Oh! what had happened? She felt Armand's fate trembling in the balance . . . she feared—now with a deadly fear—that Chauvelin *had* failed, and that the mysterious Scarlet Pimpernel had proved elusive once more; then she knew that she need hope for no pity, no mercy, from him.

He had pronounced his "Either—or—" and nothing less would content him: he was very spiteful, and would affect the belief that she had wilfully misled him, and having failed to trap the eagle once again, his revengeful mind would be content with the humble prey—Armand!

Yet she had done her best; had strained every nerve for Armand's sake. She could not bear to think that all had failed. She could not sit still; she wanted to go and hear the worst at once; she wondered even that Chauvelin had not come yet, to vent his wrath and satire upon her.

Lord Grenville himself came presently to tell her that her coach was ready, and that Sir Percy was already waiting for her—ribbons in hand. Marguerite said "Farewell" to her distinguished host; many of her friends stopped her, as she crossed the rooms, to talk to her, and exchange pleasant *au revoirs*.

The Minister only took final leave of beautiful Lady Blakeney on the top of the stairs; below, on the landing, a veritable army of gallant gentlemen were waiting to bid "Good-bye" to the queen of beauty and fashion, whilst outside, under the massive portico, Sir Percy's magnificent bays were impatiently pawing the ground.

At the top of the stairs, just after she had taken final leave of her host, she suddenly saw Chauvelin; he was coming up the stairs slowly, and rubbing his thin hands very softly together.

There was a curious look on his mobile face, partly amused and wholly puzzled, and as his keen eyes met Marguerite's they became strangely sarcastic.

"M. Chauvelin," she said, as he stopped on the top of the stairs, bowing elaborately before her, "my coach is outside; may I claim your arm?"

As gallant as ever, he offered her his arm and led her downstairs. The crowd was very great, some of the Minister's guests were departing, others were leaning against the banisters watching the throng as it filed up and down the wide staircase.

"Chauvelin," she said at last desperately, "I must know what has happened."

"What has happened, dear lady?" he said, with affected surprise. "Where? When?"

"You are torturing me, Chauvelin. I have helped you to-night . . . surely I have the right to know. What happened in the dining-room at one o'clock just now?"

She spoke in a whisper, trusting that in the general hubbub of the crowd her words would remain unheeded by all, save the man at her side.

"Quiet and peace reigned supreme, fair lady; at that hour I was asleep in the corner of one sofa and Sir Percy Blakeney in another."

"Nobody came into the room at all?"

"Nobody."

"Then we have failed, you and I? . . ."

"Yes! we have failed—perhaps . . ."

"But Armand?" she pleaded.

"Ah! Armand St. Just's chances hang on a thread . . . pray heaven, dear lady, that that thread may not snap."

"Chauvelin, I worked for you, sincerely, earnestly . . . remember. . . ."

"I remember my promise," he said quietly. "The day that the Scarlet Pimpernel and I meet on French soil, St. Just will be in the arms of his charming sister."

"Which means that a brave man's blood will be on my hands," she said, with a shudder.

"His blood, or that of your brother. Surely at the present moment you must hope, as I do, that the enigmatical Scarlet Pimpernel will start for Calais to-day—"

"I am only conscious of one hope, citoyen."

"And that is?"

"That Satan, your master, will have need of you elsewhere, before the sun rises to-day."

"You flatter me, citoyenne."

She had detained him for a while, mid-way down the stairs, trying to get at the thoughts which lay beyond that thin, fox-like mask. But Chauvelin remained urbane, sarcastic, mysterious; not a line betrayed to the poor, anxious woman whether she need fear or whether she dared to hope.

Downstairs on the landing she was soon surrounded. Lady Blakeney never stepped from any house into her coach, without an escort of fluttering human moths around the dazzling light of her beauty. But before she finally turned away from Chauvelin, she held out a tiny hand to him, with that pretty gesture of childish appeal which was so essentially her own.

"Give me some hope, my little Chauvelin," she pleaded.

With perfect gallantry he bowed over that tiny hand, which looked so dainty and white through the delicately transparent black lace mitten, and kissing the tips of the rosy fingers:—

"Pray heaven that the thread may not snap," he repeated, with his enigmatic smile.

And stepping aside, he allowed the moths to flutter more closely round the candle, and the brilliant throng of the *jeunesse dorée,* eagerly attentive to Lady Blakeney's every movement, hid the keen, fox-like face from her view.

16

RICHMOND

A few minutes later she was sitting, wrapped in cozy furs, near Sir Percy Blakeney on the box-seat of his magnificent coach, and the four splendid bays had thundered down the quiet steet.

The night was warm in spite of the gentle breeze which fanned Marguerite's burning cheeks. Soon London houses were left behind, and rattling over old Hammersmith Bridge, Sir Percy was driving his bays rapidly towards Richmond.

The river wound in and out in its pretty delicate curves, looking like a silver serpent beneath the glittering rays of the moon. Long shadows from overhanging trees spread occasional deep palls right across the road. The bays were rushing along at breakneck speed, held but slightly back by Sir Percy's strong, unerring hands.

These nightly drives after balls and suppers in London were a source of perpetual delight to Marguerite, and she appreciated her husband's eccentricity keenly, which caused him to adopt this mode of taking her home every night, to their beautiful home by the river, instead of living in a stuffy London house. He loved driving his spirited horses along the lonely, moonlit roads, and she loved to sit on the box-seat, with the soft air of an English late summer's night fanning her face after the hot atmosphere of a ball or supper-party. The drive was not a long one—less than an hour, some-

times, when the bays were very fresh, and Sir Percy
gave them full rein.

To-night he seemed to have a very devil in his fingers, and the coach seemed to fly along the road, beside
the river. As usual, he did not speak to her, but stared
straight in front of him, the ribbons seeming to lie quite
loosely in his slender, white hands. Marguerite looked
at him tentatively once or twice; she could see his handsome profile, and one lazy eye, with its straight fine
brow and drooping heavy lid.

The face in the moonlight looked singularly earnest,
and recalled to Marguerite's aching heart those happy
days of courtship, before he had become the lazy nincompoop, the effete fop, whose life seemed spent in
card and supper rooms.

But now, in the moonlight, she could not catch the
expression of the lazy blue eyes; she could only see the
outline of the firm chin, the corner of the strong
mouth, the well-cut massive shape of the forehead;
truly, nature had meant well by Sir Percy; his faults
must all be laid at the door of that poor, half-crazy
mother, and of the distracted heart-broken father, neither of whom had cared for the young life which was
sprouting up between them, and which, perhaps, their
very carelessness was already beginning to wreck.

Marguerite suddenly felt intense sympathy for her
husband. The moral crisis she had just gone through
made her feel indulgent towards the faults, the delin-
quencies, of others.

How thoroughly a human being can be buffeted and
overmastered by Fate, had been borne in upon her with
appalling force. Had anyone told her a week ago that
she would stoop to spy upon her friends, that she

would betray a brave and unsuspecting man into the hands of a relentless enemy, she would have laughed the idea to scorn.

Yet she had done these things; anon, perhaps the death of that brave man would be at her door, just as two years ago the Marquis de St. Cyr had perished through a thoughtless words of hers; but in that case she was morally innocent—she had meant no serious harm—fate merely had stepped in. But this time she had done a thing that obviously was base, had done it deliberately, for a motive which, perhaps, high moralists would not even appreciate.

And as she felt her husband's strong arm beside her, she also felt how much more he would dislike and despise her, if he knew of this night's work. Thus human beings judge of one another, superficially, casually, throwing contempt on one another, with but little reason, and no charity. She despised her husband for his inanities and vulgar, unintellectual occupations; and he, she felt, would despise her still worse, because she had not been strong enough to do right for right's sake, and to sacrifice her brother to the dictates of her conscience.

Buried in her thoughts, Marguerite had found this hour in the breezy summer night all too brief; and it was with a feeling of keen disappointment, that she suddenly realised that the bays had turned into the massive gates of her beautiful English home.

Sir Percy Blakeney's house on the river had become a historic one: palatial in its dimensions, it stands in the midst of exquisitely laid-out gardens, with a picturesque terrace and frontage to the river. Built in Tudor days, the old red brick of the walls looks eminently picturesque in the midst of a bower of green, the beautiful lawn, with its old sun-dial, adding the true note of harmony to its foreground. Great secular trees lent cool shadows to the grounds, and now, on this warm early autumn night, the leaves slightly turned to russets and gold, the old garden looked singularly poetic and peaceful in the moonlight.

With unerring precision, Sir Percy had brought the four bays to a standstill immediately in front of the fine Elizabethan entrance hall; in spite of the lateness of the hour, an army of grooms seemed to have emerged from the very ground, as the coach had thundered up, and were standing respectfully round.

Sir Percy jumped down quickly, then helped Marguerite to alight. She lingered outside a moment, whilst he gave a few orders to one of his men. She skirted the house, and stepped on to the lawn, looking out dreamily into the silvery landscape. Nature seemed exquisitely at peace, in comparison with the tumultuous emotions she had gone through: she could faintly hear the ripple of the river and the occasional soft and ghost-like fall of a dead leaf from a tree.

All else was quiet round her. She had heard the horses prancing as they were being led away to their distant stables, the hurrying of servant's feet as they had all gone within to rest: the house also was quite still. In two separate suites of apartments, just above the magnificent reception-rooms, lights were still burning, they were her rooms, and his, well divided from each other by the whole width of the house, as far apart as their own lives had become. Involuntarily she sighed—at that moment she could really not have told why.

She was suffering from unconquerable heartache. Deeply and achingly she was sorry for herself. Never had she felt so pitiably lonely, so bitterly in want of comfort and of sympathy. With another sigh she turned away from the river towards the house, vaguely wondering if, after such a night, she could ever find rest and sleep.

Suddenly, before she reached the terrace, she heard a firm step upon the crisp gravel, and the next moment her husband's figure emerged out of the shadow. He too, had skirted the house, and was wandering along the lawn, towards the river. He still wore his heavy driving coat with the numerous lapels and collars he himself had set in fashion, but he had thrown it well back, burying his hands as was his wont, in the deep pockets of his satin breeches: the gorgeous white costume he had worn at Lord Grenville's ball, with its jabot of priceless lace, looked strangely ghostly against the dark background of the house.

He apparently did not notice her, for, after a few moments pause, he presently turned back towards the house, and walked straight up to the terrace.

"Sir Percy!"

He already had one foot on the lowest of the terrace steps, but at her voice he started, and paused, then looked searchingly into the shadows whence she had called to him.

She came forward quickly into the moonlight, and, as soon as he saw her, he said, with that air of consummate gallantry he always wore when speaking to her,—

"At your service, Madame!"

But his foot was still on the step, and in his whole attitude there was a remote suggestion, distinctly visible to her, that he wished to go, and had no desire for a midnight interview.

"The air is deliciously cool," she said, "the moonlight peaceful and poetic, and the garden inviting. Will you not stay in it awhile; the hour is not yet late, or is my company so distasteful to you, that you are in a hurry to rid yourself of it?"

"Nay, Madame," he rejoined placidly, "but 'tis on the other foot the shoe happens to be, and I'll warrant you'll find the midnight air more poetic without my company: no doubt the sooner I remove the obstruction the better your ladyship will like it."

He turned once more to go.

"I protest you mistake me, Sir Percy," she said hurriedly, and drawing a little closer to him; "the estrangement, which, alas! has arisen between us, was none of my making, remember."

"Begad! you must pardon me there, Madame!" he protested coldly, "my memory was always of the shortest."

He looked her straight in the eyes, with that lazy nonchalance which had become second nature to him. She returned his gaze for a moment, then her eyes softened, as she came up quite close to him, to the foot of the terrace steps.

"Of the shortest, Sir Percy! Faith! how it must have altered! Was it three years ago or four that you saw me for one hour in Paris, on your way to the East? When you came back two years later you had not forgotten me."

She looked divinely pretty as she stood there in the moonlight, with the fur-cloak sliding off her beautiful shoulders, the gold embroidery on her dress shimmering around her, her childlike blue eyes turned up fully at him.

He stood for a moment, rigid and still, but for the clenching of his hand against the stone balustrade of the terrace.

"You desired my presence, Madame," he said frigidly. "I take it that it was not with a view to indulging in tender reminiscences."

His voice certainly was cold and uncompromising: his attitude before her, stiff and unbending. Womanly decorum would have suggested that Marguerite should return coldness for coldness, and should sweep past him without another word, only with a curt nod of her head: but womanly instinct suggested that she should remain—that keen instinct, which makes a beautiful woman conscious of her powers long to bring to her knees the one man who pays her no homage. She stretched out her hand to him.

"Nay, Sir Percy, why not? the present is not so glorious but that I should not wish to dwell a little in the past."

He bent his tall figure, and taking hold of the extreme tip of the fingers which she still held out to him, he kissed them ceremoniously.

"I' faith, Madame," he said, "then you will pardon me, if my dull wits cannot accompany you there."

Once again he attempted to go, once more her voice, sweet, childlike, almost tender, called him back.

"Sir Percy."

"Your servant, Madame."

"Is it possible that love can die?" she said with sudden, unreasoning vehemence. "Methought that the passion which you once felt for me would outlast the span of human life. Is there nothing left of that love, Percy . . . which might help you . . . to bridge over that sad estrangement?"

His massive figure seemed, while she spoke thus to him, to stiffen still more, the strong mouth hardened, a look of relentless obstinacy crept into the habitually lazy blue eyes.

"With what object, I pray you, Madame?" he asked coldly.

"I do not understand you."

"Yet 'tis simple enough," he said with sudden bitterness, which seemed literally to surge through his words, though he was making visible efforts to suppress it, "I humbly put the question to you, for my slow wits are unable to grasp the cause of this, your ladyship's sudden new mood. Is it that you have the taste to renew the devilish sport which you played so successfully last year? Do you wish to see me once more a love-sick suppliant at your feet, so that you might again have the pleasure of kicking me aside, like a troublesome lap-dog?"

She had succeeded in rousing him for the moment: and again she looked straight at him, for it was thus she remembered him a year ago.

"Percy! I entreat you!" she whispered, "can we not bury the past?"

"Pardon me, Madame, but I understood you to say that your desire was to dwell in it."

"Nay! I spoke not of *that* past, Percy!" she said, while a tone of tenderness crept into her voice. "Rather did I speak of the time when you loved me still! and I . . . oh! I was vain and frivolous; your wealth and position allured me: I married you, hoping in my heart that your great love for me would beget in me a love for you . . . but, alas! . . ."

The moon had sunk low down behind a bank of clouds. In the east a soft grey light was beginning to chase away the heavy mantle of the night. He could only see her graceful outline now, the small queenly head, with its wealth of reddish golden curls, and the glittering gems forming the small, star-shaped, red flower which she wore as a diadem in her hair.

"Twenty-four hours after our marriage, Madame, the Marquis de St. Cyr and all his family perished on the guillotine, and the popular rumour reached me that it was the wife of Sir Percy Blakeney who helped to send them there."

"Nay! I myself told you the truth of that odious tale."

"Not till after it had been recounted to me by strangers, with all its horrible details."

"And you believed them then and there," she said with great vehemence, "without a proof or question— you believed that I, whom you vowed you loved more than life, whom you professed you worshipped, that *I* could do a thing so base as these *strangers* chose to re-count. You thought I meant to deceive you about it all—that I ought to have spoken before I married you: yet, had you listened, I would have told you that up to the very morning on which St. Cyr went to the guillotine, I was straining every nerve, using every influence I possessed, to save him and his family. But my pride sealed my lips, when your love seemed to perish, as if under the knife of that same guillotine. Yet I would have told you how I was duped! Aye! I, whom that same popular rumour had endowed with the sharpest wits in France! I was tricked into doing this thing, by men who knew how to play upon my love for an only brother, and my desire for revenge. Was it unnatural?"

Her voice became choked with tears. She paused for a moment or two, trying to regain some sort of composure. She looked appealingly at him, almost as if he were her judge. He had allowed her to speak on in her own vehement, impassioned way, offering no comment, no word of sympathy: and now, while she paused, trying to swallow down the hot tears that gushed to her eyes, he waited, impassive and still. The dim, grey light of early dawn seemed to make his tall form look taller and more rigid. The lazy, good-natured face looked strangely altered. Marguerite, excited, as she was, could see that the eyes were no longer languid, the mouth no longer good-humoured and inane. A curious look of intense passion seemed to glow from beneath his drooping lids, the mouth was tightly closed, the lips compressed, as if the will alone held that surging passion in check.

Marguerite Blakeney was, above all, a woman, with all a woman's fascinating foibles, all a woman's most lovable sins. She knew in a moment that for the past few months she had been mistaken: that this man who stood here before her, cold as a statue, when her musical voice struck upon his ear, loved her, as he had loved her a year ago: that his passion might have been dormant, but that it was there, as strong, as intense, as overwhelming, as when first her lips met his in one long, maddening kiss.

Pride had kept him from her, and, woman-like, she meant to win back that conquest which had been hers before. Suddenly it seemed to her that the only happiness life could ever hold for her again would be in feeling that man's kiss once more upon her lips.

"Listen to the tale, Sir Percy," she said, and her voice now was low, sweet, infinitely tender. "Armand was all in all to me! We had no parents, and brought one another up. He was my little father, and I, his tiny mother; we loved one another so. Then one day—do you mind me, Sir Percy? the Marquis de St. Cyr had my brother Armand thrashed—thrashed by his lacqueys—that brother whom I loved better than all the world! And his offence? That he, a plebeian, had dared to love the daughter of the aristocrat; for that he was waylaid and thrashed . . . thrashed like a dog within an inch of his life! Oh, how I suffered! his humiliation had eaten into my very soul! When the opportunity occurred, and I was able to take my revenge, I took it. But I only thought to bring that proud marquis to trouble and humiliation. He plotted with Austria against his own country. Chance gave me knowledge of this; I spoke of it, but I did not know—how could I guess?— they trapped and duped me. When I realised what I had done, it was too late."

"It is perhaps a little difficult, Madame," said Sir Percy, after a moment of silence between them, "to go back over the past. I have confessed to you that my memory is short, but the thought certainly lingered in my mind that, at the time of the Marquis' death, I entreated you for an explanation of those same noisome popular rumours. If that same memory does not, even now, play me a trick, I fancy that you refused me *all* explanation then, and demanded of my love a humiliating allegiance it was not prepared to give."

"I wished to test your love for me, and it did not bear the test. You used to tell me that you drew the very breath of life but for me, and for love of me."

"And to probe that love, you demanded that I should forfeit mine honour," he said, whilst gradually his impassiveness seemed to leave him, his rigidity to relax; "that I should accept without murmur or question, as a dumb and submissive slave, every action of my mistress. My heart overflowing with love and passion, I *asked* for no explanation—I *waited* for one, not doubting—only hoping. Had you spoken but one word, from you I would have accepted any explanation and believed it. But you left me without a word, beyond a bald confession of the actual horrible facts; proudly you returned to your brother's house, and left me alone . . . for weeks . . . not knowing, now, in whom to believe, since the shrine, which contained my one illusion, lay shattered to earth at my feet."

She need not complain now that he was cold and impassive; his very voice shook with an intensity of passion, which he was making superhuman efforts to keep in check.

"Aye! the madness of my pride!" she said sadly. "Hardly had I gone, already I had repented. But when I returned, I found you, oh, so altered! wearing already that mask of somnolent indifference which you have never laid aside until . . . until now."

She was so close to him that her soft, loose hair was wafted against his cheek; her eyes, glowing with tears, maddened him, the music in her voice sent fire through his veins. But he would not yield to the magic charm of this woman whom he had so deeply loved, and at whose hands his pride had suffered so bitterly. He closed his eyes to shut out the dainty vision of that sweet face, of that snow-white neck and graceful figure, round which the faint rosy light of dawn was just beginning to hover playfully.

"Nay, Madame, it is not mask," he said icily; "I swore to you . . . once, that my life was yours. For months now it has been your plaything . . . it has served its purpose."

But now she knew that that very coldness was a mask. The trouble, the sorrow she had gone through last night, suddenly came back to her mind, but no longer with bitterness, rather with a feeling that this man who loved her, would help her to bear the burden.

"Sir Percy," she said impulsively, "Heaven knows you have been at pains to make the task, which I had set to myself, terribly difficult to accomplish. You spoke of my mood just now; well! we will call it that, if you will. I wished to speak to you . . . because . . . because I was in trouble . . . and had need . . . of your sympathy."

"It is yours to command, Madame."

"How cold you are!" she sighed. "Faith! I can scarce believe that but a few months ago one tear in my eye had set you well-nigh crazy. Now I come to you . . . with a half-broken heart . . . and . . . and . . ."

"I pray you, Madame," he said, whilst his voice shook almost as much as hers, "in what way can I serve you?"

"Percy!—Armand is in deadly danger. A letter of his . . . rash, impetuous, as were all his actions, and written to Sir Andrew Ffoulkes, has fallen into the hands of a fanatic. Armand is hopelessly compromised . . . to-morrow, perhaps he will be arrested . . . after that the guillotine . . . unless . . . unless . . . oh! it is horrible!" . . . she said, with a sudden wail of anguish, as all the events of the past night came rushing back to her mind, "horrible! . . . and you do not understand . . . you cannot . . . and I have no one to whom I can turn . . . for help . . . or even for sympathy. . . ."

Tears now refused to be held back. All her trouble, her struggles, the awful uncertainty of Armand's fate overwhelmed her. She tottered, ready to fall, and leaning against the stone balustrade, she buried her face in her hands and sobbed bitterly.

At first mention of Armand St. Just's name and of the peril in which he stood, Sir Percy's face had become a shade more pale; and the look of determination and obstinacy appeared more marked than ever between his eyes. However, he said nothing for the moment, but watched her, as her delicate frame was shaken with sobs, watched her until unconsciously his face softened, and what looked almost like tears seemed to glisten in his eyes.

"And so," he said with bitter sarcasm, "the murderous dog of the revolution is turning upon the very hands that fed it? . . . Begad, Madame," he added very gently, as Marguerite continued to sob hysterically, "will you dry your tears? . . . I never could bear to see a pretty woman cry, and I . . ."

Instinctively, with sudden overmastering passion at sight of her helplessness and of her grief, he stretched out his arms, and the next, would have seized her and held her to him, protected from every evil with his very life, his very heart's blood. . . . But pride had the better of it in this struggle once again; he restrained himself with a tremendous effort of will, and said coldly, though still very gently,—

"Will you not turn to me, Madame, and tell me in what way I may have the honour to serve you?"

She made a violent effort to control herself, and turning her tear-stained face to him, she once more held out her hand, which he kissed with the same punctillious gallantry; but Marguerite's fingers, this time, lingered in his hand for a second or two longer than was absolutely necessary, and this was because she had felt that his hand trembled perceptibly and was burning hot, whilst his lips felt as cold as marble.

"Can you do aught for Armand?" she said sweetly and simply. "You have so much influence at court . . . so many friends . . ."

"Nay, Madame, should you not rather seek the influence of your French friend, M. Chauvelin? His extends, if I mistake not, even as far as the Republican Government of France."

"I cannot ask him, Percy. . . . Oh! I wish I dared to tell you . . . but . . . but . . . he has put a price on my brother's head, which . . ."

She would have given worlds if she had felt the courage then to tell him everything . . . all she had done that night—how she had suffered and how her hand had been forced. But she dared not give way to that impulse . . . not now, when she was just beginning to feel that he still loved her, when she hoped that she could win him back. She dared not make another confession to him. After all, he might not understand; he might not sympathise with her struggles and temptation. His love still dormant might sleep the sleep of death.

Perhaps he divined what was passing in her mind. His whole attitude was one of intense longing—a veritable prayer for that confidence, which her foolish pride withheld from him. When she remained silent he sighed, and said with marked coldness—

"Faith, Madame, since it distresses you, we will not speak of it. . . . As for Armand, I pray you have no fear. I pledge you my word that he shall be safe. Now, have I your permission to go? The hour is getting late, and . . ."

"You will at least accept my gratitude?" she said, as she drew quite close to him, and speaking with real tenderness.

With a quick, almost involuntary effort he would have taken her then in his arms, for her eyes were swimming in tears, which he longed to kiss away; but she had lured him once, just like this, then cast him aside like an ill-fitting glove. He thought this was but a mood, a caprice, and he was too proud to lend himself to it once again.

"It is too soon, Madame!" he said quietly; "I have done nothing as yet. The hour is late, and you must be fatigued. Your women will be waiting for you upstairs."

He stood aside to allow her to pass. She sighed, a quick sigh of disappointment. His pride and her beauty had been in direct conflict, and his pride had remained the conqueror. Perhaps, after all, she had been deceived just now; what she took to be the light of love in his eyes might only have been the passion of pride or, who knows, of hatred instead of love. She stood looking at him for a moment or two longer. He was again as rigid, as impassive, as before. Pride had conquered, and he cared naught for her. The grey of dawn was gradually yielding to the rosy light of the rising sun. Birds began to twitter; Nature awakened, smiling in happy response to the warmth of this glorious October morning. Only between these two hearts there lay a strong, impassable barrier, built up of pride on both sides, which neither of them cared to be the first to demolish.

He had bent his tall figure in a low ceremonious bow, as she finally, with another bitter little sigh, began to mount the terrace steps.

The long train of her gold-embroidered gown swept the dead leaves off the steps, making a faint harmonious sh—sh—sh as she glided up, with one hand resting on the balustrade, the rosy light of dawn making an aureole of gold round her hair, and causing the rubies on her head and arms to sparkle. She reached the tall glass doors which led into the house. Before entering, she paused once again to look at him, hoping against hope to see his arms stretched out to her, and to hear his voice calling her back. But he had not moved; his massive figure looked the very personification of unbending pride, of fierce obstinacy.

Hot tears again surged to her eyes, and as she would not let him see them, she turned quickly within, and ran as fast as she could up to her own rooms.

Had she but turned back then, and looked out once more on to the rose-lit garden, she would have seen that which would have made her own sufferings seem but light and easy to bear—a strong man, overwhelmed with his own passion and his own despair. Pride had given way at last, obstinacy was gone: the will was powerless. He was but a man madly, blindly, passionately in love, and as soon as her light footsteps had died away within the house, he knelt down upon the terrace steps, and in the very madness of his love he kissed one by one the places where her small foot had trodden, and the stone balustrade there, where her tiny hand had rested last.

17

Farewell

When Marguerite reached her room, she found her maid terribly anxious about her.

"Your ladyship will be so tired," said the poor woman, whose own eyes were half closed with sleep. "It is past five o'clock."

"Ah, yes, Louise, I daresay I shall be tired presently," said Marguerite, kindly; "but you are very tired now, so go to bed at once. I'll get into bed alone."

"But, my lady . . ."

"Now, don't argue, Louise, but go to bed. Give me a wrap, and leave me alone."

Louise was only too glad to obey. She took off her mistress's gorgeous ball-dress, and wrapped her up in a soft billowy gown.

"Does your ladyship wish for anything else?" she asked, when that was done.

"No, nothing more. Put out the lights as you go out."

"Yes, my lady. Good-night, my lady."

"Good-night, Louise."

When the maid was gone, Marguerite drew aside the curtains and threw open the windows. The garden and the river beyond were flooded with rosy light. Far away to the east, the rays of the rising sun had changed the rose into vivid gold. The lawn was deserted now, and Marguerite looked down upon the terrace where she had stood a few moments ago trying vainly to win back a man's love, which once had been so wholly hers.

It was strange that through all her troubles, all her anxiety for Armand, she was mostly conscious at the present moment of a keen and bitter heartache.

Her very limbs seemed to ache with longing for the love of a man who had spurned her, who had resisted her tenderness, remained cold to her appeals, and had not responded to the glow of passion, which had caused her to feel and hope that those happy olden days in Paris were not all dead and forgotten.

How strange it all was! She loved him still. And now that she looked back upon the last few months of misunderstandings and of loneliness, she realised that she had never ceased to love him; that deep down in her heart she had always vaguely felt that his foolish inanities, his empty laugh, his lazy nonchalance were nothing but a mask; that the real man, strong, passionate, wilful, was there still—the man she had loved, whose intensity had fascinated her, whose personality attracted her, since she always felt that behind his apparently slow wits there was a certain something, which he kept hidden from all the world, and most especially from her.

A woman's heart is such a complex problem—the owner thereof is often most incompetent to find the solution of this puzzle.

Did Marguerite Blakeney, "the cleverest woman in Europe," really love a fool? Was it love that she had felt for him a year ago when she married him? Was it love she felt for him now that she realised that he still loved her, but that he would not become her slave, her passionate, ardent lover once again? Nay! Marguerite herself could not have told that. Not at this moment at any rate; perhaps her pride had sealed her mind against a better understanding of her own heart. But this she did know—that she meant to capture that obstinate heart back again. That she would conquer once more . . . and then, that she would never lose him. . . . She would keep him, keep his love, deserve it, and cherish it; for this much was certain, that there was no longer any happiness possible for her without that one man's love.

Thus the most contradictory thoughts and emotions rushed madly through her mind. Absorbed in them, she had allowed time to slip by; perhaps, tired out with long excitement, she had actually closed her eyes and sunk into a troubled sleep, wherein quickly fleeting dreams seemed but the continuation of her anxious thoughts—when suddenly she was roused, from dream or meditation, by the noise of footsteps outside her door.

Nervously she jumped up and listened; the house itself was as still as ever; the footsteps had retreated. Through her wide-open window the brilliant rays of the morning sun were flooding her room with light. She looked up at the clock; it was half-past six—too early for any of the household to be already astir.

She certainly must have dropped asleep, quite unconsciously. The noise of the footsteps, also of hushed subdued voices had awakened her—what could they be?

Gently, on tip-toe, she crossed the room and opened the door to listen; not a sound—that peculiar stillness of the early morning when sleep with all mankind is at its heaviest. But the noise had made her nervous, and when, suddenly, at her feet, on the very doorstep, she saw something white lying there—a letter evidently—she hardly dared touch it. It seemed so ghostlike. It certainly was not there when she came upstairs; had

Louise dropped it? or was some tantalising spook at play, showing her fairy letters where none existed?

At last she stooped to pick it up, and, amazed, puzzled beyond measure, she saw that the letter was addressed to herself in her husband's large, businesslike-looking hand. What could he have to say to her, in the middle of the night, which could not be put off until the morning?

She tore open the envelope and read:—

"A most unforeseen circumstance forces me to leave for the North immediately, so I beg your ladyship's pardon if I do not avail myself of the honour of bidding you good-bye. My business may keep me employed for about a week, so I shall not have the privilege of being present at your ladyship's water-party on Wednesday. I remain your ladyship's most humble and most obedient servant,

Percy Blakeney."

Marguerite must suddenly have been imbued with her husband's slowness of intellect, for she had perforce to read the few simple lines over and over again, before she could fully grasp their meaning.

She stood on the landing, turning over and over in her hand this curt and mysterious epistle, her mind a blank, her nerves strained with agitation and a presentiment she could not very well have explained.

Sir Percy owned considerable property in the North, certainly, and he had often before gone there alone and stayed away a week at a time; but it seemed so very strange that circumstances should have arisen between five and six o'clock in the morning that compelled him to start in this extreme hurry.

Vainly she tried to shake off an unaccustomed feeling of nervousness: she was trembling from head to foot. A wild, unconquerable desire seized her to see her husband again, at once, if only he had not already started.

Forgetting the fact that she was only very lightly clad in a morning wrap, and that her hair lay loosely about her shoulders, she flew down the stairs, right through the hall towards the front door.

It was as usual barred and bolted, for the indoor servants were not yet up; but her keen ears had detected the sound of voices and the pawing of a horse's hoof against the flag-stones.

With nervous, trembling fingers Marguerite undid the bolts one by one, bruising her hands, hurting her nails, for the locks were heavy and stiff. But she did not care; her whole frame shook with anxiety at the very thought that she might be too late; that he might have gone without her seeing him and bidding him "God-speed!"

At last, she had turned the key and thrown open the door. Her ears had not deceived her. A groom was standing close by holding a couple of horses; one of these was Sultan, Sir Percy's favourite and swiftest horse, saddled ready for a journey.

The next moment Sir Percy himself appeared round the further corner of the house and came quickly towards the horses. He had changed his gorgeous ball costume, but was as usual irreproachably and richly apparelled in a suit of fine cloth, with lace jabot and ruffles, high top-boots, and riding breeches.

Marguerite went forward a few steps. He looked up and saw her. A slight frown appeared between his eyes.

"You are going?" she said quickly and feverishly. "Whither?"

"As I have had the honour of informing your lady-ship, urgent, most unexpected business calls me to the North this morning," he said, in his usual cold, drawly manner.

"But . . . your guests to-morrow . . ."

"I have prayed your ladyship to offer my humble ex-cuses to His Royal Highness. You are such a perfect hostess, I do not think that I shall be missed."

"But surely you might have waited for your jour-ney . . . until after our water-party . . ." she said, still speaking quickly and nervously. "Surely the business is not so urgent . . . and you said nothing about it—just now."

"My business, as I had the honour to tell you, Madame, is as unexpected as it is urgent. . . . May I therefore crave your permission to go. . . . Can I do aught for you in town? . . . on my way back?"

"No . . . no . . . thanks . . . nothing . . . But you will be back soon?"

"Very soon."

"Before the end of the week?"

"I cannot say."

He was evidently trying to get away, whilst she was straining every nerve to keep him back for a moment or two.

"Percy," she said, "will you not tell me why you go to-day? Surely I, as your wife, have the right to know. You have *not* been called away to the North. I know it. There were no letters, no couriers from there before we left for the opera last night, and nothing was waiting for you when we returned from the ball. . . . You are *not* going to the North, I feel convinced. . . . There is some mystery . . . and . . ."

"Nay, there is no mystery, Madame," he replied, with a slight tone of impatience. "My business has to do with Armand . . . there! Now, have I your leave to depart?"

"With Armand? . . . But you will run no danger?"

"Danger? I? . . . Nay, Madame, your solicitude does me honour. As you say, I have some influence; my intention is to exert it before it be too late."

"Will you allow me to thank you at least?"

"Nay, Madame," he said coldly, "there is no need for that. My life is at your service, and I am already more than repaid."

"And mine will be at yours, Sir Percy, if you will but accept it, in exchange for what you do for Armand," she said, as, impulsively, she stretched out both her hands to him. "There! I will not detain you . . . my thoughts go with you . . . Farewell! . . ."

How lovely she looked in this morning sunlight, with her ardent hair streaming around her shoulders. He bowed very low and kissed her hand; she felt the burning kiss and her heart thrilled with joy and hope.

"You will come back?" she said tenderly.

"Very soon!" he replied, looking longingly into her blue eyes.

"And . . . you will remember? . . ." she asked as her eyes, in response to his look, gave him an infinity of promise.

"I will always remember, Madame, that you have honoured me by commanding my services."

The words were cold and formal, but they did not chill her this time. Her woman's heart had read his, beneath the impassive mask his pride still forced him to wear.

He bowed to her again, then begged her leave to depart. She stood on one side whilst he jumped on to Sultan's back, then, as he galloped out of the gates, she waved him a final "Adieu."

A bend in the road soon hid him from view; his confidential groom had some difficulty in keeping pace with him, for Sultan flew along in response to his master's excited mood. Marguerite, with a sigh that was almost a happy one, turned and went within. She went back to her room, for suddenly, like a tired child, she felt quite sleepy.

Her heart seemed all at once to be in complete peace, and, though it still ached with undefined longing, a vague and delicious hope soothed it as with a balm.

She felt no longer anxious about Armand. The man who had just ridden away, bent on helping her brother, inspired her with complete confidence in his strength and in his power. She marvelled at herself for having ever looked upon him as an inane fool; of course, *that* was a mask worn to hide the bitter wound she had dealt to his faith and to his love. His passion would have overmastered him, and he would not let her see how much he still cared and how deeply he suffered.

But now all would be well: she would crush her own pride, humble it before him, tell him everything, trust him in everything; and those happy days would come back, when they used to wander off together in the forests of Fontainebleau, when they spoke little—for he was always a silent man—but when she felt that against that strong heart she would always find rest and happiness.

The more she thought of the events of the past night,

the less fear had she of Chauvelin and his schemes. He had failed to discover the identity of the Scarlet Pimpernel, of that she felt sure. Both Lord Fancourt and Chauvelin himself had assured her that no one had been in the dining-room at one o'clock except the Frenchman himself and Percy—Yes!—Percy! she might have asked him, had she thought of it! Anyway, she had no fears that the unknown and brave hero would fall in Chauvelin's trap; his death at any rate would not be at her door.

Armand certainly was still in danger, but Percy had pledged his word that Armand would be safe, and somehow, as Marguerite had seen him riding away, the possibility that he could fail in whatever he undertook never even remotely crossed her mind. When Armand was safely over in England she would not allow him to go back to France.

She felt almost happy now, and, drawing the curtains closely together again to shut out the piercing sun, she went to bed at last, laid her head upon the pillow, and, like a wearied child, soon fell into a peaceful and dreamless sleep.

18

The Mysterious Device

The day was well advanced when Marguerite woke, refreshed by her long sleep. Louise had brought her some fresh milk and a dish of fruit, and she partook of this frugal breakfast with hearty appetite.

Thoughts crowded thick and fast in her mind as she munched her grapes; most of them went galloping away after the tall, erect figure of her husband, whom she had watched riding out of sight more than five hours ago.

In answer to her eager inquiries, Louise brought back the news that the groom had come home with Sultan, having left Sir Percy in London. The groom thought that his master was about to get on board his schooner, which was lying off just below London Bridge. Sir Percy had ridden thus far, had then met Briggs, the skipper of the *Day Dream,* and had sent the groom back to Richmond with Sultan and the empty saddle.

This news puzzled Marguerite more than ever. Where could Sir Percy be going just now in the *Day Dream?* On Armand's behalf, he had said. Well! Sir Percy had influential friends everywhere. Perhaps he was going to Greenwich, or . . . but Marguerite ceased to conjecture; all would be explained anon: he said that he would come back, and that he would remember.

A long, idle day lay before Marguerite. She was expecting the visit of her old school-fellow, little Suzanne de Tournay. With all the merry mischief at her command, she had tendered her request for Suzanne's company to the Comtesse in the Presence of the Prince of Wales last night. His Royal Highness had loudly applauded the notion, and declared that he would give himself the pleasure of calling on the two ladies in the course of the afternoon. The Comtesse had not dared to refuse, and then and there was entrapped into a promise to send little Suzanne to spend a long and happy day at Richmond with her friend.

Marguerite expected her eagerly; she longed for a chat about old schooldays with the child; she felt that she would prefer Suzanne's company to that of anyone else, and together they would roam through the fine old garden and rich deer park, or stroll along the river.

But Suzanne had not come yet, and Marguerite being dressed, prepared to go downstairs. She looked quite a girl this morning in her simple muslin frock, with a broad blue sash round her slim waist, and the dainty cross-over fichu into which, at her bosom, she had fastened a few late crimson roses.

She crossed the landing outside her own suite of apartments, and stood still for a moment at the head of the fine oak staircase, which led to the lower floor. On her left were her husband's apartments, a suite of rooms which she practically never entered.

They consisted of bedroom, dressing and reception room, and, at the extreme end of the landing, of a small study, which, when Sir Percy did not use it, was always kept locked. His own special and confidential valet, Frank, had charge of this room. No one was ever allowed to go inside. My lady had never cared to do so, and the other servants, had, of course, not dared to break this hard-and-fast rule.

Marguerite had often, with that good-natured contempt which she had recently adopted towards her husband, chaffed him about this secrecy which surrounded
his private study. Laughingly she had always declared
that he strictly excluded all prying eyes from his sanctum for fear they should detect how very little "study"
went on within its four walls: a comfortable arm-chair
for Sir Percy's sweet slumbers was, no doubt, its most
conspicuous piece of furniture.

Marguerite thought of all this on this bright October
morning as she glanced along the corridor. Frank was
evidently busy with his master's rooms, for most of the
doors stood open, that of the study amongst the others.

A sudden, burning, childish curiosity seized her to
have a peep at Sir Percy's sanctum. The restriction, of
course, did not apply to her, and Frank would, of
course, not dare to oppose her. Still, she hoped that the
valet would be busy in one of the other rooms, that she
might have that one quick peep in secret, and unmo-
lested.

Gently, on tip-toe, she crossed the landing and, like
Blue Beard's wife, trembling half with excitement and
wonder, she paused a moment on the threshold,
strangely perturbed and irresolute.

The door was ajar, and she could not see anything
within. She pushed it open tentatively: there was no
sound: Frank was evidently not there, and she walked
boldly in.

At once she was struck by the severe simplicity of
everything around her: the dark and heavy hangings,
the massive oak furniture, the one or two maps on the
wall, in no way recalled to her mind the lazy man about
town, the lover of race-courses, the dandified leader of

fashion, that was the outward representation of Sir Percy Blakeney.

There was no sign here, at any rate, of hurried departure. Everything was in its place, not a scrap of paper littered the floor, not a cupboard or drawer was left open. The curtains were drawn aside, and through the open window the fresh morning air was streaming in.

Facing the window, and well into the centre of the room, stood a ponderous business-like desk, which looked as if it had seen much service. On the wall to the left of the desk, reaching almost from floor to ceiling, was a large full-length portrait of a woman, magnificently framed, exquisitely painted, and signed with the name of Boucher. It was Percy's mother.

Marguerite knew very little about her, except that she had died abroad, ailing in body as well as in mind, when Percy was still a lad. She must have been a very beautiful woman once, when Boucher painted her, and as Marguerite looked at the portrait, she could not but be struck by the extraordinary resemblance which must have existed between mother and son. There was the same low, square forehead, crowned with thick, fair hair, smooth and heavy; the same deep-set, somewhat lazy blue eyes beneath firmly marked, straight brows; and in those eyes there was the same intensity behind that apparent laziness, the same latent passion which used to light up Percy's face in the olden days before his marriage, and which Marguerite had again noted, last night at dawn, when she had come quite close to him, and had allowed a note of tenderness to creep into her voice.

Marguerite studied the portrait, for it interested her: after that she turned and looked again at the ponderous desk. It was covered with a mass of papers, all neatly tied and docketed, which looked like accounts and receipts arrayed with perfect method. It had never before struck Marguerite—nor had she, alas! found it worth while to inquire—as to how Sir Percy, whom all the world had credited with a total lack of brains, administered the vast fortune which his father had left him.

Since she had entered this neat, orderly room, she had been taken so much by surprise, that this obvious proof of her husband's strong business capacities did not cause her more than a passing thought of wonder. But it also strengthened her in the now certain knowledge that, with his worldly inanities, his foppish ways, and foolish talk, he was not only wearing a mask, but was playing a deliberate and studied part.

Marguerite wondered again. Why should he take all this trouble? Why should he—who was obviously a serious, earnest man—wish to appear before his fellowmen as an empty-headed nincompoop?

He may have wished to hide his love for a wife who held him in contempt . . . but surely such an object could have been gained at less sacrifice, and with far less trouble than constant incessant acting of an unnatural part.

She looked round her quite aimlessly now: she was horribly puzzled, and a nameless dread, before all this strange, unaccountable mystery, had begun to seize upon her. She felt cold and uncomfortable suddenly in this severe and dark room. There were no pictures on the wall, save the fine Boucher portrait, only a couple of maps, both of parts of France, one of the North coast and the other of the environs of Paris. What did Sir Percy want with those, she wondered.

Her head began to ache, she turned away from this strange Blue Beard's chamber, which she had entered, and which she did not understand. She did not wish Frank to find her here, and with a last look round, she once more turned to the door. As she did so, her foot knocked against a small object, which had apparently been lying close to the desk, on the carpet, and which now went rolling, right across the room.

She stooped to pick it up. It was a solid gold ring, with a flat shield, on which was engraved a small device.

Marguerite turned it over in her fingers, and then studied the engraving on the shield. It represented a small star-shaped flower, of a shape she had seen so distinctly twice before: once at the opera, and once at Lord Grenville's ball.

19

The Scarlet Pimpernel

At what particular moment the strange doubt first crept into Marguerite's mind, she could not herself afterwards have said. With the ring tightly clutched in her hand, she had run out of the room, down the stairs, and out into the garden, where, in complete seclusion, alone with the flowers, and the river and the birds, she could look again at the ring, and study that device more closely.

Stupidly, senselessly, now, sitting beneath the shade of an overhanging sycamore, she was looking at the plain gold shield, with the star-shaped little flower engraved upon it.

Bah! It was ridiculous! she was dreaming! her nerves were overwrought, and she saw signs and mysteries in the most trivial coincidences. Had not everybody about town recently made a point of affecting the device of that mysterious and heroic Scarlet Pimpernel?

Did she not herself wear it embroidered on her gowns? set in gems and enamel in her hair? What was there strange in the fact that Sir Percy should have chosen to use the device as a seal-ring? He might easily have done that . . . yes . . . quite easily . . . and . . . besides . . . what connection could there be between her exquisite dandy of a husband, with his fine clothes and refined, lazy ways, and the daring plotter who rescued French victims from beneath the very eyes of the leaders of a bloodthirsty revolution?

Her thoughts were in a whirl—her mind a blank . . .
She did not see anything that was going on around her,
and was quite startled when a fresh young voice called
to her across the garden.

"*Chérie!—chérie!* where are you?" and little Suzanne,
fresh as a rosebud, with eyes dancing with glee, and
brown curls fluttering in the soft morning breeze, came
running across the lawn.

"They told me you were in the garden," she went on
prattling merrily, and throwing herself with pretty, girlish impulse into Marguerite's arms, "so I ran out to
give you a surprise. You did not expect me quite so
soon, did you, my darling little Margot *chérie?*"

Marguerite, who had hastily concealed the ring in the
folds of her kerchief, tried to respond gaily and unconcernedly to the young girl's impulsiveness.

"Indeed, sweet one," she said with a smile, "it is de-
lightful to have you all to myself, and for a nice whole
long day. . . . You won't be bored?"

"Oh! bored! Margot, how *can* you say such a wicked
thing. Why! when we were in the dear old convent together, we were always happy when we were allowed to
be alone together."

"And to talk secrets."

The two young girls had linked their arms in one another's and began wandering round the garden.

"Oh! how lovely your home is, Margot, darling," said
little Suzanne, enthusiastically, "and how happy you
must be!"

"Aye, indeed! I ought to be happy—oughtn't I, sweet
one?" said Marguerite, with a wistful little sigh.

"How sadly you say it, *chérie.* . . . Ah, well, I suppose
now that you are a married woman you won't care to

talk secrets with me any longer. Oh! what lots and lots of secrets we used to have at school! Do you remember?—some we did not even confide to Sister Theresa of the Holy Angels—though she was such a dear."

"And now you have one all-important secret, eh, little one?" said Marguerite, merrily, "which you are forthwith going to confide to me. Nay, you need not blush, *chérie,*" she added, as she saw Suzanne's pretty little face crimson with blushes. "Faith, there's naught to be ashamed of! He is a noble and true man, and one to be proud of as a lover, and . . . as a husband."

"Indeed, *chérie,* I am not ashamed," rejoined Suzanne, softly; "and it makes me very, very proud to hear you speak so well of him. I think maman will consent," she added thoughtfully, "And I shall be—oh! so happy—but, of course, nothing is to be thought of until papa is safe . . ."

Marguerite started. Suzanne's father! the Comte de Tournay!—one of those whose life would be jeopardised if Chauvelin succeeded in establishing the identity of the Scarlet Pimpernel.

She had understood all along from the Comtesse, and also from one or two of the members of the league, that their mysterious leader had pledged his honour to bring the fugitive Comte de Tournay safely out of France. Whilst little Suzanne—unconscious of all—save her own all-important little secret, went prattling on, Marguerite's thoughts went back to the events of the past night.

Armand's peril, Chauvelin's threat, his cruel "Either—or—" which she had accepted.

And then her own work in the matter, which should have culminated at one o'clock in Lord Grenville's dining-room, when the relentless agent of the French Government would finally learn who was this mysterious Scarlet Pimpernel, who so openly defied an army of spies and placed himself so boldly, and for mere sport, on the side of the enemies of France.

Since then she had heard nothing from Chauvelin. She had concluded that he had failed, and yet, she had not felt anxious about Armand, because her husband had promised her that Armand would be safe.

But now, suddenly, as Suzanne prattled merrily along, an awful horror came upon her for what she had done. Chauvelin had told her nothing, it was true; but she remembered how sarcastic and evil he looked when she took final leave of him after the ball. Had he discovered something then? Had he already laid his plans for catching the daring plotter, red-handed, in France, and sending him to the guillotine without compunction or delay?

Marguerite turned sick with horror, and her hand convulsively clutched the ring in her dress.

"You are not listening, *chérie,*" said Suzanne, reproachfully, as she paused in her long, highly interesting narrative.

"Yes, yes, darling—indeed I am," said Marguerite with an effort, forcing herself to smile. "I love to hear you talking . . . and your happiness makes me so very glad. . . . Have no fear, we will manage to propitiate maman. Sir Andrew Ffoulkes is a noble English gentleman; he has money and position, the Comtesse will not refuse her consent. . . . But . . . now, little one . . . tell me . . . what is the latest news about your father?"

"Oh!" said Suzanne, with mad glee, "the best we could possibly hear. My Lord Hastings came to see maman early this morning. He said that all is now well with dear papa, and we may safely expect him here in England in less than four days."

"Yes," said Marguerite, whose glowing eyes were fastened on Suzanne's lips, as she continued merrily:

"Oh, we have no fear now! You don't know, *chérie,* that that great and noble Scarlet Pimpernel himself has gone to save papa. He has gone, *chérie* . . . actually gone . . ." added Suzanne excitedly, "He was in London this morning; he will be in Calais, perhaps, to-morrow . . . where he will meet papa . . . and then . . . and then . . ."

The blow had fallen. She had expected it all along, though she had tried for the last half-hour to delude herself and to cheat her fears. He had gone to Calais, had been in London this morning . . . he . . . the Scarlet Pimpernel . . . Percy Blakeney . . . her husband . . . whom she had betrayed last night to Chauvelin.

Percy . . . Percy . . . her husband . . . the Scarlet Pimpernel . . . Oh! how could she have been so blind? She understood it now—all at once . . . that part he played—the mask he wore . . . in order to throw dust in everybody's eyes.

And all for sheer sport and devilry of course!—saving men, women and children from death, as other men destroy and kill animals for the excitement, the love of the thing. The idle, rich man wanted some aim in life— he, and the few young bucks he enrolled under his banner, had amused themselves for months in risking their lives for the sake of an innocent few.

Perhaps he had meant to tell her when they were first married; and then the story of the Marquis de St. Cyr had come to his ears, and he had suddenly turned from her, thinking, no doubt, that she might some day betray him and his comrades, who had sworn to follow him; and so he had tricked her, as he tricked all others, whilst hundreds now owed their lives to him, and many families owed him both life and happiness.

The mask of the inane fop had been a good one, and the part consummately well played. No wonder that Chauvelin's spies had failed to detect, in the apparently brainless nincompoop, the man whose reckless daring and resourceful ingenuity had baffled the keenest French spies, both in France and in England. Even last night when Chauvelin went to Lord Grenville's dining-room to seek that daring Scarlet Pimpernel, he only saw that inane Sir Percy Blakeney fast asleep in a corner of the sofa.

Had his astute mind guessed the secret, then? Here lay the whole awful, horrible, amazing puzzle. In betraying a nameless stranger to his fate in order to save her brother, had Marguerite Blakeney sent her husband to his death?

No! no! no! a thousand times no! Surely Fate could not deal a blow like that: Nature itself would rise in revolt: her hand, when it held that tiny scrap of paper last night, would surely have been struck numb ere it committed a deed so appalling and so terrible.

"But what is it, *chérie?*" said little Suzanne, now genuinely alarmed, for Marguerite's colour had become dull and ashen. "Are you ill, Marguerite? What is it?"

"Nothing, nothing, child," she murmured, as in a dream. "Wait a moment . . . let me think . . . think! . . . You said . . . the Scarlet Pimpernel had gone today. . . . ?"

"Marguerite, *chérie,* what is it? You frighten me. . . ."

"It is nothing, child, I tell you . . . nothing . . . I must be alone a minute—and—dear one . . . I may have to curtail our time together to-day. . . . I may have to go away—you'll understand?"

"I understand that something has happened, *chérie*, and that you want to be alone. I won't be a hindrance to you. Don't think of me. My maid, Lucile, has not yet gone . . . we will go back together . . . don't think of me."

She threw her arms impulsively round Marguerite. Child as she was, she felt the poignancy of her friend's grief, and with the infinite tact of her girlish tenderness, she did not try to pry into it, but was ready to efface herself.

She kissed Marguerite again and again, then walked sadly back across the lawn. Marguerite did not move, she remained there, thinking . . . wondering what was to be done.

Just as little Suzanne was about to mount the terrace steps, a groom came running round the house towards his mistress. He carried a sealed letter in his hand. Suzanne instinctively turned back; her heart told her that here perhaps was further ill news for her friend, and she felt that her poor Margot was not in a fit state to bear any more.

The groom stood respectfully beside his mistress, then he handed her the sealed letter.

"What is that?" asked Marguerite.

"Just come by runner, my lady."

Marguerite took the letter mechanically, and turned it over in her trembling fingers.

"Who sent it?" she said.

"The runner said, my lady," replied the groom, "that his orders were to deliver this, and that your ladyship would understand from whom it came."

Marguerite tore open the envelope. Already her instinct had told her what it contained, and her eyes only glanced at it mechanically.

It was a letter written by Armand St. Just to Sir Andrew Ffoulkes—the letter which Chauvelin's spies had stolen at "The Fisherman's Rest," and which Chauvelin had held as a rod over her to enforce her obedience.

Now he had kept his word—he had sent her back St. Just's compromising letter . . . for he was on the track of the Scarlet Pimpernel.

Marguerite's senses reeled, her very soul seemed to be leaving her body; she tottered, and would have fallen but for Suzanne's arm round her waist. With superhuman effort she regained control over herself—there was yet much to be done.

"Bring that runner here to me," she said to the servant, with much calm. "He has not gone?"

"No, my lady."

The groom went, and Marguerite turned to Suzanne. "And you, child, run within. Tell Lucile to get ready. I fear that I must send you home, child. And—stay, tell one of the maids to prepare a travelling dress and cloak for me."

Suzanne made no reply. She kissed Marguerite tenderly, and obeyed without a word; the child was overawed by the terrible, nameless misery in her friend's face.

A minute later the groom returned, followed by the runner who had brought the letter.

"Who gave you this packet?" asked Marguerite.

"A gentleman, my lady," replied the man, "at 'The Rose and Thistle' inn opposite Charing Cross. He said you would understand."

"At 'The Rose and Thistle'? What was he doing?"

"He was waiting for the coach, your ladyship, which he had ordered."

"The coach?"

"Yes, my lady. A special coach he had ordered. I understood from his man that he was posting straight to Dover."

"That's enough. You may go." Then she turned to the groom: "My coach and the four swiftest horses in the stables, to be ready at once."

The groom and runner both went quickly off to obey. Marguerite remained standing for a moment on the lawn quite alone. Her graceful figure was as rigid as a statue, her eyes were fixed, her hands were tightly clasped across her breast; her lips moved as they murmured with pathetic heart-breaking persistence,—

"What's to be done? What's to be done? Where to find him?—Oh, God! grant me light."

But this was not the moment for remorse and despair. She had done—unwittingly—an awful and terrible thing—the very worst crime, in her eyes, that woman ever committed—she saw it in all its horror. Her very blindness in not having guessed her husband's secret seemed now to her another deadly sin. She ought to have known! she ought to have known!

How could she imagine that a man who could love with so much intensity as Percy Blakeney had loved her from the first—how could such a man be the brainless idiot he chose to appear? She, at least, ought to have known that he was wearing a mask, and having found that out, she should have torn it from his face, whenever they were alone together.

Her love for him had been paltry and weak, easily crushed by her own pride; and she, too, had worn a mask in assuming a contempt for him, whilst, as a matter of fact, she completely misunderstood him.

But there was no time now to go over the past. By her own blindness she had sinned; now she must repay, not by empty remorse, but by prompt and useful action.

Percy had started for Calais, utterly unconscious of the fact that his most relentless enemy was on his heels. He had set sail early that morning from London Bridge. Provided he had a favourable wind, he would no doubt be in France within twenty-four hours; no doubt he had reckoned on the wind and chosen this route.

Chauvelin, on the other hand, would post to Dover, charter a vessel there, and undoubtedly reach Calais much about the same time. Once in Calais, Percy would meet all those who were eagerly waiting for the noble and brave Scarlet Pimpernell, who had come to rescue them from horrible and unmerited death. With Chauvelin's eyes now fixed upon his every movement, Percy would thus not only be endangering his own life, but that of Suzanne's father, the old Comte de Tournay, and of those other fugitives who were waiting for him and trusting in him. There was also Armand, who had gone to meet de Tournay, secure in the knowledge that the Scarlet Pimpernell was watching over his safety.

All these lives and that of her husband, lay in Marguerite's hands; these she must save, if human pluck and ingenuity were equal to the task.

Unfortunately, she could not do all this quite alone. Once in Calais she would not know where to find her husband, whilst Chauvelin, in stealing the papers at Dover, had obtained the whole itinerary. Above every thing, she wished to warn Percy.

She knew enough about him by now to understand that he would never abandon those who trusted in him, that he would not turn back from danger, and leave the Comte de Tournay to fall into the bloodthirsty hands that knew of no mercy. But if he were warned, he might form new plans, be more wary, more prudent. Unconsciously, he might fall into a cunning trap, but—once warned—he might yet succeed.

And if he failed—if indeed Fate, and Chauvelin, with all the resources at his command, proved too strong for the daring plotter after all—then at least she would be there by his side, to comfort, love and cherish, to cheat death perhaps at the last by making it seem sweet, if they died both together, locked in each other's arms, with the supreme happiness of knowing that passion had responded to passion, and that all misunderstandings were at an end.

Her whole body stiffened as with a great and firm resolution. This she meant to do, if God gave her wits and strength. Her eyes lost their fixed look; they glowed with inward fire at the thought of meeting him again so soon, in the very midst of most deadly perils; they sparkled with the joy of sharing these dangers with him—of helping him perhaps—of being with him at the last—if she failed.

The childlike sweet face had become hard and set,

the curved mouth was closed tightly over her clenched teeth. She meant to do or die, with him and for his sake. A frown, which spoke of an iron will and unbending resolution, appeared between the two straight brows; already her plans were formed. She would go and find Sir Andrew Ffoulkes first; he was Percy's best friend, and Marguerite remembered, with a thrill, with what blind enthusiasm the young man always spoke of his mysterious leader.

He would help her where she needed help; her coach was ready. A change of raiment, and a farewell to little Suzanne, and she could be on her way.

Without haste, but without hesitation, she walked quietly into the house.

20

THE FRIEND

Less than half an hour later, Marguerite, buried in thoughts, sat inside her coach, which was bearing her swiftly to London.

She had taken an affectionate farewell of little Suzanne, and seen the child safely started with her maid, and in her own coach, back to town. She had sent one courier with a respectful letter of excuse to His Royal Highness, begging for a postponement of the august visit on account of pressing and urgent business, and another on ahead to bespeak a fresh relay of horses at Faversham.

Then she had changed her muslin frock for a dark traveling costume and mantle, had provided herself with money—which her husband's lavishness always placed fully at her disposal—and had started on her way.

She did not attempt to delude herself with any vain and futile hopes; the safety of her brother Armand was to have been conditional on the imminent capture of the Scarlet Pimpernel. As Chauvelin had sent her back Armand's compromising letter, there was no doubt that he was quite satisfied in his own mind that Percy Blakeney was the man whose death he had sworn to bring about.

No! there was no room for any fond delusions! Percy, the husband whom she loved with all the ardour which her admiration for his bravery had kindled, was in immediate, deadly peril, through her hand. She had betrayed him to his enemy—unwittingly 'tis true—but she *had* betrayed him, and if Chauvelin succeeded in trapping him, who so far was unaware of his danger, then his death would be at her door. His death! when with her very heart's blood, she would have defended him and given willingly her life for his.

She had ordered her coach to drive her to the "Crown" inn; once there, she told her coachman to give the horses food and rest. Then she ordered a chair, and had herself carried to the house in Pall Mall where Sir Andrew Ffoulkes lived.

Among all Percy's friends who were enrolled under his daring banner, she felt that she would prefer to confide in Sir Andrew Ffoulkes. He had always been her friend, and now his love for little Suzanne had brought him closer to her still. Had he been away from home, gone on the mad errand with Percy, perhaps, then she would have called on Lord Hastings or Lord Tony—for she wanted the help of one of these young men, or she would be indeed powerless to save her husband.

Sir Andrew Ffoulkes, however, was at home, and his servant introduced her ladyship immediately. She went upstairs to the young man's comfortable bachelor's chambers, and was shown into a small, though luxuriously furnished, dining-room. A moment or two later Sir Andrew himself appeared.

He had evidently been much startled when he heard who his lady visitor was, for he looked anxiously—even suspiciously—at Marguerite, whilst performing the elaborate bows before her, which the rigid etiquette of the time demanded.

Marguerite had laid aside every vestige of nervousness; she was perfectly calm, and having returned the young man's elaborate salute, she began very calmly,—

"Sir Andrew, I have no desire to waste valuable time in much talk. You must take certain things I am going to tell you for granted. These will be of no importance. What is important is that your leader and comrade, the Scarlet Pimpernel . . . my husband . . . Percy Blakeney . . . is in deadly peril."

Had she had the remotest doubt of the correctness of her deductions, she would have had them confirmed now, for Sir Andrew, completely taken by surprise, had grown very pale, and was quite incapable of making the slightest attempt at clever parrying.

"No matter how I know this, Sir Andrew," she continued quietly, "thank God that I do, and that perhaps it is not too late to save him. Unfortunately, I cannot do this quite alone, and therefore have come to you for help."

"Lady Blakeney," said the young man, trying to recover himself, "I . . ."

"Will you hear me first?" she interrupted. "This is how the matter stands. When the agent of the French Government stole your papers that night in Dover, he found amongst them certain plans, which you or your leader meant to carry out for the rescue of the Comte de Tournay and others. The Scarlet Pimpernel—Percy, my husband—has gone on this errand himself to-day. Chauvelin knows that the Scarlet Pimpernel and Percy Blakeney are one and the same person. He will follow him to Calais, and there will lay hands on him. You know as well as I do the fate that awaits him at the hands of the Revolutionary Government of France. No interference from England—from King George himself—would save him. Robespierre and his gang would see to it that the interference came too late. But not only that, the much-trusted leader will also have been unconsciously the means of revealing the hiding-place of the Comte de Tournay and of all those who, even now, are placing their hopes in him."

She had spoken quietly, dispassionately, and with firm, unbending resolution. Her purpose was to make that young man trust and help her, for she could do nothing without him.

"I do not understand," he repeated, trying to gain time, to think what was best to be done.

"Aye! but I think you do, Sir Andrew. You must know that I am speaking the truth. Look these facts straight in the face. Percy has sailed for Calais, I presume for some lonely part of the coast, and Chauvelin is on his track. *He* has posted for Dover, and will cross the Channel probably to-night. What do you think will happen?"

The young man was silent.

"Percy will arrive at his destination: unconscious of being followed he will seek out de Tournay and the others—among these is Armand St. Just my brother—he will seek them out, one after another, probably, not knowing that the sharpest eyes in the world are watching his every movement. When he has thus unconsciously betrayed those who blindly trust in him, when nothing can be gained from him, and he is ready to come back to England, with those whom he has gone so bravely to save, the doors of the trap will close upon him, and he will be sent to end his noble life upon the guillotine."

Still Sir Andrew was silent.

"You do not trust me," she said passionately. "Oh God! cannot you see that I am in deadly earnest? Man, man," she added, while, with her tiny hands she seized the young man suddenly by the shoulders, forcing him to look straight at her, "tell me, do I look like that vilest thing on earth—a woman who would betray her own husband?"

"God forbid, Lady Blakeney," said the young man at last, "that I should attribute such evil motives to you, but . . ."

"But what? . . . tell me . . . Quick, man! . . . the very seconds are precious!"

"Will you tell me," he asked resolutely, and looking searchingly into her blue eyes, "whose hand helped to guide M. Chauvelin to the knowledge which you say he possesses?"

"Mine," she said quietly, "I own it—I will not lie to you, for I wish you to trust me absolutely. But I had no idea—how *could* I have?—of the identity of the Scarlet Pimpernel . . . and my brother's safety was to be my prize if I succeeded."

"In helping Chauvelin to track the Scarlet Pimpernel?"

She nodded.

"It is no use telling you how he forced my hand. Armand is more than a brother to me, and . . . and . . . how *could* I guess? . . . But we waste time, Sir Andrew . . . every second is precious . . . in the name of God! . . . my husband is in peril . . . your friend!—your comrade!—Help me to save him."

Sir Andrew felt his position to be a very awkward one. The oath he had taken before his leader and comrade was one of obedience and secrecy; and yet the beautiful woman, who was asking him to trust her, was undoubtedly in earnest; his friend and leader was equally undoubtedly in imminent danger and . . .

"Lady Blakeney," he said at last, "God knows you have perplexed me, so that I do not know which way my duty lies. Tell me what you wish me to do. There are nineteen of us ready to lay down our lives for the Scarlet Pimpernell if he is in danger."

"There is no need for lives just now, my friend," she said drily; "my wits and four swift horses will serve the necessary purpose. But I must know where to find him. See," she added, while her eyes filled with tears, "I have humbled myself before you, I have owned my fault to you; shall I also confess my weakness?—My husband and I have been estranged, because he did not trust me, and because I was too blind to understand. You must confess that the bandage which he put over my eyes was a very thick one. Is it small wonder that I did not see through it? But last night, after I led him unwittingly into such deadly peril, it suddenly fell from my eyes. If you will not help me, Sir Andrew, I would still strive to save my husband. I would still exert every faculty I possess for his sake; but I might be powerless, for I might arrive too late, and nothing would be left for you but lifelong remorse, and . . . and . . . for me, a broken heart."

"But, Lady Blakeney," said the young man, touched by the gentle earnestness of this exquisitely beautiful woman, "do you know that what you propose doing is man's work?—you cannot possibly journey to Calais alone. You would be running the greatest possible risks to yourself, and your chances of finding your husband now—were I to direct you ever so carefully—are infinitely remote."

"Oh, I hope there are risks!" she murmured softly. "I hope there are dangers, too!—I have so much to atone for. But I fear you are mistaken. Chauvelin's eyes are fixed upon you all, he will scarce notice me. Quick, Sir Andrew!—the coach is ready, and there is not a moment to be lost. . . . I *must* get to him! I *must!*" she repeated with almost savage energy, "to warn him that that man is on his track. . . . Can't you see—can't you see, that I *must* get to him . . . even . . . even if it be too late to save him . . . at least . . . to be by his side . . . at the last."

"Faith, Madame, you must command me. Gladly would I or any of my comrades lay down our lives for your husband. If you *will* go yourself . . ."

"Nay, friend, do you not see that I would go mad if I let you go without me." She stretched out her hand to him. "You *will* trust me?"

"I await your orders," he said simply.

"Listen, then. My coach is ready to take me to Dover. Do you follow me, as swiftly as horses will take you. We meet at nightfall at 'The Fisherman's Rest.' Chauvelin would avoid it, as he is known there, and I think it would be the safest. I will gladly accept your escort to Calais . . . as you say, I might miss Sir Percy were you to direct me ever so carefully. We'll charter a schooner at Dover and cross over during the night. Disguised, if you will agree to it, as my lacquey, you will, I think, escape detection."

"I am entirely at your service, Madame," rejoined the young man earnestly. "I trust to God that you will

sight the *Day Dream* before we reach Calais. With
Chauvelin at his heels, every step the Scarlet Pimpernel
takes on French soil is fraught with danger."

"God grant it, Sir Andrew. But now, farewell. We
meet to-night at Dover! It will be a race between Chauvelin and me across the Channel to-night—and the
prize—the life of the Scarlet Pimpernel."

He kissed her hand, and then escorted her to her
chair. A quarter of an hour later she was back at the
"Crown" inn, where her coach and horses were ready
and waiting for her. The next moment they thundered
along the London streets, and then straight on to the
Dover road at maddening speed.

She had no time for despair now. She was up and
doing and had no leisure to think. With Sir Andrew
Ffoulkes as her companion and ally, hope had once
again revived in her heart.

God would be merciful. He would not allow so appalling a crime to be committed, as the death of a brave
man, through the hand of a woman who loved him, and
worshipped him, and who would gladly have died for
his sake.

Marguerite's thoughts flew back to him, the mysterious hero, whom she had always unconsciously loved,
when his identity was still unknown to her. Laughingly,
in the olden days, she used to call him the shadowy
king of her heart, and now she had suddenly found that
this enigmatic personality whom she had worshipped,
and the man who loved her so passionately, were one
and the same: what wonder that one or two happier Visions began to force their way before her mind? She
vaguely wondered what she would say to him when first
they would stand face to face.

She had had so many anxieties, so much excitement during the past few hours, that she allowed herself the luxury of nursing these few more hopeful, brighter thoughts. Gradually the rumble of the coach wheels, with its incessant monotony, acted soothingly on her nerves: her eyes, aching with fatigue and many shed and unshed tears, closed involuntarily, and she fell into a troubled sleep.

21

SUSPENSE

It was late into the night when she at last reached "The Fisherman's Rest." She had done the whole journey in less than eight hours, thanks to innumerable changes of horses at the various coaching stations, for which she always paid lavishly, thus obtaining the very best and swiftest that could be had.

Her coachman, too, had been indefatigible; the promise of special and rich reward had no doubt helped to keep him up, and he had literally burned the ground beneath his mistress' coach wheels.

The arrival of Lady Blakeney in the middle of the night caused a considerable flutter at "The Fisherman's Rest." Sally jumped hastily out of bed, and Mr. Jellyband was at great pains how to make his important guest comfortable.

Both these good folk were far too well drilled in the manners appertaining to innkeepers, to exhibit the slightest surprise at Lady Blakeney's arrival, alone, at this extraordinary hour. No doubt they thought all the more, but Marguerite was far too absorbed in the importance—the deadly earnestness—of her journey, to stop and ponder over trifles of that sort.

The coffee-room—the scene lately of the dastardly outrage on two English gentlemen—was quite deserted. Mr. Jellyband hastily relit the lamp, rekindled a cheerful bit of fire in the great hearth, and then wheeled

a comfortable chair by it, into which Marguerite grate-
fully sank.

"Will your ladyship stay the night?" asked pretty
Miss Sally, who was already busy laying a snow-white
cloth on the table, preparatory to providing a simple
supper for her ladyship.

"No! not the whole night," replied Marguerite. "At
any rate, I shall not want any room but this, if I can
have it to myself for an hour or two."

"It is at your ladyship's service," said honest Jellyband, whose rubicund face was set in its tightest folds,
lest it should betray before "the quality" that boundless
astonishment which the worthy fellow had begun to feel.

"I shall be crossing over at the first turn of the tide,"
said Marguerite, "and in the first schooner I can get.
But my coachman and men will stay the night, and
probably several days longer, so I hope you will make
them comfortable."

"Yes, my lady; I'll look after them. Shall Sally bring
your ladyship some supper?"

"Yes, please. Put something cold on the table, and as
soon as Sir Andrew Ffoulkes comes, show him in
here."

"Yes, my lady."

Honest Jellyband's face now expressed distress in
spite of himself. He had great regard for Sir Percy Blakeney, and did not like to see his lady running away with
young Sir Andrew. Of course, it was no business of his,
and Mr. Jellyband was no gossip. Still, in his heart, he
recollected that her ladyship was after all only one of
them "furriners"; what wonder that she was immoral
like the rest of them?

"Don't sit up, honest Jellyband," continued Marguerite kindly, "nor you either, Mistress Sally. Sir Andrew may be late."

Jellyband was only too willing that Sally should go to bed. He was beginning not to like these goings-on at all. Still, Lady Blakeney would pay handsomely for the accommodation, and it certainly was no business of his.

Sally arranged a simple supper of cold meat, wine, and fruit on the table, then with a respectful curtsey, she retired, wondering in her little mind why her ladyship looked so serious, when she was about to elope with her gallant.

Then commenced a period of weary waiting for Marguerite. She knew that Sir Andrew—who would have to provide himself with clothes befitting a lacquey—could not possibly reach Dover for at least a couple of hours. He was a splendid horseman of course, and would make light in such an emergency of the seventy odd miles between London and Dover. He would, too, literally burn the ground beneath his horse's hoofs, but he might not always get very good remounts, and in any case, he could not have started from London until at least an hour after she did.

She had seen nothing of Chauvelin on the road. Her coachman, whom she questioned, had not seen anyone answering the description his mistress gave him of the wizened figure of the little Frenchman.

Evidently, therefore, he had been ahead of her all the time. She had not dared to question the people at the various inns, where they had stopped to change horses. She feared that Chauvelin had spies all along the route, who might overhear her questions, then outdistance her and warn her enemy of her approach.

Now she wondered at what inn he might be stopping, or whether he had had the good luck of chartering a vessel already, and was now himself on the way to France. That thought gripped her at the heart as with an iron vice. If indeed she should be too late already!

The loneliness of the room overwhelmed her; everything within was so horribly still; the ticking of the grandfather's clock—dreadfully slow and measured— was the only sound which broke this awful loneliness.

Marguerite had need of all her energy, all her steadfastness of purpose, to keep up her courage through this weary midnight waiting.

Everyone else in the house but herself must have been asleep. She had heard Sally go upstairs. Mr. Jellyband had gone to see to her coachman and men, and then had returned and taken up a position under the porch outside, just where Marguerite had first met Chauvelin about a week ago. He evidently meant to wait up for Sir Andrew Ffoulkes, but was soon overcome by sweet slumbers, for presently—in addition to the slow ticking of the clock—Marguerite could hear the monotonous and dulcet tones of the worthy fellow's breathing.

For some time now, she had realised that the beautiful warm October's day, so happily begun, had turned into a rough and cold night. She had felt very chilly, and was glad of the cheerful blaze in the hearth: but gradually, as time wore on, the weather became more rough, and the sound of the great breakers against the Admiralty Pier, though some distance from the inn, came to her as the noise of muffled thunder.

The wind was becoming boisterous, rattling the lead windows and the massive doors of the old-fashioned house: it shook the trees outside and roared down the vast chimney. Marguerite wondered if the wind would be favourable for her journey. She had no fear of the storm, and would have braved worse risks sooner than delay the crossing by an hour.

A sudden commotion outside roused her from her meditations. Evidently it was Sir Andrew Ffoulkes, just arrived in mad haste, for she heard his horse's hoofs thundering on the flag-stones outside, then Mr. Jellyband's sleepy, yet cheerful tones bidding him welcome.

For a moment, then, the awkwardness of her position struck Marguerite; alone at this hour, in a place where she was well known, and having made an assignation with a young cavalier equally well known, and who arrived in disguise! What food for gossip to those mischievously inclined.

The idea struck Marguerite chiefly from its humorous side: there was such quaint contrast between the seriousness of her errand, and the construction which would naturally be put on her actions by honest Mr. Jellyband, that, for the first time since many hours, a little smile began playing round the corners of her childlike mouth, and when, presently, Sir Andrew, almost unrecognisable in his lacquey-like garb, entered the coffee-room, she was able to greet him with quite a merry laugh.

"Faith! Monsieur, my lacquey," she said, "I am satisfied with your appearance!"

Mr. Jellyband had followed Sir Andrew, looking strangely perplexed. The young gallant's disguise had confirmed his worst suspicions. Without a smile upon his jovial face, he drew the cork from the bottle of wine, set the chairs ready, and prepared to wait.

"Thanks, honest friend," said Marguerite, who was still smiling at the thought of what the worthy fellow must be thinking at that very moment, "we shall require nothing more; and here's for all the trouble you have been put to on our account."

She handed two or three gold pieces to Jellyband, who took them respectfully, and with becoming gratitude.

"Stay, Lady Blakeney," interposed Sir Andrew, as Jellyband was about to retire, "I am afraid we shall require something more of my friend Jelly's hospitality. I am sorry to say we cannot cross over to-night."

"Not cross over to-night?" she repeated in amazement. "But we must, Sir Andrew, we must! There can be no question of cannot, and whatever it may cost, we must get a vessel to-night."

But the young man shook his head sadly.

"I am afraid it is not a question of cost, Lady Blakeney. There is a nasty storm blowing from France, the wind is dead against us, we cannot possibly sail until it has changed."

Marguerite became deadly pale. She had not foreseen this. Nature herself was playing her a horrible, cruel trick. Percy was in danger, and she could not go to him, because the wind happened to blow from the coast of France.

"But we must go!—we must!" she repeated with strange, persistent energy, "you know, we must go!—can't you find a way?"

"I have been down to the shore already," he said, "and had a talk to one or two skippers. It is quite impossible to set sail to-night, so every sailor assured me. No one," he added, looking significantly at Marguerite, *"no one* could possibly put out of Dover to-night."

Marguerite at once understood what he meant. *No one* included Chauvelin as well as herself. She nodded pleasantly to Jellyband.

"Well, then, I must resign myself," she said to him. "Have you a room for me?"

"Oh, yes, your ladyship. A nice, bright, airy room. I'll see to it at once. . . . And there is another one for Sir Andrew—both quite ready."

"That's brave now, mine honest Jelly," said Sir Andrew, gaily, and clapping his worthy host vigorously on the back. "You unlock both those rooms, and leave our candles here on the dresser. I vow you are dead with sleep, and her ladyship must have some supper before she retires. There, have no fear, friend of the rueful countenance, her ladyship's visit, though at this unusual hour, is a great honour to thy house, and Sir Percy Blakeney will reward thee doubly, if thou seest well to her privacy and comfort."

Sir Andrew had no doubt guessed the many conflicting doubts and fears which raged in honest Jellyband's head; and, as he was a gallant gentleman, he tried by this brave hint to allay some of the worthy innkeeper's suspicions. He had the satisfaction of seeing that he had partially succeeded. Jellyband's rubicund countenance brightened somewhat, at mention of Sir Percy's name.

"I'll go and see to it at once, sir," he said with alacrity, and with less frigidity in his manner. "Has her ladyship everything she wants for supper?"

"Everything, thanks, honest friend, and as I am famished and dead with fatigue, I pray you see to the rooms."

"Now tell me," she said eagerly, as soon as Jellyband had gone from the room, "tell me all your news."

"There is nothing else much to tell you, Lady Blakeney," replied the young man. "The storm makes it quite impossible for any vessel to put out of Dover this tide. But, what seemed to you at first a terrible calamity is really a blessing in disguise. If we cannot cross over to France to-night, Chauvelin is in the same quandary."

"He may have left before the storm broke out."

"God grant he may," said Sir Andrew, merrily, "for very likely then he'll have been driven out of his course! Who knows? He may now even be lying at the bottom of the sea, for there is a furious storm raging, and it will fare ill with all small craft which happen to be out. But I fear me we cannot build our hopes upon the shipwreck of that cunning devil, and of all his murderous plans. The sailors I spoke to, all assured me that no schooner had put out of Dover for several hours: on the other hand, I ascertained that a stranger had arrived by coach this afternoon, and had, like myself, made some inquiries about crossing over to France."

"Then Chauvelin is still in Dover?"

"Undoubtedly. Shall I go waylay him and run my sword through him? That were indeed the quickest way out of the difficulty."

"Nay! Sir Andrew, do not jest! Alas! I have often since last night caught myself wishing for that fiend's death. But what you suggest is impossible! The laws of this country do not permit of murder! It is only in our beautiful France that wholesale slaughter is done lawfully, in the name of Liberty and of brotherly love."

Sir Andrew had persuaded her to sit down to the table, to partake of some supper and to drink a little wine. This enforced rest of at least twelve hours, until the next tide, was sure to be terribly difficult to bear in the state of intense excitement in which she was. Obedient in these small matters like a child, Marguerite tried to eat and drink.

Sir Andrew, with that profound sympathy born in all those who are in love, made her almost happy by talking to her about her husband. He recounted to her some of the daring escapes the brave Scarlet Pimpernel had contrived for the poor French fugitives, whom a relentless and bloody revolution was driving out of their country. He made her eyes glow with enthusiasm by telling her of his bravery, his ingenuity, his resourcefulness, when it meant snatching the lives of men, women, and even children from beneath the very edge of that murderous, everready guillotine.

He even made her smile quite merrily by telling her of the Scarlet Pimpernel's quaint and many disguises, through which he had baffled the strictest watch set against him at the barricades of Paris. This last time, the escape of the Comtesse de Tournay and her children had been a veritable masterpiece—Blakeney disguised as a hideous old market-woman, in filthy cap and straggling grey locks, was a sight fit to make the gods laugh.

Marguerite laughed heartily as Sir Andrew tried to describe Blakeney's appearance, whose gravest difficulty always consisted in his great height, which in France made disguise doubly difficult.

Thus an hour wore on. There were many more to spend in enforced inactivity in Dover. Marguerite rose from the table with an impatient sigh. She looked forward with dread to the night in the bed upstairs, with terribly anxious thoughts to keep her company, and the howling of the storm to help chase sleep away.

She wondered where Percy was now. The *Day Dream* was a strong, well-built, sea-going yacht. Sir Andrew had expressed the opinion that no doubt she had got in the lee of the wind before the storm broke out, or else perhaps had not ventured into the open at all, but was lying quietly at Gravesend.

Briggs was an expert skipper, and Sir Percy handled a schooner as well as any master mariner. There was no danger for them from the storm.

It was long past midnight when at last Marguerite retired to rest. As she had feared, sleep sedulously avoided her eyes. Her thoughts were of the blackest during these long, weary hours, whilst that incessant storm raged which was keeping her away from Percy. The sound of the distant breakers made her heart ache with melancholy. She was in the mood when the sea has a saddening effect upon the nerves. It is only when we are very happy, that we can bear to gaze merrily upon the vast and limitless expanse of water, rolling on and on with such persistent, irritating monotony, to the accompaniment of our thoughts, whether grave or gay. When they are gay, the waves echo their gaiety; but when they are sad, then every breaker, as it rolls, seems to bring additional sadness, and to speak to us of hopelessness and of the pettiness of all our joys.

22

Calais

The weariest nights, the longest days, sooner or later must perforce come to an end.

Marguerite had spent over fifteen hours in such acute mental torture as well-nigh drove her crazy. After a sleepless night, she rose early, wild with excitement, dying to start on her journey, terrified lest further obstacles lay in her way. She rose before anyone else in the house was astir, so frightened was she, lest she should miss the one golden opportunity of making a start.

When she came downstairs, she found Sir Andrew Ffoulkes sitting in the coffee-room. He had been out half an hour earlier, and had gone to the Admiralty Pier, only to find that neither the French packet nor any privately chartered vessel could put out of Dover yet. The storm was then at its fullest, and the tide was on the turn. If the wind did not abate or change, they would perforce have to wait another ten or twelve hours until the next tide, before a start could be made. And the storm had not abated, the wind had not changed, and the tide was rapidly drawing out.

Marguerite felt the sickness of despair when she heard this melancholy news. Only the most firm resolution kept her from totally breaking down, and thus adding to the young man's anxiety, which evidently had become very keen.

Though he tried to disguise it, Marguerite could see

that Sir Andrew was just as anxious as she was to reach his comrade and friend. This enforced inactivity was terrible to them both.

How they spent that wearisome day at Dover, Marguerite could never afterwards say. She was in terror of showing herself, lest Chauvelin's spies happened to be about, so she had a private sitting-room, and she and Sir Andrew sat there hour after hour, trying to take, at long intervals, some perfunctory meals, which little Sally would bring them, with nothing to do but to think, to conjecture, and only occasionally to hope.

The storm had abated just too late; the tide was by then too far out to allow a vessel to put off to sea. The wind had changed, and was settling down to a comfortable north-westerly breeze—a veritable godsend for a speedy passage across to France.

And there those two waited, wondering if the hour would ever come when they could finally make a start. There had been one happy interval in this long weary day, and that was when Sir Andrew went down once again to the pier, and presently came back to tell Marguerite that he had chartered a quick schooner, whose skipper was ready to put to sea the moment the tide was favourable.

From that moment the hours seemed less wearisome; there was less hopelessness in the waiting; and at last, at five o'clock in the afternoon, Marguerite, closely veiled and followed by Sir Andrew Ffoulkes, who, in the guise of her lacquey, was carrying a number of impedimenta, found her way down to the pier.

Once on board, the keen, fresh sea-air revived her, the breeze was just strong enough to nicely swell the sails of the *Foam Crest,* as she cut her way merrily towards the open.

The sunset was glorious after the storm, and Marguerite, as she watched the white cliffs of Dover gradually disappearing from view, felt more at peace and once more almost hopeful.

Sir Andrew was full of kind attentions, and she felt how lucky she had been to have him by her side in this, her great trouble.

Gradually the grey coast of France began to emerge from the fast-gathering evening mists. One or two lights could be seen flickering, and the spires of several churches to rise out of the surrounding haze.

Half an hour later Marguerite had landed upon French shore. She was back in that country where at this very moment men slaughtered their fellow-creatures by the hundreds, and sent innocent women and children in thousands to the block.

The very aspect of the country and its people, even in this remote sea-coast town, spoke of that seething revolution, three hundred miles away, in beautiful Paris, now rendered hideous by the constant flow of the blood of her noblest sons, by the wailing of the widows, and the cries of fatherless children.

The men all wore red caps—in various stages of cleanliness—but all with the tricolor cockade pinned on the left-hand side. Marguerite noticed with a shudder that, instead of the laughing, merry countenance habitual to her own countrymen, their faces now invariably wore a look of sly distrust.

Every man nowadays was a spy upon his fellows: the most innocent word uttered in jest might at any time be brought up as a proof of aristocratic tendencies, or of treachery against the people. Even the women went about with a curious look of fear and of hate lurking in their brown eyes; and all watched Marguerite as she stepped on shore, followed by Sir Andrew, and murmured as she passed along: *"Sacrés aristos!"* or else *"Sacrés Anglais!"*

Otherwise their presence excited no further comment. Calais, even in those days, was in constant business communication with England, and English merchants were often to be seen on this coast. It was well known that in view of the heavy duties in England, a vast deal of French wines and brandies were smuggled across. This pleased the French *bourgeois* immensely; he liked to see the English Government and the English king, both of whom he hated, cheated out of their revenues; and an English smuggler was always a welcome guest at the tumble-down taverns of Calais and Boulogne.

So, perhaps, as Sir Andrew gradually directed Marguerite through the tortuous streets of Calais, many of the population, who turned with an oath to look at the strangers clad in the English fashion, thought that they were bent on purchasing dutiable articles for their own fog-ridden country, and gave them no more than a passing thought.

Marguerite, however, wondered how her husband's tall, massive figure could have passed through Calais unobserved: she marvelled what disguise he assumed to do his noble work, without exciting too much attention.

Without exchanging more than a few words, Sir Andrew was leading her right across the town, to the other side from that where they had landed, and the way to-

wards Cap Gris Nez. The streets were narrow, tortuous, and mostly evil-smelling, with a mixture of stale
fish and damp cellar odours. There had been heavy rain
here during the storm last night, and sometimes Marguerite sank ankle-deep in the mud, for the roads were
not lighted save by the occasional glimmer from a lamp
inside a house.

But she did not heed any of these petty discomforts:
"We may meet Blakeney at the 'Chat Gris,'" Sir Andrew had said, when they landed, and she was walking
as if on a carpet of rose-leaves, for she was going to
meet him almost at once.

At last they reached their destination. Sir Andrew evidently knew the road, for he had walked unerringly in
the dark, and had not asked his way from anyone. It
was too dark then for Marguerite to notice the outside
aspect of this house. The "Chat Gris," as Sir Andrew
had called it, was evidently a small wayside inn on the
outskirts of Calais, and on the way to Gris Nez. It lay
some little distance from the coast, for the sound of the
sea seemed to come from afar.

Sir Andrew knocked at the door with the knob of his
cane, and from within Marguerite heard a sort of grunt
and the muttering of a number of oaths. Sir Andrew
knocked again, this time more peremptorily: more
oaths were heard, and then shuffling steps seemed to
draw near the door. Presently this was thrown open,
and Marguerite found herself on the threshold of the
most dilapidated, most squalid room she had ever seen
in all her life.

The paper, such as it was, was hanging from the
walls in strips; there did not seem to be a single piece of
furniture in the room that could, by the wildest stretch

of imagination, be called "whole." Most of the chairs had broken backs, others had no seats to them, one corner of the table was propped up with a bundle of faggots, there where the fourth leg had been broken.

In one corner of the room there was a huge hearth, over which hung a stock-pot, with a not altogether unpalatable odour of hot soup emanating therefrom. On one side of the room, high up in the wall, there was a species of loft, before which hung a tattered blue-and-white checked curtain. A rickety set of steps led up to this loft.

On the great bare walls, with their colourless paper, all stained with varied filth, there were chalked up at intervals in great bold characters, the words: "Liberté—Egalité—Fraternité."

The whole of this sordid abode was dimly lighted by an evil-smelling oil-lamp, which hung from the rickety rafters of the ceiling. It all looked so horribly squalid, so dirty and uninviting, that Marguerite hardly dared to cross the threshold.

Sir Andrew, however, had stepped unhesitatingly forward.

"English travellers, citoyen!" he said boldly, and speaking in French.

The individual who had come to the door in response to Sir Andrew's knock, and who, presumably, was the owner of this squalid abode, was an elderly, heavily-built peasant, dressed in a dirty blue blouse, heavy sabots, from which wisps of straw protruded all round, shabby blue trousers, and the inevitable red cap with the tricolour cockade, that proclaimed his momentary political views. He carried a short wooden pipe, from which the odour of rank tobacco emanated.

He looked with some suspicion and a great deal of contempt at the two travellers, muttered "*Sacrrrés Anglais!*" and spat upon the ground to further show his independence of spirit, but, nevertheless, he stood aside to let them enter, no doubt well aware that these same *sacrés Anglais* always had well-filled purses.

"Oh, lud!" said Marguerite, as she advanced into the room, holding her handkerchief to her dainty nose, "what a dreadful hole! Are you sure this is the place?"

"Aye! 'tis the place, sure enough," replied the young man as, with his lace-edged, fashionable handkerchief, he dusted a chair for Marguerite to sit on; "but I vow I never saw a more villainous hole."

"Faith!" she said, looking round with some curiosity and a great deal of horror at the dilapidated walls, the broken chairs, the rickety table, "it certainly does not look inviting."

The landlord of the "Chat Gris"—by name, Brogard—had taken no further notice of his guests; he concluded that presently they would order supper, and in the meanwhile it was not for a free citizen to show deference, or even courtesy, to anyone, however smartly they might be dressed.

By the hearth sat a huddled-up figure clad, seemingly, mostly in rags: that figure was apparently a woman, although even that would have been hard to distinguish, except for the cap, which had once been white, and for what looked like the semblance of a petticoat. She was sitting mumbling to herself, and from time to time stirring the brew in her stock-pot.

"Hey, my friend!" said Sir Andrew at last, "we should like some supper. . . . The citoyenne there," he added, pointing to the huddled-up bundle of rags by

the hearth, "is concocting some delicious soup, I'll warrant, and my mistress has not tasted food for several
hours."

It took Brogard some few moments to consider the
question. A free citizen does not respond too readily to
the wishes of those who happen to require something
of him.

"*Sacrrrés aristos!*" he murmured, and once more spat
upon the ground.

Then he went very slowly up to a dresser which
stood in a corner of the room; from this he took an old
pewter soup-tureen and slowly, and without a word,
he handed it to his better-half, who, in the same silence, began filling the tureen with the soup out of her
stockpot.

Marguerite had watched all these preparations with
absolute horror; were it not for the earnestness of her
purpose, she would incontinently have fled from this
abode of dirt and evil smells.

"Faith! our host and hostess are not cheerful
people," said Sir Andrew, seeing the look of horror on
Marguerite's face. "I would I could offer you a more
hearty and more appetising meal . . . but I think you
will find the soup eatable and the wine good; these people wallow in dirt, but live well as a rule."

"Nay! I pray you, Sir Andrew," she said gently, "be
not anxious about me. My mind is scarce inclined to
dwell on thoughts of supper."

Brogard was slowly pursuing his gruesome preparations; he had placed a couple of spoons, also two
glasses on the table, both of which Sir Andrew took the
precaution of wiping carefully.

Brogard had also produced a bottle of wine and some

bread, and Marguerite made an effort to draw her chair to the table and to make some pretence at eating. Sir Andrew, as befitting his *rôle* of lacquey, stood behind her chair.

"Nay, Madame, I pray you," he said, seeing that Marguerite seemed quite unable to eat, "I beg of you to try and swallow some food—remember you have need of all your strength."

The soup certainly was not bad; it smelt and tasted good. Marguerite might have enjoyed it, but for the horrible surroundings. She broke the bread, however, and drank some of the wine.

"Nay, Sir Andrew," she said, "I do not like to see you standing. You have need of food just as much as I have. This creature will only think that I am an eccentric Englishwoman eloping with her lacquey, if you'll sit down and partake of this semblance of supper beside me."

Indeed, Brogard having placed what was strictly necessary upon the table, seemed not to trouble himself any further about his guests. The Mère Brogard had quietly shuffled out of the room, and the man stood and lounged about, smoking his evil-smelling pipe, sometimes under Marguerite's very nose, as any free-born citizen who was anybody's equal should do.

"Confound the brute!" said Sir Andrew, with native British wrath, as Brogard leant up against the table, smoking and looking down superciliously at these two *sacrrrés Anglais*.

"In Heaven's name, man," admonished Marguerite, hurriedly, seeing that Sir Andrew, with British-born instinct, was ominously clenching his fist, "remember that you are in France, and that in this year of grace this is the temper of the people."

"I'd like to scrag the brute!" muttered Sir Andrew, savagely.

He had taken Marguerite's advice and sat next to her at table, and they were both making noble efforts to deceive one another, by pretending to eat and drink.

"I pray you," said Marguerite, "keep the creature in a good temper, so that he may answer the questions we must put to him."

"I'll do my best, but, begad! I'd sooner scrag him than question him. Hey! my friend," he said pleasantly in French, and tapping Brogard lightly on the shoulder, "do you see many of our quality along these parts? Many English travellers, I mean?"

Brogard looked round at him, over his near shoulder, puffed away at his pipe for a moment or two as he was in no hurry, then muttered,—

"Heu!—sometimes!"

"Ah!" said Sir Andrew, carelessly, "English travellers always know where they can get good wine, eh! my friend?—Now, tell me, my lady was desiring to know if by any chance you happen to have seen a great friend of hers, an English gentleman, who often comes to Calais on business; he is tall, and recently was on his way to Paris—my lady hoped to have met him in Calais."

Marguerite tried not to look at Brogard, lest she should betray before him the burning anxiety with which she waited for his reply. But a free-born French citizen is never in any hurry to answer questions: Brogard took his time, then he said very slowly,—

"Tall Englishman?—To-day!—Yes."

"You have seen him?" asked Sir Andrew, carelessly.

"Yes, to-day," muttered Brogard, sullenly. Then he quietly took Sir Andrew's hat from a chair close by, put it on his own head, tugged at his dirty blouse, and generally tried to express in pantomime that the individual in question wore very fine clothes. *"Sacrré aristo!"* he muttered, "that tall Englishman!"

Marguerite could scarce repress a scream.

"It's Sir Percy right enough," she murmured, "and not even in disguise!"

She smiled, in the midst of all her anxiety and through her gathering tears, at thought of "the ruling passion strong in death"; of Percy running into the wildest, maddest dangers, with the latest-cut coat upon his back, and the laces of his jabot unruffled.

"Oh! the foolhardiness of it!" she sighed. "Quick, Sir Andrew! ask the man when he went."

"Ah, yes, my friend," said Sir Andrew, addressing Brogard, with the same assumption of carelessness, "my lord always wears beautiful clothes; the tall Englishman you saw, was certainly my lady's friend. And he has gone, you say?"

"He went . . . yes . . . but he's coming back . . . here—he ordered supper . . ."

Sir Andrew put his hand with a quick gesture of warning upon Marguerite's arm; it came none too soon, for the next moment her wild, mad joy would have betrayed her. He was safe and well, was coming back here presently, she would see him in a few moments perhaps. . . . Oh! the wildness of her joy seemed almost more than she could bear.

"Here!" she said to Brogard, who seemed suddenly to have been transformed in her eyes into some heavenborn messenger of bliss. "Here!—did you say the English gentleman was coming back here?"

The heaven-born messenger of bliss spat upon the floor, to express his contempt for all and sundry *aristos,* who chose to haunt the "Chat Gris."

"Heu!" he muttered, "he ordered supper—he will come back. . . . *Sacré Anglais!*" he added, by way of protest against all this fuss for a mere Englishman.

"But where is he now?—Do you know?" she asked eagerly, placing her dainty white hand upon the dirty sleeve of his blue blouse.

"He went to get a horse and cart," said Brogard, laconically, as, with a surly gesture, he shook off from his arm that pretty hand which princes had been proud to kiss.

"At what time did he go?"

But Brogard had evidently had enough of these questionings. He did not think that it was fitting for a citizen—who was the equal of anybody—to be thus catechised by these *sacrés aristos,* even though they were rich English ones. It was distinctly more fitting to his newborn dignity to be as rude as possible; it was a sure sign of servility to meekly reply to civil questions.

"I don't know," he said surlily. "I have said enough, *voyons, les aristos!* . . . He came to-day. He ordered supper. He went out.—He'll come back. *Voilà!*"

And with this parting assertion of his rights as a citizen and a free man, to be as rude as he well pleased, Brogard shuffled out of the room, banging the door after him.

23

HOPE

"Faith, Madame!" said Sir Andrew, seeing that Marguerite seemed desirous to call her surly host back again, "I think we'd better leave him alone. We shall not get anything more out of him, and we might arouse his suspicions. One never knows what spies may be lurking around these God-forsaken places."

"What care I?" she replied lightly, "now I know that my husband is safe, and that I shall see him almost directly!"

"Hush!" he said in genuine alarm, for she had talked quite loudly, in the fulness of her glee, "the very walls have ears in France, these days."

He rose quickly from the table, and walked round the bare, squalid room, listening attentively at the door, through which Brogard had just disappeared, and whence only muttered oaths and shuffling footsteps could be heard. He also ran up the rickety steps that led to the attic, to assure himself that there were no spies of Chauvelin's about the place.

"Are we alone, Monsieur, my lacquey?" said Marguerite, gaily, as the young man once more sat down beside her. "May we talk?"

"As cautiously as possible!" he entreated.

"Faith, man! but you wear a glum face! As for me, I could dance with joy! Surely there is no longer any cause for fear. Our boat is on the beach, the *Foam Crest* not two miles out at sea, and my husband will be here, under this very roof, within the next half hour perhaps. Sure! there is naught to hinder us. Chauvelin and his gang have not yet arrived."

"Nay, madam! that I fear we do not know."

"What do you mean?"

"He was at Dover at the same time that we were."

"Held up by the same storm, which kept us from starting."

"Exactly. But—I did not speak of it before, for I feared to alarm you—I saw him on the beach not five minutes before we embarked. At least, I swore to myself at the time that it was himself; he was disguised as a *curé*, so that Satan, his own guardian, would scarce have known him. But I heard him then, bargaining for a vessel to take him swiftly to Calais; and he must have set sail less than an hour after we did."

Marguerite's face had quickly lost its look of joy. The terrible danger in which Percy stood, now that he was actually on French soil, became suddenly and horribly clear to her. Chauvelin was close upon his heels; here in Calais, the astute diplomatist was all-powerful; a word from him and Percy could be tracked and arrested and . . .

Every drop of blood seemed to freeze in her veins; not even during the moments of her wildest anguish in England had she so completely realised the imminence of the peril in which her husband stood. Chauvelin had sworn to bring the Scarlet Pimpernel to the guillotine, and now the daring plotter, whose anonymity hitherto had been his safeguard, stood revealed through her own hand, to his most bitter, most relentless enemy.

Chauvelin—when he waylaid Lord Tony and Sir Andrew Ffoulkes in the coffee-room of "The Fisherman's

Rest"—had obtained possession of all the plans of this latest expedition. Armand St. Just, the Comte de Tournay and other fugitive royalists were to have met the Scarlet Pimpernel—or rather, as it had been originally arranged, two of his emissaries—on this day, the 2nd of October, at a place evidently known to the league, and vaguely alluded to as the "Père Blanchard's hut."

Armand, whose connection with the Scarlet Pimpernel and disavowal of the brutal policy of the Reign of Terror was still unknown to his countrymen, had left England a little more than a week ago, carrying with him the necessary instructions, which would enable him to meet the other fugitives and to convey them to this place of safety.

This much Marguerite had fully understood from the first, and Sir Andrew Ffoulkes had confirmed her surmises. She knew, too, that when Sir Percy realized that his own plans and his directions to his lieutenants had been stolen by Chauvelin, it was too late to communicate with Armand, or to send fresh instructions to the fugitives.

They would, of necessity, be at the appointed time and place, not knowing how grave was the danger which now awaited their brave rescuer.

Blakeney, who as usual had planned and organized the whole expedition, would not allow any of his younger comrades to run the risk of almost certain capture. Hence his hurried note to them at Lord Grenville's ball—"Start myself to-morrow—alone."

And now with his identity known to his most bitter enemy, his every step would be dogged, the moment he set foot in France. He would be tracked by Chauvelin's emissaries, followed until he reached that mysterious hut where the fugitives were waiting for him, and there the trap would be closed on him and on them.

There was but one hour—the hour's start which Marguerite and Sir Andrew had of their enemy—in which to warn Percy of the imminence of his danger, and to persuade him to give up the foolhardy expedition, which could only end in his own death.

But there *was* that one hour.

"Chauvelin knows of this inn, from the papers he stole," said Sir Andrew, earnestly, "and on landing will make straight for it."

"He has not landed yet," she said, "we have an hour's start on him, and Percy will be here directly. We shall be mid-Channel ere Chauvelin has realised that we have slipped through his fingers."

She spoke excitedly and eagerly, wishing to infuse into her young friend some of that buoyant hope which still clung to her heart. But he shook his head sadly.

"Silent again, Sir Andrew?" she said with some impatience. "Why do you shake your head and look so glum?"

"Faith, Madame," he replied, " 'tis only because in making your rose-coloured plans, you are forgetting the most important factor."

"What in the world do you mean?—I am forgetting nothing. . . . What factor do you mean?" she added with more impatience.

"It stands six foot odd high," replied Sir Andrew, quietly, "and hath name Percy Blakeney."

"I don't understand," she murmured.

"Do you think that Blakeney would leave Calais without having accomplished what he set out to do?"

"You mean . . . ?"

"There's the old Comte de Tournay . . ."

"The Comte . . . ?" she murmured.

"And St. Just . . . and others . . ."

"My brother!" she said with a heart-broken sob of anguish. "Heaven help me, but I fear I had forgotten."

"Fugitives as they are, these men at this moment await with perfect confidence and unshaken faith the arrival of the Scarlet Pimpernel, who has pledged his honour to take them safely across the Channel."

Indeed, she had forgotten! With the sublime selfishness of a woman who loves with her whole heart, she had in the last twenty-four hours had no thought save for him. His precious, noble life, his danger—he, the loved one, the brave hero, he alone dwelt in her mind.

"My brother!" she murmured, as one by one the heavy tears gathered in her eyes, as memory came back to her of Armand, the companion and darling of her childhood, the man for whom she had committed the deadly sin, which had so hopelessly imperilled her brave husband's life.

"Sir Percy Blakeney would not be the trusted, honoured leader of a score of English gentlemen," said Sir Andrew, proudly, "if he abandoned those who placed their trust in him. As for breaking his word, the very thought is preposterous!"

There was silence for a moment or two. Marguerite had buried her face in her hands, and was letting the tears slowly trickle through her trembling fingers. The young man said nothing; his heart ached for this beautiful woman in her awful grief. All along he had felt the terrible *impasse* in which her own rash act had plunged them all. He knew his friend and leader so well, with his reckless daring, his mad bravery, his worship of his

own word of honour. Sir Andrew knew that Blakeney
would brave any danger, run the wildest risks sooner
than break it, and with Chauvelin at his very heels,
would make a final attempt, however desperate, to rescue those who trusted in him.

"Faith, Sir Andrew," said Marguerite at last, making
brave efforts to dry her tears, "you are right, and I
would not now shame myself by trying to dissuade him
from doing his duty. As you say, I should plead in vain.
God grant him strength and ability," she added fervently and resolutely, "to outwit his pursuers. He will
not refuse to take you with him, perhaps, when he
starts on his noble work; between you, you will have
cunning as well as valour! God guard you both! In the
meanwhile I think we should lose no time. I still believe
that his safety depends upon his knowing that Chauvelin is on his track."

"Undoubtedly. He has wonderful resources at his
command. As soon as he is aware of his danger he
will exercise more caution: his ingenuity is a veritable
miracle."

"Then, what say you to a voyage of reconnaissance in
the village whilst I wait here against his coming!—You
might come across Percy's track and thus save valuable
time. If you find him, tell him to beware!—his bitterest
enemy is on his heels!"

"But this is such a villainous hole for you to wait in."

"Nay, that I do not mind!—But you might ask our
surly host if he could let me wait in another room,
where I could be safer from the prying eyes of any
chance traveller. Offer him some ready money, so that
he should not fail to give me word the moment the tall
Englishman returns."

She spoke quite calmly, even cheerfully now, thinking out her plans, ready for the worst if need be; she
would show no more weakness, she would prove herself
worthy of him, who was about to give his life for the
sake of his fellow-men.

Sir Andrew obeyed her without further comment. Instinctively he felt that hers now was the stronger mind;
he was willing to give himself over to her guidance, to
become the hand, whilst she was the directing head.

He went to the door of the inner room, through
which Brogard and his wife had disappeared before,
and knocked; as usual, he was answered by a salvo of
muttered oaths.

"Hey! friend Brogard!" said the young man peremptorily, "my lady would wish to rest here awhile. Could
you give her the use of another room? She would wish
to be alone."

He took some money out of his pocket, and allowed
it to jingle significantly in his hand. Brogard had
opened the door, and listened, with his usual surly ap-
athy, to the young man's request. At sight of the gold,
however, his lazy attitude relaxed slightly; he took his
pipe from his mouth and shuffled into the room.

He then pointed over his shoulder at the attic up in
the wall.

"She can wait up there!" he said with a grunt. "It's
comfortable, and I have no other room."

"Nothing could better," said Marguerite in English;
she at once realised the advantages such a position hidden from view would give her. "Give him the money,
Sir Andrew; I shall be quite happy up there, and can
see everything without being seen."

She nodded to Brogard, who condescended to go up

to the attic, and to shake up the straw that lay on the floor.

"May I entreat you, madam, to do nothing rash," said Sir Andrew, as Marguerite prepared in her turn to ascend the rickety flight of steps. "Remember this place is infested with spies. Do not, I beg of you, reveal yourself to Sir Percy, unless you are absolutely certain that you are alone with him."

Even as he spoke, he felt how unnecessary was this caution: Marguerite was as calm, as clear-headed as any man. There was no fear of her doing anything that was rash.

"Nay," she said with a slight attempt at cheerfulness, "that can I faithfully promise you. I would not jeopardise my husband's life, nor yet his plans, by speaking to him before strangers. Have no fear, I will watch my opportunity, and serve him in the manner I think he needs it most."

Brogard had come down the steps again, and Marguerite was ready to go up to her safe retreat.

"I dare not kiss your hand, madam," said Sir Andrew, as she began to mount the steps, "since I am your lacquey, but I pray you be of good cheer. If I do not come across Blakeney in half an hour, I shall return, expecting to find him here."

"Yes, that will be best. We can afford to wait for half an hour. Chauvelin cannot possibly be here before that. God grant that either you or I may have seen Percy by then. Good luck to you, friend! Have no fear for me."

Lightly she mounted the rickety wooden steps that led to the attic. Brogard was taking no further heed of her. She could make herself comfortable there or not as she chose. Sir Andrew watched her until she had reached the loft and sat down upon the straw. She pulled the tattered curtains across, and the young man noted that she was singularly well placed there, for seeing and hearing, whilst remaining unobserved.

He had paid Brogard well; the surly old innkeeper would have no object in betraying her. Then Sir Andrew prepared to go. At the door he turned once again and looked up at the loft. Through the ragged curtains Marguerite's sweet face was peeping down at him, and the young man rejoiced to see that it looked serene, and even gently smiling. With a final nod of farewell to her, he walked out into the night.

24

The Death-Trap

The next quarter of an hour went by swiftly and noiselessly. In the room downstairs, Brogard had for a while busied himself with clearing the table, and re-arranging it for another guest.

It was because she watched these preparations that Marguerite found the time slipping by more pleasantly. It was for Percy that this semblance of supper was being got ready. Evidently Brogard had a certain amount of respect for the tall Englishman, as he seemed to take some trouble in making the place look a trifle less uninviting than it had done before.

He even produced, from some hidden recess in the old dresser, what actually looked like a table-cloth; and when he spread it out, and saw it was full of holes, he shook his head dubiously for a while, then was at much pains so to spread it over the table as to hide most of its blemishes.

Then he got out a serviette, also old and ragged, but possessing some measure of cleanliness, and with this he carefully wiped the glasses, spoons and plates, which he put on the table.

Marguerite could not help smiling to herself as she watched all these preparations, which Brogard accomplished to an accompaniment of muttered oaths. Clearly the great height and bulk of the Englishman, or perhaps the weight of his fist, had overawed this free-

born citizen of France, or he would never have been at
such trouble for any *sacrré aristo.*

When the table was set—such as it was—Brogard
surveyed it with evident satisfaction. He then dusted
one of the chairs with the corner of his blouse, gave a
stir to the stock-pot, threw a fresh bundle of faggots on
to the fire, and slouched out of the room.

Marguerite was left alone with her reflections. She
had spread her travelling cloak over the straw, and was
sitting fairly comfortably, as the straw was fresh, and
the evil odours from below came up to her only in a
modified form.

But, momentarily, she was almost happy; happy because, when she peeped through the tattered curtains,
she could see a rickety chair, a torn table-cloth, a glass,
a plate and a spoon; that was all. But those mute and
ugly things seemed to say to her that they were waiting
for Percy; that soon, very soon, he would be here, that
the squalid room being still empty, they would be alone
together.

That thought was so heavenly, that Marguerite
closed her eyes in order to shut out everything but that.
In a few minutes she would be alone with him; she
would run down the ladder, and let him see her; then
he would take her in his arms, and she would let him
see that, after that, she would gladly die for him, and
with him, for earth could hold no greater happiness
than that.

And then what would happen? She could not even
remotely conjecture. She knew, of course, that Sir Andrew was right, that Percy would do everything he had
set out to accomplish; that she—now she was here—

could do nothing, beyond warning him to be cautious, since Chauvelin himself was on his track. After having cautioned him, she would perforce have to see him go off upon his terrible and daring mission; she could not even with a word or look, attempt to keep him back. She would have to obey, whatever he told her to do, even perhaps have to efface herself, and wait, in indescribable agony, whilst he, perhaps, went to his death.

But even that seemed less terrible to bear than the thought that he should never know how much she loved him—that at any rate would be spared her; the squalid room itself, which seemed to be waiting for him, told her that he would be here soon.

Suddenly her over-sensitive ears caught the sound of distant footsteps drawing near; her heart gave a wild leap of joy! Was it Percy at last? No! the step did not seem quite as long, nor quite as firm as his; she also thought that she could hear two distinct sets of footsteps. Yes! that was it! two men were coming this way. Two strangers perhaps, to get a drink, or . . .

But she had not time to conjecture, for presently there was a peremptory call at the door, and the next moment it was violently thrown open from the outside, whilst a rough, commanding voice shouted,—

"Hey! Citoyen Brogard! Holá!"

Marguerite could not see the newcomers, but, through a hole in one of the curtains, she could observe one portion of the room below.

She heard Brogard's shuffling footsteps, as he came out of the inner room, muttering his usual string of oaths. On seeing the strangers, however, he paused in the middle of the room, well within range of Mar-

guerite's vision, looked at them, with even more withering contempt than he had bestowed upon his former
guests, and muttered, *"Sacrrrée soutane!"*

Marguerite's heart seemed all at once to stop beating; her eyes, large and dilated, had fastened on one of
the newcomers, who, at this point, had taken a quick
step forward towards Brogard. He was dressed in the
soutane, broad-brimmed hat and buckled shoes habitual to the French *curé,* but as he stood opposite the
innkeeper, he threw open his soutane for a moment,
displaying the tricolour scarf of officialism, which sight
immediately had the effect of transforming Brogard's
attitude of contempt, into one of cringing obsequious-
ness.

It was the sight of this French *curé,* which seemed to
freeze the very blood in Marguerite's veins. She could
not see his face, which was shaded by his broad-
brimmed hat, but she recognized the thin, bony hands,
the slight stoop, the whole gait of the man! It was
Chauvelin!

The horror of the situation struck her as with a physical blow; the awful disappointment, the dread of what
was to come, made her very senses reel, and she needed
almost superhuman effort, not to fall senseless beneath
it all.

"A plate of soup and a bottle of wine," said Chauvelin imperiously to Brogard, "then clear out of here—
understand? I want to be alone."

Silently, and without any muttering this time, Brogard obeyed. Chauvelin sat down at the table, which had
been prepared for the tall Englishman, and the
innkeeper busied himself obsequiously round him,
dishing up the soup and pouring out the wine. The

man who had entered with Chauvelin and whom Marguerite could not see, stood waiting close by the door.

At a brusque sign from Chauvelin, Brogard had hurried back to the inner room, and the former now beckoned to the man who had accompanied him.

In him Marguerite at once recognised Desgas, Chauvelin's secretary and confidential factotum, whom she had often seen in Paris, in the days gone by. He crossed the room, and for a moment or two listened attentively at the Brogards' door.

"Not listening?" asked Chauvelin, curtly.

"No, citoyen."

For a second Marguerite dreaded lest Chauvelin should order Desgas to search the place; what would happen if she were to be discovered, she hardly dared to imagine. Fortunately, however, Chauvelin seemed more impatient to talk to his secretary than afraid of spies, for he called Desgas quickly back to his side.

"The English schooner?" he asked.

"She was lost sight of at sundown, citoyen," replied Desgas, "but was then making west, towards Cap Gris Nez."

"Ah!—good!—" muttered Chauvelin, "and now, about Captain Jutley?—what did he say?"

"He assured me that all the orders you sent him last week have been implicitly obeyed. All the roads which converge to this place have been patrolled night and day ever since: and the beach and cliffs have been most rigorously searched and guarded."

"Does he know where this 'Père Blanchard's' hut is?"

"No, citoyen, nobody seems to know of it by that name. There are any amount of fishermen's huts all along the coast, of course . . . but . . ."

"That'll do. Now about tonight?" interrupted Chauvelin, impatiently.

"The roads and the beach are patrolled as usual, citoyen, and Captain Jutley awaits further orders."

"Go back to him at once, then. Tell him to send reinforcements to the various patrols; and especially to those along the beach—you understand?"

Chauvelin spoke curtly and to the point, and every word he uttered struck at Marguerite's heart like the death-knell of her fondest hopes.

"The men," he continued, "are to keep the sharpest possible look-out for any stranger who may be walking, riding, or driving, along the road or the beach, more especially for a tall stranger, whom I need not describe further, as probably he will be disguised; but he cannot very well conceal his height, except by stooping. You understand?"

"Perfectly, citoyen," replied Desgas.

"As soon as any of the men have sighted a stranger, two of them are to keep him in view. The man who loses sight of the tall stranger, after he is once seen, will pay for his negligence with his life; but one man is to ride straight back here and report to me. Is that clear?"

"Absolutely clear, citoyen."

"Very well, then. Go and see Jutley at once. See the reinforcements start off for the patrol duty, then ask the captain to let you have half-a-dozen more men and bring them here with you. You can be back in ten minutes. Go—"

Desgas saluted and went to the door.

As Marguerite, sick with horror, listened to Chauvelin's directions to his underling, the whole of the plan for the capture of the Scarlet Pimpernel became appallingly clear to her. Chauvelin wished that the fugitives should be left in false security waiting in their hidden retreat until Percy joined them. Then the daring plotter was to be surrounded and caught red-handed, in the very act of aiding and abetting royalists, who were traitors to the republic. Thus, if his capture were noised abroad, even the British Government could not legally protest in his favour; having plotted with the enemies of the French Government, France had the right to put him to death.

Escape for him and them would be impossible. All the roads patrolled and watched, the trap well set, the net, wide at present, but drawing together tighter and tighter, until it closed upon the daring plotter, whose superhuman cunning even could not rescue him from its meshes now.

Desgas was about to go, but Chauvelin once more called him back. Marguerite vaguely wondered what further devilish plans he could have formed, in order to entrap one brave man, alone, against two-score of others. She looked at him as he turned to speak to Desgas; she could just see his face beneath the broad-brimmed *curé's* hat. There was at that moment so much deadly hatred, such fiendish malice in the thin face and pale, small eyes, that Marguerite's last hope died in her heart, for she felt that from this man she could expect no mercy.

"I had forgotten," repeated Chauvelin, with a weird chuckle, as he rubbed his bony, talon-like hands one against the other, with a gesture of fiendish satisfaction. "The tall stranger may show fight. In any case no shooting, remember, except as a last resort. I want that tall stranger alive . . . if possible."

He laughed, as Dante has told us that the devils laugh at sight of the torture of the damned. Marguerite had thought that by now she had lived through the whole gamut of horror and anguish that human heart could bear; yet now, when Desgas left the house, and she remained alone in this lonely, squalid room, with that fiend for company, she felt as if all that she had suffered was nothing compared with this. He continued to laugh and chuckle to himself for a while, rubbing his hands together in anticipation of his triumph.

His plans were well laid, and he might well triumph! Not a loophole was left, through which the bravest, the most cunning man might escape. Every road guarded, every corner watched, and in that lonely hut somewhere on the coast, a small band of fugitives waiting for their rescuer, and leading him to his death—nay! to worse than death. That fiend there, in a holy man's garb, was too much of a devil to allow a brave man to die the quick, sudden death of a soldier at the post of duty.

He, above all, longed to have the cunning enemy, who had so long baffled him, helpless in his power; he wished to gloat over him, to enjoy his downfall, to inflict upon him what moral and mental torture a deadly hatred alone can devise. The brave eagle, captured, and with noble wings clipped, was doomed to endure the gnawing of the rat. And she, his wife, who loved him, and who had brought him to this, could do nothing to help him.

Nothing, save to hope for death by his side, and for one brief moment in which to tell him that her love— whole, true and passionate—was entirely his.

Chauvelin was now sitting close to the table; he had

taken off his hat, and Marguerite could just see the outline of his thin profile and pointed chin, as he bent over his meagre supper. He was evidently quite contented, and awaited events with perfect calm; he even seemed to enjoy Brogard's unsavoury fare. Marguerite wondered how so much hatred could lurk in one human being against another.

Suddenly, as she watched Chauvelin, a sound caught her ear, which turned her very heart to stone. And yet that sound was not calculated to inspire anyone with horror, for it was merely the cheerful sound of a gay, fresh voice singing lustily, "God save the King!"

25

The Eagle and the Fox

Marguerite's breath stopped short; she seemed to feel her very life standing still momentarily whilst she listened to that voice and to that song. In the singer she had recognised her husband. Chauvelin, too, had heard it, for he darted a quick glance towards the door, then hurriedly took up his broad-brimmed hat and clapped it over his head.

The voice drew nearer; for one brief second the wild desire seized Marguerite to rush down the steps and fly across the room, to stop that song at any cost, to beg the cheerful singer to fly—fly for his life, before it be too late. She checked the impulse just in time. Chauvelin would stop her before she reached the door, and, moreover, she had no idea if he had any soldiers posted within his call. Her impetuous act might prove the death-signal of the man she would have died to save.

"Long to reign over us, God save the King!"

sang the voice more lustily than ever. The next moment the door was thrown open and there was dead silence for a second or so.

Marguerite could not see the door: she held her breath, trying to imagine what was happening.

Percy Blakeney on entering had, of course, at once caught sight of the *curé* at the table; his hesitation lasted less than five seconds, the next moment, Marguerite saw his tall figure crossing the room, whilst he called in a loud, cheerful voice,—

"Hello, there! no one about? Where's that fool Brogard?"

He wore the magnificent coat and riding-suit which he had on when Marguerite last saw him at Richmond, so many hours ago. As usual, his get-up was absolutely irreproachable, the fine Mechlin lace at his neck and wrists was immaculate in its gossamer daintiness, his hands looked slender and white, his fair hair was carefully brushed, and he carried his eyeglass with his usual affected gesture. In fact, at this moment, Sir Percy Blakeney, Bart., might have been on his way to a garden-party at the Prince of Wales', instead of deliberately, cold-bloodedly running his head in a trap, set for him by his deadliest enemy.

He stood for a moment in the middle of the room, whilst Marguerite, absolutely paralysed with horror, seemed unable even to breathe.

Every moment she expected that Chauvelin would give a signal, that the place would fill with soldiers, that she would rush down and help Percy to sell his life dearly. As he stood there, suavely unconscious, she very nearly screamed out to him,—

"Fly, Percy!—'tis your deadly enemy!—fly before it be too late!"

But she had not time even to do that, for the next moment Blakeney quietly walked to the table, and, jovially clapping the *curé* on the back, said in his own drawly, affected way,—

"Odd's fish! . . . er . . . M. Chauvelin. I vow I never thought of meeting you here."

Chauvelin, who had been in the very act of convey-

ing soup to his mouth, fairly choked. His thin face became absolutely purple, and a violent fit of coughing
saved this cunning representative of France from betraying the most boundless surprise he had ever experienced. There was no doubt that this bold move on the
part of the enemy had been wholly unexpected, as far
as he was concerned: and the daring impudence of it
completely nonplussed him for the moment.

Obviously he had not taken the precaution of having
the inn surrounded with soldiers. Blakeney had evidently guessed that much, and no doubt his resourceful
brain had already formed some plan by which he could
turn this unexpected interview to account.

Marguerite up in the loft had not moved. She had
made a solemn promise to Sir Andrew not to speak to
her husband before strangers, and she had sufficient
self-control not to throw herself unreasoningly and impulsively across his plans. To sit still and watch these
two men together was a terrible trial of fortitude. Marguerite had heard Chauvelin give the orders for the patrolling of all the roads. She knew that if Percy now left
the "Chat Gris"—in whichever direction he happened
to go—he could not go far without being sighted by
some of Captain Jutley's men on patrol. On the other
hand, if he stayed, then Desgas would have time to
come back with the half-dozen men Chauvelin had specially ordered.

The trap was closing in, and Marguerite could do
nothing but watch and wonder. The two men looked
such a strange contrast, and of the two it was Chauvelin who exhibited a slight touch of fear. Marguerite
knew him well enough to guess what was passing in his
mind. He had no fear for his own person, although he

certainly was alone in a lonely inn with a man who was powerfully built, and who was daring and reckless beyond the bounds of probability. She knew that Chauvelin would willingly have braved perilous encounters for the sake of the cause he had at heart, but what he did fear was that this impudent Englishman would, by knocking him down, double his own chances of escape; his underlings might not succeed so well in capturing the Scarlet Pimpernel, when not directed by the cunning hand and the shrewd brain, which had deadly hate for an incentive.

Evidently, however, the representative of the French Government had nothing to fear for the moment, at the hands of his powerful adversary. Blakeney, with his most inane laugh and pleasant good-nature, was solemnly patting him on the back.

"I am so demmed sorry . . ." he was saying cheerfully, "so very sorry . . . I seem to have upset you . . . eating soup, too . . . nasty, awkward thing, soup . . . er . . . Begad!—a friend of mine died once . . . er . . . choked . . . just like you . . . with a spoonful of soup."

And he smiled shyly, good-humouredly, down at Chauvelin.

"Odd's life!" he continued, as soon as the latter had somewhat recovered himself, "beastly hole this . . . ain't it now? La! you don't mind?" he added, apologetically, as he sat down on a chair close to the table and drew the soup tureen towards him. "That fool Brogard seems to be asleep or something."

There was a second plate on the table, and he calmly helped himself to soup, then poured himself out a glass of wine.

For a moment Marguerite wondered what Chauvelin

would do. His disguise was so good that perhaps he meant, on recovering himself, to deny his identity: but Chauvelin was too astute to make such an obviously false and childish move, and already he too had stretched out his hand and said pleasantly,—

"I am indeed charmed to see you, Sir Percy. You must excuse me—h'm—I thought you the other side of the Channel. Sudden surprise almost took my breath away."

"La!" said Sir Percy, with a good-humoured grin, "it did that quite, didn't it—er—M.—er—Chaubertin?"

"Pardon me—Chauvelin."

"I beg pardon—a thousand times. Yes—Chauvelin of course. . . . Er . . . I never could cotton to foreign names. . . ."

He was calmly eating his soup, laughing with pleasant good-humour, as if he had come all the way to Calais for the express purpose of enjoying supper at this filthy inn, in the company of his arch-enemy.

For the moment Marguerite wondered why Percy did not knock the little Frenchman down then and there—and no doubt something of the sort must have darted through his mind, for every now and then his lazy eyes seemed to flash ominously, as they rested on the slight figure of Chauvelin, who had now quite recovered himself and was also calmly eating his soup.

But the keen brain, which had planned and carried through so many daring plots, was too far-seeing to take unnecessary risks. This place, after all, might be infested with spies; the innkeeper might be in Chauvelin's pay. One call on Chauvelin's part might bring twenty men about Blakeney's ears for aught he knew, and he might be caught and trapped before he could help or, at least, warn the fugitives. This he would not risk; he meant to help the others, to get *them* safely away; for he had pledged his word to them, and his word he *would* keep. And whilst he ate and chatted, he thought and planned, whilst, up in the loft, the poor, anxious woman racked her brain as to what she should do, and endured agonies of longing to rush down to him, yet not daring to move for fear of upsetting his plans.

"I didn't know," Blakeney was saying jovially, "that you . . . er . . . were in holy orders."

"I . . . er . . . hem . . ." stammered Chauvelin. The calm impudence of his antagonist had evidently thrown him off his usual balance.

"But, la! I should have known you anywhere," continued Sir Percy, placidly, as he poured himself out another glass of wine, "although the wig and hat have changed you a bit."

"Do you think so?"

"Lud! they alter a man so. . . but . . . begad! I hope you don't mind my having made the remark? . . . Demmed bad form making remarks. . . . I hope you don't mind?"

"No, no, not at all—hem! I hope Lady Blakeney is well," said Chauvelin, hurriedly changing the topic of conversation.

Blakeney, with much deliberation, finished his plate of soup, drank his glass of wine, and, momentarily, it seemed to Marguerite as if he glanced quickly all round the room.

"Quite well, thank you," he said at last, drily. There was a pause, during which Marguerite could watch these two antagonists who, evidently in their minds, were measuring themselves against one another. She could see Percy almost full face where he sat at the table not ten yards from where she herself was crouching, puzzled, not knowing what to do, or what she should think. She had quite controlled her impulse by now of rushing down and disclosing herself to her husband. A man capable of acting a part, in the way he was doing at the present moment, did not need a woman's word to warn him to be cautious.

Marguerite indulged in the luxury, dear to every tender woman's heart, of looking at the man she loved. She looked through the tattered curtain, across at the handsome face of her husband, in whose lazy blue eyes, and behind whose inane smile, she could now so plainly see the strength, energy, and resourcefulness which had caused the Scarlet Pimpernel to be reverenced and trusted by his followers. "There are nineteen of us ready to lay down our lives for your husband, Lady Blakeney," Sir Andrew had said to her; and as she looked at the forehead, low, but square and broad, the eyes, blue, yet deepset and intense, the whole aspect of the man, of indomitable energy, hiding, behind a perfectly acted comedy, his almost superhuman strength of will and marvellous ingenuity, she understood the fascination which he exercised over his followers, for had he not also cast his spells over her heart and her imagination?

Chauvelin, who was trying to conceal his impatience beneath his usual urbane manner, took a quick look at his watch. Desgas should not be long: another two or three minutes, and this impudent Englishman would be secure in the keeping of half a dozen of Captain Jutley's most trusted men.

"You are on your way to Paris, Sir Percy?" he asked carelessly.

"Odd's life, no," replied Blakeney, with a laugh. "Only as far as Lille—not Paris for me . . . beastly uncomfortable place Paris, just now . . . eh, Monsieur Chaubertin . . . beg pardon . . . Chauvelin!"

"Not for an English gentleman like yourself, Sir Percy," rejoined Chauvelin, sarcastically, "who takes no interest in the conflict that is raging there."

"La! you see it's no business of mine, and our demmed government is all on your side of the business. Old Pitt daren't say 'Bo' to a goose. You are in a hurry, sir," he added, as Chauvelin once again took out his watch; "an appointment, perhaps. . . . I pray you take no heed of me. . . . My time's my own."

He rose from the table and dragged a chair to the hearth. Once more Marguerite was terribly tempted to go to him, for time was getting on; Desgas might be back at any moment with his men. Percy did not know that and . . . oh! how horrible it all was—and how helpless she felt.

"I am in no hurry," continued Percy, pleasantly, "but, la! I don't want to spend any more time than I can help in this God-forsaken hole! But, begad! sir," he added, as Chauvelin had surreptitiously looked at his watch for the third time, "that watch of yours won't go any faster for all the looking you give it. You are expecting a friend, maybe?"

"Aye—a friend!"

"Not a lady—I trust, Monsieur l'Abbé," laughed Blakeney; "surely the holy Church does not allow? . . . eh? . . . what! But, I say, come by the fire . . . it's getting demmed cold."

He kicked the fire with the heel of his boot, making the logs blaze in the old hearth. He seemed in no hurry to go, and apparently was quite unconscious of his immediate danger. He dragged another chair to the fire, and Chauvelin, whose impatience was by now quite beyond control, sat down beside the hearth, in such a way as to command a view of the door. Desgas had been gone nearly a quarter of an hour. It was quite plain to Marguerite's aching senses that as soon as he arrived, Chauvelin would abandon all his other plans with regard to the fugitives, and capture this impudent Scarlet Pimpernel at once.

"Hey, M. Chauvelin," the latter was saying arily, "tell me, I pray you, is your friend pretty? Demmed smart these little French women sometimes—what? But I protest I need not ask," he added, as he carelessly strode back towards the supper-table. "In matters of taste the Church has never been backward. . . . Eh?"

But Chauvelin was not listening. His every faculty was now concentrated on that door through which presently Desgas would enter. Marguerite's thoughts, too, were centered there, for her ears had suddenly caught, through the stillness of the night, the sound of numerous and measured treads some distance away.

It was Desgas and his men. Another three minutes and they would be here! Another three minutes and the awful thing would have occurred: the brave eagle would have fallen in the ferret's trap! She would have moved now and screamed, but she dared not; for whilst she heard the soldiers approaching, she was looking at Percy and watching his every movement. He was standing by the table whereon the remnants of the supper, plates, glasses, spoons, salt and pepper-pots were scattered pell-mell. His back was turned to Chauvelin and he was still prattling along in his own affected and inane way, but from his pocket he had taken his snuff-box, and quickly and suddenly he emptied the contents of the pepper-pot into it.

Then he again turned with an inane laugh to Chauvelin,—

"Eh? Did you speak, sir?"

Chauvelin had been too intent on listening to the sound of those approaching footsteps, to notice what his cunning adversary had been doing. He now pulled himself together, trying to look unconcerned in the very midst of his anticipated triumph.

"No," he said presently, "that is—as you were saying, Sir Percy—?"

"I was saying," said Blakeney, going up to Chauvelin, by the fire, "that the Jew in Piccadilly has sold me better snuff this time than I have ever tasted. Will you honour me, Monsieur l'Abbé?"

He stood close to Chauvelin in his own careless, débonnaire way, holding out his snuff-box to his archenemy.

Chauvelin, who, as he told Marguerite once, had seen a trick or two in his day, had never dreamed of this one. With one ear fixed on those fast-approaching footsteps, one eye turned to that door where Desgas and his men would presently appear, lulled into false security by the impudent Englishman's airy manner, he never even remotely guessed the trick which was being played upon him.

He took a pinch of snuff.

Only he, who has ever by accident sniffed vigorously a dose of pepper, can have the faintest conception of the hopeless condition in which such a sniff would reduce any human being.

Chauvelin felt as if his head would burst—sneeze after sneeze seemed nearly to choke him; he was blind, deaf, and dumb for the moment, and during that moment Blakeney quietly, without the slightest haste, took up his hat, took some money out of his pocket, which he left on the table, then calmly stalked out of the room!

It took Marguerite some time to collect her scattered
senses; the whole of this last short episode had taken
place in less than a minute, and Desgas and the soldiers
were still about two hundred yards away from the
"Chat Gris."

When she realised what had happened, a curious
mixture of joy and wonder filled her heart. It all was so
neat, so ingenious. Chauvelin was still absolutely helpless, far more so than he could even have been under a
blow from the fist, for now he could neither see, nor
hear, nor speak, whilst his cunning adversary had quietly slipped through his fingers.

Blakeney was gone, obviously to try and join the fugitives at the Père Blanchard's hut. For the moment,
true, Chauvelin was helpless; for the moment the daring Scarlet Pimpernel had not been caught by Desgas
and his men. But all the roads and the beach were patrolled. Every place was watched, and every stranger
kept in sight. How far could Percy go, thus arrayed in
his gorgeous clothes, without being sighted and followed?

Now she blamed herself terribly for not having gone
down to him sooner, and given him that word of warning and of love which, perhaps, after all, he needed. He
could not know of the orders which Chauvelin had
given for his capture, and even now, perhaps . . .

But before all these horrible thoughts had taken concrete form in her brain, she heard the grounding of arms outside, close to the door, and Desgas' voice shouting "Halt!" to his men.

Chauvelin had partially recovered; his sneezing had become less violent, and he had struggled to his feet. He managed to reach the door just as Desgas' knock was heard on the outside.

Chauvelin threw open the door, and before his secretary could say a word, he had managed to stammer between two sneezes—

"The tall stranger—quick!did any of you see him?"

"Where, citoyen?" asked Desgas, in surprise.

"Here, man! through that door! not five minutes ago."

"We saw nothing, citoyen! The moon is not yet up, and . . ."

"And you are just five minutes too late, my friend," said Chauvelin, with concentrated fury.

"Citoyen . . . I . . ."

"You did what I ordered you to do," said Chauvelin, with impatience. "I know that, but you were a precious long time about it. Fortunately, there's not much harm done, or it had fared ill with you, Citoyen Desgas."

Desgas turned a little pale. There was so much rage and hatred in his superior's whole attitude.

"The tall stranger, citoyen—" he stammered.

"Was here, in this room, five minutes ago, having supper at that table. Damn his impudence! For obvious reasons, I dared not tackle him alone. Brogard is too big a fool, and that cursed Englishman appears to have the strength of a bullock, and so he slipped away under your very nose."

"He cannot go far without being sighted, citoyen."

"Ah?"

"Captain Jutley sent forty men as reinforcements for the patrol duty: twenty went down to the beach. He again assured me that the watch has been constant all day, and that no stranger could possibly get to the beach, or reach a boat, without being sighted."

"That's good.—Do the men know their work?"

"They have had very clear orders, citoyen: and I myself spoke to those who were about to start. They are to shadow—as secretly as possible—any stranger they may see, especially if he be tall, or stoop as if he would disguise his height."

"In no case to detain such a person, of course," said Chauvelin, eagerly. "That impudent Scarlet Pimpernel would slip through clumsy fingers. We must let him get to the Père Blanchard's hut now; there surround and capture him."

"The men understand that, citoyen, and also that, as soon as a tall stranger has been sighted, he must be shadowed, whilst one man is to turn straight back and report to you."

"That is right," said Chauvelin, rubbing his hands, well pleased.

"I have further news for you, citoyen."

"What is it?"

"A tall Englishman had a long conversation about three-quarters of an hour ago with a Jew, Reuben by name, who lives not ten paces from here."

"Yes—and?" queried Chauvelin, impatiently.

"The conversation was all about a horse and cart, which the tall Englishman wished to hire, and which was to have been ready for him by eleven o'clock."

"It is past that now. Where does that Reuben live?"

"A few minutes' walk from this door."

"Send one of the men to find out if the stranger has driven off in Reuben's cart."

"Yes, citoyen."

Desgas went to give the necessary orders to one of the men. Not a word of this conversation between him and Chauvelin had escaped Marguerite, and every word they had spoken seemed to strike at her heart, with terrible hopelessness and dark foreboding.

She had come all this way, and with such high hopes and firm determination to help her husband, and so far she had been able to do nothing, but to watch, with a heart breaking with anguish, the meshes of the deadly net closing round the daring Scarlet Pimpernel.

He could not now advance many steps, without spying eyes to track and denounce him. Her own helplessness struck her with the terrible sense of utter disappointment. The possibility of being of the slightest use to her husband had become almost *nil*, and her only hope rested in being allowed to share his fate, whatever it might ultimately be.

For the moment, even her chance of ever seeing the man she loved again, had become a remote one. Still, she was determined to keep a close watch over his enemy, and a vague hope filled her heart, that whilst she kept Chauvelin in sight, Percy's fate might still be hanging in the balance.

Desgas had left Chauvelin moodily pacing up and down the room, whilst he himself waited outside for the return of the man whom he had sent in search of Reuben. Thus several minutes went by. Chauvelin was evidently devoured with impatience. Apparently he trusted no one: this last trick played upon him by the daring Scarlet Pimpernel had made him suddenly doubtful of success, unless he himself was there to watch, direct and superintend the capture of this impudent Englishman.

About five minutes later, Desgas returned, followed by an elderly Jew, in a dirty, threadbare gaberdine, worn greasy across the shoulders. His red hair, which he wore after the fashion of the Polish Jews, with the corkscrew curls each side of his face, was plentifully sprinkled with grey—a general coating of grime, about his cheeks and his chin, gave him a peculiarly dirty and loathsome appearance. He had the habitual stoop, those of his race affected in mock humility in past centuries, before the dawn of equality and freedom in matters of faith, and he walked behind Desgas with the peculiar shuffling gait which has remained the characteristic of the Jew trader in continental Europe to this day.

Chauvelin, who had all the Frenchman's prejudice against the despised race, motioned to the fellow to keep at a respectful distance. The group of the three men were standing just underneath the hanging oil-lamp, and Marguerite had a clear view of them all.

"Is this the man?" asked Chauvelin.

"No, citoyen," replied Desgas, "Reuben could not be found, so presumably his cart has gone with the stranger; but this man here seems to know something, which he is willing to sell for a consideration."

"Ah!" said Chauvelin, turning away with disgust from the loathsome specimen of humanity before him.

The Jew, with characteristic patience, stood humbly on one side, leaning on a thick knotted staff, his greasy, broad-brimmed hat casting a deep shadow over his grimy face, waiting for the noble Excellency to deign to put some questions to him.

"The citoyen tells me," said Chauvelin peremptorily to him, "that you know something of my friend, the tall Englishman, whom I desire to meet. . . . *Morbleu!* keep your distance, man," he added hurriedly, as the Jew took a quick and eager step forward.

"Yes, your Excellency," replied the Jew, who spoke the language with that peculiar lisp which denotes Eastern origin, "I and Reuben Goldstein met a tall Englishman, on the road, close by here this evening."

"Did you speak to him?"

"He spoke to us, your Excellency. He wanted to know if he could hire a horse and cart to go down along the St. Martin Road, to a place he wanted to reach tonight."

"What did you say?"

"I did not say anything," said the Jew in an injured tone, "Reuben Goldstein, that accursed traitor, that son of Belial . . ."

"Cut that short, man," interrupted Chauvelin, roughly, "and go on with your story."

"He took the words out of my mouth, your Excellency: when I was about to offer the wealthy Englishman my horse and cart, to take him wheresoever he chose, Reuben had already spoken, and offered his half-starved nag, and his broken-down cart."

"And what did the Englishman do?"

"He listened to Reuben Goldstein, your Excellency, and put his hand in his pocket then and there, and took out a handful of gold, which he showed to that descendant of Beelzebub, telling him that all that would be his, if the horse and cart were ready for him by eleven o'clock."

"And, of course, the horse and cart were ready?"

"Well! they were ready in a manner, so to speak, your Excellency. Reuben's nag was lame as usual; she refused to budge at first. It was only after a time and with plenty of kicks, that she at last could be made to move," said the Jew with a malicious chuckle.

"Then they started?"

"Yes, they started about five minutes ago. I was disgusted with that stranger's folly. An Englishman too!— He ought to have known Reuben's nag was not fit to drive."

"But if he had no choice?"

"No choice, your Excellency?" protested the Jew, in a rasping voice, "did I not repeat to him a dozen times, that my horse and cart would take him quicker, and more comfortably than Reuben's bag of bones. He would not listen. Reuben is such a liar, and has such insinuating ways. The stranger was deceived. If he was in a hurry, he would have had better value for his money by taking my cart."

"You have a horse and cart too, then?" asked Chauvelin, peremptorily.

"Aye! that I have, your Excellency, and if your Excellency wants to drive . . ."

"Do you happen to know which way my friend went in Reuben Goldstein's cart?"

Thoughtfully the Jew rubbed his dirty chin. Marguerite's heart was beating well-nigh to bursting. She had heard the peremptory question; she looked anxiously at the Jew, but could not read his face beneath the shadow of his broad-brimmed hat. Vaguely she felt somehow as if he held Percy's fate in his long, dirty hands.

There was a long pause, whilst Chauvelin frowned impatiently at the stooping figure before him: at last the Jew slowly put his hand in his breast pocket, and drew out from its capacious depths a number of silver coins. He gazed at them thoughtfully, then remarked, in a quiet tone of voice,—

"This is what the tall stranger gave me, when he drove away with Reuben, for holding my tongue about him, and his doings."

Chauvelin shrugged his shoulders impatiently.

"How much is there there?" he asked.

"Twenty francs, your Excellency," replied the Jew, "and I have been an honest man all my life."

Chauvelin without further comment took a few pieces of gold out of his own pocket, and leaving them in the palm of his hand, he allowed them to jingle as he held them out towards the Jew.

"How many gold pieces are there in the palm of my hand?" he asked quietly.

Evidently he had no desire to terrorize the man, but to conciliate him, for his own purposes, for his manner was pleasant and suave. No doubt he feared that threats of the guillotine, and various other persuasive methods of that type, might addle the old man's brains, and that he would be more likely to be useful through greed of gain, than through terror of death.

The eyes of the Jew shot a quick, keen glance at the gold in his interlocutor's hand.

"At least five, I should say, your Excellency," he replied obsequiously.

"Enough, do you think, to loosen that honest tongue of yours?"

"What does your Excellency wish to know?"

"Whether your horse and cart can take me to where I can find my friend the tall stranger, who has driven off in Reuben Goldstein's cart?"

"My horse and cart can take your Honour there, where you please."

"To a place called the Père Blanchard's hut?"

"Your Honour has guessed?" said the Jew in astonishment.

"You know the place?"

"I know it, your Honour."

"Which road leads to it?"

"The St. Martin Road, your Honour, then a footpath from there to the cliffs."

"You know the road?" repeated Chauvelin, roughly.

"Every stone, every blade of grass, your Honour," replied the Jew quietly.

Chauvelin without another word threw the five pieces of gold one by one before the Jew, who knelt down, and on his hands and knees struggled to collect them. One rolled away, and he had some trouble to get it, for it had lodged underneath the dresser. Chauvelin quietly waited while the old man scrambled on the floor, to find the piece of gold.

When the Jew was again on his feet, Chauvelin said,—

"How soon can your horse and cart be ready?"

"They are ready now, your Honour."

"Where?"

"Not ten meters from this door. Will your Excellency deign to look."

"I don't want to see it. How far can you drive me in it?"

"As far as the Père Blanchard's hut, your Honour,

and further than Reuben's nag took your friend. I am
sure that, not two leagues from here, we shall come
across that wily Reuben, his nag, his cart and the tall
stranger all in a heap in the middle of the road."

"How far is the nearest village from here?"

"On the road which the Englishman took, Miquelon
is the nearest village, not two leagues from here."

"There he could get fresh conveyance, if he wanted
to go further?"

"He could—if he ever got so far."

"Can you?"

"Will your Excellency try?" said the Jew simply.

"That is my intention," said Chauvelin very quietly,
"but remember, if you have deceived me, I shall tell off
two of my most stalwart soldiers to give you such a
beating, that your breath will perhaps leave your ugly
body for ever. But if we find my friend the tall Englishman, either on the road or at the Père Blanchard's hut,
there will be ten more gold pieces for you. Do you accept the bargain?"

The Jew again thoughtfully rubbed his chin. He
looked at the money in his hand, then at his stern interlocutor, and at Desgas, who had stood silently behind him all this while. After a moment's pause, he said
deliberately,—

"I accept."

"Go and wait outside then," said Chauvelin, "and
remember to stick to your bargain, or by Heaven, I will
keep to mine."

With a final, most abject and cringing bow, the old
Jew shuffled out of the room. Chauvelin seemed
pleased with his interview, for he rubbed his hands to-

gether, with that usual gesture of his, of malignant satisfaction.

"My coat and boots," he said to Desgas at last.

Desgas went to the door, and apparently gave the necessary orders, for presently a soldier entered, carrying Chauvelin's coat, boots, and hat.

He took off his soutane, beneath which he was wearing close-fitting breeches and a cloth waistcoat, and began changing his attire.

"You, citoyen, in the meanwhile," he said to Desgas, "go back to Captain Jutley as fast as you can, and tell him to let you have another dozen men, and bring them with you along the St. Martin Road, where I daresay you will soon overtake the Jew's cart with myself in it. There will be hot work presently, if I mistake not, in the Père Blanchard's hut. We shall corner our game there, I'll warrant, for this impudent Scarlet Pimpernell has had the audacity—or the stupidity, I hardly know which—to adhere to his original plans. He has gone to meet de Tournay, St. Just and the other traitors, which for the moment, I thought, perhaps, he did not intend to do. When we find them, there will be a band of desperate men at bay. Some of our men will, I presume, be put *hors de combat*. These royalists are good swordsmen, and the Englishman is devilish cunning, and looks very powerful. Still, we shall be five against one at least. You can follow the cart closely with your men, all along the St. Martin Road, through Miquelon. The Englishman is ahead of us, and not likely to look behind him."

Whilst he gave these curt and concise orders, he had completed his change of attire. The priest's costume had been laid aside, and he was once more dressed in his usual dark, tight-fitting clothes. At last he took up his hat.

"I shall have an interesting prisoner to deliver into your hands," he said with a chuckle, as with unwonted familiarity he took Desgas' arm, and led him towards the door. "We won't kill him outright, eh, friend Desgas? The Père Blanchard's hut is—an I mistake not—a lonely spot upon the beach, and our men will enjoy a bit of rough sport there with the wounded fox. Choose your men well, friend Desgas . . . of the sort who would enjoy that type of sport—eh? We must see that Scarlet Pimpernel wither a bit—what?—shrink and tremble, eh? . . . before we finally . . ." He made an expressive gesture, whilst he laughed a low, evil laugh, which filled Marguerite's soul with sickening horror.

"Choose your men well, Citoyen Desgas," he said once more, as he led his secretary finally out of the room.

27

On the Track

Never for a moment did Marguerite Blakeney hesitate. The last sounds outside the "Chat Gris" had died away in the night. She had heard Desgas giving orders to his men, and then starting off towards the fort, to get a re-inforcement of a dozen more men: six were not thought sufficient to capture the cunning Englishman, whose resourceful brain was even more dangerous than his valour and his strength.

Then a few minutes later, she heard the Jew's husky voice again, evidently shouting to his nag, then the rumble of wheels, and noise of a rickety cart bumping over the rough road.

Inside the inn, everything was still. Brogard and his wife, terrified of Chauvelin, had given no sign of life; they hoped to be forgotten, and at any rate to remain unperceived: Marguerite could not even hear their usual volleys of muttered oaths.

She waited a moment or two longer, then she quietly slipped down the broken stairs, wrapped her dark cloak closely round her and slipped out of the inn.

The night was fairly dark, sufficiently so at any rate to hide her dark figure from view, whilst her keen ears kept count of the sound of the cart going on ahead. She hoped by keeping well within the shadow of the ditches which lined the road, that she would not be seen by Desgas' men, when they approached, or by the patrols, which she concluded were still on duty.

Thus she started to do this, the last stage of her weary journey, alone, at night, and on foot. Nearly three leagues to Miquelon, and then on to the Père Blanchard's hut, wherever that fatal spot might be, probably over rough roads: she cared not.

The Jew's nag could not get on very fast, and though she was weary with mental fatigue and nerve strain, she knew that she could easily keep up with it, on a hilly road, where the poor beast, who was sure to be half-starved, would have to be allowed long and frequent rests. The road lay some distance from the sea, bordered on either side by shrubs and stunted trees, sparsely covered with meagre foliage, all turning away from the North, with their branches looking in the semi-darkness, like stiff, ghostly hair, blown by a perpetual wind.

Fortunately, the moon showed no desire to peep between the clouds, and Marguerite hugging the edge of the road, and keeping close to the low line of shrubs, was fairly safe from view. Everything around her was so still: only from far, very far away, there came like a long soft moan, the sound of the distant sea.

The air was keen and full of brine; after that enforced period of inactivity, inside the evil-smelling, squalid inn, Marguerite would have enjoyed the sweet scent of this autumnal night, and the distant melancholy rumble of the waves; she would have revelled in the calm and stillness of this lonely spot, a calm, broken only at intervals by the strident and mournful cry of some distant gull, and by the creaking of the wheels, some way down the road: she would have loved the cool atmosphere, the peaceful immensity of Nature, in this lonely part of the coast: but her heart was too full of cruel foreboding, of a great ache and longing for a being who had become infinitely dear to her.

Her feet slipped on the grassy bank, for she thought it safest not to walk near the centre of the road, and she found it difficult to keep up a sharp pace along the muddy incline. She even thought it best not to keep too near to the cart; everything was so still, that the rumble of the wheels could not fail to be a safe guide.

The loneliness was absolute. Already the few dim lights of Calais lay far behind, and on this road there was not a sign of human habitation, not even the hut of a fisherman or of a woodcutter anywhere near; far away on her right was the edge of the cliff, below it the rough beach, against which the incoming tide was dashing itself with its constant, distant murmur. And ahead the rumble of the wheels, bearing an implacable enemy to his triumph.

Marguerite wondered at what particular spot, on this lonely coast, Percy could be at this moment. Not very far surely, for he had had less than a quarter of an hour's start of Chauvelin. She wondered if he knew that in this cool, ocean-scented bit of France, there lurked many spies, all eager to sight his tall figure, to track him to where his unsuspecting friends waited for him, and then, to close the net over him and them.

Chauvelin, on ahead, jolted and jostled in the Jew's vehicle, was nursing comfortable thoughts. He rubbed his hands together, with content, as he thought of the web which he had woven, and through which that ubiquitous and daring Englishman could not hope to escape. As the time went on, and the old Jew drove him leisurely but surely along the dark road, he felt more and more eager for the grand finale of this exciting chase after the mysterious Scarlet Pimpernel.

The capture of the audacious plotter would be the finest leaf in Citoyen Chauvelin's wreath of glory. Caught, red-handed, on the spot, in the very act of aiding and abetting the traitors against the Republic of France, the Englishman could claim no protection from his own country. Chauvelin had, in any case, fully made up his mind that all intervention should come too late.

Never for a moment did the slightest remorse enter his heart, as to the terrible position in which he had placed the unfortunate wife, who had unconsciously betrayed her husband. As a matter of fact, Chauvelin had ceased even to think of her: she had been a useful tool, that was all.

The Jew's lean nag did little more than walk. She was going along at a slow jog trot, and her driver had to give her long and frequent halts.

"Are we a long way yet from Miquelon?" asked Chauvelin from time to time.

"Not very far, your Honour," was the uniform placid reply.

"We have not yet come across your friend and mine, lying in a heap in the roadway," was Chauvelin's sarcastic comment.

"Patience, noble Excellency," rejoined the son of Moses, "they are ahead of us. I can see the imprint of the cart wheels, driven by that traitor, that son of the Amalekite."

"You are sure of the road?"

"As sure as I am of the presence of those ten gold

pieces in the noble Excellency's pockets, which I trust will presently be mine."

"As soon as I have shaken hands with my friend the tall stranger, they will certainly be yours."

"Hark, what was that?" said the Jew suddenly.

Through the stillness, which had been absolute, there could now be heard distinctly the sound of horses' hoofs on the muddy road.

"They are soldiers," he added in an awed whisper.

"Stop a moment, I want to hear," said Chauvelin.

Marguerite had also heard the sound of galloping hoofs, coming towards the cart, and towards herself. For some time she had been on the alert thinking that Desgas and his squad would soon overtake them, but these came from the opposite direction, presumably from Miquelon. The darkness lent her sufficient cover. She had perceived that the cart had stopped, and with utmost caution, treading noiselessly on the soft road, she crept a little nearer.

Her heart was beating fast, she was trembling in every limb; already she had guessed what news these mounted men would bring. "Every stranger on these roads or on the beach must be shadowed, especially if he be tall or stoops as if he would disguise his height; when sighted a mounted messenger must at once ride back and report." Those had been Chauvelin's orders. Had then the tall stranger been sighted, and was this the mounted messenger, come to bring the great news, that the hunted hare had run its head into the noose at last?

Marguerite, realizing that the cart had come to a standstill, managed to slip nearer to it in the darkness; she crept close up, hoping to get within earshot, to hear what the messenger had to say.

She heard the quick words of challenge—

"Liberté, Fraternité, Egalité!" then Chauvelin's quick query:—

"What news?"

Two men on horseback had halted beside the vehicle.

Marguerite could see them silhouetted against the midnight sky. She could hear their voices, and the snorting of their horses, and now, behind her, some little distance off, the regular and measured tread of a body of advancing men: Desgas and his soldiers.

There had been a long pause, during which, no doubt, Chauvelin satisfied the men as to his identity, for presently, questions and answers followed each other in quick succession.

"You have seen the stranger?" asked Chauvelin, eagerly.

"No, citoyen, we have seen no tall stranger; we came by the edge of the cliff."

"Then?"

"Less than a quarter of a league beyond Miquelon, we came across a rough construction of wood, which looked like the hut of a fisherman, where he might keep his tools and nets. When we first sighted it, it seemed to be empty, and, at first we thought that there was nothing suspicious about, until we saw some smoke issuing through an aperture at the side. I dismounted and crept close to it. It was then empty, but in one corner of the hut, there was a charcoal fire, and a couple of stools were also in the hut. I consulted with my comrades, and we decided that they should take cover with the horses, well out of sight, and that I should remain on the watch, which I did."

"Well! and did you see anything?"

"About half an hour later, I heard voices, citoyen, and presently, two men came along towards the edge of the cliff; they seemed to me to have come from the Lille Road. One was young, the other quite old. They were talking in a whisper, to one another, and I could not hear what they said."

One was young, the other quite old. Marguerite's aching heart almost stopped beating as she listened: was the young one Armand?—her brother?—and the old one de Tournay—were they the two fugitives who, unconsciously, were used as a decoy, to entrap their fearless and noble rescuer.

"The two men presently went into the hut," continued the soldier, whilst Marguerite's aching nerves seemed to catch the sound of Chauvelin's triumphant chuckle, "and I crept nearer to it then. The hut is very roughly built, and I caught snatches of their conversation."

"Yes?—Quick!—What did you hear?"

"The old man asked the young one if he were sure that was the right place. 'Oh, yes,' he replied, ' 'tis the place sure enough,' and by the light of the charcoal fire he showed to his companion a paper, which he carried. 'Here is the plan,' he said, 'which he gave me before I left London. We were to adhere strictly to that plan, unless I had contrary orders, and I have had none. Here is the road we followed, see . . . here the fork . . . here we cut across the St. Martin Road . . . and here is the footpath which brought us to the edge of the cliff.' I must have made a slight noise then, for the young man came to the door of the hut, and peered anxiously all round him. When he again joined his companion, they whispered so low, that I could no longer hear them."

"Well?—and?" asked Chauvelin, impatiently.

"There were six of us altogether, patrolling that part of the beach, so we consulted together, and thought it best that four should remain behind and keep the hut in sight, and I and my comrade rode back at once to make report of what we had seen."

"You saw nothing of the tall stranger?"

"Nothing, citoyen."

"If your comrades see him, what would they do?"

"Not lose sight of him for a moment, and if he showed signs of escape, or any boat came in sight, they would close in on him, and, if necessary, they would shoot: the firing would bring the rest of the patrol to the spot. In any case they would not let the stranger go."

"Aye! but I did not want the stranger hurt—not just yet," murmured Chauvelin, savagely, "but there, you've done your best. The Fates grant that I may not be too late . . ."

"We met half a dozen men just now, who have been patrolling this road for several hours."

"Well?"

"They have seen no stranger either."

"Yet he is on ahead somewhere, in a cart or else . . . Here! there is not a moment to lose. How far is that hut from here?"

"About a couple of leagues, citoyen."

"You can find it again?—at once?—without hesitation?"

"I have absolutely no doubt, citoyen."

"The footpath, to the edge of the cliff?—Even in the dark?"

"It is not a dark night, citoyen, and I know I can find my way," repeated the soldier firmly.

"Fall in behind then. Let your comrade take both your horses back to Calais. You won't want them. Keep beside the cart, and direct the Jew to drive straight ahead; then stop him, within a quarter of a league of the footpath; see that he takes the most direct road."

Whilst Chauvelin spoke, Desgas and his men were fast approaching, and Marguerite could hear their footsteps within a hundred yards behind her now. She thought it unsafe to stay where she was, and unnecessary too, as she had heard enough. She seemed suddenly to have lost all faculty even for suffering: her heart, her nerves, her brain seemed to have become numb after all these hours of ceaseless anguish, culminating in this awful despair.

For now there was absolutely not the faintest hope. Within two short leagues of this spot, the fugitives were waiting for their brave deliverer. He was on his way, somewhere on this lonely road, and presently he would join them; then the well-laid trap would close, two dozen men, led by one whose hatred was as deadly as his cunning was malicious, would close round the small band of fugitives, and their daring leader. They would all be captured. Armand, according to Chauvelin's pledged word would be restored to her, but her husband, Percy, whom with every breath she drew she seemed to love and worship more and more, he would fall into the hands of a remorseless enemy, who had no pity for a brave heart, no admiration for the courage of a noble soul, who would show nothing but hatred for the cunning antagonist, who had baffled him so long.

She heard the soldier giving a few brief directions to the Jew, then she retired quickly to the edge of the road, and cowered behind some low shrubs, whilst Desgas and his men came up.

All fell in noiselessly behind the cart, and slowly they all started down the dark road. Marguerite waited until she reckoned that they were well outside the range of earshot, then, she too in the darkness, which suddenly seemed to have become more intense, crept noiselessly along.

28

THE PÈRE BLANCHARD'S HUT

As in a dream, Marguerite followed on; the web was drawing more and more tightly every moment round the beloved life, which had become dearer than all. To see her husband once again, to tell him how she had suffered, how much she had wronged, and how little understood him, had become now her only aim. She had abandoned all hope of saving him: she saw him gradually hemmed in on all sides, and, in despair, she gazed round her into the darkness, and wondered whence he would presently come, to fall into the death-trap which his relentless enemy had prepared for him.

The distant roar of the waves now made her shudder; the occasional dismal cry of an owl, or a sea-gull, filled her with unspeakable horror. She thought of the ravenous beasts—in human shape—who lay in wait for their prey, and destroyed them, as mercilessly as any hungry wolf, for the satisfaction of their own appetite of hate. Marguerite was not afraid of the darkness, she only feared that man, on ahead, who was sitting at the bottom of a rough wooden cart, nursing thoughts of vengeance, which would have made the very demons in hell chuckle with delight.

Her feet were sore. Her knees shook under her, from sheer bodily fatigue. For days now she had lived in a wild turmoil of excitement; she had not had a quiet rest for three nights; now, she had walked on a slippery road for nearly two hours, and yet her determination never swerved for a moment. She would see her husband, tell him all, and, if he was ready to forgive the crime, which she had committed in her blind ignorance, she would yet have the happiness of dying by his side.

She must have walked on almost in a trance, instinct alone keeping her up, and guiding her in the wake of the enemy, when suddenly her ears, attuned to the slightest sound, by that same blind instinct, told her that the cart had stopped, and that the soldiers had halted. They had come to their destination. No doubt on the right, somewhere close ahead, was the footpath that led to the edge of the cliff and to the hut.

Heedless of any risks, she crept quite close up to where Chauvelin stood, surrounded by his little troop: he had descended from the cart, and was giving some orders to the men. These she wanted to hear: what little chance she yet had, of being useful to Percy, consisted in hearing absolutely every word of his enemy's plans.

The spot where all the party had halted must have lain some eight hundred meters from the coast; the sound of the sea came only very faintly, as from a distance. Chauvelin and Desgas, followed by the soldiers, had turned off sharply to the right of the road, apparently on to the footpath, which led to the cliffs. The Jew had remained on the road, with his cart and nag.

Marguerite, with infinite caution, and literally crawling on her hands and knees, had also turned off to the right: to accomplish this she had to creep through the rough, low shrubs, trying to make as little noise as possible as she went along, tearing her face and hands against the dry twigs, intent only upon hearing without being seen or heard. Fortunately—as is usual in this part of France—the footpath was bordered by a low rough hedge, beyond which was a dry ditch, filled with coarse grass. In this Marguerite managed to find shelter; she was quite hidden from view, yet could contrive to get within three yards of where Chauvelin stood, giving orders to his men.

"Now," he was saying in a low and peremptory whisper, "where is the Pére Blanchard's hut?"

"About eight hundred meters from here, along the footpath," said the soldier who had lately been directing the party, "and half-way down the cliff."

"Very good. You shall lead us. Before we begin to descend the cliff, you shall creep down to the hut, as noiselessly as possible, and ascertain if the traitor royalists are there? Do you understand?"

"I understand, citoyen."

"Now listen very attentively, all of you," continued Chauvelin, impressively, and addressing the soldiers collectively, "for after this we may not be able to exchange another word, so remember every syllable I utter, as if your very lives depended on your memory. Perhaps they do," he added drily.

"We listen, citoyen," said Desgas, "and a soldier of the Republic never forgets an order."

"You, who have crept up to the hut, will try to peep inside. If an Englishman is there with those traitors, a man who is tall above the average, or who stoops as if he would disguise his height, then give a sharp, quick whistle as a signal to your comrades. All of you," he added, once more speaking to the soldiers collectively, "then quickly surround and rush into the hut, and each seize one of the men there, before they have time to draw their firearms; if any of them struggle, shoot at their legs or arms, but on no account kill the tall man. Do you understand?"

"We understand, citoyen."

"The man who is tall above the average is probably also strong above the average; it will take four or five of you at least to overpower him."

There was a little pause, then Chauvelin continued,—

"If the royalist traitors are still alone, which is more than likely to be the case, then warn your comrades who are lying in wait there, and all of you creep and take cover behind the rocks and boulders round the hut, and wait there, in dead silence, until the tall Englishman arrives; then only rush the hut, when he is safely within its doors. But remember that you must be as silent as the wolf is at night, when he prowls around the pens. I do not wish those royalists to be on the alert—the firing of a pistol, a shriek or call on their part would be sufficient, perhaps, to warn the tall personage to keep clear of the cliffs, and of the hut, and," he added emphatically, "it is the tall Englishman whom it is your duty to capture tonight."

"You shall be implicitly obeyed, citoyen."

"Then get along as noiselessly as possible, and I will follow you."

"What about the Jew, citoyen?" asked Desgas, as silently like noiseless shadows, one by one the soldiers began to creep along the rough and narrow footpath.

"Ah, yes; I had forgotten the Jew," said Chauvelin, and, turning towards the Jew, he called him peremptorily.

"Here, you . . . Aaron, Moses, Abraham, or whatever

your confounded name may be," he said to the old man, who had quietly stood beside his lean nag, as far away from the soldiers as possible.

"Benjamin Rosenbaum, so it please your Honour," he replied humbly.

"It does not please me to hear your voice, but it does please me to give you certain orders, which you will find it wise to obey."

"So please your Honour . . ."

"Hold your confounded tongue. You shall stay here, do you hear? with your horse and cart until our return. You are on no account to utter the faintest sound, or to even breathe louder than you can help; nor are you, on any consideration whatever, to leave your post, until I give you orders to do so. Do you understand?"

"But your Honour—" protested the Jew pitiably.

"There is no question of 'but' or of any argument," said Chauvelin, in a tone that made the timid old man tremble from head to foot. "If, when I return, I do not find you here, I most solemnly assure you that, wherever you may try to hide yourself, I can find you, and that punishment swift, sure and terrible, will sooner or later overtake you. Do you hear me?"

"But your Excellency . . ."

"I said, do you hear me?"

The soldiers had all crept away; the three men stood alone together in the dark and lonely road, with Marguerite there, behind the hedge, listening to Chauvelin's orders, as she would to her own death sentence.

"I heard your Honour," protested the Jew again, while he tried to draw nearer to Chauvelin, "and I swear by Abraham, Isaac and Jacob that I would obey your Honour most absolutely, and that I would not

move from this place until your Honour once more
deigned to shed the light of your countenance upon
your humble servant; but remember, your Honour, I
am a poor old man; my nerves are not as strong as
those of a young soldier. If midnight marauders should
come prowling round this lonely road, I might scream
or run in my fright! And is my life to be forfeit, is some
terrible punishment to come on my poor old head for
that which I cannot help?"

The Jew seemed in real distress; he was shaking from
head to foot. Clearly he was not the man to be left by
himself on this lonely road. The man spoke truly; he
might unwittingly, in sheer terror, utter the shriek that
might prove a warning to the wily Scarlet Pimpernel.

Chauvelin reflected for a moment.

"Will your horse and cart be safe alone, here, do you
think?" he asked roughly.

"I fancy, citoyen," here interposed Desgas, "that
they will be safer without that dirty, cowardly Jew than
with him. There seems no doubt that, if he gets scared,
he will either make a bolt of it, or shriek his head off."

"But what am I to do with the brute?"

"Will you send him back to Calais, citoyen?"

"No, for we shall want him to drive back the
wounded presently," said Chauvelin, with grim significance.

There was a pause again—Desgas waiting for the
decision of his chief, and the old Jew whining beside
his nag.

"Well, you lazy, lumbering old coward," said Chauvelin at last, "you had better shuffle along behind us.
Here, Citoyen Desgas, tie this handkerchief tightly
round the fellow's mouth."

Chauvelin handed a scarf to Desgas, who solemnly began winding it round the Jew's mouth. Meekly Benjamin Rosenbaum allowed himself to be gagged; he, evidently, preferred this uncomfortable state to that of being left alone, on the dark St. Martin Road. Then the three men fell in line.

"Quick!" said Chauvelin, impatiently, "we have already wasted much valuable time."

And the firm footsteps of Chauvelin and Desgas, the shuffling gait of the old Jew, soon died away along the footpath.

Marguerite had not lost a single one of Chauvelin's words of command. Her every nerve was strained to completely grasp the situation first, then to make a final appeal to those wits which had so often been called the sharpest in Europe, and which alone might be of service now.

Certainly the situation was desperate enough; a tiny band of unsuspecting men, quietly awaiting the arrival of their rescuer, who was equally unconscious of the trap laid for them all. It seemed so horrible, this net, as it were drawn in a circle, at dead of night, on a lonely beach, round a few defenceless men, defenceless because they were tricked and unsuspecting; of these one was the husband she idolised, another the brother she loved. She vaguely wondered who the others were, who were also calmly waiting for the Scarlet Pimpernel, while death lurked behind every boulder of the cliffs.

For the moment she could do nothing but follow the soldiers and Chauvelin. She feared to lose her way, or she would have rushed forward and found that wooden hut, and perhaps been in time to warn the fugitives and their brave deliverer yet.

For a second, the thought flashed through her mind of uttering the piercing shrieks, which Chauvelin seemed to dread, as a possible warning to the Scarlet Pimpernel and his friends—in the wild hope that they would hear, and have yet time to escape before it was too late. But she did not know how far from the edge of the cliff she was; she did not know if her shrieks would reach the ears of the doomed men. Her effort might be premature, and she would never be allowed to make another. Her mouth would be securely gagged, like that of the Jew, and she, a helpless prisoner in the hands of Chauvelin's men.

Like a ghost she flitted noiselessly behind that hedge: she had taken her shoes off, and her stockings were by now torn off her feet. She felt neither soreness nor weariness; indomitable will to reach her husband in spite of adverse Fate, and of a cunning enemy, killed all sense of bodily pain within her, and rendered her instincts doubly acute.

She heard nothing save the soft and measured footsteps of Percy's enemies on in front; she saw nothing but—in her mind's eye—that wooden hut, and he, her husband, walking blindly to his doom.

Suddenly, those same keen instincts within her made her pause in her mad haste, and cower still further within the shadow of the hedge. The moon, which had proved a friend to her by remaining hidden behind a bank of clouds, now emerged in all the glory of an early autumn night, and in a moment flooded the weird and lonely landscape with a rush of brilliant light.

There, not two hundred mètres ahead, was the edge of the cliff, and below, stretching far away to free and

happy England, the sea rolled on smoothly and peace-
ably. Marguerite's gaze rested for an instant on the brilliant, silvery waters; and as she gazed, her heart, which
had been numb with pain for all these hours, seemed to
soften and distend, and her eyes filled with hot tears:
not three miles away, with white sails set, a graceful
schooner lay in wait.

Marguerite had guessed rather than recognized her.
It was the *Day Dream*, Percy's favourite yacht, with old
Briggs, that prince of skippers, aboard, and all her crew
of British sailors: her white sails, glistening in the
moonlight, seemed to convey a message to Marguerite
of joy and hope, which yet she feared could never be.
She waited there, out at sea, waited for her master, like
a beautiful white bird all ready to take flight, and he
would never reach her, never see her smooth deck
again, never gaze any more on the white cliffs of England, the land of liberty and of hope.

The sight of the schooner seemed to infuse into the
poor, wearied woman the superhuman strength of despair. There was the edge of the cliff, and some way
below was the hut, where presently, her husband would
meet his death. But the moon was out: she could see
her way now: she would see the hut from a distance,
run to it, rouse them all, warn them at any rate to be
prepared and to sell their lives dearly, rather than be
caught like so many rats in a hole.

She stumbled on behind the hedge in the low, thick
grass of the ditch. She must have run on very fast, and
had outdistanced Chauvelin and Desgas, for presently
she reached the edge of the cliff, and heard their footsteps distinctly behind her. But only a very few yards

away, and now the moonlight was full upon her, her figure must have been distinctly silhouetted against the silvery background of the sea.

Only for a moment, though; the next she had cowered, like some animal doubled up within itself. She peeped down the great rugged cliffs—the descent would be easy enough, as they were not precipitous, and the great boulders afforded plenty of foothold. Suddenly, as she gazed, she saw at some little distance on her left, and about midway down the cliffs, a rough wooden construction, through the walls of which a tiny red light glimmered like a beacon. Her very heart seemed to stand still, the eagerness of joy was so great that it felt like an awful pain.

She could not gauge how distant the hut was, but without hesitation she began the steep descent, creeping from boulder to boulder, caring nothing for the enemy behind, or for the soldiers, who evidently had all taken cover since the tall Englishman had not yet appeared.

On she pressed, forgetting the deadly foe on her track, running, stumbling, foot-sore, half-dazed, but still on . . . When, suddenly, a crevice, or stone, or slippery bit of rock, threw her violently to the ground. She struggled again to her feet, and started running forward once more to give them that timely warning, to beg them to flee before he came, and to tell him to keep away—away from this death-trap—away from this awful doom. But now she realised that other steps, quicker than her own, were already close at her heels. The next instant a hand dragged at her skirt, and she was down on her knees again, whilst something was wound round her mouth to prevent her uttering a scream.

Bewildered, half frantic with the bitterness of disappointment, she looked round her helplessly, and, bending down quite close to her, she saw through the mist, which seemed to gather round her, a pair of keen, malicious eyes, which appeared to her excited brain to have a weird, supernatural green light in them.

She lay in the shadow of a great boulder; Chauvelin could not see her features, but he passed his thin, white fingers over her face.

"A woman!" he whispered, "by all the Saints in the calendar."

"We cannot let her loose, that's certain," he muttered to himself. "I wonder now . . ."

Suddenly he paused, and after a few seconds of deadly silence, he gave forth a long, low, curious chuckle, while once again Marguerite felt, with a horrible shudder, his thin fingers wandering over her face.

"Dear me! dear me!" he whispered, with affected gallantry, "this is indeed a charming surprise," and Marguerite felt her resistless hand raised to Chauvelin's thin, mocking lips.

The situation was indeed grotesque, had it not been at the same time so fearfully tragic: the poor, weary woman, broken in spirit, and half frantic with the bitterness of her disappointment, receiving on her knees the *banal* gallantries of her deadly enemy.

Her senses were leaving her; half choked with the tight grip round her mouth, she had no strength to move or to utter the faintest sound. The excitement which all along had kept up her delicate body seemed at once to have subsided, and the feeling of blank despair to have completely paralyzed her brain and nerves.

Chauvelin must have given some directions, which she was too dazed to hear, for she felt herself lifted from off her feet: the bandage round her mouth was made more secure, and a pair of strong arms carried her towards that tiny, red light, on ahead, which she had looked upon as a beacon and the last faint glimmer of hope.

29

Trapped

She did not know how long she was thus carried along, she had lost all notion of time and space, and for a few seconds tired nature, mercifully, deprived her of consciousness.

When she once more realised her state, she felt that she was placed with some degree of comfort upon a man's coat, with her back resting against a fragment of rock. The moon was hidden again behind some clouds, and the darkness seemed in comparison more intense. The sea was roaring some two hundred feet below her, and on looking all round she could no longer see any vestige of the tiny glimmer of red light.

That the end of the journey had been reached, she gathered from the fact that she heard rapid questions and answers spoken in a whisper quite close to her.

"There are four men in there, citoyen; they are sitting by the fire, and seem to be waiting quietly."

"The hour?"

"Nearly two o'clock."

"The tide?"

"Coming in quickly."

"The schooner?"

"Obviously an English one, lying some three kilometers out. But we cannot see her boat."

"Have the men taken cover?"

"Yes, citoyen."

"They will not blunder?"

"They will not stir until the tall Englishman comes, then they will surround and overpower the five men."

"Right. And the lady?"

"Still dazed, I fancy. She's close beside you, citoyen."

"And the Jew?"

"He's gagged, and his legs strapped together. He cannot move or scream."

"Good. Then have your gun ready, in case you want it. Get close to the hut and leave me to look after the lady."

Desgas evidently obeyed, for Marguerite heard him creeping away along the stony cliff, then she felt that a pair of warm, thin, talon-like hands took hold of both her own, and held them in a grip of steel.

"Before that handkerchief is removed from your pretty mouth, fair lady," whispered Chauvelin close to her ear, "I think it right to give you one small word of warning. What has procured me the honour of being followed across the Channel by so charming a companion, I cannot, of course, conceive, but, if I mistake not, the purpose of this flattering attention is not one that would commend itself to my vanity and I think that I am right in surmising, moreover, that the first sound which your pretty lips would utter, as soon as the cruel gag is removed, would be one that would perhaps prove a warning to the cunning fox, which I have been at such pains to track to his lair."

He paused a moment, while the steel-like grasp seemed to tighten round her wrist; then he resumed in the same hurried whisper:—

"Inside that hut, if again I am not mistaken, your brother, Armand St. Just, waits with that traitor de

Tournay, and two other men unknown to you, for the arrival of the mysterious rescuer, whose identity has for so long puzzled our Committee of Public Safety—the audacious Scarlet Pimpernel. No doubt if you scream, if there is a scuffle here, if shots are fired, it is more than likely that the same long legs that brought this scarlet enigma here, will as quickly take him to some place of safety. The purpose then, for which I have travelled all these miles, will remain unaccomplished. On the other hand it only rests with yourself that your brother—Armand—shall be free to go off with you to-night if you like, to England, or any other place of safety."

Marguerite could not utter a sound, as the handkerchief was wound very tightly round her mouth, but Chauvelin was peering through the darkness very closely into her face; no doubt too her hand gave a responsive appeal to his last suggestion, for presently he continued:—

"What I want you to do to ensure Armand's safety is a very simple thing, dear lady."

"What is it?" Marguerite's hand seemed to convey to his, in response.

"To remain—on this spot, without uttering a sound, until I give you leave to speak. Ah! but I think you will obey," he added, with that funny dry chuckle of his as Marguerite's whole figure seemed to stiffen, in defiance of this order, "for let me tell you that if you scream, nay! if you utter one sound, or attempt to move from here, my men—there are thirty of them about—will seize St. Just, de Tournay, and their two friends, and shoot them here—by my orders—before your eyes."

Marguerite had listened to her implacable enemy's

speech with ever-increasing terror. Numbed with physical pain, she yet had sufficient mental vitality in her to
realize the full horror of this terrible "either—or" he
was once more putting before her; "either—or" ten
thousand times more appalling and horrible, than the
one he had suggested to her that fatal night at the ball.

This time it meant that she should keep still, and
allow the husband she worshipped to walk unconsciously to his death, or that she should, by trying to
give him a word of warning, which perhaps might even
be unavailing, actually give the signal for her own
brother's death, and that of three other unsuspecting
men.

She could not see Chauvelin, but she could almost
feel those keen, pale eyes of his fixed maliciously upon
her helpless form, and his hurried, whispered words
reached her ear, as the death-knell of her last faint, lingering hope.

"Nay, fair lady," he added urbanely, "you can have
no interest in anyone save in St. Just, and all you need
do for his safety is to remain where you are, and to keep
silent. My men have strict orders to spare him in every
way. As for that enigmatic Scarlet Pimpernel, what is
he to you? Believe me, no warning from you could possibly save him. And now dear lady, let me remove this
unpleasant coercion, which has been placed before
your pretty mouth. You see I wish you to be perfectly
free, in the choice which you are about to make."

Her thoughts in a whirl, her temples aching, her
nerves paralyzed, her body numb with pain, Marguerite
sat there, in the darkness which surrounded her as with
a pall. From where she sat she could not see the sea,

but she heard the incessant mournful murmur of the incoming tide, which spoke of her dead hopes, her lost love, the husband she had with her own hand betrayed, and sent to his death.

Chauvelin removed the handkerchief from her mouth. She certainly did not scream: at that moment, she had no strength to do anything but barely to hold herself upright, and to force herself to think.

Oh! think! think! think! of what she should do. The minutes flew on; in this awful stillness she could not tell how fast or how slowly; she heard nothing, she saw nothing: she did not feel the sweet-smelling autumn air, scented with the briny odour of the sea, she no longer heard the murmur of the waves, the occasional rattling of a pebble, as it rolled down some steep incline. More and more unreal did the whole situation seem. It was impossible that she, Marguerite Blakeney, the queen of London society, should actually be sitting here on this bit of lonely coast, in the middle of the night, side by side with a most bitter enemy: and oh! it was not possible that somewhere, not many hundred feet away perhaps, from where she stood, the being she had once despised, but who now, in every moment of this weird, dreamlike life, became more and more dear—it was not possible that *he* was unconsciously, even now walking to his doom, whilst she did nothing to save him.

Why did she not with unearthly screams, that would re-echo from one end of the lonely beach to the other, send out a warning to him to desist, to retrace his steps, for death lurked here whilst he advanced? Once or twice the screams rose to her throat—as if by instinct:

then, before her eyes there stood the awful alternative: her brother and those three men shot before her eyes, practically by her orders: she their murderer.

Oh! that fiend in human shape, next to her, knew human—female—nature well. He had played upon her feelings as a skilful musician plays upon an instrument. He had gauged her very thoughts to a nicety.

She could not give that signal—for she was weak, and she was a woman. How could she deliberately order Armand to be shot before her eyes, to have his dear blood upon her head, he dying perhaps with a curse on her, upon his lips. And little Suzanne's father, too! he, an old man; and the others!—oh! it was all too, too horrible.

Wait! wait! wait! how long? The early morning hours sped on, and yet it was not dawn: the sea continued its incessant mournful murmur, the autumnal breeze sighed gently in the night: the lonely beach was silent, even as the grave.

Suddenly from somewhere, not very far away, a cheerful, strong voice was heard singing "God save the King!"

30

THE SCHOONER

Marguerite's aching heart stood still. She felt, more than she heard, the men on the watch preparing for the fight. Her senses told her that each, with sword in hand, was crouching, ready for the spring.

The voice came nearer and nearer; in the vast immensity of these lonely cliffs, with the loud murmur of the sea below, it was impossible to say how near, or how far, not yet from which direction came that cheerful singer, who sang to God to save his King, whilst he himself was in such deadly danger. Faint at first, the voice grew louder and louder; from time to time a small pebble detached itself apparently from beneath the firm tread of the singer, and went rolling down the rocky cliffs to the beach below.

Marguerite as she heard, felt that her very life was slipping away, as if when that voice drew nearer, when that singer became entrapped . . .

She distinctly heard the click of Desgas' gun close to her. . . .

No! no! no! no! Oh, God in heaven! this cannot be! let Armand's blood then be upon her own head! let her be branded as his murderer! let even he, whom she loved, despise and loathe her for this, but God! oh God save him at any cost!

With a wild shriek, she sprang to her feet, and darted round the rock, against which she had been cowering; she saw the little red gleam through the chinks of the hut; she ran up to it and fell against its wooden walls, which she began to hammer with clenched fists in an almost maniacal frenzy, while she shouted,—

"Armand! Armand! for God's sake fire! your leader is near! he is coming! he is betrayed! Armand! Armand! fire in Heaven's name!"

She was seized and thrown to the ground. She lay there moaning, bruised, not caring, but still half-sobbing, half-shrieking,—

"Percy, my husband, for God's sake fly! Armand! Armand! why don't you fire?"

"One of you stop that woman screaming," hissed Chauvelin, who hardly could refrain from striking her.

Something was thrown over her face; she could not breathe, and perforce she was silent.

The bold singer, too, had become silent, warned, no doubt, of his impending danger by Marguerite's frantic shrieks. The men had sprung to their feet, there was no need for further silence on their part; the very cliffs echoed the poor, heart-broken woman's screams.

Chauvelin, with a muttered oath, which boded no good to her, who had dared to upset his most cherished plans, had hastily shouted the word of command,—

"Into it, my men, and let no one escape from that hut alive!"

The moon had once more emerged from between the clouds: the darkness on the cliffs had gone, giving place once more to brilliant, silvery light. Some of the soldiers had rushed to the rough, wooden door of the hut, whilst one of them kept guard over Marguerite.

The door was partially open; one of the soldiers pushed it further, but within all was darkness, the charcoal fire only lighting with a dim, red light the furthest corner of the hut. The soldiers paused automatically at the door, like machines waiting for further orders.

Chauvelin, who was prepared for a violent onslaught from within, and for a vigorous resistance from the four fugitives, under cover of the darkness, was for the moment paralyzed with astonishment when he saw the soldiers standing there at attention, like sentries on guard, whilst not a sound proceeded from the hut.

Filled with strange, anxious foreboding, he, too, went to the door of the hut, and peering into the gloom, he asked quickly,—

"What is the meaning of this?"

"I think, citoyen, that there is no one there now," replied one of the soldiers imperturbably.

"You have not let those four men go?" thundered Chauvelin, menacingly. "I ordered you to let no man escape alive! —Quick, after them all of you! Quick, in every direction!"

The men, obedient as machines, rushed down the rocky incline towards the beach, some going off to right and left, as fast as their feet could carry them.

"You and your men will pay with your lives for this blunder, citoyen sergeant," said Chauvelin viciously to the sergeant who had been in charge of the men; "and you, too, citoyen," he added turning with a snarl to Desgas, "for disobeying my orders."

"You ordered us to wait, citoyen, until the tall Englishman arrived and joined the four men in the hut. No one came," said the sergeant sullenly.

"But I ordered you just now, when the woman screamed, to rush in and let no one escape."

"But, citoyen, the four men who were there before had been gone some time, I think . . ."

"You think?—You? . . ." said Chauvelin, almost choking with fury, "and you let them go . . ."

"You ordered us to wait, citoyen," protested the sergeant, "and to implicitly obey your commands on pain of death. We waited.

"I heard the men creep out of the hut, not many minutes after we took cover, and long before the woman screamed," he added, as Chauvelin seemed still quite speechless with rage.

"Hark!" said Desgas suddenly.

In the distance the sound of repeated firing was heard. Chauvelin tried to peer along the beach below, but as luck would have it, the fitful moon once more hid her light behind a bank of clouds, and he could see nothing.

"One of you go into the hut and strike a light," he stammered at last.

Stolidly the sergeant obeyed: he went up to the charcoal fire and lit the small lantern he carried in his belt; it was evident that the hut was quite empty.

"Which way did they go?" asked Chauvelin.

"I could not tell, citoyen," said the sergeant; "they went straight down the cliff first, then disappeared behind some boulders."

"Hush! what was that?"

All three men listened attentively. In the far, very far distance, could be heard faintly echoing and already dying away, the quick, sharp splash of half a dozen oars. Chauvelin took out his handkerchief and wiped the perspiration from his forehead.

"The schooner's boat!" was all he gasped.

Evidently Armand St. Just and his three companions had managed to creep along the side of the cliffs, whilst the men, like true soldiers of the well-drilled Republican army, had with blind obedience, and in fear of their lives, implicitly obeyed Chauvelin's orders—to wait for the tall Englishman, who was the important capture.

They had no doubt reached one of the creeks which jut far out to sea on this coast at intervals; behind this, the boat of the *Day Dream* must have been on the lookout for them, and they were by now safely on board the British schooner.

As if to confirm this last supposition, the dull boom of a gun was heard from out at sea.

"The schooner, citoyen," said Desgas, quietly; "she's off."

It needed all Chauvelin's nerve and presence of mind not to give way to a useless and undignified access of rage. There was no doubt now, that once again, that accursed British head had completely outwitted him. How he had contrived to reach the hut, without being seen by one of the thirty soldiers who guarded the spot, was more than Chauvelin could conceive. That he had done so before the thirty men had arrived on the cliff was, of course, fairly clear, but how he had come over in Reuben Goldstein's cart, all the way from Calais, without being sighted by the various patrols on duty was impossible of explanation. It really seemed as if some potent Fate watched over that daring Scarlet Pimpernel, and his astute enemy almost felt a superstitious shudder pass through him, as he looked round at the towering cliffs, and the loneliness of this outlying coast.

But surely this was reality! and the year of grace 1792: there were no fairies and hobgoblins about. Chauvelin and his thirty men had all heard with their own ears that accursed voice singing "God save the King," fully twenty minutes *after* they had all taken cover around the hut; by that time the four fugitives must have reached the creek, and got into the boat, and the nearest creek was more than a mile from the hut.

Where had that daring singer got to? Unless Satan himself had lent him wings, he could not have covered that mile on a rocky cliff in the space of two minutes; and only two minutes had elapsed between his song and the sound of the boat's oars away at sea. He must have remained behind, and was even now hiding somewhere about the cliffs; the patrols were still about, he would still be sighted, no doubt. Chauvelin felt hopeful once again.

One or two of the men, who had run after the fugitives, were now slowly working their way up the cliff: one of them reached Chauvelin's side, at the very moment that this hope arose in the astute diplomatist's heart.

"We were too late, citoyen," the soldier said, "we reached the beach just before the moon was hidden by that bank of clouds. The boat had undoubtedly been on the look-out behind that first creek, a mile off, but she had shoved off some time ago, when we got to the beach, and was already some way out to sea. We fired after her, but of course, it was no good. She was making straight and quickly for the schooner. We saw her very clearly in the moonlight."

"Yes," said Chauvelin, with eager impatience, "she had shoved off some time ago, you said, and the nearest creek is a mile further on."

"Yes, citoyen! I ran all the way, straight to the beach, though I guessed the boat would have waited some-

where near the creek, as the tide would reach there earliest. The boat must have shoved off some minutes before the woman began to scream."

Some minutes before the woman began to scream!
Then Chauvelin's hopes had not deceived him. The
Scarlet Pimpernel may have contrived to send the fugitives on ahead by the boat, but he himself had not had
time to reach it; he was still on shore, and all the roads
were well patrolled. At any rate, all was not yet lost,
and would not be, whilst that impudent Britisher was
still on French soil.

"Bring the light in here!" he commanded eagerly, as
he once more entered the hut.

The sergeant brought his lantern, and together the
two men explored the little place: with a rapid glance
Chauvelin noted its contents: the cauldron placed close
under an aperture in the wall, and containing the last
few dying embers of burned charcoal, a couple of
stools, overturned as if in the haste of sudden departure, then the fisherman's tools and his nets lying in
one corner, and beside them, something small and
white.

"Pick that up," said Chauvelin to the sergeant, pointing to this white scrap, "and bring it to me."

It was a crumpled piece of paper, evidently forgotten
there by the fugitives, in their hurry to get away. The
sergeant, much awed by the citoyen's obvious rage and
impatience, picked the paper up and handed it respectfully to Chauvelin.

"Read it, sergeant," said the latter curtly.

"It is almost illegible, citoyen . . . a fearful scrawl. . . ."

"I ordered you to read it," repeated Chauvelin, viciously.

The sergeant, by the light of his lantern, began deciphering the few hastily scrawled words.

"I cannot quite reach you, without risking your lives and endangering the success of your rescue. When you receive this, wait two minutes, then creep out of the hut one by one, turn to your left sharply, and creep cautiously down the cliff; keep to the left all the time, till you reach the first rock, which you see jutting far out to sea—behind it in the creek the boat is on the look-out for you—give a long, sharp whistle—she will come up—get into her—my men will row you to the schooner, and thence to England and safety—once on board the *Day Dream* send the boat back for me, tell my men that I shall be at the creek, which is in a direct line opposite the 'Chat Gris' near Calais. They know it. I shall be there as soon as possible—they must wait for me at a safe distance out at sea, till they hear the usual signal. Do not delay—and obey these instructions implicitly."

"Then there is the signature, citoyen," added the sergeant, as he handed the paper back to Chauvelin.

But the latter had not waited an instant. One phrase of the momentous scrawl had caught his ear. "I shall be at the creek which is in a direct line opposite the 'Chat Gris' near Calais": that phrase might yet mean victory for him.

"Which of you knows this coast well?" he shouted to his men who now one by one had all returned from their fruitless run, and were all assembled once more round the hut.

"I do, citoyen," said one of them, "I was born in Calais, and know every stone of these cliffs."

"There is a creek in a direct line from the 'Chat Gris'?"

"There is, citoyen. I know it well."

"The Englishman is hoping to reach that creek. He does *not* know every stone of these cliffs, he may go there by the longest way round, and in any case he will proceed cautiously for fear of the patrols. At any rate, there is a chance to get him yet. A thousand francs to each man who gets to that creek before that long-legged Englishman."

"I know a short cut across the cliffs," said the soldier, and with an enthusiastic shout, he rushed forward, followed closely by his comrades.

Within a few minutes their running footsteps had died away in the distance. Chauvelin listened to them for a moment; the promise of the reward was lending spurs to the soldiers of the Republic. The gleam of hate and anticipated triumph was once more apparent on his face.

Close to him Desgas still stood mute and impassive, waiting for further orders, whilst two soldiers were kneeling beside the prostrate form of Marguerite. Chauvelin gave his secretary a vicious look. His well-laid plan had failed, its sequel was problematical; there was still a great chance now that the Scarlet Pimpernel might yet escape, and Chauvelin, with that unreasoning fury, which sometimes assails a strong nature, was longing to vent his rage on somebody.

The soldiers were holding Marguerite pinioned to the ground, though she, poor soul, was not making the faintest struggle. Overwrought nature had at last peremptorily asserted herself, and she lay there in a dead swoon: her eyes circled by deep purple lines, that told of long, sleepless nights, her hair matted and damp round her forehead, her lips parted in a sharp curve that spoke of physical pain.

The cleverest woman in Europe, the elegant and fashionable Lady Blakeney, who had dazzled London society with her beauty, her wit and her extravagances, presented a very pathetic picture of tired-out, suffering womanhood, which would have appealed to any, but the hard, vengeful heart of her baffled enemy.

"It is no use mounting guard over a woman who is half dead," he said spitefully to the soldiers, "when you have allowed five men who were very much alive to escape."

Obediently the soldiers rose to their feet.

"You'd better try and find that footpath again for me, and that broken-down cart we left on the road."

Then suddenly a bright idea seemed to strike him.

"Ah! by-the-bye! where is the Jew?"

"Close by here, citoyen," said Desgas; "I gagged him and tied his legs together as you commanded."

From the immediate vicinity, a plaintive moan reached Chauvelin's ears. He followed his secretary, who led the way to the other side of the hut, where, fallen into an absolute heap of dejection, with his legs tightly pinioned together and his mouth gagged, lay the unfortunate descendant of Israel.

His face in the silvery light of the moon looked positively ghastly with terror: his eyes were wide open and almost glassy, and his whole body was trembling, as if with ague, while a piteous wail escaped his bloodless lips. The rope which had originally been wound round his shoulders and arms had evidently given way, for it lay in a tangle about his body, but he seemed quite unconscious of this, for he had not made the slightest attempt to move from the place where Desgas had originally put him: like a terrified chicken which looks upon a line of white chalk, drawn on a table, as on a string which paralyzes its movements.

"Bring the cowardly brute here," commanded Chauvelin.

He certainly felt exceedingly vicious, and since he had no reasonable grounds for venting his ill-humour on the soldiers who had but too punctually obeyed his orders, he felt that the son of the despised race would prove an excellent butt. With true French contempt of the Jew, which has survived the lapse of centuries even to this day, he would not go too near him, but said with biting sarcasm, as the wretched old man was brought in full light of the moon by the two soldiers,—

"I suppose now, that being a Jew, you have a good memory for bargains?"

"Answer!" he again commanded, as the Jew with trembling lips seemed too frightened to speak.

"Yes, your Honour," stammered the poor wretch.

"You remember, then, the one you and I made together in Calais, when you undertook to overtake Reuben Goldstein, his nag and my friend the tall stranger? Eh?"

"B . . . b . . . but . . . your Honour . . ."

"There is no 'but.' I said, do you remember?"

"Y . . . y . . . y . . . yes . . . your Honour!"

"What was the bargain?"

There was dead silence. The unfortunate man looked round at the great cliffs, the moon above, the stolid faces of the soldiers, and even at the poor, prostrate, inanimate woman close by, but said nothing.

"Will you speak?" thundered Chauvelin, menacingly.

He did try, poor wretch, but, obviously, he could not. There was no doubt, however, that he knew what to expect from the stern man before him.

"Your Honour . . ." he ventured imploringly.

"Since your terror seems to have paralyzed your tongue," said Chauvelin, sarcastically, "I must needs refresh your memory. It was agreed between us, that if we overtook my friend the tall stranger, before he reached this place, you were to have ten pieces of gold."

A low moan escaped from the Jew's trembling lips.

"But," added Chauvelin, with slow emphasis, "if you deceived me in your promise, you were to have a sound beating, one that would teach you not to tell lies."

"I did not, your Honour; I swear it by Abraham . . ."

"And by all the other patriarchs, I know. Unfortunately, they are still in Hades, I believe, according to your creed, and cannot help you much in your present trouble. Now, you did not fulfil your share of the bargain, but I am ready to fulfil mine. Here," he added, turning to the soldiers, "the buckle-end of your two belts to this confounded Jew."

As the soldiers obediently unbuckled their heavy leather belts, the Jew set up a howl that surely would have been enough to bring all the patriarchs out of Hades and elsewhere, to defend their descendant from the brutality of this French official.

"I think I can rely on you, citoyen soldiers," laughed Chauvelin, maliciously, "to give this old liar the best and soundest beating he has ever experienced. But don't kill him," he added drily.

"We will obey, citoyen," replied the soldiers as imperturbably as ever.

He did not wait to see his orders carried out: he knew that he could trust these soldiers—who were still smarting under his rebuke—not to mince matters, when given a free hand to belabour a third party.

"When that lumbering coward has had his punishment," he said to Desgas, "the men can guide us as far as the cart, and one of them can drive us in it back to Calais. The Jew and the woman can look after each other," he added roughly, "until we can send somebody for them in the morning. They can't run away very far, in their present condition, and we cannot be troubled with them just now."

Chauvelin had not given up all hope. His men, he knew, were spurred on by the hope of the reward. That enigmatic and audacious Scarlet Pimpernel, alone and with thirty men at his heels, could not reasonably be expected to escape a second time.

But he felt less sure now: the Englishman's audacity had baffled him once, whilst the wooden-headed stupidity of the soldiers, and the interference of a woman had turned his hand, which held all the trumps, into a losing one. If Marguerite had not taken up his time, if the soldiers had had a grain of intelligence, if . . . it was a long "if," and Chauvelin stood for a moment quite still, and enrolled thirty odd people in one long, overwhelming anathema. Nature, poetic, silent, balmy, the bright moon, the calm, silvery sea spoke of beauty and of rest, and Chauvelin cursed nature, cursed man and woman, and above all, he cursed all long-legged, meddlesome British enigmas with one gigantic curse.

The howls of the Jew behind him, undergoing his punishment sent a balm through his heart, overburdened as it was with revengeful malice. He smiled. It eased his mind to think that some human being at least was, like himself, not altogether at peace with mankind.

He turned and took a last look at the lonely bit of coast, where stood the wooden hut, now bathed in moonlight, the scene of the greatest discomfiture ever experienced by a leading member of the Committee of Public Safety.

Against a rock, on a hard bed of stone, lay the unconscious figure of Marguerite Blakeney, while some few paces further on, the unfortunate Jew was receiving on his broad back the blows of two stout leather belts, wielded by the stolid arms of two sturdy soldiers of the Republic. The howls of Benjamin Rosenbaum were fit to make the dead rise from their graves. They must have wakened all the gulls from sleep, and made them look down with great interest at the doings of the lords of the creation.

"That will do," commanded Chauvelin, as the Jew's moans became more feeble, and the poor wretch seemed to have fainted away, "we don't want to kill him."

Obediently the soldiers buckled on their belts, one of them viciously kicking the Jew to one side.

"Leave him there," said Chauvelin, "and lead the way now quickly to the cart. I'll follow."

He walked up to where Marguerite lay, and looked down into her face. She had evidently recovered consciousness, and was making feeble efforts to raise herself. Her large, blue eyes were looking at the moonlit scene round her with a scared and terrified look; they rested with a mixture of horror and pity on the Jew, whose luckless fate and wild howls had been the first signs that struck her, with her returning senses; then she caught sight of Chauvelin, in his neat, dark clothes, which seemed hardly crumpled after the stirring events of the last few hours. He was smiling sarcastically, and his pale eyes peered down at her with a look of intense malice.

With mock gallantry, he stooped and raised her icy-cold hand to his lips, which sent a thrill of indescribable loathing through Marguerite's weary frame.

"I much regret, fair lady," he said in his most suave tones, "that circumstances, over which I have no control, compel me to leave you here for the moment. But I go away, secure in the knowledge that I do not leave you unprotected. Our friend Benjamin here, though a trifle the worse for wear at the present moment, will prove a gallant defender of your fair person, I have no doubt. At dawn I will send an escort for you; until then, I feel sure that you will find him devoted, though perhaps a trifle slow."

Marguerite only had the strength to turn her head away. Her heart was broken with cruel anguish. One awful thought had returned to her mind, together with gathering consciousness: "What had become of Percy?—What of Armand?"

She knew nothing of what had happened after she heard the cheerful song, "God save the King," which she believed to be the signal of death.

"I, myself," concluded Chauvelin, "must now very reluctantly leave you. *Au revoir,* fair lady. We meet, I hope, soon in London. Shall I see you at the Prince of Wales' garden party?—No?—Ah, well, *au revoir!*—Remember me, I pray, to Sir Percy Blakeney."

And, with a last ironical smile and bow, he once more kissed her hand, and disappeared down the footpath in the wake of the soldiers, and followed by the imperturbable Desgas.

31

The Escape

Marguerite listened—half-dazed as she was—to the fast-retreating, firm footsteps of the four men.

All nature was so still that she, lying with her ear close to the ground, could distinctly trace the sound of their tread, as they ultimately turned into the road, and presently the faint echo of the old cart-wheels, the halting gait of the lean nag, told her that her enemy was a quarter of a league away. How long she lay there she knew not. She had lost count of time; dreamily she looked up at the moonlit sky, and listened to the monotonous roll of the waves.

The invigorating scent of the sea was nectar to her wearied body, the immensity of the lonely cliffs was silent and dreamlike. Her brain only remained conscious of its ceaseless, its intolerable torture of uncertainty.

She did not know!—

She did not know whether Percy was even now, at this moment, in the hands of the soldiers of the Republic, enduring—as she had done herself—the gibes and jeers of his malicious enemy. She did not know, on the other hand, whether Armand's lifeless body did not lie there, in the hut, whilst Percy had escaped, only to hear that his wife's hands had guided the human bloodhounds to the murder of Armand and his friends.

The physical pain of utter weariness was so great, that she hoped confidently her tired body could rest here for ever, after all the turmoil, the passion, and the intrigues of the last few days—here, beneath that clear sky, within sound of the sea, and with this balmy autumn breeze whispering to her a last lullaby. All was so solitary, so silent, like unto dreamland. Even the last faint echo of the distant cart had long ago died away, afar.

Suddenly . . . a sound . . . the strangest, undoubtedly, that these lonely cliffs of France had ever heard, broke the silent solemnity of the shore.

So strange a sound was it that the gentle breeze ceased to murmur, the tiny pebbles to roll down the steep incline! So strange, that Marguerite, wearied, overwrought as she was, thought that the beneficial unconsciousness of the approach of death was playing her half-sleeping senses a weird and elusive trick.

It was the sound of a good, solid, absolutely British "Damn!"

The sea gulls in their nests awoke and looked round in astonishment; a distant and solitary owl set up a midnight hoot, the tall cliffs frowned down majestically at the strange, unheard-of sacrilege.

Marguerite did not trust her ears. Half-raising herself on her hands, she strained every sense to see or hear, to know the meaning of this very earthly sound.

All was still again for the space of a few seconds; the same silence once more fell upon the great and lonely vastness.

Then Marguerite, who had listened as in a trance, who felt she must be dreaming with that cool, magnetic moonlight overhead, heard again; and this time her heart stood still, her eyes large and dilated, looked round her, not daring to trust to her other sense.

"Odd's life! but I wish those demmed fellows had not hit quite so hard!"

This time it was quite unmistakable, only one particular pair of essentially British lips could have uttered those words, in sleepy, drawly, affected tones.

"Damn!" repeated those same British lips, emphatically. "Zounds! but I'm as weak as a rat!"

In a moment Marguerite was on her feet.

Was she dreaming? Were those great, stony cliffs the gates of paradise? Was the fragrant breath of the breeze suddenly caused by the flutter of angels' wings, bringing tidings of unearthly joys to her, after all her suffering, or—faint and ill—was she the prey of delirium?

She listened again, and once again she heard the same very earthly sounds of good, honest British language, not the least akin to whisperings from paradise or flutter of angels' wings.

She looked round her eagerly at the tall cliffs, the lonely hut, the great stretch of rocky beach. Somewhere there, above or below her, behind a boulder or inside a crevice, but still hidden from her longing, feverish eyes, must be the owner of that voice, which once used to irritate her, but which now would make her the happiest woman in Europe, if only she could locate it.

"Percy! Percy!" she shrieked hysterically, tortured between doubt and hope, "I am here! Come to me! Where are you? Percy! Percy! . . ."

"It's all very well calling me, m'dear!" said the same sleepy, drawly voice, "but odd's life, I cannot come to you: those demmed frog-eaters have trussed me like a goose on a spit, and I am as weak as a mouse . . . I cannot get away."

And still Marguerite did not understand. She did not realise for at least another ten seconds whence came that voice, so drawly, so dear, but alas! with a strange accent of weakness and of suffering. There was no one within sight . . . except by that rock . . . Great God! . . . the Jew! . . . Was she mad or dreaming? . . .

His back was against the pale moonlight, he was half crouching, trying vainly to raise himself with his arms tightly pinioned. Marguerite ran up to him, took his head in both her hands . . . and looked straight into a pair of blue eyes, good-natured, even a trifle amused— shining out of the weird and distorted mask of the Jew.

"Percy! . . . Percy! . . . my husband!" she gasped, faint with the fulness of her joy. "Thank God! Thank God!"

"La! m'dear," he rejoined good-humouredly, "we will both do that anon, an you think you can loosen these demmed ropes, and release me from my inelegant attitude."

She had no knife, her fingers were numb and weak, but she worked away with her teeth, while great welcome tears poured from her eyes, onto those poor, pinioned hands.

"Odd's life!" he said, when at last, after frantic efforts on her part, the ropes seemed at last to be giving way, "but I marvel whether it has ever happened before, that an English gentleman allowed himself to be licked by a demmed foreigner, and made no attempt to give as good as he got."

It was very obvious that he was exhausted from sheer physical pain, and when at last the rope gave way, he fell in a heap against the rock.

Marguerite looked helplessly round her.

"Oh! for a drop of water on this awful beach!" she cried in agony, seeing that he was ready to faint again.

"Nay, m'dear," he murmured with his good-humoured smile, "personally I should prefer a drop of good French brandy! an you'll dive in the pocket of this dirty old garment, you'll find my flask. . . . I am demmed if I can move."

When he had drunk some brandy, he forced Marguerite to do likewise.

"La! that's better now! Eh! little woman?" he said, with a sigh of satisfaction. "Heigh-ho! but this is a queer rig-up for Sir Percy Blakeney, Bart., to be found in by his lady, and no mistake. Begad!" he added, passing his hand over his chin, "I haven't been shaved for nearly twenty hours: I must look a disgusting object. As for these curls . . ."

And laughingly he took off the disfiguring wig and curls, and stretched out his long limbs, which were cramped from many hours' stooping. Then he bent forward and looked long and searchingly into his wife's blue eyes.

"Percy," she whispered, while a deep blush suffused her delicate cheeks and neck, "if you only knew . . ."

"I do know, dear . . . everything," he said with infinite gentleness.

"And can you ever forgive?"

"I have naught to forgive, sweetheart; your heroism, your devotion, which I, alas! so little deserved, have more than atoned for that unfortunate episode at the ball."

"Then you knew? . . . " she whispered, "all the time . . ."

"Yes!" he replied tenderly, "I knew . . . all the time.
. . . But, begad! had I but known what a noble heart
yours was, my Margot, I should have trusted you, as
you deserved to be trusted, and you would not have
had to undergo the terrible sufferings of the past few
hours, in order to run after a husband, who has done so
much that needs forgiveness."

They were sitting side by side, leaning up against a
rock, and he had rested his aching head on her shoulder. She certainly now deserved the name of "the happiest woman in Europe."

"It is a case of the blind leading the lame, sweetheart,
is it not?" he said with his good-natured smile of old.
"Odd's life! but I do not know which are the more sore,
my shoulders or your little feet."

He bent forward to kiss them, for they peeped out
through her torn stockings, and bore pathetic witness
to her endurance and devotion.

"But Armand . . ." she said, with sudden terror and
remorse, as in the midst of her happiness the image of
the beloved brother, for whose sake she had so deeply
sinned, rose now before her mind.

"Oh! have no fear for Armand, sweetheart," he said
tenderly, "did I not pledge you my word that he should
be safe? He with de Tournay and the others are even
now on board the *Day Dream*."

"But how?" she gasped, "I do not understand."

"Yet, 'tis simple enough, m'dear," he said with that
funny, half-shy, half-inane laugh of his, "you see! when
I found that that brute Chauvelin meant to stick to me
like a leech, I thought the best thing I could do, as I
could not shake him off, was to take him along with
me. I had to get to Armand and the others somehow,

and all the roads were patrolled, and every one on the look-out for your humble servant. I knew that when I slipped through Chauvelin's fingers at the 'Chat Gris,' that he would lie in wait for me here, whichever way I took. I wanted to keep an eye on him and his doings, and a British head is as good as a French one any day."

Indeed it had proved to be infinitely better, and Marguerite's heart was filled with joy and marvel, as he continued to recount to her the daring manner in which he had snatched the fugitives away, right from under Chauvelin's very nose.

"Dressed as the dirty old Jew," he said gaily, "I knew I should not be recognized. I had met Reuben Goldstein in Calais earlier in the evening. For a few gold pieces he supplied me with this rig-out, and undertook to bury himself out of sight of everybody, whilst he lent me his cart and nag."

"But if Chauvelin had discovered you," she gasped excitedly, "your disguise was good . . . but he is so sharp."

"Odd's fish!" he rejoined quietly, "then certainly the game would have been up. I could but take the risk. I know human nature pretty well by now," he added, with a note of sadness in his cheery, young voice, "and I know these Frenchmen out and out. They so loathe a Jew, that they never come nearer than a couple of yards of him, and begad! I fancy that I contrived to make myself look about as loathsome an object as it is possible to conceive."

"Yes!—and then?" she asked eagerly.

"Zooks!—then I carried out my little plan: that is to say, at first I only determined to leave everything to chance, but when I heard Chauvelin giving his orders to the soldiers, I thought that Fate and I were going to work together after all. I reckoned on the blind obedience of the soldiers. Chauvelin had ordered them on pain of death not to stir until the tall Englishman came. Desgas had thrown me down in a heap quite close to the hut; the soldiers took no notice of the Jew, who had driven Citoyen Chauvelin to this spot. I managed to free my hands from the ropes, with which the brute had trussed me; I always carry pencil and paper with me wherever I go, and I hastily scrawled a few important instructions on a scrap of paper; then I looked about me. I crawled up to the hut, under the very noses of the soldiers, who lay under cover without stirring, just as Chauvelin had ordered them to do, then I dropped my little note into the hut, through a chink in the wall, and waited. In this note I told the fugitives to walk noiselessly out of the hut, creep down the cliffs, keep to the left until they came to the first creek, to give a certain signal, when the boat of the *Day Dream*, which lay in wait not far out to sea, would pick them up. They obeyed implicitly, fortunately for them and for me. The soldiers who saw them were equally obedient to Chauvelin's orders. They did not stir! I waited for nearly half an hour; when I knew that the fugitives were safe I gave the signal, which caused so much stir."

And that was the whole story. It seemed so simple! and Marguerite could but marvel at the wonderful ingenuity, the boundless pluck and audacity which had evolved and helped to carry out this daring plan.

"But those brutes struck you!" she gasped in horror, at the bare recollection of the fearful indignity.

"Well! that could not be helped," he said gently, "whilst my little wife's fate was so uncertain, I had to remain here by her side. Odd's life!" he added merrily, "never fear! Chauvelin will lose nothing by waiting, I warrant! Wait till I get him back to England!—La! he shall pay for the thrashing he gave me with compound interest, I promise you."

Marguerite laughed. It was so good to be beside him, to hear his cheery voice, to watch that good-humoured twinkle in his blue eyes, as he stretched out his strong arms, in longing for that foe, and anticipation of his well-deserved punishment.

Suddenly, however, she started: the happy blush left her cheek, the light of joy died out of her eyes: she had heard a stealthy footfall overhead, and a stone had rolled down from the top of the cliffs right down to the beach below.

"What's that?" she whispered in horror and alarm.

"Oh! nothing, m'dear," he muttered with a pleasant laugh, "only a trifle you happened to have forgotten . . . my friend, Ffoulkes . . ."

"Sir Andrew!" she gasped.

Indeed, she had wholly forgotten the devoted friend and companion, who had trusted and stood by her during all these hours of anxiety and suffering. She remembered him now, tardily and with a pang of remorse.

"Aye! you had forgotten him, hadn't you, m'dear?" said Sir Percy, merrily. "Fortunately, I met him, not far from the 'Chat Gris,' before I had that interesting supper party, with my friend Chauvelin. . . . Odd's life! but I have a score to settle with that young reprobate!—but in the meanwhile, I told him of a very long, very round-about road, that would bring him here by a very circuitous road which Chauvelin's men would never suspect, just about the time when we are ready for him, eh, little woman?"

"And he obeyed?" asked Marguerite, in utter astonishment.

"Without word or question. See, here he comes. He was not in the way when I did not want him, and now he arrives in the nick of time. Ah! he will make pretty little Suzanne a most admirable and methodical husband."

In the meanwhile Sir Andrew Ffoulkes had cautiously worked his way down the cliffs: he stopped once or twice, pausing to listen for the whispered words, which would guide him to Blakeney's hiding-place.

"Blakeney!" he ventured to say at last cautiously, "Blakeney! are you there?"

The next moment he rounded the rock against which Sir Percy and Marguerite were leaning, and seeing the weird figure still clad in the Jew's long gaberdine, he paused in sudden, complete bewilderment.

But already Blakeney had struggled to his feet.

"Here I am, friend," he said with his funny, inane laugh, "all alive! though I do look a begad scarecrow in these demmed things."

"Zooks!" ejaculated Sir Andrew in boundless astonishment as he recognized his leader, "of all the . . ."

The young man had seen Marguerite, and happily checked the forcible language that rose to his lips, at sight of the exquisite Sir Percy in this weird and dirty garb.

"Yes!" said Blakeney, calmly, "of all the . . . hem! . . . My friend!—I have not yet had time to ask you what you were doing in France, when I ordered you to remain in London? Insubordination? What? Wait till my shoulders are less sore, and, by Gad, see the punishment you'll get."

"Odd's fish! I'll bear it," said Sir Andrew, with a merry laugh, "seeing that you are alive to give it. . . . Would you have had me allow Lady Blakeney to do the journey alone? But, in the name of heaven, man, where did you get these extraordinary clothes?"

"Lud! they are a bit quaint, ain't they?" laughed Sir Percy, jovially. "But, odd's fish!" he added, with sudden earnestness and authority, "now you are here, Ffoulkes, we must lose no more time: that brute Chauvelin may send some one to look after us."

Marguerite was so happy, she could have stayed here for ever, hearing his voice, asking a hundred questions. But at mention of Chauvelin's name she started in quick alarm, afraid for the dear life she would have died to save.

"But how can we get back?" she gasped; "the roads are full of soldiers between here and Calais, and . . ."

"We are not going back to Calais, sweetheart," he said, "but just the other side of Gris Nez, not half a league from here. The boat of the *Day Dream* will meet us there."

"The boat of the *Day Dream?*"

"Yes!" he said, with a merry laugh; "another little trick of mine. I should have told you before that when I slipped that note into the hut, I also added another for Armand, which I directed him to leave behind, and which has sent Chauvelin and his men running full tilt back to the 'Chat Gris' after me; but the first little note contained my real instructions, including those to old Briggs. He had my orders to go out further to sea, and then towards the west. When well out of sight of Calais, he will send the galley to a little creek he and I know of, just beyond Gris Nez. The men will look out for me—we have a preconcerted signal, and we will all be safely aboard, whilst Chauvelin and his men solemnly sit and watch the creek which is 'just opposite the "Chat Gris." ' "

"The other side of Gris Nez? But I . . . I cannot walk, Percy," she moaned helplessly as, trying to struggle to her tired feet, she found herself unable even to stand.

"I will carry you, dear," he said simply; "the blind leading the lame, you know."

Sir Andrew was ready, too, to help with the precious burden, but Sir Percy would not entrust his beloved to any arms but his own.

"When you and she are both safely on board the *Day Dream,*" he said to his young comrade, "and I feel that Mlle. Suzanne's eyes will not greet me in England with reproachful looks, then it will be my turn to rest."

And his arms, still vigorous in spite of fatigue and suffering, closed round Marguerite's poor, weary body, and lifted her as gently as if she had been a feather.

Then, as Sir Andrew discreetly kept out of earshot, there were many things said, or rather whispered, which even the autumn breeze did not catch, for it had gone to rest.

All his fatigue was forgotten; his shoulders must have been very sore, for the soldiers had hit hard, but the man's muscles seemed made of steel, and his energy was almost supernatural. It was a weary tramp, half a league along the stony side of the cliffs, but never for a moment did his courage give way or his muscles yield to fatigue. On he tramped, with firm footstep, his vigorous arms encircling the precious burden, and . . . no doubt, as she lay, quiet and happy, at times lulled to momentary drowsiness, at others watching, through the slowly gathering morning light, the pleasant face with the lazy, drooping blue eyes, ever cheerful, ever illumined with a good-humoured smile, she whispered many things, which helped to shorten the weary road, and acted as a soothing balsam to his aching sinews.

The many-hued light of dawn was breaking in the east, when at last they reached the creek beyond Gris Nez. The galley lay in wait: in answer to a signal from Sir Percy, she drew near, and two sturdy British sailors had the honour of carrying my lady into the boat.

Half an hour later, they were on board the *Day Dream*. The crew, who of necessity were in their master's secrets, and who were devoted to him heart and soul, were not surprised to see him arriving in so extraordinary a disguise.

Armand St. Just and the other fugitives were eagerly awaiting the advent of their brave rescuer; he would not stay to hear the expressions of their gratitude, but found the way to his private cabin as quickly as he could, leaving Marguerite quite happy in the arms of her brother.

Everything on board the *Day Dream* was fitted with that exquisite luxury, so dear to Sir Percy Blakeney's heart, and by the time they all landed at Dover he had found time to get into some of the sumptuous clothes which he loved, and of which he always kept a supply on board his yacht.

The difficulty was to provide Marguerite with a pair of shoes, and great was the little middy's joy when my lady found that she could put foot on English shore in his best pair.

The rest is silence!—silence and joy for those who had endured so much suffering, yet found at last a great and lasting happiness.

But it is on record that at the brilliant wedding of Sir Andrew Ffoulkes, Bart., with Mlle. Suzanne de Tournay de Basserive, a function at which H.R.H. the Prince of Wales and all the *élite* of fashionable society were present, the most beautiful woman there was unquestionably Lady Blakeney, whilst the clothes Sir Percy Blakeney wore were the talk of the *jeunesse dorée* of London for many days.

It is also a fact that M. Chauvelin, the accredited agent of the French Republican Government, was not present at that or any other social function in London, after that memorable evening at Lord Grenville's ball.

Some other Puffin Classics

AROUND THE WORLD IN EIGHTY DAYS
Jules Verne

For a bet, Phileas Fogg sets out with his servant Passepartout to achieve an incredible journey—from London to Paris, Brindisi, Suez, Bombay, Calcutta, Singapore, Hong Kong, San Francisco, New York and back to London again, all in just eighty days! There are many alarms and surprises along the way—and a last-minute setback that makes all the difference between winning and losing.

THE ADVENTURES OF TOM SAWYER
Mark Twain

Tom skips school and has some incredible adventures with his friends Huckleberry Finn and Joe Harper—some real enough, others not quite. They go off and live like pirates on an island, are presumed dead, and return just in time for their own funeral. They witness a murder, and discover treasure beyond their wildest dreams.

THE PHANTOM OF THE OPERA
Gaston Leroux

The legendary rumors of an "opera ghost" take on a terrifying reality when the beautiful young singer Christine Daaé suddenly disappears after her triumphant appearance. An ever increasing pattern of fear and violence pervades the dim backstage areas and subterranean passages of the glorious Opera House as the phantom threatens to strike once more.

FRANKENSTEIN
Mary Shelley

Victor Frankenstein, a Swiss scientist, has a great ambition: to create intelligent life. But when his creature first stirs, he realizes he has made a monster. A monster which, abandoned by its maker and shunned by everyone who sees it, dogs Dr. Frankenstein with murder and horrors to the very ends of the earth . . .

PENGUIN BOOKS

ARE YOU READY FO█ ██HE C█████Y

Peter Doggett was born in 1957. He█ █as be█ █iting about
music for twenty years, has interviewed hundr█ █f rock and
country stars in Britain and America, and was █ █editor of
Record Collector magazine from 1982 to 1999. Int█duced to
country by the late '60s recordings of Bob Dylan an█ █d Gram█
Parsons, he has become a passionate champion of all fo█ █rms of
music, from bluegrass to alternative country.

AR YOU READY

FOR THE COUNTRY
PETER DOGGETT

PENGUIN BOOKS

PENGUIN BOOKS

Published by the Penguin Group
Penguin Putnam Inc., 375 Hudson Street,
New York, New York 10014, U.S.A.
Penguin Books Ltd, 27 Wrights Lane,
London W8 5TZ, England
Penguin Books Australia Ltd, Ringwood,
Victoria, Australia
Penguin Books Canada Ltd, 10 Alcorn Avenue,
Toronto, Ontario, Canada M4V 3B2
Penguin Books (N.Z.) Ltd, 182–190 Wairau Road,
Auckland 10, New Zealand

Penguin Books Ltd, Registered Offices:
Harmondsworth, Middlesex, England

First published in Great Britain in Viking (UK) 2000
Published in Penguin Books (USA) 2001

10 9 8 7 6 5 4 3 2 1

Copyright © Peter Doggett, 2000
All rights reserved

CIP data available
ISBN 0 14 20.0016 7

Printed in the United States of America
Set in Sabon

To Louise Cripps, who set out with me
on this trip into the country

Contents

Introduction – The Rise and Fall of Lonesome Rhodes

Marcia Jefferies finds him languishing in an Arkansas prison, and names him 'Lonesome' Rhodes. She gives him a slot on her radio station, so he can spout small-town philosophy and the white man's blues over the pulse of his battered guitar. TV executives in Memphis sniff him out, and before long he is in New York and on the cover of *Life* magazine. 'I'm just a country boy,' he says apologetically, and viewers across America take him to their hearts.

Rhodes calls his TV show *Just Plain Folks*. 'I'm not just an entertainer,' he muses, 'I'm a force.' To prove it he concocts another television vehicle – *Lonesome Rhodes' Cracker Barrel*, trading on his 'grass roots wisdom', and his support for the ambitions of a fast-rising Senator. 'He wants me to be Senator for National Morale,' the singer boasts. 'Rednecks, crackers, hillbillies, hausfraus, pea-pickers – they're mine. I own 'em. They're even more stupid than I am, so I gotta think for them.' Marcia Jefferies watches in appalled silence. With every boost to his ratings, Rhodes' contempt for his audience grows. During a commercial break, a microphone is left open, and the nation hears him laugh at 'those morons out there . . . a cage full of guinea pigs, a lot of trained seals. I throw them a wet fish and they flip their flippers.' Outraged viewers jam the switchboard; the network throws him off the air; the Senator searches for another way to boost national morale. In a Manhattan office, 'Lonesome' Rhodes' manager grooms a replacement. 'I'm just a country boy,' the new kid smirks, lighting a cigar.

'Lonesome' Rhodes only existed on the cinema screen, as the focus of Elia Kazan's 1957 movie *A Face In The Crowd*. It was no coincidence that this cynical tale was released soon after another

hillbilly emerged out of the American South with a blues voice
and a battered guitar. Rhodes was played by Andy Griffith,
the Southern comedian who three years earlier had gaped in
amazement as Elvis Presley reduced an audience to hysteria with
his blend of hillbilly music and black R&B.

The scenario of *A Face In The Crowd* haunted the music
industry every time that country music – or hillbilly, as it was still
called in the mid-1950s – collided with the pop mainstream. In the
eyes of the country community, the moral of the film was that
'Lonesome' Rhodes had been corrupted by East Coast immorality.
Pop executives in New York and California shuddered at the ease
with which his rural values were accepted as the voice of the
people.

That suspicion, bordering on hatred, has shadowed every
encounter between country and rock since the 1950s. From Elvis
Presley through Bob Dylan and Willie Nelson to Garth Brooks, the
result has been not just a merging of musical styles, but a clash of
cultures – all the more intense because the protagonists know that
they are close cousins. The troubled relationship between country
and rock has its roots in an American divide which was created by
the Civil War of the 1860s, and which has never quite healed. The
rhetoric that fuelled the battles between the Confederate South
and the Union troops of the North was set in stone after the
Confederacy was defeated in 1865. As the victors, the North set the
agenda for the future, and the United States of America grew out
of the uneasy agreement that the South alone stood for slavery and
racial discrimination – evils which were held to be rooted in its
soil, no matter how rigorously the ground was weeded. Even US
Presidents have not been immune to the cultural taint. Lyndon B.
Johnson, the Texan who assumed office after the assassination of
John F. Kennedy, wrote in his memoirs of 'a disdain for the South
that seems to be woven into the fabric of Northern experience . . .
an automatic reflex, unconscious or deliberate, on the part of
opinion holders of the North and East in the press and television'.
From the opposite camp, Californian rock critic Greil Marcus
admits that 'although my parents were very liberal people who
made it clear to us that no form of bigotry was acceptable, I still
got the idea that the one group of people it was acceptable to

project your disdain and contempt on were white Southerners. That prejudice came out of the culture, out of the media, and it seemed to be shared by everyone I knew.'

These twin layers of prejudice met in the 1960s, when Johnson was President: civil rights legislation freed America from institutional discrimination on racial grounds, while a new prosperity granted the South the regeneration which had been its dream since the Civil War. In the midst of this cultural confusion, performers such as Bob Dylan, Gram Parsons and Michael Nesmith began to infiltrate country influences into the mainstream of rock music. This fertilization was apparent as early as 1966; by 1968, albums by the Byrds, the Beau Brummels and the Everly Brothers signalled that a musical flirtation was becoming a movement.

This strange cultural hybrid only became a commercial force in 1969, after Bob Dylan issued an album of unexpectedly traditional country-flavoured music, *Nashville Skyline*. As the album was released, he returned to Nashville to guest on the television show hosted by the most iconic country performer of the era, Johnny Cash – a union which sent shock-waves through both the rock and country communities.

Dylan's approval paved the way for what became known as 'country-rock' to become the dominant American rock style of the 1970s. In the hands of the Eagles, Poco and a host of imitators, country-rock gradually shed all recognizable traces of its hillbilly origins, and mutated into little more than a parody of its mid-sixties roots.

Part I of *Are You Ready For The Country* portrays that turbulent era. It tracks the simultaneous flowering of country-rock across various spheres of rock culture between 1966 and 1976, and documents both the dominant figures of the genre and other, less likely participants, from Californian acid-rockers to British pop singers.

While Part I deals with country entering the world of rock, Part II reverses the perspective, explaining how country music became the unwitting vehicle for the birth of rock'n'roll in the 1950s. Over the next twenty years, country engaged in a relentless cycle of infatuation and disgust with the pop and rock industry, sending out confused signals that came close to destroying the identity of the music.

Part III surveys the strange debris left by the collisions of country and rock over the last twenty-five years, as the music business has fragmented and a dozen parallel traditions have struggled with the same dilemmas that haunted the career of 'Lonesome' Rhodes. Can country, the music of the white American South, reach across America, and out into the world, without losing its soul? And can rock music feed off the fertility of country without becoming trapped in the culture from which it originated? Throughout its fifty-year history, the rock industry has struggled to face the question posed by Neil Young: Are you ready for the country?

PART I
COUNTRY-ROCK

1 Nashville Skyline Rag
Bob Dylan and Johnny Cash in Nashville, May 1969

An anonymous trail of motels, malls and drive-away auto lots leads out of Nashville towards the lake, which is flanked by forests and marshland crawling with copperheads. On the edge of the waterfront, discreetly obscured from the nearby town of Hendersonville, are scattered mansions, columned in the style of the Old South. In 1969, as today, this exclusive district housed the *ancien régime* of country music. The narrow roads held trucks laden with pigs or maize, stretched limos and the ragged procession of coaches which carried tourists on a voyeur's itinerary of security gates and barbed-wire fences. Singer Ray Stevens rapidly tired of the buses which blocked his driveway, spilling out fans anxious for a glimpse of the guitar-shaped pool built by his neighbour, fifties star Webb Pierce. 'Serves him right for moving next to a real legend,' Pierce snapped when Stevens complained.

Roy Orbison and Johnny Cash were near neighbours on the lake shore, their properties barely visible from each other. The snows of February 1969 coated their mansions with a layer of privacy, grounding the tour buses and casting an eerie silence around the lakeside. Alone in Orbison's house were his mother, and his fiancée, the 17-year-old German schoolgirl Barbara Wellnoener-Jacobs.

'I'd just moved to the States,' she recalls. 'Roy was off touring in Canada, and we were completely snowed in. But one day somebody knocked at the door. I was really scared. I looked out, and all I could see was a face I didn't recognize. So I opened it up, and there was this guy calling to see Roy. I asked him how far he'd walked, and he told me he was staying out at John Cash's house. He said he came from Minnesota, and he was used to the snow.'

The visitor was Bob Dylan, a regular guest at Johnny Cash's

home that spring. Cash's 12-year-old stepdaughter Carlene Carter was too young to be overawed by the shy figure who drifted through the house, or the other out-of-town guests who mingled uneasily with Nashville's hippest writers. 'We used to have these parties,' she remembered, 'where they'd sit and pass a guitar around and everyone would sing a new song. One night Dylan sang "Lay Lady Lay", and Joni Mitchell sang "Both Sides Now", Graham Nash sang "Marrakesh Express" and James Taylor was there singing "Sweet Baby James". It wasn't strange at all, it seemed real normal.' Stoking the legend, Cash insists that his guests that night also included Shel Silverstein, showing off his satirical cowboy saga 'A Boy Named Sue', and Kris Kristofferson, who regaled the company with 'Me And Bobby McGee'. 'They were all there to meet Bob,' Cash explained. 'He did a couple of songs. Then I did a couple. Then I said, "Let's sing 'Girl Of The North Country', like we did it on the record", just for the hell of it.'

The next day they sang it again, at the mother church of country music – the Ryman Auditorium, a one-time mission hall in downtown Nashville. It took its name from a sea captain who survived a fearsome storm off the Gulf of Mexico, and repaid his Deliverer by selling his home and handing the proceeds to the church.

Like a sinner's penance, the Ryman was austere, its wooden benches harsh, its roof offering no respite from the sapping summer heat. It was the weekend home of the *Grand Ole Opry*, a country radio show regarded as a sacred monument. The broadcast hooked across America's radio networks, transmitting the traditions of Tennessee to the Pacific and Atlantic coasts.

The *Opry* was revered by all who loved country music for its authority and grandeur, yet it was interrupted every few minutes by downhome commercials. Musical pioneers such as Hank Snow or Bill Monroe would introduce half-hour slots on behalf of the manufacturers of sickly-sweet chocolate bars, or insurance companies preying on the fears of the working man. Then they'd slide seamlessly into a gospel hymn, as if advertising and salvation were twin reflexes of the same impulse.

What better location for a TV show that signalled mainstream

America's acceptance of a hillbilly superstar? *The Johnny Cash Show* ran for two seasons in 1969 and 1970, dulling the stark emotions of his music to fit a Hollywood format. The programme eventually fell foul of the network's prejudices, but during its first series Cash was allowed to proselytize strands of American folk and country that were rarely aired in the mainstream, and mix guests from clashing genres.

Into this forum in spring 1969 stepped the enigmatic figure of Bob Dylan – scarcely seen in public since his turbulent world tour of 1966. 'I asked Bob if he'd be a guest,' Cash explained before the inaugural edition was taped. 'I had a lot of friends I wanted to be on the show. And he agreed to do it. He hasn't done TV in years. He doesn't intend to do any more TV, either.' To relax his guest, Johnny took him fishing on the lake the day before rehearsals.

At the Ryman, there was an immediate collision of cultures. To illustrate that Cash was a Southerner, the set was dressed in rural fashion. 'When Bob went out to rehearse,' Cash recalled wearily, 'they had an old shack hanging from wires behind him to try to give it a backwoods look. He came off stage upset. He said, "I'm gonna be the laughing stock of the business. My fans are gonna laugh in my face over that thing."'

'What would you like?' Cash asked his troubled guest.

'Have them get that set out of the way,' Dylan mumbled back. 'Just put me out there by myself.'

It was an *Opry* tradition that stars and journalists mingled as equals backstage at the Ryman. Dylan was no respecter of tradition. 'Bob asked me to keep the reporters away,' Cash recounted. 'But Red O'Donnell from the *Nashville Banner* wouldn't give up. He kept saying, "Why can't I talk with Bob Dylan? Ask him again if he won't talk to me." So I went back to the dressing-room and said, "Bob, this Red O'Donnell won't give up. Any way you want to communicate with him at all?" He said, "Have him write out three questions he wants to ask me and I'll answer them on paper."'

That wasn't how they conducted business in Nashville. Wearing down Cash with his credentials, O'Donnell talked his way into Dylan's presence. 'Why are you so shy?' he fired at the singer, who avoided his gaze. After a lengthy pause, Dylan muttered: 'Let me think about that.' 'All right,' the reporter resumed, 'but first, how do you explain your appeal to people? I know some people think you're a religion.'

Dylan glanced at his inquisitor, then lowered his eyes. 'I wish I knew.' Then he relented. 'He started talking about his songs,' O'Donnell reported, 'how he gets sparks and hears phrases. But he never explained why he was so shy.' The journalist fired off another impatient query: 'Do you have any friends?' Dylan slipped wordlessly out of the room. Outside, he reported the encounter to Bob Johnston, Columbia Records' staff producer in Nashville who handled Dylan and Cash. Johnston immediately confronted O'Donnell. 'Why the hell did you ask him that? You acted like he was some weirdo.'

Red O'Donnell wasn't the only outsider seeking Dylan's attention that afternoon. 'Some kid got through security,' Bill Carruthers, the show's executive producer, explained to the surviving press corps, 'and forced himself on Bob. There was a scene where the police had to throw the kid out of the theatre. Bob felt badly about it. He was the centre of attention, and he hates it. I can only tell you that the string is very taut at the moment regarding Bob Dylan even doing the show. He's on the edge. He's only sticking it out because of Johnny.'

Photographers also expected open access. 'No cameras, please,' Dylan begged Carruthers. 'I look bad.' It was an unusual request for a TV show. 'The man is so very human,' noted his fellow guest, Cajun fiddler Doug Kershaw. 'You have to realize that he's afraid. Deathly afraid.'

May Day, 1969. At 9 a.m., security around the entrance to the Ryman was doubled. Through the morning, the guest stars trickled in. Doug Kershaw announced that he and Dylan had spent the previous evening in their Nashville motel, writing songs. Joni Mitchell arrived with her boyfriend, rock musician Graham Nash, and their manager, Elliott Roberts. 'In the hotel, we've been treated fantastically,' she cooed. 'But the boys went out to get me a bouquet of flowers. They said everybody was hostile to them. People yelled, called them shaggy-hairs and hippies. They felt unsafe.'

Meanwhile, the crop-haired Dylan remained in seclusion at Cash's Hendersonville mansion. As the rehearsals proceeded, his absence soured the atmosphere inside the Ryman. Cash described him coolly as 'scared, or a little embarrassed'. Bill Carruthers pointed to his 'little bit of fear', but opined that 'he's trying to change'. 'I don't really know what his plans are,' Cash added.

Thirty minutes behind schedule, a cab deposited Dylan, his wife Sara and young son Jesse outside the Ryman. They were ushered through a rear entrance, away from the eager audience standing in line outside the Auditorium, *Opry* style. A lensman for the daily *Tennessean* snapped the queue; the picture was captioned 'Subjects wait to see their king'. The metaphor stuck: the paper's headline the next day declared, 'New Monarch At Opry Tabernacle'. *Rolling Stone* reporter Patrick Thomas surveyed the crowd: 'Businessmen and their wives, country boys, bald heads and acid heads, bee-hive bouffant blondes, drawling teenyboppers and other assorted travelling wonders'.

Inside, their reluctant ruler edged through a soundcheck. 'He didn't look at ease,' noted onlooker Carol Botwin. 'He went through his number woodenly, raising his guitar as if it was a burden. He looked faintly happy only when it was over.' In his sober suit, open collar and week-old beard, Dylan could have been a defrocked priest or a salesman on the skids. 'He's not a hippie or anything,' noted a bewildered TV technician. 'He's got a kind of bluesy, country sound.'

The final element now in place, the producer signalled for the audience to be admitted. In filed the hippies and hillbillies, to take their place alongside Sara and Jesse Dylan. From Cash, they anticipated an aura of tradition – a voice that spoke for the ordinary man with the booming resonance of an Old Testament prophet. He was a sinner justified, by fame and marriage: the saga of his addiction to artificial stimulants, and his salvation via the redeeming love of his latest wife, June Carter, had already passed into legend. His persona could stretch from the eerie menace of 'Folsom Prison Blues' ('I shot a man in Reno, just to watch him die') to the sheer inanity of 'Egg-Sucking Dog'. Duetting with his wife on Dylan's 'It Ain't Me Babe', Cash wrapped this five-year-old disavowal into his tapestry of Americana.

With Dylan, there were no such certainties. The rock community had digested his move from folk protest to psychedelic wordplay. But his most recent incarnation as an apologetic country crooner had proved more elusive. His *Nashville Skyline* album, featuring an erratic duet with Cash, had been on sale for just three weeks. Unwilling to believe that the rock icon could have assumed the identity of a Nashville balladeer without irony, Dylan's audience still regarded him as a seer.

Dylan shyly delivered 'I Threw It All Away', a text that required no translation. But the song's gentle lament for lost love was hidden beneath the dull thud of Kenneth Buttrey's drumkit. The rest of the seasoned Nashville sessionmen were, like Dylan, virtually unamplified for all but the TV microphones, heightening the surrealism of the moment. Then a new song, albeit one which conjured up distant memories – was that an old hit by Jerry Lee Lewis? No: it was Dylan's 'Living The Blues', a dry and delicious country rocker designed to hit the stores the day after *The Johnny Cash Show* aired.

His host reappeared, to reprise their *Nashville Skyline* duet. 'We did it at rehearsal,' Cash commented wryly after the taping. 'I knew my lines, he knew his. I didn't feel anything about it. But everybody said it was the most magnetic, powerful thing they ever heard in their life. They were just raving about electricity and magnetism. And all I did was just sit there hitting G chords.'

Cash and Dylan sat uneasily on a giant wooden block, dropped into a stage set that was Hollywood's idea of an American living room. Dylan's face was trapped in a mask of discomfort. 'Bob just really doesn't believe who he is,' compère T. Tommy Carter had told the audience. Then Cash strained credulity by announcing that Dylan had enjoyed the experience so much that he was willing to repeat it, this time with full amplification. At the end of a third run-through of 'Living The Blues', the haunted glaze of his eyes had begun to soften. He turned to Cash and whispered an aside. 'Bob says you're a great audience,' his host announced proudly.

'I was scared to death,' Dylan confessed to a photographer as he left the Ryman. With Cash, June Carter, Joni Mitchell and Graham Nash, he repaired to Printer's Alley, Nashville's dingy Sunset Strip, to watch Doug Kershaw conjure up the Cajun blues at the Black Poodle. 'We try to keep everybody away,' June Carter admitted, 'because we respect Bob's privacy. John wants Bob to be comfortable.' But down in Printer's Alley, the select crowd grew restless: they wanted a cameo from their star. So Johnny Cash bowed to their wishes, and pulled his wife up on stage to sing with Kershaw. The guy with the beard? Just some friend Cash had brought along for the show. No one approached him for an autograph.

2 Country Pie
Bob Dylan and country music, 1962–1970

Bob Dylan's appearance on *The Johnny Cash Show* echoed the message of the album he'd released a few weeks earlier. The most daredevil spirit of the rock era was now content to perform gentle country music. Such was Dylan's iconic power that, far from alienating his audience by this volte-face, he was able to drag them along in his wake. Before *Nashville Skyline*, pioneering country-rock projects by the Byrds and the Beau Brummels had aroused no more than mild curiosity. Now that same uneasy hybrid of styles entered the American mainstream, where it remained for almost a decade.

Not that Dylan had any evangelical purpose in recording *Nashville Skyline*: his motives were strictly expedient. Fourteen months after the release of *John Wesley Harding*, he was coming under discreet pressure from Columbia Records to deliver another album. The crack Nashville musicians assembled by his producer, Bob Johnston, could make the process relatively painless.

Nor was this agenda-setting album meticulously planned. Dylan arrived in the country music capital in February 1969 with just four songs – among them the lubricious 'Lay Lady Lay', which had been written for the movie *Midnight Cowboy*. It was the only substantial piece cut during the first session. That night, Dylan hurriedly composed three more tunes in his motel room. 'Bob would come in with songs,' sessionman Charlie Daniels recalls. 'We'd sit and listen to what he had, and throw together an arrangement, almost immediately.'

Bob Johnston has often been criticized for his ethos as a producer. 'I don't do nothing,' he once remarked, 'I just let the tapes roll.' But he approached Dylan's visit to Nashville with more foresight than his artist. Booking an afternoon slot for the third day of recording, Johnston invited another of his clients, Johnny

Cash, to fill the vacant evening session – and ensured that he arrived early.

His strategy coincided with the grand design of Columbia Records boss Clive Davis. After the Byrds had cut a country album the previous year, Davis had suggested that they should collaborate with none other than Johnny Cash. In organizing the 'accidental' meeting of Cash and Dylan in February 1969, Johnston was hoping to milk the commercial potential of a duet between the most potent performers in rock and country. He may also have hoped that Cash's presence might embarrass Dylan into a show of creativity.

Neither objective was immediately fulfilled, as the two stars romped through spontaneous renditions of each other's songs. A camera crew were present, working on a documentary about Cash's transformation from drug addict to American legend. They filmed Dylan and Cash crooning Bob's 'One Too Many Mornings' like cows on heat, then breaking up when they heard the playback.

'We just sat down and started doing some songs,' Dylan explained. 'But you know how these things are. You get into a room with someone, you start playing and singing, and you sort of forget after a while what you're there for!'

That was only too apparent when Dylan and Cash resumed the next day. Within three hours, they taped around fifteen shambolic tunes – mostly Cash's own songs, plus some hillbilly standards and a couple of Dylan compositions. In honour of rockabilly legend Carl Perkins, now playing guitar in Cash's band, they revived his fifties rock favourite, 'Matchbox'.

So relaxed was the atmosphere that two songs were composed in the studio. Cash and Dylan collaborated on 'Wanted Man', a sly parody of Cash's familiar style which was little more than a gazetteer of American cities. Then Perkins and Dylan concocted the equally playful 'Champaign, Illinois', named after a stop on the railroad line between Frankfort and Normal.

Reviewing the week's work, Dylan reckoned he could fill an album, albeit a short one, if he used one of the Cash collaborations as a makeweight. Their disarmingly bucolic rendition of the once-beautiful 'Girl Of The North Country' was duly selected. Programming the record like a traditional country show, Dylan

opened the album with an instrumental, then featured his guest
star, before providing a third and final introduction with 'To Be
Alone With You', edited to begin with his question to Johnston: 'Is
it rolling, Bob?' It was, at last.

Johnston confided to the media that Columbia would soon be
releasing an album of Dylan/Cash duets. But at least one of the
participants recognized the material's shortcomings. 'If there was
an album,' Dylan speculated, 'we would have to go back to the
studio and record some more songs. If they wanted a joint album,
they could probably get a lot more material with a broader range.
That didn't happen this time.'

Nor would it again. Instead of uniting Columbia's rock and
country divisions, the Dylan/Cash sessions reminded both camps
that their working methods – and, more importantly, their
audiences – might be mutually exclusive.

Columbia Records boss Clive Davis was acutely aware of the
danger when Dylan chose to name his record *Nashville Skyline*. 'I
was wary of the title,' he wrote in his autobiography. 'I tried to get
him to change it . . . I felt there was considerably greater
universality on the album than a country-oriented title would
suggest – the "Nashville" idea might be a turn-off to great
numbers of city people.'

In Davis's account, Dylan himself was uncertain about his
decision. The album covers had already been printed when he
contacted the Columbia boss: 'He said he'd been thinking a great
deal about the album's title. Maybe it should be changed. But it
was too late. He asked if there was any way of holding up the
shipment. I said no. Did I *really* think the title would hurt sales? I
said I'd stand on my statement: it was a *limiting* title. But if the
album got good reviews, and we were able to break out a single,
sales would undoubtedly be good, though no one could tell what it
might have sold.'

In a playful interview with *Rolling Stone* editor Jann Wenner,
Dylan joked that he'd toyed with other names – *John Wesley
Harding Vol. 2*, perhaps, or some coy amalgam of song titles like
Tell Me That It Isn't Peggy Day.

But *Nashville Skyline* was his first choice, even before the
February recording sessions were completed, when he

commissioned a photographer to shoot the city's featureless vista through early morning haze. The eventual design emerged only by accident, as lensman Elliott Landy recalled: 'He called me to come over and do a picture for the back of his new album, because he had the cover already picked out. We didn't know what to do. We had no concepts, we just winged it. It started out terribly painful and hard. We couldn't get anything good. He was uncomfortable being photographed, and I was uncomfortable. We just stayed with it and we got a moment that was very special.'

Landy's picture revealed no hint of tension. It might have been conceived in advance for an album that eschewed complexity, and an artist keen to present himself as a benevolent troubadour. Eagle-eyed scholars noticed the similarity between Dylan's pose and the artwork for a record by folksinger Ric Von Schmidt, visible on the cover of Dylan's *Bringing It All Back Home*. But that 'coincidence' said less than the portrait of an uncomplicated man with a cowboy hat and a country guitar, the ideal persona for the creator of *Nashville Skyline*.

That simplicity was intentional. In December 1968, Dylan had told a *Los Angeles Free Press* reporter that he could now 'see the whole thing' in his songwriting; 'Now I can go from line to line, whereas yesterday it was from thought to thought. Now I'm more concise. I am not interested in taking up that much of anybody's time.'

True to his word, *Nashville Skyline* ran for scarcely twenty-eight minutes – barely half the length of *Bringing It All Back Home* or *Highway 61 Revisited*. Nowhere in its songwriting was there a hint of the allegories or surrealism of his previous work. Indeed, Dylan's lyrics seemed to be transparent. 'The new songs are easy to sing,' he explained. 'There aren't too many words to remember.' In the words of critic Robert Christgau, 'The songs are so daringly one-dimensional that they seem contrived.'

Even when Dylan did lapse into imagery, the strokes were bold and precise. 'Once I had mountains in the palm of my hand,' he sang on 'I Threw It All Away', a rare acknowledgement of his mythic power, 'and rivers that ran through ev'ryday'. In a couplet from 'Lay Lady Lay', he teased his audience with a reminder of his vintage wordplay: 'Whatever colors you have in your mind, I'll show them to you and you'll see them shine'.

Nashville Skyline fulfilled none of that psychedelic promise. On 'Country Pie', his dexterity was purely playful: 'Raspberry, strawberry, lemon and lime, what do I care? Blueberry, apple, cherry, pumpkin and plum, call me for dinner, honey, I'll be there.'

The most shocking element of Dylan's writing was its familiarity. The man credited with destroying the common currency of the popular song was now purring clichés such as 'Love is all there is, it makes the world go round', 'Night-time is the right time' and 'He's tall, dark and handsome, and you're holding his hand'.

Equally alarming for many observers was his satisfaction with his new style. 'These are the type of songs that I always felt like writing when I've been alone to do so,' Dylan commented as the album was released. 'The songs reflect more of the inner me than the songs of the past. They're more to my base than *John Wesley Harding*. There I felt everyone expected me to be a poet, so that's what I tried to be. But the smallest line in this album means more to me than some of the songs on any of the previous records I've made . . . I feel like writing a whole lot more of them, too.'

Nashville Skyline subverted expectations in another way; a way requiring no analysis. Even *Time* magazine, which failed to notice the album's country sound, couldn't ignore it. 'Dylan is definitely doing something that can be called singing,' their reviewer sneered, noting that his voice had 'a brassy, unstrained quality that suits his light-hearted material perfectly'.

Village Voice critic Robert Christgau, writing from within the rock community, located the precise nature of the change: 'All of those leaks from Nashville: we all knew for certain what it would be, we even knew the details of the duet, and yet when we put it on the turntable, there was one bug: Dylan wasn't singing. It was somebody else, some cowboy tenor who sounded familiar.' Christgau was driven to speculate that the shift of style was emblematic: 'By the mere trick of changing his voice, Dylan has crossed us up once again. *Nashville Skyline* is as much a switcheroo as *John Wesley Harding*. It is touching that everyone wants to believe that Bobby Dylan has settled down, but don't count on it. All those protestations of easy innocence may be just one more shuck. Or maybe they're not. Which would make them the biggest shuck of all.'

In the absence of explanation from the artist – who commented merely that 'I was just sitting down trying to write some notes on where the songs came from and I couldn't figure it out myself' – reporters were left to speculate about his motives. At their most simplistic, they sided with Ritchie Yorke in the *New Musical Express*, who decided that 'If the content of the songs are any indication of the composer's present state of mind, Dylan is carefree and careless.' Others saw *Nashville Skyline* as nothing more sinister than a celebration of married life, from a man whose Woodstock home already held a wife and four children.

In 1969, when faultlines ran through the American psyche, political interpretations were inevitable. Tom Smucker in *Fusion* spoke for much of the rock community in his review of *Nashville Skyline*: 'It's cast in the reactionary, Wallace-for-President, traditionally repressed cultural form of country music.' But Smucker was able to see beyond his instinctive distaste, and recognize that country 'seems to be the one non-middle-class musical form that speaks for working people . . . It's a very traditional form in many ways. And it's a form that bears the brunt of a lot of middle-class scorn.'

Smucker was also quick to appreciate the effect that Dylan's 'conversion' would have: 'The fact that the number one hip rock poet goes to honky Nashville to record . . . has automatically made Nashville and country music human to a whole milieu that would have thought otherwise last year. This has neither made Johnny Cash a hippie nor Bob Dylan a country and western artist, but I think it has lent new respectability to both.'

There was a generosity in this account which escaped other critics. In the *Village Voice*, Robert Christgau could see only the surface: 'A year and a half ago, remember, Dylan released his most political album in years, *John Wesley Harding*, he also put in a rare public appearance at a Woody Guthrie memorial. Now, after *Nashville Skyline*, he guests for Johnny Cash, an enthusiastic Nixon supporter.' Christgau saw country as 'naturally conservative . . . intensely chauvinistic, racist, majority-oriented and anti-aristocratic in the worst as well as the best sense'.

If Dylan had a political intent, then it was not his first challenge to liberal expectations. After President Kennedy's assassination, he'd dared to identify with the chief suspect, Lee Harvey Oswald. 'Only A Pawn In Their Game' had described not the murder of a civil rights activist, but the culture which had moulded his killer: 'The poor white man's used in the hands of them all like a tool . . . But it ain't him to blame, he's only a pawn in their game'. Unlike other 'protest' singers, Dylan refused to parrot liberal platitudes, or reflect the prejudices of his audience.

But *Nashville Skyline* may have had a simpler genesis. Dylan told *Newsweek* that 'The people who shaped my style were performers like Elvis Presley, Buddy Holly, Hank Thompson.' Presley and Holly were acknowledged forefathers of rock'n'roll, but Hank Thompson? No rock icon had ever credited the fifties honky-tonk star as a guiding influence. It wasn't a mischievous statement. Dylan was merely stating the truth: that he'd loved country music before rock'n'roll had been invented.

In 1969, Bonnie Beecher listened to *Nashville Skyline* with incredulity. 'I was startled,' she said. 'I thought he had lost that sweet voice forever.' A close friend of Dylan's from Minneapolis, she recognized the way he'd sounded before he adopted the nasal whine which became his trademark.

In 1960, as in 1969, Dylan's vocal style reflected his self-image. 'Bob Dylan' was a persona he'd adopted in the final months of 1959, when he moved to Minneapolis. Once he'd shed his 'real' identity as Bob Zimmerman from Hibbing, Minnesota, he could construct a physical presence to match his new name.

Only one tape documents the first stage of his transition. In May 1960, he finished his nightly gig at the Purple Onion Pizza Parlor in St Paul, and walked to the apartment of his friend Karen Wallace, where he captured his repertoire on tape. The traditional folksongs, spirituals and Guthrie ballads resembled what he played in New York the next winter. But for anyone familiar with *Nashville Skyline*, there is an immediate shock of recognition: the teenage folksinger carries the seed of Dylan's 1969 incarnation.

Though biographer Clinton Heylin asserts that 'the recording shows a singer whose voice resembles more the country twang of Hank Williams than the harsh nasal sound of Woody Guthrie', there was little affinity in Dylan's 1960 repertoire with the hillbilly tradition. At that time, there was a strict delineation between 'folk' music and commercial country. Musicians now celebrated as country pioneers – the Carter Family, Jimmie Rodgers, Bill Monroe – were viewed as folk performers, because their work exhibited none of the surface gloss of the records being made in Nashville.

Despite his obvious affection for the western swing and honky-tonk ballads of Hank Thompson, plus rock'n'roll and blues, the young Dylan maintained a purist's attitude to the folk scene. He spurned the commercialism of folk-pop singers such as the Kingston Trio in favour of performers whose music sounded as if it was coming from the heart. Foremost amongst those was Hank Williams, whose laments had seized Dylan's attention in 1954. 'I used to sing his songs way back,' he recalled, 'even before I played rock'n'roll as a teenager.' Until he was won over by the teen-oriented escapades of Chuck Berry and Little Richard, Dylan soaked himself in whatever music he could find. Adolescent exuberance led him to rock'n'roll, but he never stopped listening to R&B, bluegrass, folk, country and adult pop.

Once he left Hibbing, Dylan stumbled for a style to match the clamour in his head. In Minneapolis, he and blues singer Spider John Koerner performed duets, echoing the close harmonies of the country duos. 'I could always hear my voice sounding better as a harmony singer,' he recalled. 'The Delmore Brothers – God, I really love them. I think they've influenced every harmony I've ever tried to sing.'

When Dylan headed East in search of the folk community in Greenwich Village, he found that the soul of the city was eclecticism: 'There could be 20 different things happening in the same kitchen. There could be 200 bands in one part of New York: 15 jug bands, 5 bluegrass bands and an old crummy string band, 20 Irish confederate groups, a Southern mountain band, folksingers of all kinds and colors, singing John Henry work songs.' But these strands rarely mingled. 'Folk music was a strict and rigid establishment,' Dylan told Cameron Crowe. 'If you sang Southern blues, you didn't sing Southern mountain ballads and you didn't sing city blues. If you sang Texas cowboy songs, you didn't play English ballads. It was really pathetic. If you sang folksongs from the thirties, you didn't do bluegrass tunes or Appalachian ballads. I didn't ever pay too much attention to that.' Slipping across stylistic borders with the same ease as he'd shed his name, Dylan instinctively combined his influences. In September 1961, *New York Times* reviewer Robert Shelton recognized that this 'cross between a choir boy and a beatnik' was 'consciously trying to recapture the rude beauty of a Southern field hand musing in the melody on his porch'.

His début album was dominated by traditional tunes, such as 'Freight Train Blues', which he claimed to have learned from *Grand Ole Opry* star Roy Acuff. In April 1962, he cut an exuberant version of Hank Williams' 'I Heard That Lonesome Whistle' for his *Freewheelin'* album, but left it off the record. Gradually the country songs, and the material he'd borrowed from Woody Guthrie, were filtered out of his repertoire in favour of original compositions.

His debt to Southern rock'n'roll was apparent when he recorded a rockabilly romp, 'Mixed Up Confusion', in late 1962. The same spirit fired much of the electric music on 1965's *Bringing It All Back Home*. But the public Dylan was a folkie, and more pertinently a protest singer, declaiming polemics which had no apparent connection with Hank Williams, the Delmore Brothers or Carl Perkins.

Another artist who spanned folk and country encouraged Dylan's career. When Columbia A&R man John Hammond was pilloried by the label's executives for signing such an unpromising artist, Johnny Cash used his commercial power to insist that Dylan should not be dropped. 'We just became friends like any two songwriters might,' he explained, 'through mutual admiration for each other's work.'

When the magazine *Broadside* declared in 1965 that Dylan had 'sold out' by playing electric rock music, Cash leaped to his defence with a Whitmanesque prose poem. Some of his testimony was oblique: 'I got hung but didn't choke . . . Bob Dylan slung his rope. I sat down and listened quick . . . Gravy from that brain is quick.' But a message gradually emerged: 'Came a Poet Troubadour, Singing fine familiar things. Sang a hundred thousand lyrics, Right as Rain, Sweet as Sleep, Words to thrill you . . . And to kill you. Don't bad-mouth him, till you hear him, Let him start by continuing, He's almost brand new, SHUT UP! . . . AND LET HIM SING!'

Right as Rain, Sweet as Sleep, Dylan and Cash were now as thick as thieves. In May 1966, after Bob had recorded *Blonde On Blonde* in Nashville, the two men's tour schedules collided. Both were wired on a soup of chemicals, but together they stumbled through Cash's 'I Still Miss Someone' backstage in London. 'I know Bob very well,' Cash commented during that tour. 'Some of his stuff is weird, but I can't knock him. I like his first albums better, but I do like the new things. Lots of people don't understand him, but he's a real nice guy.' Dylan was equally enthusiastic: 'I have Johnny Cash in my film,' he boasted to John Lennon a few days later. 'Are you gonna shit yourself when you see it. He moves great, like all good people. Like prizefighters.'

Those 1966 tours were propelled at a pace which could not be sustained. Dylan fled the merry-go-round of rock stardom by falling off his motorcycle. Cash staggered through another year of chaos before taking solace in marriage. Dylan recuperated in Woodstock, romping through Cash's hits with his tour band. Meanwhile, Cash cut a steady flow of Dylan songs. By 1969, their careers had drifted on to near-parallel lines, as restless explorers of folk traditions and celebrants of romantic bliss. Uniting them in Columbia's Nashville studio, Bob Johnston was simply renewing an old rapport.

Johnston had been appointed as Dylan's producer in 1965. Though he was based at Columbia's New York office, he also handled sessions in Nashville, where he'd struck up firm relationships with the city's leading studio musicians.

Among them was Charlie McCoy, a canny, personable harmonica-player who has graced thousands of Nashville recordings since the early sixties. Equally adept on bass and rhythm guitar, McCoy was a first-call sessionman by 1965.

That summer, he took a vacation in New York. 'I wanted to go to the World's Fair,' he remembers, 'and I called up my friend Bob Johnston, who had told me that if I ever came to the East Coast, he'd get me some Broadway theatre tickets. I asked him what he was doing that afternoon, and he said he was recording a song with Bob Dylan. "In fact," he said, "I'm sure Bob would like to meet you."'

Johnston had just completed two days of sessions for Dylan's *Highway 61 Revisited* album. From his predecessor, Tom Wilson, he'd inherited an artist fired by the potential of electric rock'n'roll, but unschooled in the mechanics of working with a studio band. Alongside Dylan were inspired but rough-edged musicians like Al Kooper and Mike Bloomfield, who patterned their demeanour after Dylan's mercurial arrogance. More comfortable with the dispassionate competence of professional sessionmen, Johnston relished the opportunity to throw a Nashville pro into Dylan's creative process.

'When I arrived,' McCoy continues, 'Dylan told me that he had one of my records, which I was really amazed about. Then he suggested I should stick around and play. I asked him what instrument I should play, and Bob said, "Play guitar". And that was "Desolation Row".'

The twelve minutes of Dylan's astonishing dystopia convinced Johnston that a single Nashville sessionman would not be enough to tame his artist. Rather than smoothing out Dylan's idiosyncrasies, McCoy was intoxicated by the same liberated spirit, conjuring ragged swathes of sound out of his electric guitar like Bo Diddley impersonating a jet aircraft. It was the comparatively untrained Mike Bloomfield who provided the elegant acoustic flourishes on the final version of 'Desolation Row' a few days later. McCoy returned to Nashville; Dylan toured with an electric band. By October 1965, he was working with the Hawks, four Canadians and an Arkansas sharecropper's son who'd been on the road with rockabilly singer Ronnie Hawkins since the late fifties. Through late 1965 and into 1966, Dylan and the Hawks performed perhaps the most celebrated series of concerts in rock history. Fuelled on adrenalin and chemicals, they transformed the brittleness of Dylan's studio recordings into a wave of passion, noise and frenzy.

Little of that spirit survived when Dylan took the Hawks into the studio. After unproductive sessions in New York, Bob Johnston persuaded Dylan to abandon his road band – and his familiar habitat. In February 1966, the singer, his manager Albert Grossman, Hawks guitarist Robbie Robertson and Al Kooper arrived in Nashville. 'Dylan wasn't sure it was a good idea,' recalls Kooper, 'so he brought me and Robbie along, to have part of his past there.'

'It was Bob Johnston who talked him into coming down here to do *Blonde On Blonde*,' Charlie McCoy confirms. 'To begin with, Dylan was a little bit reluctant, but Johnston was really pushing him towards it. He also used the fact that Dylan and I had got along so good up there in New York. Finally Dylan said, "OK, I'll go try it . . ."'

He was entering a community that paid little attention to music outside its own sphere. 'To be honest with you,' McCoy says, 'the whole thing was kinda hush-hush the first time he came. A lot of people in this town who were heavily into the country music industry didn't really know much about Bob Dylan.'

Johnston assembled Nashville's hottest session talents, most of them little older than Dylan. Jerry Kennedy was a guitarist who doubled as Mercury's A&R man, in which guise he had the unenviable task of controlling Jerry Lee Lewis. Blind piano-player 'Pig' Robbins was equally at home with country and R&B, while Joe South also flitted between genres, writing hit singles for soul groups such as the Tams between session commitments in Nashville and Muscle Shoals.

Guitarist Wayne Moss was another musician who could switch comfortably between country and blues. But that diversity still didn't prepare him for working on *Blonde On Blonde*: 'I soon noticed that recording with Dylan was more relaxing and more enjoyable than the usual country things we did. He altered a lot of the studio techniques that we had been familiar with.'

Nashville ran on tightly structured three-hour sessions, each expected to produce at least four – and sometimes as many as ten – completed masters. Not during the *Blonde On Blonde* sessions: the musicians were left to play cards or table tennis, while the studio clocks ticked into overtime. 'I played ping-pong with Albert

Grossman,' recalls Billy Swan, a songwriter who was working at Columbia as a studio assistant. 'I remember him asking me, "Do you know Thelonious Monk?" I said I'd heard the name, but I didn't *know* him. "Well, he's a good ping-pong player," said Albert.' While his manager teased the musicians, Dylan was spewing out screeds of words on to hotel notepaper. Then he'd seclude himself in a back room with Robertson or Kooper, translating his visions into the skeletons of songs.

'We'd record all night,' Kooper explains, 'then he'd sleep, get up and call me over to his room. I was his cassette player. He'd teach me a song, and I'd play it over and over again, and he'd write the lyrics. He had a piano in his room. Then I'd go to the session an hour before him, and teach the band the songs that I knew, so they'd be ready to go when he came in.'

'The second night,' McCoy remembers, 'we were booked in the studio at 6 o'clock, and he said, "You all just wait. I haven't finished writing the song yet." We started recording at 4 a.m. the next morning. That was "Sad-Eyed Lady Of The Lowlands". The hardest thing to do that night was stay awake. We were there thinking, "Well, any minute now he's gonna call us. We better be ready." That was something bizarre in Nashville at that time.' Equally unexpected was the scale of the material: 'Sad-Eyed Lady' stretched out for eleven minutes, the Nashville sessioneers assuming that each chorus must surely be the last. 'After about five or six minutes of this stuff,' drummer Kenny Buttrey recalls, 'we started looking at the clock. We'd built to a peak, and bang, there goes another harmonica solo, and we'd drop down into another verse. After about ten minutes of this thing, we were cracking up at each other, at what we were doing. I mean, we peaked five minutes ago. Where do we go from here? How does this thing peak some more?'

The musicians were left to puzzle out the answers. Al Kooper was the liaison between Dylan and the studio musicians, but he wasn't at liberty to divulge the artist's intentions; Bob hadn't told him, either. To the Nashville sessionmen, Dylan's self-effacement was puzzling.

'He was a real quiet kinda guy,' Charlie McCoy muses. 'He wasn't the kind of guy who would go around and have small talk with the rest of the band. He just didn't do that. He really had very little to say to anybody. You would ask him, "What do you think about me playing like this?" and he would say, "I don't know, what do you think?" ' Billy Swan remembers Dylan's disarming habit of approaching him out of the blue to ask what he thought of the song in progress. 'I wasn't sure what he wanted me to say,' Swan says, 'so I just said, "It sounds good to me," and he'd walk away.'

McCoy claims that he saw no evidence of drug use, which might have heightened Dylan's alienation, during the sessions. But as Moss admits, 'We were green as far as the dope culture was concerned. All we knew was that Dylan looked very strange to us. We were still what you'd call rednecks.'

Only once does McCoy remember Dylan showing any overt emotion. For 'Rainy Day Women #12 & 35', Bob demanded a 'Salvation Army thing' from a trumpet and trombone. 'I could do the trumpet,' the versatile McCoy says, 'and I called in a buddy of mine to do the trombone. We were just goofing off. I picked up the bass, which was something I did on stage, and I was playing the trumpet at the same time. Bob saw me, and said, "Yeah, let's record it like that!" '

Years later, Dylan commented that 'The closest I ever got to the sound I hear in my mind was on . . . the *Blonde On Blonde* album. It's that thin, that wild mercury sound.' Critic Jon Landau described his use of Nashville musicians as 'an act of genius. Those musicians showed themselves capable of the kind of fluid yet structured sound that Dylan utilized so brilliantly when just performing alone.' But much of what Landau called 'a genuine artistic tension' arose from a cultural divide, between the bemused professionalism of the musicians and the decadent symbolism of the songs. What is most notable about *Blonde On Blonde* is its singularity of vision – the way in which Dylan drew what he wanted from the session musicians without submitting himself to any vestige of their trademark 'Nashville Sound'. There's nothing 'country' about the musicianship on *Blonde On Blonde*: the 'wild mercury sound' is closer to the jaded hothouse of Andy Warhol's Factory than the production-line mentality of Nashville's Music Row.

'I really enjoyed the professionalism that the Nashville guys exhibited,' Al Kooper admits. 'It was so slovenly in New York, and that's exactly the difference between *Highway 61 Revisited* and *Blonde On Blonde*. *Highway 61* is just the guys slogging through it, while *Blonde On Blonde* sounded like a *record*, for the first time. Finally Dylan was in the situation where he could take the songs and really do them justice – get a "record" sound without having to overdub.'

As *Blonde On Blonde* was released, Bob Dylan was caught up in the surreal intensity of his 1966 world tour. He escaped only when he slipped off his motorcycle near his Woodstock home, and suffered injuries serious enough to allow him to cancel all his outstanding commitments.

His months of recuperation fundamentally altered the man and his music. Eighteen months after *Blonde On Blonde*, a new Bob Dylan was heard on the *John Wesley Harding* album – unrecognizable as the frenzied seer who'd inhabited a tornado of noise on his most recent tour.

The transformation would have seemed less extreme, though no less puzzling, had Dylan's audience been party to the music he'd made in private during the summer of 1967. Reassembling the members of his touring band, he devoted months to exploring the limits of American roots music. The so-called 'Basement Tapes', sampled only in part by a retrospective album in 1975, allowed Dylan and the musicians who would become famous as the Band to indulge themselves with playful re-creations of Hank Williams and Jerry Lee Lewis, Johnny Cash and the Carter Family – and then to tap those same sources for original songs which evoked every impulse from drunken satire to haunting spirituality. Whether Dylan was parodying a Bobbie Gentry country hit ('Ode To Billie Joe', revamped as 'Clothes Line Saga') or examining man's inescapable burden of guilt ('Tears Of Rage'), he displayed a verbal conciseness and artistic certainty that was maintained on the starker, less-ebullient sessions for *John Wesley Harding*.

Only one element linked *Blonde On Blonde* with the new album: both were recorded in Nashville. For the *John Wesley Harding* sessions, Bob Johnston gathered the sparsest of studio bands.

Aside from some steel guitar flourishes from Pete Drake, the entire album was cut with just two local musicians. 'I'd heard the sound that Gordon Lightfoot was getting with Charlie McCoy and Kenneth Buttrey,' Dylan recounted in 1969. 'I'd used Charlie and Kenny before, and I figured if he could get that sound, I could. But we couldn't get it. It was an attempt to get it, but it didn't come off. We got a different sound . . . a muffled sound.'

The self-deprecation in those words was a deliberate strategy, part of the process of demystification that led inexorably to the *Self Portrait* album in 1970. Contemporary critics marvelled at the precision of the musicianship on *John Wesley Harding*. 'Buttrey is a great drummer,' wrote Jon Landau in *Crawdaddy*, 'and McCoy's bass playing is without flaw. It must astound people that these two crackers (that's what McCoy calls his new band) have just been floating around Nashville spending their talents on studio sessions.' No one in Nashville was astounded: the city revolved around such sessions. But they obviously weren't Landau's 'people'.

'There was something really different about Dylan,' McCoy recalls with a slightly baffled air. He grasps for statistics to quantify the change: 'On *Blonde On Blonde*, we went on and on and on. On *John Wesley Harding*, we did the whole album in nine and a half hours.' Three sessions were neatly spaced in October and November 1967, the first coming just two weeks after the death of Woody Guthrie, the man Dylan described as 'my first hero'. Producer Bob Johnston booked Columbia's Studio B in Nashville a week in advance. Dylan apparently boarded a train in New York in mid-October, and disembarked in mid-Tennessee a day later with the manuscripts for three songs, 'Drifter's Escape', 'I Dreamed I Saw St Augustine' and 'The Ballad Of Frankie Lee And Judas Priest'. The remainder of the album was written with similar haste before the November sessions.

The bare textures of the record hinted at Dylan's roots in folk and rockabilly, but there was no escaping the inspiration for the final track, 'I'll Be Your Baby Tonight': Nashville country music. On an album that was rich in biblical imagery and the flawed heroism of Shakespearian tragedy, that song was jarring in its unfeigned warmth. It looked ahead to the verbal simplicity of

Nashville Skyline, as if offering Dylan relief from the strict moral dilemmas that filled the record. But Dylan had already opened the album with a substantial clue that his relationship to the mythology of country music, and the American South, was altogether more complex.

The title track of *John Wesley Harding* purported to tell the story of a legendary figure in nineteenth-century American history. But when he added a single letter to the name of the Texas outlaw John Wesley Hardin, Dylan signalled that he was switching from fact to fiction. Hardin had already inspired at least three country songs, each claiming to offer the authentic history of this ruthless killer. Naming his 1965 album *Ballads Of The True West*, Johnny Cash staked his claim to the role of historian. He prefaced 'Hardin Wouldn't Run' with an ambiguous anecdote about the outlaw's moral code: 'John Wesley Hardin lost his roll shootin' dice in the Gem Saloon in El Paso one night back in '95. For a while, he sat there and watched the game: brooding, mad. Then he drew a pistol and said, "Gimme my money back." And the timid soul handling the cash for the house said, "Take it all, Mr Hardin, it belongs to you." Hardin got arrested for it the next day, but nobody thought to ask him to return the money. He did get told not to play that way anymore.' No one would have told the hero of Jimmie Skinner's 'John Wesley Hardin' how to shoot dice: 'John Wesley Hardin was a bad bad man, Carried two guns every day, He shot a man dead at the age of 15'. His first victim was black, but Hardin was no racist: by the age of 21 he'd killed a dozen Texans, regardless of their colour.

Leon Payne, a country writer capable of spanning sentimental ballads ('I Love You Because') and Gothic nightmares ('Psycho'), dramatized the legend in 'Don't Make It Fifty-Four: The Fate Of John Wesley Hardin'. After revealing that the gunman was named after the Methodist preacher John Wesley, Payne noted that he had a distinctive way of passing on the gospel message: 'He removed men from temptation, but he did it Texas style'.

His Hardin had the style of a refugee from Dylan's *Blonde On Blonde* album: 'He sure had a method but he was no Methodist, A double-action six-gun and a double-jointed wrist'. But Payne's attempt to understand what drives a man to the life of an outlaw was strictly sixties liberal: 'He was a tender-hearted kid, but easy to get mad, The times he grew up in are what drove him to mad'.

Dylan had no interest in deciphering whether, in a phrase from one of his earlier songs, Hardin had been 'bent out of shape by society's pliers'. Neither did he care to broaden the legend. His 'John Wesley Harding' portrayed the invention of the myth: it was an outlaw ballad *about* an outlaw ballad (or three). 'All across the telegraph,' he sang, 'his name it did resound', and later across the radio as well, thanks to Cash, Skinner and Payne. To undercut the 'True Ballad' tradition of a thousand country songs, Dylan manipulated the 'facts' to the point where they contradicted the historical Hardin. 'John Wesley Harding was a friend to the poor,' he began, 'always known to lend a helping hand'. 'He never was known to make a foolish move,' the song contended, though the 'real' Hardin was captured by a Texas Ranger in 1878 and served sixteen years in an Austin prison. He devoted his imprisonment to studying theology and law, and emerged in 1894 to write a self-serving autobiography, boasting of his power over women and his facility with a gun. 'There was no man around who could track or chain him down', claimed Dylan's equally unrealistic account. But John Wesley Hardin was shot in August 1895 by an El Paso constable, riled because the outlaw had insulted his son. His killer was in turn murdered, Jack Ruby style, before he could stand trial. 'To live outside the law you must be honest', Dylan wrote in another *John Wesley Harding* song, but the moral of the title track was that honesty was purely subjective.

Six weeks elapsed between the final session for *John Wesley Harding* and the album's release, two days after Christmas 1967. During that time, Dylan played the tapes to Robbie Robertson and Garth Hudson of the Band, suggesting that they could flesh out the sound. Both parties eventually concurred that the additions were unnecessary.

At the end of a year in which sonic exploration, not to mention gimmickry, had become the guiding ethos of rock, *John Wesley Harding* had the stark impact of silence after an explosion. *Rolling Stone* magazine highlighted its leaning on traditional country blues, as a corrective to 'the new electric music'. Record producer Phil Spector, the master of the Wagnerian crescendo, appreciated the drama of what Dylan had done: 'He is so honest that it's just like going into the studio with twelve of Stephen Foster's songs.' It was the quietness of *John Wesley Harding* that left its mark, more than the instant Americana of its lyrics. Without needing to utter a word of protest, Dylan clearly distanced himself from psychedelia, mind excursions and the studio trickery of *Sgt Pepper's Lonely Hearts Club Band*. Years later, he was more explicit: 'I thought *Sgt Pepper* was a very indulgent album. I didn't think all that production was necessary. There was a lotta stuff happening that I just didn't understand at that period. None of us did.'

For the next year, Dylan remained silent, allowing time for his innovation to be digested. His former playmates in the Band disseminated the spirit of the 'Basement Tapes' and *John Wesley Harding* on their 1968 début album, *Music From Big Pink*. Gradually, the major players of sixties rock – the Beatles, the Stones, the Beach Boys, the Byrds – began to echo Dylan's musical simplicity. None of them was prepared for his next move: an album of uncomplicated country music, which rejected any attempt to lend it artistic weight.

'When he sent me the *Nashville Skyline* tapes,' wrote Columbia Records boss Clive Davis, 'I decided immediately that "Lay Lady Lay" was the best release. It was vintage Dylan, and it had a bite to it – a strong melody and appealing sexuality. I also thought that it might cross over to middle-of-the-road listeners.'

Dylan was unconvinced: 'Clive Davis begged to release it as a single. I begged and pleaded with him not to. I never felt too close to the song, or felt it was representative of anything I do. He thought it was a hit single, and he was right.'

'Lay Lady Lay', and *Nashville Skyline*, sold Dylan to an audience who had resisted his earlier work. The cracked whine of his earlier records had given way to a smooth purr. If the surrealism of his lyrics had once been a barrier, *Nashville Skyline* offered a cosy bed of familiar sentiments. Long-term admirers puzzled over the secret agenda which they assumed must be buried in its grooves. New York Dylanologist A. J. Weberman combed its clichés for 'clues' about the singer's supposed heroin addiction. But casual listeners who hadn't registered the birth of country-rock flocked to its comfortable pleasures. *Nashville Skyline* was one of America's best-selling albums in the summer of 1969, far outstripping rivals by the Byrds, the Flying Burrito Brothers, Poco and Dillard & Clark. Dylan's celebrity achieved what the pioneering efforts of Gram Parsons, Chris Hillman and Gene Clark could not: mass appeal for a blend of two uneasy partners, country and rock.

His success inspired dozens of acts to experiment with the same raw materials. But in musical terms, it was a dead end. No other rock performer dared follow Dylan into easy-listening country. Even he was to discover that rock fans could grow tired of the lush Nashville textures that now dominated his music.

In April 1969, Dylan returned to the country music capital. Besides appearing on Johnny Cash's TV show, he recorded local standards such as Hank Snow's 'A Fool Such As I' and Cash's 'Ring Of Fire' and 'Folsom Prison Blues'. He even attempted 'Blue Moon', once an eerie cowboy ballad in the hands of Elvis Presley, now wrapped in a furry warmth that banished any thought of irony.

As an album, these songs would have banished something else – his fanbase. Delaying his plan of finding a home in Nashville, Dylan stepped back from his latest recordings. Though he teased *Rolling Stone* editor Jann Wenner that 'I was thinking about introducing [veteran country stars] Marvin Rainwater and Slim Whitman to my audience', he stayed out of the studio for almost a year. During that time, he made only one major public appearance, in Britain, headlining the Isle of Wight rock festival in August. While his hippie audience shivered in tie-dyes and cheesecloth, Dylan donned a white suit and delivered his anthem 'Like A Rolling Stone' in his *Nashville Skyline* voice.

The dissatisfaction engendered by that performance paled alongside the reaction to his next album. In June 1970, he released a double-LP set, pointedly titled *Self Portrait*. As a sarcastic commentary on its contents, the cover was a *faux naïf* Dylan painting of a clown face.

Self Portrait mystified, appalled and angered those who

regarded the singer as a poet and a prophet. *Rolling Stone*, the counter-culture journal named after Dylan's most famous rock song, ran a lengthy analysis of the set, which began: 'What is this shit?' Dylan's self-portrait consisted of borrowed tunes, instrumentals, blatant rewrites of traditional material, and desultory performances from the Isle of Wight. If the title was meant literally, it seemed like a declaration of creative bankruptcy.

His offended followers would have been even more perturbed if they'd known how the album was completed. During three days of New York sessions in March 1970, Dylan recorded around twenty songs, some solo, others with a small band. Bob Johnston then carried the solo tapes to Nashville, where bassist Charlie McCoy and drummer Kenny Buttrey added their overdubs. Dylan wasn't present.

'Johnston had a tape full of what I took to be demos that Bob had done with just guitar or piano and voice,' McCoy recalls. 'We just overdubbed them – separately, because our session commitments meant that me and Kenny couldn't be there at the same time.' McCoy did what he was hired to do, but remains puzzled by this episode: 'I'm not quite sure that the *Self Portrait* album was necessarily a mutual agreement project. Bob did a couple of sessions here that ended up on the album, but he wasn't here for the whole thing. Either he told Bob Johnston, "Well, here, just go ahead and finish it up, take these demos and patch them up," or maybe Bob Johnston had so many sides left on his production contract with Dylan and he just did them on his own account.'

Having already outraged the Byrds in 1969 by overdubbing their version of 'Lay Lady Lay' without their consent, Johnston was certainly capable of working behind Dylan's back. But why did the artist issue the results? Dylan's explanation hinged around his desire to shed his responsibilities: 'I said, fuck it, I wish these people would just *forget* about me. I wanna do something they *can't* possibly like, they can't relate to. They'll see it, and they'll listen, and they'll say, "Well, let's go on to the next person. He ain't saying it no more. He ain't giving us what we want." They'll go on to somebody else. But the whole idea backfired. The album went out there, and the people said, "*This* ain't what we want," and they got more resentful.'

Dylan's popularity ensured that *Self Portrait* still sold in enormous quantities, and his Machiavellian plan was undermined when he released the more orthodox *New Morning* four months later. *Rolling Stone*'s Ralph Gleason duly crowed: 'We've got Bob Dylan back again.' Dylan's feelings are undocumented.

In any case, his retrospective account of his motives is suspect. Even before *Self Portrait* had been released, Dylan had returned to the studio. There was talk of a project with Ringo Starr, who visited Nashville that summer to cut his own country album. Then Columbia's Clive Davis arranged for Dylan to record with the Byrds, who were still suffering commercially from their decision to concentrate on country-tinged rock. However, through mutual misunderstanding and a clash of egos, Dylan was left stranded in Columbia's New York studios while the Byrds flew back to Los Angeles. The possibility of some hybrid of *Sweetheart Of The Rodeo* and *New Morning* passed away. Instead, Dylan worked with a compact unit led by Al Kooper – and devoted most of the sessions to taping yet more covers, including country standards like 'Mr Bojangles', 'Long Black Veil' and 'I Forgot To Remember To Forget'. 'He's so sure in the studio,' noted guitarist Ron Cornelius, who played on those recordings. 'He knows exactly what he wants, and if he doesn't get it, he moves on to something else.' And eventually he moved on to the songs which filled *New Morning*.

Though that album retained its country seasoning, it ended Dylan's four-year courtship of Nashville. After taping *John Wesley Harding* and *Nashville Skyline* there, plus substantial parts of *Blonde On Blonde* and *Self Portrait*, he abandoned the city as a recording venue. He dismissed Bob Johnston as his producer; he cut his connections with Music City's session community.

But the experience left its mark. Recalling the sessions for *Nashville Skyline*, he explained: 'We just take a song. I play it and everyone else just sort of fills in behind it. No sooner you got that done, and at the same time, there's someone in the control booth who's turning all those dials. And then it's done. Just like that.'

For Nashville musicians, that was second nature; the city thrived on improvisation within strictly defined limits. After he left Nashville, Dylan insisted on retaining that approach to recording, with musicians who weren't so disciplined. He complained in the late eighties that, 'My records never seem to turn out the way I expect them to. The musicians never quite pick up on what I want.' Maybe he was pining for Charlie McCoy, Kenny Buttrey and the rest of the crew who'd supported him through the least-troubled sessions of his career.

3 I Am a Pilgrim
Country-rock roots, 1962–1967: the Kentucky Colonels; Chris Hillman and the Byrds; the Dillards; Peter Rowan; the Charlatans; the Lovin' Spoonful; Buffalo Springfield

Bob Dylan's *John Wesley Harding* clouded the psychedelic sunshine of 1967. The album was widely regarded as a corrective to the excesses of the Summer of Love, and so shocking was its austerity and stark imagery that it propelled artists like the Beatles and the Rolling Stones back towards their musical roots.

Critic Greil Marcus believes the album had a more specific impact, crediting it as the prime influence on country-rock in 1968: 'People were just imitating *John Wesley Harding*, that's all. They suddenly thought, "Bob Dylan says we shouldn't be doing *Pepper*-style sound effects, we should be doing simple roots music about the soil." ' Given Dylan's vice-like hold over the rock aristocracy in the sixties, that's an easy assumption to make. But it presumes that *John Wesley Harding* came out of a vacuum, and that the lunge towards 'simple roots music' was a cynical shift into an alien tradition. In fact, the premier American rock bands of the mid-sixties had been schooled in both hillbilly and pop. For the Byrds, the Grateful Dead, the Lovin' Spoonful, Buffalo Springfield and many more, country music wasn't foreign territory, but the core of their own heritage.

'If I had known then what I do now,' Bob Dylan admitted in 1978, 'I probably would have taken off when I was 12 and followed Bill Monroe.' The same fantasy was shared by the Grateful Dead's Jerry Garcia, whose first wife, Sara Ruppenthal, recalls: 'What he really wanted to do was to play with Bill Monroe. That would have been the pinnacle of success.'

Bill Monroe was the founding father of bluegrass music, an offspring of the hillbilly string-band tradition which was built on rigid discipline and instrumental dexterity. Monroe defined bluegrass in the image of his Blue Grass Boys: playing banjo, mandolin, acoustic bass and guitar, they swapped solos with the ingenuity of jazzmen, but never strayed outside strictly defined musical structures. On to this background, Monroe and his band layered three-part vocal harmonies, which echoed across the decades the music of the first immigrant settlers in the Appalachian mountains.

California was 2,500 miles removed from Monroe's Kentucky, but distance didn't diminish his power. In San Francisco, Jerry Garcia and Robert Hunter formed their first bluegrass band in 1960, maintaining absolute fidelity to their hero's design. Down the coast in Los Angeles, Clarence White and his brothers Roland and Eric formed their own band in the Monroe tradition – the Kentucky Colonels.

The Whites came from neither Kentucky nor California. As Clarence explained: 'I'm from Maine. People tend to think I'm from the South, because I've been playing bluegrass music since I was a kid. Me and my brothers learned a lot of old-time Canadian jigs and fiddle music from my father, who's Canadian. I started on guitar when I was six years old, and when I was ten, I began travelling with my brothers. We called ourselves the Three Little Country Boys.'

In 1962, the Country Boys became the Kentucky Colonels, claiming a fabricated allegiance to Monroe's home state. On their first album, *The New Sound Of Bluegrass America*, they simply regurgitated what they'd learned from their elders. *Appalachian Swing* (1964) broke with tradition, via the exploratory verve of Clarence White's guitar playing. Extending Monroe's boundaries, White tossed off licks that were borrowed from Chuck Berry or Django Reinhardt. The Colonels' repertoire didn't transgress the purists' rules – 'I Am A Pilgrim', 'Sally Goodin', 'John Henry' and 'Clinch Mountain Backstep' wouldn't have raised hackles at any bluegrass festival – but White's daring improvisations thrilled those who were frustrated by Monroe's narrow vision.

Among Californian bluegrass players, this maverick approach spawned a sympathetic cult. 'I was in several bluegrass bands back then,' recalled David Lindley, who later formed the psychedelic band Kaleidoscope. 'There was the Dry City Scat Band, and the Mad Mountain Ramblers. I was working with Chris Darrow, Richard Greene – a whole lot of people who went on to do other things. Chris Hillman was on the same LA bluegrass trip. It was regarded as a real oddity at the time, because everyone else was playing folk music. In the middle of all that, there was a whole Clarence White-inspired bluegrass movement. We were considered lunatics, because it seemed so uncommercial.'

Darrow, Greene and Lindley worked together briefly, Darrow even daring to venture that 'we were one of the best bluegrass bands in California concurrent with the Kentucky Colonels. They were more traditionally minded, while we were stretching out a bit.' But Clarence White had already moved beyond the imagination of his imitators. 'Vanguard and Elektra [record companies] had been bidding for me to do a guitar album for them, and I'd started getting material,' he revealed shortly before his death. 'The first demo I received was "Mr Tambourine Man", by Bob Dylan and Ramblin' Jack Elliott.'

Unable to convince the other Colonels that the sumptuous imagery of Dylan's song could be translated into bluegrass, White turned the demo down. It was then offered to another Los Angeles band with bluegrass roots: the Byrds. Lauded as pioneers of folk-rock, or electric folk, after they recorded 'Mr Tambourine Man' in 1965, they betrayed only hints of a wider influence on their early albums – though their second LP, *Turn! Turn! Turn!*, did feature a smooth rendition of a country tune, 'Satisfied Mind'. 'That was a Porter Wagoner song,' Byrds bassist Chris Hillman recalls, 'and it was my idea to cut that. I was always trying to get the band to play country songs. But David Crosby always objected. I used to get so angry with him. We'd be driving in the car, and he'd go on and on about the sitar – how it was unique, the way it used sliding scales, and had no frets. So I'd say, "Listen to this," and I'd hit the radio dial until I found a Nashville station, and a steel guitar. And Crosby would shout, "I hate that, I hate that corny shit . . ." Of course, five years later he had Jerry Garcia playing steel on CSNY's "Teach Your Children". That's Crosby.'

In 1965, media attention focused on the Byrds' singers and songwriters, Gene Clark, Jim McGuinn and David Crosby, all veterans of the Greenwich Village folk scene in New York. Chained to a bass guitar behind them was the awkward, anonymous figure of Hillman – who in fact had the longest professional pedigree of them all. As a teenage mandolin player, he'd formed the Scottsville Squirrel Barkers in 1958, together with Kenny Wertz (later with the Flying Burrito Brothers) and Larry Murray (founder of Hearts & Flowers). Future Eagles guitarist Bernie Leadon replaced Wertz in 1962, in time for the group to promote its only album, a traditional affair called *The Best Of Bluegrass Favorites*.

Hillman re-emerged as one of the Golden State Boys, alongside seventies country star Vern Gosdin and his brother Rex. 'They were my window on authenticity,' he says. 'They came right out of the South. I was a middle-class white kid from Southern California, a surfer, and I'd never been around people from the South before. That's when I heard the "n" word [nigger] – not from the Gosdins, but from people who were around the perimeter of the band, because we would play all these weird clubs in California that were really for all the transplanted Southerners, who would have been more at home in Alabama.' In bluegrass as in folk, a fluid identity ensured multiple bookings at the same venue, so the Golden State Boys masqueraded as the Blue Diamond Boys and, in deference to their mandolinist's stubborn will, the Hillmen.

Even before Clarence White heard 'Mr Tambourine Man', the Hillmen had recorded two Bob Dylan songs – 'When The Ship Comes In' and 'Farewell'. Dylan was accepted as part of the folk tradition by 1964, but these strict bluegrass interpretations of his songs startled the Hillmen's contemporaries.

The group had auditioned at World Pacific Studios in Los Angeles for Jim Dickson, who had produced the early albums by another young band of folk/bluegrass adventurers, the Dillards. Doug and Rodney Dillard arrived in California from the Ozark community of Salem, Missouri. Drawn to California by the lustre of the folk revival, they softened their bluegrass harmonies and satirized their rural upbringing to become nightclub favourites in Los Angeles. Impresario Fred Weintraub soon dubbed them 'the first pop bluegrass singing group'.

Learning their craft from their father, old-time fiddle player Homer Dillard, Doug and Rodney initially applied themselves to maintaining 'the feeling of the campfires and the log cabins and lonely candlelight burning in the wilderness', according to the romanticized notes on their début album. Evocatively titled *Back Porch Bluegrass*, it introduced the quartet as purists with an iconoclastic edge – more audible on their next album, *Live! Almost!* in 1964.

Bassist Mitch Jayne won an immediate laugh from the nightclub audience at the Mecca in Los Angeles by announcing: 'We're all hillbillies'. His laconic introductions satirized the brothers' rural background, but didn't overshadow their breakneck musicianship and bluegrass harmonies. Amid traditional material like 'Old Blue' and 'Pretty Polly', both of which resurfaced in the Byrds' repertoire five years and many incarnations later, the Dillards slipped in a tune by a young writer who, said Jayne, 'has a voice like a dog with his leg caught in barbed wire'.

Jim Dickson had introduced the Dillards to Bob Dylan's 'Walkin' Down The Line', and he was soon ushering the Hillmen along the same path. 'What Jim had,' Chris Hillman explains, 'and what he carried into the Byrds, was a great sense of song – how important the lyric was. He said, "Why are you guys doing all these traditional bluegrass songs? Everybody does them. Why don't you try something else?" He played us "When The Ship Comes In", and encouraged Vern and Rex to write more.'

Dickson had a particular affection for the shy mandolin-player, so when he was approached by a trio of folkie Beatles fans called the Jet Set, he recognized their commercial potential and suggested that Chris Hillman should join them. Inevitably, he also persuaded the group – soon renamed the Byrds – that they should tackle some Dylan material. Lining up alongside Jim McGuinn, Gene Clark and David Crosby proved a lucrative career move for Hillman, but he was so soaked in bluegrass culture that he felt alienated by their folk-pop music. 'When I joined the Byrds,' he admits, 'I didn't fully understand where the other guys were coming from. I'd heard the Beatles, of course, and I'd loved rock'n'roll in the fifties. But when the Top 40 became inundated with all those Italian crooners, like Frankie Avalon, I was drawn into folk music, and then country. So when the other guys were watching *A Hard Day's Night*, I was playing these weird country clubs.'

'Satisfied Mind' aside, Hillman's country roots were suppressed on the Byrds' early records. Jim Dickson did briefly attempt to promote another of his clients, and widen the Byrds' horizons, but his pleas that they should let Doug Dillard play banjo on 'Mr Tambourine Man' went unheard. The manager pursued his aim more subtly thereafter, teaming the Byrds with the Dillards for two American tours in early 1966. At one show in Louisiana, teenage Byrds fan Don Henley was introduced to country music by the rousing bluegrass harmonies and collegiate humour of the Dillard brothers' band.

Initially overshadowed within the Byrds, Chris Hillman found creative gratification elsewhere. He didn't lose contact with his contemporaries from the LA bluegrass scene: early in 1966, he produced a single for the Gosdin Brothers, with Clarence White on guitar – electric lead guitar. 'It was like learning a completely different instrument,' White commented. 'I bought a Telecaster and started playing country music, getting more power and using bigger amps – just like rock'n'roll.'

Freed from the bluegrass purism of the Kentucky Colonels, he was able to conjure several strands of American music into a distinctive style of picking. His lead lines wound around the Gosdins' 'One Hundred Years From Now', impressing Hillman sufficiently for White to guest on the Byrds' 'Time Between' a few months later. On both songs, White transformed melodic country tunes into the harbinger of a new genre: country-rock.

'A lot of cats from the West would go on this pilgrimage,' explained Peter Rowan, whose pedigree stretches from Bill Monroe's Blue Grass Boys to psychedelic rock. 'You get in your car and you go to Pennsylvania and you have a meeting there of Jerry Garcia from California and David Grisman from New York, who'd come to hear bluegrass in the only place where you could hear it.'

Garcia, Grisman, Rowan and their peers were the first generation of bluegrass musicians raised on Elvis Presley as well as Bill Monroe. But by the early sixties, little of the confrontational glee of mid-fifties rockabilly and R&B was audible on Top 40 radio. Bluegrass offered its own levels of initiates and converts, with the puritan Monroe as high priest. As Sandy Rothman, then playing in a band with Jerry Garcia, recalled, Monroe exerted a forbidding command over his followers: 'We had this dream that was never verbalized: we could get a job playing with Bill Monroe.' They drove halfway across America to the Brown County Jamboree in Indiana to see him perform: 'Before the show, Monroe was signing autographs and talking to people. We positioned ourselves right in his line of vision, about eight or ten feet away. We had our instrument cases standing upright and we were sort of leaning on them. We were too scared to say anything. We thought he was going to take pity on us and come over and talk to us. But he never did.'

Garcia's longtime lyricist, Robert Hunter, remembers: 'Sandy Rothman went out to New York, and eventually ended up playing with Bill Monroe. That was one of the tested and approved routes to bluegrass sainthood, to get into Monroe's band. Bill Keith made it first: he was the best of all, I guess.'

An associate of Clarence White and the Kentucky Colonels, mandolinist Bill Keith began the subtle infiltration of the rock'n'roll generation into Monroe's élite. The rural South-Eastern musicians who had been Blue Grass Boys since the early forties were gradually replaced by more cosmopolitan, middle-class players, who'd come to bluegrass as students.

By late 1966, Monroe's band included Peter Rowan, an Elvis fan from Boston, and the classically trained fiddle-player Richard Greene. Both had learned as much from the records of the Kentucky Colonels as from Monroe's back catalogue. Monroe wasn't immune to the Colonels' musicianship; he briefly allowed Clarence White's guitarist brother Roland into his band. Rowan, Monroe and Indian sitar virtuoso Ravi Shankar once jammed together, uniting the musics of the Appalachians and the Himalayas. Like Monroe, Shankar left his mark on a generation of American folk/rock experimentalists, from the Byrds to Earth Opera.

Ultimately these younger musicians took more from their mentor than they gave. Monroe's music remained virtually unchanged; his disciples graduated from the Blue Grass Boys with a grounding in tempo and technique that proved vital when they began to explore the outer boundaries of country-rock later in the decade.

For musicians like Jerry Garcia, whose tastes ran beyond bluegrass, Bill Monroe's puritanism had its limitations. In 1964, he abandoned his fruitless quest for the ultimate San Francisco bluegrass band and threw himself into a less demanding, more egalitarian style. Jug-band music condensed a bunch of 'ethnic' genres – folk, country blues, electric R&B, honky-tonk country and old-time string-band music – into an uneasy hybrid. This bastard creation removed the taint of poverty and suffering from its working-man's laments, turning the blues into nostalgic entertainment.

From West Coast to East, the jug style was a popular live attraction on the mid-sixties folk scene – never more so than in the hands of the Lovin' Spoonful in New York, who translated their jug-band music into commercially viable folk-rock. But even before the Spoonful cut their first record, a group from San Francisco used the jug sound to fertilize the seeds of Californian acid culture. The Charlatans, credited as the city's first psychedelic band, also christened one of the most pervasive myths of the next decade: rock stars as cowboy outlaws. They evaded the San Francisco police, and compensated for the city's lack of live venues, by taking their music and their drugs to the virtual ghost town of Virginia City, Nevada, several hundred miles inland.

Besides its isolation, the town held a symbolic significance: it had been the site of the Comstock Lode silver-rush in 1859, attracting bounty-hunters who'd missed the Californian gold-rush a decade earlier. Stripped of its silver, the proceeds from which kept the Union states' treasury afloat during the Civil War, Virginia City maintained only a sparse population of miners and farmers – joined, after June 1965, by the first wave of what became known as hippies.

The town's deserted streets sparked the imagination of the Charlatans, who drew on its folk memory of gun battles and western imagery. 'We wanted to dress sharp,' guitarist Mike

Wilhelm explained, 'so we'd go round thrift stores and find old Victorian clothes which actually looked very modern. We started carrying pistols and guns, mostly because the locals objected to our long hair. Everybody up there carried pistols, because there's miles and miles of desert, and you can't holler for a policeman if someone hassles you.' On 29 June 1965, the Charlatans reopened a disused bar called the Red Dog Saloon. For the next year, the band conjured up the spirit of the Old West with the music of the New, teasing their renditions of blues, country and folk standards into extended improvisations that exuded the scent of marijuana. 'A lot of groups picked up on our hip dress,' Wilhelm noted. Among them were the Quicksilver Messenger Service and the Grateful Dead, who by the late sixties were clad in an unruly mix of Hell's Angels' uniforms, cowboy garb and the working-man's chic also favoured by the Band. In the early seventies, the Eagles adopted the Charlatans' image wholesale for their *Desperado* album.

The Charlatans billed themselves as 'The Limit Of The Marvelous', and their frontier spirit was heightened as the psychedelic drug LSD entered their milieu early in 1966. But when they returned to San Francisco that summer, their country-based material seemed, appositely enough, like a relic from a far-flung era alongside the full-blown acid-rock of the Grateful Dead and Jefferson Airplane. The San Francisco rock scene was slowly distancing itself from its country roots.

In New York, John Sebastian was leading the Lovin' Spoonful out of the folk ghetto and into the pop charts. Even when they acknowledged their previous incarnation, on a tune like 'Blues In The Bottle', Sebastian's blues slipped into comedy, as he drawled his words like a cotton farmer chewing tobacco.

But the Spoonful couldn't expel all the country air from their music. Lead guitarist Zally Yanovsky showed off his Carl Perkins licks on delicious country chugs like 'It's Not Time Now' and 'Butchie's Tune'. The chord changes might have edged closer to jazz than Nashville honky-tonk, but Yanovsky's playing was the missing link between fifties rockabilly and sixties folk-rock. This hybrid flowered on 'Darlin' Companion', a gentle jogtrot under an unbroken Southern sky – so convincing that Johnny Cash and his bride-to-be, June Carter, adopted it as a public pledge of their wedding vows.

As the band's chief songwriter, Sebastian maintained a fashionable ambiguity towards hillbilly music. On 'Boredom', he evoked the deadening landscape of ennui with a country lament. Whereas a Nashville writer would have compared the big city and the rural small town and found the metropolis wanting, Sebastian pined for the comforts of New York – marooned as he was in a 'one-channel town . . . feeling 'bout as local as a fish in a tree'. Sebastian's fondest tribute to country music exposed his distance. 'Nashville Cats' lapsed into a pastiche of Southern slang as condescending as any minstrel black-face: gee, these Tennessee boys mighn't have no learning, but they can play guitar twice as better than I will. At the height of psychedelia, however, there was a glorious defiance in the Spoonful's tribute to the 'thirteen hundred and fifty-two guitar-pickers in Nashville', who played 'clean as country water' while their rock counterparts were refuelling on acid and grass. Sebastian recalled his teenage conversion, 'blasted sky high' by those 'yellow Sun records from Nashville'. Memphis, actually, but either way he was told, 'up North there ain't nobody buys 'em, and I said, "But I will" '.

The man who could write 'Summer In The City' was never going to convince anyone as a Tennessee farmhand. But the Lovin' Spoonful's acceptance of Nashville licks helped smooth the dirt road that brought hillbilly rhythms into rock.

Another unheralded catalyst was Stephen Stills, guitarist and songwriter for the Los Angeles-based folk-rock group, Buffalo Springfield. Born in Texas, and raised across the Southern states and in Costa Rica, Stills ingested everything from big-band jazz to Latin dance rhythms. Though his deepest love was the blues, he was equally at home with country and folk, and in the early seventies he channelled all these influences into Manassas, one of the great lost forces of American rock.

Buffalo Springfield's 1966 début album was a blend of contemporary echoes, and two Stills songs wandered across the border into country. 'Pay The Price' carried a 'sin causes suffering' message that could have come from Hank Williams, while the

Beatlesque 'Go And Say Goodbye' was hooked around an old bluegrass lick from a tune called 'Salt Creek'. Like Sebastian, Stills was simply borrowing anything he could find in the quest for novelty and honesty. It took another Texan, Michael Nesmith, to merge country and rock in a self-conscious search for a form that could do justice to them both.

4 Good Clean Fun
Michael Nesmith and the Monkees, 1966–1969

'Some people think I'm moody and difficult,' Michael Nesmith informed the members of the Monkees Fan Club in 1967. 'Well, I come from the South.'

Moody and Southern were built into his role as 'Mike Nesmith', the wool-hatted guitar-picker and Texas troublemaker who was one-quarter of a manufactured rock group called the Monkees. They were assembled in early 1966 by the Hollywood TV company Screen-Gems Columbia, as a conscious attempt to mimic the teen appeal of the Beatles. Their scripts were based on the zaniness of *A Hard Day's Night*, while the characters of the four Monkees were modelled squarely on their Liverpool counterparts.

Davy Jones was the pretty boy McCartney figure, Micky Dolenz the brash and witty Lennon and Peter Tork the dumb, lovable Ringo Starr: which left Nesmith to fill the role of George Harrison, laconic, slow but not stupid, and more eloquent with guitar chords than vocal cords. The writers drew on a full palette of stereotypes: encouraged to stretch out his slight Dallas drawl, Nesmith was cast as a rural savant, wise beyond his own comprehension.

The Monkees project was an instant success around the world. The four actors grew into their roles as pop stars – to the disgust of 'real' musicians, who denounced the group for not playing on their own records and acting like Hollywood puppets. 'We all had musical experience,' Nesmith notes. 'I'd been playing and performing for ten years. But everyone in the press and in the hippie movement had got us into their target window as being illegitimate, and not worthy of consideration as a musical force. We were under seige. The rabid element of hatred that was engendered is almost impossible to describe. It lingers to this day among people of my own age.'

Lambasted by the media as 'fakes', but legally prevented from creating their own music, the Monkees – led by the fearlessly stubborn Nesmith – mounted a coup. Calling a press conference, they announced their intention to control their own destinies – or quit. The Nesmith rebels won the battle, but their TV show was cancelled at the end of 1967, and the group began to disintegrate a year later.

Only when they had vanished as a threat to the precious 'authenticity' of rock culture was any attention paid to their music. In 1970, Nesmith emerged as the leader of the First National Band, an idiosyncratic country-rock combo who swore devotion to Jerry Lee Lewis, Jimmie Rodgers and Hank Williams, while being equally at home with musical surrealism and impressionistic sound-pictures. Belatedly, Nesmith was greeted as a maverick, and an honourable one at that, who'd been subverting Hollywood's TV industry from within. Rock critics who'd lampooned the Monkees returned to their records and discovered that these 'imitation' pop stars had been pioneers in the use of the Moog synthesizer. Another synthesis was also apparent: Michael Nesmith's unique blend of country-rock. 'Of course, country-rock didn't exist then,' Nesmith insists. 'They were country and rock, two distinct institutions. I first butted heads with the rock'n'roll scene with the early Monkees records, when I sort of fell into this countryish mode. Before that, there wasn't really anyone who was toying with what you could call country-rock, unless you count James Burton playing guitar on Ricky Nelson singles. In the Monkees, I suddenly had the power and the money to hire James to play guitar for us, so I was aware of trying to create a marriage of the two styles. I figured that if we got closer to playing country, we'd be creating something that was more honest, that was closer to country blues. But I wasn't doing it within a landscape where people were waiting for me and saying, "Boy, you've finally moved into that country-rock sound."'

As early as June 1966 – five months before the Byrds first invited bluegrass guitarist Clarence White to play country licks on their records – Nesmith was producing sessions that were, ostensibly at least, intended for the Monkees. 'When I signed up to do the show,' he explains, 'I was told, "You're supposed to be the guitar-player in this fictional band, and you're supposed to have certain characteristics. We will pay you a certain amount of money to do that.'' Then they asked me if I wrote songs, ''because if you do, we'd be interested to see what you have''. So I would write the songs and bring them forward, and they would say, ''Well, no, that's too country. No, that's too obscure. We don't wanna do anything like that.'' '

In an attempt to marshal Nesmith's undoubted talents, he was teamed with the prestigious New York writing duo of Gerry Goffin and Carole King. Together, they concocted 'Sweet Young Thing', which Nesmith recorded – with the aid of Hollywood session aces like James Burton, Glen Campbell, Larry Knechtel and Hal Blaine – in July 1966. Though he still decries the process whereby the song evolved ('I hated being thrown in a room with other people and told to write songs with them'), 'Sweet Young Thing' is as convincing a starting-point for country-rock as any. On a more prestigious record, Nesmith's juxtaposition of a country fiddle and freak-out fuzz guitar would have aroused more comment. Hidden on an album by a 'manufactured' group aimed at teenyboppers, its radicalism passed unnoticed.

'That was a sensational platform,' Nesmith says of these sessions. But he could contribute one or at most two songs to the Monkees' albums. 'That's when it got tough,' he recalls. 'I went outside the job description and said, ''No, wait a minute, I'm gonna go home. I'm not gonna be a part of this. We have an opportunity to do good music, and if we're not gonna do that, then I'm outta here.'' Anyone who'd made that kind of ultimatum before had been pushed to the side, so the TV show could go forward. But it was the sixties, and people were perhaps more open to ideas from outside than before or since.'

For their third album, *Headquarters*, the Monkees elected to play, and wherever possible write, everything on the record. Nesmith had been taking steel guitar lessons from 'Red' Rhodes in Hollywood, and his first experiments with the bar and pedal surfaced on 'I'll Spend My Life With You'.

For most of 1967, though, Nesmith sublimated the country elements of his work in favour of an exotic blend of folk-rock, psychedelia and sonic trickery. An exception was 'What Am I Doing Hangin' Round', which didn't follow strict Bakersfield procedures – 'It was like a new-wave country song,' Nesmith judges, 'with its minor-chord changes; Buck Owens wouldn't have done anything like that' – but which did introduce to a wider audience two Texan writers called Michael Martin Murphey and Owens Castleman, the precursors of the Austin 'alternative' country scene in the early seventies.

Eager to experiment, Nesmith had accumulated a backlog of equally oblique country songs by the end of the year. While Bob Dylan was recording *John Wesley Harding* in Nashville, the Monkee was assembling a big band to cut unwieldy country-jazz instrumentals under the pseudonym of the Wichita Train Whistle. Six months later, Nesmith followed Dylan and the Byrds to Nashville, taping a dozen tracks with musicians like Kenny Buttrey and Wayne Moss (both veterans of Dylan's trips to the city), Norbert Putnam, David Briggs, Felton Jarvis – and Lloyd Green, the sole link between these songs and the Byrds' Nashville recordings a few weeks earlier.

Nesmith remembers the week's events with pride: 'If anybody was going to ask me at what point the marriage of country and rock became a viable form, that is the exact session. It wasn't just a mixture of two different things, it became a separate style in its own right, borrowed from the gene pool of each organism.'

The Nashville musicians were stretched beyond the three- or four-chord regularities of earlier country-rock crossovers, as Nesmith recalls: 'They were playing these extraordinary parts that they'd never played before. They weren't playing country parts. These were hardcore country guys – I mean, look at Lloyd Green. He played the steel, and you couldn't be more of a Nashville cat than that. There's a stereotype of a good ol' boy from Tennessee, which is a caricature but has an element of truth to it. And that was him. But he loved playing this music. They all did.'

Among the songs recorded that week was 'I've Just Begun To Care' – or, as Nesmith insisted on titling it, 'Propinquity'. 'Once you give a country record a title like that, you know you're not going to get too many cover versions,' he smiles. That song's elegiac aura did at least owe something to the tradition of Nashville songwriting. 'St Matthew' (or, in Nesmith-speak, 'Effervescent Popsicle') was an altogether more elusive concept, lyrically oblique, and intended, so its creator now explains, as a response to Bob Dylan's 'She Belongs To Me'. Then there was 'Listen To The Band', composed by reversing the chord sequence of another Nesmith country song, 'Nine Times Blue', and then given an arrangement that owed more to Duke Ellington than to Johnny Cash. 'That song was fascinating to me,' Nesmith boasts, 'because the musicians just lapped it up. We recorded that in the morning, and after that the session just fell apart, because all we did for the rest of the day was send out for food and listen to the track, over and over again.'

While the Nashville exploits of the Byrds spawned hordes of imitators, Nesmith's more adventurous music influenced only himself. Its impact was muffled by the decay of the Monkees' career. Augmented with an anthemic brass section which replicated what Lloyd Green had played on the original track, 'Listen To The Band' was issued as a single in April 1969, but flopped. Otherwise, only two of the Nashville songs, 'Don't Wait For Me' and the deliberately obtuse 'Good Clean Fun' (a phrase which neither described the music nor appeared in the lyrics), were released at the time.

'The Monkees were important to me, if only because they gave me the chance to make music like that,' Nesmith says today. 'I've heard those country-rock recordings described as subversive, because I was using the Monkees' name and money to make them, but that wasn't my intention. Conscious subversion never works: the saboteur is always blown up by his own bomb. I was just pursuing a personal crusade.' When the debris of the Monkees cleared at the end of the sixties, Nesmith was able to make a more telling contribution to the history of country-rock.

5 Pretty Boy Floyd

Gram Parsons, 1963–1968; the Shilos; the International Submarine Band; the Byrds

'I've some sort of "rep" for starting what (I think) has turned out t'be pretty much of a "country-rock" (ugh!) plastic dry-fuck,' Gram Parsons wrote to a friend in late 1972. A year later, he was dead. His posthumous curse was to be remembered as the creator of a genre for which he felt only contempt. 'He hated country-rock,' his singing partner Emmylou Harris confirms. 'He thought that bands like the Eagles were pretty much missing the point.'

Parsons won his dubious accolade for his brief adventures with three late-sixties Los Angeles outfits – the International Submarine Band, the Byrds and the Flying Burrito Brothers. Their flirtations with country music attracted only cult acclaim, but they provided the inspiration for a style which became the trademark of Californian rock by the early seventies. A decade earlier, as Parsons slipped from adolescent rock'n'roll into a new identity as a folksinger, his fantasy was stardom, not influence. Throughout his career, he was able to match his surroundings like a chameleon. A child of the South, he deepened or mellowed his accent at will. He borrowed the poverty-racked persona of Merle Haggard, hiding the fact that he could fall back on family wealth. Dropped into the milieu of the Rolling Stones, he aped Mick Jagger.

With the Shilos, the South Carolina outfit that was his first serious vehicle on the path to fame, he metamorphosed into a painfully earnest college folkie. Sober-suited, but with hair that daringly clipped the top of their ears, the quartet oozed respectability with just a faint scent of bohemianism.

Captured on tape in 1964, the Shilos were interchangeable with any other middle-class folk combo. Their harmonies were rounded and pure; their voices echoed with a righteous vibrato. Delivering a tale of bravery in San Antone, Parsons sang 'Mary Don't You Weep' as if he'd never wandered further South than Harvard Square. His own 'Zah's Blues' was even more telling: this exquisitely crooned ballad was built on jazzy minor chords, over which he boasted that once 'I wore my youth like a crown'. Every over-signified syllable betrayed the touch of the actor.

In May 1965, when Bob Dylan's first electric album, *Bringing It All Back Home*, exposed the pomposity of the folk scene, Parsons was awakened to the flaws in the Shilos' approach. 'if we want to make it as a group we're going to have to do some serious rearranging,' he wrote to bandmate Paul Surratt, dropping his capitals like e.e. cummings. 'the people want a really different sound and ours isn't different enough yet . . . i'm sure that my music is going to be as big as dylans . . . we are going to have to cash in on this thing dylan's started.'

The Shilos were forgotten when Parsons moved to Boston in the late summer of 1965, ostensibly to enrol as a Harvard student. Instead, he dallied on a folk scene which was just beginning to comprehend electricity. By Christmas, he had gathered together a band – John Nuese, Mickey Gauvin and a British emigrant, Ian Dunlop. The quartet named themselves the International Submarine Band, after a combo in the *Little Rascals* TV show.

Drawn away from country by the earnestness of folk, Parsons was reminded of his roots by John Nuese's enthusiasm. 'I'd almost been ashamed of country for a while,' Parsons admitted shortly before his death. Nuese confirmed that 'Gram didn't know what was going on in country music. He knew no Buck Owens or Merle Haggard.' Under this influence, Parsons began to unveil tender ballads like 'Brass Buttons', which added genuine emotion to the melodicism of the Shilos.

Neither song fitted comfortably into the International Submarine Band's relentlessly uptempo repertoire. Barry Tashian of the Boston punk band the Remains recalls hearing the ISB playing rock'n'roll arrangements of Buck Owens tunes like 'Together Again', alongside Jerry Lee Lewis and Little Richard classics. But when they taped their first studio demos in early 1966, the ISB betrayed only an uncomfortable array of pop influences –

garage-rock, Bob Dylan, even Sonny Bono, but certainly not a hint of country.

That changed when Gram's actor friend, Brandon de Wilde, enabled the ISB to record the theme for Norman Jewison's movie *The Russians Are Coming*. On the flipside was Terry Fell's truckers' anthem, 'Truck Driving Man'. 'That was the first one that we really got to hard rock, or rhythm and blues and country music at the same time,' Gram recalled. 'Nobody understood it.' Playing country songs with the energy of a rock group set the Submarine Band out of step with New York; the country records that Parsons and Nuese loved were coming out of Bakersfield, California. In late 1966, the International Submarine Band moved to the West Coast, where de Wilde introduced them to Hollywood's in-house hippie, Peter Fonda. He recruited the ISB for his psychedelic exploitation movie *The Trip*, and even recorded Parsons' 'November Nights'. Meanwhile, Gram had discovered the Palomino, LA's premier country haunt. Located on Lankershim Boulevard in North Hollywood, down the street from the legendary cowboy outfitters, Nudie's Rodeo Tailors, the Palomino staged weekly talent contests. Parsons chose to put himself through the demeaning routine of competing with other country hopefuls, week after week, 'to show them that a guy with long hair could be accepted'.

His Damascene conversion to country music polarized the Submarine Band. Soon after arriving in California, they ran into Barry Tashian and his Remains colleague, Billy Briggs. 'I was looking to play some different music,' Tashian recalls, 'and so were Ian Dunlop and Mickey Gauvin. Ian came up with this idea for a club band called the Flying Burrito Brothers. One night Billy and I lined up alongside Ian and Mickey – and Gram was there too. We just went out to this club and played every old song we could remember, from "Bony Moronie" to "Truck Driving Man". That was the first night of the Flying Burrito Brothers.' Or, as Gram recalled, 'The Remains Of The International Main Street Flying Burrito Brothers Blues Band'.

The Burritos' blend of rock, soul and country enticed Dunlop and Gauvin away from the Submarine Band. Parsons was tempted to follow, but he was pulled back by his loyalty to a more traditional country sound. With Nuese, he revamped the ISB, adding Jon Corneal on drums, Chris Ethridge on bass and Bob Buchanan on guitar.

In the summer of 1967, they recorded a single for LHI, the small label run by Phoenix producer, entrepreneur and sometime duet partner of Nancy Sinatra, Lee Hazlewood. 'Luxury Liner' illustrated the extent of Gram's conversion. Like a Johnny Cash story-song, it rolled along a freewheeling train rhythm which was undermined by the chorus: 'You think I'm lonesome? So do I.'

It was a theme repeated when the ISB cut their only album in November 1967. With California's leading pedal-steel player, J. D. Maness, and with Nashville pianist Earl Ball lending support, Parsons shaped a close approximation of the Bakersfield country sound. The result was *Safe At Home* – often cited as the first country-rock album.

'The cover depicted a typical rock group, four smiling long-hairs, but inside was skillful country music,' wrote *Village Voice* critic Robert Christgau a year later – when it was possible to gain some perspective on what Parsons and the ISB had achieved. 'The album was an assertion of continuity from Arthur Crudup to Gram Parsons,' Christgau continued, 'with country music and all its simple virtues square in the center. In retrospect, it seems a good record and a brilliant conception. Yet at the time I listened twice and filed it in the closet.'

Christgau's explanation was that 'Parsons, with his deep respect for country music, played it too straight. He needed the canted approach of the Byrds, who combine respect with critical distance.' He was writing in the aftermath of Parsons' – and the Byrds' – next release: *Sweetheart Of The Rodeo*.

With another three decades' hindsight, *Safe At Home* sounds timeless – or at least divorced from its time. It was certainly removed from rock chronology, left untouched by advances in production and songwriting. Its very lack of elegance, of irony, of Christgau's 'critical distance', was a manifesto of sorts. It represented a rejection of the trappings of psychedelia. In fact, *Safe At Home* came from a world in which rock'n'roll had stood still since Elvis Presley and Johnny Cash left Sun Records. Stylistically, it owed more to the Everly Brothers' early-sixties exhumation of *Great Country Songs* than to any of the experimental hybrids of country and rock that were emerging in 1967. 'It's probably the best country album that I've done,' Gram noted in 1972, 'because it had a lot of really quick-shuffle, brilliant-sounding country.'

Even in his own writing, Parsons attempted nothing that wasn't on Merle Haggard's records. His terrain was the bittersweet brutality of romance. There was none of the emotional complexity that had begun to infiltrate rock music by the mid-sixties, none of Dylan's sexual ambiguity or Lennon's ironic ennui. Parsons' lovers could never have handled the uneasy morality of David Crosby's 'Triad', recorded by the Byrds while the International Submarine Band were making *Safe At Home*. Betraying more than it intended, the title of *Safe At Home* reflected the ethos of the entire record. It was not a clarion-call to any kind of revolution: nobody followed the ISB's example, not just because the record didn't sell, but because there was nowhere to follow.

Ironically, the same isolation from the times which marked *Safe At Home* as a historical dead-end is its greatest artistic strength. Parsons set out to reflect his love of Sun rockabilly and Bakersfield country, and *Safe At Home* matches that ambition perfectly. On another label (and with shorter hair), the Gram Parsons Band might have registered a minor footnote in the history of California country. To reach a national audience, Parsons needed to refract his music through the distorting prism of rock'n'roll.

'I loved the Byrds from "Mr Tambourine Man" onwards,' remembers Parsons' first biographer, Sid Griffin. 'In 1968, I was in hospital with a serious illness, and when I got out, my sister told my uncle to buy me their new album.

'That was how I heard *Sweetheart Of The Rodeo*. I loved the cover from the start, but when I played it the first few times, I just didn't get it. I didn't even identify it as a country and western album. I began to wonder if it was a comedy record. Finally, it was the lyrics to "Hickory Wind" that drew me in.

'Down South, the local TV station would air all these country and western TV shows – the Wilburn Brothers, Porter Wagoner and Dolly Parton, guys like that. And there would always be one from your hometown. The local guy with grease in his hair who just did covers of George Jones would have a half-hour show on Saturday afternoons at 5.30 p.m. I hated those shows – until I heard *Sweetheart*. Then I did an about face. I started listening to this music, and I began to adore it. I remember looking at Dolly Parton and thinking, "Gee, she's great, but she'll never make it in the rest of America." It was like a local secret which the Byrds had locked onto.'

Since 'Mr Tambourine Man' in 1965, the Byrds had assumed the status of gurus, apparently incapable of a false move. After translating Bob Dylan's epic imagery into electric folk-rock, they unveiled a dazzling array of new styles – space-rock, raga-rock, psychedelia and beyond – each performed with artistic nerve and arrogant self-belief.

Their growth was matched only by their internal attrition, as each musical shift spawned a jockeying for power. Gene Clark, their chief songwriter in 1965, was the first casualty, prey to the naked ambition of David Crosby and Roger McGuinn. The survivors battled for dominance over the next two years, Crosby holding sway until he was toppled by an alliance between McGuinn and the band's previously low-key bassist, Chris Hillman. These dramas ensured that by the time each Byrds album appeared, the group had already lurched forward into a new phase.

In April 1968, *The Notorious Byrd Brothers* was released in Europe. The album was a stunning essay in electronic experimentation, drawing on the spirit of psychedelia at the same time as it pronounced its death sentence. The Byrds were booked to appear at a London club called Middle Earth, the bastion of the underground. Running several months behind American time, hip London nightlife was a hazy mist of swirling slide shows and the sweet scent of grass. The beautiful people arrived for a night of candles, incense and musical mind-blowing.

Minds were indeed blown when the Byrds took the stage. Instead of the kaftans and kaleidoscopic cloaks sported by their adoring fans, the psychedelic explorers were dressed like farm-hands. There was no chaotic explosion of sound, simply the gentle burr of acoustic guitars, fiddle and banjo. Worse still, the only recognizable members of the band, McGuinn and Hillman, appeared to have been sidelined by a country boy with a cherubic face and a hillbilly twang.

'Graham Parsons', as he was invariably described, had been a member of the Byrds for just over two months. Three months later, he had gone. But that brief collision was enough to remake the group in his image, and set the course for the rest of their career. It produced an album which introduced a generation of rock fans to country music for the first time. And it created a myth around the previously unheralded Parsons which survives to this day.

Roger McGuinn struggled for two years to wrest control of the Byrds from his colleagues: it took less than a month for him to lose it. In mid-February 1968, Gram Parsons was delivered to his first Byrds rehearsal. By mid-March, America's champions of space-rock were performing on the flagship country music show, the *Grand Ole Opry*, with Parsons as their unchallenged leader.

How did Parsons pull it off? It had nothing to do with *Safe At Home*, the International Submarine Band's album, which was released around the time that Gram met Chris Hillman at a Los Angeles bank. Parsons had already realized that *Safe At Home* – crippled by limited distribution – was doomed to, at best, cult acceptance. For a man still convinced his music would be as popular as 'dylans', that wasn't reward enough.

Friends recall him saying that the way to reach a larger audience was to join an established group. In the Byrds, he'd stumbled across an internationally popular act reduced to the two-man core of McGuinn and Hillman. The latter knew Parsons' work with the International Submarine Band, and shared his passion for country music.

Hillman introduced Parsons to McGuinn and the band's newly acquired drummer, Kevin Kelley (Hillman's cousin, no less). McGuinn was impressed by Gram's Southern politeness, his rapport with Hillman, and his piano-playing, so he agreed to hire him as a second-string Byrd, a sideman to join Kelley.

As McGuinn memorably recounted, his evaluation of Gram wasn't entirely accurate: 'He turned out to be a monster in sheep's clothing. And he exploded out of this sheep's clothing. God! It's George Jones! In a sequin suit!'

There was a place for George Jones, sequin suit or not, in the 1968 Byrds. McGuinn had formulated an ambitious concept for their next project: nothing less than a history of white American music, from country roots to electronic sound. 'My original idea for *Sweetheart Of The Rodeo*', he explained to *Rolling Stone* in 1970, 'was to do a double-album, a chronological album, starting out with old-timey music – not bluegrass, but pre-bluegrass, dulcimers and nasal Appalachian stuff. Then to get into the advanced 1930s version of it, and move it up to modern country, the forties and fifties, with steel guitar and pedal steel guitar – do the evolution of that kind of music. Then cut it there and bring it up into electronic music and a kind of space music, and going into futuristic music.'

Chris Hillman agreed the concept, but the arrival of Parsons rekindled an old love. 'Gram reminded me how much I loved country music,' he says. 'We'd always played a little country with the Byrds, but with two of us in the band, the obvious thing was to bring out that influence in our music.'

For the moment, the three men's subtly different plans coincided. In early March, the Byrds flew to Nashville, to work with producer Gary Usher in the same studio in which Bob Dylan had recorded most of *Blonde On Blonde*. Clarence White, by now a regular at Byrds sessions, was on call; so, at Parsons' suggestion, were two veterans of *Safe At Home*, steel-player J. D. Maness and pianist Earl Ball. Nashville session bassist Roy Huskey and steelman Lloyd Green completed the line-up.

Columbia used their power as Nashville's leading record label to buy the Byrds a slot on the *Grand Ole Opry*. 'We were the first rock group ever to play there,' Roger McGuinn recalled. Broadcast across the nation on Friday and Saturday nights, the *Opry* was an institution heavily resistant to change. Drummers were restricted to a single snare and brushes; Western swing legend Bob Wills was refused permission to use his horn players on the show.

Conservatively clad, their hair trimmed for the occasion, the Byrds immediately realized they were on enemy territory. 'Just to let us know how hostile the audience felt towards us,' Hillman recalled, 'they were shouting stuff like "tweet tweet" and "cut your hair".' *Opry* regular Lloyd Green helped to smooth their path: 'It took a lot of balls,' Hillman added, 'to get up on stage with a band of long-haired weirdo strangers in town, knowing that his friends and peers were so antagonistic towards us.'

Byrds fans who caught the broadcast wouldn't have recognized the band. Nothing connected their brief set with the group's latest album – not the material, the style or even the singer, for it was Gram Parsons who assumed leadership of the Byrds. 'He took the reins,' Hillman recalled. 'He was right smack into that – "Here I am on the *Opry*! I'm Hank Williams" – so he went with it. He played the whole role out.' As with the Shilos four years earlier, Parsons became the man that the occasion required. First he led the Byrds through Merle Haggard's recent hit, 'Sing Me Back Home'. Next on the cue sheet was a second Haggard tune, 'Life In Prison', but Parsons had no time for *Opry* etiquette. Hillman explained: 'Out came Tompall Glaser to make the intro: "Well, thank you boys, and now you're going to do another Merle Haggard song, aren't you?" Then Gram suddenly got hold of the microphone and said, "No, I'm going to sing 'Hickory Wind' for my grandmother in Tennessee."'

Gram's nostalgic ballad painted rural South Carolina as a utopian refuge from 'a faraway city, with a faraway feel'. It was cut early in the Nashville sessions, alongside two other Parsons tunes, 'One Hundred Years From Now' and 'Lazy Days'. In fact, as the week progressed, it became clear that he now saw the Byrds as his group. Happy to be playing country, Hillman didn't protest. McGuinn clung to his grand design, convinced he could regain control once the location reverted to California and the music to electric or even electronic rock.

First, the revamped Byrds had a college tour to fulfil, which consolidated Parsons' status. With J. D. Maness in tow, they opened their sets with a fully countrified arrangement of Bob Dylan's 'You Ain't Goin' Nowhere', and then veered back and forth between vintage Byrds hits and their new repertoire.

Interviewed during the tour, McGuinn explained that their album was now half-completed. 'Gram has added a whole hunk of country,' he explained, 'and we're going to let him do his thing.

But Chris and I are still there. I think we are the containers for the
"old" sound, and the new members augment that sound.'

The exact nature of that augmentation became apparent when
they resumed recording in Hollywood. With the Nashville tapes
mixed to Parsons' satisfaction, Gram and Chris announced that as
far as they were concerned, the record was finished. Neither was
keen to proceed with McGuinn's plan: the chronological history of
American music was jettisoned, and the Byrds were now a country
band. 'Gram thought we could win over the country audience,'
McGuinn explained. 'He figured that once they dig you, they never
let you go.'

The European tour proceeded as planned in May; two months
later, the Byrds were back in London for a charity show, prior to a
potentially controversial visit to South Africa. This allowed
Parsons to visit an acquaintance he'd made in May – Keith
Richard of the Rolling Stones. 'I went out to visit the Byrds when
they came to England,' Richard recalled. 'I was really going to see
Roger. Gram was with him, and we just hit it off right away.'
Hillman adds: 'Gram immediately fell in with Mick and Keith. He
was obsessed with the idea of being *with* the Rolling Stones, if not
actually in the band.'

When they met again, Keith Richard asked Parsons: 'Why are
you going to South Africa? We wouldn't go there. Nobody goes
there.' None of the Byrds was enthusiastic about visiting a country
ruled by apartheid; for Gram, disapproval from a Rolling Stone
tipped the balance. When the band assembled in August for the
flight to Johannesburg, Parsons was missing. 'Hillman wanted to
kill him,' Byrds roadie Jim Seiter told Sid Griffin. 'I heard he was
down at the motel banging on Gram's door, saying he'd better not
split the group.' Parsons held firm, and while the Byrds flew to
Johannesburg, he returned to England, and Keith Richard's Sussex
mansion.

Later that month, *Sweetheart Of The Rodeo* was released.
Country music critics weren't impressed: 'They try to sing
country, I think,' sneered one British writer. 'Hope they don't try it
again.' The leading American rock paper, *Rolling Stone*, was no
more encouraging: 'The Byrds do not sound like Buck Owens and
his Buckaroos. They aren't that good.'

McGuinn attempted to explain the shift in direction: 'We've always dabbled in country music, but then we ran into Gram Parsons, who wants to be the world champion country singer, and he hung out with us for a couple of months. He was going to be in the group, but it didn't work out. While he was with us, he led us into this direction headlong, which we would never have done. We were afraid to commit ourselves. It was a little foreign to us.'

There was only the barest of hints about McGuinn's original concept: 'We might even go so far as to put the synthesizer into country music, in such a way that it won't be foreign but will blend with it. Our next album is going to be all electronic music.' And he offered some retrospective justification for the change of approach: 'It's sort of a backlash from the psychedelic scene, which I'm personally saturated with. Everyone's jumping on the bandwagon, so we wanted to get off and clear the slate for a while.'

In its completed form, *Sweetheart* was an epic of self-effacement on McGuinn's part. Having co-written virtually all of *The Notorious Byrd Brothers*, he contributed not a single new song to this album. Even the title came from the advertising agency who'd designed the cover.

McGuinn asserted himself in other ways. In a symbol of continuity with the Byrds' heritage, the album began and ended with Bob Dylan songs. 'You Ain't Goin' Nowhere' smoothed the clip-clop pace of Dylan's 'Basement Tapes' demo into a space-age ride, powered by the instrumental hook of Lloyd Green's pedal steel – mirroring McGuinn's guitar lick on 'Mr Tambourine Man' three years earlier.

Steel guitar was the album's unifying force, but the variety of lead voices reflected the differing ideals of the participants. Parsons acted out 'Hickory Wind' like a confessional, while Hillman's delivery of the traditional gospel tune 'I Am A Pilgrim' rang with humility.

But McGuinn's was the dominant voice, and he told another story. In a year of riots and assassinations, the idea of a rock group singing 'I Like The Christian Life' inevitably reeked of satire – especially when McGuinn invested the song with the naïvety of a cowhand adrift on Sunset Strip. And cynicism was built into

Woody Guthrie's ballad 'Pretty Boy Floyd'. The album cover celebrated the myth of the cowboy outlaw; 'Pretty Boy Floyd' destroyed it.

As Parsons added some country standards, and McGuinn traced soul's country roots through William Bell's hit, 'You Don't Miss Your Water', *Sweetheart* matched McGuinn's boast that 'it's a departure for the Byrds, but not a departure from my music'.

It wasn't supposed to be that way. Once Parsons was free from the Byrds, he complained that *Sweetheart* had little in common with the album he'd worked on. Two of his vocal performances, 'Lazy Days' and Tim Hardin's 'Reputation', had been struck from the record.

More telling was the substitution of McGuinn's vocals for Parsons' on 'The Christian Life' and 'You Don't Miss Your Water'. 'He erased them and did the vocals himself and fucked it up', Gram complained. The accusations didn't end there: 'They pulled a few things out of the can that weren't supposed to be used, like "Life In Prison" and "You're Still On My Mind",' he added. 'We just did them as warm-up numbers. We could've done them a lot better.'

Certain he'd been wronged, but confused about the circumstances, Parsons lashed out blindly. The débâcle was McGuinn's fault, he alleged, or maybe producer Gary Usher's. Hillman was probably to blame as well. McGuinn and Hillman retorted that the culprit was Parsons, who'd failed to alert Columbia to the fact that he was still under contract to Lee Hazlewood's LHI when the Byrds' album was made.

The official account of this sorry saga, as told ever since by McGuinn, is that LHI threatened legal action against Columbia, who in turn instructed the Byrds to delete Parsons' lead vocals. Then the parties settled, just before Gram's voice had been stripped off 'Hickory Wind', and two Parsons rehearsals were added at short notice to reinstate his presence on the album.

McGuinn's explanation held water, until late-eighties archive work located the Parsons masters of 'Reputation' and 'Lazy Days' in Columbia's vaults, begging the question of why they hadn't been added to the final album. Roger didn't help his case when he revealed that he had also dubbed a vocal on to 'Hickory Wind', but elected to use the original instead. Presumably Parsons' renditions of 'You Don't Miss Your Water' and 'The Christian Life' could also have been included.

Twenty years after the sessions, Gary Usher rekindled the controversy. In his revised account, LHI's claim had been raised during the March 1968 sessions in Nashville. It had long been settled by the time that he and McGuinn assembled the final album. Roger, he was suggesting, had acted on purely artistic – or political – grounds when he retrospectively altered the power balance.

'I thought it was time for a serious country album,' Parsons reflected shortly before his death. That description suited *Safe At Home*, but not the released version of *Sweetheart Of The Rodeo*. The original *Sweetheart* might have been a more 'serious' country record, but maybe not a country-rock album. McGuinn's version opened up Merle Haggard, the Louvin Brothers and, indeed, Gram Parsons to an audience who might not have been ready for Gram's unalloyed authenticity. The slyness and satire that Parsons hated were exactly what made *Sweetheart* an influential record. The irony is that McGuinn's chicanery not only 'rescued' his group from Gram's outside intervention, but also prepared the way for Parsons to leave as lasting an impact on rock history as McGuinn himself.

6 Sin City

Los Angeles, 1968–1970: Buffalo Springfield; the Dillards; Dillard & Clark; the Byrds; the Flying Burrito Brothers; the Rolling Stones; Gram Parsons

The sound of a steel guitar drifted from the radio, while an unfamiliar voice crooned a tune about South Carolina. 'It's the Byrds,' insisted a woman. 'That's not the Byrds,' her companion replied. And so the argument continued, until the commercial ended with a smooth voiceover: 'The Byrds take eleven trips to the country. Why not fly with them?'

Madison Avenue and *Sweetheart Of The Rodeo*: it was no more of a mismatch than Gram Parsons and the Byrds' audience. *Sweetheart*, the country con-trick which Parsons had played on one of America's most prestigious groups, was released in August 1968, and duly became the Byrds' least successful album to date. Its pioneering spirit passed unnoticed, and it languished outside the US Top 50, an ignominious position for the group once tagged America's answer to the Beatles.

Sweetheart Of The Rodeo was outsold by an album from a band who'd broken up five months earlier – Buffalo Springfield's *Last Time Around*. Both albums assumed retrospective importance, as the trigger for a distinctly Californian brand of country-rock.

While Parsons imposed his hillbilly vision on the Byrds, the Springfield's more gentle country style was the almost accidental creation of Richie Furay (overshadowed as a songwriter by his bandmates Stephen Stills and Neil Young), and engineer/bassist Jim Messina.

Messina was rooted in Florida surf music, Furay in wholesome folk harmonies; together they concocted a sleepy sound that was glazed with marijuana smoke and sunshine. 'Carefree Country Day' was their stoner's anthem; 'Kind Woman' set the mood for the decade ahead. Over the slowest of chord changes, Furay evoked country without the pain, fuelling the assumption that country-rock and the mellow spirit of seventies California were interchangeable.

The pioneers of what was fast becoming a country-rock community were caught in shifting alliances in the summer of 1968. Ego battles had already killed the Springfield, and *Sweetheart* seemed likely to become the epitaph for the Byrds, who had struggled through a wretched tour of South Africa without Gram Parsons. Meanwhile, that deserter was attempting to form a new band. He approached former bluegrass guitarist Clarence White, whom he'd met during the *Sweetheart* sessions, and who was now playing in a Los Angeles club band dubbed Nashville West. Their repertoire – drawn from recent hits by Merle Haggard and Glen Campbell plus old Chuck Berry tunes – was enlivened by White's miraculous guitar playing, as he weaved tapestries of sound around the strictly formulaic arrangements.

Confusing country-rock historians for eternity, Gram Parsons also wanted to enlist Nashville West's multi-instrumentalist drummer, Gene Parsons. But it was White's call, and he rejected Gram in favour of Roger McGuinn, who invited him to join the Byrds. It was a shortlived arrangement: within a month, Chris Hillman – dispirited by the South African débâcle – quit. His first port of call was the man who'd abandoned the Byrds on the verge of that controversial tour.

Gram sold Hillman on the vision of a mighty crossover of soul and country – 'Cosmic American Music', he called it. In England with Keith Richard that autumn, he told a reporter that 'My new group is already formed. It's basically a Southern soul group playing country and gospel-oriented music with a steel guitar.' It was an exaggerated account of a half-assembled unit that included only the reluctant Hillman, and bassist Chris Ethridge.

Parsons was confident enough to turn down an offer from none other than Richie Furay, himself floundering for a new direction. Furay and Jimmy Messina were assembling a country-rock outfit, initially called Pogo – too close to mainstream rock, Parsons complained, to hold his interest, which suggested he hadn't listened too closely to *Last Time Around*. 'I like Richie Furay's singing a lot,' Gram noted, 'but I don't see that the two of us have anything in common more than a steel guitar.'

Not that Hillman and Parsons held any guarantee of commercial acceptance. The track record for ex-Byrds wasn't encouraging. David Crosby, sacked in 1967, had effectively vanished from the recording scene. And Gene Clark, the creative leader of the 1965 Byrds, was languishing in semi-obscurity on the Los Angeles club circuit.

Through the latter half of the 1960s, two dozen country-minded musicians on the West Coast tumbled through a baffling series of encounters, many destined to pass undocumented. Gene Clark's family tree was more incestuous than most. After quitting the Byrds in late 1965, he had embarked on an ambitious project with Vern and Rex Gosdin, former bluegrass buddies of Chris Hillman. The ex-Byrds and the Gosdins were reunited at the sessions for *Gene Clark & The Gosdin Brothers*, an astonishingly mature but commercially disastrous record which combined pop orchestrations, Byrdsian folk-rock and uptempo country – sometimes on the same song, as in the Lovin' Spoonful-flavoured 'Keep On Pushing'.

Clark's album also featured Doug Dillard, signalling his distance from his family band, the Dillards. Though that bluegrass outfit were anxious to extend their appeal beyond the LA coffeehouses, their idealism held them back from overt commercialism. The graph of their career closely tracked that of the Byrds through the mid-sixties. They were competing for smaller stakes: the Byrds were rivals to the Beatles, while the Dillards had no higher expectation than dominating the West Coast bluegrass scene. But after peaking commercially in 1965/66, both bands steered gradually away from the mainstream. In 1968, not just their trajectories matched, but their goals – a viable blend of country and rock. *Sweetheart Of The Rodeo* may have threatened the Byrds' status as rock luminaries, but its financial – and musical – impact was still far beyond the Dillards' reach. Two years earlier, they had abandoned an attempt to electrify their sound, symbolically handing over their amplifiers and PA system to Buffalo Springfield. But their 1968 album *Wheatstraw Suite* represented a change of heart. It was recognizably the work of country musicians, but in laying down their acoustic instruments in favour of electric dobros and pedal steels, the Dillards had shed their traditional values.

Like their contemporaries Hearts & Flowers, they borrowed songs from young writers like Tim Hardin and Jesse Lee Kincaid; they also ran a bluegrass wash across the Beatles' 'I've Just Seen A Face', which needed only the most delicate of nudges to slip from pop into country. Even their massed acappella harmonies on the country spiritual 'I'll Fly Away' seemed closer to the LA tradition of the Beach Boys and the Association than Bill Monroe's Blue Grass Boys.

One musician was noticeably absent from *Wheatstraw Suite*: Doug Dillard. In an ironic twist, Doug had quit the group to pursue a more flexible direction, just as the rest of the Dillards were preparing to abandon their strict acoustic approach. He guested on *Sweetheart Of The Rodeo*, then toured North America and Europe with Gram Parsons' shortlived line-up of the Byrds. At psychedelic clubs like Middle Earth in London, he gamely picked bluegrass banjo while the decaying aristocrats of folk-rock debunked the expectations of London hippiedom. When the Byrds switched from their new country repertoire to their vintage rock hits, Dillard was like a cyclist struggling to keep pace with a sports car.

This bizarre experiment ended with Parsons' departure, which sent aftershocks through the entire Los Angeles country-rock community. It ended Doug Dillard's sojourn with the Byrds, and reunited him with Gene Clark – whose career had briefly soared when he rejoined the Byrds in 1967, then collapsed when their unique internal politics refuelled the neurosis which had forced his departure two years earlier. In the summer of 1968, with the Byrds grounded and Gram Parsons preoccupied with the Rolling Stones' court, Dillard & Clark provided the main activity on the Los Angeles country-rock scene. Early Byrds biographer Bud Scoppa set the scene: 'A typical session started with all the boys pouring as much beer inside them as they could hold; then they'd get down to some serious playing. It was a full-fledged attempt to regain the loose, relaxed state of mind that the rigors of the music business had ground out of them.'

The Fantastic Expedition Of Dillard & Clark was a stunning collection of original country-rock material, shaped by Gene Clark's unique imagination but coloured by the influence of bluegrass and white gospel. Songs like 'She Darked The Sun' and 'Train Leaves Here This Morning' matched anything in the Byrds' own catalogue, but *The Fantastic Expedition* maintained the invisible profile of Clark's first solo album. (Of all the musicians tangled in the tale of Los Angeles country-rock, Gene Clark may have been the unluckiest. None of his fellow Byrds members, including Roger McGuinn, who controlled the group during that period, matched his consistent creativity between 1966 and 1973. But whilst McGuinn, Chris Hillman, David Crosby and even to some extent Gram Parsons and Michael Clarke tasted the fruits of stardom, Gene enjoyed nothing more fulfilling than a cult reputation.)

Doug and Gene struggled through the summer of 1969, recording the wearily titled *Through The Morning, Through The Night*. Clark's contributions were less remarkable than on their début, though his interpretations of material as diverse as John Lennon's 'Don't Let Me Down' and the Everly Brothers' 'So Sad' displayed no lack of creativity. But by late 1969, the camaraderie between Dillard and Clark had become strained. Doug had insisted on using vocalist Donna Washburn on the second album; Gene accused him of being more interested in her body than her voice. His antipathy lent his duets with Washburn a certain tension. The irony is that, having lost key members of his group to Gram Parsons, he also sacrificed his place in history to the same man. The tenor of the Clark/Washburn harmonies clearly anticipated the fragile beauty of Gram's duets with Emmylou Harris in 1973.

By December 1969, the Dillard & Clark group had dissolved. Doug Dillard wandered into a dead-end career of solo banjo albums. Gene Clark cut a superb record called *White Light*, which revitalized the spirit of Bob Dylan's mid-sixties acoustic work, before he began to assemble a collection of songs that would examine man's spiritual quest within the context of country-rock settings. Cosmic American Music, indeed . . .

*

Despite the departure of Parsons and Hillman, the Byrds promoted *Sweetheart Of The Rodeo* as if nothing had happened. Roger McGuinn was the only survivor of the *Sweetheart* sessions, but he betrayed none of his horror at Parsons' brief domination of his group. Instead, he emphasized the Byrds' groundbreaking spirit: 'I think the people who did what we did right after we did it were opportunists. We were trendsetters.' Now unopposed within the group, McGuinn could have revived his infatuation with electronic music. But the identity of his new recruits suggested that he was comfortable to coast as a country-rock pioneer. Bassist John York was culled from one of Gene Clark's shortlived touring bands, while Clarence White and Gene Parsons were poached from Nashville West.

Columbia Records made surprisingly little effort to persuade the Byrds to rejoin the rock mainstream. As McGuinn noted, 'One guy called me in and told me that we were doing great in the country thing. How would we like to do a joint album with another Columbia artist?' McGuinn's preference was Bob Dylan, but the executive countered: 'How about Johnny Cash?'

Instead, the Byrds chose to record with Dylan's and Cash's producer Bob Johnston: 'He comes across so strong, so country-like,' McGuinn gushed. Johnston flew to Los Angeles for the sessions, and was entrusted with the final mix while the Byrds went on the road. Muddy and cluttered, *Dr Byrds And Mr Hyde* was aeons away from the crystal clarity of *Sweetheart*, or the gemlike precision of the Byrds' earlier work. One moment they were a bar-room blues band, vamping through Jimmy Reed's 'Baby What You Want Me To Do'. The next they were Dylanesque rockers, with Clarence White vainly attempting to master psychedelia on 'This Wheel's On Fire'. McGuinn's only country tune on the record (co-written with Gram Parsons) was 'Drug Store Truck Driving Man' – an assault on the Nashville ethos, as epitomized by celebrity DJ Ralph Emery.

During their March 1968 visit to Nashville, Emery had sounded off about these out-of-town intruders (on the same network which aired the Byrds' *Grand Ole Opry* appearance). According to McGuinn, the normally urbane and personable DJ attacked the band 'in right-wing, fascist' language, calling them 'hippies, complete undesirables and even possibly dangerous'. Then he broke for a truck commercial, a juxtaposition which evolved into McGuinn's caricature of a drug-store truck driving man, 'the head of the Ku Klux Klan'. 'This one's for you, Ralph,' he called sarcastically over the final chords.

His performance demonstrated the extent to which he'd now mastered the country idiom. In a final twist of the knife, McGuinn sent the tape to Lloyd Green in Nashville, who overdubbed his trademark pedal steel guitar. Now it was an authentic country tune, assaulting an authentic country hero. The Byrds didn't return to Nashville until 1990, by which time Chris Hillman was himself a country star, Ralph Emery hosted the city's top TV show, and memories of 'Drug Store Truck Driving Man' had dimmed.

There was a strange postscript to the making of *Dr Byrds And Mr Hyde*, and to the brief rapport between the Byrds and Bob Johnston. In early March 1969, Columbia Records president Clive Davis received the master tapes for Bob Dylan's *Nashville Skyline*. Davis was immediately entranced by 'Lay Lady Lay', and lobbied Dylan to release it as a single. Dylan initially refused, and by the time he relented, Bob Johnston had already sold the idea to McGuinn and the Byrds.

They tackled the song in late March, after which Johnston added the same blend of female voices that he later overdubbed on to Dylan's *Self Portrait*. McGuinn claimed he didn't hear the finished mix until the record was being pressed, whereupon he declared himself 'embarrassed', and retrospectively decided he hated Johnston's work on *Dr Byrds And Mr Hyde* as well.

Between the completion of that album and the 'Lay Lady Lay' débâcle, the 1969 Byrds line-up was briefly reunited with the major players of 1968, Gram Parsons and Chris Hillman. At the Boston Tea Party in late February, McGuinn's crew were booked as headliners. Supporting them were an untested California outfit: the Flying Burrito Brothers.

'The original Flying Burrito Brothers was a name that Ian Dunlop thought up for a club band,' according to bluegrass singer and Gram Parsons associate Barry Tashian. Dunlop offered work to

Tashian's garage band, the Remains, and refugees from Parsons' International Submarine Band. Local sessionmen such as saxophonist Bobby Keyes and guitarist Jesse Ed Davis also gravitated towards the group, which continued to mutate through the early months of 1968.

'After about ten months of playing clubs in LA, thinking about putting together a horn band to play soul music, we realized it wasn't happening,' Tashian continues. 'So Billy Briggs and I went back home to Boston, and started the Flying Burrito Brothers East. A soul band in Boston: we must have been mad! So those Burritos didn't exactly fly, either.' The West Coast franchise of the Burritos collapsed when Ian Dunlop migrated to Cornwall, leaving the name in abeyance. Meanwhile, Gram Parsons had drifted on to the Los Angeles club circuit. 'I was playing the country nightclubs, like the Palomino and the Lazy X,' recalled steel guitarist 'Sneaky' Pete Kleinow. 'Gram Parsons, Chris Hillman and all these people used to hang out there with country songwriters like Roger Miller. Sometimes I would sit in with them.' Gradually Kleinow and bassist Chris Ethridge were amalgamated into Chris and Gram's unnamed band – the 'Southern soul group playing country and gospel-oriented music' that Parsons had already trumpeted to the British press.

He wasn't alone in his quest for a hybrid of country, gospel and soul. That elusive phantom shadowed the Los Angeles club scene in late 1968, enticing musicians such as Delaney & Bonnie, Leon Russell, J. J. Cale and even the Byrds' Roger McGuinn, who opined that the underground movement was 'a white soul backlash. There's been a black soul predominance for the past year, and now the white kids are saying, "Wait! There's soul in white music too!", and country music has it.'

If Bob Dylan's *John Wesley Harding* had signalled one solution to the psychedelic overload of 1967, the soul records cut in Memphis and Muscle Shoals suggested another. This was the golden era of Southern soul, a style as heady as the climate from which it came. While most of the American record industry ran on racially segregated lines, white and black musicians, engineers and artists worked together across the South, mingling their blues and country traditions. On records by Aretha Franklin, Percy Sledge and Dusty Springfield, boundaries of race and genre faded into a blur.

To tap into that spirit, Parsons and Hillman required musicians who stepped outside the stereotype. Sneaky Pete Kleinow fitted the bill. 'He's different,' reckoned Nashville pedal steel ace Buddy Emmons, 'because he has got a tone most steel players try not to get, the one we all started out with. But he makes it work.' Introduced to hillbilly music in the mid-thirties, the electric steel performed a dual role – signposting the fact that you were listening to a country record, and capturing the 'lonesomeness' at the heart of the hillbilly experience.

Kleinow never imitated the polite melancholy of the acknowledged steel masters. Instead, his instrument rasped like a car-horn. In his hands, the hillbilly emblem became a freak flag, prompting press hyperbole that Kleinow was 'the Jimi Hendrix of the steel guitar'.

Over-amplified to be heard above Parsons and his cohorts, Kleinow's steel became the Burritos' instrumental hallmark. But their core identity was forged by the partnership of Parsons and Hillman – and the songs they composed during the final months of 1968. The Burritos rented a house in Resada, California, and established a strict regime, rising early every morning to write. 'We set out to merge R&B and country,' Hillman says. 'We knew what we were up to. We were trying to combine the white blues and black blues.'

Within a few weeks, Parsons and Hillman had assembled most of the songs on which the Burritos' reputation rests. 'My Uncle', a comic addition to what writer Stanley Booth called 'the great hillbilly tradition of draft-dodging', was inspired when Parsons was sent call-up papers. 'Juanita' was a tribute to a girl at the Troubadour; 'Wheels' an ode to the motorbikes on which they explored the fringes of the California desert. 'Sin City' lambasted Larry Spector, who'd once managed both the Byrds and the International Submarine Band; 'Christine's Tune' satirized a groupie who'd teased the Burritos at LA parties. Around October 1968, Parsons borrowed back the Burritos' name from Ian Dunlop, and began to shop around for a deal. Columbia Records weren't interested in the masterminds behind the Byrds' worst-selling record, but Warner Brothers were intrigued when Gram let slip that Keith Richard had promised to produce their album. 'Mo Ostin from Warners called me,' Parsons recalled, 'and said, "Yeah, I sure like some of this stuff you've been writing and Joan Baez has just recorded 'Hickory Wind', and wouldn't you like to do something for us?"' A&M were equally enthusiastic, and when they agreed to finance the group's equipment, the Burritos joined Dillard & Clark on the company's roster. Four years later, Parsons maintained that the Keith Richard tale wasn't merely bait for naïve record companies: 'Keith really was going to produce that Burrito thing, but then it worked out that he was going to be doing something else. That's the way it always is with the Stones.'

Hillman remains more sceptical: 'I think that's what Gram wanted, short of actually being asked to join the Stones. But I certainly don't remember any promise from Keith, or even any discussion with him.'

Stoned or Stone-less, the Burritos received a sizeable cheque from A&M's Jerry Moss, which they promptly blew on suits from Nudie's, the hillbilly tailor on Lankershim Boulevard. They weren't Nudie's only rockstar clients that month: Monkees guitarist Michael Nesmith was fitted with a gloriously kitsch outfit for the TV special they were about to film.

But it was the Flying Burrito Brothers who established the Nudie suit as a flag of rock'n'roll decadence. For their cover shoot, they took some groupies out to Pearl Blossom in the Mojave Desert, and were photographed in various states of jaded excess – their extravagance restrained only by the winter chill. While Chris Hillman posed awkwardly, like a farmhand exposed to a camera for the first time in his life, Gram Parsons carried himself like Elvis. In one shot, he grasped a groupie with one hand, while with the other he eased down the waistband of his trousers in a promise of carnal delight.

There were only four Burritos on the cover of *The Gilded Palace Of Sin*, because there were only four full-time musicians in the band. Drummer Eddie Hoh was recruited from Barry Goldberg's Reunion; 'Eddie just wanted to get the advance money,' Parsons quipped, 'and then he left town. He was smart to do that, I guess.' Sam Goldstein and Popeye Phillips filled the vacant role, until

Parsons' friend from the International Submarine Band, Jon Corneal, was persuaded to sit in.

Whoever played drums, the sessions were quick and haphazard. 'We cut the album without any rehearsals,' remembered Sneaky Pete Kleinow. Hillman adds: 'It wasn't quite live in the studio, but it was done with the minimum of takes. I never really liked the way it sounded.'

Jerry Moss told Parsons: 'You're a second-album group. Don't expect your first album is going to be the greatest thing in the world.' Gram didn't decode that remark until after he'd left the band: '[Jerry] was probably thinking things like the fact that Chris Ethridge isn't a country bass player. I didn't realize it. It should have been obvious to me, but he didn't know it either. He was part of the group. He was the person who persuaded me to come back from England when I had split from the Byrds. He told me, "Oh man, we got to get something together." And it just blew my mind when [I realized] he wasn't the right bass player.'

Parsons was no more enthralled by Sneaky Pete Kleinow: 'He wasn't the right pedal steel player for the group. I wanted Tom Brumley [Buck Owens' steel player] deep inside, and when it came down to it, I just settled for anybody who could play flying guitar with pedals on it.'

Mutually suspicious and unsettled, the band still completed the album in less than a month. *The Gilded Palace Of Sin* was rush-released in March 1969. Having failed with Dillard & Clark's début, A&M's marketing department decided that this strange country–rock–soul hybrid required a new kind of promotion. Journalists received the album in parcels stuffed with hay. Many packages were impounded by the US Postal Service, responding to a tip-off that the plant-life was another kind of grass entirely.

'God bless A&M,' Parsons said without a hint of irony in 1972. 'Man, they were really excited about us and they had no reason to be. Nobody had ever heard of the Flying Burrito Brothers. A&M bought some record spots on underground radio stations. But nobody had ever heard anything we'd done. We were playing with groups like Savoy Brown, groups that had big teenybopper followings, and people loved us. I was used to people being very cold to country music, and from the moment we started, it got really exciting.'

'It was a rather painful time in a lot of ways,' Pete Kleinow recalled. 'I wouldn't like to live it all over again, because it was a lot of struggle. There wasn't much acceptance for the Burritos at that time.'

That was an understatement: despite the presence of two ex-Byrds and a rave review from Parsons' fellow Georgian Stanley Booth in the underground bible *Rolling Stone*, *The Gilded Palace Of Sin* steadfastly refused to sell. It registered briefly – just – as one of the Top 200 best-selling albums in America, peaking at No. 164 on the *Billboard* chart. It was no compensation that the Byrds' latest, *Dr Byrds And Mr Hyde*, had proved no more successful. The great country-rock explosion wasn't so much muffled as defused. But some people were listening. 'Boy, I love them,' Bob Dylan said when the Burritos' name was raised. 'Their record knocked me out!' Keith Richard, who tried unsuccessfully to recruit Gram for the Stones' *Rock'n'Roll Circus* TV special, was equally enamoured of the record that Parsons had wanted him to produce.

Their respect wasn't misplaced. From its provocatively decadent cover to the apocalyptic vision of 'Sin City', *The Gilded Palace* acted as a Gothic critique of the city which gave it birth. The sixties had been a Californian decade, as the entertainment industry sold the state's hedonistic culture and climate to the world. Los Angeles had been the unrivalled capital of Californian music until the San Francisco acid-rock sound exposed the plasticity – or commercial nous – of its southern neighbour. From within Los Angeles came dissenting voices – Stephen Stills spotlighting Sunset Strip politics on Buffalo Springfield's 'For What It's Worth', Neil Young tracing the city's faultline with the eve-of-inferno 'LA' (written in 1968 but unreleased until 1973).

Parsons and Hillman caught the same *fin de siècle* ambience, with their satirical jabs at ex-managers and businessmen in green mohair suits. 'A gold-plated door on the 31st floor,' they sang on 'Sin City', accurately locating Larry Spector's office, 'won't keep out the Lord's burning rain.' It was Barry McGuire's 'Eve Of

Destruction' visited on a single community, from a band whose album cover, and lifestyle, seemed to bite a thumb in the face of the apocalypse.

'Christine's Tune' directed the same venom at an individual, with the aggressive sexism that typified the late sixties. Miss Christine, a stalwart of the groupie-singers the GTOs, died within a year, whereupon the Burritos remorsefully renamed their song 'Devil In Disguise'.

Macho theatrics rose to the surface on 'Wheels', where Hillman and Parsons boasted, 'We're not afraid to ride, We're not afraid to die', while Kleinow conjured the roar of the tarmac from his pedal steel.

The group's country-soul ambitions were spotlighted as they tackled two Southern Soul classics, James Carr's 'Dark End Of The Street' and Aretha Franklin's 'Do Right Woman'. 'We loved that soul music,' Hillman asserts, and the magical union of their voices on 'Do Right Woman' (supported by a soaring harmony from ex-Byrd David Crosby) proved the point.

While soul was treated with reverence, the country tradition was dealt a mischievous blow. The album cover mocked those country stars – Porter Wagoner and Hank Snow among them – who wore Nudie suits without a protective coating of irony; and the same amused distance powered the final track, 'Hippie Boy'. With Chris Hillman playing the role of the wide-eyed preacher facing civilization's decay, the Burritos took on the whole heritage of the country monologue – Hank Williams' recitations as 'Luke The Drifter', Wink Martindale's 'Deck Of Cards', Tex Ritter's 'Hillbilly Heaven'. 'That poor little hippie boy on his way to town!' chuckled Bob Dylan when he heard the song.

Hillman has rightfully been keen to stake his claim to the Burritos ('Gram and I started the band together') and the songs on *The Gilded Palace Of Sin* ('people think they're all Gram's tunes, but we wrote them together, face to face'). As with Lennon and McCartney, the surviving partner has been overshadowed by the death of his colleague.

But the two most durable songs on the Burritos' début album came from another team: Gram Parsons and Chris Ethridge. Their contributions were 'Hot Burrito #1' and 'Hot Burrito #2' – a

plaintive ballad and a driving rock song, which demanded two
contrasting but equally remarkable vocal performances from
Gram.

More familiarly known as 'I'm Your Toy', '#1' was the ballad.
Dedicated to Nancy Ross, the mother of Gram's child, it expressed
a romantic commitment that he could never achieve in real life.
'#2' flipped the coin, as love decayed into contempt. 'You better
love me,' Parsons cried, 'Jesus Christ'. This was no call for a
saviour: he already knew his cause was lost. The violence of the
music, powered by strident piano chords and Sneaky Pete's
howling steel, was his only compensation.

In the spring of 1969 the Burritos played several gigs at the
1,000-capacity Boston Tea Party. 'One time,' recalls Barry
Tashian, 'Gram's line-up of the Flying Burrito Brothers came into
town, and we were still running the Flying Burrito Brothers East.
We ended up being booked on to the same bill at the Tea Party, so
there were two different sets of Burritos playing that night!'

In late February, the West Coast Burritos – hailed in *Rolling
Stone* as 'a newly-formed group comprised entirely of people who
have either gigged with or were at one time members of the Byrds'
– played four nights as support for the band which Parsons and
Hillman had left the previous year. By this point, they'd recruited a
third ex-Byrd, Michael Clarke, as their drummer. 'We have more
Byrds than the Byrds,' noted Chris Ethridge dryly. *Rolling Stone*
virtually ignored the Burritos' performance, except when the two
bands combined resources for a lengthy encore. Parsons reprised
his *Sweetheart Of The Rodeo* gem 'Hickory Wind', and finally got
to sing 'You Don't Miss Your Water' in public with the Byrds.
'Gram seemed to be entranced,' wrote reviewer Jon Landau, 'and
in touch with his music in a way that he is not with the Burritos.'
Chris Hillman's reaction can only be imagined.

The Burritos were acquiring a reputation as an erratic live act.
Bernie Leadon remembers seeing them at the Troubadour and
thinking, 'Great image, lousy band. They couldn't sing, they
couldn't play. All they could do was look good.' As their roadie,
Jim Seiter, told Parsons' biographer Sid Griffin: 'Gram had a
phenomenal way of putting emotion into a song. He'd make

people cry. And it used to piss us off so bad when he wouldn't do it, and we'd have to drag it out of him.'

The group were locked into a gruelling circuit of LA club gigs, at the Troubadour, the Palomino and the Corral. Occasional East Coast visits were good for their collective ego, but didn't alleviate their precarious financial position. So the Burritos had to accept work that was less than dignified, like their support slot behind harmony pop band Three Dog Night and the Beatles' *Magical Mystery Tour* movie at colleges across the Southern states. Meanwhile, airplay for their record was minimal. 'The rock and roll stations said we were too country,' Hillman explained, 'and the country stations said we were too rock and roll. You know why? Because we had more emphasis on bass and drums. That was the R&B influence.'

A&M maintained faith in the band: Jerry Moss was still insistent that they were 'a second-album group', while the label's reputation as a haven for country-rock artists was boosted when they signed folkie Steve Young. Formerly a member of the delightfully named but artistically insignificant Stone Country, Young established an instant rapport with the Burritos, and with Parsons in particular: 'We were both from Georgia and in the strange land of LA, out on some kind of new limb. It was a lonely and somewhat unique place to be, so we had an unspoken bond and kinship.'

Both Parsons and Gene Clark guested on Young's 1969 album *Rock, Salt And Nails*. Gram must have relished the song selection – an Otis Redding blues to open, then cowboy ballads, Marvin Rainwater country hits, and Young's own 'Seven Bridges Road', a precursor of the Eagles' romantic mythology.

Not that Young was ever a serious rival to Parsons' musical adventurism. Supping whiskey on a cross-country railroad ride from one club gig to the next, Gram and Chris Hillman composed 'The Train Song'. Back in Los Angeles, they approached fifties R&B rocker Larry Williams, the creator of hits like 'Dizzy Miss Lizzy' and 'Bony Maronie', to produce the track, hoping to match the white soul brew of Gram's old friends Delaney and Bonnie. Williams was no stranger to excess: the year before, he'd cut a devilish rock tune with Kaleidoscope, which dissolved the boundaries between R&B, psychedelia and Middle Eastern music. After that, country soul was a pushover, especially with Leon Russell and Clarence White in support. But predictably the single wasn't a hit.

Michael Clarke, who had moonlighted with a soul band in Hawaii, relished that session. But it didn't take Parsons long to decide that 'Michael wasn't the right drummer for the Burritos. He's not a country drummer. I always thought that the Burritos had a drummer problem.'

Parsons was now harbouring doubts about three of the five-man Burritos line-up, so perhaps it was a relief when Chris Ethridge quit the band in July 1969. 'Chris was a country person,' Gram noted later, 'but like so many people from the country, they turn the other way, turned his back on it. I'm sure he cried when Hank Williams died, but he never really studied that kind of music. He didn't want to play it.' Then, in an aside that shed light on the Burritos' activities that year, he added: 'There wasn't much money in the South, anyway, ten bucks a night.' And Parsons was the only Burrito who could fall back on a family trust fund.

Ethridge's replacement was Bernie Leadon, the veteran of Hearts & Flowers and, more pertinently, Dillard & Clark. He brought a country sensibility, plus the writing talent that had sparked two of D&C's finest songs, 'She Darked The Sun' and 'Train Leaves Here This Morning'. The Burritos were certainly in need of creative input. Aside from 'The Train Song', of which Hillman declared 'I hate it, and I *wrote* half of it', the Parsons/Hillman team had composed precisely nothing since their stay in Resada in late 1968. Parsons' recreational drug use was scarcely unusual for the era, but it dissipated the energy that could have been devoted to music. The only additions to the group's repertoire in 1969 were country standards like Mel Tillis's 'Mental Revenge' and the truckers' anthem 'Six Days On The Road'; their first sessions after the début album produced lacklustre covers of a dozen such tunes.

Calculating the sales of *The Gilded Palace Of Sin*, then offsetting the recording and promotion costs, A&M decided that the Burritos were more than $100,000 in debt. 'What made us angry,' Chris Hillman reveals, 'was that Gram was seduced by all the trappings of fame – and he hadn't earned them. He'd say, "I'm gonna get a limousine". Why? We're going to a bar, to play five shows, what are you talking about? But he had all this money, so it was OK for him.' At Hillman's suggestion, Jim Dickson, the former manager and mentor of the Byrds, the Hillmen and the Dillards, was appointed to oversee the sessions.

'We didn't have anything ready for that album,' Sneaky Pete Kleinow admitted. 'We just came in and fooled around.' As in 1964, Dickson's automatic response to a shortage of material was to suggest that they should cover Dylan. 'If You Gotta Go' was suitably obscure, but the Burritos signalled their contempt for the idea by trouncing the song in a mêlée of harmonies and guitar licks.

Gram Parsons was only too keen to apportion blame: 'The second album was a death knell for the Burritos. It was a mistake to get Dickson involved. We should have been more careful than that. He was trying to make it commercial. I didn't listen to him. But Chris always listens to what Jim says. I guess it goes back to "Mr Tambourine Man".' For once, Gram was aware he might have been part of the problem: 'I can't even claim to have participated. I did what was asked of me and that was it. It's a pretty lousy thing to have to admit.'

Such riches as were apparent on *The Gilded Palace Of Sin* – the country-soul hybrid, the aching commitment of the 'Hot Burrito' songs, the ambiguous flirtation with LA decadence – were all missing from the follow-up. 'She calls me the man in the fog', Parsons wrote for a Leadon melody, and that was how the album sounded. The band were reduced to retrieving unused songs from the *Gilded Palace* sessions ('High Fashion Queen') and even the *Sweetheart* offcuts ('Lazy Days'), and reviving the spiritual, 'Farther Along'. The Byrds dutifully named an equally lacklustre album after that same song two years later. The degree of Parsons' involvement in *Burrito Deluxe* is illustrated by the fact that he was sitting on a backlog of song fragments. Titles like 'I Was So Near To Being Right' and 'You've Been Gone So Long, I Don't Miss You' simply rewrote orthodox country formulas. But amid the scrawled capitals and surreal doodles in his 1969 workbook were lyrics that hinted at his inner turmoil. 'I been living, I know, like two sides,' ran one unfinished song, 'somehow a change is due . . . Please, oh please, contact me, I need to know more.' The scribbled lyrics held other clues to Gram's state of mind. Before the *Burrito Deluxe* sessions began, he sketched a self-help 'Chart For Start', with the manifesto: 'Ought to get together'. To that end, he wrote: 'Let's get that feeling. Vital essences make you warm (*chills must come*).'

After transcribing the first line of Joni Mitchell's 'For Free', he changed tack and – alongside an erratic drawing of a star, bearing the announcement 'Here It Is . . .' – began to delve into speculative philosophy: 'Ontology. St Gregory the Great. Vision of the Principle. Apprehension of the Metaphysical Object. The Eternal (dual)/The Successive. Trancended [*sic*] through or rather by "Funklein" spark (Apex of the Soul). Prof Pratt – Lewin. Fredrich Von Hügel. Anima – trancendental self.' Below ran the first verse of a lyric about 'old blind Casey Jones, the one who hears the music . . . how much it hurts to be alone'.

In Parsons' workbook, the pages of unfinished verses and scattered notes suddenly give way to the lyrics of 'Wild Horses' – the saving grace of *Burrito Deluxe*, and the song which reminded the world of the relationship between Gram Parsons and the Rolling Stones. Mick Jagger and Keith Richard still dispute the authorship of this beautiful country ballad. Keith claims that the title line was his; Mick that Marianne Faithfull's first words when she regained consciousness after a 1969 suicide attempt were 'Wild horses wouldn't drag me away from you'.

Either way, the Rolling Stones recorded 'Wild Horses' in December 1969 at Muscle Shoals studios in Alabama. They experimented with an electric slide guitar, but recognized that a country tune required a trademark. Keith Richard passed the tape to Gram, with the request that Sneaky Pete Kleinow should add a pedal steel line. Gram asked if the Burritos could record 'Wild Horses' themselves, and thereafter boasted that Jagger and Richard had hand-crafted the tune for him.

This renewed encounter with the Stones dazzled the starstruck Parsons, who ingratiated himself firmly into the group's entourage. 'It was embarrassing,' notes Chris Hillman. 'He would rather play at being a rock star with the Rolling Stones than make music with the Burritos.' 'Gram was showing up late for rehearsals,' added roadie Jim Seiter, 'and everyone was pissed off about it. He wanted to hang out with Keith all the time.' To Parsons' undoubted delight, the attraction proved to be mutual. The Stones had first met Gram with the Byrds in April 1968. Drug busts and the gradual disintegration of guitarist Brian Jones had halted their challenge to the Beatles' artistic supremacy. With Jones effectively crippled as a musical force, the weight fell entirely on Mick Jagger and Keith Richard.

Parsons slipped into their close-knit society at its most uncertain moment. After he and Keith had swapped stories and guitar tunings for a couple of days, a new texture entered the Stones' work. The sessions for *Beggars Banquet* directly reflected Gram's inspiration, as illustrated by the country blues of 'Prodigal Son', the affectionate hillbilly satire of 'Dear Doctor', and the self-explanatory 'I'm Just A Country Boy'.

When *Beggars Banquet* was released at the end of 1968, *Rolling Stone* editor Jann Wenner was perceptive enough to notice its 'steel guitar and piano, much of it directly from the country and western tradition in rock and roll'. Keith Richard's interest in that tradition had been fired by his house guest that summer. 'I always loved country music,' Keith reflected, 'to me it's one of the essential ingredients of what's now called rock'n'roll. But Gram taught me the mechanics, the different styles – the Nashville style as against the Bakersfield style.' He also introduced the Stones' guitarist to 'Nashville tuning': replacing three strings of an acoustic guitar with their 12-string equivalents, which sound an octave higher. The result is a chime of low and high frequencies, which has permeated Keith Richard's acoustic playing ever since.

That sound entered the Stones' canon on 'Country Honk', their blueprint for the hit single, 'Honky Tonk Women'. 'That was written in the Mato Grosso in Brazil,' Keith Richard recalled. 'Mick and I were on a ranch in the middle of nowhere. We had an acoustic guitar and we just bashed it out. The other version is the "urban" version, where we got back to civilization.'

The 'urban' arrangement was the single, a swaggering piece of blues theatre more overtly American than anything they'd recorded before. Jagger rolled the words around his palate before drawling them out like a Georgia hustler in a heatwave.

After that, Southern became Jagger's natural language, as if he'd been born on the banks of the Mississippi, not the Thames. 'Mick's Southern accent and my English accent,' Gram Parsons laughed. 'What does it all tell you? It's the same.'

That same transplanted whine inhabited 'Country Honk'. Slipped on to their *Let It Bleed* album late in the year, it sounded as if the Stones were joking with the genre. But they were deadly serious, asking Parsons to select a fiddle-player for the solo, and shipping the tape to California so Byron Berline could overdub his part.

'Mick knows a lot about country music,' Gram noted at the time, 'and so does Keith, but he says that Jagger knows more, so I'll take his word for it.' He found Jagger difficult to read, 'a mystery unto himself', though the Stones' frontman seems to have made his resentment of Parsons' friendship with Keith Richard clear. 'Mick was rude to Gram,' Richard remembered. 'It didn't matter whether he wanted to be Mick's friend. Mick's attitude was, "You can have him".'

Nonetheless, Parsons was ecstatic when the Stones' US touring schedule in the final weeks of 1969 allowed him to tag along, part camp follower, part guru. 'Gram was special,' Keith recalls. 'If he was in a room, everybody else became sweet.' His obvious kinship with the Stones' guitarist ensured him VIP treatment. But Mick Jagger wasn't the only person who was suspicious of their relationship.

'He was like a groupie to the Stones,' Burritos roadie Jim Seiter figured. 'The times I picked him up at Keith Richard's were a little strange. They'd come out skipping like little kids.' Keith invited Sneaky Pete Kleinow to a jam session, but the steel-player refused to go, scared that the Stones might brainwash him the way they had Gram.

Kleinow's fears weren't entirely unjustified. Parsons talked the Burritos on to the bill of the Stones' most blatant display of hubris – a giant free festival planned for Golden Gate Park in San Francisco. Two days before the show, the venue was switched to a desolate racetrack, the Altamont Speedway. After Woodstock's 'three days of love, peace and music', Altamont brought down the curtain on 1960s idealism. The Hell's Angels recruited to steward the event murdered one of the spectators; as the documentary movie *Gimme Shelter* reveals, the concert was a freakshow of arrogance, incompetence and psychic terror. The Burritos escaped unharmed, and were only glimpsed briefly in the film – from behind, as if to protect their identities.

At least Parsons salvaged 'Wild Horses' from the tour. He sang the plaintive melody like a man so familiar with emotional extremes that he no longer noticed them. Leon Russell's piano added a blues edge to the tune, the only track on *Burrito Deluxe* which approached the intensity of their first album.

'It's a logical combination between our music and their music,' Parsons declared. 'It's something that Mick Jagger can accept and I can accept. My way of doing it is not necessarily where it's at, but it's certainly the way I feel it, and not the way he feels it.' Jagger responded in the most eloquent way possible. On *Sticky Fingers*, the album which included the Stones' rendition of 'Wild Horses', he contributed a straight country tune called 'Dead Flowers', which he delivered in a cracker's chewed-up sneer. Transplanting the musical dialect of Bakersfield into the hothouse of the LA rock scene, it was the perfect continuation of *The Gilded Palace Of Sin* – the jaded aftermath to the orgy promised by that album's cover.

The psychic communication between Jagger and Parsons didn't pass unnoticed. 'I think Gram wants to be Mick Jagger now', smirked Roger McGuinn. 'Roger shouldn't say things like that,' Parsons responded. 'Mick Jagger? *No.*' But in the spring of 1970 the Burritos filmed a clip to promote 'Older Guys', a single from *Burrito Deluxe*. It was a laughable concept, with the band miming on a yacht. While Hillman and Kleinow and the rest peered at the camera like schoolboys in the annual class photo, Gram strutted around the deck, throwing jabs into the air, mincing with his hands on his hips, pointing at some invisible 'chick' on the shore – the parade of gestures that were Mick Jagger's stage persona. It was the dance of the chameleon: the folkie with the Harvard vibrato, the country boy with the Georgia drawl, and now the rock star with everything intact – except the stardom.

*

'It started slipping away when the Stones came to town,' Jim Seiter sighed. Chris Hillman was more dismissive: 'When the going got rough, Gram would disappear.'

As the Burritos' career slid further from its early promise, Parsons' commitment waned. That process was accelerated in May 1970. Riding with his friend John Phillips, former leader of the Mamas and the Papas, Gram's Harley disintegrated at 50mph, throwing him full-length on to the tarmac. Phillips drove back to find him swathed in blood, and apparently close to death.

In the workbook Gram used for his lyrics that year, one of his girlfriends who witnessed the aftermath of the crash wrote this poetic account: 'Graham said "John, take me for a long white ride", on Sunday afternoon after he crashed on his Harley bleeding like a great WARRIOR, a river of scarlet blood, braver than Scarlett O'Hara. Blood in Graham's hair, we should have gone to the funfair. His shoes are broken, there's a hole in his knees. He never says, "What is going to happen to me?" Everyone hates the hospital. Tony is mystical and brings Graham a change of clothes. "Life goes up and down like a see saw." Tony cares. He knows that Graham likes what we wears. I hope he's dreaming of a picnic in a meadow with a gondolier from Venus who is a girl in disguise. I hope Graham's getting wiser than wise. I hope he's getting better and time can wait, put it in your pocket and hesitate. Graham is so pretty. I hope he hasn't hurt his face. Graham is made of lace, stardust can't rust. I hate fate. Destiny's child has got to be wild. A river of blood running down the road. Graham's got a mouth like Elvis.' And underneath she inked a self-portrait, with tears streaming through her wispy hair. Alongside was a heart, punctured by Cupid's arrow, with the words: 'Everybody loves G.P.' When he returned from hospital, Gram pencilled 'sp.' in the margin like a weary teacher every time she misspelled his name.

The adoration of his devotee wasn't echoed by the Flying Burrito Brothers. When he had recuperated, he rejoined the band for some gigs in late June 1970. 'I waited to see if the album was going to be a freak,' he explained, 'and then split' – in style. Deliberately flunking verses and missing cues, he roused Chris Hillman into smashing Gram's guitar backstage.

With that, his time as a Burrito was over. In the group, there was simply relief. 'We didn't think we were lost at all,' recalled Sneaky Pete. 'We were actually somewhat relieved, because Gram had been a constant problem, being very difficult to work with – and having quite a little personal problem with drug use. The sets started to go much smoother after that.' So did their music. With his departure, the rough-hewn honky-tonk that he'd brought to the International Submarine Band and the Byrds vanished from the Burritos' repertoire. They became a country-influenced soft-rock group, perhaps the best of their kind. But their link with Parsons' Cosmic American Music was shattered.

While the Burritos fulfilled their tour schedule, Gram hung out in Hollywood bars and made some new friends. Among them was the former Byrds producer, Terry Melcher, who volunteered to help him make a solo album. Gram wanted to call it *These Blues Have Made A Nigger Out Of Me*. Between drunken carousing and cocaine binges, he cut a pile of country standards – 'I Fall To Pieces', 'She Thinks I Still Care' and the ironically apt 'White Line Fever' among them. But none of the fragments in his workbook would translate into songs. From his distant past, before he'd conceived the International Submarine Band, he retrieved a gorgeous ballad called 'Brass Buttons'. His cosmic vision produced nothing else that summer.

When the Melcher sessions collapsed, so did Gram's deal with A&M. He fell in with guitarist Jesse Ed Davis, who shared his lust for chemical stimulation. Together they cut several songs, reprising the covers he'd tackled with Melcher. 'It all fell through,' remembered Moon Martin, who played on the sessions. 'Gram was doing a lot of cocaine, and I didn't think he could really sing that well. Jesse took the basic tracks, and put them out with his own voice, like "White Line Fever" on *Ululu*.'

'Gram was very self-destructive,' added songwriter Walter Egan, who met him around this time. 'To see him as a person, as opposed to a performer or a singer, was disappointing. To hear him sing was amazing.'

Looking back two years later, Gram had convinced himself that after he left the Burritos, 'I just started doing better things'. These included a prolonged period of heroin use, exacerbated when he travelled to France in the late spring of 1971. There he rejoined the extended entourage of the Rolling Stones, who were recording *Exile On Main Street* at Keith Richard's villa in Villefranche.

The 1971 sessions caught the Stones at a peak of creative inspiration and chemical self-indulgence. Beneath their trademark bluster, *Exile On Main Street* was choked with references to fraility and self-doubt, its songs peopled by men who were physically impotent and psychically adrift. Parsons provided the Stones' guitarist with a foothold within the whirlwind of excess.

While the rest of the band slept or escaped the villa for a breath of sanity, Parsons coached Richard through a crash course in country music. 'He knew some of the old-time stuff,' Gram explained, 'but I was the one who really turned him on to Merle Haggard, George Jones and Waylon Jennings.' With his ballads of sin and guilt, Jones was a touchstone for Richard's music during the *Exile* sessions. Alongside the songs of Hank Williams, Jones' repertoire became a secret refuge for the guitarist; in moments of crisis, he'd turn to the piano, and moan his way through 'She Thinks I Still Care' or 'I'm So Lonesome I Could Cry'.

Nothing that direct surfaced on *Exile*: the stark beauty of those tunes was filtered through the Stones' vision, and emerged as 'Sweet Virginia', a deliciously ramshackle and dirty country stomp to which Gram lent a harmony vocal. 'Got to scrape the shit right off your shoes,' Jagger and Richard swaggered, a sentiment Hank Williams could have recognized, if not sung.

Like many outsiders who'd attempted to match the Stones' sensory appetites, Parsons was unable to stay the course. Long before the *Exile On Main Street* sessions ended, he had fled to England in an attempt to ride out his increasing dependence on heroin. Throughout his stay in France, he'd waited patiently for Keith Richard to offer him a deal with the Stones' newly formed record company, maybe even to suggest a duet album, but Richard and Jagger hadn't achieved mythic status by putting others' needs before their own. Recuperating on the Cornwall farm owned by Ian Dunlop, the man who'd originally named the Flying Burrito Brothers, Parsons was effectively an outcast from the music he'd helped to create.

7 King Harvest
The Band and the spirit of 1968

'Country is the gimmick of the year,' wrote *Village Voice* critic Robert Christgau in November 1968. 'The industry is trend-hungry, and the best-hyped new thing of the year is America's rediscovery – the prefix is of dubious specificity – of country and western.' After country-based albums by the Byrds and the Beau Brummels, and the genre's overt influence on the Band, Bob Dylan, and even the Rolling Stones, the hype had become self-fulfilling.

Christgau claimed to have anticipated this development in 1965, when he noticed that the jukebox at New York rock club CBGB's carried nothing but country singles. The trigger, he considered, was Bob Dylan's *John Wesley Harding*, 'which I take as signalling, if not actually causing, the whole present boomlet'.

With hindsight, fellow critic Greil Marcus remains a sceptic. 'I remember reading at the time an article saying that when you get a press release for a new band [the Flying Burrito Brothers] and when you open the envelope a handful of straw falls out, then you know something's really happening. But my reaction was quite the opposite. Nothing was happening.' He is unimpressed by the bluegrass or country roots shared by many country-rock pioneers: 'Authenticity proves nothing. You can't fall back on saying, "Well, my daddy was a farmer." As an artist, you have to make the world real in your art. You can't come back afterwards and say that even if we weren't convinced, we ought to have been.' But authenticity was exactly what country, and country-rock, seemed to be offering in 1968. 'Its traditional honesty . . . accounts for the current wave,' Christgau argued. 'Country and western seems unspoiled. It has the feel of mass-cult folk music, just like rock and roll before its promotion into rock, or rhythm and blues before its elevation into soul.' *Rolling Stone* editor Jann Wenner bought wholesale into country's realism and honesty: 'Country and western music is the soul music of white people . . . in its highest moments (Cash, Otis, Dylan) it is intensely heartfelt, intensely soulful and intensely close to people.'

Wenner tagged country 'the music of reconciliation', another factor in its acceptance. The shift away from the utopianism of acid-rock, and the political activism of 1968, were fuelled by those familiar fractures in American culture – the Vietnam War, the assassinations of Martin Luther King and Robert Kennedy, the crusade for black civil rights, the victory of Republican candidate (and country music fan) Richard Nixon in the November 1968 election.

Politically oriented rock musicians in 1968 ranged from liberal Democrats to unashamed revolutionaries. On this simplistic ideological map, country musicians represented the enemy – white Southerners, conservatives; at best apologists for intervention in Vietnam, at worst racists and bigots. For large elements of Southern society, that was not just a stereotype but a badge of pride.

Country music emblazoned its cultural roots, so there was an almost instinctive shudder of revulsion from many rock fans when they stumbled across the whine of a steel guitar or a cracked hillbilly voice. To the rest of young America, the white South was a foreign land. Hence the double-pronged assault on taboos and tradition. First, country stars like Merle Haggard, Johnny Cash and Waylon Jennings were claimed as progressive forces – conservatives by party allegiance, perhaps, but with an inherent sympathy for the working man. 'In 1968, it became cool among people I knew to listen to Johnny Cash,' recalls Greil Marcus. 'So I listened to him, and I tried to convince myself that I really liked him, even though I didn't really.' Marcus was a rare dissenter: as a champion of the oppressed, Cash enjoyed heroic status in the late sixties. The barren terrain of his music, with its poverty and despair, smoothed his passage from country star to poet of – and for – America. At the same time, country was draped across the landscape of rock as rural decoration. 'The line between high camp and real country music is often nonexistent,' Robert Christgau astutely noted as early as 1968. Incorporating a banjo or a blare of bluegrass harmonies became a self-conscious totem of American identity, a statement that the artist was speaking for a nation, not a youth movement or cultural élite. Three years earlier, black rhythm and blues had been adopted by rock bands as a badge of emotional authenticity. Now another minority culture provided a banner to wave.

Writing in the folk music journal *Sing Out!* at the end of 1968, guitarist Artie Traum viewed this facile assumption of outside values with suspicion. Looking back over the previous five years, he noted: 'This music of the abandoned (blues, mountain music, etc.) was quickly absorbed by the middle class who, after all, could pick better than any "cracker" or sing better than any "nigger". The exploitative aspects of Rock, which is essentially progressive, are generally overlooked, and maybe it's just as well.'

'We were going to call ourselves the Crackers,' says drummer Levon Helm. 'I was proud to come out of an Arkansas farm, and the other guys weren't exactly rich, either. So we thought we should tell it like it is. And then we figured, no, maybe it will piss people off. Sometimes I wish we had gone with the Crackers, just to push it in their faces.' Instead, Helm, Robbie Robertson, Rick Danko, Richard Manuel and Garth Hudson – one Southern farmer's son and four Canadians – became the Band. No one represented Artie Traum's 'music of the abandoned' with such fidelity in 1968. And few albums have left such an immediate mark on the rock community as their début, *Music From Big Pink*. 'Everyone I have played it to has flipped,' Eric Clapton raved that August. 'Since I heard all this stuff, all my values have changed.' Clapton credited the Band with inspiring him to dissolve his extravagant power trio, Cream, and concentrate on more 'organic' playing and songwriting. Even the Beatles were affected by what they heard. 'On this one, I'm trying to sound like the Band,' George Harrison told the rest of his group as they struggled through his song 'All Things Must Pass' during a January 1969 recording session. 'I have been for all of them,' John Lennon retorted.

Reviewing the album in *Rolling Stone*, Blood, Sweat & Tears leader Al Kooper recognized a scrum of styles competing for space:

'I hear the Beach Boys, the Coasters, Hank Williams, the Association, the Swan Silvertones as well as obviously Dylan and the Beatles.' In the *Village Voice*, Robert Christgau made the pertinent observation that *Music From Big Pink* 'captures country-soul feeling without imitating it'.

'Out of all the idle scheming,' wrote Richard Manuel on the album's 'In A Station', 'can't we have something to feel?' Or, as Robbie Robertson put it: 'Everybody was getting really loud, psychedelic, flashy; and we went the other way. This was never discussed, you understand, it was just a constant reaction through the years.'

Robertson's comment mirrored Bob Dylan's reaction to the Beatles' *Sgt Pepper*. When that record was released, in June 1967, Dylan, Robertson, Danko, Manuel and Hudson (but not Levon Helm, who was on a year's vacation from the group) were in Woodstock, upstate New York. Every day, they would gather at a house called Big Pink, and retire to the basement with crates of beer. There they recorded the music that is now known as the 'Basement Tapes' – not just the official 1975 CBS album of the sessions, but hours of tape reels filled with new Dylan material, plus spontaneous covers of folk and country standards, and raucous carousing inspired more by alcohol than by artistic inspiration.

As Robbie Robertson explains, the ambience of their surroundings left its mark: 'When we moved to Big Pink, everybody was in a little huddle. If you played too loud, it was annoying. Also, the basement was kind of a hard surface, all the concrete and the furnace and everything down there. It didn't sound good if you were loud.'

Robertson also pinpoints aesthetic reasons for the change: 'There was more intricacy going into the songs. I felt like playing more subtle things, little things that would happen just in the nick of time, that would be sexier. I just evolved into a different place.' The legend of the Basement Tapes spread through the early months of 1968, when selected Dylan songs were distributed to artists who might be interested in covering them. Word spread that the musicians on these downhome recordings were the same people who'd accompanied Dylan on his 1966 world tour. When their début album was released with a cover painting by Dylan and three new songs from the master, critical respect was guaranteed.

'It was instantly obvious,' wrote rock critic Ralph J. Gleason, 'that this was no Hollywood studio group in buckskin and beads playing what they had learned off Carter Family records. Whatever this band played was real.' Here were five musicians who seemed to be immersed in American roots music. While their contemporaries were obsessed with stretching boundaries – competing among themselves to play louder, faster or longer, exploding lyrical boundaries in free-form chaos, pressing for excess, excess, excess – the Band rarely took a solo, and played with, rather than against, each other. It was impossible to miss the sense of community in their music, as they swapped phrases and filled each other's pauses. To borrow the title of their first hit single, the Band insisted that 'The Weight' should be shared amongst us all. In the turbulent political climate of 1968, that was a comforting ideal.

The songwriting on *Music From Big Pink* came out of that 'country-soul feeling' that Robert Christgau noticed, but lyrically it was closer to the conversational surrealism of Dylan's Basement Tapes – and hence to the pre-twentieth-century folk tradition – than to sixties rock, hillbilly or R&B culture. It was their second album, originally titled *America* by Robbie Robertson, which narrowed their focus.

'Like Henry Fonda walking down the road at the beginning of *Grapes Of Wrath*,' wrote Ralph Gleason as *The Band* was released, 'it says volumes in a phrase . . . It has the sound of familiarity in every new line because it is ringing changes on the basic truths of life.' Like CSNY's *Déjà Vu*, the album was wrapped in a sepia-tinted cover that provoked instant nostalgia for a mythic American past. The five musicians, clad in working man's clothes with scraggly beards and moustaches, could have passed as a gang of railroad pioneers from the 1850s, or outlaws bustling along the Western frontier. And the songs, especially those penned by Robbie Robertson, were soaked in the essence of the past. 'I was so surprised that Robbie wrote that stuff,' confessed rockabilly veteran Ronnie Hawkins in 1969 – four years after the Hawks, as these musicians had been named in his honour, were poached by Bob Dylan. 'They were a rhythm and blues act. And they didn't like country music. We even had a few arguments about that in the old days. I wanted to play country to people, and they wouldn't play it. Then the album came out, and I was shocked, man, because they were definitely country roots.'

The Band's chief songwriter had immersed himself in a Southern heritage so rich and fertile it could only have been fictional. His introduction to the South, when he was called down from Canada by Ronnie Hawkins at the end of the fifties, had the air of romantic intoxication: 'I thought, "I'm here, I made it." I was a little kid realizing this dream. And everything – the smell of the air, the movement of the river, the way people talked – it all worked perfectly for me.'

Long before he met Ronnie Hawkins, though, Robertson had been inhaling the spirit of the South, and of country music. As his mother was a Native American, Robbie spent his summer vacations on the Six Nations Reservation. Undercutting every western-movie stereotype, 'the people on the Reservation used to sit around and play country songs – Hank Williams, Lefty Frizzell, that kind of stuff', Robertson recalls. 'Just because it was Indian country didn't mean it was a timewarp. It wasn't like the movies, with all these guys singing traditional songs. They were folk who lived in the country, so they would listen to country music. They thought Hank Williams was good at what he did.'

Ironically, Robertson's own Native heritage was one aspect of North American culture which didn't find its way into *Music From Big Pink* or *The Band*. 'I was brought up to think that if you want to get ahead in this world, you've got to forget this Indian business,' he explains. 'I would never have felt natural imposing that heritage on the other guys in the Band. It was too personal.'

Instead, Robertson wrote himself a fictional past. On 'King Harvest (Has Surely Come)', he caught the rustle of the wind that brought potential ruin to farming communities. 'Rocking Chair' and 'Jawbone' sounded like tales from some impossibly aged veteran of a previous century. As Helm, Danko and Hudson conjured up the spirit of 1920s string bands with fiddle, mandolin and tuba, Robertson provided unsettling folk wisdom that might have been passed down the generations.

Like Robertson, Rick Danko and Richard Manuel were outsiders in the American South. 'Richard and Rick don't sing about the South,' Robertson insisted in 1971. 'It works for Levon because he's from Arkansas. The only songs we do in relation to the South are all sung by Levon.' The most enduring was 'The Night They Drove Old Dixie Down'. From the Tennessee bulwark of the defeated Confederate Army, a proud veteran called Virgil Caine looks back at the days in 1865 when 'we were hungry, just barely alive'. What sticks in his memory is not the death of his brother, 'just eighteen, proud and brave', but the sound of the bells, celebrating the arrival of the Union Army in Richmond, Virginia. 'The people were singing,' he recalls, Helm's Deep South voice whittling away the last hundred years, and this stark moment of failure is transformed into a memory of comradeship. 'You can't raise a Caine back up when he's in defeat', Helm sings, but every triumphant syllable declares that he's wrong, that the South will rise again.

8 A Trip in the Country

Country-rock crosses America, 1966–1973: Joan Baez; Country Joe McDonald; Area Code 615; Barefoot Jerry; Seatrain; Janis Joplin; Doug Sahm; Creedence Clearwater Revival; Leon Russell; the Beau Brummels; the Everly Brothers; Neil Young; James Taylor; John Stewart; Phil Ochs

Bob Dylan's journey from New York to Nashville inspired other musicians to step outside their native milieu. While Dylan led the procession South from the East Coast bastion of folk music, white Southerners were deserting their traditional home for the liberal climate of California. Consciously or not, they were retracing the paths of earlier generations, who'd abandoned the rural desolation of the dustbowl during the Great Depression for the oasis of the Pacific Coast. Reaching San Francisco and Los Angeles, these refugees fell into the company of native Californians who were eager to ingest their experience of the South, but who preferred to make a purely imaginative pilgrimage to the home of bluegrass and honky-tonk music. Meanwhile, across the Atlantic Ocean, British songwriters also began to draw inspiration from a version of Southern culture which existed only in their minds.

The revelation that Bob Dylan had recorded *Blonde On Blonde* in Nashville transformed the city's reputation. 'History will tell us that Bob Dylan coming here was one of the biggest things that ever happened to this town,' reckons Charlie McCoy. 'It opened the door for all those other people that came – Joan Baez and the Byrds, Buffy Sainte-Marie, Simon and Garfunkel. It was like, "Hey, if it's OK with Bob Dylan, then it must be OK down there."' McCoy and other recent Dylan cohorts like drummer Kenny Buttrey and bassist Henry Strzelecki were soon invited to reprise their contributions to *Blonde On Blonde*, when jazz vibesman Gary Burton arrived in town to cut *Tennessee Firebird*, a strange country/jazz hybrid. 'New projects began to spring up that couldn't have happened before,' Wayne Moss adds. 'It seemed like Nashville was suddenly fashionable.' The city was attracting some unlikely tourists. When Joan Baez decided to record an album of Dylan songs, Vanguard Records packed her off to work with the veterans of *Blonde On Blonde*. 'The first thing I saw when I arrived at the studio,' she recalls, 'was a "George Wallace For President" sticker. So I knew what I was walking into. They were poker-faced, and didn't let anything show at first. But I figured they were expecting me to be this Commie hippie. One of them even told me that he hadn't recognized me when I arrived, because he'd assumed I was going to be wearing motorcycle boots.'

Bob Dylan, they told her after a few days of sullen jousting, had been a 'slob', but she was 'real ladylike'. Baez adds modestly: 'They were all pleasantly surprised to find that I had a sense of humour and that I was attractive. That just knocked their teeth out.' The sessions proved so productive that in five days they had completed the double-set of Dylan tunes, *Any Day Now*, and moved on to another project. *David's Album* was a gift of some mellow country songs for Baez's husband, the imprisoned anti-Vietnam-War protestor David Harris. Wisely, Baez refrained from discussing the cause which had landed Harris behind bars. 'We communicated through music,' she says. 'Politics never came into it.'

As the barriers between the rock and country communities crumbled, the collaborations became ever more outlandish. Who could have imagined that Country Joe McDonald, creator of the infamous 'Fish Cheer' and assorted anti-LBJ anthems, could have cut two albums in Nashville? To heighten the absurdity, much of McDonald's Nashville stay was devoted to songs by Woody Guthrie, the folksinger who had stepped outside mainstream American culture a generation earlier. McDonald claims that he was aided by ignorance: 'They had no idea about Woody. What happened was that we went to Nashville to cut a country and western album, *Tonight I'm Singing Just For You*. We had three days booked in the studio, but because the musicians played those songs all the time, we had some time left over. So we thought, let's make a Woody Guthrie album.

'The players were very conservative: they didn't know who

Woody was. But they related to the lyrics because they were working-class. There's nothing radical about those songs – I mean, we did "This Land Is Your Land", plus this stuff about "we're poor, we're on the road, on the bum", whatever. The musicians said they'd heard the tunes before, but not with those lyrics.' McDonald denies any hint of political conflict during the sessions: 'There might have been some if they'd known who Woody was. But it wasn't the twenties or thirties or forties anymore. It was the sixties. Those guys just sat there all day long, doing their best for whatever client comes in. Now, maybe if I'd made them play some Country Joe songs, they might have gone a little fucking wacko on me. But Woody Guthrie was quite passé, even then.'

As critic Robert Christgau observed, it was coming to something when a Cree Indian – Buffy Sainte-Marie – could thrive in Nashville. But she was so impressed by the musicianship displayed by Floyd Cramer, Lloyd Green, Roy Huskey and Grady Martin on her 1968 album *I'm Gonna Be A Country Girl Again* that she took up residence in the city. By the early seventies, as Charlie McCoy explains, Nashville had lost its exoticism: 'Everybody came into town eventually. And there were never any problems. People here realized how much money was coming in, and that every time a rock star cut an album here, it meant more work in the future. Pretty soon, guys from overseas were coming here, like Johnny Hallyday and Eddy Mitchell from France.'

By then, McCoy and his cohorts had transcended their status as sessionmen. Jazz sidemen had been attracting cult attention since the mid-fifties, but it was only in the late sixties that this attitude extended into rock. Leon Russell's transition from studio regular to international superstar convinced session bassists in New York and LA that reliability and a modicum of technique might translate into charisma.

McCoy's crew had no such illusions, but they were itching to escape their formulaic studio routine. Charlie's ties with Wayne Moss, Kenny Buttrey and guitarist Mac Guyden stretched back to their rock'n'roll apprenticeship in the early sixties. Forced together for endless sessions in Nashville, they slid easily into old habits.

'Between takes,' Wayne Moss explained, 'we'd sit around and jam, adding dirty lyrics to songs we knew, or just working them out instrumentally. Eventually we had some rough tapes together, which we played to a producer, Elliot Mazer. He dug them, and suggested that a group of us should stick together. For a while, we backed up other singers – Linda Ronstadt, Joan Baez, Al Kooper – but eventually we decided to form our own band. We added Buddy Spicher on fiddle and Bobby Thompson on banjo.'

Charlie McCoy remembers that, 'We went into the studio together three or four times, but nothing was happening. We were just about to abandon the whole idea, when Bobby and Buddy started messing around with the Beatles' "Hey Jude" with just banjo and fiddle. When we heard them doing that, the wheels started to turn. So we decided that instead of rock guys playing country, or country guys playing rock, everyone should just do what they normally did and see what happened when we fitted it together. And it worked.' After eighteen sessions – unaccustomed luxury for these musicians – they had completed an album which avoided the torpor that affected much country-rock. A medley of Ray Price's two-step anthem 'Crazy Arms' and the Beatles' 'Get Back', acted as a manifesto, and Wayne Moss's arrangement of Dylan's 'Just Like A Woman' repaid a debt from the *Blonde On Blonde* sessions. 'We sold it to Polydor,' steel guitarist Weldon Myrick explained, 'and we were able to get a good budget for our next album.'

The musicians submerged their identities into Area Code 615, after Nashville's local phone code. But they won little attention in their adopted hometown. It was the rock market that responded to Area Code 615, astonished that these faceless hired-guns could create valid music. 'We hadn't planned to play live,' Charlie McCoy admits, 'because we were still working as session players. But the record was so well received that we did agree to one engagement – four nights at the Fillmore West in San Francisco.'

'If you look at the cover of our second album,' Wayne Moss notes, 'you'll see us all outside the Fillmore. We were supporting Country Joe and the Fish, and the promoter, Bill Graham, got the audience really primed for us. Visually, no one knew what to make of us. I guess we all had short hair. McCoy was wearing dress pants and a windbreaker, and I had on a pair of white sneakers, and we all had the cowboy shirts.' McCoy remembers the ambience as 'really kind of freaky'; but the band's performances, which featured guest spots from Linda Ronstadt, were ecstatically received. Weaned on the sprawling, haphazard and imperfect jams of the Grateful Dead, the Fillmore crowd were stunned by the lightning-fast interplay of Area Code 615. 'We were simply doing our job as musicians,' McCoy says. 'Any band of good country pickers could have done that.'

A second album followed, pointedly called *A Trip In The Country*. But by then, the sales figures for the début were in, and Polydor were ready to drop the band – unless they agreed to tour. 'Most of us were sessionmen and couldn't leave town,' Weldon Myrick explained. 'It was impossible for us to go on the road,' McCoy concurs, 'so we had to give the group up.' As compensation, his harmonica instrumental 'Stone Fox Chase' became the theme tune for BBC-TV's long-running rock show *The Old Grey Whistle Test*. Henceforth, Area Code 615 was nothing more than a phone number, but for Wayne Moss, Kenny Buttrey and Mac Guyden, the prospect of a permanent band remained tantalizing. Adding keyboard player John Harris, they retired to Guyden's home in the Tennessee mountains, emerging only to make flying visits to Barefoot Jerry's Grocery down the hill. In 1971, Barefoot Jerry became a band and an album, the latter uncompromisingly subtitled *Southern Delight*. They'd retained the Code's virtuosity, but channelled it into songs which boldly reflected the ethos of the counter-culture. Their record was an unashamed advertisement for the joys of the weed: in 'The Hospitality Song', they advised their friends to 'Light up a pipe, pass it round', while 'Quit While You're A Head' and 'Smokies' told their own story. Even 'I'm Proud To Be A Redneck' evaded cultural certainties: these crackers were farming 'a batch of Tennessee green'. Like a hillbilly Cheech and Chong, Barefoot Jerry continued to inhale for the rest of the decade – finally dragging Tennessee up to speed with the drug culture which had dominated the San Francisco rock scene since the mid-sixties.

In 1966, San Francisco was the hippie capital of the universe, bloated with journalists and innocents searching for the mirage of flower-power. The transformation of Haight-Ashbury from an artistic playground into a beacon for teenage America radically altered the city's culture. But this loss of innocence left little impact on the music that pulsed from the city's dancehalls. San Francisco remained a bastion of white rhythm and blues, extended and perverted to mirror the cosmic fantasies of an acid trip.

Even those local musicians who'd been raised on the bluegrass of Bill Monroe submerged themselves within the psychedelic ethos. Country music was only aired in the dancehalls as a novelty. Visitors like Johnny Cash were greeted as exotic specimens, every bit as kitsch as the falsettoed Tiny Tim reviving the age of Rudy Vallee with his ukulele. When Cash played the Fillmore, the acid-rock ballroom was barely a quarter full.

In San Francisco, as elsewhere across America, this attitude changed in 1969, when *Nashville Skyline* filled the airwaves and bluegrass veteran Jerry Garcia began to rekindle his roots with the New Riders Of The Purple Sage. Before then, the only Fillmore West regulars who dared to expose their hillbilly leanings were Clover. Bassist Johnny Ciambotti recalled that, 'John McFee from our band was playing pedal steel way before anyone else. He started before Garcia, at least in public, but Clover weren't as well known as the Dead, so Garcia got all the thunder.'

Another West Coast band who incorporated country musicians were Seatrain. Their 1969 début album used the fiddle playing of ex-Bill Monroe sideman Richard Greene as textural decoration for their jazzy rock excursions. They soon added another Monroe graduate, Peter Rowan: 'Seatrain was really interesting,' he reminisced, 'because they were classical musicians. There was no fooling around. It was back to the strict tempo approach that we'd used with Bill Monroe.'

The British paper *Melody Maker* greeted their 1971 album, cunningly titled *Seatrain* (as against their début, *Sea Train*) as 'the best country album since *The Band*'. Flautist Andy Kulberg explained: 'The music we play is sort of bluegrass, because the thing that stands out is Richard's violin.' But it was Peter Rowan who completed the transition. He encouraged Greene to pump his fiddle through a wah-wah pedal on '13 Questions', which teamed CSNY-style harmonies with the rhythmic feel of the country Dead, emerging with the blueprint for late-seventies album-oriented rock (AOR). More emblematic was the way Rowan segued 'Oh My Love' into a staple of Bill Monroe's bluegrass repertoire, 'Sally Goodin'.

Suddenly these throwbacks were everywhere. When the Allman Brothers Band unleashed a forty-five-minute 'Mountain Jam' at the Fillmore East in New York, lead guitarist Duane Allman toyed with the familiar melody line of the Carter Family's pre-war standard, 'Will The Circle Be Unbroken'. Mike Bloomfield, giant of the white blues guitar, also began to incorporate country licks into his solos. When Janis Joplin, the Dead, the Band and Delaney & Bonnie boarded the Festival Express across Canada in the summer of 1970, they filled the journey by getting high and chorusing country tunes such as 'Silver Threads And Golden Needles' and 'Honeysuckle Rose'. For one passenger on that train, their repertoire was a reminder of the music that she'd learned in Texas, almost a decade earlier.

The once independent state of Texas still wears its distance from the United States with pride. 'Texas gets weirder the further west you fetch,' says Sonny Curtis of the Crickets. 'West Texas is flat. That's all it is. It's a good place to be from, but it's also a good place to get away from.' Janis Joplin, raised in middle-class Port Arthur, would have concurred with that sentiment. 'I got treated very badly in Texas,' she recalled from the relative sanctuary of San Francisco in 1968. 'They don't treat beatniks too good there.'

Texas State University is based in Austin, a haven of bohemian ideals in a vast sweep of conservatism. Joplin was a student there in 1961, when the campaign for civil rights had infiltrated the university, if not the rest of Texas. In a show of empathy, student activists based themselves in a downtown apartment they dubbed The Ghetto. Their second home was Threadgill's, a gas station converted into a bar by Kenneth Threadgill in 1933. That was the year Travis County citizens voted to overturn the Prohibition on alcohol consumption, whereupon Threadgill's became a haunt for TSU students.

Thirty years on, the bar doubled as a hub of political agitation, and East Austin's bastion of hillbilly music. While civil rights campaigners planned their marches, they were entertained by the

Waller Creek Boys – among whom, their name notwithstanding, was Janis Joplin. 'She was a wonderful old gal, just good common country people,' Threadgill recalled. 'But she was just a kid. She came up to Austin to go to school, and she worked part-time as a key-punch operator to pay expenses.' At night, she strummed an autoharp, and sang in what the clubowner called 'a high, shrill, bluegrass kind of sound. She didn't go over so well around there.'

Voted the 'Ugliest Man on Campus' by her Texas State contemporaries, Joplin escaped for the West Coast, where future Electric Flag guitarist Nick Gravenites saw her in the San Francisco suburbs around 1963: 'She was at the Coffee Gallery in North Beach, way before she joined Big Brother. She was playing autoharp and singing country blues, and country music in general.' Though Southern soul and gutbucket R&B dominated her singing once she became a rock star in 1967, her country roots weren't entirely eradicated. Viewing her triumphant début at the Monterey festival in 1967, critic Robert Christgau described her voice as 'two-thirds [R&B singer] Willie Mae Thornton and one-third [country pioneer] Kitty Wells'.

Among Joplin's train-ride repertoire was Kris Kristofferson's 'Me And Bobby McGee'. 'Freedom's just another word for nothing left to lose', ran the chorus line, which appealed to a woman slowly sinking beneath the burden of fame. She'd been taught the song by her friend Bob Neuwirth, a painter and sometime musician who turned the ability to hang out with superstars into a sixties art-form. His own attempts to cut a straight country album in 1968 had foundered, but he generously encouraged any young writers who seemed capable of matching up to Bob Dylan and Jim Morrison.

Joplin sang 'Me And Bobby McGee' at a gig in Nashville, which awoke the interest of the Tennessee press – and of Kris Kristofferson, who became a close friend in her final months. She duly recorded the song, taking it for a fast ride down a bumpy road. 'Me And Bobby McGee' reached No. 1 after her death, but few in the rock audience connected the song with its composer, or with Joplin's passion for country music. After all, female country stars were meant to be victims, like Tammy Wynette and Loretta Lynn – or Janis Joplin, who never achieved the grace under pressure that was second nature to her country counterparts.

The town Joplin deserted was a bastion of tolerance: 'Hell,' exclaimed songwriter Jerry Jeff Walker, 'I don't live in Texas, I live in Austin.' But as Ed Gunn of local psychedelic band the Conqueroo reflected, 'People are really weird back there. It's tough for a long-hair. They treat long-hairs just like they treat coloureds.'

The longest hair in Texas belonged to Doug Sahm – the original Texas Tornado, a non-conformist and musical explorer since the early fifties. He encompassed all the cultural currents of his state, drawing on bluesmen like Junior Parker and T-Bone Walker, the hillbilly of Hank Williams and Lefty Frizzell, Bob Wills' cross of jazz and country, and the lazy rock'n'roll of Ray Sharpe.

'He really is an icon of Texas and hippiedom,' says his erstwhile manager Denny Bruce. 'He's hell on wheels. Maybe it has something to do with the fact that he was a child prodigy on steel guitar, opening for guys like Hank Williams.' By the age of 6, Sahm could handle steel, mandolin and fiddle. As Little Doug, aged 12, he cut hillbilly records in the early fifties, and was offered a spot on the *Grand Ole Opry* in Nashville. He regularly slipped off to R&B clubs in Austin to catch Bobby Bland or Jimmy Reed, or soaked up the Mexican rhythms pulsing in the air of his hometown, San Antonio.

In the mid-sixties, Sahm fronted the Sir Douglas Quintet, who recorded the Tex-Mex garage-punk anthem 'She's About A Mover'. With their seamless blend of country, blues and rock, fuelled equally by marijuana and Austin's killer brew, Shiner Bock, the Quintet were the quintessential Texas rock band. But a dope bust in Corpus Christi and police harassment drove them out to California. 'All the heat out of Austin, that did it,' Sahm explained. 'Everybody who could do it had to split to San Francisco, man, 'cos it was beautiful there.'

His move to the West Coast heightened his Texan identity, as he teased at the clash of cultures between San Antonio and San Francisco. One minute he was a hillbilly, the next a psychedelic prankster. If there was a dividing line between redneck and hippie, Doug Sahm erased it.

By 1969, he was based in the acid-rock scene, but still liable to interrupt a freak-out with a Hank Williams tune. That summer, he cut a magical album called *Mendocino*, which held the essence of every bar he'd filled from Dallas to the Haight. The extent of that journey permeated the whole album, from 'At The Crossroads' (with its manifesto, 'You just can't live in Texas if you don't have a lot of soul') to 'Texas Me', in which the San Antone kid puzzled over the fog in the San Francisco bay, while a fiddle and pedal steel carried the echo of his hometown.

'I wonder what happened to the man inside, the real old Texas me,' Sahm mused. The title track offered an answer, as he lauded the Northern Californian shoreline, where 'life's such a groove you blow your mind in the morning'. But most of the record subverted that stoned naïvety. Two years after Scott McKenzie had hymned (and thereby killed) the city as a hippie paradise in his anthem, 'San Francisco', Sahm aimed a blast of downhome wisdom at the global capital of psychedelia.

In the album's key moment, he played an innocent hayseed adrift: 'Lawd I'm Just A Country Boy In This Great Big Freaky City'. Against the backdrop of a disoriented hillbilly stomp, Sahm's voice crackled with pride. 'Thought I'd stroll on up to Haight-Ashbury,' he sang like the survivor of an earthquake. 'There's a whole bunch of things I wanted to see.' Then the landscape began to dissolve before his eyes: 'Met a little girl with strange notions, went to the doctor, gave me funny potions'. The cowboy was never the same again: 'Sure did mess up my mind'. All he knew was that he was still a country boy, and the city was still big – and freaky.

'This propaganda that San Francisco was a free city, that you could dress or do anything anyway you wanted to, smoke dope without a lot of trouble, that's what brought them out here,' said Sahm's fellow refugee Tracy Nelson. But Doug knew that Texans could never become Californians, and by 1971 he'd returned to Austin. He found the city wreathed in marijuana smoke, with its own rival to the San Francisco dancehalls – the Armadillo World Headquarters. The era of the Cosmic Cowboy was about to begin; the original of the species had come home.

No one in San Francisco rock leaned more heavily on country music, and its bastard children, than John Fogerty, the unashamedly autocratic singer, guitarist, keyboardist, songwriter and producer behind Creedence Clearwater Revival.

Fogerty and elder brother Tom worked in fifties vocal groups, sixties frat-rock combos, mid-sixties garage bands and ultimately the Golliwogs, usually with the stolid rhythm section of Doug Clifford and Stu Cook. While the Golliwogs kept pace with the starburst of British beat into psychedelia, John Fogerty never drifted far from the Memphis rockabilly of Elvis Presley and Carl Perkins. Even when Creedence, as the band were renamed in 1968, embarked on their tentative trips into acid-rock improvisation, Fogerty's solos never wandered far from the country licks of Perkins and Elvis's guitarist, Scotty Moore.

As brother Tom conceded, 'John had a *voice*'. He roared like a cross between a Mississippi bullfrog and a mountain lion, a fearsome sheet of sound that twisted every vowel into a Southern twang. Creedence's music provided a more exact location: the Louisiana swamps, breeding ground of musicians who couldn't tell country from soul. But Fogerty had never even been to the South when Creedence Clearwater Revival cut their Delta anthems. 'Our music is not Bayou music,' he insisted in 1970. 'It's not based on any real geographical influence. The only thing that's weird about it is that I'm from here [California] and not there. Most of the people I really liked came from there.' And he namechecked the forefathers of rock'n'roll: the Sun rockabillies Fats Domino, Little Richard and Chuck Berry.

On their *Willie & The Poor Boys* LP, Creedence stepped back from the frenetic R&B of their earlier albums. For the cover, they posed with acoustic instruments like a thirties string band. The record followed suit, churning jug-band music, folk, hillbilly and country blues into a compelling restatement of Fogerty's political values. 'There was definitely a message on that album,' he says. 'I was using country and blues music the way Jimmie Rodgers or Woody Guthrie might have done.' 'Don't Look Now, It Ain't You Or Me' utilized rockabilly to convey the working man's need for self-respect. 'Who takes the coal from the mines?' he sang. 'Who takes the salt from the earth?' In an interview, he slammed home his message: 'We're all so ethnic now, with our long hair and shit. But when it comes to doing the real crap that civilization needs to keep it going, who's going to be the garbage collector? None of *us* will.'

Creedence imploded in 1972, after Fogerty was persuaded to hand over a democratic proportion of their final album to his bassist and drummer. In keeping with their destiny as Nashville session musicians, they turned in the anonymous country-rock of *Mardi Gras*. By then, Fogerty had already slipped into the legal morass that would asphyxiate his career. 'I stopped writing songs,' he says today, 'because I knew that if I did write, I'd lose the publishing on them.' Instead, he made an album of cover versions. Masquerading as the Blue Ridge Rangers, he worked as a one-man-band, ensuring that democracy wasn't even an issue.

For his material, he turned back to country – not the rockabilly that was Creedence's terrain, but the mid-fifties honky-tonk of Webb Pierce, George Jones and Lefty Frizzell. 'This was my exercise to maintain sanity,' he explains. 'I needed to do something, or else I would be going crazy. Cutting those country songs was a relaxation, and also a step away from Creedence. They're lovely songs, and I like the arrangements. But then I ruined it by playing everything myself. I find a lot of fault with it. I don't regard it as a good record.' For Fogerty, *The Blue Ridge Rangers* was a way of escaping his own persona. It was his *Self Portrait*, Bob Dylan's attempt to fake an autobiography. But just as Dylan couldn't help leaving his personality on even the sloppiest of his Nashville cover versions, *The Blue Ridge Rangers* held enough of Fogerty's trademarks to defeat his own purpose. Leon Russell, who worked with Dylan the year after *Self Portrait*, learned from their examples. The top-hatted, flaxen-haired sessionman turned superstar had been born Russell Bridges, but created 'Leon' when he became a singer – of sorts – in the mid-sixties. His voice sounded as if his oxygen supply was about to be cut, but Russell was a superb keyboardist and an occasionally inspired songwriter.

He was also, according to his producer Denny Cordell, 'an Okie. Until the Beatles, country music was the main musical thrust in his life. I've seen him get up in front of country folks who thought he was a rock and roll star, and sing something like

"Crazy Arms". They'd say, "Goddamn, you're a country-singing son of a bitch."'

In the days before David Allan Coe and Willie Nelson made waist-length hair acceptable for male country stars, Leon Russell realized that Nashville stardom was destined not to be his. But respect was attainable, especially given his friendship with Willie Nelson. Willie tipped the nod to Music Row's session community that this boy might look and talk like a hippie, but he was just good folks, like you and me.

Russell titled his 1973 collection of hillbilly standards *Hank Wilson's Back*. He even became Hank Wilson for the duration, in the hope that naïve country DJs might fall for the disguise. That didn't work, but naïve rock journalists greeted Hank Wilson as a pioneer. *Rolling Stone* even voted him the most promising new country artist of the year. In truth, *Hank Wilson's Back* was Nashville by numbers, with a well-trained session crew strolling through companionable renditions of 'I'm So Lonesome I Could Cry' and 'Jambalaya'. A genre that could make a star out of Ernest Tubb would never baulk at Leon Russell's voice, and the entire enterprise was a success – and pretty much an irrelevance.

Hank Wilson reappeared when Russell's career was in deep difficulties in 1984. Sadly, *Hank Wilson No. 2* could muster neither the surprise nor the chic value of the original album. Neither did Paradise Records, Leon's belated shot at running a country label, live up to its name. But one project did indulge Russell's country leanings to the full: *The Live Album*, which teamed him with bluegrass experimentalists New Grass Revival. Alongside the familiar chestnuts of the genre, Russell brought in songs from the Beatles and the Stones, and used them as the raw material for music that stretched beyond country to encompass rock, soul and Broadway standards. In 1973, that might have made him a country-rock superstar. A decade later, his valiant crossbreed of bluegrass and R&B passed virtually unnoticed.

Down the California coastline, the tangled heritage of the Byrds dominated the history of Los Angeles country-rock in the sixties, disseminating their blend of bluegrass and Bakersfield around the world. But other LA figures in the late sixties approached country with more eclectic, not to mention ironic, impulses. For the luminaries at Warner-Reprise's Burbank offices, like Jack Nitzsche, Van Dyke Parks and Lenny Waronker, country was merely another shade in a spectacular palette. What was someone such as Hank Williams to Parks, who had George Gershwin and Charles Ives in his sights? When he sketched the Gothic textures of his 1967 *Song Cycle*, he employed Steve Young to open the album with a hillbilly romp, as a reminder of the all too corporeal America outside his sanctuary. 'That was the past,' the traditional folk tune seemed to say; 'thank goodness those inelegant days are behind us.'

Arranger, producer and composer Jack Nitzsche contrived a less decadent approach. He'd survived an apprenticeship with the maniacal Phil Spector, then cultivated the young Rolling Stones. By the mid-sixties, he was a maverick at large, uncertain whether he should be tackling Chopin or the Crystals.

Instead, he was enlisted to find material for the Everly Brothers. Nitzsche was rooming with Neil Young of Buffalo Springfield, so Don and Phil, the missing link between country duos such as the Louvin Brothers and the Beatles, were turned towards Young's cynical examination of stardom, 'Mr Soul'. 'Is it strange I should change?' they sang, over an exquisite country-pop arrangement.

For a few magical years, Warner Brothers' Hollywood operation was open to anyone who could convince the incumbents of his or her genius. The more uncompromising they were, the better. So it was that Warners played host not only to Parks and Nitzsche but to Randy Newman, Ry Cooder, even Tiny Tim – anyone who could offer an edge of ambiguity. As late as the mid-seventies, a vestige of this beautiful madness survived in WB's Burbank headquarters, when Ian Whitcomb and Andy Wickham assembled a collection of gloriously knowing country singers for a determined assault on Nashville. Among Warners' starlets were Debbie Dawn, who crooned 'Hands', a ditty about a massage parlour, and Kenni Husky, whose 'Gimme That Western Swing' saw her ditching Elton John as her date in favour of Bob Wills (possibly a wise move). The fact that Whitcomb and Wickham also signed acts called Cowboy Colin and Narvis Reptile suggests that irony may have played some small part in their scheme.

That was history repeated as farce. In the 1960s, Warners had courageously believed that genius might translate into profit. If ecstatic reviews could have been measured financially, they would have been right.

Even when Warners signed a known commodity, they encouraged them to ignore the obvious. In 1966, they bought up the Beau Brummels, San Francisco's answer to the Beatles, who'd outpaced the Byrds into the stores with their folk-rock harmonies. Going against type, Warners forced them into cutting an album of contemporary hits; then, as if racked by guilt, they urged the band to experiment with the label's money.

In the person of songwriter Ron Elliott, the Beau Brummels responded with two of the most impressive, and least profitable, albums of the sixties. *Triangle* (1967) epitomized Warners' technique. Elegant, archly beautiful, cunningly deceptive, it only yielded up its treasures after careful scrutiny. Elliott penned a series of delicate and lyrical songs, supported by arrangements that merged baroque and hillbilly. The album ended with Randy Newman's 'My Old Kentucky Home', a country tune coated in protective irony.

In spring 1968, just after the Byrds had recorded *Sweetheart Of The Rodeo* in Nashville, the Beau Brummels flew to Tennessee, and the Mount Juliet studio run by veteran producer Owen Bradley. Their album was named after the location: *Bradley's Barn*. It placed the gorgeous voice of Sal Valentino against the solid perfectionism of Nashville's rhythm aces – the same musicians who were now working with anyone from Bob Dylan to Roy Acuff. For this project, Elliott assembled his most enticing collection of songs. Whereas the Byrds delivered their country material with a degree of emotional distance, Elliott crafted that distance into his songs, and then recorded them without a hint of satire.

So delighted was Warners' A&R head Lenny Waronker that, before *Bradley's Barn* was released, he recruited Ron Elliott to guide the Everly Brothers through an album. Adrift in the age of psychedelia, the Everlys had taken only tentative steps towards the rock audience, scared of alienating their traditional fans. The cunningly titled *Roots* was intended to bridge that divide, rejuvenating the country harmonies that were their *métier*.

Waronker wrapped the album in vintage tapes of *The Everly Family Show*, a Kentucky radio delight from the fifties which found father Ike Everly welcoming his 'neighbours' to some downhome music, 'family style and country style'. Pop and Mom and Don and baby Phil would chime their voices around an old folksong, then break off to plug a dance on Saturday night or sing the virtues of some patent medicine.

Alongside these winsome radio transcriptions, Waronker revealed just how far country music had travelled. The Everlys might have sung Jimmie Rodgers' 'T For Texas' on their radio show, but never with wah-wah guitar. They returned to the flipside of their first hit, 'I Wonder If I Care As Much', but now their vocal precision was set within a landscape of electronic sound. Nowhere was the definition of *Roots* stretched as far as on 'You Done Me Wrong', an early fifties hit for honky-tonk pioneer Ray Price. In its new setting, Van Dyke Parks (of course) acted as an instrumental Jackson Pollock, splashing tuba, violin, castanets, bells, even a marching band, over the brothers' vocals.

A selection of Ron Elliott songs completed the transition, shifting the Everlys as far from home as 'Illinois'. On 'Ventura Blvd', they spoke as refugees from the big city, returned home to the country: 'Everyone says I was gone too long'. Their old friends from the farm watched them with suspicion – which mirrored the reaction of the Everlys' audience. Despite a series of equally adventurous singles, the Everlys were forced to abandon innovation for the certainties of Las Vegas and a TV variety show.

At a time when the Byrds and the Beau Brummels, pop stars within recent memory, were struggling to find a home for their country-rock experiments, the Everly Brothers' failure was unsurprising. Another act signed to the Warners corporation in 1968 achieved more success.

Since the demise of Buffalo Springfield, only their guitarist Stephen Stills had grabbed the public's attention, via his work on Al Kooper's *Super Session*. Outside Los Angeles, there was little demand for Neil Young to launch a solo career. But even his limited exposure on the Springfield's albums had illustrated the unpredictability of his musical vision. With Jack Nitzsche, Young devoted several months that summer to creating an eponymous album that carried a large painting of his face on the cover, then hid his identity. Not only did the artwork omit his name, but Young ensured that his voice was buried deep in Nitzsche's textured production.

Bob Dylan opened his deceptively titled *Self Portrait* with a track on which he didn't sing; but Neil Young beat him to the trick. His album began with two minutes of country MOR, as a string section carried a bland melody. It was called 'The Emperor Of Wyoming', and it could have come from the westerns that Young devoured as a child. To the polio-stricken Canadian, the mid-fifties were the era not only of Elvis Presley, but also of *Rawhide* and Frankie Laine. Before his illness, he'd learned 'church dancing', waltzing reverently around the hall to the sound of Kitty Wells or Hank Williams. 'I loved that stuff,' he boasted years later. 'I used to identify with those cowboy heroes.' The faint tinge of Indian blood running through his veins was enough to shroud his response to Hollywood westerns. The same ambiguity coloured his irregular dabblings with country music.

'The Emperor Of Wyoming' didn't come close to a synopsis of his début album. But by using his Buffalo Springfield colleague Jim Messina, plus two other members of Messina's new band, Poco, Young did sprinkle a little LA country-rock ambience across the record. His namesake Rusty Young decorated several songs with wavering lines of pedal steel – the instrument that came closest to aping the lonesome whine of Neil's voice. Some people are just born to be country singers.

Country-rock turned from a Californian speciality to a national trend during 1969. It was the year when a wealthy East Coast college drop-out, one who'd survived a flirtation with heroin and a spell in a mental institution, staked his claim to reflect the inner turmoil of American youth and was snatched up as a generational icon.

James Taylor fought no political battles, preferring to craft gentle songs of love and loneliness with an acoustic guitar. His confessional lyrics were assumed to be purely autobiographical, and every lost soul and would-be poet in America greeted him as (to quote the media hype of 1970) 'the Messiah of rock'. There was a bitter poignancy to the phrase, which echoed the idealism once reserved for the doomed Kennedy brothers. Like them, Taylor uttered clipped Bostonian vowels, but when he emphasized a line for humorous or dramatic effect, he lapsed into a broad Southern drawl.

On his breakthrough album, *Sweet Baby James*, Taylor played up the country resonances, with the help of Californian luminaries such as Randy Meisner (Poco) and John London and Red Rhodes (Michael Nesmith's First National Band). The title track flirted with one of the most pervasive images of the decade to come – the rock star as cowboy – while 'Country Road' carried its own message. But for Taylor, the country wasn't a place, let alone an American region, and least of all the old Confederate states of the South: it was where the city ended, and a man might find his feet on solid ground – 'Anywhere Like Heaven', as another song put it. For all the subtle fluency of his vocal phrasing and guitar work, James Taylor was no more a country singer than a country boy. But the intimacy and quiet emotion of his work left its mark on the country music industry, long after he'd been discarded by the rock mainstream.

In an alternative universe, James Taylor's role might have been played by John Stewart. While Taylor travelled from Boston to California to pretend he came from the South, Stewart left California for Nashville and emerged sounding like a Boston folkie. He'd been a member of the Kingston Trio, the harmony threesome who brought fresh-scrubbed cheeks and sober suits to the open-necked world of folk. Before he joined, they'd turned murder ballads like 'Tom Dooley' into mass entertainment. That was a world Stewart could understand, as he spent the late fifties with the Cumberland Three, carefully cutting albums of Civil War songs from both sides of the great divide.

In 1967, he wrote 'Never Goin' Back (To Nashville Anymore)', which was snapped up by the Lovin' Spoonful; in 1969, the same month that Bob Dylan recorded *Nashville Skyline*, Stewart contradicted himself by winding up in a Music City studio with

Charlie McCoy and Kenny Buttrey (both also working with Dylan), Lloyd Green (who'd played with the Byrds) and other veteran sessionmen.

Dylan's album title paid tribute to the site of its creation, but Stewart emerged with *California Bloodlines*. Cut off from his roots, he seemed to gain perspective on his home state, ensuring that this was one of the rare country-tinged albums of the era that didn't pledge allegiance to the tradition of Hank Williams, Jimmie Rodgers or Bob Wills. It was never likely to attract imitators, and even Stewart failed to repeat this experiment.

In Phil Ochs, the cultural transplantation of country music reached its apotheosis. He'd been the quintessential East Coast folkie in the early sixties, all passion and sincerity, who was scarred by the mind games he endured from Bob Dylan and his entourage. No other performer clung so fiercely to the idealism surrounding the Kennedys, and Robert Kennedy's murder in 1968 seemed to catapult Ochs into another personality. Relocating to California, he eschewed political activism in favour of dense metaphorical mazes, then refashioned himself in a gold lamé suit as the shadow of Elvis Presley, outraging the remnants of his liberal audience.

On his ironically titled album *Greatest Hits*, Ochs revised his image again, emerging as a country troubadour for 'Chords Of Fame' – a brilliantly incisive critique of his own doomed career. Under the inevitable supervision of Van Dyke Parks, Ochs gathered together musicians from Nashville, Bakersfield and Los Angeles country-rock, among them members of the Byrds and the Burritos – a last defiant celebration of a maverick LA spirit which had fuelled some of the most glorious commercial failures in rock history.

9 Sing Me Back Home
Jerry Garcia and the Grateful Dead, 1960–1995

Most of the rock musicians entranced by country in 1969 were
exploring foreign territory. For Jerry Garcia, lead guitarist and
creative fulcrum of the Grateful Dead, the stylistic shift was a
homecoming.

Garcia came from a San Francisco bluegrass scene peopled by
groups whose names evoked their music – the Thunder Mountain
Tub-Thumpers, the Heart Valley Drifters, the Black Mountain
Boys. 'When I got turned on to bluegrass in about 1960,' he
recalled, 'the first time I *really* heard it, it was like, "Whoa, what
is this?" The banjo just made me crazy. It was the same way
rock'n'roll had affected me when I was 15.'

The harsh harmonies of bluegrass music often repelled those
raised on pop radio, but Garcia was no stranger to the sounds of
the South: 'My grandmother was a big *Grand Ole Opry* fan. This
was in San Francisco, a long way from Tennessee, but they used to
have the *Opry* on the radio every Saturday night. My grandmother
listened to it religiously. I heard Bill Monroe hundreds of times
without knowing who he was.'

In 1960, the year when Bob Dylan shed his icy Minnesota
heritage and reinvented himself as an Okie balladeer, Garcia too
immersed himself in another culture. 'I got into old-time
string-band music,' he explained in 1971, 'and in order to play
that, you have to have a band.' Toting his five-string banjo to folk
clubs and student bars, he identified kindred spirits – among them
guitarist David Nelson, and budding poet Robert Hunter.

'Garcia had a band,' Hunter remembered, 'and they were
lacking a mandolin player, so he asked me to play. I'd never played
one before, so I practised very hard all that day to be at my first gig
that night.' Hunter lacked Garcia's dedication to his instrument,

but their intellectual rapport allowed his musical failings to be overlooked.

'I had somewhat of a Bill Monroe capability to my voice in those days,' Hunter claimed. Likewise Garcia, whose imposing frame and dominating personality were belied by his strangled Appalachian whine. Bluegrass offered a natural home to his fragile vocal sound. Rock'n'roll could encompass musical incompetence, but bluegrass demanded proficiency and self-improvement. 'Bluegrass bands are hard to put together,' Garcia noted, 'because you have to have good musicians to play. I was frustrated insofar as I never really had a *good* band.'

Hunter survived alongside Garcia in the Wildwood Boys, but when Jerry formed the Black Mountain Boys, the amateurs and professionals were quickly divided. 'I only played with them once,' Hunter admitted. 'Everyone was interested in making a serious living out of music, and I was not going to break my butt learning to play mandolin properly.' David Nelson recalls the crucial argument: 'Garcia said, "You're really going to have to get serious or I'm going to have to get another mandolin player." Bluegrass is a staunch kind of music. If you don't dedicate yourself, you'll never make it. So Hunter just quit.' Though Garcia was able to drag a few committed souls into his orbit, his demands were too stringent for the San Francisco scene: 'There weren't many real musicians around, not enough to keep a band playing.' So in 1963, the Black Mountain Boys gave way to Mother McCree's Uptown Jug Champions, a unit broad enough to hold blues singer Ron 'Pigpen' McKernan, rock drummer Bill Kreutzmann, and teenage guitar student Bob Weir. Like the Lovin' Spoonful in New York, they blended blues, country, folk and Chuck Berry's rock'n'roll into a chaotic whole, in which entertainment ranked higher than virtuosity.

Not that Garcia entirely abandoned his bluegrass purism: the Heart Valley Drifters were revived for the Monterey Folk Festival in 1964, Jerry sporting a flamboyant cowboy hat for the occasion. But when the Uptown Jug Champions became the Warlocks, and then the Grateful Dead, Bill Monroe's influence was audible only in the tumbling fluency of his guitar playing.

The Dead shared another quality with the classic bluegrass bands: musical communication. In the late sixties, they were the masters of West Coast psychedelia, as unpredictable as an acid trip. Their expansive jams could become marooned in flatlands, until their collective unconscious sprang into three-dimensional splendour. Their inspiration could last for hours, or just as easily splinter within seconds. Songs were elongated to test the limits of the Dead's competence and comradeship: two-minute R&B classics like 'In The Midnight Hour' or 'Dancing In The Street' could run for half an hour, while each musician teased out the potential of the moment.

The strict ethic of bluegrass sat uneasily within this psychedelic milieu, with its acid tests, light shows and hippie ideology. But like Garcia, Robert Hunter bridged the gulf. He was recruited to provide a lyrical evocation of the LSD experience, establishing a writing partnership with Garcia which survived for three decades.

Neither man entirely forgot his adolescence. When Bob Dylan's *Nashville Skyline* was released in April 1969, Garcia responded with glee: 'After hearing Dylan's country, it was soon, "Hey, we can pull good ole country music into our act!" Too much!' That month, the Dead added the Nashville standard 'Silver Threads And Golden Needles' to their repertoire. Played without a hint of irony, it inaugurated a new era of Dead music.

For the next twenty-five years, no Dead set was complete without one of Bob Weir's enthusiastic forays into commercial Americana – Merle Haggard's 'Mama Tried' (one of the few overly country tunes performed at the Woodstock festival in August 1969), Marty Robbins' 'El Paso' or Johnny Cash's 'Big River'.

For some shows, Weir became Bobby Ace, while the Dead were The Cards From The Bottom Of The Deck – a country bar band churning out erratic covers of Joe South's 'Games People Play', Buck Owens' 'I've Got A Tiger By The Tail', the Everly Brothers' 'Cathy's Clown' and George Jones' 'The Race Is On'. They'd have been laughed out of Nashville or Bakersfield, but to an audience newly awakened to the potency of country, Ace and his Cards sounded authentic enough.

Typically, Garcia responded in more academic fashion. With

the dedication that he'd once applied to the banjo and guitar, he learned pedal steel – one of the totems of a 'real' country sound. He unveiled his new obsession on, suitably enough, 'The Farm', an ambiguous foray into country-rock by the Dead's acid-rock compadres Jefferson Airplane. But his most significant steel playing was the melodic lick he added to 'Teach Your Children', a hit single for Crosby, Stills, Nash and Young in 1970.

Exposure to CSNY's tightly structured harmonies inspired the Dead to create a synthesis of their acid-rock tradition and their enthusiasm for country. 'Crosby and those guys were hanging around a lot,' Garcia explained in 1972, 'and nothing turns you onto singing more than three guys who can really sing good. They'd start singing, and we'd think, "Wow! Why don't we try making a simple record?"'

Voices were the Dead's weakness: Pigpen could shout a blues tune, but Weir and Garcia's pipes were strictly functional. It took weeks of rehearsal for them to mimic the flawless harmonies of CSNY. The effort was apparent when the Dead débuted Garcia/Hunter's 'Uncle John's Band' on the *Workingman's Dead* album in spring 1970. They sounded less like choirboys than cowboys, their voices clashing as they stretched into unfamiliar octaves. But the erratic singing matched the enigma of the song, which seemed to belong to a forgotten skirmish of the Civil War: 'Goddamn, well I declare, Have you seen the like? Their walls are built of cannonballs, Their motto is "Don't tread on me".'

Robert Hunter was steeped in folk heritage and western myth, and he relished the opportunity to invent a cast of American archetypes. On *Workingman's Dead* (its title an admission that the band equated country music with the common people), he even borrowed a twentieth-century legend. John Luther 'Casey' Jones was a train driver, killed in a crash near Vaughan, Mississippi in 1906. His conduct had been ambivalent: an inquiry blamed him for the wreck, while two popular ballads lauded him as a hero. The truth was obscure, allowing Hunter to recreate Jones as a hippie adventurer, 'Drivin' that train, High on cocaine'.

That spirit invested the whole album. 'We were into a much more relaxed thing,' Garcia explained. 'We weren't feeling so much like an experimental music group but more like a good old band.' Nowhere was that more apparent than on 'Cumberland Blues', which glazed Elvis Presley's 'Mystery Train' in marijuana smoke. Hunter later wrote: 'The best compliment I ever had was from an old guy who'd worked at the Cumberland mine. He said, "I wonder what the guy who wrote this song would've thought if he'd ever known the Grateful Dead was gonna do it"!'

Other songs carried more contemporary weight, songs such as 'New Speedway Boogie' – a response to the disastrous free festival at Altamont in December 1969. 'The only song that failed on that record is "High Time",' Garcia noted later. 'I was not able to sing it worth a shit.' He sounded like a farmer exhausted by the burden of the land: 'The wheels are muddy, got a ton of hay . . . I'm having a hard time, living the good life'. There were no instant utopias on *Workingman's Dead*.

Neither, at least in Garcia's eyes, was there more than a veneer of country on a record that has come to epitomize country-rock. 'The only thing country about that album is "Dire Wolf",' he claimed, 'because it has a pedal steel. And even that song was like a folksong, rather than a country and western number.' For Bob Weir, the distinction was minimal: 'Lots of rock'n'roll guys evolved out of being folkies, which is real close to being a country musician.' But for Garcia, country implied some sort of professionalism, which the Dead's lifestyle precluded: 'Country musicians are used to being competent, rather than getting high and blowing everyone's minds. It's just a difference in ethos. A country audience goes wild when a band plays tight and clean. That sound is something you can live with from day to day. It doesn't require that you listen to it with great concentration.'

By his own admission, *American Beauty*, which followed close on the heels of *Workingman's Dead*, was the product of just such a sensibility: 'The emphasis is on the vocals and the songs, the music being more or less incidental.' Smoother than its predecessor, it shed the aura of doom which hung over 'Dire Wolf' and 'New Speedway Boogie'. It was as if the Dead had fallen for the dubious equation which saw country-rock as a guarantee of 'good times' (or even high times, perhaps).

Garcia revealed later that 'it was raining down on us while that record was going on'; his mother was dying, as was the father of bassist Phil Lesh, and the band's legal affairs were slipping into a morass. Lesh's father was serenaded with 'Box Of Rain', while the same transcendental hippie philosophy (tinged with Zen mysticism) fuelled 'Ripple' and 'Brokedown Palace'.

Even the album title connoted acceptance rather than struggle. If *Workingman's Dead* was a nod to an American everyman, then *American Beauty* was strictly idealistic. Only two songs escaped the slickness: 'Friend Of The Devil', a mythic Hunter parable, and 'Truckin'', a celebration of life on the road, dope busts and all.

As the band realized, *American Beauty* was a dead end, its logical conclusion a reincarnation as Poco or the Eagles, purveying fantasies for college students. Accidentally or not, they had already created an escape route: a side project dubbed (in homage to Hollywood cowboy movies) the New Riders Of The Purple Sage.

At the heart of this band was Dave Nelson, Garcia's cohort from the bluegrass years. He had remained within the acoustic tradition, hawking his New Delhi River Band round San Francisco clubs. By 1969, he had enlisted John 'Marmaduke' Dawson, Bob Matthews, Dave Torbert, Robert Hunter – and Jerry Garcia, for whom the New Riders acted as a rehearsal room for his pedal steel playing.

Other members of the Dead joined the escapade. 'I wanted to learn about country and western,' drummer Mickey Hart recalled, 'so we set up a workshop in my barn.' Briefly, Garcia, Hart and Phil Lesh were all New Riders. 'For us to go on the Dead's tour,' Marmaduke Dawson noted sardonically, 'Jerry only needed two more tickets. Everyone else was already in the band. For the price of two tickets, he got a new five-piece band to open for the Dead.' The classically trained Lesh quickly ticked off 'country' on his lifetime's list of experiences, and quit, but Hart and Garcia stayed the course. Not so Robert Hunter: 'I learned all the material but never performed with them. I felt I was in the New Riders, and Nelson, Marmaduke and I did sit down and write "Friend Of The Devil". Then they started performing, and suddenly I wasn't in the band.'

In the summer of 1970, the New Riders became the Dead's support act. 'It was the New Riders, then the acoustic Dead, and then the full Dead set,' Mickey Hart explained. 'I loved it, but do you know how many hours a night that was?' He also struggled with the transition from the New Riders' country to the Dead's psychedelia: 'Being in the Dead was like being in a spacesuit, and being in the New Riders was like wearing a new pair of jeans. I couldn't go back and forth in one evening.' Hart and then Garcia removed themselves from the New Riders, who pursued a rambling career in country-rock for the next decade and beyond, filling their albums with tuneful tales of hippie escapades.

Garcia soon began to tire of the pedal steel: 'I really got into it, but it became an either/or situation. I found it very hard to play half the night with a pedal steel and a bar in my left hand, and then switch to straight guitar. It was painful to the muscles. It got to where I couldn't play either of them very well, so I realized it wouldn't work.'

Workingman's Dead and *American Beauty* also exhausted Garcia's enthusiasm for comfortable 'country-rock' material. Though the Dead still added country standards to their live set, like Merle Haggard's 'Sing Me Back Home', or Garcia's stroll through Hank Williams' 'You Win Again', the new songs on 1971's *Grateful Dead* and the epic *Europe '72* moved beyond genre into what Elvis Costello calls 'that whole Americana feel. They're quite timeless. They represent a thread in American music that stretches from Hoagy Carmichael through Mose Allison, Charles Ives and Van Dyke Parks.' The *Europe '72* transition from a rousing 'Truckin'' into a suite of almost ambient psychedelia opened another dimension in the Dead's music.

Yet the purity of bluegrass remained, in Garcia's words, 'an itch I'd had for a long time'. He enlisted fellow survivors from the early-sixties club scene – fiddler Richard Greene and guitarist Peter Rowan, refugees from Bill Monroe's Blue Grass Boys who'd later merged hillbilly and psychedelia in Seatrain; mandolin virtuoso David Grisman, a colleague of Rowan's in another late-sixties combo, Earth Opera; and stand-up bassist John Kahn. 'Jerry wanted me to be leader,' Grisman noted, 'because I was always more of a disciplinarian, wanting to get things tight. Bluegrass is precision music.'

'We got together to see what would happen,' Garcia explained in the spring of 1973, 'and thought, "Shit, why don't we play a few bars?"' Greene soon dropped out, but Garcia enlisted fiddle veteran Vassar Clements as a replacement. 'Vassar was at the height of his powers,' Grisman recalled wistfully. 'It was like being next to Charlie Parker in his prime.' 'That was the bluegrass band I'd always wanted,' Garcia reflected. 'I was flattered to be in such fast company. I was only sorry that my banjo chops were never what they had been when I was playing continually.'

The band was dubbed Old And In The Way, after a sardonic Grisman tune. 'I think that was the nicest Vassar's played,' Garcia beamed when their live album was belatedly released in 1975. 'With us, he came up with the maximum of mind-blowing but beautifully tasty stuff – more than he does normally.' But Garcia had to struggle with an unaccustomed problem: 'Bluegrass is like chamber music, it's very quiet. If the audience got at all enthusiastic during the tune, it would drown out the band, and we couldn't hear each other.'

Old And In The Way was never built to last: too much money rested on the Grateful Dead. The concept was revived in 1974, under the guise of the Great American String Band; two years later, Garcia smuggled another bluegrass outfit, the Good Old Boys, on to the Dead's record label. Thereafter, for more than a decade, Garcia abandoned the music of his youth. Not until 1988 did he assemble another acoustic group, the nostalgically named Black Mountain Boys '88, whose repertoire encompassed folk, blues and Americana, but nothing that either Merle Haggard or Bill Monroe would have recognized as his own.

In his final years, Garcia reunited with David Grisman for a series of sessions that disintegrated any lingering distinctions between American music genres. A 1991 collaboration locked their mandolin and guitar around tunes that came from Hoagy Carmichael, Irving Berlin, B. B. King and – an elegaic 'Friend Of The Devil' – even the Grateful Dead. At a time when heroin addiction was blighting his performances with the Dead, *Jerry Garcia/David Grisman* acted as a purgative, stripping away layers of rockstar bullshit and psychological torment to reveal the pure musician beneath. In Bob Dylan's phrase, Garcia was 'the very spirit personified of whatever is muddy river country at its core and screams up into the spheres'.

10 England Swings
Rockabilly and country-rock in Britain, 1963–1975: the Beatles; the Rolling Stones; Ian Matthews; pub-rock; Elton John

In 1985, Tennessee rockabilly veteran Carl Perkins hosted a London TV special. To gain admission, fans had to present themselves at a local radio station, dressed in the drapes, bootlace tie and winkle-picker shoes of a Teddy Boy. Then they queued outside the windswept TV complex, watching as Perkins' superstar guests absorbed their pre-gig nerves with judicious quantities of alcohol. Into their view stumbled a short, squat figure who, in another world, might have been lined outside with the fans. 'There he is,' spat one of the draped rockers as he recognized Ringo Starr, 'there's one of the bastards who killed rock'n'roll.'

Few deserved that accusation less than Starr, whose respect for Perkins' music – expressed in several Beatles' cover versions – helped to maintain his hero's royalties when his commercial profile had slipped below eye-level. Like the other Beatles, Starr's devotion stretched beyond rockabilly to encompass the traditional country music from which it emerged. When country legend Hank Snow toured Britain in the late sixties, Starr was the only rock musician who went backstage to shake his hand. In 1970, he even cut a country album in Nashville.

'Ringo was always into country and western, and blues,' Paul McCartney told Spencer Leigh. 'He had a lot of mates who were seamen, who'd come back from New Orleans and New York and the other big American ports, and they'd bring back these great records. So Ringo used to have a lot of country and western stuff. In fact, we were all quite big country fans. And we loved people whose roots were in country, like Carl Perkins, Buddy Holly, Eddie Cochran, Jerry Lee Lewis – who were all really country singers, who'd gone over to rock'n'roll.' The Atlantic crossing fuelled the imagination of another future Beatle: George Harrison recalls his father returning from the Merchant Navy with such exotica as brittle shellac records by the Singing Brakeman, Jimmie Rodgers.

For anyone raised in the austere climate of Britain between the Second World War and the advent of Beatlemania, American culture gleamed with a surreal glamour. Britain was cowed by food rationing, poverty and the greyness that infested everything from suits to the killer fogs of the 1950s. Its people couldn't help but be bewitched by street-wide Cadillac saloons, and the gaudy, almost dreamlike colours of Hollywood.

Those who'd been charged by the high-voltage currents of American rock'n'roll never forgot their debt, and the spirit of Elvis, Chuck, Jerry Lee and Little Richard was preserved into the sixties by young British musicians. Some kept the faith silently, while playing trad jazz, straight pop or blues, as the times demanded. Future Rolling Stones guitarist Keith Richards (he later dropped the final 's', although he has since reinstated it) even bided his time in a suburban London country band, waiting for his friend Mick Jagger to offer an escape route.

For the Beatles, and their contemporaries across the country, the breakneck rhythms and Southern swagger of Memphis rockabilly remained a formative influence. By the early sixties, their minds were crowded with other sounds – Brill Building pop, Motown soul, New Orleans R&B. But the country twang of Carl Perkins was fundamental for Ringo Starr, and for George Harrison, whose early guitar solos with the Beatles were inspired by Perkins' licks on 'Blue Suede Shoes' and 'Boppin' The Blues'.

In June 1964, Perkins watched as the Beatles recorded 'Matchbox', the Blind Lemon Jefferson blues that he'd transformed into a rockabilly standard. Later, they taped two more of his songs, 'Everybody's Trying To Be My Baby' and 'Honey Don't'. Perkins' reaction was mercenary: 'Their versions are OK,' he told a reporter in 1969, 'but the royalty cheques are nicer'. But as he grew older and more sentimental, he waxed lyrical about the generosity and love of 'those boys'. The three surviving Beatles contributed to his final album, *Go, Cat, Go*, and both sides reckoned it an honour.

*

As fledgling songwriters, John Lennon and Paul McCartney depended on simple formulas. The standard four-chord progression of doo-wop was one model; another was provided by the three-chord trick which was at the root of both rock'n'roll and Hank Williams' country tunes. Several of their earliest songs, such as 'What Goes On' and 'Won't You Please Say Goodbye', were built around familiar country progressions.

Their triumphant tours of the United States in the mid-sixties exposed them to the latest developments in soul and country. (Bizarrely, their initial foray coincided with a rival crusade from country luminaries Wesley Rose and Roy Acuff, who travelled to London in February 1964 to boost the popularity of Nashville's output in Britain.) The Beatles returned home with a bunch of albums by Buck Owens, and hints of his Bakersfield sound were soon audible in their own music. Lennon's 'I'll Cry Instead' and 'I Don't Want To Spoil The Party' both displayed a clear debt to country, and the winsome mood of the *Beatles For Sale* album was shaped by their exploration of the genre.

In June 1965, Ringo Starr was even permitted to record a Buck Owens hit, 'Act Naturally', for the *Help!* LP. Fans assumed that the song had been chosen for its lyrics – 'they're gonna put me in the movies' chimed with a film soundtrack album – but it was also an admission that Owens was a personal favourite. So entrenched was Starr's regard for country that when he first attempted to write songs he found it impossible to escape its pull. 'I used to write new words to other people's tunes, and never know,' he recalled, and on a hilarious composing tape from 1966 Ringo improvises banal lyrics to a succession of Johnny Cash melodies.

When he finally completed an acceptable song, it was, unsurprisingly, a country tune. 'Don't Pass Me By' duly appeared on *The Beatles*, just as the Los Angeles élite was beginning to succumb to the first wave of country-rock. 'We weren't aware of the country kick coming in,' Lennon pleaded; so cocooned were the Beatles in 1968 that he was probably speaking the truth.

George Harrison spent the final weeks of that year with Bob Dylan in Woodstock, and returned for the troubled *Let It Be* sessions haunted by the melodies of Dylan's new country songs. The two musicians met again in 1969 and 1970, collaborating on an attractive country-pop melody ('I'd Have You Anytime') and sharing a recording session. Sadly, their combined assault on the cowboy ballad 'Ghost Riders In The Sky' and Carl Perkins' 'Matchbox' didn't even rival the turgid results of the Dylan/Cash liaison a year earlier. More significant was Harrison's encounter in New York with steel guitarist Pete Drake. When he began work on his *All Things Must Pass* album, he flew Drake in to play on 'I'd Have You Anytime' and a poignant tribute to Dylan, 'Behind That Closed Door'. Also present at those sessions was Ringo Starr, who was considering a country project of his own. He'd contacted Dylan's producer, Bob Johnston: 'I phoned him to say, "Do you wanna come over and bring about 12 guys with you?" He said, "How long do you think it will take?", and because of my experience making albums with the Beatles, I said, "Just come over for a month or two". He said, "Are you crazy? It only took a day and a half to do Dylan's one!" And I thought, "Christ! A day and a half! Incredible!" But he wanted a lot of bread, so I decided not to do it with him.'

Keen to save money at every opportunity, Starr himself drove Pete Drake from the airport to the Beatles' central London studio. 'We got talking about country music,' Ringo recalled. 'I was surprised to discover how much Ringo knew,' Drake added. As the sessions progressed, Starr enlisted the steel player's help with his own album project. 'I said, "Why don't you fetch in a crowd of guys?" and he said, "Well, if you wanna do a country album, the best place is Nashville." So I said, "How long will it take?" and he said, "Three or four days. In a week, we can have it all finished." I said, "You're putting me on," and he said, "No, I promise you. I'll have the studios and the musicians organized."' In late June 1970, Starr flew to Nashville: 'For three days, we searched for songs. We played a lot of tapes, and picked out the ones we liked. Then on the Thursday, in the morning, I learned five songs and I did them that night. We did five the next night, and then on Saturday I did three more, plus one I wrote. In three days, I did a double-album, because I've got an album which I've never put out, just jamming with all the guys there.'

Starr's naïvety is quite touching. His second album would have comprised twenty-five minutes of the virtually tuneless 'Hoochie

Coochie' – rarely has one chord been so thoroughly exhausted – and another twenty minutes of 'Nashville Jam', a time-filling exercise no self-respecting country producer would have committed to tape. But the record that he did release that summer, *Beaucoups Of Blues*, proved to be a charming genre exercise. Starr coped manfully with his vocal limitations, crack sessionmen like Jerry Reed, Scotty Moore and D. J. Fontana ran through their paces, and only the strictly functional songwriting disappointed. Nashville took to the lugubrious drummer, in his Sears-Roebuck dungarees and red bandanna; Ringo returned the compliment.

All the Beatles flirted with country stylings on their solo records – Lennon via rockabilly, Harrison as a tribute to Dylan, Starr from the heart, and McCartney as a master of pastiche. In 1974, McCartney's band Wings continued the cultural tourism which had already seen them record in Nigeria and New Orleans, and arrived on Music Row, Nashville. There they recorded 'Sally G', a wholesome ditty which picked up a little local airplay. The visit was more memorable for sentimental reasons, as McCartney explained: 'I got to know Chet Atkins there, who'd been a real big hero of mine. Down at the Cavern in Liverpool, Colin Manley from the Remo Four was the finest guitarist in the city at that time, because he could play Chet's pieces, like "Trambone". That's how I was introduced to Chet's music. We got talking about our dads, and I said, "We should do this song that my dad wrote and make a record of it." So we called ourselves the Country Hams, and I played washboard and bass. To them, using a washboard was so comical – it reminded them of when they were little kids. But we'd used it in our skiffle band when we were teenagers.'

In the 1990s, it seems obligatory for rising Nashville stars to pay homage to the Beatles, but their heritage was less familiar to an earlier generation of musicians, as George Hamilton IV explains: 'When I was in Nashville recording Paul McCartney's song "Mull Of Kintyre", we passed around the chord sheets. One of the leading Nashville musicians looked at the sheet and said, "Hey, man, you've misspelled this." I said, "Misspelled what?" He said, "On this lead sheet, here. Mule of Kintyre. You've got 2 L's in it."'

*

Even after Ringo Starr's visit to Nashville, the British music industry could find little connection between country and rock. *Melody Maker* journalist Chris Welch spoke for most rock fans when he reviewed a country single in 1971: 'It was not enough that we had to suffer Hank Williams. There is now apparently a Hank Williams Jr, just as bent on producing wailing, self-pitying, maudlin sentiment. White American country music must be the worst music the world has yet produced.'

Not if you were to believe Larry Adams, first editor of Britain's leading country journal, *Country Music People*. 'Rock was an intelligent music started mainly by country artists,' he asserted in 1970, before slipping into invective: 'The fact that Rock finds difficulty in struggling for acceptance today is because its main champions have turned back to Country music, albeit in a more advanced and popular form. Those left in the Hard Rock field are so musically inept, sartorially unkempt and socially disgusting as to deserve the increasing disinterest in their activities. As regards a "new culture", I've greater respect for pigs in a pigsty.' Elsewhere, Adams lamented 'the hordes of pop groups whose only claim to "fame" is the ability to come up with more repugnant group names than their competitors, while generally being unable to play more than two chords and incapable of singing in key, let alone in harmony'.

In that climate, it took courage to merge the two traditions. Only in Liverpool was it respectable to perform an overt country-rock hybrid. At the height of the Merseybeat boom, Sonny Webb and the Cascades revived George Jones songs like 'Who Shot Sam' and 'White Lightning' without alarming audiences at the Cavern Club. The Cascades later became the Hillsiders, Britain's top country band of the sixties; when they toured America in 1967, their Liverpool accents ensured them a sympathetic hearing, via an imagined link with the Beatles.

Outside Liverpool, an occasional breath of country air wafted across the beatgroup scene. Among their R&B covers, the Rolling Stones also performed Hank Snow's train song, 'I'm Movin' On', though they'd learned it from bluesman Ray Charles. In June 1964, during their first American tour, they were given a first-hand lesson in the emotional power of country music. 'We played a state fair in San Antonio, Texas,' recalls Bill Wyman. 'We stood on a big box about as big as a room, and played to these cowboys who were wandering about, looking at the rodeo or the agricultural displays. We shared the bill with Bobby Vee, who we thought was a bit of a joke. His band were all wearing Bermuda shorts on stage. But also on the bill was George Jones, and I've been a fan ever since. Every time I hear a song, my hair goes up on end. Mick and Keith loved him as well.'

Elsewhere on the purist London R&B scene, only eternal mavericks like the Downliners Sect could afford to flirt with the music of the white South. When they cut an album of recent Nashville hits, they persuaded Bob Morgan, head of A&R at Epic's Tennessee office, to boast: 'This package sounds more authentic than the *Grand Ole Opry*.'

Country was foreign territory to most British rock bands in the sixties. In the era of civil rights protests, there was more glamour and 'authenticity' to be had from the descendants of nineteenth-century slaves than from what was perceived as the music of their slavemasters. The snobbery which led British rock writer Steve Burgess to note that 'country audiences suffer from a total lack of the ability to be discriminating' imposed the same 'total lack' on rock fans, who seemed unable to perceive any difference between the bluegrass of Bill Monroe, the social realism of Merle Haggard and the mellifluous ballads of Jim Reeves.

There were momentary exceptions. 'Run For Your Life' and 'What Goes On' on the Beatles' *Rubber Soul* in late 1965 were a final reminder of the group's rockabilly roots; John Lennon even borrowed a few lines from Elvis Presley's 'Baby Let's Play House'. A few months later, the Rolling Stones recorded 'High And Dry', pitched midway between hillbilly and country blues. Pete Townshend toyed with a loping cowboy rhythm during the Who's mini-rock opera, 'A Quick One While He's Away'; while the Kinks' Ray Davies regularly exposed the family links between American string-band music and the British music-hall novelties of George Formby.

But the dominant rhythms of British rock in 1966 came from black America; and 1967's 'Summer Of Love' combined the spirit of San Francisco's hippies with a typically English whimsy borrowed from Lewis Carroll and Edward Lear.

Branded by its perceived links with Southern racism, the very accent of country music became a laughing-stock in mid-sixties Britain. The rare images of the American South which crossed the Atlantic carried an uncompromising sting: freedom marchers being attacked by white racists; TV's *Beverly Hillbillies*, in which a family of gormless rednecks was thrust into the heart of Hollywood sophistication (the series inspired Ray Davies to name a Kinks album *Muswell Hillbillies*); and movies like *In The Heat Of The Night*, in which Rod Steiger's bullnecked sheriff epitomized the hollow brutality assumed to be at the heart of Southern culture. It was all too easy to imagine Steiger relaxing after a hard day's lynching to the comforting sound of the *Grand Ole Opry*.

Until America's country heritage was reclaimed for the youth audience by the Byrds and Bob Dylan, similar experiments in Britain came from outside the rock and pop mainstream. The commercial success that balladeers like Tom Jones and Engelbert Humperdinck found with contemporary Nashville songs, such as 'Green Green Grass Of Home', 'Detroit City' and 'Release Me', convinced rock musicians that the country heritage was best ignored or denied.

Britain's rivals to Michael Nesmith, Gram Parsons and Chris Hillman were less fêted, and less influential. Gordon Huntley was the nation's nearest equivalent to Lloyd Green or J. D. Maness, the American steel players who dared to tangle with rock in the mid-sixties. He was leading a straitlaced dance band called the Hawaiian Serenaders when he met Jon Derek, and discovered a shared admiration for the western swing of Bob Wills. Together they formed Johnny and the Hounders, who developed into the Flintlocks, and briefly became Britain's answer to Buck Owens' Buckaroos. Jon Derek and his friend Jed Kelly passed through a succession of bands until 1968, when they formed Britain's first authentic country-rock combo, Country Fever, with ex-R&B musicians Albert Lee and Pat Donaldson. Meanwhile, Huntley had encountered the thin but vital strand of British country-folk –

led by the Strawbs, who as the Strawberry Hill Boys had played the Club Folksville in Putney, south London, billed as a 'famous country music trio'. Within a few months they'd switched allegiance to traditional folk, but never quite abandoned their country roots. More significant were Fairport Convention. Their role as the pioneers of electric folk-rock has been well documented. Equally renowned is their shift from contemporary material towards traditional fare, linking sixties rock to themes and tunes which had been passed from parent to child for centuries.

The original Fairport line-up included singer Ian Matthews. While his colleagues were infatuated by Britain's folk heritage, he was entranced by American traditions. 'Towards the end of my time with Fairport,' he explained, 'I was listening to Merle Haggard and Rick Nelson's country stuff, and the Byrds' *Sweetheart Of The Rodeo*.'

Matthews and Huntley combined forces in Matthews Southern Comfort, a deceptively modest band who drew together British folk and American country into a soft-rock style reminiscent of Crosby, Stills and Nash. Matthews supplied the rock sensibility, Huntley the trademark pedal steel; albums such as *Second Spring* and *Later That Same Year* won acclaim from both country and rock critics. Matthews boasted that 'You don't have to chew straw and wear a cowboy hat to play country music.'

Matthews Southern Comfort cracked under the pressures of success after scoring an unexpected hit with a smooth cover of Joni Mitchell's 'Woodstock'. In their wake, other British bands were inspired by the Band and the Burritos, and sought to prove that a credible amalgam of American roots influences was possible at long distance.

These outfits graduated towards the Nashville Room, a club situated next to a west London train station. Besides hosting stars from Nashville and Bakersfield, it showcased emerging country-rock artists. Its design mirrored the uncertainty of the London country scene: traditional western imagery, of cowboys, steeds and pursuing Indians, was swathed in psychedelic colours, painted with acid-flash extravagance. That uneasy marriage of psychedelic rock and country was evident on some of the pirate radio stations which broadcast in the late sixties. These provided an outlet for American music too controversial for the staid playlists of the BBC, but they also allowed country DJs like David Allan and Stephen West to spin singles by Merle Haggard, Tammy Wynette and Buck Owens, who were equally absent from BBC programming.

Typifying Britain's confusion were the activities of Country Fever. In Albert Lee, they boasted the finest country-rock guitarist ever to emerge east of the Atlantic. He was a one-man combination of James Burton, Clarence White and Carl Perkins, but such dexterity was wasted on backing American artists like Guy Mitchell, which is how the band earned their wages in 1968. Equally unrewarding was their liaison with Britain's first country label. Entrepreneur Gordon Smith assembled the talent, then nearly scuppered the venture by dubbing the label Confederate Records. He was gently advised that this might not be a diplomatic way of winning American friends, and Confederate duly became Lucky. Only in name, though: Lucky boasted Britain's finest guitar talent, but it had no idea what to do with him. Fortunately, Lee escaped in 1970 to form Head, Hands & Feet, who not only had a major label deal but also the confidence to tackle American roots from a uniquely British perspective.

Among Lee's contemporaries, only pedal steel ace B. J. Cole was able to escape the pull of America. Like Head, Hands & Feet, his early-seventies band Cochise were clearly influenced by the Band, but Cole's at times almost ambient playing ensured that they retained some flavour of their homeland. Over subsequent decades, he was in constant demand from British country performers, but he regularly sought out more challenging assignments, collaborating with such unlikely partners as John Cale and the Verve.

In August 1974, the Nashville Room discontinued its policy of booking nothing but country-based artists, just in time to welcome the burgeoning pub-rock and punk movements. Ironically, that decision coincided with another brief flurry of British country-rock. Orange Blossom picked up the mantle of Manassas and the Flying Burrito Brothers. Starry-Eyed And Laughing (named after a line from Bob Dylan's 'Chimes Of Freedom') updated the Byrds' 12-string jangle, but proved closer to *Mr Tambourine Man* than *Sweetheart Of The Rodeo*. Chilli Willi and the Red Hot Peppers were evidence of an ongoing British infatuation with western swing, but weren't as successful on record as in a sweaty London club. Kenny Johnson, a veteran of Merseybeat's Sonny Webb and the Cascades and the Hillsiders, formed his own National Band, sounding less like Michael Nesmith than a Liverpudlian Eagles. And still they kept coming: Meal Ticket, Prairie Oyster, all workmanlike club fare, but lacking anything resembling a mass audience. Most bizarre was the sight of TV wrestling star Brian Maxine attracting a bevy of Fairport Convention veterans to support him on two country albums in the mid-seventies.

British or American accents, songs about Kent or Kentucky, country style or country content? The British country-rock movement never found satisfactory answers. Critics who applauded Mick Jagger for his authentic Southern blues moan laughed at the idea of a cockney country singer.

Few performers managed to evade this prejudice. Olivia Newton-John turned to country after previous career routes in mainstream pop had petered out. Subsequent hits with unashamedly country material like 'Banks Of The Ohio' and 'Take Me Home, Country Roads' secured her status in Britain. Then, in 1973, she recorded 'Let Me Be There', a rousing pop confection tailored for Nashville tastes by its composer and producer, John Farrar, and by 1975 she had become the best-selling female country artist in America. While Olivia Newton-John never disguised her origins, Elton John had no qualms about shifting personae. On his self-titled 1970 album, he sometimes sang like a sensitive London suburbanite, sometimes like an Alabama boy who'd learned to speak from Rolling Stones records. 'No Shoestrings On Louise' echoed the Mick Jagger who'd adopted the voice of a tobacco-chewin' cracker for the Stones' 'Prodigal Son'. When John sang phrases like 'boss man's cow', you could trace the lineage back through three generations of Jagger's vocal identity (polite middle-class English, rough-necked working-class cockney, devilish Deep South farmhand) into an entirely mythical America.

No British album of the period evoked the American South as boldly as Elton John's *Tumbleweed Connection*. As the mouthpiece for lyricist Bernie Taupin, John had to play an apologist for the Confederate cause in the Civil War. 'I'll take my horse and I'll ride the Northern plain,' he sang on 'My Father's Gun', 'to wear the colour of the greys and join the fight again.' Taupin's ideal South didn't include racial discrimination or slavery: 'As soon as this is over we'll go home, to plant the seeds of justice in our bones . . . There'll be laughter when the bells of freedom ring.' Laughter was in short supply on either side of the great divide; as for the seeds of justice, they were still in dispute a century later.

Was Taupin imagining an alternative history, like Hank Williams Jr's rabble-rousing 'If The South Woulda Won'? More likely he was so entranced by his role model for *Tumbleweed Connection*, the Band's second album, that he forgot that politics could run deeper than a poem. All across the album were images that pastiched Robbie Robertson's, when they weren't stealing from Bob Dylan. 'I hung my head in shame', John sang on 'Ballad Of A Well-Known Gun', but Taupin was the guilty man, purloining the key line from Dylan's 'Lo And Behold'.

So whole-hearted was John and Taupin's adoption of their borrowed garb that outrage became irrelevant. Their American South was no more realistic than their frontier railroad-station on the cover artwork, which on closer examination proved to date from Victorian England. ('Driving Through Mythical America' was the phrase that lyricist Clive James coined for an album by British singer Pete Atkin around the same time.) The conceit was handled with impressive aplomb. Beyond the pleasure of spotting the homages to *The Band* – the horns from 'Dixie', the farmer's lament from 'King Harvest' – the album delivered a forty-minute baptism in foreign waters. Gordon Huntley, on loan from Matthews Southern Comfort, laced a beautiful steel solo through 'Country Comfort', and in the same song, Taupin hit on a celebratory couplet that Robbie Robertson might have relished. Country music, Elton John sang, was 'the sweetest sound my ears have ever known, just an old-fashioned feeling fully-grown'.

With words and voices, British artists could only approach

country as actors – a generation further removed from the American rock artists who donned rural garb at the start of the seventies. As Sid Griffin, leader of the transatlantic country-rock band, the Coal Porters, points out, 'Musical notes do not respect international borders. You have to sing in your native tongue. But you certainly don't have to play in it.'

11 Tantamount to Treason
Michael Nesmith, 1969–1992

Michael Nesmith came closer than anyone to meeting the demands of Gram Parsons' Cosmic American Music. 'Coming from Texas,' he explained in 1970, 'my roots are in R&B but somehow I feel more comfortable in country and western.' Today, he takes a broader view: 'As you mature, you find out more about yourself. Growing up in the Tex-Mex culture, I realize Latin music rhythm patterns had a tremendous effect on the way I thought about music and the way I wrote.'

Through the seventies, Nesmith explored the links and tensions between these three styles. His late-sixties experimentation in Nashville had passed virtually unnoticed, so his formation of the First National Band in 1969 was greeted as a stunning reinvention. But the transition from the Monkees' country-rock sessions was entirely seamless: the only fracture was in the mind of the spectators, who had to adjust their preconceptions of Nesmith's capabilities.

The First National Band was a gathering of old allies. Drummer John Ware and bassist John London had played behind Linda Ronstadt in the Corvettes. Ronstadt's mild success with Nesmith songs like 'Different Drum' and 'Some Of Shelly's Blues' during her liaison with the Stone Poneys cemented the relationship.

Completing the line-up was steel player O. J. 'Red' Rhodes. 'He and I were very compatible musically, right from the start,' Nesmith confirms. 'He was the guy who first schooled me in playing the pedal steel, during the early Monkees sessions. His steel guitar gave my music a mellifluous, smooth quality, and I was always surprised how few of my contemporaries – people like Poco – picked up on that. Other people quickly moved on from steel to bottleneck. But steel has its own sound. For instance, it's the driving instrument on Sheryl Crow's "All I Wanna Do" – not played very well, admittedly, but it lends that record a quality that it otherwise wouldn't have.'

Within a year of leaving the Monkees, Nesmith recorded a trilogy of albums with the First National Band: *Magnetic South*, *Loose Salute* and *Nevada Fighter*. They boasted generic artwork, conceived by California cult figure Dean Torrence (of the surf duo Jan and Dean). *Magnetic South* – its title a statement of pride – placed the American eagle in an emblematic tapestry; by the end of the trilogy, the eagle had trapped a Native American warrior and some flowing stems of greenery beneath its claws. The defender of the national spirit had become a pillager of the land and its occupants. Meanwhile, *Loose Salute* offered a caricature of a bloated, beaten army general (was the resemblance to President Lyndon Johnson accidental?), taking the ceremonial salute on the back of a mouse. Nesmith's Cosmic America was a distorted reflection of its forefathers' ideals: it was no coincidence that *Nevada Fighter* was 'dedicated to the Great People of the Navajo'.

The three albums displayed a conceptual integrity that exposed Nesmith as country-rock's resident intellectual. The music on *Magnetic South* lived up to his claim that 'Hank Williams, Jerry Lee Lewis and Jimmie Rodgers are to me something of a musical triumvirate. Somehow I always get back to them. They, like Dylan, Presley, Cash and the Beatles, had, and have, a clearly defined musical position – a pure approach to what they have sung and written – free from euphemisms and alive with their own emotions.' But there was an emotional distance in Nesmith's voice which left him less a participant than a commentator.

Indeed, his stance anticipated post-modernism. As Nesmith bravely revived the yodel, missing from country music for years, he passed judgement on the genre from which that archaic sound had come. 'I love it here on the range,' he sang in the Jerry Lee-style 'Mama Nantucket', but 'I would love it more if it changed'.

Loose Salute was released just three months later. The least adventurous and most homogeneous of the trilogy, it compressed all the stylistic chaos of his Monkees experiments into concise songs, bridging folk, traditional country, rock'n'roll, Latin and LA country-rock. 'Listen To The Band' was delivered from its original incarnation as a country/big band hybrid into a simple hillbilly hoedown; Patsy Cline's 'I Fall To Pieces' fitted as well in this company as Nesmith's appropriately wordy 'Conversations'.

Having stumbled across a coherent style, most musicians would have camped there. Instead, Nesmith quickly distorted the neat picture of *Loose Salute*. During the sessions for *Nevada Fighter*, the First National Band imploded, and Nesmith finished the record with Rhodes and several members of Elvis Presley's band, including James Burton, Ronnie Tutt and Glen Hardin. All three men were later recruited by Gram Parsons for his *GP* sessions. *Nevada Fighter* was a transitional work, which Nesmith filled with borrowed tunes, including the cowboy ballad 'Tumblin' Tumbleweeds', first recorded by the Sons Of The Pioneers in the 1930s. Nesmith's vocal floated through the track like a spacewalker drifting away from his ship. Echoed, shifted out of phase, cloaked in distortion, it added an eerie context to the breeze that swayed the desert tumbleweeds.

That track was a preview of *Tantamount To Treason* – 'a very strange record', as Nesmith admits. It was the sole incarnation of the Second (and last) National Band, a unit with a built-in knowledge of its own imminent demise. 'I knew that I wasn't going to be able to keep the band going anymore,' Nesmith explains. 'The LA music scene for country had absolutely dried up. That might sound strange, because it was the time that the Burritos and Poco and the Eagles were all working. But they weren't playing the country music that I was. They mutated away from the National Band style. I stayed pretty much in that pocket, because I was listening to Jimmie Rodgers as an influence, but those other guys were listening to me! It wasn't like they were going back to the roots of the music and drawing from that. All they were doing was recycling the LA music scene. So because I was aware that our time was limited, I wanted to push out the boat and see what would happen.'

Tantamount to treason indeed, especially for anyone who looked to country-rock for stability amidst the fall-out of psychedelia. Nesmith's lyrics had always tended towards the conceptual – not for him the working-man's solidarity that was country's common language – but now he began to rely on abstract imagery, sounding a death-knell to his commercial expectations. 'That was naturally the way I wrote,' he says today, 'but I was also aware that it was new for country music. And I knew I would pay a price. It absolutely shut off the possibility of selling large quantities of records.' The album included 'In The Afternoon', probably the first country song ever to use the word 'domicile'. 'Yeah, in country music that's a double-wide trailer!' Nesmith laughs. 'I don't know whether or not I regret using language like that, but I couldn't have done it any differently. I couldn't have spelled it out, and written about car-wrecks and how I felt about daddy.'

Language wasn't the only barrier on *Tantamount To Treason*. The music constantly shifted perspective: one moment, Nesmith was delivering a wonderfully affectionate 'Bonaparte's Retreat', signing up to a tradition of folk and country standards. The next, the orthodox country-rock scenery of 'Lazy Lady' was decaying around him, like celluloid melting in the projector.

There is nothing in the entire history of country music like the album's strangest outing, a trip down 'Highway 99 With Mélange'. Nesmith sketches the landscape: 'That's a song about sexual tension that develops between a guy and a friend's wife with whom he's driving to San Francisco, up Highway 99 through Bakersfield, which of course is the heart of California country territory. So we played with that in-car sensibility. Once we hit on that, we could put the windows down, and listen to what was going on outside.' And outside was the palette of nature, which flowed into a country boogie on the car radio. Then time collapsed: the music slipped and surged like a tape machine fed by a variable current. There was no horizon to offer a sense of balance, just a constant inversion of dimensions and surfaces. 'I apologize for being pretentious,' Nesmith says, 'but I think we created a kind of sonic poetry there.' Cosmic American Music, without a doubt, but it echoed the central dilemma of modernism: after you've deconstructed an art-form, what do you put in its place?

There was no road back from *Tantamount To Treason* to the safety of *Loose Salute*. Neither was there a commercial demand for Nesmith to pursue his aural adventures. 'RCA had unrealistic hopes of what my records would sell,' Nesmith admits, 'based on the fact I had been in the Monkees.' His deal had two albums to run, but Nesmith had to finance the records himself. He sardonically titled one offering *And The Hits Just Keep On Comin'*; the next *Pretty Much Your Standard Ranch Stash*.

And The Hits didn't come close to matching the commercial promise of its title, but Nesmith did solve the mystery of how to replace his National Bands. Using just his own guitar and voice, and the pedal steel of Red Rhodes, he constructed a set of meditative songs only loosely utilizing the melodic structures of country. Lyrically, they were closer to William Wordsworth than Hank Williams: 'While lightly perusing my state of affairs,' he sang on 'Harmony Constant', 'With nothing apparently wrong, A silent and quiet restoration occurs, Of emotions forgotten and gone.' But Nesmith hadn't forgotten his ambiguous heritage as a Southern Man. Inside the gatefold sleeve he posed in a sumptuous mansion, a quartet of beautiful women (black and white: lovers? slaves?) at his side. On his knee wasn't a shotgun or a bullwhip but a book: *Bury My Heart At Wounded Knee*, the account of the white man's betrayal of the Native American.

In the mid-seventies, Nesmith founded his Pacific Arts Corporation, and shed most of his remaining audience with a weighty concept album, *The Prison*. He retained his links with country, producing albums for Red Rhodes and the English folk-pop singer, Ian Matthews. By his own account, he was still setting the pace for the LA aristocracy: 'I made a record with Ian called *Valley Hi*, which included "Seven Bridges Road". Ian and I were putting on harmony parts, and on one of them I got the notes slightly wrong, but it worked, so we left it. Years later, the Eagles sang the same song, and they took that arrangement, every last note. It was so exact that they even copied my mistake.'

The Latin-flavoured 'Rio' finally brought Nesmith a worldwide hit single in the late seventies. With inspired wilfulness, he cut that record, and its eclectic album, *From An Engine To The Photon Wing*, in Nashville. 'That was the one time in my life that I hit any opposition from the Nashville musicians,' he recalls. 'In the sixties, they managed to deal with the fact that I wanted to use banjos and fiddles on a rock'n'roll song. In fact, they relished the experience. But with *Photon Wing*, I ran into a full-on rebellion, with the guys virtually refusing to play.

'David Briggs put a band of first-rate session players together. But I used my own bass player: I brought in this white guy to explain reggae to them. I figured they would never understand it if I just told them about it: they had to hear it. And if I'd brought a black bassist into Nashville, they'd have run him out of town. That was OK, just about, until I told them I wanted to do the old cowboy song "Navajo Trail" with a reggae rhythm. They thought I'd lost my mind.'

After touring with what Nesmith calls 'a straight-up, no-nonsense country-rock band' in the late seventies, he abandoned the genre and record-making. Instead, he became a video pioneer, selling the concept for MTV to Warner Brothers and American Express, and eventually emerging as a movie producer.

Not until 1992 did he resurface as an active country-rocker, signing the guitar collective the Hellecasters to his record label, and fronting the band on the road. 'We revived all these First National Band tunes,' he recalls, 'and that's when I really locked into hardcore Latin music.' Nashville might finally have been ready for the First National Band in the early nineties, but connecting with the times was never close to a priority for Michael Nesmith.

12 Pickin' Up the Pieces
Country-rock reaches the California mainstream, 1968–1972: Linda
Ronstadt; Poco; Rick Nelson; the Flying Burrito Brothers; Emmylou Harris;
Gram Parsons

In the summer of 1968, Los Angeles rock was in stasis. The Byrds
were floundering; Buffalo Springfield had split; everyone else was
marking time. The inactivity proved to be merely a pause for
breath. By winter, the LA aristocracy had regrouped into
impromptu units, which were cemented in spring 1969. For the
next three years, these groups – the revamped Byrds, the Burritos,
Crosby, Stills and Nash, Poco, Dillard & Clark – traded members
and reputations, every shift of allegiance analysed by the emerging
rock press. Too many critics had revered the Byrds and the
Springfield for their fall-out to be ignored. There was a spurious
glamour by association for every cast-off from a name band, a
process which led inevitably to the personality-free 'supergroups'
of the seventies – the belief that throwing together someone who'd
once played bass with the Byrds, a former Poco guitarist and Linda
Ronstadt's ex-boyfriend might spark something more creative
than avarice.

In 1968, Los Angeles was still untouched by this cynicism, and
each amalgam of talent flowered with optimism. The influence of
Bob Dylan's *John Wesley Harding* and the anti-politics of the
Diggers guided them towards music that was simple, acoustic and
attuned to the sensibility of the earth. Respect for the planet
encouraged a vague environmentalism; equally pervasive was the
feeling that country, the sound of the soil, echoed this shift in
perception.

Los Angeles was where these idealistic missionaries for a new
age collided with transplanted Southerners, for whom country was
a heritage, not a symbol. Pedal steel player Al Perkins, whose
country-rock history stretches from the Flying Burrito Brothers to

Emmylou Harris's Nash Ramblers, was one of those drawn west. He was raised in West Texas, where, he says, 'there's nothing much but oilfields, drilling rigs and sand-dunes'. While California revelled in new technology, Perkins recalls that his father 'would put a wire from our old radio into the ground. In certain atmospheric conditions, we could pick up the *Louisiana Hayride*. I recall liking what I called hillbilly, but which was actually bluegrass. I called everything hillbilly back then. I realize that I loved the edge that guys like George Jones and Webb Pierce had, and Buck Owens. When they started putting strings on their records, I thought they'd sold out to pop, and I didn't care for that.' Around 1968, Perkins was playing with a band called Foxx: 'We played the Rickshaw Club in north Dallas. Groups ended up there on a Saturday night after they'd played other clubs. This band Felicity used to ask us to play country songs, because they really loved the Dillards, and the Byrds, that early country-rock stuff.' Impressed that Perkins owned a steel guitar, Felicity invited him to their rehearsal room, 'an old house in the woods up in East Texas. I went up there and fell in love with country all over again. I had tears in my eyes, because of how it made me feel to play it. There were these long-hair guys playing real country music, but with a little different flair.'

Felicity and Perkins relocated to California, renaming themselves Shiloh after the battleground that witnessed one of the South's most valiant defeats in the Civil War. They were enticed to the coast by country-pop star Kenny Rogers, who'd agreed to produce them, and in 1970 they cut an unassuming country-rock album for Amos Records. Perkins notes: 'The label was started by Jimmy Bowen, who ended up as one of the most important producers and executives in country music history. The guy he chose to look after us was Bruce Hinton, who was the head of MCA in the nineties. Our keyboard player was Jim Ed Norman, who wound up running Warner Brothers' Nashville Division in the nineties. And our drummer was Don Henley.'

Shiloh became regulars at the Troubadour. 'One night,' recalled Linda Ronstadt, 'I was on my way to the bathroom there, and this band Shiloh come on and start doing an exact version of "Silver Threads And Golden Needles". I was flabbergasted.'

Ronstadt was another West Coast pilgrim. She was born in Tucson, Arizona, sixty miles from the Mexican border, and raised on a stew of country, bluegrass, folk and mariachi music. She bought into the California myth of a teen paradise, and wound up on the LA folk circuit, hanging out with the guys who formed the Doors, plus songwriters Bobby Kimmel and Kenny Edwards. With them, she formed the Stone Poneys – an arty folk trio named after a Charley Patton blues song. But Ronstadt wasn't comfortable with either style: 'I was fighting to do country all along. I sang with Hearts & Flowers on their records, because we had the same producer, and they'd let me sing country. But my manager, Herb Cohen, who also handled Frank Zappa, used to say, "Country music – don't be stupid! You're too country for pop, and too pop for country, so you'll end up nowhere."'

She found solace at the Palomino, a Los Angeles country venue where Gram Parsons was amusing himself by signing up for the weekly talent contests. There she met California country legend Merle Haggard. 'She was a fan of mine,' he remembered, 'but she was too young to get into the club. Somebody came to the stage and said, "There's this girl who's just signed with Capitol. She's back in the kitchen because they won't let her into the cocktail area since she's under age." So I went back into the kitchen and there was Linda. I never forgot her. I think she's the best singer I've ever heard.'

Freed from the Stone Poneys in early 1968, Ronstadt recorded *Hand Sown . . . Home Grown* with producer Chip Douglas, who tried to hustle her towards pop. The tension highlighted the uncertain marriage between country and rock. On 'Silver Threads And Golden Needles', the country standard which she had learned from a Dusty Springfield record, Ronstadt couldn't escape the vocal purity of her folk heritage. Behind her clashed the banshee wail of an electric violin and a fuzz guitar. Stylistically displaced, the track didn't convince on any level.

Elsewhere, Ronstadt was the most country element on show – as on 'Break My Mind', where she anticipated the way that Emmylou Harris would bite down on a syllable midway through a line. She delivered 'We Need A Whole Lot More Of Jesus (And A Lot Less Rock & Roll)' without a hint of the irony that Roger McGuinn had brought to the Byrds' '(I Like) The Christian Life'. Loretta Lynn would have been proud of her.

Travelling to Nashville to record 1970's *Silk Purse*, Ronstadt belatedly realized that 'there's such an enormous difference between country music in Nashville and country music in California. They have a different concept of rhythm section down there. They can make an album in three days, just assembly line stuff.' To resist that flow, an artist had to jam something in the machinery – a vision, a concept, even a personality. Instead, Ronstadt was a spectator as the Tennessee record machine churned out rhythm tracks by the yard, reducing even Dillard & Clark's eerie evocation of the Gothic folk tradition, 'She Darked The Sun', to three minutes of emotional absence. The album cover portrayed Ronstadt as a hillbilly simpleton, happy with the hogs; Nashville's finest didn't do anything to alter that impression.

Back at the Troubadour, Ronstadt licked the hogs' mud out of her wounds. She'd assembled a band who shared her love for traditional country, and could translate it for a rock audience. Through the Corvettes passed musicians like John London and John Ware (both of whom later joined Mike Nesmith), Jeff Hanna (en route to the Nitty Gritty Dirt Band) and Chris Darrow. Dazzled by Shiloh's performance at the Troubadour, she teased away their drummer, Don Henley. Her boyfriend, John David Souther, had his own country-rock band, Longbranch Pennywhistle: their guitarist, Glenn Frey, joined Linda's touring unit. When Bernie Leadon quit the Flying Burrito Brothers, he too needed a job. Bassist Randy Meisner was stolen from Rick Nelson's Stone Canyon Band.

The *Linda Ronstadt* album was built around this core, and it presented an altogether more certain singer. The record was soaked in lazy bluegrass harmonies inspired by the perfectionism of Crosby, Stills and Nash. It was the sound of Los Angeles, 1971 – a sound shared with those who'd taken a similar route along the borders of rock and country.

The originators of the seventies LA country-rock style were Poco, formed by Richie Furay and Jim Messina after the collapse of Buffalo Springfield. Poco achieved a democratic spirit that had proved impossible for the Springfield, and Furay and Messina shared the creative weight with Randy Meisner, George Grantham and Rusty Young.

Like Al Perkins and Sneaky Pete Kleinow, Young migrated to Los Angeles to capitalize on the city's lack of pedal steel virtuosos. In summer 1968 he was invited to audition by Gram Parsons, who claimed he was about to launch a band called the Flying Burrito Brothers. When Young discovered that Parsons was the new group's only member, he opted to join Furay and Messina. Furay then approached Parsons to join Poco, and was rejected in turn.

Instead, Young, Messina and Furay expanded into a quintet. Though, as Young recalls, 'we all liked country music', Poco never masqueraded as honky-tonk cowboys or hillbillies. Instead, they built on the gentle melancholy which had been Furay's trademark in Buffalo Springfield, topped with effervescent harmonies and a disposition that was pure southern California.

Their sunshine smiles didn't survive their début album, *Pickin' Up The Pieces*, as Randy Meisner quit when he was excluded from the mixdown sessions. But there was no trace of antagonism in the music. This was country-rock for people who didn't like country, sparkling with instrumental and vocal dexterity.

The title track set the tone, with its fantasy image of cowboys round the campfire, 'happy sittin', pickin' and a-grinnin''. Furay's good-time feel was irresistible: 'Somebody yelled out at me, "Hey, country music and harmony kind of make it, on a Sunday afternoon."' It was a promise of togetherness, of repairing the fractures in American society, of (sure enough) *Pickin' Up The Pieces*.

Any album dedicated to 'the backwoods of meadows and memories', and launched on Furay's exultant cry, 'It's a good morning and I feel fine!' ought to have been marketed as a universal panacea. In the wake of *Nashville Skyline*, Poco's début did register in the best-seller lists, and it outsold the Burritos' *The Gilded Palace Of Sin* by two-to-one. But, as Randy Meisner observed, 'When it came out, there wasn't really a market for it. You had to play either country or rock.' Unless, of course, you were Bob Dylan.

Leaving Poco, Randy Meisner joined forces with a man who

very much wanted to be Bob Dylan: former fifties teen idol and sixties soft-pop star Rick Nelson. He had literally grown up in public, on his family's TV show, which became the launch pad for his career as a singer in 1957. Despite having the legendary session guitarist James Burton at his disposal, the teenage Ricky was quickly ushered away from his first love, Carl Perkins' mean-eyed brand of rockabilly, towards a mellower style.

By the mid-sixties, Nelson was marooned in premature middle-age, offering sentimental ballads to an audience ripe for the Rolling Stones. 'I went through about four years not knowing what I wanted to do,' he admitted in 1971. 'I was playing night-clubs, and I wasn't digging it one bit. Eventually I decided that I'd rather work in a gas station than carry on with that trip, so about a year and a half ago I sat down and thought about where I was going. It was all about clearing my mind and going back to basics. Randy Meisner was looking for something to do, and he came to me.'

Nelson introduced his Stone Canyon Band via a series of Hollywood club gigs, mixing countrified versions of his vintage hits with copious Dylan tunes. Their easy-paced renditions of 'She Belongs To Me', 'If You Gotta Go' and 'I Shall Be Released' recalled the Flying Burrito Brothers, though Nelson's voice sounded anonymous alongside Gram Parsons' or even Richie Furay's. Drawn back to the nostalgia circuit by the lure of money, Nelson outraged a sell-out audience at New York's Madison Square Garden with his new country-rock sound – a collision which he recounted on 'Garden Party', a surprise No. 1 in 1972. It was by far the biggest-selling single of the country-rock era and, so it transpired, also a dead end, as within five years Nelson was reduced to playing oldies gigs alongside other fifties veterans who had never dared to take a similar leap of faith.

To replace Randy Meisner, Poco enlisted Timothy Schmit from the band Glad (what heritage could be more appropriate for a member of this sunny-eyed group?). Like the Burritos, they embarked on their second album at the end of 1969. While Gram Parsons and Chris Hillman's vision encompassed traditional gospel tunes and Rolling Stones songs, Poco usually set themselves stricter limits, only stumbling when they ignored their own rules. Nearly half of the 1970 LP *Poco* was devoted to an instrumental, 'El Tonto De Nadie Regresa'. 'We were rehearsing at the Troubadour,' explained George Grantham, 'and we just started going with it.' The fiery musical interplay of their début was soon dissipated: Poco merely revealed that they lacked the spontaneity to match the extended jams of the Grateful Dead or Quicksilver Messenger Service. It was an experiment they never repeated.

Although their first album had been well received, many critics held Poco in growing contempt. 'I didn't really think they existed,' says Greil Marcus today. 'They were just a blip on a trend, slavishly following what Dylan had done. Groups like that were horrible.'

After 1970, Poco (indeed, the whole Los Angeles country-rock industry) were the victims of a prolonged media assault, inspired as much by their geographical base as by their music. *Rolling Stone*, published in San Francisco, set the era's critical agenda, and its staff (of whom Marcus was one) grew increasingly impatient with the LA vibe. The media treatment of Crosby, Stills, Nash and Young exemplified the process. Over the course of summer 1970, their reputation declined from spokesmen for rock's radical left to purveyors of self-obsessed soft-rock. And this was the band whom most of the country-rockers took as their model.

What angered the San Francisco critics was the audible shift in LA rock away from roots music. Many LA bands were now incorporating elements of country, but the genre's awkward edges were smoothed into something seamless and, at worst, anonymous. Each fresh wave of country-rockers slipped further away from the source.

Nobody illustrated that shift more clearly than the standard-bearers of Cosmic American Music – the Flying Burrito Brothers. Stripped of their cheerleader, Gram Parsons, in the summer of 1970, the Burritos stumbled on as a quartet for several months.

They'd lost an erratic but visionary songwriter; in his place, they recruited Rick Roberts, an amiable singer rooted in the Byrds, not Buck Owens. 'I had been trying unsuccessfully to get a solo deal together,' he recalled. 'I had already bought my ticket back from

Los Angeles to Colorado when I gave it one more try, and went with a friend of mine to see Columbia Records. The guy I saw there was Ed Tickner.' He was in the unusual position of managing the Burritos from his desk at a rival company. Loyalty to his band came first, and Roberts was sent for a rehearsal. 'They weren't really looking for another singer,' he says, 'and I wasn't looking for a band, but it fell together real nice so we decided to go along with it.'

As Roberts saw it, 'I wasn't a direct replacement for Gram.' But without Parsons, the band were bereft of new material: 'They didn't have an active songwriter, as Chris Hillman was not writing much.' Roberts arrived with a sackful of ideas, and at least one classic soft-rock ballad, dedicated to his home state of Colorado. Through early 1971, the Burritos cut a self-titled album as well-crafted as any Los Angeles record of that decade.

Full of subtle pleasures, *The Flying Burrito Brothers* was a perfect blend of the city's pop heritage and the new singer-songwriter movement. As Rick Roberts admitted, 'I was writing songs that were not so honky-tonk country as Gram Parsons had been writing.'

Even when the revamped Burritos offered country, with the trucker's anthem 'White Line Fever', they managed all the hillbilly passion of James Taylor. No wonder Parsons regarded their activities as a betrayal: 'My first reaction was like when a mother loses one of her young. My eggs were broken, you know. I felt jealousy that Chris [Hillman] could prostitute himself in such a way.' In retrospect, Hillman is keen to distance himself from the record: 'That's not an album I'm particularly fond of.' The Burritos weren't even making a good whore's wages: their third album followed the altogether inferior *Burrito Deluxe* into commercial insignificance.

Even before it was released, steel player Sneaky Pete Kleinow quit, tired of the constant travelling. As before, Ed Tickner found a replacement: Al Perkins, from Shiloh. 'Ed heard me on Kenny Rogers' records,' Perkins explains, 'and called me to audition. That was Friday, and they wanted me to start on Monday. I'd never even heard their stuff, so they gave me some records to listen to. Within three days, we were out on the road.'

Over the next nine months, the Burritos jettisoned all their remaining connections with Gram Parsons' group. By December 1971, Rick Roberts was the longest-serving member, a veteran of fifteen months' standing. The band served their final months as the Hot Burrito Revue, incorporating Country Gazette – an aggregation of bluegrass virtuosos such as Byron Berline, Alan Munde, Roger Bush and Kenny Wertz, whose breakneck renditions of 'Orange Blossom Special' and 'Foggy Mountain Breakdown' were more convincing than Roberts' efforts to play a double role as Parsons and Hillman.

'It got to the point,' Hillman explains, 'as with the Byrds, that I just wasn't enjoying being in the band. Bernie Leadon left a little while before me, and when he went, my interest vanished as well. I shouldn't have stayed long enough to do the *Last Of The Red Hot Burritos* live album, though it was OK, I guess. But I was getting no pleasure from playing with those guys. Nothing against them as people or musicians, it just wasn't what I wanted to do.'

As the Hot Burrito Revue slowly cooled, Rick Roberts and Chris Hillman toyed with the idea of recruiting a female singer. They approached Linda Ronstadt, but she had more of a career to lose than the Burritos. In the final weeks of 1971, Roberts and Kenny Wertz stepped into a bar in Washington, DC, led by a friend who demanded they hear the resident singer. 'I was on a break,' she says, 'but they asked me to get back on stage. I wasn't too enthusiastic, but I did "It Wasn't God Who Made Honky-Tonk Angels", one of the first country songs I ever learned. Rick and Kenny liked it, and the next night they brought Chris Hillman with them.' Hillman only attended under duress, but then sat open-mouthed. 'I told you so,' said Roberts.

The singer was Emmylou Harris, a single mother whose aspirations of rivalling Joni Mitchell had been squashed by her initial exposure to the music business. 'When I hit my teenage years, I got into folk,' she says, 'and through that into bluegrass and mountain music. My brother was a big country fan, so I heard Hank Williams and Buck Owens through him. But folk was what I really loved, and what I wanted to sing.' A subscriber to *Sing Out!* magazine, her idols included folksingers Joan Baez, Judy Collins, Pete Seeger and Tom Rush.

She set out for Greenwich Village in 1967, and won a regular opening spot at Gerde's Folk City, one of the venues that could claim to have launched Bob Dylan. In 1969 she was offered a recording contract by the tiny Jubilee label. 'I thought that was it,' she says. 'Once I'd made a record, what could go wrong?' But between the intention and the act came expediency: 'The guy who was managing me signed Jubilee to produce me, which I didn't know anything about. The album was thrown together in nine hours. It was not exactly a joyful experience for me.'

The *Gliding Bird* album, a misfiring vehicle for her illusions about country and folk, didn't sell; Harris's marriage to songwriter Tom Slocum collapsed; and with her baby daughter she returned to her parents' home in Washington. By day, she exhibited show homes to young families in more secure situations than her own. At night, she sang cover versions in bars, while her parents minded her child. Apart from a one-off single disguised as 'Hannah Brown', there was nothing to suggest that Harris would ever escape the club circuit.

Without making any promises, the Burritos invited her to a series of East Coast gigs. 'Next they asked me to join the band,' she recalled, 'and I said yes, but they disbanded a couple of days later.'

Harris's recollection is only partially accurate. The Burritos survived, albeit in ragged style, for another three months, but the departure of Chris Hillman and Al Perkins robbed them of their credibility. Both musicians had been enticed into a new unit, as Perkins explains: 'We'd been travelling up and down the north-east coast, doing university shows, and we kept running into Stephen Stills, who was touring with the Memphis Horns. He wanted to record a multi-faceted concept album, presenting a different form of music on each side, and he suggested that the Burritos should help him make the country side. He was recording in Florida, so we arranged to go down and work with him. We did that for a couple of weeks, and then he proposed that we form a band. It was then he let slip that Chris and I were the only ones he was interested in.'

Fired by Stills' enthusiasm, Hillman and Perkins quit the Burritos. The unnamed band played their first acoustic gig at the

Cellar Door club in Washington with a female singer: Emmylou Harris.

'At that point,' Perkins recalls, 'Chris was still telling me and the Burritos' manager, Ed Tickner, that he wanted to work with Emmy. He was so sure about it that he even wrote to Gram Parsons, saying he'd discovered this amazing girl singer, and they were going to work together. Then Chris and I got sucked into Stephen Stills' band, who were now called Manassas, full-time, and Emmy just went by the board. That's when Gram suddenly reappeared, and took over where Chris's intentions had left off.'

Perkins makes it sound like robbery; Hillman insisted that he begged Parsons to pay Harris a visit. 'I had to damn near break his arm to call her,' he said.

Gram didn't call, but turned up unannounced at Clyde's, her Washington hangout on Monday nights. By this time, Harris was presumably immune to the shock of finding ex-Byrds and Burritos in her tiny audience. She wasn't immediately impressed: Parsons had been drinking, and she didn't trust his motives. But when he revealed that Hillman had suggested he should meet her, she relented: 'We went down to the cellar, sat among the beer crates and worked up "I Fall To Pieces" and "That's All It Took". It was a rainy night and only about five people were in the audience. We just did the two numbers, then chatted and exchanged phone numbers. Gram said he would be in touch.' She didn't see him again for a year, but regularly he'd call and promise that he was about to start work on an album. After a while, she grew sceptical, the phone calls further apart. Emmylou Harris kept playing at Clyde's, convinced that her promised land was a mirage.

'Merle Haggard is a great artist and a great person, a great human being. Great everything,' Gram Parsons told A&M's Chuck Casell in the spring of 1972, during a rambling interview designed to provide copy for *Last Of The Red Hot Burritos* – a live album on which Parsons didn't even appear.

Haggard was Parsons' country-music hero. He had lived out the persona that Johnny Cash impersonated: the ex-con whose psyche was scarred by the years he'd wasted behind bars. For Haggard, jailhouse tales like 'Life In Prison' and 'Sing Me Back Home' were real life edited into verse and chorus. When Parsons sang those tunes with the Byrds and Burritos, aping every nuance of Merle's weary precision, rock audiences took him at face value. They didn't realize that Haggard was a fantasy figure for Gram. As Chris Hillman put it succinctly, 'Gram was into playing out the rock lifestyle. He was into playing out the role of Hank Williams.' When Gram sang Merle, the two roles were combined.

At the end of 1971, when Parsons realized that he was not about to become an honorary member of the Rolling Stones, he made a conciliatory call to the Burritos' manager Ed Tickner. Gram's deal with A&M had collapsed after his abortive 1970 sessions, but Tickner remembered Warner Brothers' enthusiasm for the Burritos four years earlier, and contacted their president, Mo Ostin.

By January 1972 Gram Parsons had signed his final deal, pledging to deliver two albums over the next two years. Tickner then pulled another master-stroke: he arranged for Parsons to meet Merle Haggard.

'We were talking about the concept of him doing an album with me,' Gram explained a few months later. 'And then, we both figured we didn't have enough time. If we were going to do it together it would be sort of difficult.' Or, as Chris Hillman put it, 'Gram was drunk. So Merle quit.' Haggard wasn't unfamiliar with alcohol – he had recorded 'Tonight The Bottle Let Me Down' and 'Think I'll Just Stay Here And Drink', after all – but getting sloppy in the studio wasn't the way to make records. Why should the poet of the American working man waste time on a hippie who wanted to be a country star?

In 1968, the Byrds and the British rock band Family appeared at a rock festival in Rome. Flying back to London, Parsons met Rick Grech, Family's violinist and bass player. Both men loved country music, but that wasn't their only connection. 'One of them had a bottle of tequila, one a bottle of vodka. And that was how their lovely relationship began,' says Grech's widow Jenny, with the grim irony of a woman who has watched her husband drug himself to death.

The two men became friends, hanging out in London before the Byrds flew home to LA, and again when Grech – now with Blind Faith – toured the West Coast in 1969. Parsons visited the Grech family in 1971; in the summer of 1972, sidelined by the collapse of the Haggard sessions, he responded immediately when Rick requested his assistance in a recording project.

'Rick was making a country album with a doctor friend, Sam Hutt [alias Hank Wangford],' Jenny Grech explains. 'Gram and his wife Gretchen hung out at the farm with us. It was like a re-bonding of kindred spirits – they'd ride go-karts around the roads, pass out in the fields drunk.' Parsons also encouraged Grech to resume his occasional heroin use. 'The drug thing was a huge problem,' Jenny admits, 'and I had to battle Rick with it, probably until the day he died. I didn't win, I certainly didn't win. He and Gram were so similar. They could not be saved.'

Between the bottle and the straitjacket of heroin, Grech and Parsons played music. 'Rick was classically trained,' says his widow, 'but he had this Ukrainian blood, and he found a link between eastern European folk music and country. Gram pushed him further towards the American end of that spectrum. He was genteel, well-mannered, sympathetic, spiritual, totally mad, and persuasive as hell. Whatever he believed in, he'd push at you, 100 per cent of the time. And all he could talk about was the way that Tammy Wynette sang with George Jones.' Parsons informed the Grechs that he'd discovered a duet partner called Emmylou, and that they were about to record together.

'Rick was writing an autobiographical tune called "Kiss The Children",' says Jenny Grech. It was a country song without a hint of his rock heritage, inspired by late-night phone calls to his family across a continent. 'Rick played his fiddle, Gram had his guitars, and they decided that they were going to make an album – not with Sam Hutt, but together, and in Los Angeles.'

When he reached California, Parsons contacted Emmylou Harris on the opposite coast. 'It had become almost a routine,' she explains, 'for Gram to phone me up every month or two and promise me that he wanted me to make an album with him. Then the trail would go cold. And a month later he'd be on the phone again, spinning the same line. When he finally arrived, I was amazed, to say the least.'

Harris wasn't Parsons' only call. That spring, he'd assembled his ideal band for the Haggard sessions, then had to let them go. Now he invited his old friend Barry Tashian, and some musicians he'd met years earlier in Los Angeles – among them former Rick Nelson guitarist James Burton, Crickets pianist Glen D. Hardin and drummer Ronnie Tutt. In 1972, all three were committed to touring with Elvis Presley, but Gram's recording schedule coincided with Elvis's vacation, so they agreed to show up at Wally Heider's studio in Hollywood.

At the Bel Air Sands hotel, Parsons and Grech commandeered a suite and – between increasingly eccentric demands from room service – began to assemble the bare bones of an album. Gram described the next few days as a 'pickin' and pukin' party', as they matched their musical output with a voracious appetite for hard liquor. 'The first guy they asked down was Byron Berline, the fiddle-player,' remembers Jenny Grech. 'He was a wonderful musician, but he was so totally straight alongside Gram and Rick. He came out of country, not rock'n'roll. It was funny to see them playing together, like a visual gag.' When the Sands management politely suggested they should move elsewhere, they relocated to the equally expensive but more libertarian Château Marmont – a regular party haunt for rock stars. It was there that they summoned Emmylou Harris.

'That was a completely new experience for me,' she admitted. 'I was a little wary at first, because of Los Angeles and Hollywood and all, and I was very much East Coast orientated. So I was on my guard, but Gram was a very real person and I always felt that I was in some kind of protective bubble.'

For all his excessive intake of alcohol and chemicals, Parsons impressed almost every musician who worked with him as a supremely congenial man. Al Perkins also participated in the sessions: 'Gram was very easy to work with. During my time with the Burritos I had heard all these stories about what a wild guy he could be, but in the studio he was the perfect Southern gentleman. He chose people whose work he appreciated, and then let them do what they did best. If someone else had an idea, he'd go with it. He would acquiesce to anyone's feel for the way the song should be played.'

Perhaps Parsons was more malleable because the man he'd flown over from England as his co-producer was absent from the early sessions. Rick Grech had collapsed with stomach pains: 'He ended up passing a kidney stone,' says his widow, 'so he had to miss a few days of recording. When he came back, he was playing bass and singing harmony, but he hadn't got clearance from the Musicians' Union, so he could only be credited on the album as producer.' His contribution wasn't always appreciated by the other sessionmen: 'None of the Americans were really prepared to admit that a Brit could write a decent country tune,' says Jenny Grech. ' "Kiss The Children" was his song, entirely. He'd written it before Gram had come to see us in England, but everyone seemed to assume that Gram had actually composed it.' So did Parsons, who claimed it as his own in a contemporary interview.

Vital though the Parsons/Grech combination was, it wasn't the most significant pairing at the sessions. With Emmylou Harris, Parsons forged duets that were sometimes erratic, often spontaneous, but always built on an almost supernatural empathy. 'Sometimes I felt that we were like Fred Astaire and Ginger Rogers,' she observes, 'because I would just jump in, and he would never tell me which note to sing. I'd never done duet singing before. I didn't know the tenor from the baritone. I just followed his lead. He might go as far as to say, "Why don't you go down and sing a low part rather than a high part," but that was as close as we ever got to constructing the harmonies. We just sang together, constantly. After a while, I instinctively knew what he was going to do.'

Everyone who watched the chrysalis of this partnership was struck by the chasm between their musical roots. Songwriter Walter Egan, who'd met both Harris and Parsons before the sessions began, recalled that he had had to 'teach her some of Gram's songs. I was much more into Gram than she was. She came out of a whole other tradition. It was kind of ironic, their meeting in their minds as performers.' Or, as Parsons himself explained: 'Emmylou is so much better than those straight Nashville session cats because she hasn't been conditioned to sing in any particular style. There just ain't no way that she's not going to break your heart.'

In three weeks, the *GP* album evolved. 'We can sing anything,' Gram had boasted, 'from a George and Tammy tune to songs by the Louvins, the Everlys, even hard-nosed rock'n'roll.' But only one tune matched that final claim, Parsons' self-mocking 'Big Mouth Blues', and Harris didn't sing on it. After his conscious attempt at Cosmic American Music on *The Gilded Palace Of Sin*, crossing country, soul and the lyrical ethos of rock, he reverted on *GP* to the allegiance he'd shown with the International Submarine Band and the Byrds.

Was Parsons closer to rock or country? 'I think it was even,' Harris says tactfully. 'He really loved both musics, but country was his real home. He really was a country boy, a yes ma'am, no ma'am genuine Southern boy, but he also had the soul of a rocker. He wasn't trying to recreate old country music: he brought poetry to the genre, like he was pouring new blood into the stew.'

Back at the Bel Air Sands, Gram had toyed with a song he'd scrawled in his workbook a couple of years earlier. 'Ain't no Beatle, ain't no Rolling Stone,' he'd written, less a boast than a source of regret. Then he raised his flag: 'You can make a trip to England, with your hair all down your back. I can save you the trouble, come inside my Southern shack.' Byron Berline would have been able to identify with that.

Previewing the album, Gram talked boldly about conquering both the pop and country markets: 'The pop single is going to be a song I wrote with Chris Ethridge called "She". And the country single is going to be a song that's going to be billed as a classic country duet, "That's All It Took".' But country radio had never heard of Parsons, and pop DJs couldn't relate to a message of love sung in a voice so lonely that it was the antithesis of the Top 40 ethos.

GP stumbled into the same divide, and rapidly vanished. Though it carried the name of a former Byrd on its cover, it was unashamedly a country album, and a traditional one at that. 'Those record company thugs are the ones most responsible for what goes down,' Gram sneered to a friend as the album was released, but no company on the planet could have marketed *GP* as the sound of 1973. Why, it wasn't even country-rock. It didn't sound anything like the Eagles.

13 Take it Easy
The birth of the Eagles, 1968–1972

'The Eagles' music is bubblegum. It's got too much sugar in it. Life is tougher than they make it out to be.' Gram Parsons said that. When he died, the Eagles wrote him a song: 'My Man'. But being their man was never on his agenda.

Nor was he alone. The Eagles mapped out the landscape for Californian rock in the seventies; however, their critical reputation slumped as soon as the *Village Voice* reviewed their début album. 'They are the tightest and most accomplished rock band to emerge since Neil Young's Crazy Horse', wrote Robert Christgau. 'They are the culmination of the vaguely country-oriented mainstream of American rock. Most such bands either seem to undermine their popularity with purism . . . or seem to design their music for broadcast into elevators. In contrast, the Eagles have a basic commitment to rock and roll.'

But – with the Eagles there was always a 'but' – Christgau added: 'Another thing that interests me is that I hate them . . . Do I hate music that has been giving me pleasure all weekend, made by four human beings I've never met? Yeah, I think so. Listening to the Eagles has left me feeling alienated from things I used to love.'

That alienation was partly political; the Eagles epitomized the individualism which inevitably succeeded the doomed collectivism of sixties counter-culture. They were Californians by adoption, who'd swallowed every frame of those beach movies which promised beautiful airheads in bikinis for every boy.

They were Californians in another way: they'd learned their Southern culture second-hand. No matter that most of the Eagles were transplanted Southerners; they received their education in country music via the distorting prism of country-rock. It made perfect sense that they should coalesce as the backing group for Linda Ronstadt, whose style emerged from the same process.

Together, Ronstadt and the Eagles created what the world came to know as 'country-rock' – a lie Christgau perceptively nailed as early as June 1972. 'It's no accident,' he wrote, 'that the Eagles' hip country music excises precisely what is deepest and most gripping about country music – its adult working-class pain, its paradoxically rigid ethics – and leaves bluegrass-sounding good feelin' . . . The music, the lyrics and the distribution machine are all suave and synthetic. Brilliant stuff – but false.'

'I always hated the Eagles,' concurs critic Greil Marcus. 'I like *Hotel California*, sure. That's proof that even slimeballs can do great things. The Eagles are too good at what they did not to make a good record along the way, but as a group of people, they're really horrible.' He pauses for a second. 'I've never met any of them.'

Christgau's hatred and Marcus's contempt were triggered by precisely what sold the Eagles to those who'd ignored the country Byrds and the Burritos. By 1972, when the Eagles' first album was released, most of the idealism of the sixties had dissolved. The US Army was nearing a decade of inconclusive involvement in the South-East Asian war. Years of organized opposition to the Nixon administration were about to be rewarded by his re-election, with an increased popular mandate. Initiatives on civil rights, feminism and environmentalism were dissipated, as the broad left/liberal coalition dissolved into disputes between increasingly irrelevant factions.

By the early seventies, the link between radical politics and rock music which had flowered between 1965 and 1969 had effectively vanished. Crosby, Stills, Nash and Young were the last rock group of the sixties who dared to act as standard-bearers. Their collapse amid the clatter of bruised egos mirrored the decay of their ideals.

Other American artists who might have carried the weight of the times rejected the responsibility. The Byrds were still active, but their intuitive command of the *Zeitgeist* had vanished. Even a reunion of the original line-up failed to command any iconic power. Bob Dylan had followed his espousal of country music with a long period of silence. The Grateful Dead and Jefferson Airplane were grounded, Janis Joplin, Jim Morrison and Jimi

Hendrix were dead, the Beach Boys irrelevant, the other crusaders of sixties rock little more than self-caricatures.

In their place had arisen two strands of music that were entirely at odds. Bombastic bands like Chicago and Grand Funk Railroad used the language of the sixties revolution without any of its meaning. They were cartoon replicas of their predecessors, loud, empty and complacent.

The antithesis of these hard rockers were the singer-songwriters. They were the voice of a quiet revolution, in which knowledge of one's own psyche was the ultimate goal. James Taylor, Carole King, Joni Mitchell and their ilk – sensitive men and women cut to the same design, with varying degrees of poetic insight – were lauded as beacons of honesty and compassion. The leaders of the genre were deeper than their public realized: Taylor was schooled in folk, blues and country, and boasted a sly wit which didn't fit the stereotype, while Mitchell's jazzy structures and dazzling imagery were beyond the grasp of her imitators. The audience which had looked to the sixties icons for content as well as style was willing to trade the exhilarating rush of rock music for the delicate insights of these acoustic bards.

There was music of intelligence, integrity, passion and artistic daring in early-seventies America, but it was being made by black artists – Curtis Mayfield, Marvin Gaye, Sly Stone, Miles Davis. Few within the rock audience were willing to concede that the era's most creative and experimental records might come from the ghetto marked 'R&B'.

So there was a niche for a band who could combine the mythic power of 'classic' rock with the lyrical sensitivity of the singer-songwriters, and span the increasingly divided markets for singles and albums. Maybe they could boogie as hard as Grand Funk and sing as sweetly as CSNY. Maybe they could be named after a national symbol. Maybe they could be the Eagles.

In the summer of 1971, Glenn Frey, Don Henley, Bernie Leadon and Randy Meisner were the Corvettes – the smooth country-rock band who supported Linda Ronstadt. For Frey and Henley, this was unexpected fame; for Leadon and Meisner, who'd licked the skin of stardom with the Burritos and Poco, it was better than mulling over missed opportunities at the Troubadour.

Of the quartet, Glenn Frey had the clearest agenda. Since his teenage years in Detroit, he'd clung to the fantasy of California: 'I saw *Surfer* magazine, I got the Beach Boys' albums. I took acid and bought the first Buffalo Springfield album and got chillibumps and had to lay on the floor. I got into this whole California consciousness. I saw the articles about people taking marijuana and LSD and going to Golden Gate Park. I was a victim of the media in the same way everybody else was.'

Arriving in Los Angeles in 1968, he met John David Souther, with whom he formed the country-rock duo Longbranch Pennywhistle. In late 1969, they cut an album for the same label as Shiloh, Don Henley's band, featuring many musicians (James Burton, Joe Osborn, Jim Gordon, Larry Knechtel) who'd worked with the artists they hoped to emulate – Gram Parsons, Michael Nesmith, Rick Nelson. The duo didn't survive, but their friendship did. Through another songwriter, Jackson Browne, they were introduced to the feisty manager of Crosby, Stills, Nash and Young: David Geffen. 'He told me point blank,' Frey admitted, 'that I shouldn't make a record by myself, and that maybe I should join a band.'

A year later, Geffen and Frey found their vehicle. Promising to handle their careers with the shark-like instincts he'd demonstrated for CSNY, Geffen persuaded the quartet to abandon Ronstadt. Not yet ready to face the cynical Hollywood media, they relocated to Aspen, Colorado, which had become a retreat for country-rockers, including various ex-members of the Burritos and the core of Stephen Stills' new band, Manassas.

Aspen provided a soft playpen for the newly named Eagles, who could experiment in local clubs like the Gallery before audiences not expecting the new Byrds or CSNY. 'We did four sets a night for a month,' Randy Meisner explained, 'playing as many originals as we'd written, and filled out with just about every other song we knew – loads of Chuck Berry, some Neil Young. It tightened the group up pretty well. We learned how to play with each other.'

The Eagles shared more than a manager with CSNY. As Bernie

Leadon explains, their philosophy was taken directly from their mentors: 'The idea was that we would be four entirely equal partners, all of whom wrote, could take centre-stage, and would be prepared to support whichever was up front. There would be no leader, no second-string members. It was supposed to be a total democracy.' As Frey noted, 'We'd watched bands like Poco and the Flying Burrito Brothers lose their initial momentum. We were determined not to make the same mistakes. We didn't just want to be another LA band.'

Once they'd hardened their musical rapport, David Geffen arranged for the band to play a club in Boulder, and flew out English producer Glyn Johns, a passionate country fan. Though he loved the Eagles' harmonies and melodies, 'he didn't think we could rock and roll', as Frey remembered.

When producer and band assembled in England in February 1972, Johns' task was to accentuate the Eagles' rock leanings while retaining the country-rock harmonies. 'We wanted a producer who could handle folkie stuff and rock'n'roll,' Leadon explained at the time, and Johns fitted the bill.

With its desert iconography showing the band stoned and snuggled round a campfire, *The Eagles* literally wore its marketing strategy on its sleeve. The desert suggested loneliness; hippies were a symbol of community; the band's name encompassed America. For anyone mourning lost ideals, searching for somewhere to belong, this was a way back home. Exactly what kind of refuge was on offer emerged from the first Eagles song aired in public – 'Take It Easy'. It could hardly have been a more prominent signpost to the band's desires. The smooth flow of the music evoked timeless Californian images of freedom, but whereas Jan and Dean's 'Surf City' offered 'two girls for every boy', the Eagles' landscape was more challenging. 'I was driving down the road trying to loosen my load,' Frey sang, 'seven women on my mind.' If the rewards had increased since Jan and Dean's day, so had the responsibilities. The 'loosen my load' line served as a subtle reminder of that generational anthem, the Band's 'The Weight'. See, there were still people out there who *believed*!

Their harmonies perfectly pitched, the Eagles' voices were an exact replica of Poco or the post-Parsons line-up of the Flying

Burrito Brothers. Their music had an urgency beneath the finesse, which transformed 'Take It Easy' from country-rock into something with Top 40 potential.

Nothing mapped out the course of LA country-rock more plainly than the song's title. 'Take It Easy' might have been the manifesto of seventies California. When it was followed by the equally mellifluous 'Peaceful Easy Feeling', there was no mistaking the Eagles' intention.

'We were judged by our early work,' Don Henley complained years later. 'Our early stuff was country-rock, and so we were immediately labelled a country-rock band. I knew we would never escape that category.'

But what is most striking about *The Eagles* is its absence of country. Admittedly, Meisner and Leadon's 'Earlybird' chimed with bluegrass references, via a banjo and a backwoods edge to the stacks of harmonies. It was Leadon who supplied 'Train Leaves Here This Morning', retrieved from its original hiding-place on Dillard & Clark's first album. The song applied the rhetoric of rock culture ('I watched as the smoker passed it on') to a tale of romantic despair familiar from a thousand Nashville lyrics.

That was as country as *The Eagles* cared to go. The haunting self-doubt that became Don Henley's trademark was a reflection of a world in which James Taylor was king. Their complaint that 'Most Of Us Are Sad' was merely a recasting of Taylor's 'Hey Mister, That's Me Up On The Jukebox'. Gee, it's tough to be a rock star, 'specially if you have feelings and all. Thank God for the chance to 'Chug All Night', or dig down into the Louisiana swamps in search of a 'Witchy Woman'. 'High up on his own, the eagle flies alone and he is free', they sang in 'Earlybird'. But, as Merle Haggard could have told them, the working man still had rent to pay.

14 Back to the Garden
The Diggers and the return to the land, 1966–1972

The slide towards country-rock in the late sixties held symbolic importance for musicians and audiences alike. For some, merging country and rock was an act of political *rapprochement*, welding Southern and Northern cultures. Others viewed country as the white man's blues, a way of tacking some notion of 'authenticity' on to the overt commercialism of rock'n'roll. For those raised on crackly broadcasts of the *Grand Ole Opry* and scratched Jimmie Rodgers 78s, country-rock was a homecoming, a reconcilation between generations. Or it might be nothing more complex than a reaction against the sonic excesses of acid-rock and psychedelia, a way of regaining some kind of simplicity in a world of kaleidoscopic studio trickery.

Within the teeming counter-culture of Haight-Ashbury, in San Francisco, the rise of country-rock chimed with the almost puritan ethic of the Diggers. In late 1966, as 'flower power' and 'mind expansion' began to drift into the American mainstream, the most idealistic denizens of San Francisco's underground formed a loose-knit community designed to maintain a vigilant eye from within.

The Diggers repudiated any compromise with 'straight' society, and were repelled by the sight of (in John Lennon's phrase) 'day trippers' experimenting with hippiedom on the weekend and returning to capitalist greed at 9 a.m. on Monday morning. Although the city had been the site and seed of the LSD revolution, they feared its 'silent-crowded uptight sidewalks', through which hippies had to wander with 'pockets full of absurdity and compromise between cowardice and illusion'.

From beyond the city came the call of the land, an Edenic paradise in which acid-trippers could experience the wonder of psychedelic experimentation, in harmony with the pure spirit of nature. It was a deliberate avoidance of responsibility, for duty involved organization and organization required the curse of leadership.

'The return to the land is happening,' trumpeted an anonymous writer in the San Francisco underground paper *The Oracle* in February 1967. Under the enigmatic banner of 'Sounds From The Seed-Power Sitar', the Digger proclaimed that 'Land is being made available at a time when many of us in the Haight-Ashbury and elsewhere are voicing our need to return to the soil, to straighten our heads in a natural environment, to straighten our bodies with healthier food and Pan's work, toe to toe with the physical world.' As radical historian David Zane Mairowitz noted, 'Nature was acting as a purifier, exorcizing city demons you'd picked up hanging out in corrupt vicinities.'

For healthier food, the Diggers needed to farm – not the back-breaking torment under a ruthless sun familiar to generations of Southerners in the Cotton Belt, but a utopian vision of communal living, with crops being harvested for everyone, even city dwellers, to share, free of charge, and the natural round of rural life interrupted only by reflection and chemical stimulation.

With the back-to-the-land idealism came a fetishism of natural objects. As Haight-Ashbury historian Charles Perry noted: 'Even people who tolerated technology collected *objets de nature* such as rocks, flowers, driftwood, fur and feathers for the beauty of their spontaneous forms. Such objects were considered "gentle" because they suggested the bounty of nature rather than the regimentation of society.'

For the underground, which had previously viewed technology as a useful tool to draw out mankind's potential for bliss, this rural idealism triggered a refocusing of energy. The Diggers didn't reject technology, but they suggested a means whereby one could live without it. They emphasized the importance of personal rather than mass communication. It was but a short ideological step to rejecting the complexities of electric and electronic music in favour of the 'naturalness' of 'real' instruments, and the ethnic richness of traditional forms.

Like a brief reprise of the late-fifties folk revival, elements of the underground were drawn towards acoustic sounds, played on instruments carved lovingly from wood which could gather the music of the spheres. There was no apparent link between this naïve idealism and the clear-eyed realism of a Johnny Cash or a Merle Haggard: what connected them was the suggestion that country music, folk and bluegrass might in some way be closer to the Diggers' spirit than the compromised hybrid of rock and roll.

Inevitably, the rhetoric flooded back into the city: why else would a band like Crosby, Stills, Nash and Young refer lovingly to their acoustic sets as 'wooden music'? Based securely within corporate America, self-confessed revolutionary musicians of the late sixties could idealize the pull of the land – 'we've got to get ourselves back to the Garden', as Joni Mitchell put it, and she wasn't talking about Madison Square – at the same time as they milked multi-national corporatism for all the riches it could offer.

This impulse inevitably left its mark on those exploring country roots in the late sixties and early seventies. The 'reality' of rural existence became as much a symbol of counter-cultural philosophy as the identification of dope-smoking hippies with outlaws and cowboys. By the early seventies, when the utopian demands of 1968 had dissipated into a sullen hatred for the Nixon administration, the land – or more particularly, preserving it – became a central issue for what remained of the counter-culture. David Zane Mairowitz saw the growth of the ecology movement not as a continuation of sixties radicalism but as a step away from it: 'People were experimenting with narrowing their utopias, unhinging their "attachments", moderating their desires, helping themselves.'

That was a pithy encapsulation of the shift in California radicalism from 1968 to 1975 – the death of revolutionary zeal, and its replacement by a woolly code of self-improvement: heal the planet, so that I can feel better about myself. This solipsism infected Californian society, and nowhere was it more apparent than in rock culture. In 1969, Jefferson Airplane could still call for revolutionary 'Volunteers'; by 1971, the self-absorption of the singer-songwriter movement held sway. Gradually, even the trappings of radicalism disappeared. By the late seventies, the rock ethos demanded not the satisfaction of stopping the war or saving the planet, but merely the sensual gratification of unfulfilled desires.

That age-old emblem, the American eagle, symbolized the change. In 1969, ex-Bill Monroe Blue Grass Boy Peter Rowan led the country and rock musicians of Earth Opera through a long, impassioned assault on US involvement in Vietnam, 'The Great American Eagle Tragedy'. In 1971, the national bird of America symbolized the death of the environment in the languorous country-rock of 'The Last Lonely Eagle' by the New Riders Of The Purple Sage.

A year later, the eagle gave its name to the band which came to define seventies country-rock. 'That whole movement,' reflected Eagles drummer Don Henley, 'was connected to environmentalism, because it was a music that had grown in part out of country music. It was very much connected to the earth, and everybody was wearing earthy clothes and celebrating the outdoors. It was a very natural time. And it all made sense with the music. Then in the late seventies, there was a backlash against that. The country, the natural sound that is connected with nature, has gone out of music pretty much.'

Eagles guitarist Bernie Leadon coined the name, for its spiritual power: 'It's high soaring, flying closer to the sun than any other bird, and it's spiritually the richest of them all.' But as rock critic Robert Christgau pointed out, 'The eagle roams the sky not in search of freedom and fresh air but in search of prey, which is why he is such an apt symbol of American imperial power.'

On the cover of the band's début album, the dusky sky spans a landscape of shadowed desert cacti. Inside, the four Eagles are gathered round a campfire in the wilderness, sharing stories, passing joints, not so much escaping from the world as unconscious of it. All that exists is the fire, and the smoke in their lungs: at that moment, they are the compass of the universe.

15 Desperado
Cowboy chic, 1968–1973: the Eagles; the Byrds

An alien marooned at a UK country festival in the early nineties, Chris Hillman led his Desert Rose Band through a set that reflected his heritage with the Byrds and the Flying Burrito Brothers. Before him, fans paraded in the unofficial uniform of British country: full cowboy regalia, with holsters, belts and replica pistols. Hillman's face creased with disbelief as they greeted each song with a fusillade of blanks. Backstage, he shook his head: 'What *were* those people?'

Two decades earlier, his former cohort Gram Parsons had watched the LA country-rock band the Eagles adopt a similar pose. He too had been appalled at the fate of his vision of Cosmic American Music. 'He thought they were kinda missing the point, dressing up as cowboys,' says his duet partner Emmylou Harris. 'He didn't know what that outlaw stuff had to do with the music.'

Few nineteenth-century symbols held the twentieth century in such thrall as the cowboy. Filtered through the distorting lens of Hollywood, generations of cattle herders and gunfighters were compressed into a single image: the cowboy roaming the range, a solitary man meeting his peers only for battle (a showdown at noon) or companionship (singing round the campfire at dusk). Decades of American history were distorted into the profile of John Wayne or James Stewart, facing up to What A Man's Gotta Do.

Eager for vicarious heroism, entertainers often fall prey to this fantasy. Like Ronald Reagan, uncertain of the gap between his real Second World War exploits and those of his screen personae, they confuse stereotype and legend. Not all cowboys were gunfighters; not all gunfighters were outlaws; not all outlaws were heroes. But the circle remains unbroken in rock and country mythology.

For country, the cowboy began as an uncomplicated hero.

Marty Robbins recorded *Gunfighter Ballads*; Johnny Cash promised *Ballads Of The True West*. But just as John Ford, the master of the Hollywood western, blurred the cowboy myth in *The Man Who Shot Liberty Valance*, the image began to fade. Willie Nelson sang that 'My Heroes Have Always Been Cowboys', then begged, 'Mama Don't Let Your Babies Grow Up To Be Cowboys'. Michael Martin Murphey invented the 'Cosmic Cowboy', a redneck mother with long hair. *Wanted: The Outlaws* introduced a brand of country singers who wouldn't conform to Nashville's conservatism. *Urban Cowboy* propelled the myth into a new era. The Cowboy Junkies twisted it into the mainstream of rock iconography. Donning a cowboy hat was a statement of purpose in 1990s Nashville; then it became a cliché, and Travis Tritt and Marty Stuart flaunted their outlaw status with the 'No Hats Tour'.

On the cover of 1970's *Déjà Vu*, Crosby, Stills, Nash and Young shuffled a fistful of outlaw images. Stephen Stills looked wearied by the weight of Confederate defeat. David Crosby played a haunted sharpshooter, running from a sheriff's gun. Neil Young was the frontier dandy, Graham Nash the doomed romantic. Among them stood the band's only black member, Greg Reeves, the former slave dragooned into service for a cause he could never trust. Were they meant to be Civil War veterans or gunfighters living beyond the law? CSNY couldn't have told you. But the power of that image, sepia-tinted on *Déjà Vu* for instant nostalgia, had already survived for a century.

David Crosby charted the downfall of CSNY's idealism in a song called 'Cowboy Movie', portraying his colleagues as paranoid and trigger-happy. No matter that Bob Dylan had already deconstructed cowboy mystique on *John Wesley Harding*; for Crosby, as for Pigpen of the Grateful Dead and every other rock star who posed as a gunslinger, the myth was eternal.

It was shared by the Eagles, whose second album, *Desperado*, was released in early 1973. The musicians crowded the front cover like fugitives from the law, desperate and (a standard Hollywood clue) unshaven. When the cover was flipped over, the legend decayed. The Eagles (plus associate Jackson Browne) were trussed on the ground, dead or defeated, while the victors gazed lazily at the camera. Every one of them sported David Crosby's patented 'outlaw' moustache: desperadoes indeed.

They made unconvincing corpses. Like Che Guevara (the Jim Morrison of sixties activism) on his deathbed, they looked as if they were about to stand up and smile. It wasn't that way in the real west, when the Dalton brothers of Coffeyville, Kansas, robbed two banks, and then got caught in a shoot-out. Two of them died, alongside four bystanders, and the brothers' corpses were dragged upright for the camera to record the triumph of law and order. In death, Bob and Grat Dalton were as triumphant as pellet-ridden pheasants. The all too real demise of the Dalton brothers sparked the Eagles' *Desperado* project.

'It began with a book about outlaws that was given to me by my friend Ned Doheny on my twenty-first birthday,' recalls Jackson Browne, who collaborated on the Eagles' early albums. 'It told the story of these various gangs, including the Doolin' Dalton gang.' Don Henley explained: 'We were going to do an all-encompassing album about rebels or outlaws that didn't have a time reference. The Daltons would have sufficed for that whole period.' Guitarist Joe Walsh – later to join the Eagles – had already named his hard rock combo the James Gang, after the Daltons' immediate predecessors as America's meanest armed robbers. Their exploit in robbing the Glendale Train spawned a country-rock tribute from the New Riders Of The Purple Sage. The James Gang – the rock stars, not the gunslingers – also joined Country Joe and the Fish in 'the first electric western', *Zachariah*. In its incoherence, it is rivalled in the history of rock cinema only by its thematic sequel, *Straight To Hell*. Its one rewarding facet was the Fish's impersonation of 'The Crackers', a bunch of cowboy eccentrics who wielded six-string weapons, not twelve-bores.

So the Eagles weren't alone in their affinity with western outlaws. 'Halfway through the sessions, we realized the concept was holding together,' Frey noted. 'The whole thread between outlaw and rock star that we were trying to get across with the album was working.'

Nowhere was that thread traced more boldly – or crassly – than on 'Outlaw Man', written by David Blue, a Dylan disciple swamped by his desire to emulate his mentor. Dylan would never have penned a chorus this trite: 'Woman don't try to love me, don't try to understand, A life out on the road is the life of an outlaw man.' Sexist and condescending, it exposed the arrogance which linked all these would-be cowboy heroes.

Studying their own egos over drinks at the Troubadour, the boys' club of the Eagles, Jackson Browne, John David Souther and Ned Doheny extended the concept into an album. But *Desperado* fell some way short of a rock opera. The plaintive title track and the tale of 'Doolin' Dalton' were reprised as a finale, but, aside from 'Outlaw Man', none of the tracks fitted the storyline. 'The concept that they ended up doing was not the concept that I had,' Jackson Browne is keen to stress today. 'My concept was less of a cowboy movie and more outlaw music. The song "James Dean" would have been on the album that I thought of. All the dressing up in western stuff was not part of my idea.' Even without a plot, *Desperado* attracted the attention of maverick movie director Sam Peckinpah. He optioned the rights soon after he'd completed another film which teased out comparisons between the mythical west and the icons of showbusiness: *Pat Garrett And Billy The Kid*. While Rudy Wurlitzer's screenplay subverted the Billy the Kid legend, Bob Dylan skirted around the edges of the action, playing a hollow character called Alias. Dylan also contributed a suitably anonymous soundtrack album, which added a heady blast of tequila to the conventions of country-rock.

Sam Peckinpah never made a movie of *Desperado*, though he'd probably have enjoyed blowing the Eagles away. In 1978, the idea was revived, and Glenn Frey and Don Henley considered writing some new songs for the project. At that point, their next album carried the working title *What Would Robert Mitchum Do?*. Not make a movie with the Eagles, that's for sure; and anyway, the band was disintegrating under the weight of arrogance and cocaine. They were close enough to emulating the fate of the Dalton brothers to require no fictional assistance.

Desperado wasn't country-rock's first aborted horse-opera. Four years earlier, Roger McGuinn of the Byrds had collaborated with playwright Jacques Levy on an ambitious revamping of the fairytale *Peer Gynt*. The action was transplanted from Scandinavia to American frontier territory, and the title juggled into *Gene Tryp* – the 'y' a happy etymological parallel to the Byrds' monicker.

Though McGuinn had been alarmed by the speed at which Gram Parsons had dragged the Byrds into country-rock, he was happy to remain there after Parsons' abrupt departure. In spring 1969, he and Levy composed twenty-five songs in less than eight weeks. The McGuinn/Levy libretto was offered to Broadway producers between late 1969 and 1972, at which point McGuinn admitted temporary defeat. He sporadically rekindled the idea, but by the end of the seventies he was ready to admit that 'It wouldn't work today. I've had talks with Jacques Levy and he completely puts it down on the grounds that the novelty of country-rock is over and the attitude of it is extremely male-chauvinistic. He doesn't want to even think about it.'

In its original form, *Gene Tryp* would have been a lavish, probably unstageable mélange of styles and motifs. Its circular narrative – male adventurer finds and discards love, then journeys around the world to regain it just before he dies – was the stuff of Greek legend. Its imagery was based on the same tales of the Old West which inspired the Eagles. Its episodic diversity shifted the locale from cowboy opera to science-fiction fantasy, via scenes which portrayed its hero (McGuinn fancied Bob Dylan for the role) as a gun-runner or a presidential candidate.

This was far more adventurous than anything offered by *Desperado*, and much less feasible as popular entertainment. A Byrds album of the twenty-five *Gene Tryp* songs might have been a masterpiece: instead, the likes of 'Chestnut Mare', 'I Wanna Grow Up To Be A Politician', 'Kathleen's Song' and 'All The Things' were scattered across the group's inconsistent early-seventies releases.

As McGuinn and Levy were assembling *Gene Tryp*, another project dabbling in this enticing mythology was reaching fruition. Like *Pat Garrett And Billy The Kid*, its models were legendary gunfighters from the past. While Peckinpah's movie subjected the nineteenth century to twentieth-century scrutiny, Peter Fonda and Dennis Hopper's *Easy Rider* simply recast its characters in the immediate present.

On one level, *Easy Rider* was an upgrade of the biker movies that Fonda had been making since the mid-sixties. But Fonda had a rock sensibility: he'd adored the Byrds, and sought out their company, in 1965; that summer, he'd inadvertently inspired one of John Lennon's most acidic Beatles songs, 'She Said She Said'.

Though he's never confirmed the rumour, *Easy Rider*'s portrayal of Fonda (granny specs, fatalistic optimism) and Hopper (lavish moustache, doomed idealism) mirrored the physical and psychological relationship between the Byrds' two main players, Roger McGuinn and David Crosby.

But the movie dramatizes a more vital confrontation. As the bikers journey across a mythic American landscape, they collide with the forces of tradition. 'They're gonna talk to you about individual freedom,' lawyer Jack Nicholson tells Fonda and Hopper as they share a joint, 'but they see a free individual, it's gonna scare 'em. It makes 'em dangerous.' In the brutal climax, the bikers are murdered by bigots who think they're preserving the America that Fonda and Hopper had set out to find.

The movie's been described as a battle between hippies and hillbillies, but country star Dwight Yoakam – who owns a Hollywood bar with Hopper and Fonda – corrects that impression: 'They were actually more Louisiana redneck figures; I wouldn't lay that burden on my people, the hillbillies.' As he points out, *Easy Rider*'s use of music was significant: 'It had that great soundtrack, with the Byrds, Hendrix and Steppenwolf. But they also used country music. There was a great piece for that scene where they were hanging out on the commune. Peter Fonda has always been a country music fan, which may sound ironic given his image in the film. But that's a superficial view. Country music was originally the musical voice of people that were on the outside of society, that were ostracized from city life. It was only in the sixties that it became so associated with the right-wing.'

To Roger McGuinn fell the task of writing a song to encapsulate the movie: 'The Ballad Of Easy Rider'. With assistance from Bob Dylan, he composed a conciliatory theme to follow the double murder. But when Dylan saw a rough cut, he demanded that his name be removed from the credits. 'I gave no hope to the audience,' Peter Fonda explained, 'and Mr Zimmerman [Dylan] says, "That's wrong, you have to give them hope!" I said, "OK,

Bob, what do you have in mind?" He said, "Well, reshoot the ending, and have Fonda run his bike into the truck and blow up the truck . . . How about you don't use the song and we make another movie?" I said, "No, no, how about we don't make another movie and we use the song?" He said, "The song's pretentious." I said, "He not busy being born is busy dying." He said, "Never mind that, man, have you heard my new album [*Nashville Skyline*]? It's a whole new number. We've got to give them love!" I said, "I understand that. You have to love them. But you cannot give them love." ' Dylan's name was omitted from the writing credits.

So potent was *Easy Rider* that McGuinn and the Byrds elected to wrap themselves in its lustre. Their next album was entitled *The Ballad Of Easy Rider*, and Peter Fonda wrote the sleeve-notes, a gushing prose poem that established little beyond the fact that he loved the Byrds. *Gene Tryp* would have redoubled that passion; instead, it was the Eagles who picked up the torch of *Easy Rider* and stumbled with it all the way to the bank.

16 Will the Circle Be Unbroken

Country-rock revivalists, 1969–1977: the Nitty Gritty Dirt Band; Asleep At The Wheel; Commander Cody and his Lost Planet Airmen

'Will the circle be unbroken?' runs the country gospel standard. It's a rhetorical question, a pledge of Christian faith and spiritual continuity. 'There's a better place a-waiting, in the sky, Lord, in the sky', the chorus adds, as if God needed the reassurance.

Bill Monroe occupied a status that was little short of divine in the string-band tradition, and reassurance was exactly what he lacked in 1972, when a rock group invited him to participate in a project named after that gospel tune. Their intention was to unite two generations of country musicians, but Monroe was suspicious of their motives, and his manager politely declined. 'We never got to speak to Bill personally,' admitted Jeff Hanna of the Nitty Gritty Dirt Band. 'He said he was afraid that his fans wouldn't understand.'

It's intriguing to imagine the puritanical Monroe secluding himself with a set of the Dirt Band's early albums, examining them for traces of righteousness or sin. He would have been puzzled by the gulf between the coffee-house hilarity of their first incarnation as a jug band, and their respectful country-rock of the early seventies. Even at their most arch, in 1967, the Dirt Band could find room for the traditional banjo picking of John McKuen, their in-house purist. But he had to compete with the Dirt Band's penchant for vaudeville novelties and student poetry.

The recruitment of multi-instrumentalist Jimmy Ibbotson in 1970 coincided with a decisive shift in direction. Across that year's *Uncle Charlie And His Dog* album, and 1971's more integrated *All The Good Times*, the Dirt Band began to play country-based music as if it were a vocation, not a pose. They were the only major country-rock band of the era left (virtually) untouched by the influence of Bob Dylan. Instead, their sometimes anarchic style

– Cajun mixed with bluegrass, rockabilly, old-time string band music and country blues – belonged to a world where someone like Johnny Cash might have felt at home.

That may explain why it was the Nitty Gritty Dirt Band, rather than the Byrds, Burritos or Eagles, who achieved the only major collaboration between the long-hairs who had infiltrated the country tradition and the veterans whose heritage they had borrowed. The catalyst was William McKuen, John's elder brother, who assembled hillbilly pioneers like Roy Acuff, the King of Country Music; Maybelle Carter, mother superior of the original Carter Family; Merle Travis, composer of 'Dark As A Dungeon'; and fiddler Vassar Clements. Bill Monroe wasn't the only old-timer who regarded the project with suspicion. Acuff had often sounded off about hippie musicians and their disregard for real country music, so the Dirt Band assumed that he'd be cool, if not downright hostile. 'We got along well, as it turned out,' Jeff Hanna reflected. 'He was the only one there was any tension about, and that was only because he'd made some comments about hair before.' Acuff proved to be more interested about the Dirt Band's abilities than their appearance. 'Let's do it the first time, and to hell with the rest of it,' he called out before he counted the group into the gloriously sentimental tale of 'The Precious Jewel'. When the rock musicians demonstrated themselves equal to the task, any uncertainty dissolved.

Acuff, Carter and the rest had a selfish reason for collaborating with the Dirt Band. *Will The Circle Be Unbroken* was the only album of the early seventies which found a mass audience for traditional hillbilly music. Across three records, the Dirt Band imposed none of their own personality on the music they were chronicling. The album was a last gathering of the tribe who had once defined country music, but who were gradually being eased to the margins of the picture. It documented the passing of a torch, as the generation of Roy Acuff and Mother Maybelle were exiled by self-styled 'outlaws' such as Willie Nelson and Waylon Jennings, who had been raised on their music.

The transition was peaceful, because the country music establishment always prided itself on its respect for tradition. Each fresh generation of country stars genuflected to those who went before. Beneath this polite veneer, commercial realities were often more brutal. 'In the late sixties and early seventies,' explains Ray Benson, guitarist, vocalist and leader of Asleep At The Wheel, 'there was quite a move to obliterate the roots of country music, because that was what people's parents had liked, and that was what they were trying to get away from.' A strange paradox arose: while the country mainstream tried to escape the spectre of the past a handful of threateningly long-haired rock bands emerged with the express design of maintaining – reviving, if necessary – the hillbilly tradition. They might use genteel reverence or rowdy pastiche, but in either case, the intention was the same. The Dirt Band's epic was merely one reflection of this nostalgic spirit. Ray Benson and his cohorts in Asleep At The Wheel offered an alternative approach. Distance was built into their adventures in country by sheer geography: Benson came from the hillbilly-free zone of Philadelphia, and almost every other member of the Wheel also hailed from the East Coast.

'I played bass in swing bands at high school, Count Basie and that stuff,' Benson recalls. 'All of us were playing rock'n'roll, jazz, blues, everything but country.' During his explorations into swing, Benson had come across the western variety pioneered by one Texan maverick, Bob Wills, with his Texas Playboys. 'Jazz at that time [the thirties and forties] was very black, inner-city American music,' Benson says. 'Country was redneck, Southern, racist music. Bob Wills combined these two traditions of an earlier era into his cowboy swing.'

Asleep At The Wheel were designed to revive the lost art of western swing, which had been pushed aside by the increasingly narrow confines of the Nashville Sound in the 1960s. Unremarkable in itself, that decision was lent an exotic edge by Benson's desire to recreate the Texas Playboys' sound from within the world of rock'n'roll.

'We were hippies,' he notes, 'and we were playing – well, what was it? Was that jazz? Was it country? Nobody was too sure.' This incomprehension surfaced when they toured with the Medicine Ball Caravan rock bill in 1970; no more successful was their brief existence as the Poor Boys, backing band to one of the few successful black country singers, Stoney Edwards.

In 1971, they migrated to California, where they won a residency at the Longbranch Saloon in San Francisco. They attracted a potentially incendiary mix of punters, from hippies who needed a beer chaser between tokes to rednecks who were missing their Southern roots, via urban cowboys and a scattering of bikers. Satisfying their various needs required volume, humour and the ability to maintain a ferocious tempo. Those qualities survived when they signed to United Artists in 1973, and won the approval of veteran country fiddle-player Buddy Spicher, who told them, 'I sure hope y'all bring back western swing. I've missed it sorely.' Their début album, *Comin' Right At Ya*, mixed country standards such as Hank Williams' 'I'll Never Get Out Of This World Alive' and Bob Wills' 'Take Me Back To Tulsa' with original material in the same vein.

The following year, they finally reached their spiritual home when they moved to Austin, Texas. 'There was a real scene there,' Benson recalled, 'with guys like Willie Nelson and Doug Sahm. We were all young people thinking the same, wearing long hair and cowboy hats, smoking pot and drinking beer.' Refuelled by the encounter, Asleep At The Wheel continued to experiment with Wills' blueprint, adding a horn section in the late seventies so that they could master jive tunes like 'One O'Clock Jump' and 'Ain't Nobody Here But Us Chickens', though rarely venturing outside a style that their mentor would have recognized. Their career has been a delicate balancing act, persuading purists that they're serious, newcomers that they're parodists and everyone else that they're a dance band.

Much the same task confronted another outfit who ventured into the minefield between country, rock and comedy: Commander Cody and his Lost Planet Airmen. Their path initially mimicked that of Asleep At The Wheel – a bunch of long-hairs travel from the East Coast to California. But there the similarity ended, as the Commander (actually George Frayne, born in Idaho but raised in New York) made few concessions to delicate sensibilities.

Frayne stepped west to Detroit in the late sixties, attracted by the motor city's uniquely eclectic culture. 'It's an auto plant area,' says artist/producer Don Was, who was a Detroit teenager during the sixties, 'and what you have is all these workers who came from all over, like the blues guys who came up from the South – that's how John Lee Hooker ended up in Detroit. The same highway brought a lot of white Southern migrant workers to the auto factories. There's a lot of country music there as a result. The atmosphere there was one of cross-pollination. You grew up with these incredible juxtapositions, whereby you could go and see Miles Davis's quintet play one night, Iggy and the Stooges the next, then George Clinton or the Motown groups, then Merle Haggard. The only thing was, it was dangerous for someone with long hair to go to the shows. You were taking your life in your hands. I used to tuck my hair under a cowboy hat if I was going to see Merle or George Jones.' George Frayne revelled in that turbulent wash of cultures, and in his subsequent career he seemed to welcome the danger. Anyone who could form a band called the Fabulous Surfing Beavers was never going to be a purist. When Frayne saw a late-night movie called *Lost Planet Airmen*, he figured that was an ideal name for a rock'n'roll band who could play revivalist music with a knowing wink.

By 1969, he was resident in Oakland, California, having evaded the attempts of Kama Sutra Records to turn his band into 'the next Lovin' Spoonful'. Instead, the Airmen moved on to the San Francisco ballroom circuit, delivering truckers' anthems – stripped-down, hot-wired, laconic tales of mayhem on the highway – with the same affectionate humour that the Grateful Dead reserved for 'Okie From Muskogee'.

Lost In The Ozone and *Hot Licks & Cold Steel* won them cult appreciation from both the country and rock communities, who found different but equal pleasures in songs like 'Mama Hated Diesels', 'Hot Rod Lincoln' and 'Smoke! Smoke! Smoke! (That Cigarette)'. But their prospects in Nashville were doomed by their third album, *Country Casanova*. DJ copies were stickered with a warning that one song, 'Everybody's Doin' It', had been deemed unsuitable for airplay. An error at the pressing plant ensured that when a jockey at Music City's leading country station, WSM, cued up the gospel tune 'Shall We Meet', he was greeted by Cody's rowdy tribute to the joy of sex. 'A whole bunch of stations swore that they'd never play another Commander Cody product, because of that mistake,' Frayne lamented.

Worse was to follow. 'I remember once that Paramount Records got me into this country and western station,' Frayne recalled, 'some real honky one. This guy's right there live on the air, and says, "Well, folks, you'll never guess what the cat just dragged in. Commander Cody! Scruffy old hippie." So I just walked over to the microphone and said, "Fuck you," and walked right out of there. They have never forgiven me for that, never. Those people in Nashville hardly talk to me.' Subsequent dope busts did little to improve Commander Cody's reputation in the country market, while the rock audience never recognized the band as anything more than a novelty act.

In 1977, when the Lost Planet Airmen had disbanded and Cody was back with Nicolette Larson and a boogie band, he explained: 'I decided I wanted to be a rock singer. I've pretty much alienated myself from the world of country music, through a series of me being downright obstinate and nasty and snide, and them – that is to say the Nashville establishment – being downright obstinate and nasty and snide. At one point, I was actively trying to ingratiate myself to those hillbilly chiefs. I loved them. I was really knocked out by country music. I really wanted them to accept me as a musician. I really tried! It broke my fucking heart, man, it really did.' The lesson wasn't lost on his contemporaries. It was easier to infiltrate the rock market with country music than to import traditional values into the seventies country industry, which cared more for Hollywood philosophy than hillbilly wisdom.

17 Trouble in Paradise

The death of country rock, 1973–1975: Gram Parsons; the Byrds; Clarence White; Emmylou Harris; the Eagles; Poco; the Souther Hillman Furay Band; Manassas; Gene Clark; the Flying Burrito Brothers

The delayed birth of Gram Parsons' solo career slowed the faint momentum he had retained from the Flying Burrito Brothers. Little sense of anticipation gripped the rock community when *GP* was finally released in the early spring of 1973. But the album didn't pass entirely unnoticed. 'When I heard *GP*,' says Parsons' first biographer, Sid Griffin, 'I realized that he was the guy. We hadn't produced any hip white Southerners who played any kind of anti-Vietnam dope-smoking music; Gram was our boy.'

Griffin also credits Parsons with a musical revelation: 'Students in the South had never heard that kind of country music until Gram played it, even though it came from their own backyard. They'd avoided it like the bubonic plague. It was what happened when the Rolling Stones and the Yardbirds brought Chicago blues back to America. It introduced country to a brand new audience.'

When Parsons and his Fallen Angels set out on a promotional tour in February 1973, any audience was welcome. *GP* was ignored by rock and country radio, and attention normally reserved for the Byrds was being directed at the reunion of their original line-up. Parsons' record label were reluctant to commit themselves to the project, as drummer John Ware recalled: 'Gram's manager, Eddie Tickner, tried getting Warners to put some big money behind Gram, and they just laughed at him. He told Warners, "This is probably the most important music that has come out of America in a decade."'

Parsons and his band were an erratic combination. 'That was just the embryonic stage of what was meant to be,' concedes his duet partner, Emmylou Harris. 'It was a bar band – the ultimate bar band, in a way – and I think we were on the path to something else, maybe to what I did with the Hot Band.' Concentrating on the new album, with the briefest of nods to his past affiliation with the Byrds and the Burritos, Parsons delivered sets solidly rooted in California country. His rock roots surfaced only in the ragged joy of the Fallen Angels, who lacked the slickness that even a semi-professional country band would have imposed.

Parsons felt little affinity with the rock mainstream. 'We're into the great age of nothing rock,' he noted during the tour. 'Some people call it glitter rock. I call it litter rock. I guess everybody is just out to make a buck, and if they see a chance to jump on the bandwagon, they do. When it starts to get off the ground, it's already starting to die. All they're doing is dyeing their hair and putting on make-up. Can you imagine anybody continuing to do that for ten years?'

When he began work on a second album in July 1973, he had no intention beyond promoting 'good country music'. But whereas *GP* would have passed as a Bakersfield country album, *Grievous Angel* was a more diffuse effort.

Parsons had finally found a home for several old songs – the painful tale of a '$1000 Wedding', once attempted by the Burritos; 'Ooh Las Vegas', a collaboration with Rick Grech from the *GP* sessions; and 'Brass Buttons', the sentimental ballad he'd written almost a decade earlier. His equally affecting duet with Emmylou Harris on the Everly Brothers' 'Love Hurts' signalled their emotional connection. 'Gram was in really good shape for that album,' Harris remembered, 'and we were tight from working on the road together. The band knew what they were doing, and we had the charts [i.e., the song arrangements] together by the time we got into the studio. We went in, and man, it was really fast – we did the tracks in five days and then a second five days for the vocals, which were nearly all first or second takes.'

Like 'Big Mouth Blues' on *GP*, several songs affectionately satirized his own image. The man who'd once strutted like Mick Jagger now sang Tom T. Hall's 'I Can't Dance'. As a sardonic commentary on his meagre sales figures, Parsons concocted a 'Medley From Northern Quebec' – fake 'live' recordings of the Louvin Brothers' 'Cash On The Barrelhead' and his own Byrds classic, 'Hickory Wind', overdubbed with the kind of bar-room crowd who bottled the Blues Brothers off-stage.

The Louvins' reference was not accidental, as Emmylou Harris explained: 'Gram really loved the Louvin Brothers, and had been searching for their album with "The Angels Rejoiced In Heaven Last Night" for a long time. It's just a beautiful song, and it ranks with "Love Hurts" as the best thing we ever recorded.'

Parsons set a poem he'd been given to music, and emerged with 'Return Of The Grievous Angel'. In its images of 'the truckers and the kickers and the cowboy angels', he found the company in which his image was destined to rest. But the song which carried the deepest resonance was 'In My Hour Of Darkness', a deceptively mellow account of self-destruction and despair. 'Some say he was a star, but he was just a country boy, his simple songs confess,' Parsons wrote, in what many took as a draft for his own obituary. In fact, his words were directed outwards, to a cousin from the Byrds' family tree.

Retrospection haunted the survivors of the Los Angeles country-rock boom in 1973. The year began with the release of *The Byrds*, an eagerly awaited reunion by the band's original members. Hillman, McGuinn, Clark, Clarke and Crosby had already contributed to early-seventies recordings by Roger McGuinn and Gene Clark, but only via the magic of overdubbing. After a five-year feud, a *rapprochement* between Crosby and McGuinn removed the remaining obstacle to the project. With the McGuinn-led carcass of the Byrds long overdue for burial after two mediocre albums, the reunion had the air of a resurrection, not just for the group but also for the individual participants.

Unrealistic expectations that the Byrds might revive the spirit of 'Mr Tambourine Man' and 'Eight Miles High' were tempered by their change in fortunes since this line-up had first worked together. In 1965, McGuinn and Clark had been the acknowledged leaders of the group; in 1972, Crosby boasted the highest profile, and the most powerful ego. He took control of the production, and was duly castigated when *The Byrds* sounded nothing like the psychedelic folk-rock of the mid-sixties. Instead, it carried all the traits of the Los Angeles élite in the early seventies: tight, not to mention slick, country-rock harmonies, self-satisfaction verging on arrogance, and professionalism that almost obscured the musicians' lack of urgency. 'Full Circle', 'Cowgirl In The Sand' and a majestic rendition of 'See The Sky About To Rain' easily matched the best that the West Coast could muster in 1972, but they couldn't balance the weight of anticipation.

While his former band floundered, Byrds guitarist Clarence White reacquainted himself with his past. Muleskinner was a low-key supergroup of bluegrass graduates who had ventured into the devil's parlour of rock'n'roll; men such as Richard Greene, Peter Rowan, David Grisman and Bill Keith. Their acoustic repertoire of Jimmie Rodgers standards, Chicago blues and traditional folk tunes was a perfect vehicle for White to display the dazzling licks which had established his reputation a decade earlier.

Another project reunited him with Byrds drummer Gene Parsons. Parsons' début album, *Kindling*, astonished those who had reckoned him little more than a backing musician for Roger McGuinn. Effectively a Parsons/White duet, it was a rich, rewarding trip into the acoustic roots of country-rock that ranked alongside the best that the genre had to offer. Its strength was its scale: Parsons simply reflected the tranquillity, simplicity and good humour he'd discovered in his rural retreat. *Kindling* could have reoriented the country-rock tradition at a time when many of its protagonists were merely drifting.

That record complete, White regrouped his family band, the Kentucky Colonels, before beginning a long-overdue solo album. Ahead lay the schedule for a fresh flowering of country-rock talent: a European tour involving the Kentucky Colonels, Gram Parsons and the Fallen Angels, and the inheritors of the Flying Burrito Brothers' legacy, Country Gazette. First, Clarence White had some gigs to fulfil with his brothers, Eric and Roland. In mid-July 1973, White attended a birthday party at Roger McGuinn's Malibu home. 'We were all sitting around playing music,' recalls songwriter Bob Neuwirth, 'and Clarence said, "I have to go, I have a gig with Roland. I'll come back after the gig,"' which was up the San Fernando valley, about thirty miles up the road. Now I would sit and listen to Clarence White all fucking day and night if I could. So we said, "Yeah, man, please come back."'

Clarence, Eric and Roland played the gig, then began to stow away their equipment. As Clarence stepped back from the truck, a drunk driver ploughed into him, killing him instantly.

'We were sitting at Roger's house,' Neuwirth continues, 'waiting for him to come back, and at about three or four in the morning, someone called up and said, "Clarence just got killed." We just started to cry. I was there with Roger and with Kris Kristofferson, and we didn't know what we could do – except that in country music, there has always been this tradition that when something really bad happens, you sing. That's what June Carter Cash taught me when Janis Joplin died. So we wrote a song, called "Rock'n'Roll Time". We all recorded it eventually, all three of us. Not that it was a great song: it was just our way of saying goodbye to Clarence.'

Three days later, Clarence White was buried at Lancaster, on the edge of the Mojave Desert. Many of his country-rock contemporaries were at the graveside, where Gram Parsons recalled that he and Clarence had each vowed to sing the country spiritual 'Farther Along' if the other died first. As his alcohol-slurred voice fell into the familiar verses, the other mourners joined in. The coffin was lowered into the grave, and as Parsons turned away, he spoke to his friend and roadie, Phil Kaufman. 'He told me that he didn't want this to happen to him,' Kaufman says. 'He said, "If I die, Phil, take my body out into the desert and let it burn."'

Back in Los Angeles, Parsons completed work on *Grievous Angel*, dedicating 'In My Hour Of Darkness' to the lost spirit of Clarence White. In early September, he ran into his old friend Rick Grech. 'Rick had turned down the chance to play on *Grievous Angel*,' explains his widow Jenny, 'because the two of them were lethal together, and he'd come to realize that. But he was thrilled that Gram had recorded "Ooh Las Vegas", which Rick had written and then handed over to Gram for the final touches.'

After the *GP* sessions at the end of 1972, Parsons had introduced Grech to the Crickets, who'd snapped him up as a fiddle-player and bassist. 'They were lovely people, very downhome,' Jenny Grech says, 'and for Rick, they represented safety. That was something he couldn't find with Gram. Phil Kaufman knew that: he always said that Rick was the closest person to Gram he'd ever seen – which was great on one level, and highly dangerous on another.

'Rick was due to head back to Nashville to rejoin the Crickets that September,' she continues, 'but he stopped by to see Gram before he left. Gram was in a real state, heavily back into drugs, but he said that he was going out to Joshua Tree. Rick told him, "You better get sorted out there." Then he said – and I swear this is the last thing he said to Gram – "You wanna watch it, 'cos you're going to be a legend in your own lifetime." I flew over to join Rick in Nashville a few days later, just in time to get the phone call from Phil Kaufman saying that Gram had died.'

At the Joshua Tree Inn, in the Mojave Desert, the surreal barrenness of the landscape attracted refugees from the claustrophobia of city life. By the late sixties they were reinforced by drug-dealers, preying on the regular traffic of hippies.

Parsons and some friends partied and slept, the singer taking his pleasure with regular shots of heroin, topped up with morphine, cocaine, marijuana and alcohol. Eventually he passed out in a bathtub, and his body began to turn blue: his female companion applied ice-cubes to his anus, then manually stimulated his penis, and his circulation, back to life. When he collapsed for a second time, his system was too poisoned to respond. There was a chaotic attempt at a cover-up, and the precise circumstances of the fatal hit – and the identities of the bystanders – are wrapped in a fog of confusion and deceit. One fact remained: Gram Parsons was dead. Remembering his promise two months earlier, Phil Kaufman 'stole' the body from Los Angeles airport, and returned Gram to the desert. There he torched the casket, and established a legend which has brought hundreds of musicians to Joshua Tree (notably U2, who named an album after the site) in search of an ember of Gram's inspiration and mystique.

As the self-appointed guardian of Parsons' remains, Kaufman distributed remnants to his friends. Rick Grech was entrusted with Gram's guitar, and with his workbook. 'Rick didn't want to treat it as a sacred object,' Jenny Grech explains, 'so he just carried on using it where Gram had finished off. It was a way of continuing the work that he had done.' One portion of Parsons' legacy was beyond Kaufman's control. Before his death, Gram had not yet approved a running order for *Grievous Angel*. He had, however, chosen a cover photograph: 'Gram selected a shot of him and Emmylou on a motorcycle,' Kaufman explains. 'But after he died, the choice was left to Gretchen, Gram's wife, who hated Emmylou. She persuaded Warner Brothers not to use that picture.' Kaufman threatened to dump 'fifteen pounds of chicken-shit' in Warners president Joe Smith's executive parking-space if Gram's wishes weren't upheld, but Warners bowed to the widow's instructions. Emmylou Harris's picture was absent from *Grievous Angel*, and her name relegated to the back cover.

In the weeks after Gram's death, his friends congregated in private to celebrate his life. 'Emmylou came and visited us shortly after Gram died,' recalls Barry Tashian, 'and she happened to have a tape of some of the last sessions she'd done with him, which she hadn't heard before. We were sitting around playing guitars and singing, and then we put on that tape, which had all these songs like "Brass Buttons" on it. It was as if Gram was in the room with us. It was an emotional moment.'

That gathering reflected one aspect of Parsons' character; another was captured by Phil Kaufman, who staged a commercial wake in Los Angeles. Admission was five dollars, and inside you could buy Gram Parsons T-shirts, and Gram Parsons beer with custom labels. A Johnny Cash imitator provided the country atmosphere, while a dose of Hollywood madness was supplied by sixties novelty act Bobby Pickett and the Crypt-Kickers, and Jonathan Richman and the Modern Lovers, whose quirky garage-punk might have appealed to Parsons' sense of the absurd.

Gram would have been more surprised by what happened to his reputation. *Grievous Angel* won the rave reviews that are often granted to the recently deceased, though it left only the shallowest of marks on the sales charts. But end-of-year polls proved that the album was held in high esteem, and by 1975 Parsons was close to canonization as the icon of country-rock performers.

'I get asked a lot, "Don't you feel you're the second man to

Gram Parsons?"' Chris Hillman notes soberly. 'I say, "I don't care." My wife puts it in perspective: "You're still alive!" It's OK, because death brings icon status, like with Jim Morrison of the Doors. As much press as Gram gets, I constantly remind people that Gene Clark wrote some amazing songs, and lots of them. Gram had some talent, but no discipline.'

Hillman's judgement is understandably harsh, though it's unarguable that the circumstances of Parsons' death helped to construct a myth that has allowed little room for objectivity. Hillman finds it difficult to envisage an alternative scenario, in which Parsons survives to the end of the century: 'He had really bad addictions, and he had such a history of that in his family – his mother was an alcoholic, like him – that it would have been pretty hard for him to escape it.'

Without his death to stoke the legend, Gram's career is easier to predict. *Grievous Angel* would have sold even less, he'd have been dropped by Warners, and would have slipped into the same ghetto of cult acceptance as fellow ex-Byrds Gene Clark and Gene Parsons. Emmylou Harris might never have had a solo career; and there'd have been no Hot Band to guide the tarnished spirit of country music through its late-seventies turmoil. In death, Gram Parsons achieved something he'd never managed in his lifetime: convincing the public that the collision of country and rock'n'roll could, after all, produce Cosmic American Music.

'We who must remain go on singing just the same', ran the chorus of the Eagles' 'My Man', the first song written in Parsons' memory. The tribute was composed by Bernie Leadon, who'd played alongside Gram in the Flying Burrito Brothers but who was hardly inspired to lyrical heights. 'I once knew a man, a talented guy', one verse began unassumingly, and there was little in the song that Gram would have recognized.

Closer to the mark was 'Crazy Eyes', written by Richie Furay for Poco – the band whose invitation Parsons had refused several years earlier. An epic production which pinned a lonesome banjo line against a sweeping string arrangement, it matched the romantic grandeur, if not the style, of Parsons' best work. Eerily, it had been written and recorded before Gram's death, as if Furay instinctively knew that he'd be required to summarize his friend's life.

The most heartfelt response to the tragedy came from Emmylou Harris. 'When Gram died,' she recalled, 'I felt like I'd been amputated, like my life had just been whacked off. I'd only been with him a short time, but it was like everything had become clear to me in that short period. I'd never realized what kind of music was inside me before I met Gram. Then, when I knew exactly what I wanted to do and where I was going, he was gone.' The bleak landscape of loss was the setting for 'Boulder To Birmingham', one of Harris's few original compositions. 'You really got me this time,' she wrote, with her old friend, Bill Danoff, 'and the hardest part is knowing I'll survive'. It was a mature response, but also an accurate account of the aftermath. While *Grievous Angel* was being lauded as a triumphant farewell, Harris was rebuilding her career from the roots.

'I returned to Washington after Gram died,' she explains, 'and I decided to keep working. So I formed the Angel Band with my friend Tom Guidera. We toured around all these bluegrass clubs in Maryland and Washington.'

After her contributions to *Grievous Angel* began to receive as much attention as Parsons', her manager Eddie Tickner was able to persuade Warner Brothers to consider her as a solo act. 'They sort of wanted to sign me,' she remembered, 'and sort of didn't want to sign me at the same time, because ladies were regarded as a liability. You know – "they get pregnant and they freak out on the road, they're unreliable and they don't sell".' With Gram's roadie Phil Kaufman on hand to ensure that all freaking-out would be strictly intentional, that problem could be overcome. But Warners weren't interested in signing the Angel Band, only Harris. With regret, she had to let her club band go.

'Warners said, "Look, we would like to propose that you get a hot band and we'll fund it for you," ' she explained. 'So I figured, "What have I got to lose?" ' She approached the musicians who had proved too expensive for Parsons eighteen months earlier: James Burton, Glen D. Hardin, Ronnie Tutt (all veterans of the Elvis Presley touring band) and Emory Gordy. They duly became the Hot Band. 'I was definitely gathering up everything that Gram had touched,' she admits, 'like they were holy relics. I had just started to find my musical identity and my voice, but it was so closely associated with what he was doing. Then I was left in the lurch. So I figured, "OK, Gram picked this band to record with him, so they must be an important part of it!" I had to use them. And I had to keep singing the songs we had sung together.'

Distanced from California, Emmylou Harris was also removed from the musicians who'd grown up alongside Gram Parsons. One of the many ironies of his death is that it coincided with the moment when country-rock, or the music known by that name, became the currency of the West Coast – just as it shed its overt country roots.

On The Border, the Eagles album which contained their Parsons tribute, signalled the subtle shift in mood. They began the sessions with Glyn Johns, the producer of The Eagles and Desperado, but after a few weeks the band fired him. Instead, they hired Bill Szymczyk, on the reputation of his blues-rock productions for Joe Walsh and the James Gang. 'I saw through the Eagles as far as their acoustic, cowboy elements went,' Szymczyk explained. 'I saw them as rockers who were dying and screaming to get out, and I think I helped them.'

Rock session-guitarist Don Felder was recruited as a full-time Eagle, and On The Border was pumped up with rock adrenalin, though the trademark harmonies were retained as a link to the past. Concocting a tribute to 'James Dean', the band signposted their rejection of the emotional complexities of adult relationships in favour of adolescent gesturing. In retrospect, Glenn Frey claimed that the shift away from country was inevitable: 'When we went out on those early tours with bands like Jethro Tull and Yes, we were taking a beating out there. Don Henley and I kept visualizing that we needed this kick-ass segment to our live show, something at the end to just take off with. We needed a little more fire power.' Sacrificed in return was the bluegrass finesse of Bernie Leadon. As Don Henley admitted: 'He never really understood how to get that dirty rock and roll sound.'

Leadon's final stand with the Eagles was One Of These Nights. The album's biggest single was the purest country song they'd ever written, 'Lyin' Eyes ' – its smooth harmonies wedded to a structure that anyone in Nashville would have relished. On the same album was 'Journey To The Sorcerer', a space voyage in sound that grew from country banjo and fiddles to incorporate backwards guitar, and a vast orchestra. It seemed like the ultimate perversion of Bernie Leadon's hillbilly tradition – but 'Journey To The Sorcerer' was his composition, while the traditional values of 'Lyin' Eyes' came from Henley, Frey and Felder, the Eagles who were keenest to leave their country heritage behind.

When they staked their future on the dynamics of arena rock, the Eagles were following the example of their LA predecessors Poco. After the good-time bluegrass of their début album, Richie Furay and Jim Messina's band opened themselves up to a tougher sound. Pedal steel player Rusty Young was encouraged to create sonic textures beyond the imagination of strictly country musicians: 'I think we led the way in getting the sound of the organ through the steel guitar,' Furay reflected. Messina's departure in late 1970 to form a soft-rock duo with Kenny Loggins tilted Poco a few more degrees away from the country-rock axis.

His replacement was Paul Cotton, from rock band Illinois Speed Press. 'I had to learn a whole other way of playing,' Cotton admitted, 'but after a while, I just threw the fingerpicks away, because what they really needed me for was the rock'n'roll. That's my background, and they needed more strength in that area.'

Though Messina's departure cut one of Poco's ties to Buffalo Springfield, Cotton's songwriting ability more than compensated. After a false start on the patchy *From The Inside*, the new line-up flowered on *A Good Feelin' To Know*, recorded in the summer of 1972. 'I thought that album had everything anybody could want,' Furay admitted, and its mix of crafted songs, exhilarating harmonies and Rusty Young's creative steel playing was a landmark in Los Angeles rock history. But it failed to enliven Poco's mediocre commercial showing, and the failure crushed Furay's enthusiasm.

His bitterness was understandable. Of his former colleagues, Stephen Stills and Neil Young had become superstars via CSNY; Randy Meisner had left Poco for the Eagles, who were now outselling Furay's band; even Loggins and Messina held more cachet than Poco.

Furay agreed to record one more album with the band, *Crazy Eyes*, and then departed – enticed away by the prospect of a Los Angeles extravaganza which would reunite the original members of the Byrds, Buffalo Springfield and Crosby, Stills, Nash and Young on the same bill.

The architect of this grandiose plan was David Geffen, the one-time agent for Poco who had become the most powerful figure in Los Angeles rock. Either as a manager or as the owner of the Asylum label, he had handled the careers of CSNY, Poco, the Eagles, Linda Ronstadt and Joni Mitchell. Only the maverick sensibility of musicians like Stephen Stills and Neil Young, arrogant and utopian enough to demand control over their own destinies, thwarted his proposal, which was eventually downsized to a stadium tour by CSNY. That mammoth series of gigs in summer 1974 signalled that one of the most intriguing experiments of the era had failed. In Manassas, Stephen Stills had created a band worthy of the heritage of the Byrds and Buffalo Springfield. Though their full potential was never captured on record, Manassas provided an antithesis to the common LA belief that country-tinged rock was the only viable successor to the eclecticism of the sixties.

Country-rock was certainly an essential ingredient of the Manassas concept, but Stills wasn't satisfied with mastering a single genre. Instead, he envisaged a band that could switch at will from country to blues, to Latin jazz, to acoustic folk and back to driving rock'n'roll. It was a vast, possibly foolhardy, enterprise – an amalgam of every style that the Byrds and the Springfield had embraced in the sixties. Few musicians were arrogant enough to attempt something so expansive; fewer still could have come so close to succeeding. At the core of Manassas were the musicians that Stills had borrowed from the decaying Flying Burrito Brothers in late 1971 – Chris Hillman and Al Perkins. Byron Berline was on hand whenever a country fiddle was required, while Joe Lala provided the Latin rhythms and bursts of Spanish rhetoric. After some acoustic shows which featured the unknown Emmylou

Harris as an honorary member, the band played their official début at the Concertgebouw in Amsterdam – always a sympathetic venue for the Californian country-rock fraternity. The initial reviews were ecstatic – one British critic described Manassas as 'the greatest band I've ever seen in my life' – and their repertoire of old Springfield and Byrds tunes, plus almost two dozen new songs, suggested that they carried as much potential as the much-hyped CSNY supergroup.

Much of that promise was fulfilled on *Stephen Stills/Manassas*, a double-album issued in the summer of 1972. 'I like the whole album,' said Chris Hillman later, 'I think it's great. It's rare for me to come from a project and say, "That's wonderful".'

The album cover explained the origin of the group's name, as the seven key musicians posed on the platform at Manassas Junction railroad station. Stills claimed that they'd held the photo session there by accident, and that the station sign had provided a fortuitous title for his ensemble. 'No, we went there on purpose,' reveals Al Perkins. 'Manassas was the site of two Civil War battles, and Stephen was a big Civil War buff, so he took us there deliberately. He had already come up with the name.' Not only was Manassas a battleground: it marked the site of the Bull-Runs, where the Confederate Army had defeated the Union forces as part of their bid to drive the Northern troops back to the Atlantic coast. Once a Southerner, it seems, always a Southerner . . .

Nothing on the album was quite so politically loaded; there was barely a hint of the anti-establishment preaching which had been part of Stills' music for the last five years. Instead, Manassas made their statement via the universality of music, commanding genres which were frequently seen as antagonistic (notably hard rock and country) with dazzling skill. Joe Lala provided the line which bonded Latin America with the mountain music of Kentucky: 'Música Latina es Cuban bluegrass,' he chanted, as the timbales rattled. Stills offered more conventional wisdom, opting for the sanity of nature above the claustrophobia of the city: 'California dreamin' nearly put me down for good, Colorado Rocky Mountains saved my senses.'

With one side of the album – symbolically titled 'The Wilderness' – devoted to country and bluegrass, and another

('Consider') to variations on reflective country-rock, *Manassas* was pitched into the tradition of *Sweetheart Of The Rodeo*, *The Gilded Palace Of Sin* and *The Flying Burrito Brothers*. 'That band could cover anything, from hardcore salsa to traditional bluegrass,' says Chris Hillman. But although Hillman's bluegrass roots helped to authenticate the portrayal of 'The Wilderness', this was very much Stills' project.

Anticipating the Christian country-rock excursions of the early eighties, in which both Hillman and Al Perkins would be active, Stills used the almost spiritual sparseness of country gospel to proclaim that 'Jesus Gave Love Away For Free'. 'Out of everyone I've known in rock'n'roll,' Hillman claims, 'Stills really understood country music. He knew what it was, and what it wasn't.' Another song, 'Fallen Eagle', used the tools of Bill Monroe's bluegrass to make his one comment on the state of contemporary America under the domain of Richard Nixon. 'Fly on up to Canada,' Stills entreated, using the eagle as a double symbol of American power and individual freedom, 'this country isn't safe anymore.'

In keeping with the ferocious pace at which Stills dealt with his life in the early seventies – suitably fuelled studio sessions lasting several days weren't uncommon – Manassas could only maintain their momentum for a few months. Following their spectacular début tour, Stills seems to have sacrificed their collective spirit in favour of his own career, and after a desultory second album, *Down The Road*, on which their bluegrass leanings were virtually ignored, the band disintegrated.

David Geffen didn't get his way. The lukewarm reception of the Byrds' reunion album prohibited their involvement in any 1974 concerts, and Stephen Stills and Neil Young soon realized there were riches to be reaped from a CSNY tour, without any need for a regrouping of Buffalo Springfield.

The Asylum Records supremo had a reserve plan. He brought together Poco refugee Richie Furay, Manassas cast-off Chris Hillman and solo songwriter John David Souther, who'd contributed some of the best material to recent albums by his girlfriend, Linda Ronstadt. In keeping with the ego-friendly billing of CSNY, they became the Souther Hillman Furay Band: the ultimate LA country-rock supergroup.

What followed was a symptom of the genre's terminal decline, and also a major contributory factor in that change of fortune. Despite Furay and Hillman's experience in the Byrds, the Burritos, the Springfield and Poco, neither man had the personality to impose his will on the others; Souther was an unknown quantity as far as the public were concerned. 'He was a very gifted writer,' Hillman admits, 'but not necessarily a person that should be in a band, as a team-player.' Their self-titled début album in 1974 was a solid, unpretentious piece of LA product, but it was entirely lacking in urgency – or indeed anything more gripping than the silence of a movement standing still. Hillman's 'Rise And Fall' provided an unwitting epitaph: 'After all these years of trying, tell me is it really worth it all?' He was merely echoing Richie Furay's comment during an abortive early rehearsal: 'Why did I leave Poco for this?'

The Souther Hillman Furay Band proved to be adept at such inadvertent self-criticism. 'Greetings from Glamour City!' screamed the inner artwork on their début album, belying its contents. Hillman even had the nerve to title one song 'Safe At Home', which not only underscored the complacency at the heart of the project but borrowed the name of Gram Parsons' far more vital record with the International Submarine Band seven years earlier. It was Souther who composed the group's obituary, with his title track for their mediocre second album: 'Trouble In Paradise'. By then, this country-rock band were dividing their attention between lame hard-rock riffs and the polished white disco which was the soundtrack for Los Angeles in the second half of the 1970s. 'We were going nowhere fast,' Hillman admits, 'and by the time we made that second album, we knew it.'

In the weeks after Gram Parsons' death, another refugee from the Byrds completed the album that came closest to fulfilling his vision of Cosmic American Music. Gene Clark was the only original Byrd to emerge from their reunion project with his creative energies renewed. The band's brief refuelling had interrupted his sessions for a country-rock album – eventually issued as *Roadmaster* –

which added nothing to the spartan textures of the Dillard & Clark records. The artistic tension and critical failure of *The Byrds* punctured the self-confidence of Clark's colleagues. But like a musical vampire, he was able to feed off their collective heritage when he threw himself into the lengthy recording process for his finest work: *No Other*.

Elements of the Byrds' tradition soaked Clark's album, from the David Crosby-style wordless harmonies of 'Strength Of Strings' to the McGuinnesque fusion of gospel and country that powered 'Life's Greatest Fool'. While the other Byrds were sinking into Californian decadence by the mid-seventies, Clark could still control a rich palette of genres and metaphors. Producer Thomas Jefferson Kaye marshalled a huge cast of session players and singers, creating vast landscapes of sound that Phil Spector might have envied. The album was rooted in country-rock, but never limited by it.

Clark had immersed himself in Zen Buddhism, and through *No Other* ran the motif of change, of faith in the inevitable shifts of fate. It must have been a comforting doctrine for a man who had regularly seen stardom evade his grasp since his departure from the Byrds. Maybe Clark felt an ironic sense of justice when he sang, 'What's been flying high must sometimes touch the ground.' But his agenda was wider than settling scores with his former bandmates. Just as his music used country-rock as the foundation for grand experiments in sound, so Clark extended the verbal territory of the genre. The true precursor of a song like 'Strength Of Strings' was less Gram Parsons, or even Bob Dylan, than a poem like Coleridge's 'The Eolian Harp'.

As Michael Nesmith had already discovered, the audience for country-rock was too small to encompass flights of lyrical abstraction. An album which ought to have admitted Clark to the rock immortals was mistrusted – why was he wearing make-up and twelve-inch flares on the cover? – and mostly ignored. Admired only in retrospect, *No Other* influenced no one; Gene Clark never dared to match its adventurous zeal again.

The commercial failure of *No Other* symbolized the death of the utopian ideals that had ignited the country-rock movement nearly a decade earlier. They were replaced by the arrogant, lazy self-belief engendered by Hollywood's drug of choice, cocaine. The indulgence was fuelled by a record industry on the verge of sharp decline. During the remainder of the seventies, excess baggage was jettisoned from company rosters to the point that no member of the Byrds had a secure solo deal with a major label by 1980. It was as if every line of coke was repaid by a fractured career, as the generation of 1972 was pared to the minimum. Only those who had continued to grow as artists were able to survive – Neil Young, Joni Mitchell, Jackson Browne and, to everyone's surprise, Linda Ronstadt, who rode each wave from LA funk to disco to punk with practised ease. The rest were cast aside to the oblivion of the nostalgia circuit, or the ignominy of hand-to-mouth existence on an indie label.

As if they were unable to believe that their nirvana had a limited lifespan, the main casualties continued to struggle their way through the late seventies. There were solo albums from Chris Hillman, J. D. Souther, Richie Furay and the rest, but they sold to an increasingly limited audience.

For anyone who had followed the saga since the days of the International Submarine Band, no episode carried more symbolic weight than the ill-fated decision to relaunch the Flying Burrito Brothers. Gram Parsons was dead, Chris Hillman busy with Furay and Souther, Bernie Leadon was battling for his place in the Eagles, and even Rick Roberts was unavailable, caught midway between his solo career and another intended LA supergroup, Firefall. So the burden of reviving Parsons and Hillman's vehicle fell to steel guitarist Sneaky Pete Kleinow and bassist Chris Ethridge. They enlisted Gene Parsons from the late-period Byrds and Gib Guilbeau, who'd played alongside Parsons and Clarence White a decade earlier in bands like Nashville West and Cajun Gib & Gene.

'Eddie Tickner asked us around 1974 if we'd like to get a group together,' explained Kleinow, 'and go to Europe for a Burritos tour. I said, "Yeah, that's a good idea," and so we got together. When we were rehearsing, we found it sounded pretty good, so we decided to make a permanent thing of it.'

The reformed Burritos made two disappointing albums for

Columbia; Ethridge stayed long enough to appear on the first, *Flying Again*, but then baled out before the erroneously titled *Airborne*. Skip Battin, Gene Parsons' one-time partner in the Byrds' rhythm section, took his place. 'Chris Ethridge told me that he left because he couldn't stand it,' Chris Hillman explained in the late seventies. His view of the venture was harsh, but scarcely surprising: 'Maybe I wouldn't feel so bad if they had been really good, but they weren't. They were neither good vocally nor instrumentally. They took the Flying Burrito Brothers' name when they should have let it rest, and they were even singing songs that Gram and I wrote.'

The accusation cut Kleinow to the quick: 'We do get requests for the old songs,' he admitted, 'but not as much as we used to. I think we're gradually coming out of that handicap – which it is, because we are not that old group. If it was up to me, if we could do exactly what we pleased, we'd probably change the name, but for political reasons it's not really that easy to do.' So Gram Parsons' vehicle for Cosmic American Music became the subject of ridicule and dispute; and the stream of Los Angeles country-rock ran dry.

Ricky Skaggs: God's Hands Were on the Beatles

I was influenced by the Beatles and the Stones. The Beatles sounded like the Everly Brothers, who sounded like the Louvin Brothers, who sounded like the Stanley Brothers, who sounded like the Monroe Brothers. It just goes right back, all the way to the Delmore Brothers.

There was a sound about the Beatles that made the whole world stand on its ears. The way I look at things, nothing is just by accident, and God has His hand on everything. I believe that the Beatles were anointed, called forth by God, to do what they did. In the beginning of their career, at least, the hand of God was on them.

There is no way that men can create new rhythms, new music, new lyrics, new recording techniques, new videos, new sound systems. That comes from the creativity of God. And I really do believe with all my heart that God wanted to use those four guys to influence a whole generation of young men and women.

I'm convinced that God wanted the church to embrace those guys. Every one of the Beatles was looking for a spiritual experience. They all needed something. And because the church rejected them so bad, and hurt them, they started looking for whatever would embrace them – Hare Krishna, all the Eastern religions, anything that would satisfy that need. They tried to fill that void in their lives. What they heard was that you're your own God. It's New Age philosophy, and they believed it.

Back in the beginning, God anointed them to usher in a charismatic revival. There was a big revival in the sixties – the whole Jesus movement – and thousands of hippies and teenage kids came to the Lord. I'll never believe anything else but that the Beatles were divinely ordered, to represent the works of God. But they forfeited their inheritance, they forfeited their calling, when they got into drugs and all that other philosophy. All of a sudden, they were scoring points for the other team.

Ricky Skaggs, Nashville, 1992

PART II
COUNTRY INTO ROCK

18 My Kind of Carryin' On
The birth of Memphis rockabilly, 1953–1957: Elvis Presley, Carl Perkins and Sun Records

All he could think about was Hank Williams. A haze of flashbulbs washed across his eyes, streaking his view of the Saturday night crowd. But he wasn't even trying to focus on the rings of wooden pews, or the distant blur of the Confederate Balcony. He searched for something solid amid the cloud of images. Always he came back to Hank Williams, who'd trodden the same route through the claustrophobic maze of dressing-rooms to reach the bare boards of the *Grand Ole Opry* stage.

Then it was over, and Hank Snow – Hank Snow! – was requesting a hand for this young boy from Memphis, Tennessee, won't you show some appreciation for Elvis Presley, always a pleasure to greet a new face to the *Opry*. A wave of respectful applause reached the stage, then ebbed away, as the crowd readied themselves for Snow to sing. Scotty Moore and Bill Black whooped and slapped his back as they slipped past the wooden chairs that filled the wings. From the mass of singers and stagehands backstage came the familiar face of Sam Phillips, his recording manager, beaming with satisfaction. Alongside him was a dark-suited figure whose generous jowls, greased-down hairline and perfectly poised handkerchief signified a successful businessman. Elvis stammered his thanks as *Opry* manager Jim Denny offered polite congratulations. But Denny kept on talking. The *Opry* was a country show, he said soberly, and he intended to keep it that way. 'Have you been singing long?' he asked the teenager, who was almost twitching with embarrassment. 'No sir,' Elvis replied. 'What were you doing before that?' 'Well, sir, I used to drive a truck.' 'That's a good trade, son,' Denny noted, fixing the singer with an emotionless stare. 'Maybe you should think about going back to it one day.' And with a nod to Phillips, Denny turned away, to focus attention on the real *Opry* stars, such as Ernest Tubb or Webb Pierce. 'Forget him,' Sam Phillips whispered to Elvis. 'That man threw Hank off the *Opry*, too.'

Exposure on the *Opry* was an honour. As Elvis's home-town paper, the *Commercial Appeal*, noted, 'It is unprecedented for the *Grand Ole Opry* to take a performer on the basis of a single record, which is what Presley had until two weeks ago.' In Sam Phillips' account, it took a bravura performance to win over the reluctant Jim Denny: 'I knew Jim, so I went over to play him the record. He said, "I've heard it, Sam, I just better not put him on right now because we might do something to the *Grand Ole Opry*, and it's so traditional." I told him I understood, and then I went into this bit about younger people and I said, "These people that used to drive to town in a wagon – well, the world has changed, we got jet aeroplanes!" He said, "The door is not closed. I think it's an interesting record but I don't wanna get sponsors cancelled."'

All the jet aeroplanes in the world wouldn't have touched Jim Denny's heart: his concern was the future of the *Opry*. But by late September 1954, that 'interesting record' – Elvis Presley's double-headed monster, 'That's All Right'/'Blue Moon Of Kentucky' – was sweeping across the South. Already the best-selling country record in Memphis, it was starting to show up on stations in Nashville and New Orleans. Denny had also heard the testimony of his friend Webb Pierce. On 10 August, Pierce had been scheduled to follow Elvis on stage at Overton Park in Memphis. But the reaction to the teenager, whose routine was all noise and swagger, was so overwhelming that Pierce realized there was no point in even bothering to sing. 'Sunnuvabitch,' he whistled in amazement as he watched the crowd – *his* crowd – erupt in a howl of approval.

So Denny booked Elvis and his Blue Moon Boys, guitarist Scotty Moore and bass fiddle player Bill Black, for a one-off spot on the *Opry* – the coveted prize for any country musician in 1954. 'It was a big thing to be on the *Opry* stage,' Moore remembered. 'I remember Bill and I saying, "What are we gonna do now? This is as high as you can go."' Not that the audience who squeezed into Nashville's Ryman Auditorium were too impressed. 'The *Opry* crowd were polite,' Moore recalled. 'They didn't boo, hiss or anything. They didn't jump up and down in their seats, either, but they didn't do that for anybody. But Elvis was disappointed. The crowds at the *Opry* weren't from here in town, and the records hadn't gotten out further. Only a handful of people that night had heard it.' Elvis was never invited back to the *Opry*; neither was Hank Williams after he was kicked off the show's roster in August 1952 for unreliable conduct. Five months later, Hank was dead, and Jim Denny, who'd administered that blow, was one of the pall-bearers. Legend has it that when Elvis returned to Nashville in 1955, now a recognized country star, Denny voiced his belief that he'd always known the kid would make it. For once, Elvis's innate politeness failed him. In 1956, Denny himself was sacked from the *Opry* management for alleged misconduct. By then, Elvis was too big for any radio show. Indeed, he was too big for country music.

'A lot of country stars don't want to be known as country,' reckoned Marty Robbins – best known for cowboy songs like 'El Paso', but one of the earliest performers to recognize the potential of Elvis Presley's music. 'Elvis told me when he was getting started that Hank Snow and I were his favourite singers. Well, Elvis got real big, and then he was interviewed and said his favourites were Frank Sinatra and Perry Como. I think Colonel Parker was involved in that, because I don't think he wanted Elvis to be associated with country.'

Parker won management rights over the young singer's career in 1955, ousting contenders like Scotty Moore and Memphis promoter Bob Neal. Late that year, Presley left the local label run by Sam Phillips and signed with RCA, a major company centred in New York. By early 1956, Parker had pulled Elvis away from hillbilly jamborees. No longer would Presley line up alongside Hank Snow and Marty Robbins: now he was the sole attraction, and the under-bill was filled with jugglers, hack comedians and clowns.

'Colonel' Tom Parker (the honour was self-bestowed) was a Dutch illegal immigrant posing as a good ol' boy, a leftover from the old Southern culture of carnivals and medicine shows. He won Elvis's trust because he was the manager of Hank Snow, who was renowned for his integrity. Snow deserves much credit for shepherding the teenage singer through his initial year in showbusiness.

Part scheming Svengali, part bumbling booster, Parker asserted total control over Presley's career after 1955. He's the ultimate hero or villain, depending on whether you view Presley's Progress as a triumph or tragedy. But there seems to have been no cultural motive for steering Elvis away from country, no desire to strip the adjective from the Hillbilly Cat. Parker's goal was money, and he realized the folly of caging a teenage sensation in the South. He judged that Presley could work the same magic on adolescent girls in New York as he had in hillbilly centres like Shreveport and Dallas.

Parker faced no opposition from his client. Elvis wasn't lying when he pledged allegiance to Snow and Robbins; like most kids in the American South, he'd grown up with the *Opry*. Hillbilly giants like Roy Acuff, Bill Monroe and Hank Williams soundtracked the lives of every rock'n'roller who came out of Tennessee, Arkansas, Mississippi or Texas in the mid-1950s. But Presley was no purist. His prime ambition had been to join a gospel quartet, like the Blackwoods. In August 1954, he was invited to join their junior combo, the Songfellows – an offer he would have accepted had he not signed a deal with Sun Records just a few weeks earlier.

Spiritual and secular, this diet of gospel and hillbilly was common ground in the South. But Elvis also responded to different pulses – like the black R&B artists he heard on WHBQ in Memphis, where Dewey Phillips (no relation to Sam) filled the airwaves every night with his *Red Hot And Blue* show. Dewey was possessed like a Southern preacher, but his gospel was the blues – preferably loud and lascivious. In the early fifties, an obsession with Bobby Bland and Joe Turner linked a secret society, which stretched from the young Robert Zimmerman in the icy landscape of Minnesota down to Jerry Lee Lewis amid the copperheads and cottonfields of Louisiana. DJs like Dewey Phillips fuelled their private obsessions.

To this regimen of country and R&B, Presley added another ingredient. He envied the amused sophistication of Dean Martin, aped the controlled hysterics of Johnnie Ray, echoed the operatic rotundity of Mario Lanza. Despite the grinding poverty of his upbringing, the sparkle of showbusiness was in his blood. Years before terms like 'crossover' were ever imagined, Elvis was a bridge waiting to be opened.

Uncertain of his ambitions and his talent, Presley searched for directions in the early fifties. In May 1953, he hitchhiked 250 miles to Meridian, Mississippi, for the Jimmie Rodgers 'Father Of Country Music' festival – honouring another Southern pioneer who didn't recognize boundaries. There he entered a talent contest, and finished second. He sang in class, to the amusement of his schoolmates. He tried out for gospel groups, strummed a guitar in front of his apartment block, but mostly just dreamed of a brighter future. In the late summer of 1953, he walked into the Memphis Recording Service, a custom operation which boasted that 'We Record Anything – Anywhere – Anytime'. It doubled as the headquarters of Sun Records. This barely thriving concern was run by a white man, Sam Phillips, whose forte was creating black blues records which lacked the smoothness demanded by major labels.

Subsequent events constitute the first rock'n'roll legend, a creation story that exists in several forms. When he first arrived at Phillips' HQ, the owner wasn't home, so Elvis's request to cut a record – for his mother, or maybe to satisfy his own curiosity – passed to Sam's assistant, Marion Keisker. 'Who do you sound like?' she asked the awkward teenage boy. 'I don't sound like nobody,' ran his mythic reply. 'Are you hillbilly?' 'Yeah, I sing hillbilly,' Presley mumbled. 'But I don't sound like nobody.'

Keisker went to her grave disputing what happened next, but less than a year later, Presley was back inside Sun Studios – this time with two of Phillips' musicians, Scotty Moore and Bill Black. They were members of the Starlite Wranglers, whom Moore describes as 'honky-tonk. We'd play clubs, whatever was popular on the jukebox.'

Older than Presley, and with fewer fantasies about their prospects, Moore and Black had cut a record earlier that year, behind hillbilly Doug Poindexter. The lugubrious 'My Kind Of Carryin' On' proved that, even when it came to hedonism,

Poindexter couldn't escape a sense of failure. Moore and Black's accompaniment was equally restrained, but as they slipped into the first verse, Moore liberated a flurry of electric guitar notes, a signal that some kind of escape might be possible.

Sam Phillips provided the key, though only after Sun's other country band, the Ripley Cotton Choppers, declined to accompany the untried Presley. So it was that Elvis, Scotty and Bill set out on the path to – well, nobody, least of all Presley, had any idea. They warmed up with some country hits, like 'I Don't Hurt Anymore' and 'I Really Don't Want To Know'. Hours passed as Elvis reached back to Dean Martin and Mario Lanza, emitting a ghostly croon as he floated through pop standards like 'Blue Moon' and 'Harbor Lights'. Only when they thought Mr Phillips wasn't listening did they lighten up, skipping through a decade-old blues hit. 'Elvis just started singing this song and acting the fool,' Moore remembered, 'and then Bill picked up his bass and he started acting the fool, too, and I started playing with them. Sam, I think, had the door to the control booth open, and he stuck his head out and said, "What are you doing?" And we said, "We don't know." "Well, back up," he said, "and try to find a place to start, and do it again."'

In the hands of Arthur 'Big Boy' Crudup, 'That's All Right' was a weary blues tune that undercut its title with every stumbling chord. Presley set the pace at uptempo hillbilly, Bill Black slapped his bass fiddle as if he were pumping water, and Moore's electric lead doubled as pulse-beat and decoration. 'I was thinking about horns when I played that lead,' he explained years later. 'Once I discovered I could do that, I started playing it on every song – mixing up some rhythm and some lead, throwing in everything I knew.'

His voice loosened by the moment, Elvis shed his self-conscious theatrics and snapped into the lyrics, spitting them out with a lustful disdain that he had never expressed in real life. In that moment he became himself. But what was he? Looking back, Sam Phillips remembered he'd been looking for a white man who could sing black music – not as a cultural experiment, but as a way of translating the passion he found in the blues. 'He never mentioned anything like that to us,' Scotty Moore comments. 'Maybe in the back of his mind that's what he was looking for, but I can't recall any songs Elvis sang where Sam said, "That's a black man singing!"'

'That's All Right' was pure excitement, honed over a series of takes into something – nobody knew quite what – that might have commercial potential. Elvis might have drifted back into the safety of his ballads. But Phillips nagged him to find another vehicle for that joyful shedding of inhibition.

The trio found it in an unlikely source: a maudlin country waltz by Bill Monroe, the grim-faced puritan of bluegrass music. He sang 'Blue Moon Of Kentucky' like a religious anthem; Presley's vocal hopped like a stallion on heat. 'We thought it was exciting, but what was it?' Moore recalls. 'It was just so completely different. It really flipped Sam. He felt it really had something. We just sort of shook our heads and said, "Well, that's fine, but good God, they'll run us out of town!"' Sam Phillips knew exactly what it had. 'Hell,' he exclaimed as another take of 'Blue Moon Of Kentucky' careered to a standstill, 'that's a pop song now!'

On 7 July 1954, Sam Phillips delivered dubs of 'That's All Right'/ 'Blue Moon Of Kentucky' to three Memphis DJs – Dewey Phillips at WHBQ, Sleepy-Eyed John Lepley at WHHM, and Uncle Richard at WMPS. That night, all three aired Sam's new discovery. Sleepy-Eyed John and Uncle Richard slipped 'Blue Moon Of Kentucky' into their hillbilly playlists, while Phillips threw aside his regular blues offerings and replayed 'That's All Right' over and over, opening the phone-lines for reactions and even interviewing the timid Presley on air.

As *Country Song Round-Up* magazine noted a year later, 'The disc represented something new: the unusual pairing of an R&B number with a country standard.' When the single reached the national trade mags, *Cashbox* recognized 'a potent new chanter who can sock over a tune for either the country or R&B markets'. Back in Memphis, they fought shy of the word 'country', and 'hillbilly' sounded like an insult, so they parcelled Presley as a 'folk' singer. Sun's Marion Keisker told the local paper in July

1954, 'The odd thing is that both sides seem to be equally popular on popular, folk and race record programmes. This boy has something that seems to appeal to everybody.'

The racial divide that ran through Southern culture in 1954 precluded everyone but mavericks like Dewey Phillips from straying across the border. Elvis, Scotty and Bill couldn't be marketed as a blues act, so they were sold as country. Sam Phillips talked Bob Neal into slipping Elvis on to an open-air show on 30 July. The headliner was Slim Whitman, billed as 'one of the top-ranking rural rhythm experts . . . currently hitting the top with a variety of rustic records'. It was eleven days since 'Ellis Presley', as the advance publicity put it, had released his first single, enough to pick up a smattering of hometown fans. Whitman was sufficiently impressed by this brief appearance to recommend Elvis to Horace Logan, boss of country's second-ranked radio barn dance, the *Louisiana Hayride*. Two weeks later, Presley was at Overton Park, reducing Webb Pierce to incoherent amazement. 'Blue Moon Of Kentucky' registered on the list of country best-sellers in Memphis, behind Hank Snow's 'I Don't Hurt Anymore'. By early September, it had outstripped its rivals and was spreading across state borders like spilt water.

Bob Neal recognized a phenomenon, and latched on to Presley as his adviser and agent. He suggested that Scotty and Bill tag themselves 'The Blue Moon Boys'. They were an ungainly trio: Moore and Black sported their Starlite Wranglers cowboy shirts and bootlace ties while Presley sweated under a sports jacket. Shutting his eyes as he sang, Elvis's legs twitched to Black's pumping rhythm, and the 19-year-old who could scarcely meet a woman's eyes off stage mimed the bump and grind of sexual innuendo before a crowd of strangers.

'We were used to playing with more musicians,' Scotty Moore reflected, trying to grasp the essence of being a Blue Moon Boy. 'Whether it was country or pop, you had a piano player, a sax, a fiddle. You played whatever was popular. If you had a country band, you'd play a pop song with country instruments, and vice versa. Everyone just wanted to dance. As long as you made music they could dance to, they didn't care.'

With just three pieces, Elvis, Scotty and Bill sounded almost fragile. Presley's fingering was suspect, and his acoustic rhythm was more percussive than melodic. When Scotty laid back for a solo, all that fuelled the band was the failsafe thrust of Bill Black's bass. But that nakedness forced attention on to Elvis's voice.

Back at Sun in September, his chemical energy powered another blues tune, Roy Brown's 'Good Rockin' Tonight'. 'Tonight I'll be a mighty mighty man,' he swaggered, and Scotty and Bill caught the moment. Sensing he'd found a formula, Sam Phillips encouraged the trio to rock up a country tune. Instead, Elvis dipped into his reservoir of Dean Martin songs for 'I Don't Care If The Sun Don't Shine'. Given the 'Blue Moon Of Kentucky' treatment, it lured country DJs into giving Presley more exposure. Now they'd seen proof that Elvis was white, they were prepared to push their format to the limit. It was 'Good Rockin' Tonight' that showed up as the most popular country song in Memphis in late November 1954.

By then, Tennessee couldn't hold him. On 2 October, he collided with the one format that wouldn't bend, the *Grand Ole Opry*. Backstage, he was embarrassed to meet the composer of 'Blue Moon Of Kentucky', Bill Monroe. 'If ol' Bill hears this,' Tennessee Ernie Ford had quipped a few weeks earlier, 'he'll take his little ol' country band and head back for the hills.' But Monroe had other ideas: 'I thought Elvis had a beautiful voice. He came into the dressing-room at the *Opry* and apologized for the way he changed "Blue Moon Of Kentucky". I told him, "Well, if it gives you your start, then it's all right with me." And I was glad he picked it as his first number.' Glad enough, in fact, for Monroe to recut 'Kentucky' himself – starting in his original waltz tempo, and then echoing Presley's propulsion. 'We moved it on up faster, breakin' it over,' Monroe explained. 'It's more like bluegrass now.'

'Before that show, I thought he was black,' Marty Robbins reflected. 'But he didn't do too well that night. Country people weren't that acquainted with what he was doing.' Jim Denny's parting shot about truck-driving left Elvis crushed, but his obligations for the day weren't over. The *Opry* stars adjourned to Ernest Tubb's Record Store on Nashville's Broadway for another live radio show, the more relaxed *Midnight Jamboree*.

In the company of these hillbilly giants, Elvis Presley was still pulsing with nerves. He sought out Tubb for some more advice. 'What do you want me to sing, Mr Tubb,' he begged, '"Blue Moon Of Kentucky" or "That's All Right"?' 'Sing "Blue Moon Of Kentucky", son', Tubb replied. 'That's what I hoped you'd say, sir,' Elvis stammered, 'but the people at my record company tell me that if I'm gonna make any money, I've got to sing "That's All Right".' 'Do you need the money?' the veteran asked. 'I sure do,' Elvis admitted. 'I've been poor all my life.' 'So go ahead and do what they tell you,' Tubb countered. 'Make your money, and then you can sing country music, or love ballads, or anything else you want to sing.'

Two weeks later, Elvis, Scotty and Bill were in Shreveport, home of the *Louisiana Hayride*. In 1952, the *Hayride* had provided refuge for the battered spirit of Hank Williams. Now the barn dance offered the same sanctuary to another child of the South.

From New Mexico to Florida, 190 stations carried the signal across the cotton belt every Saturday night, in direct competition with the *Opry*. Presley was booked on to the Lucky Strike Guest Time segment, a weekly showcase for fledgling talent. 'He is only nineteen years old,' boasted announcer Frank Page. 'He has a new, distinctive style. Let's give him a nice hand.' Elvis announced his first song to the Confederate nation, cracking his vowels like a caricature. 'I'd like to say how happy we are to be out here,' he said. 'It's a real honour for us to appear on the *Louisiana Hayride*.' And with that he snapped into an explosive 'That's All Right', all subtlety lost in the static of the airwaves. All that carried across the wires was the crisp clatter of Scotty Moore's guitar riffs, and that keening, primeval voice.

Frank Page knew exactly what was going on. 'How did you arrive on that rhythm and blues style?' he asked. Elvis told the truth: 'We just stumbled on it.' 'Well,' said Page generously, 'they've been looking for something new in the folk music field for some time, and I think you've got it.' To make certain, Elvis, Scotty and Bill bopped up their Bill Monroe tune, torching the old certainties of hillbilly music with two minutes of incendiary rock'n'roll.

The *Hayride*'s boss, Horace Logan, immediately grabbed Elvis for a return engagement. On 6 November 1954, he signed the trio to a one-year contract, which required that they pledge to 'perform in a competent and pains-taking manner'. Presley kept his word, slotting thirty-five *Hayride* performances into his touring schedule over the next twelve months. By Christmas 1954, he had a second record to plug, and the nerve to slip a rowdy blues tune like LaVern Baker's 'Tweedlee Dee' into his repertoire. Besides Scotty and Bill, he was backed by the *Hayride's* drummer and pianist D. J. Fontana and Floyd Cramer, plus stand-by steel player, Jimmy Day. 'Elvis wanted to use me on a record,' Day revealed. 'I said, "Man, you got a sound going. You don't want to spoil it with steel guitar because it would make you automatically country, and you're going down a different road."' Not that Elvis's road had a name. When he signed up for tours under the *Hayride* banner, he was billed as the Newest Country Sensation in the Land, or the King Of Western Bop. In an inspired moment, the show's publicist tagged him the Hillbilly Cat, and that monicker stuck.

'I didn't know what he was,' recalls Waylon Jennings, who first met Elvis in late 1954. 'But I knew I liked what he did. We considered him country, and he was on a country music show. He sang me all these songs backstage. One of them was "Tweedlee Dee", which he said was going to be his next single. But the guys on the show didn't like him, because he was tearing the audience up, driving them crazy. So they moved him away from country as soon as they could. What I remember most was how he looked. He was wearing charcoal pants and a pink jacket – and he had a pink car waiting for him outside. Nobody else on a country show was dressed like that.'

Charlie Louvin and his brother Ira headlined some of those first Presley tours: 'Off stage he was a good guy,' Charlie maintains, 'but on stage he kinda got carried away – whatever it takes to please the people up front. That's his business, and I didn't blame him for that.' Comedian and actor Andy Griffith watched an early show from backstage, his mouth open in awe and horror. He turned to a friend, and drawled laconically: 'It's a reg-u-lar or-gy.'

In Memphis, Elvis showed up in country popularity polls, but outside Tennessee, the public was more suspicious of his revolutionary ways. Duane Eddy recalled that his producer, Lee Hazlewood, 'was a DJ in the mid-fifties. He was the first guy in Phoenix to play Elvis's Sun records, and he got a strange reaction. People would call up the station, and say, "Why are you playing that kind of music? That's not country!"'

'He was making a big stir in about four or five states,' reckoned Jimmie Rodgers Snow – Hank Snow's son, who pledged himself to the rock'n'roll cause before catching religion and denouncing Western Bop as the Devil's music. 'Once you left Memphis, Louisiana, Mississippi, Alabama and part of Texas, no one knew who Elvis Presley was. He was as different as daylight and dark, compared to the rest of country music.'

This strange fruit was exposed on package tours through early 1955. He had little in common with headliners such as Jim Edward & Maxine Brown, or Mother Maybelle and the Carter Sisters, and it was soon apparent that he drew a teenage audience, enticed by his sexual presence.

In May 1955, Tom Parker and Hank Snow promoted a three-week tour, billed as 'Hank Snow's All-Star Jamboree'. The line-up matched the hyperbole: besides the perennially popular Snow and his son, it offered Slim Whitman, Faron Young, the Wilburn Brothers, the Davis Sisters and the Carter Sisters.

'My dad was drawing the crowds in those days, not Elvis,' Jimmie Rodgers Snow reported. 'People came in and saw the photos of Elvis, and they'd say, "Who's he?" He would always go on before the midway part of the show, while Dad would do the last half, because he was the star. But when Elvis performed, the audience went crazy. It'd take forever to get him off the stage. So Dad, who was a traditional country singer, began to realize that it was making him look terrible. He had ballads and slower songs where people would clap and enjoy it, but they didn't go into a frenzy and get excited with that electricity Elvis had. Dad started putting him on last, then let him go on as long as he wanted to.'

Midway through the tour, there was a show in Jacksonville, Florida – where, so the press reported, the stage was invaded and lustful teenage girls robbed Elvis of most of his clothing. Conveniently, Colonel Parker was waiting off stage with a brand-new sports coat to replace the one that had been destroyed.

The tale spread through the country press, though local disc jockey Johnny Tillotson reported that he'd noticed no hint of a riot. Parker was certainly capable of hyperbole, but there was nothing fictitious about the way he assumed command of Presley's career. Outflanking both Bob Neal and Hank Snow, Parker won control of Elvis by late June 1955. Ostensibly, Presley was signed to a management deal with Hank Snow Enterprises, but the Colonel swiftly isolated himself from his veteran client, and concentrated on steering Elvis away from the restricted market for country and western.

Three further singles on Sun consolidated Presley's hold on the South, but Parker had ambitions further afield. In October 1955, he booked Bill Haley and the Comets, America's dominant rock'n'roll act, and sent out Elvis as their support. He hyped it as a battle, with 'the Nation's No. 1 Rhythm & Blues Artist' pitched against 'the King Of Western Bop'. This package attracted a teen audience who would have ignored a straight country show, and allowed Elvis to show that he was sharper, sexier and a decade younger than the tubby Haley. Thereafter, Parker ensured that Presley would never tour as anything but a headliner. Fifties pop icon Pat Boone witnessed one of Elvis's earliest ventures out of the South, at an October 1955 show in Cleveland, Ohio. As Boone tells it, there was an immediate culture clash: 'The high-school kids didn't know what to make of him. He looked like some of them, with the turned-up collar and the hair a little too long and greased. He seemed like the kinda guy who would be on a motorcycle. Plus he had a hillbilly kind of a twang. These kids were looking at him and covering their mouths with their hands, snickering. But when he began to sing again, there was an electricity about him, which won them over.'

In November 1955, Elvis travelled to Nashville to collect an award as the Most Promising New Artist from the Country Music Disc Jockeys Convention. While the country mags garlanded him with superlatives, Colonel Parker met with record company executives who wanted to sever Elvis's last ties with the country industry. Atlantic Records, New York's most prestigious R&B label, laid out its terms for buying Elvis out of his Sun contract; it offered a signing-on fee of $10,000. Columbia's Mitch Miller topped that figure by 50 per cent. He had in mind not R&B or rock'n'roll ('It's not music, it's a disease,' he once quipped) but a switch from country-blues into mainstream pop.

It was RCA, in the person of Steve Sholes, that outbid its rivals. Sholes registered the increasing impact of Elvis's Sun singles, as 'Milkcow Blues Boogie', 'Baby Let's Play House' and 'Mystery Train' (each rooted in R&B, but backed by a country side) broadened his fan base. With the assistance of producer Chet Atkins, Sholes masterminded an experiment to expand that market potential.

At RCA, the raw three-piece sound of Elvis, Scotty and Bill was fattened and smoothed by Nashville sessionmen – Atkins, Hank Garland, pianist Floyd Cramer, and the barbershop harmonies of the Jordanaires. Elvis had been allowed unlimited studio time by Sam Phillips, but Sholes and Atkins demanded a professional turnround of material, with a minimum of four songs from each three-hour session. There was no time for styles to collide and then coalesce: the direction was determined from the start. Strands of country and R&B still filtered through, but they were stripped of their roots. The essential constituents of the Sun Records sound were reduced to decoration: crossover was king, and pop stardom the eventual goal.

The break from Sam Phillips is often seen as an irreparable fracture in Presley's career. This theory holds that once Elvis left Sun, music lost out to marketing. Sam Phillips had teased him into creating sounds beyond his own imagination; now RCA's analysts made those decisions in advance.

But even among Presley's immediate peers, there were dissenting voices. 'He had to have another style of song,' Marty Robbins reflected, 'and he got it in "Heartbreak Hotel" [his RCA début]. Colonel Parker had the right idea. It was the best move for Elvis, because at that time country music was as far down in the dungeon as it could be thrown. Nobody was buying it.'

Parker signalled the shift of priorities when he abandoned the package tours which had broken Elvis across the South. No longer would Elvis be competing with established hillbilly stars. Rock'n'rollers were also off-limits, after an incident witnessed by would-be Elvis imitator, Gene Vincent: 'We were playing Memphis one night, me, Carl Perkins and Elvis. Carl came out and done "Blue Suede Shoes", and Elvis came after him and started doing "Blue Moon Of Kentucky", and they started cheering for Carl Perkins. Elvis came backstage, put his foot on the guitar, smashed it and said, "I shall never play with another rock'n'roller again". And from that day to this, he hasn't.'

A few weeks later, Elvis visited San Diego on a bill which featured a balladeer, a team of acrobats, a comic of no certain humour and a xylophone act. 'The Presley part of the show was brief,' complained a reviewer, but the reaction was as hysterical as ever. Colonel Parker now wanted Presley to endear himself to the parents of those lusting teens. In April 1956, he negotiated a two-week engagement at the Frontier hotel in America's capital of adult entertainment, Las Vegas. The booking had the air of a scientific experiment: place one rampant Southern kid in front of middle-aged vacationers, then leave to congeal. There were no explosions: instead of the barbed wave of screams which usually greeted his performance, the Vegas crowd offered only gentle applause.

Faced with an audience stoically waiting for the next juggler, Elvis blathered in embarrassment. The ancient one-liners he'd been delivering for two years collapsed in front of these urban sophisticates. Presley discovered exactly where he stood when he went through the Vegas ritual of pointing out the stars who were in the house. Actors Ray Bulger and Phil Silvers drew a generous round of applause, but there was silence when Elvis called the name of the King of Country Music, Roy Acuff. Elvis had one more man on his list: 'And my daddy . . .,' he mumbled, before cracking the band into 'Blue Suede Shoes'. If they didn't recognize Acuff, what price an uneducated ex-con from Mississippi who'd sired a rock'n'roll revolutionary?

The Vegas fiasco, and Parker's careful coaching, slowly altered Elvis's self-perception. When a journalist dared to call him 'the Marlon Brando of the mountain music set', the singer responded with a denial worthy of St Peter: 'I'm no hillbilly singer.' Could he describe himself more accurately? 'No, I don't dare,' the now rootless Presley replied. 'I'm scared, know what I mean, honey? Real scared.'

Steve Sholes shared his terror in the early weeks of 1956. No country artist in history had sparked such a bidding war, and there were RCA executives waiting for Sholes' protégé to fail. As he'd hoped, the hottest record of the moment came from a country boy discovered by Sam Phillips and launched by Sun Records. Only it wasn't Elvis Presley's 'Heartbreak Hotel' which became the first record to rack up airplay in the pop, country and R&B markets, but a song by another of Phillips' Southern titans: Carl Perkins.

'Steve Sholes called me,' Phillips recalled, 'and said, "Man, I don't know whether I bought the wrong person or not. That damn 'Blue Suede Shoes' is the hottest thing, it's breaking all over New York and everywhere I go." I told him he hadn't bought the wrong person. He asked if he could put "Blue Suede Shoes" out by Elvis because he couldn't get "Heartbreak Hotel" to do a damn thing. I said to Steve, "Look, man, if y'all put that out on Elvis . . . Elvis has some momentum going. You know we talked about keeping things simple and not getting overly wrought and going too far country . . ."'

Phillips' not entirely selfless persuasion counted for nothing: Sholes encouraged Presley to cover 'Blue Suede Shoes', and it followed Perkins' original up the charts. But Elvis's treatment of the song signalled his drift away from hillbilly music.

' "Blue Suede Shoes" is the most country song ever written,' its composer believed, and Perkins had some homespun philosophy to back his assertion: 'There never was a man who appreciated a pair of shoes like an ol' country boy, and them city boys don't drink liquor out of an old fruit jar. That's country.'

For Perkins, 'Blue Suede Shoes' was a conversation on the dancefloor. In Elvis's hands, it was a whirlwind. The shoes and the liquor were mere props: what counted was the bolt lightning that hot-wired the rhythm. It was the difference between wary middle-age and the daredevilry of youth; the difference, in fact, between Perkins and the kid just three years, but a whole generation, younger.

Like most of the Sun rockabillies, Carl Perkins had been drawn to Sam Phillips by the sound of Elvis, Scotty and Bill. According to Carl's well-rehearsed legend, it was his wife Valda who noted the similarity between the nascent rock'n'roll of the Hillbilly Cat and the stomping boogie purveyed by the ragged but righteous Perkins Brothers Band.

Carl and his brothers had been raised a step closer to the dirt than Presley. While Elvis grew up in the city, the Perkins boys toiled for sixteen-hour days in the cottonfields, caught in a union of drudgery with the descendants of slaves. If Carl's background sometimes reads like a fable, it's because he established the myth. That potent tale of a gnarled black bluesman passing secrets to an eager white disciple was simple truth for a man who emerged from poverty so severe that it's difficult to imagine in twentieth-century America.

'I would take the country songs I'd heard and put to them the kind of rhythm I'd listen to every day in the fields. I just adapted the black man's rhythm to the white man's country songs.' That was Perkins' naïve explanation for his music, after he'd heard a thousand analysts tell him it had happened that way. But none of the initial flurry of rockabilly artists was that calculating. The only man with the vision to imagine a collision of styles was Sam Phillips, and he couldn't make it happen; he could only recognize it when it did. More accurate is Perkins' assertion that when he heard Elvis on his radio, 'It sounded just like the stuff we did. I sang "Blue Moon Of Kentucky" the same way. Elvis didn't copy me, or me him. It's just that a lot of people in that part of the country were doing music that way.'

Presley biographer Peter Guralnick made the same point: 'When Elvis first recorded, there was no name for the music he was playing. It was just the sort of thing you heard at roadhouses and country fairs all through Mississippi, Arkansas and Tennessee.'

Or take the word of Curtis Gordon, who followed Presley into rockabilly in 1956, but cut sides like 'Rompin' And Stompin' for the same label, RCA, three years earlier: 'I have really been playing rock'n'roll and rockabilly for as long as I can remember. I played in a country band out of Moultrie, Georgia. We always did a lot of uptempo stuff. I always liked to play the blues, with the saxes doing the little riff in the background. I loved it all – country, rock'n'roll, western swing.'

In the eyes of Larry Manuel, whose father Joe ran the *Saturday Night Jamboree* barn dance in Memphis, 'The rockabillies drew on the same influences. There were elements of western swing or fast-paced country in an almost borderline bluegrass vein, but the R&B element I didn't notice so much until after Elvis's first record came out. Elvis made it acceptable to play black music in front of a white audience. Over a period of three to six months, you had this sound developing strongly – from hardly anything to a strong recognizable sound. The Presley phenomenon was the catalyst, and made a lot of people feel like they could do it, too.'

Before he'd even heard of Elvis Presley, Sam Phillips told the *Press-Scimitar* in Memphis that he loved 'genuine, untutored negro jazz' – alias the blues, not the urbane music that bandleaders like Duke Ellington concocted for a predominantly white audience. In 1940s Alabama and then Tennessee, Phillips was one of the few white DJs dedicated to exposing black music. Another was his namesake, Dewey Phillips, with whom he launched a record label – Phillips Records, no less – in 1950. They billed themselves as 'The Hottest Thing in the Country', but sold just 350 copies of their only release, by bluesman Joe Hill Louis.

Thereafter Phillips worked as an independent consultant for more flourishing labels, such as Chess and Modern. He cut fifties sides with B. B. King and Howlin' Wolf, and produced the R&B single that many claim as the first rock'n'roll record: Jackie Brenston's 'Rocket 88' in 1951.

The following February, Sam Phillips invested his earnings in another label: Sun Records. For its first eighteen months, Sun issued nothing but blues and gospel. Its early ventures into hillbilly music displayed no emotional commitment.

In May 1954, Sun finally showed some recognition of what Bill Haley and his Comets had achieved. Hardrock Gunter's 'Gonna Dance All Night' was a descendant of Tennessee Ernie's jump boogie sides, played with a carefree rhythm that bordered on mayhem. 'We're gonna rock and roll while they dance all night,'

Gunter boasted, as the steel player hammered explosive block chords. In execution, if not intent, Hardrock Gunter was Sun's first rock'n'roller.

The Sun roster sidestepped the prevailing currents of early-fifties country music: there were none of the Hank Williams or Lefty Frizzell copyists found on other labels. What excited Sam Phillips was individuality, and that summer he found it in Gunter – and in Harmonica Frank Floyd. Few Sun releases were less timely than 'The Great Medical Menagerist', in which Floyd played a nineteenth-century confidence-man, hawking pills, potions and medical miracles to a gullible audience of small-town hicks. It was fine comedy, but it was hardly likely to spark a jukebox into life.

On the same record, Harmonica Frank had an even stranger tale to unfold. 'Rockin' Chair Daddy' was a white blues tune, which seemed to tap into the future. 'I'm gonna rock all day and rock all night,' Floyd whined, as if he could invent electricity with a piece of wood and some strings. What powered the track was a wheezing harmonica, romping around the chords. Nine years later, exactly these ingredients – a small-town white hillbilly singer, obsessed with black country blues, pouring out his soul into the skeleton keys of a mouth organ – filled one of the best-selling albums of the sixties: *The Freewheelin' Bob Dylan*.

Dylan is unlikely to have heard Harmonica Frank, at least until the Sun catalogue was reissued in the 1970s, but he did respond to Phillips' next country release: Elvis Presley's 'Blue Moon Of Kentucky'. That record aroused surprised recognition across the Southern states, not just from Carl Perkins and his wife, but from scores of unsung and probably unrecorded country boogie merchants, who'd added a backbeat to drag drinkers away from their barstools.

The telescopic gaze of history distorts what happened at Sun in the mid-fifties. In retrospect, Phillips seems to have assembled a generation of rockabilly giants overnight: Presley, Perkins, Roy Orbison, Johnny Cash, Jerry Lee Lewis, Charlie Rich, Charlie Feathers, Malcolm Yelvington, Warren Smith, Billy Riley, Sonny Burgess – not to mention those whom he rejected, such as Johnny Burnette, Conway Twitty, and would-be rockers Mel Tillis and Webb Pierce.

But Sun's output was virtually halted by Presley's success. For a small label, a hit record is often the catalyst of ruin. Receipts crawl into the bank, while distributors and retailers cry out for fresh supplies of the hit song. Elvis's first single spread slowly across the South, which at least allowed Sam Phillips time to pay for his expansion, but its continued sales distracted him from his label's other business for the rest of 1954.

When future rockabilly Malcolm Yelvington issued a Sun single that November, it was anything but an imitation of Elvis. Yelvington followed his example by tackling a rhythm and blues song – 'Drinkin' Wine Spo-Dee-O-Dee', based on a salty sailors' chant – but clearly had no conception of how Elvis had achieved 'Good Rockin' Tonight'. This was a country singer playing the blues, not some unholy blend of both styles, and it seemed to belong to a different century from that of Presley's Sun singles.

A couple of months later, Phillips bowed to almost a year of insistent pressure from a kid called Charlie Feathers, and allowed him to record – not for Sun, but its hillbilly subsidiary, Flip Records. 'Charlie was in and out of Sam's studios,' recalls Scotty Moore. 'You'd see him all the time.' Feathers, who stoked his cult reputation with increasingly flamboyant claims, was eager to take credit for Sun rockabilly. He told Peter Guralnick that 'I arranged all of Elvis's stuff, definitely'; more specifically, he declared that 'Blue Moon Of Kentucky' and 'That's All Right' evolved not by chance, but followed a blueprint which he'd already suggested to Sam Phillips. He also alleged that he cut 'Good Rockin' Tonight' at Sun months before Elvis tackled the song, and that Phillips has deliberately concealed the tapes ever since.

In 1956, Feathers taped some of the most visceral rockabilly of the era; but for a pioneer, his Sun recordings are surprisingly tame. His Flip début revived memories of Hank Williams ('I've Been Deceived'); and even when he skipped into a faster tempo, nothing suggested he'd heard Presley's singles, let alone arranged them.

But another Flip artist came from the same mould as Elvis Presley. 'Rockabilly music, ain't nothin' to it,' Carl Perkins wrote four decades later. 'It's just a hopped-up country song.' He might have been remembering his début single, 'Movie Magg'. The way Perkins hustled through the verses, his voice impatient for the release of the chorus, he could have been a cotton-picker with a wife and five children at home, and a waitress on hold outside the picture house in town. If Elvis was a young stallion wired on speed, then Carl was a workhorse who knew a shortcut to illicit bliss.

Elvis, Scotty and Bill may have invented rockabilly, but Carl Perkins lived it. He was 23 in 1955, cadaverously thin from years of semi-starvation, and his hair was coming loose in tufts. He was a hard drinker and a family man, for whom the exhilaration of rock'n'roll could never be divorced from the burden of adulthood.

Perkins carried that weight throughout a life dogged by disappointment. Most rockabilly music was a cry of liberation, but Carl bowed under the knowledge that what happened on Saturday night had consequences for Sunday morning. Not only that: Carl Lee Perkins wrote his own songs. He was the Hank Williams of rockabilly, the man who coined the language of a new land.

First, he had to shed the past. 'Movie Magg' exposed the traditions at war in his soul. 'That double-barrel behind the door, it waits for me, I know,' he sang, as if he was condemned to perish in a pool of whiskey and a blast from a shotgun. 'So let's climb aboard ol' Becky's back,' he continued, 'and let's go to the picture show.' But even in Jackson, Tennessee, nobody rode their horse to the movies in 1955.

While his words mixed historical fantasy and grim reality, Perkins' music struggled to escape the legacy of Hank Williams. 'Let The Jukebox Keep Playing', pleaded the title of his second single, but no matter how many quarters he dropped in the slot, only hillbilly came out of the speaker. Even 'Gone, Gone, Gone' tiptoed where Elvis would have swaggered. With Presley en route to New York, Sam Phillips groomed Perkins as his next star. In December 1955, local DJs received two singles, one aimed at teens, the other at those honky-tonk jukeboxes. The country coupling teamed Carl and his brother Jay, their voices clashing like a shovel on stone. 'Let's give old Tennessee credit for music,' they sang on 'Tennessee', 'as they play it in that ol' hillbilly way.' By the end, Carl was scouring around for anything to which the state could lay claim. 'They built the first atomic bomb in Tennessee,' he wrote, refuelling a country tradition which had spawned Cold War gems like Little Jimmy Dickens' 'They Locked God Outside The Iron

Curtain' and the Louvin Brothers' 'From Mother's Arms To Korea'. Or, as Elton Britt sang proudly, 'The Red That We Want Is The Red That We've Got (In The Old Red, White And Blue)'.

'Blue Suede Shoes' used a different palette of colours. It pulled Carl Perkins one irreversible step over the line between country and rock'n'roll. Backed by the equally hopped-up 'Honey Don't', it was the first three-way hit of the rock era – close to topping the country, pop and R&B sales charts at the same time.

'Perkins contributes a lively reading on a gay rhythm ditty with strong R&B styled packing,' opined *Billboard* magazine, struggling to adjust to the new sound. 'Fine for the jukes,' it concluded, but the song spilled out in every direction. Within three months, there were cover versions galore – not just from country singers Roy Hall, Cliffie Stone and Boyd Bennett, but also pop idol Jim Lowe and bandleader Lawrence Welk.

'Blue Suede Shoes' was a career record, and Perkins must have imagined he might never top it. But its success liberated his music: the tentative country rocker of 1955 became the full-fledged rockabilly of 1956. 'Boppin' The Blues', 'All Mama's Children', 'Everybody's Tryin' To Be My Baby': out of half-remembered blues tunes, teen romances and sheer adrenalin, Perkins conjured up a bunch of rockabilly classics during a March 1956 Sun session.

One tune outpaced them all. 'Put Your Cat Clothes On' wasn't even considered for release in 1956: there was no place on radio for a performance so tightly wound. Two decades later it was uncovered like an Egyptian mummy, and entranced a new generation with its unsweetened essence of a lost era. Carl had doomed the song commercially when he sang, 'I slick up myself till I look like a dilly, Then I run downstairs and pick up my female hillbilly.' That would never play in New York.

Perkins was scheduled to do just that, as he was heading for a guest spot on TV's *Perry Como Show* – now, *there* would have been a culture clash – when his car was involved in a wreck near Dover, Delaware. His brother Jay suffered the worse injuries, but Carl himself was held in hospital long enough to miss the Como show, and watch the momentum of his crossover hit melt away. (Contrary to legend, though, he did not have to watch something even more galling: Elvis Presley 'stealing' his 'Blue Suede Shoes' on national TV. Presley had already done him that honour six weeks earlier.)

Out of the hospital in April 1956, Carl created the wildest music of his life. Nothing he ever recorded laid him as bare – bare as barbed wire – as 'Dixie Fried'. It wasn't in the tempo, which caught a midpace boogie rhythm and held it steady. 'Dixie Fried' didn't need rocket fuel: it ran on a heady brew of alcohol, violence and Southern pride. At a time when rock'n'roll concerts were being banned because they attracted juvenile delinquents, here was a newly crowned king of the genre, spitting out lines like these: 'Now Dan got happy and he started ravin', Jerked out his razor but he wasn't shavin', And all the cats knew to jump and hop, 'Cause he was borned and raised in a butcher shop.' Carl hollered out his warcry in each chorus: 'Rave on children, I'm with ya . . . Let's all get Dixie fried.'

Sam Phillips waved goodbye to the *Perry Como Show* when he issued 'Dixie Fried' as a single. It sold across the South, but sank Perkins' pop career. It also exhausted everything he had to say about bars, women, and the hot blood that alcohol sent speeding through his veins. Carl spent another year at Sun, cutting 'Matchbox' with Jerry Lee Lewis the day that Elvis Presley and Johnny Cash came to call. A few months later, the lingering memory of 'Blue Suede Shoes' won him a cameo in the movie *Jamboree*. The film-makers delivered two demos, and asked him to choose his song: 'Great Balls Of Fire', or 'Glad All Over'. Perkins hated them both, but rejected 'Great Balls Of Fire', which duly became the biggest-selling record in Sun's history for the kid piano-player he'd used on 'Matchbox'. By then, Carl had decided to leave Sun, figuring that Sam Phillips was too infatuated with Jerry Lee Lewis to spare him any time. Like his friend Johnny Cash, he signed with Columbia; unlike Cash, who was free to record everything from gospel to protest songs, Carl found his new label was a foreign country. Worse still, no one had written a phrasebook to translate his rural rockabilly into the slicked-up urban rock they demanded. His new hosts assumed that Carl could be smoothed into an international teen idol. The hillbilly roots were extracted from his music, and he was forced to cut banal ditties – 'Jive After Five', 'Pop Let Me Have The Car',

'Pointed Toe Shoes' – better-suited to a teen idol like Rick Nelson. By the early sixties, the purest rockabilly singer of them all was a half-forgotten alcoholic peddling country pop. And before every show, Carl made sure he got Dixie fried. 'If I had a bottle in my back pocket,' he noted in his autobiography, 'then I was me. I thought I was total then. There was an arm gone, there was a limp in my walk, there was a slowness in everything I did without it.'

It was a connection of sorts with home – the only one left when he was cut off from his family by the demands of the road, from his music by the loss of his audience, from ambition by the dull realization that this was his life, this and nothing more.

'When you're a country boy, just a month from the plough,' he admitted in 1968, 'and suddenly you're a star with money in your pocket, cars, women, big cities, crowds, the change is just too fast. You're the same person inside, but you're a star outside, so you don't know how to act. You're embarrassed about the way you talk, the way you eat. You can't take the strain without a crutch. For me it was booze – I've seen the bottom of a lot of bottles. I was a mess, a wreck for years.' Carl Perkins lived out every scene of Hank Williams' life but one. Instead of spewing away his life in the back of a rented Cadillac, he threw his bottles of whiskey into the Pacific Ocean, submerged his ego as Johnny Cash's lead guitar player, and waited for history to recognize his contribution. It all used up another decade.

19 Settin' the Woods on Fire
Hank Williams as rock'n'roll icon, 1947–1953

Two decades after Elvis Presley and Carl Perkins had first exhumed the spirit of Hank Williams, his legacy was still capable of casting a shadow over Nashville. 'The first time we played there,' recalls Elvis Costello, 'we opened with three Hank Williams songs. That didn't go down well. I was surprised. I'd thought, "Well, here we are in the home of country music." But of course, Hank didn't go down well in Nashville. I didn't know my history then.'

A year later, Costello was back in Music City, cutting country songs with veteran producer Billy Sherrill. He attacked a Hank Williams hit from 1950, 'Why Don't You Love Me?', compressing it into ninety seconds of manic ferocity. Sherrill watched laconically, then leaned into the talkback mike: 'That was Hank on the phone,' he drawled. 'He's coming right over.'

'I think Hank Williams is one of the fathers of punk,' says Evan Dando of the Lemonheads. '"Settin' The Woods On Fire" – that's one of the most punk-rock songs ever.' For guitarist Jimmy Day, Hank was 'the first of the country soul singers'. And Don Helms, steel player with Hank's Drifting Cowboys, believed that 'If Hank had lived, rock'n'roll would have been different'.

Pronounced dead on New Year's Day 1953, emaciated, drugged and destroyed by his years on the road, Hank Williams was the first fatality of the rock'n'roll era. He was just 29 when his body was pulled out of the Cadillac which was ferrying him to his next engagement. Maybe the drink killed him; maybe, as another Drifting Cowboy, Curley Henson, once claimed, Hank overdosed on 'a sex stimulant called Ampheniamide, a drug normally given to cattle for breeding purposes. Hank had received this for what he thought was heroin from a dealer in Oklahoma who was shortly afterwards arrested and jailed for peddling dope.'

It was Hank's life that killed him – a decade of drink, drugs, marital warfare, financial insecurity and, finally, the ostracism of his peers. 'I suppose you just might call me a saddist,' he once told *Grand Ole Opry* compère Grant Turner, and he's passed into legend as the bard of romantic disappointment. But there was an element of sado-masochism in the way he sought out trouble. No wonder that others who flirted with annihilation, from Gram Parsons to Kurt Cobain, responded to Hank's image.

The electors of the Rock and Roll Hall of Fame recognized a kindred spirit, inducting him in 1987 despite the fact that he died before rock'n'roll was invented. The post-modernist group the Residents tackled Hank in their *American Composer Series*, alongside George Gershwin, James Brown and John Philip Sousa. Since the mid-fifties, Southern rock'n'rollers from Jerry Lee Lewis to Jason and the Scorchers have reclaimed his songs as their own. And more than four decades after his death, artists as diverse as British post-punk composer Matt Johnson (alias The The) and Detroit funk-rocker Don Was (with Orqestra Was) have constructed albums around Williams' material.

'He wrote some of the greatest poetry you'll ever read,' says Was, who reset Hank's lyrics to music that spanned jazz, soul and rock. 'He distilled complex emotional issues down to a simple, but brilliant, form. It transcends any cultural barriers between human beings. He deals with universal emotional themes.'

Hank's musical baptism echoed the lives of the fifties rock'n'rollers: 'I learned to play guitar from an old coloured man in the streets of Montgomery. He played in a street band. They had a washtub bass. I was shining shoes and selling newspapers and following this old negro around to get him to teach me how to play guitar.'

The blend of hillbilly and blues traditions existed long before Elvis Presley arrived at Sun Records, or Bill Haley covered R&B dance tunes. It's not just simplistic but inaccurate to assume that, before the early fifties, there'd been no mingling of black and white styles. Before the Second World War, the Singing Brakeman, Jimmie Rodgers, had cut hillbilly blues tunes with jazz pioneer Louis Armstrong. In 1949, the year Hank Williams topped the *Billboard* folk chart for the first time, R&B singer Roy Brown also registered with the hillbilly audience, by cutting a bluesy rendition of the country tune "Fore Day In The Morning'.

Williams wouldn't have recognized the terms of this debate. He called himself a 'folk singer', and told reporter Ralph Gleason in 1952: 'Folk music is sincere. There's nothing phoney about it. When a folk singer sings a sad song, he's sad. He means it.'

Williams' achievement was to persuade his audience that, by living out their sorrows, he could wipe them away. The messianic image isn't misplaced for a singer who has been sanctified and saluted as the patron saint of country music. Whether they stretch their vowels like Deep South shitkickers or smooth them with strings and choirs, country singers always bow at the altar of Hank Williams. It's a simple statement of faith in the tradition he inspired.

As the unifying force behind country music, it's not surprising that Hank has also been claimed as the creator of rock'n'roll. Don Helms worked with him for almost a decade: 'I'm not too sure that Hank didn't start the whole rock movement,' he considered. 'Country music, up to that time, was mostly about "take me back to the old cabin". But Hank actually started singing about being in the doghouse, and in the honky-tonks, and things like that. And putting a beat with it. That was the beginning of what evolved into rock'n'roll.'

Hank's son, country star Hank Williams Jr, credits his father with bridging country and pop: 'Jimmie Rodgers started the whole thing but Daddy took it downtown and got the pop artists to start cutting the songs. He took a little of the corn out of it, if you know what I mean. His songs can be done in any style.'

Hank Jr also made a more specific claim: 'Daddy's "Move It On Over" and Bill Haley's "Rock Around The Clock" – there could be a good copyright suit on those two, when you listen to them.'

'Move It On Over' was Williams' début single for MGM, in June 1947, but a month earlier the indie label Sterling Records let loose a spoiler. Jukebox listeners could now punch in a dime to hear Hank's country boogie tune, 'Pan American'.

For anyone raised on rock'n'roll, 'Pan American' is an exercise in frustration. Everyone on the record sounds as if they'd be violating their parole if they dared to pick up the tempo. For nearly three minutes, they keep their foot on the brake, the fiddle taking the strain when the rhythm guitar can't hold back any longer; and all the time Hank toys with the accelerator, every snap of his voice threatening to send the vehicle out of control. Reversing the usual trend, it was the major label which freed Williams and the Drifting Cowboys. A drummer joined the party for 'Move It On Over', the bassist slapped a few measures double-time, and Hank bopped his way through verse after verse of swaggering self-confidence. 'Move over skinny dog,' sneered the most cadaverous singer in country music, 'cos the fat dog's movin' in.'

It wasn't 'Rock Around The Clock', but it was a beacon for Bill Haley and any other country boy out to fill a dancefloor. 'Move It On Over' made the best-sellers' lists for a month. But 'Lovesick Blues' topped the chart for sixteen weeks. A pop tune written by a Russian immigrant and a professional composer from Cincinnati, it reached country music via the black-face minstrel Emmett Miller in the twenties. Williams had performed the song for a decade, relishing the chance to stretch a word like 'blues' out to a dozen syllables like a reincarnation of Jimmie Rodgers.

That was the song Hank chose for his début at the *Opry*. In the church of country music, he twitched his pelvis like a promise, his bones nearly slicing through his suit. He was called back for six encores, and the legend of Hank Williams – skeletal sex symbol, the hottest star in hillbilly – was born.

Ralph Gleason, who met Williams in 1952, recalled: 'When he sang, he looked like he squeezed himself to get the notes out. He made them scream when he sang, and the audience was shipped right up from the Deep South intact. There were lots of those blondes you see at country and western affairs, the kind of hair that mother never had and nature never grew, and the tight skirts that won't quit and the guys looking barbershop neat but still with a coat of dust on them. Shitkicker dances, the outside world called them then.' That was a jazz critic writing for a rock audience in 1969, and there are layers of prejudice to strip from his account – 'the outside world', indeed, as if the South were a jungle left untouched by civilization. But Gleason identified Hank's people, and during the four years between the singer's *Opry* début and his death, there was no one to match his popularity among the country audience.

Williams mapped out their emotional traumas through songs like 'Long Gone Lonesome Blues' and 'My Son Calls Another Man Daddy'. Meanwhile he slipped ever closer to the border of rock'n'roll. In 1949, he effectively reprised 'Move It On Over' with a new set of words, as 'Mind Your Own Business'. Like its ancestor, it lived out the lines Hank wrote in 'I'm A Long Gone Daddy': 'I'm gonna do some rockin' on the midnight train, I'm takin' everything but my ball and chain.'

With 'Why Don't You Love Me?', the scene of Elvis Costello's flash-fire three decades later, Hank delivered a rock'n'roll record at half-speed, teasing his listeners with a glimpse of the future. The same eerie sense of time expanding cloaks two of his biggest hits, 'Moanin' The Blues' and 'Hey, Good Lookin''. But it was 'Settin' The Woods On Fire' that demonstrated how much Hank knew about what would happen, both to himself and to country music. 'You sing loud and I'll sing louder,' he boasted, 'tonight we're settin' the woods on fire.' Through the verses skipped the hint of a rockabilly guitar, while with a match in his hand, Hank gloated over a vision of Southern culture waiting to burn. But he didn't strike the spark. After cutting 'Kaw-Liga', a callous cartoon of Native American life, Williams set out on his final tour, a comedy of accident and excess that ended when he overloaded his frail system once too often.

His funeral was a jamboree, rivalled in country history only by the memorial for Tammy Wynette. His legend immediately began to bloat, as the doubters who'd kicked him off the *Opry* started to reel back their words.

As rockabilly and rock'n'roll knocked the country industry off track, so Hank's legacy was seized by other voices. Jerry Lee Lewis dabbled with most of his catalogue during late-night sprees at Sun Records. Elvis Presley played with 'Your Cheatin' Heart' in 1958, slurring the words like Marlon Brando, while guitarist Scotty Moore skipped up and down the scales as if he were running a dance-class. New Orleans R&B star Fats Domino showed more respect, creating rock'n'roll magic out of 'Jambalaya'. Across the

South, generations raised on Hank's records found their own way to set the woods on fire.

'Are You Sure Hank Done It This Way?' asked Waylon Jennings in the mid-seventies, when he was accused of perverting country's good name. It was a question that begged the answer 'Yes', but Don Helms wasn't convinced that Hank would have slipped all the way into rock'n'roll: 'I'm not sure. But he would have made some changes. Maybe rock'n'roll as it did later come would have been a little bit different if he'd stayed alive and been the pioneer of it. They might not have called it rock'n'roll.'

But Hank's son has no difficulty in imagining him in the rock'n'roll era: 'His voice would fit anything. He could have sung any of those songs I sung. Daddy could do it all. They found that out when they put strings on some of his old records, for the people downtown in Chicago and London that don't want to get too corny. Daddy never recorded with strings, but his music still sounded good that way. Watch that film of him they have at the Country Music Hall of Fame: he could have sung Elvis Presley off stage.' It was an obligation that Hank Williams Jr was to take on his own shoulders. But long before then, Hank's hillbilly boogie was ignited by a less likely arsonist: Bill Haley.

20 Real Rock Drive
Bill Haley and hillbilly boogie, 1945–1956

Stern-faced and stetsoned, a young hillbilly singer posed for a publicity photo in the early weeks of 1951. He was no Hank Williams: even the skeletal sideburns which slid from under his hat couldn't carve his pudgy features into Hank's cadaverous visage. But the spotlight cast a shadow that hinted at melancholy in his heart.

Bill Haley had been playing hillbilly dance music for almost a decade. He'd yodelled and fiddled with the Down Homers and the Range Drifters. Clad in a flowery cowboy shirt and a coy grin, he'd guested at barn dances and state fairs. With the Four Aces of Western Swing, the Philadelphia-born country crooner had cut hackneyed sides like 'Four Leaf Clover Kisses' and 'The Covered Wagon Rolled Right Along'. Now Dave Miller, the head of the Pennsylvania-based Holiday label, advised Haley to revamp a rhythm and blues hit for the hillbilly audience. According to Miller, Haley's response was brutal: 'I don't want to play that fuckin' nigger music!' The tale paints Haley as a naïve redneck, who chanced upon the sound of the future.

'Bill Haley was a has-been country singer in Pennsylvania clubs for years before "Rock Around The Clock" came along,' recalled rock'n'roller turned evangelist Jimmie Rodgers Snow. 'They had a sax player who would climb on the bass, and the bass player would drag him around the aisles, and the people would go wild. The drummer would play his cymbals so hard he'd bust his sticks. He'd see to it that they cut his hands and the blood would get all over the drums. This was a planned thing – to always bust a stick or bleed a little bit. They were gimmicks. Elvis never had to do those things.'

Racist, a novelty act, a middle-aged caricature of a teen rocker – that's the Bill Haley that passed into history. But there was another

side to the intensely ambitious bandleader who became America's
first ambassador of rock'n'roll. When his progress as a yodeller
and balladeer stalled in the mid-forties, Haley pursued another
path as a disc jockey. Recruited to play hillbilly music, he raised
eyebrows – sometimes even hackles – when he slipped 'race'
records (black rhythm and blues) into his playlist. Bill's son John
Haley recalls that his father was regularly lambasted for
broadcasting 'jig-a-boo music' to Pennsylvania country fans.

In 1947, Haley was appointed musical director of Pennsylvania
station WPWA. He insisted on a multi-cultural programming
policy to maximize the station's audience, and tuned in himself to
the nightly blast of R&B that was *Judge Rhythm's Court*. When
Haley formed the Four Aces of Western Swing, around 1948, he
told singer Slim Allsman that 'he had heard music in other places
that was more alive than ours. It had a real kick in it. He wanted to
mix it with ours and create something really new. He said it would
be like mixing Dixieland and hillbilly. He was real excited about it.
I thought he was crazy, and I told him, "Who's gonna listen to it, if
you could do it? Why mess up good country music?"'

With Allsman supplying the Four Aces' first electric guitar,
Haley added a rhythmic spine to their hillbilly boogie numbers. He
was still being billed as 'The Singing Cowboy'; indeed, the Four
Aces cut a bunch of singles for the Cowboy label, without
betraying a hint of R&B. But when the Four Aces became the
Saddlemen in 1949, Haley maintained his vision.

'We were always looking for something different,' explained
accordionist Johnny Grande. 'We'd take a standard like "Ida",
and play it every way we could think of – fast, slow, loud, soft,
hillbilly, waltz, Dixie, progressive. Haley was like a scientist,
putting one thing after another into a test tube.' His experiments
had no ulterior motive: Haley was merely searching for a gimmick
that would fill a dancefloor, guarantee some return bookings, and
maybe shift a few Saddlemen 78s.

The way Grande recalls it, Haley would explain his musical
gumbo to the regulars at the Twin Bar in Gloucester, on the
Atlantic shore: 'All you hillbillies out there gotta go home now,
'cos we're gonna play a little something we call cowboy jive. It's a

mixture of western swing, Dixieland and hard-edge blues. And we're the only band crazy enough to play it.'

Dave Miller caught Haley and the Saddlemen at the Twin Bar in the spring of 1951, and reckoned he'd found the fissile material for a chemical experiment of his own. He'd registered the popularity of Jackie Brenston's 'Rocket 88' on jukeboxes and R&B radio shows, and wanted to offer that excitement to a white audience.

Brenston's original, powered by Ike Turner on piano, was a rock'n'roll record in all but name. But where Brenston swaggered, Haley crooned and cooed. The Saddlemen didn't hammer the backbeat, but clicked it, shuffle tempo, while a hillbilly guitar licked around the rhythm.

What Miller and Haley had created was not yet rock'n'roll. It slipped easily into a tradition that had been a mainstay of the hillbilly industry for almost a decade – country boogie. Johnny Barfield's 'Boogie Woogie' in 1939 was the first country record openly to acknowledge the rhythmic piano style that had become a jazz institution. Strict delineation between black and white traditions was restricted to radio programming and commercial marketing: the black and white blues had been bleeding into each other for decades. Dance bands like Bill Boyd's Cowboy Ramblers satisfied the demand for toe-tapping music in the mid-thirties by playing 'bop' tunes pitched across the racial boundaries.

After the Second World War, record companies like King in Cincinnati – one of the few independents to specialize in both R&B and country – encouraged a more overt crossing of currents. Blues shouters like Roy Brown recorded country hits that might otherwise have eluded the black audience. In return, King boss Sid Nathan encouraged his country roster to cut boogie tunes, mostly blatant rewrites of songs that had already caught the ear of R&B fans.

The pivotal moment in this two-way transplant came when the Delmore Brothers released 'Hillbilly Boogie' in 1945 – simultaneously naming and defining a new sound. In their wake, country boogie tunes filled the nation's jukeboxes. Sid Nathan steered Hawkshaw Hawkins through 'Pan-American Boogie' (also tackled by the Delmores) and 'Dog House Boogie'. Another King artist, Zeb Turner, offered the 'Tennessee Boogie'. The new rhythm rippled out beyond Nathan's Cincinnati headquarters. It was the perfect setting for Moon Mullican, who was billed as the King of the Hillbilly Piano Players. Jack Guthrie (cousin of folk legend Woody) brought California into line with his nostalgic 'Oakie Boogie'. Arthur Smith inspired a generation of pickers, from Chet Atkins to Chuck Berry, with his genre-hopping 'Guitar Boogie'.

For two musicians, Kentucky's Clyde 'Red' Foley and 'Tennessee' Ernie Ford, boogie was an entrée to careers which would stretch into legend. Though both men ultimately found a home in sacred music – Ford recording hymns, Foley spirituals such as 'Peace In The Valley' and 'It Is No Secret' – it was the propulsive rhythms of boogie-woogie which consolidated their fame.

Foley was no stranger to cultural collisions: in 1947, he topped the folk charts with 'New Jole Blonde', a raucous reading of the traditional (and indecipherable) Louisiana lyric, 'Jole Blon'. His second chart-topper, 'Tennessee Saturday Night', settled his course. 'Civilized people live there all right,' he boasted of his newly adopted home, 'but they all go native on a Saturday night.' Not on his record, it's true, but the arrangement was only a backbeat and a surge of adrenalin short of Sun Records rockabilly.

That was as close as Foley came to stealing Elvis Presley's place in history, though he continued to issue boogie singles for the next few years, and even attempted valiant covers of R&B hits like 'Shake A Hand' and 'Hearts Of Stone' in 1953–4. To no avail: the commercial decline in his career coincided exactly with the influx of rockabilly in 1955. Tennessee Ernie Ford suffered the same fate, albeit after the crossover pop hit 'Sixteen Tons' had lent him an autumnal glow in the final weeks of 1955. Ford had the consolation of a networked TV series, which survived for another decade. His viewers were rarely treated to anything as bohemian as 'The Shot Gun Boogie' – the biggest jukebox hit of 1951.

While Foley worked out of Nashville, Ford's base from the late forties was California, where he played with two of the hottest pickers in country history – guitarist Jimmy Bryant (an influence on musicians as diverse as rock'n'roll session giant James Burton and Deep Purple's Ritchie Blackmore) and steel ace Speedy West. With pianist Moon Mullican and guitarist/songwriter Merle Travis also on hand, Ford could hardly fail to strike a groove when he cruised into dance tunes, from 1949's 'Smokey Mountain Boogie' to 1953's 'Catfish Boogie'. 'The Shot Gun Boogie' was the exemplar, with Bryant tripping through the 'walking bass' riff double-time to force the pace. Even more than Foley, Tennessee Ernie leaned over the boundary that separated uptempo hillbilly from the earliest rock'n'roll. But despite West and Bryant nudging him on, Ford never dared to swing. The same criticism couldn't be made of another white boogie man, Merrill E. Moore, who learned his trade from pianist Freddie Slack. He borrowed two of his mentor's R&B hits, 'House Of Blue Lights' and 'Cow Cow Boogie', but never compromised his sound enough to attract more than passing attention from country fans.

There are other contenders in the frame – for example, Hardrock Gunter's 'Birmingham Bounce', or Arkie Shipley's 'Hot Rod Race', both astutely rescued from regional obscurity by Red Foley. Out in Dallas, the Star Talent label (why be modest?) specialized in hillbilly bounces from long-forgotten outfits like Freddie Burns and his Ranch Hands, and Hank Harral and his Palomino Cowboys. But even though their 'Rocket 88' didn't sell more than 10,000 copies in the summer of 1951, it was Bill Haley and the Saddlemen – soon to become the Comets – who transported country boogie into a new arena.

In April 1952, Dave Miller began to plug a tortured country lament called 'Icy Heart', a homage to Hank Williams' 'Cold, Cold Heart'. But it was the flipside which stoked the jukeboxes. 'Rock This Joint' was another twist of the boogie formula, but half the band were primed for adventure. With the double-bass pulsing out the backbeat, Haley caught the rhythm like a kid mounting a merry-go-round. The pedal steel player eased gently into his solo, as if this were just another hillbilly outing, but Danny Cedrone cut him dead with a double-timed guitar solo that was repeated, note for note, three years later on 'Rock Around The Clock'.

Typically, the Saddlemen were slow to realize what they'd done.

Several months later, now renamed the Comets, they ended 1952 with another explosion, 'Real Rock Drive'. 'They play it in a real gone way,' Haley sang, and the defiant piano-player apart, the Comets proved it.

In 1953 'Crazy Man Crazy' propelled them into the future. Their country heritage was flung aside as the snare drum stole the beat, the band chanted an inane chorus like a whiskey-fuelled R&B combo, and the entire excursion ended in a drunken fury. All that survived of Haley's hillbilly band was one line of 'Dixie', thrown into the steel solo as a satirical farewell.

'Crazy Man Crazy' may, or may not, be the first rock'n'roll record, but it undeniably introduced that sound to the national pop charts. Significantly, Haley and his Comets made no impact on the folk (or hillbilly) listings as they swept America with such rock hits as 'Shake, Rattle And Roll' and 'Rock Around The Clock'. Haley's role as John the Baptist to Elvis's Messiah ended with his revolution spiralling into self-parody, and by 1956 the Comets were no longer a significant force. Their embrace of the new may have owed as much to accident as to genius; nothing Haley cut after his initial rise to fame showed any comprehension of what he'd achieved, or how he might respond to Elvis Presley's raised stakes.

The successive waves of Haley and Presley punctured country boogie as a vehicle for commercial success. Elvis made one gesture towards the past when he treated the Comets' 'Shake, Rattle And Roll' to an incendiary cover on his first album; paying respect to his predecessor, he torched his legacy in the same moment.

During 1956, Presley and the other rock'n'rollers who had benefited from Haley's adventures could be heard right across the radio dial, on country, R&B and pop stations. But the country audience couldn't hear the hillbilly band who'd surprised themselves by becoming rock'n'roll stars. What is ironic is that the traditionally conservative world of country was prepared to welcome such hellraisers as Carl Perkins and Jerry Lee Lewis, while rejecting the 'nigger music' of Bill Haley. Perkins and Lewis conjured up a landscape of switchblades, ginsoaks and illicit sex; Haley got tagged with the same image, while insisting that 'I won't play any tune that couldn't be sung at a church festival.' That kind of proclamation killed him as a potential teenage rebel, even before his avuncular appearance stripped away his hoodlum image. Meanwhile the nationwide furore stirred up by Haley's innocent backbeats exiled him from the genre where he really belonged: not rock'n'roll, but country.

21 | Take the Devil out of Me
Rockabilly and the country backlash, 1954–1958: Marty Robbins; Webb Pierce; George Jones; Johnny Horton; Jackie Lee Cochran; Mac Curtis; the Collins Kids

The country industry didn't know whether to welcome the first wave of rockers as kindred spirits or run them out of town at gunpoint. Southern by birth, Sun Records' rockabillies came from the same culture as the established stars of country music, and respected the same heritage. There the synchronicity ended. Thrown together on package tours and radio barn dances, two generations of hillbillies were set on a collision course.

'There was no opposition at first,' said Carl Perkins, one of rockabilly's trailblazers. 'They knew I was a country boy just like them. I'd picked cotton, and I'd been raised on Hank Williams and the *Grand Ole Opry*, just like they were. But when rock'n'roll started to eat into their sales, then the mood seemed to change.'

Sonny Burgess signed with Sun two years after Perkins: 'A lot of the country artists seemed upset about rockabilly music, as they reckoned it would take their living away. But after a year or so, they realized it was helping them. We were doing what nowadays they would call country-rock – fast country, with added drums. Country stars like Marty Robbins went into the rockabilly field and discovered they could do it well.'

'I wasn't doing any good cutting country songs,' Robbins recalled. 'I wasn't getting any airplay.' He had watched Elvis Presley incite country crowds with 'That's All Right', so he added a fiddle and honky-tonk piano to Presley's arrangement, and was rewarded with a Top 10 country hit in spring 1955. It was a subtle piece of transplantation: Robbins omitted Elvis's 'da da di' chorus, the main hook for his teenage fans, and held every syllable just an instant too long. His rendition epitomized the dilemma for the country industry, which wanted to emasculate rock'n'roll and feed off it at the same moment.

Robbins stepped across racial boundaries with his next hit. In July 1955, he seized on Chuck Berry's car-race anthem, 'Maybellene', and cut it Sun style, with guitar licks flickering through the song. He hit some of the beats right on the nail, coming dangerously close to losing his self-control. But the fever was cooled by a guitar solo that shuffled like a deadbeat on a dancefloor: country stations could safely expose their listeners to this damp squib.

The next year, he tackled another black rock classic, Little Richard's 'Long Tall Sally'. This time, Nashville guitar ace Hank Garland smothered the flames into embers. Thereafter, despite the release of an album entitled *Rockin' Rollin' Robbins* in late 1956, rock'n'roll was merely a gimmick for Robbins. It was purely an accident of fate that his 1960 single, 'Don't Worry', was the first country record to feature that staple of late-sixties psychedelia, a fuzz guitar.

Few country stars were as receptive to the new music as Robbins. Sonny Curtis recalls setting out with Buddy Holly on a country tour in 1956: 'We backed up people like George Jones, Hank Locklin, Justin Tubb, Cowboy Copas and Glen Reeves. Everybody was real country on the show but for Glen Reeves, and he did a country version of "Tutti Frutti" – like "Wop bop a loo bop, wop hee haw", or something like that! Everybody else on the show said, "Oh *man*!" It really did irritate those boys.'

For someone like Porter Wagoner, whose career was built on fidelity to 'real' country, compromise with the forces of rockabilly was impossible. 'Even though I had the No. 1 song in 1955, with "A Satisfied Mind", country just wasn't making it,' he complained. 'All we could work was the little clubs, the skull orchards, the dives, for maybe $100 a night. RCA was having problems selling country records, and they wanted everybody to do more rock. Me included. Even [RCA producer and head of A&R in Nashville] Steve Sholes believed in rock and asked me to do some. I told him I couldn't, that it didn't suit my personality.'

Wagoner began to invest in the insurance business, in case the country industry collapsed. 'I was scared there would be a blast from another area of rock'n'roll,' he explained. 'Country music was dead, and rock was gigantic. Managers only wanted to handle rock acts.'

Wagoner's fears were well founded. Pedal steel ace Lloyd Green worked with one of Nashville's biggest stars: 'I quit playing with Faron Young because there was no work. The king was Elvis. He came out with "Heartbreak Hotel", and all the country singers started to think they could be him. They all tried to sing pop, and country fans stopped coming to the shows. The music reached its lowest ebb in that period. Faron was one of the top two or three in the field, but even his work became so small that he started going out solo without a band.'

Almost overnight, the structure of the music business changed. As a regular on the *Louisiana Hayride*, steel player Jimmy Day had witnessed the Elvis revolution first-hand: 'After Christmas 1955, I decided it was time to move on. Shreveport was going rock'n'roll: the *Hayride* was filled with rock'n'roll cats. A cat playing rock guitar only needed two strings, with no talent required, so I didn't feel I could further my career. I left and went to a place where I hoped they would still be playing country music, which was Nashville.'

Not that the home of country music was immune to rock'n'roll fever. As large sections of the country audience were welcoming the rockabilly artists, Nashville executives had to bend with the wind. In March 1956, the record stores whose reports made up the 'C&W Best Sellers' listing agreed that Elvis Presley's 'Heartbreak Hotel' was the hottest record of the moment. After four months, it was finally pushed aside by Ray Price's 'Crazy Arms' in June. It was the last brick in the dam: for the next two years, almost every No. 1 country record was either rock'n'roll or pop, or at least heavily infected by outside influences. Disc jockeys may have favoured Ray Price, Jim Reeves and Webb Pierce, but the public opted for Elvis, Jerry Lee Lewis, the Everly Brothers and crossover confections by Sonny James, Ferlin Husky, Bobby Helms and, of course, Marty Robbins.

Not even the DJs were united. In late-fifties Texas, future outlaw stars Willie Nelson and Waylon Jennings both hosted country shows. 'I loved a lot of that Sun rockabilly,' Waylon remembers. 'I recognized Elvis as a Southern boy like me. But I also wanted to play records by guys like Little Richard, Ray Charles and Buddy Holly. It didn't matter to me that they weren't country.' Willie Nelson was no more of a purist: 'I was a disc jockey when Carl Perkins came along with "Blue Suede Shoes",' he says, 'and I liked that. I used to play all that stuff – Elvis, Carl, Johnny Cash, Jerry Lee Lewis. Some DJs tried to turn their back on what was happening, and wouldn't play anything but the more traditional guys like Hank Snow. My idea of country wasn't as narrow as that, although I loved the traditional guys too. On my show, you could hear Hank Snow *and* Jerry Lee Lewis!'

Other elements of the country industry were disturbed by the encroachment of rock'n'roll on their territory. Writing in 1958, *Billboard* music editor Paul Ackerman revealed that 'Well-entrenched artists, talent managers and other members of the trade resented [Elvis] fiercely. One day I had two phone calls from music executives in Nashville, Tennessee. Both demanded that *The Billboard* remove Presley from the best-selling country chart on the ground that – so they said – he was not truly representative of the country field.' Ackerman refused to give way. But country support for Elvis dissipated after he returned from the US Army in 1960 and severed his links with rock'n'roll.

Back in 1956, a siege mentality darkened the country industry. *Opry* veteran Roy Acuff was forced to add electric instruments to his band to survive. Established stars including Porter Wagoner, Lefty Frizzell and Eddy Arnold struggled to maintain the sales they'd enjoyed before the emergence of rockabilly. For Eddy Arnold, 'The Tennessee Plowboy', the jolt was all the more jarring because Presley's career had been orchestrated by Colonel Tom Parker, whom Arnold had sacked because he was dubious about his manners and ethics. For Hank Snow, who'd graciously allowed Parker to take over Presley despite his own claim to a share, the reverses were less severe. But even that sturdy purist was reduced to recording novelties like 'Hula Rock' in 1956, in an attempt to match the invading forces. Many of Snow's peers reckoned that collaboration was safer than opposition. 'Just about a third of the people in Nashville either called in to see me or dropped by,' recalls Sun boss Sam Phillips. 'They wanted to be associated with Sun, because we were hot. Webb Pierce was as hot as hell for a long time, and then he cooled down just a little bit. Mel Tillis was trying to get started, but he just couldn't get anything going record-wise. They both came to try out for Sun. I told them that I just didn't think it would be fair to them. Plus I really wanted to work with people that had not made a record before.'

Few artists were as popular in the mid-fifties as Webb Pierce, who had the best-selling country record for ten months out of twelve in the year before Elvis first topped the *Billboard* chart. He refused to ignore the demand for rock'n'roll. In 1956, at the age of 30, he cut a tune called 'Teenage Boogie' – nothing more outrageous than a rewrite of his 1950 hit 'Hayride Boogie', but a useful piece of gestural politics none the less. Pierce's other move towards rock was less subtle: with Wayne Walker, he penned a rockabilly tune called 'Bop-A-Lena' for Ronnie Self (whose finest moment was a downhome rock'n'roller called 'Ain't I'm A Dog?'). No country station dared play anything so ferocious, but Pierce was not dissuaded from following the teen market. His 1957 chart-topper 'Honky Tonk Song' was, according to one reviewer, 'a rockabilly, and it really goes'. A few weeks later, Pierce covered the Everly Brothers' 'Bye Bye Love'; for a while, he even outstripped their original on the country charts.

Ferlin Husky straddled the rock'n'roll fence with equal aplomb. His career had stalled with the arrival of rock'n'roll. But Husky had an alter ego – comedian Simon Crum, who could record a rock tune, 'Bop Cat Bop', under the guise of satire. Then Husky released the biggest-selling record of his career, reviving 'Gone' – a ballad he'd originally cut under another pseudonym, Terry Preston, in 1952. This time it was arranged as a doo-wopping pop tune, which outsold every other record in country music (even Elvis and the Everly Brothers) in 1957.

Another who revelled in the new sound was Skeets McDonald, best remembered for the western tune 'Don't Let The Stars Get In Your Eyes' back in 1952. Perry Como had picked up that tune for the pop charts, but no crooner – or country veteran – would have dared touch McDonald's 1956 single, 'You Oughta See Grandma Rock'. At 41, he was approaching grandpa status himself, but he had 18-year-old Eddie Cochran on guitar to steer him right. McDonald roared through the ridiculous lyrics (penned by future Nashville luminary Harlan Howard) as if he'd just struck oil. 'Let's rock it,' he yelled as the solo approached, 'but don't ruin it.'

Pierce, Husky and even McDonald were striplings alongside Red Foley – a major country star since the 1940s, a pioneer in bringing modern recording techniques to Nashville, the artist behind standards like 'Peace In The Valley' and 'Old Shep' and (cementing his righteous image) the father-in-law of Pat Boone. Foley had dabbled in boogie and uptempo hillbilly throughout his career, and when his lengthy run of hits dried up in 1956 he was tempted to cut an ersatz rock'n'roll record called 'Shake Baby Shake'. It was based on a Hank Ballard R&B tune called 'Sexy Ways'; only Jerry Lee Lewis would have dared play that to a country crowd. Foley realized it was impolite to commend a lady on anything but 'purdy ways', but he couldn't shake off the rock'n'roll riff at the hub of the song. The 46-year-old veteran didn't sound entirely at ease, but desperation was better than waving farewell to his career.

Almost everyone in country music stuck at least a finger into the steaming waters of rock'n'roll. Some were revived by the experience; others took a painful bath. 'I can't dance,' sang Faron Young on a 1956 single of that name, proving it by the way he handled the alien rock rhythm.

The parade of hopefuls was endless: Little Jimmy Dickens ('I've Got A Hole In My Pocket'), Ernest Tubb ('Thirty Days'), Lefty Frizzell ('You're Humbuggin' Me'), Hank Thompson ('Rockin' In The Congo', a blatant derivative of Warren Smith's 'Ubangi Stomp'), Moon Mullican (the disastrous 'Honolulu Rock-A-Roll-A'), Red Sovine ('Juke Joint Johnny'), even western swing pioneer Bob Wills ('So Let's Rock'). 'I've been rockin' and rollin' for a long long time,' sang Wills' vocalist, Lee Ross, which was partly true and partly a mark of total despair.

For younger singers, the sense of self-betrayal might have been slighter, but the consequences could be absurd. Warner Mack was a regular on the *Grand Ole Opry* and *Louisiana Hayride* in his late teens, but Decca pushed him into tackling a banal pop tune, 'Rock A Chicka'. At first, country stations resignedly playlisted the record. Then, Mack recalled, 'I got a phone call from one of the big radio people to say that the record was banned. I couldn't believe it. The guy said that the girl chorus that was put on over the top made the song sound obscene. I was staggered but I went to the record player and listened to it with different ears. And he was right!' Appalled by the stupidity of the assignment, one of the chorus had subtly altered the words: not so much 'rock' as 'fuck a chicka', in fact.

No such vulgarity surfaced on the records of George Jones, but the man often described as the greatest country singer of all time also gave way to the temptation of rock'n'roll. 'I got started when rock was beginning to be big,' he recalled. 'They didn't have many stations that played country music, so I thought I'd try a rock song. I wrote one of the stupidest things I ever wrote. One side was called "Rock It" and the other was called "Dadgummit, How Come It". I used the name Thumper Jones so people wouldn't think it was me.' Anonymity was a popular strategem for embarrassed country singers: Buck Owens masqueraded as Corky Jones for the boppin' 'Hot Dog', Leon Payne as Rock Rogers on the shameless 'Little Rock Rock'. But George Jones took his apostasy more seriously. Cornered on TV by Nashville celebrity Ralph Emery, he admitted sourly: 'There wasn't much else we could do. You got to join them. We only did one record in that style. It was my own idea. One of my worst.'

Few sinners are more repentant than those truly thrilled by their sin, and Jones' bitter distaste must have been fuelled by the knowledge that he not only attempted rockabilly, but mastered it. 'I had some fun with it,' he conceded once, 'but it didn't touch my heart.' 'Rock It' suggests otherwise. Jones may have been wired on adrenalin and whiskey when he cut the tune at Pappy Dailey's Starday studio in Beaumont, Texas. But few rockabilly performances cut so close to the bone. 'Weeeeelllll,' he wailed, 'I'm going down to the Calgary, I'm gonna bop to every song,' and he hit the 'bop' like an executioner with an axe. 'I mean rock it, YEAH!' he shrieked, making Elvis sound like a choirboy, before cueing the guitar solo with a series of primeval growls and screams.

Every man gets drunk and does something he regrets, but 'Rock

It' wasn't a momentary aberration. On the other side of the record was 'How Come It', a perfect reproduction of the Carl Perkins sound. Even before Sam Phillips met Perkins or Presley, Jones had skipped through uptempo tunes such as 'No Money In The Deal' like a hillbilly cat on heat. 'I'm a tramp and a rounder and I stay out late at night,' he sang in his early anthem, 'I'm Ragged But I'm Right', and Elvis couldn't have said it better.

By 1958, rock'n'roll sounded like pure country alongside the pop arrangements that were creeping out of Nashville. Jones cut a raw rocker that year called 'White Lightning', an adult entertainment about bootleg hootch, revenue men and the kind of backwoods scenery that filled the movie *Deliverance*. The song had been written by a country DJ, J. P. Richardson, who passed himself off as the Big Bopper for one of the more lascivious rockers of the era, 'Chantilly Lace'. Jones has been singing 'White Lightning' ever since, apparently unaware that if it hadn't been a major country hit, it would have been claimed as a rockabilly classic. The saga didn't end there: Jones taped two soundalikes that veered even closer to rock, 'Who Shot Sam' and 'Revenooer Man', plus an R&B tune called 'Slave Lover' that might have been written for the Coasters. 'I did some rock,' the man said, and he wasn't lying.

Jones didn't sell his soul to the teenage kick – in the middle of his rockabilly period, he also penned a heartfelt ballad called 'Take The Devil Out Of Me'. But most of Starday's roster, Texas hillbillies to a man, learned to lean that way. Leon Payne, the composer of songs as diverse as the sentimental standard 'I Love You Because' and the serial-killer saga 'Psycho', used his 'Rock Rogers' alias to cover Elvis Presley tunes for Texas jukeboxes. Sonny Fisher, another contemporary of George Jones, had Carl Perkins in his sights even before 'Blue Suede Shoes'. 'I'm a rockin' daddy from Ding Dong, Tennessee,' he boasted on 'Rockin' Daddy', 'I'm gonna rock away all your blues.' First, he had to explain the rudiments of electricity to his guitar-picker, whose solo was so lacking in rhythm that he might have been restringing his instrument at the same time.

Starday seemed to attract these wayward spirits. There was Bill Mack, middle-aged but still eager to rock. 'I got in-laws, kinfolk crawling over me,' he complained on 'Shadow My Baby', 'living under my roof, wearing better clothes than me.' In 1955, Mack and a piano-player who might have given lessons to Jerry Lee Lewis cut a ridiculous rocker called 'Atom Bomb', which offered a fast track to the apocalypse: 'They're building an atom bomb, gonna blow me out of this place.' These raw, rural sides found a natural home in the Texas honky-tonks, where their stark imagery bolstered the alcohol-fuelled misanthropy of labourers and refinery workers.

The further the hybrid of country and rock'n'roll drifted from the urban centres of Tennessee, the fewer chains tied it down. In Lake Charles, Louisiana, on the prettily named Sulphur River, Goldband Records offered a heady brew of Cajun, country and rock'n'roll. Nashville taboos didn't apply here, so Al Ferrier could cut a rampant slice of rockabilly like 'Let's Go Boppin' Tonight' as early as 1955, one of the few genuine classics of the genre recorded before Carl Perkins' 'Blue Suede Shoes'. In 1960, when the rest of the industry had abandoned rock'n'roll, Goldband was still offering throwbacks such as Jay Chevalier. 'If you ever go to Cuba,' Chevalier sang, 'you better learn to do the Castro Rock'; an acceptance of Fidel's new administration lacking in the rest of the United States. Back in Nashville, the Maddox Brothers & Rose recorded a hopeful tune called 'The Death Of Rock'n'Roll' in 1956. But that was the year the city's major labels effectively abandoned the fight, and encouraged their entire rosters – even veterans like Red Foley and Ernest Tubb – to experiment with teenage rhythms.

For some artists, such as the 27-year-old Johnny Horton – bizarrely billed as 'The Singing Fisherman' – the step from raw-edged honky-tonk to rockabilly was barely noticeable. His breakthrough hit was 'Honky Tonk Man', as pure an exhibition of country as the mid-fifties could offer. Horton attacked it with the spirit of a rocker, which made the transition to 'Honky-Tonk Hardwood Floor' all the easier. This was rock'n'roll all the way, but without a single element that a country fan could regard as betrayal. Horton softened the blow by filling the first verse with clichés about Texas dancefloors, before slipping in the teen references to 'soda pop' and his lust for 'a honey'.

Horton was signed to Columbia, the slowest of the majors to

respond to rockabilly. By the time they made their move, signing Johnny Cash and Carl Perkins in 1958, the movement had already been filtered into a cult. Other companies were less hesitant.

Decca had already allowed Roy Hall, a prime influence on Jerry Lee Lewis, to cover Fats Domino's R&B hit 'All By Myself' in 1955 – the same year he cut the original of Jerry Lee's signature tune, 'Whole Lotta Shakin' Goin' On'. Texan rockabilly Johnny Carroll was signed to the label that year, and in April 1956 Nashville studio regulars Grady Martin, Owen Bradley and Harold Bradley accompanied him on three of the wildest rockers of the era. Decca A&R chief Paul Cohen encouraged Carroll to tackle the Joe Turner R&B hit, 'Corrine Corrina', for the country market, but 'Hot Rock' – an almost incoherent rockabilly thrash – and 'Crazy Crazy Lovin'' were wild beyond any marketing man's imagination.

In Cohen's mind, rockabilly was merely another hillbilly variation. Decca released records as ethnic as James Gallagher's 'Crazy Chicken', which sounded as if its creator had never seen a town bigger than two shacks and a mule. Until the rockabilly craze expired in 1958, Decca were gloriously shameless. So were their key artists – like Red Foley, who followed his experiment with 'Juke Joint Johnny' by delivering 'Crazy Little Guitar Man' as if he could just as easily make country hits out of the cha-cha or the watusi. Even singing cowboy Rex Allen, veteran of thirty-two western movies in seven years, donned some winklepickers beneath his spurs. His 1958 single 'Knock Knock Rattle' exemplified the gung-ho spirit of a generation adapting to survive.

For juvenile discoveries, who would once have been groomed as the next Hank Williams, the new order was more natural. Guitarist Jerry Kennedy needed little persuasion to début with 'Teenage Love Is Misery' in 1957, a decade before he encouraged Jerry Lee Lewis to abandon rock'n'roll and forge a new career as a honky-tonk balladeer.

No Decca rockabilly was younger, or more willing, than Jackie Lee Cochran. He was just 15 when he cut 'Mama Don't You Think I Know' in November 1956. Guitarist Merle Travis spent three minutes polishing up his Scotty Moore licks, while piano veteran Jimmy Pruett rinky-tinked through a solo as if it was still 1945.

Even at 15, Cochran had some tradition to lose: he'd already worked the *Big D Jamboree* in Dallas, and shared a stage with western swing stars like Spade Cooley. None of that influence survived on his solitary Decca single, which might have provided the ideal soundtrack for the period exploitation movie, *Untamed Youth*.

Mac Curtis lived out the adolescent rockabilly rebellion better than anyone. At the age of 16, he was working in Weatherford, Texas, fronting a hillbilly band. 'I heard a Marty Robbins record called "That's All Right",' he recalled, 'which I loved, because I had always wanted to do upbeat things. That was the version I knew, because the major labels had most of the jukeboxes sewn up. But one day, when I was rehearsing, a friend came in and said, "There's a guy who sounds just like you, and he's got a record on the jukebox down at the Dairy Mart". So we went down, and it was Elvis Presley. We said, "Aw, that's the way we ought to be playing it."'

A few months later, Curtis was in Fort Worth, playing at the opening of a new car lot. A local DJ told him that Ralph Bass, from King Records, was in town looking for a hillbilly bop band. 'Unknown to me,' Curtis explains, 'every record label was looking for an Elvis Presley. When we got into the studio, Bernie Pearlman, one of King's executives, had a copy of Elvis's first album. He would play a little bit of it and compare it with what we were doing, to see if we were getting close to that sound.'

They were: 'If I Had Me A Woman' matched the echo-drenched swagger of Elvis's Sun sides. No matter that the drums sounded like the clatter of chicken bones on wood, or that the guitar was playing in a different key from the rest of the band. Curtis scorched through the song as if his tail were on fire, and Ralph Bass didn't hold him back.

At 15 and 16, Jackie Lee Cochran and Mac Curtis weren't even the youngest rockabillies in town. Brenda Lee began cutting rock'n'roll when she was 12, while guitar prodigy Larry Collins turned professional just after his eleventh birthday. He and his slightly older sister, Lorrie, were the Collins Kids, who launched their recording career in February 1956, after eighteen months on the TV show *Town Hall Party*. Lorrie was an authentic vocal stylist before her fifteenth birthday, while even before he'd reached his teens, Larry was enough of a virtuoso to handle guitar duels with seasoned pros like Joe Maphis.

The West Coast record industry reckoned they were a novelty act, and swamped their naïve talent with teen confections like 'Soda Poppin' Around'. But occasionally the Collins Kids could squeeze out 'Hop, Skip And Jump' or 'Hoy Hoy', lightning rockers that matched Lorrie's hillbilly rasp with the twin-guitar rampage of Maphis and her brother. The pair also provided some of the more startling local TV images of the era, strutting round the set of *Town Hall Party* like adolescent aliens. Puberty intervened after 1958 – Lorrie fell in love with Rick Nelson, while Larry paused for his voice to break – but the Collins Kids left behind one last slice of rockabilly genius, 'Mercy'. Three years later, Lorrie briefly re-emerged to cut quintessential Bakersfield singles like 'Waitin' And Watchin'': she remains one of country music's great lost talents.

The Collins Kids, Mac Curtis, Jackie Lee Cochran, Johnny Carroll, Roy Hall, and dozens more bombarded the country industry like invaders from another dimension. (A personal favourite is Jimmy Heap, whose 'Sebbin Come Elebben' from February 1955 not only swings like a demon, but has one of the romantic chat-up lines of the century: 'You got handles, woman, just like a turnin' plough.' The fact that Heap sings as if he is in an advanced state of delirium merely adds to the appeal.)

But no matter how 'authentic' their records might have been – as hillbilly or rock'n'roll – they rarely matched the sales of those rock acts who aimed shamelessly at the mainstream pop audience. With the exception of Webb Pierce's 'Teenage Boogie', which was simply an update of a proven country formula, none of the crossovers attempted by Nashville luminaries in the mid-fifties made much impression on the charts. There was a residual loyalty to acts like Red Foley, Ernest Tubb and Little Jimmy Dickens, but that didn't mean their fans wanted to hear them sing rock'n'roll. Neither did the teenagers, who preferred their idols young, rebellious and unsullied by a decade or more of honky-tonk fame. Red Foley might have rattled through 'Juke Joint Johnny', but as a rock'n'roll icon, he couldn't rival leather-clad Lotharios like Gene Vincent or Eddie Cochran.

Nashville was losing out both ways. 'When Elvis came along,' recalls Chet Atkins, 'the country industry got in really bad shape, because people started buying him and a lot of black artists. We struggled for a while, and then we decided to just make great country songs.'

For the core audience who'd worshipped Hank Williams and Lefty Frizzell, that decision came none too soon. Disenchanted Nashville citizens had already hanged Elvis in effigy in 1956, during a demonstration against the 'nigger elements polluting our children'. In St Louis, the noose wasn't dramatic enough, so they burned a lifesize cut-out of Presley designed to promote his first movie.

The backlash against rock'n'roll whipped across the South that summer. While country stars tried to pass themselves off as teen revolutionaries, the North Alabama White Citizens Council launched a violent campaign in cities like Birmingham to rid jukeboxes of 'the basic, heavy-beat music of negroes, which appeals to the base in man, and brings out animalism and vulgarity'. The days of Hardrock Gunter and his 'Birmingham Bounce' were long gone.

Out in Texas, Sam Phillips was told that 'we don't play songs by niggers on our stations'. The 'nigger' in question was Jerry Lee Lewis, who may or may not have once stomped off stage and told Chuck Berry to 'follow that, nigger', but who was never wary of admitting the black antecedents of his music.

Chet Atkins never expressed even the barest hint of this racist rhetoric, but his move towards 'great country songs' chimed with the demands of the South's less progressive elements, not to mention those alienated by the emphasis on teenage dance fodder. Rock'n'roll was not the only outside force at work in the country industry in the mid-fifties. Its emergence capitalized on the growth of a teenage consciousness in the United States, a product of increased disposable income after the Second World War. In a post-war climate of full employment, kids suddenly had money to burn. The shape of American entertainment was irreversibly altered: every aspect of the media, from the movies to the music business, via publishing, radio and television, was alerted to the commercial potential of targeting youngsters who were earning a respectable wage but who did not yet have the financial demands of a family or a home to support.

Enter the teenage rebels – Marlon Brando, James Dean, Elvis Presley and many more, personifying the fissure between youth and adulthood that teen culture represented. Rock'n'roll was the purest musical expression of this gulf, and its success depended on its ability to heighten conflict between the generational forces. Performers like Presley, Lewis, Buddy Holly and Eddie Cochran were little older than their fans, and in their primeval state they summed up everything that one generation demanded, and the other rejected. The middle-aged Red Foley and Ernest Tubb were unrealistic teenage icons. Their shift towards the new ideology also distanced them from their existing audience. Not only generations were at war. The increased urbanization of the South had pulled millions of the region's inhabitants out of the country and into the city. New and old environments competed for their loyalty. The continued success of radio barn dances like the *Grand Ole Opry* proved that Southerners liked to be reminded of their rural past, but only within the context of an affectionate pastiche. In the New South, city dwellers wished to share in the sophistication that was beamed from TV studios on the East and West Coasts.

In musical terms, the aspirational shift was marked by a gradual rejection of those elements which had once been badges of Southern pride – harsh, nasal, mountain harmonies; the banshee screech of fiddles; lyrical imagery taken from the farmyard and the cottonfield. At the same time, the urban South still required its trademarks, and a regional accent remained the ID card of country music, even when its origins were masked by horns and strings. 'It's a sales tag,' explained Chet Atkins, 'but I suppose anytime you have background singers and musicians who are primarily from the South, they will sing with a certain sound to their voices, and play in a certain manner.'

The trick was to accommodate these contradictory urges, for country and city, Southern traditions and urban finesse. By a process of trial and error, Atkins and his fellow musicians and producers in Tennessee's Music City struck upon a solution: the Nashville Sound.

22 Great Balls of Fire
Sun Records after Elvis, 1956–1963: Roy Orbison; Sonny Burgess; Johnny Cash; Jerry Lee Lewis

'Sun Records at its peak was like punk rock at its best,' wrote rock critic Lester Bangs, 'the premise and principle of American democracy brought right back home: I/you can do it too. It was a landmark in the history of Western culture: that bunch of hillbillies in that shabby little room, some of them more than just half illiterate, changed the course of the history of the world.' One of those hillbillies, Sonny Burgess, admits: 'Man, most of those artists were all just like me. They came out of the country, and radio stations – hey, when you got on there, it was like going to the moon! None of us knew anything. Some of us Sun guys never got through high school.'

Burgess's experience speaks for them all: 'My heroes were from the country field: Ernest Tubb, Hank Williams, Lefty Frizzell, Red Foley. I started out playing country. Man, I *lived* in the country! Everything we did was country: there was no rock'n'roll back then. You needed a beat for dancing, but we had to play all different kinds of music. We were doing rhythm and blues, and fast country – but also pop songs like "Stardust". If they called for something, we had to play it, or else things could get ugly.

'Once we heard Elvis and Carl Perkins, we knew we had to be where they came from. We were from the same place, we had the same heroes, and played the same music. So we went to see Sam Phillips at Sun.

'In the studio, Sam would just get behind the board and say, "Play". It didn't have to be technically correct. If you listen to our records, all of us, we made a lot of mistakes. I'm embarrassed by some of them now, to tell you the truth. But if it had a good feeling, he kept it. The one thing that comes through on everything is that Sam had an ear for what sounded good.

'Thousands of people wanted to be on Sun. People envied us because we were signed with Sam. He only chose about eight of us. And he couldn't even promote us all. He didn't have that kind of money. But what did we know? You reached your peak when you were on a record label. That record had your name on it: that was the top. It didn't make any difference whether it sold.'

During 1955–6, Phillips was besieged by country singers who reckoned they had what it took to be Elvis Presley. Even established hillbilly stars, like 30-year-old Webb Pierce, buried their pride and applied for an audition. As the Sun roster expanded, so Phillips became harder to please. Few bands have ever matched the savagery of the Johnny Burnette Rock'n'Roll Trio, but as drummer Paul Burlison recalled, 'Sam was so stuck on Elvis at the time that he didn't want another group like that. We thought we were as good as Elvis, because every time we'd play a show and Elvis was on it, Johnny would get as much applause as he would. But Sam still turned us down. With Sun being the only studio in town, we couldn't do anything else but leave.' The Burnette trio drove to New York, and won their shot at immortality via a TV talent show.

One singer/composer who did intrigue Phillips was Roy Orbison – unique among the Sun rockabilly artists in that he had made a record for another label before arriving in Memphis. 'Roy borrowed money and went to Clovis, New Mexico,' explains his widow, Barbara, 'to the studio owned by Norman Petty. And that's where he cut "Ooby Dooby", for the Je-Wel label. They released it regionally, and then it was lost for all these years.' If Elvis Presley was the apogee of rockabilly flamboyance, with Carl Perkins a degree or two below, Orbison was way down the scale. As he proved in later decades, his forte was the operatic ballad. 'He sang country at dances early in his life,' Barbara Orbison reckons, 'but he never was country. He really wanted to be known as a great guitar player.' That was the hook of 'Ooby Dooby', both on Je-Wel and when Phillips supervised a re-recording for Sun in 1956: a simplistic set of runs and riffs that compressed a genre into a twenty-four-bar solo. 'So he did rockabilly,' Barbara Orbison continues, 'but almost immediately he surpassed it.' According to her, 'He'd been playing that ten years earlier. He was after something else.' And so was Sam Phillips, although not in the same dimension as Orbison. In the history of Sun, Roy was an eccentric: he was the label's only performer who didn't cement his style, and create his most lasting music, under Phillips' intuitive supervision. Sam could still respond to that 'something else', though: it was the common factor in all the major talents he signed between 1954 and 1957.

Phillips didn't refine his vision immediately. As he assembled a roster in 1955, he experimented with acts who didn't match his expectations. With the Miller Sisters, he cut 'Someday You Will Pay' around the time of his final Elvis sessions, but rockabilly rhythms and Andrews Sisters harmonies didn't gel. Smokey Joe's 'Signifying Monkey' demonstrated that setting a country piano-player loose on gutbucket blues didn't necessarily create rockabilly. And when hillbilly singer Slim Rhodes towed a drummer into the studio in spring 1956, his band were too embarrassed to match a song called 'Gonna Romp And Stomp'.

Warren Smith was another matter. Few rockabilly tracks were as primitive – on every level – as 'Ubangi Stomp'. Cultural historians could root a thesis in Smith's prehistoric lines about natives in the jungle and 'Red Indians' signalling: 'heap big jam session about to begin'.

What was wilder than the jungle and the pow-wow? Outer space, of course, the inspiration for Billy Riley's 'Flyin' Saucers Rock'n'Roll'. The song was written by minor Sun luminary Ray Scott, who 'saw a UFO back in 1952. I was at a drive-in movie theatre, and I was standing outside my car when I saw an object. It was all lit up and shaped like a cigar.' Much scarier than Scott's vision was Riley's nerve-shredding howl, midway between a maimed wolf and a man on fire. 'After hearing Elvis,' Riley explained, 'a lot of us guys got away from country stuff. We wanted to get with what was happening. It fit me because it was black: it was still country, but it had that black feel, which I was brought up on.'

Like Smith and Riley, Sonny Burgess's music exploded in the summer of 1956. Though he's been saddled with the 'rockabilly' tag, his finest Sun singles were pure R&B. After all, few rockabilly acts featured a trumpet-player. 'That took it straight out!' Burgess laughs. 'That made it something different. We wanted a sax player, but we had a guy called Jack Nance who played drums and trumpet. We liked the sound, and went with it. Sam Phillips didn't know where to pitch our music. There was a market for Elvis, because he was a true rockabilly, but not for us. The black stations wouldn't play us, but neither would the white stations, because it wasn't what you'd call country.'

Phillips had the commercial sense, or artistic judgement, to recognize raw talent, regardless of how it presented itself. In the final weeks of 1954, a 22-year-old air force veteran from Arkansas auditioned at Union Avenue. John Cash approached Phillips as a gospel singer, with an original song called 'Belshazzar'. 'He was weighed in the balance and found wanting,' Cash wrote of the Babylonian king. His own fate might have been similar, for the last thing Sun needed was an evangelist. But his acoustic rendition of 'Wide Open Road' had an almost biblical authority that the producer couldn't ignore.

Cash had more than a sheaf of songs to offer: like Presley, he fronted a trio, with upright bass player Marshall Grant and guitar-picker Luther Perkins. The latter was no relation to Carl, by blood or talent: take after take was abandoned when Luther strayed away from his rudimentary riffs. This incompetence was also an asset: his 'boom-chicka-boom' sound became the hallmark of all the group's best Sun recordings.

Cash's début single, 'Hey Porter', might have been rockabilly. Luther Perkins strangled that hope, and Cash's voice had a mountainous quality that rooted his music in tradition. But Johnny (as Sam dubbed him, with the teen market in mind) wasn't oblivious to commercial potential. In the summer of 1955, he started to pen songs that were capable of dual interpretation – pure hillbilly, if Cash and the Tennessee Two were at the mike, or rockabilly in more spontaneous hands. 'Mean-Eyed Cat' was backwoods poetry, worthy of Carl Perkins, while 'Rock'n'Roll Ruby' was a more contrived play for the adolescent audience. Cash had few illusions about his band. In 1955, he wrote a song for his guitar player. 'Luther Played The Boogie', it announced, with a sting in the tail: '. . . in the strangest kind of way'. As Perkins plodded through the deliberately naïve chord changes, Cash called for a solo: 'Play it strange, Luther'. Perkins couldn't do anything else.

Sun Records promoted Cash as a Country Boy, 'so simple he's almost sophisticated'. But Cash was no backwoods *ingénu*. His writing had a compelling realism that was remarkable even for country music, in which bereavement and poverty were familiar settings. Hank Williams had never painted a picture so black as 'Folsom Prison Blues', which Cash released in summer 1955. He tried out the song that spring in a gentle tenor voice (a spooky harbinger of how Bob Dylan would sound on *Self Portrait* fifteen years later). In its final form, however, 'Folsom Prison Blues' was delivered in a baritone as grim as the narrative: 'I shot a man in Reno, just to watch him die.'

The same character could have delivered Cash's biggest Sun hit, 'I Walk The Line'. 'I keep a close watch on this heart of mine,' the song began, teenage abandon already rejected. The rhythm and melody were as unwavering as a set of prison bars, and once again Cash took on the role of an outsider – a rock'n'roll rebel without the backbeat.

Plugging that record on the *Town Hall Party* barn dance, Cash unveiled a less predictable image. He mimicked 'one of the cats', bursting into 'Heartbreak Hotel' while his pelvis twitched like a frog wired to electrodes. It wasn't the only Presley move he aped. Like Elvis, he tackled Ray Charles' rhythm and blues hit 'I Got A Woman'. 'We'd like to do a country version of this song,' he claimed, 'I hope you like the way we tear it up.'

That was not the man Sun Records wanted to promote. 'When it comes to loneliness, you'd think Johnny invented the word,' claimed the liner notes on his first album. 'Naturally endowed with a rangy, big, hollow voice, John's melancholy mood comes through strong.'

In 1957, Phillips jettisoned some of his workload, allowing Memphis bandleader and songwriter Jack Clement to supervise some recording sessions. Clement struck up an immediate rapport with Cash, whom he envisaged as a pop star. 'Jack was a very creative person,' Phillips reflects, 'but he didn't follow the lines of my thinking.' Whereas Phillips preferred subtle direction, Jack

Clement imposed his own vision on Sun's skeletal sound. From 'Home Of The Blues' in August 1957, Cash's records were overdubbed with piano and a white-bread vocal chorus, in an unashamed dash at the pop charts. That November, Clement flourished his royal flush: a saccharine pop tune of his own creation, 'Ballad Of A Teenage Queen', to which was added a hubbub of voices as a Greek chorus. Cash maintained his composure, secure in the knowledge that Clement hadn't been able to pollute the flipside, 'Big River'.

The record was Cash's biggest seller to date, slipping easily into the pop charts. For the remainder of his Sun contract, which expired in summer 1958, he was steered towards the widest possible audience. Ironically, once he'd left the label, Phillips admitted in an LP sleeve-note that, 'Almost reluctantly, Johnny evolved a pop-country style in arrangement and instrumentation . . . He caused more of a revolution in pop music than in country music, as was his aim, by being one of the first country and western artists exposed on national "general entertainment" TV shows.'

Cash fled Sun Records, famed for its raw naturalism, for a major label, Columbia. Elvis Presley had been tamed and tidied by his move to a major; the same process was later tried on Carl Perkins and Jerry Lee Lewis. But Columbia allowed Cash to strip away the sonic baggage and return to an unadorned sound. Furthermore, they actively encouraged him to return to his roots, as Cash explained: 'I always loved folk music. When I was signed by Columbia, Goddard Lieberson gave me a collection of world folk music, and I listened to that for years. I heard strains of our country music in all that, in Elizabethan ballads, in Irish folk songs, in Scottish melodies. You can see how melodies and some words have been handed down. They became different songs, but still have some of that original flavour.' The final twist in this tale is that while Cash was exploring the folk heritage, Jack Clement fell out of favour with Sam Phillips – because he was too interested in folk.

Cash wasn't the only artist handled by Jack Clement in 1957–8. The producer wrote 'It'll Be Me' for a new Sun acquisition, Jerry Lee Lewis, cleaning up the original lyric (one line began, 'if you see

257 **Great Balls of Fire**

a turd floating in your toilet bowl . . .'). 'It'll Be Me' was soon
buried beneath the biggest-selling record Sun ever released: 'Whole
Lotta Shakin' Goin' On'.

'I wanted to be Jimmie Rodgers reincarnated,' Jerry Lee Lewis
shouted on stage in 1994, 'but they wouldn't let me!' More than
any other performer at Sun – or in the whole history of rock'n'roll
– Lewis wiped away borders with every touch of his piano. He was
raised on country and gospel, inhaled the blues, ate up Broadway
standards and novelty dance tunes, and was inflamed by
rock'n'rollers, black and white. No American music was beyond
his compass. His Sun career was an atomic explosion, stubbed out
by a ridiculous scandal that could only have befallen a man of
Jerry Lee's arrogance. But the prime legacy of his seven years at
Sun, which fills more than a dozen CDs, was accumulated in
private.

Sam Phillips kept the tapes rolling while Lewis sidetracked his
way through every half-remembered song fragment in his head,
pausing only to praise his own genius or argue a point of scripture.

'Sam? He's a crazy son of a bitch,' Lewis contended in a
much-repeated quote. 'He's as nutty as a fox squirrel. He's just like
me. He ain't got no sense. Me and him and Jack Clement, birds of
a feather flock together. It took all of us to get together to really
screw up the world.'

Jerry Lee screwed up the world, and himself, and anyone else
who got in his way, but still it's easy to hear why Sam Phillips gave
him free rein in the studio. Spontaneous to the point of
combustion, Lewis didn't respond to persuasion. As a 21-year-old
braggart in 1956, Jerry insisted he knew more about music than the
man who had discovered Presley, Perkins and Cash. And he knew
it intuitively. Music flowed out of Lewis like a gusher, and Phillips
recognized that his abilities were limitless – or restrained only by
the chaos which inevitably followed him.

Like his cousins, the troubled evangelist Jimmy Lee Swaggert,
and country star Mickey Gilley, Lewis hailed from Ferriday, a
small town in East Louisiana. 'We grew up in a shack,' says his
youngest sister, Linda Gail. 'We hardly had any clothes.' His
father sold bootleg whiskey – 'Daddy cooked it out back,' his sister

Frankie Jean recalled, 'we had shrubs hiding the still' – and filled his son's head with Jimmie Rodgers and Al Jolson songs. When Jerry Lee was eight, his parents sacrificed home comforts to buy the boy a piano. Within a few weeks, he was embellishing the simple tunes he'd been taught, and thereafter he played boogie-woogie, country and gospel as if they were all variations on the same theme.

His cousins shared his natural talent at the keyboard. Jerry Lee and Jimmy Lee became childhood partners in crime and Christ, whose paths tangled like mating snakes for the next five decades. Together they explored the love of God and the lure of the Devil, until they hit a fork in the road in the mid-fifties, and headed towards differing destinations.

For Lewis, the spirit and the blood were ever at war. The fervour of evangelism roused him with the same ferocity as the liquor-fuelled mayhem he witnessed at Haney's Big House, a black R&B club and drinking den across the Mississippi River in Natchez. 'Haney'd bring blues and boogie-woogie cats, the best,' Lewis recalled. 'Duke Ellington, Champion Jack Dupree, Sunnyland Slim, Albert King, B. B. King, Muddy Waters and Ray Charles, a great, great cast. Sometimes Jimmy and me, we'd get in the door of this wild negro club, and they'd be drunk, dancing and going crazy, some out cold on the floor.' At the Pentecostal Holiness Assembly of God church, that same fervour was channelled into the fear of God and Satan. 'They preached nothing but hellfire and brimstone,' recalls sister Linda Gail. 'I've been scared to death by it my whole life.' A visiting preacher in the early fifties drenched the Ferriday congregation in the awareness of their sin, and stirred up a revivalist movement that drove the teenage Jerry Lee Lewis to Bible School. He was 17 years old, and was already married to the preacher's daughter. For several months, Lewis calmed the hedonism that tingled in his blood and gave up his life to Christ – except when he bunked over the college walls to meet local girls.

In an incident which has been smoothed into a myth, Lewis's career as a preacher ended when he was invited to play 'My God Is Real' in front of the students. 'I kinda put a little feeling into it,' he explained, 'a little Louisiana boogie-woogie. The students loved it, they stamped and hollered. I felt the spirit move me so I kept going on the piano, singing as powerful as I could. The students all clapped and rose to their feet in joyous rapture. But the Dean expelled me, so I came home.'

His marriage to the preacher's daughter collapsed soon after, and before the divorce was finalized, Jerry Lee took another bride. He sold encyclopaedias door to door, spieling out hype to make housewives sign their lives away. But only music would satisfy his soul, and in 1954, approaching his nineteenth birthday, he took the bus towards Nashville, the home of the *Grand Ole Opry*. Like thousands of innocents arriving in Music City, he assumed that his talent would instantly be recognized. The few executives who allowed him to audition told him that country stars played guitar. Lewis fled for the safety of Ferriday. Nashville's rejection was understandable: they already had the self-styled King of the Hillbilly Piano Players, Aubrey 'Moon' Mullican. A stout, lugubrious figure, he played boogie riffs with a solid left hand and two dancing fingers on his right. To modern ears, he sounds like a British pub pianist, while his voice carries the weight of dampened middle-aged expectations. Jerry Lee lapped up the linguistic chaos of 'New Pretty Blonde', on which Mullican tried vainly to master Creole French, and mimicked the boogie rhythms of Moon's biggest hit, 'I'll Sail My Ship Alone'. Mullican crooned the lyric like a barstool loner; Lewis breezed through it as a declaration of independence.

The industry still wasn't ready for him. Later in 1954, he travelled to Shreveport, the home of the *Louisiana Hayride*. He auditioned for country star Slim Whitman, who had recently helped Elvis Presley win a residency on the *Hayride*. Whitman turned him down, but did arrange for the teenager to cut two country tunes at the home of the *Hayride*, station KWKH.

Around 1954–5, Lewis worked with another hillbilly piano-player, Roy Hall. The two men shared a feel for rhythm and blues, a taste for hard liquor and a line in hyperbole which expanded the truth into a cartoon. In September 1955, Hall cut a workmanlike boogie called 'Whole Lotta Shakin' Goin' On'. He claimed to have written it with a black blues musician, then cloaked his identity behind a pseudonym; Jerry Lee Lewis claims that he taught Hall the song, having written it around the skeleton of a vintage blues tune. Hall slipped into obscurity after several records failed to click. Meanwhile, Jerry Lee Lewis was two hundred miles west in Memphis, drawn by the furore surrounding Elvis Presley and Carl Perkins. The simplistic prose of the fan magazines suggested that all a country boy had to do was turn up at Union Avenue and be transformed into a star.

When Lewis arrived unannounced at the Memphis Recording Service, Phillips was on the road, delivering acetates of his new releases to radio DJs. Jerry threatened to camp outside until Mr Phillips returned, so Jack Clement, recently hired as Sun's engineer, let him audition. Like Carl Perkins and Johnny Cash before him, Lewis hardly arrived rockin': 'Jerry Lee sang "Seasons Of My Heart" and some of those old George Jones type things,' Clement recalls. 'I really dug his piano and singing, but it was straight country. I told him, "Man, this stuff ain't happening now. You ought to learn some rock and roll songs and come back."' Typically, Lewis remembers it another way: 'Jack said rock'n'roll was finished with. Elvis had got it sewn up. I disagreed and set out to prove him wrong.'

When Phillips returned, Clement played him the tape, and Sam immediately recognized a kindred spirit. As Jerry Lee remembers it, 'I went back a month later and met Jack coming out the door. He said, "Sam Phillips heard your tapes and he wants to make a record."' Not that he would produce it himself. Once again, it was Jack Clement who supervised the session: 'We brought in some guys on bass guitar and drums, and started experimenting. We spent most of the time on "My Blue Heaven", but we were just about through when I said, "Do you know 'Crazy Arms'?" He said, "Part of it."

'I told him to do what he knew and we ran it through and made one take on it. At the time, the bass player had wandered out somewhere, and the guitar player was in the bathroom. So really all it was on the record was piano and drums. And right at the end the bass player walked in and thought we were just clowning around, which we kinda were. So he picked up the guitar and hit this little chord, clink, and that was the record.

'Several days after Sam came back, we were sitting around

listening to the tape and really digging it. At first we dug "My Blue Heaven", but then we got to digging "Crazy Arms". Of course, at this time Ray Price had had a hit with "Crazy Arms", maybe five months previously. And it had been a pop hit with the Andrews Sisters, and was on its way down. But Sam heard this thing and said, "Man, put it out." He made a dub and took it up to WHVQ. And they played it on the air and started getting hundreds of calls. So we pressed it up.' 'Crazy Arms' was a bizarre choice of material, as Ray Price's original version was still at the top of the country charts. Adding a shuffle beat to the honky-tonk sound familiar from Hank Williams and Ernest Tubb, Price and his Cherokee Cowboys took a bar-room lament on to the dancefloor. It wasn't rock'n'roll, but it had an enduring effect on the country mainstream, still a recognizable influence in the nineties on artists like George Strait and Clint Black.

Lewis wasn't cowed by Price's shuffle beat. He swaggered into the song like a hoodlum entering a bar, stretching and distorting his syllables. Price's 'Crazy Arms' was a five-beer lament; Lewis sang as if the only arms that mattered were his own, digging deep boogie chords out of the piano while drummer Jimmy Van Eaton struggled to keep pace. Trade magazine *Billboard* praised his 'sock warbling' and 'powerful feeling for country blues', which was even more apparent on the flipside. As Lewis sang 'End Of The Road', adapting a pre-war blues tune, he mapped out the rest of his career right there – one long roadhouse stomp, without a worthy obstacle in his way.

Jerry Lee was like a hot-wired jukebox in the weeks after 'Crazy Arms' appeared: you poured in a drink, and out came a random selection of tunes, pulled from the recesses of his memory. Sam Phillips taped it all, aware from his experience with Presley and Perkins that inspiration might strike at any moment. So the tape machines of the Memphis Recording Service rolled while Jerry led his cohorts – Sun regulars Roland Janes, Jimmy Van Eaton and J. W. Brown – through gutbucket blues tunes, country weepers, boogie instrumentals, even 'The Marines' Hymn', while Phillips waited patiently for something that might be a hit record.

After one particularly eclectic session, in which Jerry led them from R&B swagger ('I'm a sixty-minute man') to Hank Williams heartbreak ('Cold, Cold Heart'), the crew burst into all they could remember of that Roy Hall flop, 'Whole Lotta Shakin' Goin' On'. Phillips filed the memory away, while the band returned later to craft Jack Clement's spunky pop novelty, 'It'll Be Me', into a rock'n'roll classic. Lewis had already drifted off into a tear-jerking Jimmie Rodgers song that his daddy used to play for him when Phillips reminded him about Hall's country boogie. Jerry Lee doubtless staked his claim to the tune – 'I rewrote the whole song,' he was still complaining decades later – and then set about proving it.

Hall's recording of 'Whole Lotta Shakin'' buried the keyboard beneath a scratchy guitar. Jerry Lee set the song where it belonged, on a piano riff forged in steel. Then he lived out the lyric, turning Hall's polite party invitation into a promise of an explosive night with the sixty-minute man himself.

For a few weeks, the world continued unchanged. Jerry Lee guested on the *Big D Jamboree* barn dance in Dallas, then went out on the road with Johnny Cash and the Louvin Brothers. Then, in May 1957, Sam Phillips booked Cash, Lewis and Carl Perkins on a package that swooped down from Canada to join another tour, led by pop crooner Sonny James, in Texas. The excursion began in Winnipeg, where Lewis watched moodily from the wings while Perkins and Cash wore their guitars like phalluses and drove the audience into a frenzy. 'Play standing up,' Carl suggested when Lewis complained that he was stuck behind his piano, and the following night, in Saskatoon, Jerry Lee did just that. He flung the piano stool behind him, and approached the eighty-eight keys like a butcher with a cleaver. His carefully stacked pompadour slipped down the side of his face, his features contorted with violence, and his Sun rivals watched from backstage as he stole their crowd away.

Back in the South, the police department in Beaumont, Texas, promoted a show which placed the Sun stars alongside two other youthful rock'n'rollers, Wanda Jackson and Gene Vincent. That same week, 'Whole Lotta Shakin' Goin' On' was finally released. The trade mags greeted it merely as 'a driving blues shouter in the typical Sun tradition'. But like 'Blue Suede Shoes' before it, the single spread across the radio dial, roaring from country stations to pop and R&B.

What turned a flame into an inferno was an appearance on TV's *Steve Allen Show* in July 1957. Allen's forte was comedy, and his guests were automatically involved, whether they liked it or not. The TV star had satirized the controversy around Elvis Presley's pelvic thrusts by dressing him in a tuxedo and having him serenade a bored bassett-hound called Sherlock. Jerry Lee Lewis was beyond satire. He entered millions of American homes like an invader from Mars, pumped high on adrenalin and the knowledge that he was unstoppable. Allen's audience saw the whole routine – the flying piano stool, the tumbling hair, the arrogant leer and convulsive force of Jerry Lee in full flight. They were also treated to a lavish display of lust, not often exposed on fifties network TV. When Lewis reached the line about taking the bull by the horns, he mimed the action with a masturbatory jerk of his hands: this was one horn that plainly didn't need a steer.

For the next ten months, Jerry Lee Lewis was the hottest name in rock'n'roll. 'Whole Lotta Shakin'' topped both the country and the R&B charts, only narrowly failing to match 'Blue Suede Shoes' by hitting the No. 1 pop position too. 'Great Balls Of Fire', a manufactured burst of frenzy, followed suit. At one point, Lewis had the two most popular songs on country radio, as DJs flipped 'Great Balls' to find a revival of Hank Williams' ballad 'You Win Again'.

There were movie cameos, overseas tours, residencies on prestigious rock packages, and with each new release Lewis bopped closer to the heart of rock'n'roll. Country DJs were still prepared to interrupt their diet of Ray Price and George Jones hits for a lightning bolt of 'Breathless' or 'High School Confidential'.

In May 1958, Lewis flew to London Airport, for a British tour intended to crown him as America's number one rock export. Trailing in his wake were his sister, Frankie Jean, and a shy, pubescent girl who was revealed to be Jerry's wife. He admitted as much to the press, adding with a shrug that she was 15 years old. Further questioning revealed that she was his second cousin, no more than 13, and that Lewis had neglected to divorce his second wife before bagging his third.

Lewis pleaded that teenage marriages were legal in the American South, but that merely piqued British snobbery. Questions were asked in Parliament, and the popular press incited a wave of criticism against the unrepentant rock'n'roller. After just four shows, the tour was cancelled, and Lewis and his 'bride' jetted home in disgrace.

In a rare misjudgement, Sam Phillips decided that Jerry's home crowd – some of whom had married at 13 themselves – would laugh off the controversy as Old World arrogance. Even before Lewis had reached Tennessee, Phillips allowed local DJ George Klein and Jack Clement to assemble a fake radio interview about the scandal, punctuated by 'appropriate' extracts from Jerry's records. They called it 'The Return Of Jerry Lee', and slipped it on to the flipside of his egotistical romp, 'Lewis Boogie'. 'We think it's a cute record,' Phillips said. 'It makes light of the whole British episode, which is the way we think the whole thing should be treated.' Radio ignored the record, and although Lewis could still draw an audience for his live shows, his rock'n'roll career was fatally wounded.

Country DJs remained the most loyal, flipping over his next single, 'Break Up', to find the apologetic 'I'll Make It All Up To You'. So subdued was Lewis on this track that he didn't even play piano, leaving that to the composer, new Sun signing Charlie Rich. Thereafter, a revival of Moon Mullican's 'I'll Sail My Ship Alone' proved prophetic. Jerry Lee cut consistently strong rock records into the early sixties, but only one – a 1961 revamp of Ray Charles' 'What'd I Say' – caught the attention of radio. He followed with what would once have been a surefire double-sided hit, coupling the playful pop tune 'It Won't Happen With Me' with a sublime reading of Hank Williams' 'Cold, Cold Heart'. When that failed, he waited patiently for his Sun contract to expire, which it finally did in August 1963. In the words of a song he cut at his last session with Sam Phillips, Lewis was now 'One Minute Past Eternity'.

Four years earlier, with his career disintegrating around him, Lewis still had the self-belief to pummel out an improvised statement of faith. 'Hillbilly fever goin' round,' he promised, 'Good ol' mountain music comin' down.' Then, as the tempo reached a crescendo, he spelled it out once and for all: 'This country music's goin' round, You get the feelin' boy you can't sit down.' The song careered to a halt a few seconds later, leaving Jerry to mull over his dilemma: he was the last man alive who believed that 'hillbilly fever' was still the future of rock'n'roll.

23 Let's Have a Party

The country roots of rock'n'roll, 1953–1960: the Everly Brothers: Brenda Lee; Wanda Jackson; Chuck Berry; Gene Vincent; Eddie Cochran; Buddy Holly

In the mythology of country music, family tradition is an unmixed blessing. Countless songs, from 'That Silver-Haired Daddy Of Mine' to 'Mother The Queen Of My Heart', hymn the importance of the parental gene pool. Equally potent is the almost eerie sense of unity that comes from the voices of two brothers, raised in song.

Both traditions coincided in a duo whose music caught an indefinable blend of country, rock'n'roll and pop in the late fifties. According to hillbilly myth, Don and Phil Everly should have kept alive the music of their folksinging parents, Ike and Margaret. In the rock'n'roll equivalent, they'd have torched their parents' heritage. For the Everly Brothers, the gravitational pull of their country lineage triumphed over teenage rebellion; instead, tension expanded *within* their partnership. By the time of their violent confrontation at a 1973 concert at Knotts Farm, the Everlys had ceased to communicate except at the microphone. It was as if the strain of maintaining family ties had destroyed the empathy which was their natural asset.

Ike and Margaret Everly were local heroes in the Kentucky hills, where Ike developed a guitar technique that was passed first-hand to country luminaries like Chet Atkins and Merle Travis. After the birth of a son, Don, in 1937, the family moved to Chicago, where Phil was born two years later. But it was from Shenandoah, Iowa, deep in the Mid-West farming belt, that the Everly Family's voices reached out across the central plains, via a daily show on KMA radio.

The boys began performing almost as soon as they could talk. Don showed a prodigal talent on the guitar, and Phil assumed the role of harmony singer. At first, their naïve voices were a novelty, but as they reached their teens, their precision began to outgrow the family's downhome image.

In 1954, Ike Everly called in a favour from Chet Atkins, by now a producer for RCA in Nashville. Atkins noted Don Everly's writing skills, and passed 'Thou Shalt Not Steal' to country queen Kitty Wells. He also won the brothers an audition at Columbia, who signed them in late 1955.

They were groomed as potential rivals to the Louvin Brothers, who shared their fraternal mastery of harmony. But as Don recalls, the Everlys were already looking to explore a wider seam: 'We were doing more uptempo and pop stuff. We weren't real country. But we had to cut these songs because country is what they wanted.'

Elaine Tubb, daughter of honky-tonk pioneer Ernest, handled their management, but she was unable to interest Columbia in more than one, very traditional, Everlys single. It arrived just as Elvis Presley and Carl Perkins were jolting country into a new era. 'I wanted to write like Hank Williams,' Don Everly recalls, 'so that tradition was in my blood. But we were also listening to R&B artists like Ray Charles and the Clovers.' It was the same brew that fuelled the first generation of rock'n'rollers, so it was inevitable that the Everlys should follow their example.

After a fallow year, Chet Atkins introduced them to Nashville publisher Wesley Rose. He promised them a record deal if they signed away their songwriting rights, and duly introduced them to Cadence boss Archie Bleyer.

In spring 1957, Elaine Tubb won the Everlys a place on an acoustic package headed by bluegrass legend Bill Monroe – whose song 'Blue Moon Of Kentucky' had unwittingly sparked Elvis Presley's first experiments with rockabilly. 'They had a good duet,' Monroe recalled. 'Their father was a good guitar man, too. But they wasn't with me for long until their record really went to hittin' the charts. So they had to quit the tent show, and get back playin' in country. They were more country than they would have been bluegrass.'

Don Everly has a wider vision of what they represented: 'We were always experimental. We weren't just country. We were never just rock'n'roll, either.' Their first hit, a chirpy pop tune from professional writing team Boudleaux and Felice Bryant, hinted at their range. The harmonies on 'Bye Bye Love' were pure country, the rhythm flirted with rock'n'roll, but Don's guitar playing was an unashamed hybrid. 'That opening riff came from another of my songs, called "Give Me A Future",' he says, 'but it seemed to fit on the front of "Bye Bye Love". It was a mix of different stuff. I loved those Bo Diddley R&B records, that hard, driving rhythm. But I'd also picked up something from the way Hank Williams played guitar, with real chunky chords. That's where the riff came from.' Built on harmonies so smooth that the Brothers sounded like lovers, 'Bye Bye Love' reached across the radio dial. It sold to pop, country and R&B listeners, and carried the sound of the Everlys overseas. 'The Everly Brothers were my favourite rock'n'roll duo of the 1950s,' Paul McCartney has explained, and their supernaturally tight vocal lock was a primary influence on the Beatles and the groups – British and American – who succeeded them.

The Everlys' hits, which continued unbroken into the sixties, were also quintessential Nashville recordings. Chet Atkins led the team who appeared on almost all their early sides, while other bastions of the Nashville Sound, like Floyd Cramer and Buddy Harman, were also regulars on Everlys sessions. Their records rarely slipped into the excessive sentimentality that had become a Music City trademark. Producer Archie Bleyer realized that the selling point was Don and Phil's harmonic blend, and nothing was allowed to obstruct it.

The Everlys' hits straddled the border between country and pop with such precision that they were uniquely accepted by both audiences. 'One night we'd finish up in New York City at the Paramount Theatre with the screaming teenagers,' Don Everly recalls, 'the next weekend we'd be at the *Grand Ole Opry* with the adults and young people screaming and carrying on. It was just the same response.' *Opry* managers overlooked their ruling that nobody could perform on the show with a full drumkit: previous transgressors had hidden their offending percussion behind a curtain, but the Everlys had their drummer on open display.

They followed 'Bye Bye Love' with 'Wake Up Little Susie', a

daring vignette about a teenage couple who fall asleep at the drive-in on a date. The cause of their exhaustion is never revealed, but either way, 'our reputation is shot'. It was risqué for 1957, though it still topped the country charts for two months. Don Everly emphasized the duo's breadth by borrowing the central guitar riff from the country blues tradition – since when it has recurred in the least predictable of places, from Bob Dylan's 'Fixin' To Die' to Yoko Ono's 'Don't Worry Kyoko'.

Country fans continued to respond to the brothers' teen dramas, like 'Bird Dog' and 'Til I Kissed You'. Tradition suggested that the duo would gradually slough off their hillbilly skins and concentrate on the international pop market. But the Everlys hadn't forgotten their roots.

In August 1958, Don and Phil entered RCA's Nashville studio with bassist Floyd Chance, to cut an album of folk and hillbilly standards – the music that had cradled their youth. 'It was as good a thing as we'd ever done,' Don Everly claims, 'it was true and from the heart. That's exactly where we were in those days. Those songs bring a tear to my eye sometimes.'

The album was called *Songs Our Daddy Taught Us*, and Archie Bleyer commendably resisted the temptation to decorate them with contemporary pop production. Instead, his liner notes sought to reassure fans who knew nothing of the Everlys' heritage: 'These are old, old songs, but there's the beat and rhythm of today in the wonderful way Don and Phil sing them . . . It takes a special talent like the Everly Brothers possess to bring these ageless songs of a family fireside to the jet-propelled age of today.'

'Jet-propelled', 'beat and rhythm' – that was pure fantasy. *Songs Our Daddy Taught Us* was an unashamed throwback to the 1930s, when Ike Everly was the hottest folk guitarist in Kentucky. Indeed, 'Kentucky' was the key track, a sublime, almost spiritual tribute to the state from which the Everly stock had arisen. The brothers performed the song with such reverence that they might have been plucked straight from their parents' fields. The Everlys now claim that their motives for recording this album were tangled: they were planning to leave Bleyer's label for a more lucrative deal, and didn't want to leave potential hit singles that might compete with their new product. But that didn't explain the respect they paid to their father's repertoire. *Songs Our Daddy Taught Us* stands alone in fifties rock'n'roll. Jerry Lee Lewis or Elvis Presley might have cut an occasional Hank Williams tune, but only the Everlys had the courage to strip away the trappings of success and expose their country roots to the mass audience.

The gesture wasn't repeated, although the brothers still perform 'Kentucky' to this day. They duly moved from Cadence to the Hollywood-based Warner Brothers label in 1960, and soon fell foul of one of Nashville's least appealing traditions. Wesley Rose, son of Hank Williams' mentor Fred Rose and a senior partner in the Acuff-Rose publishing concern, had exercised a near-managerial role in the Everlys' career since 1957. He encouraged both brothers to compose, in the knowledge that they were under contract to Acuff-Rose, and ruled that they should only record material owned by his company. It was the richest catalogue in Nashville, but it didn't contain 'Let It Be Me' or 'Temptation', which the Everlys insisted on issuing as singles. Open conflict ensued, and the brothers vowed not to record any Acuff-Rose copyrights – or write new material themselves – until the dispute was settled.

That consumed almost four years, during which the duo shifted their centre of operations from Nashville to California, and were forced to tackle increasingly unsuitable pop tunes. They returned to Rose and Nashville in 1964, but their career never fully recovered. Country radio had abandoned them when they signed to Warners; now pop stations followed suit. While Everlys-inspired bands like the Beatles, the Byrds and the Beach Boys enjoyed worldwide acclaim, Don and Phil were eased out of the public consciousness – until the first stirrings of country-rock in the late sixties provided a viable context for their music again.

The Everlys employed the Nashville industry as a launch pad for a career that extended far beyond country music. For another mid-fifties pioneer, acceptance by Nashville did not automatically translate into hit records on the country charts. There was no doubt about Brenda Lee's roots: 'I worked with a country band in my hometown of Atlanta, Georgia. I was maybe six years old when I started out, singing Hank Williams songs. That's the kind of stuff that my mother used to sing to me, so that was what I learned. And I sang Hank's "Jambalaya" when I was discovered by Red Foley on his *Ozark Jubilee* TV show. That was my first record.'

Well before she reached her teens, Brenda Mae Tarpley roared like a lion who smoked forty a day. After she cut a wild rocker called 'Dynamite', a publicist dubbed her Little Miss Dynamite, and the description stuck. Brenda Lee was raised on country, signed to the Nashville arm of Decca Records, and recorded with the cream of the city's sessionmen. But even after she cut 'Jambalaya' at her first session, country stations couldn't handle the raucous power of her voice. A pocket dynamo, she adapted perfectly to rockabilly, and during the late fifties she recorded some of the classics of the genre – 'Bigelow 6-200', 'Rock The Bop' and 'Let's Jump The Broomstick'.

'The community in Nashville were great to me,' she says today, 'but they wouldn't play me on the radio. They had this thing that if you started out in pop or rock, they couldn't wholly embrace you. No matter that I was singing country before I came to Tennessee. They still thought I was a rock singer.'

Lee's constant theme is that 'I just think of myself as a singer, and I like to sing every style you can show me.' Her success in the rock'n'roll market narrowed her audience. Although her sixties hits such as 'I'm Sorry' and 'All Alone Am I' were prime examples of the Nashville Sound, they weren't playlisted by country stations.

Another factor militated against success in Nashville: her extreme youth. 'On my first record,' she explains, 'they said I was nine years old. They made a point of putting that on the label. Actually I was ten, or maybe just eleven. Maybe they felt that if they said I was younger, it might be more of an attraction, but I think that the opposite was the case. People in Nashville thought I was a novelty act who would soon go away.'

Instead, Lee became the biggest-selling American female singer of the sixties. She gives the credit to Owen Bradley, the veteran producer who also guided her close friend, Patsy Cline. 'Owen was a genius,' she insists, 'he just knew the way the business worked better than anyone. He was the magic ingredient behind my hit records. Patsy loved him too. She was a real inspiration to me. She had a big personality and a kind heart, but she knew what she wanted, and she wouldn't take no for an answer. She was a strong woman at a time when there weren't that many in the record business.'

Like the Everlys, Cline was signed as a country artist, and crossed into the pop mainstream. Lee should have followed the same route: 'When I started out, I was being played on all kinds of stations. Country played me, rock'n'roll played me, rhythm and blues played me. Then they decided I was a pop act. I sold tens of millions of records in the fifties and sixties, and these days you hear them on the country oldies shows. Back then, they called them pop.'

Owen Bradley knew that rockabilly wouldn't fuel a lasting career, so he encouraged Lee to widen her horizons. If country wouldn't accept her, maybe the adult pop audience would. 'I always loved the standards,' Brenda says, 'and I cut my teeth on people like Billie Holiday, Judy Garland, Edith Piaf and Mabel Mercer. So it was our policy – mine and Owen's – that if you cut those kind of good songs on your albums, then if radio stations wouldn't play anything else, they'd always fall back on them.'

In Europe, Lee was acknowledged as a first-generation rock'n'roller: 'I used to travel in Britain with people like Gene Vincent, and we had some very successful tours. I went to Germany, too. In fact, the Beatles opened for me at the Star-Club in Hamburg. We did a couple of shows in England, too, and then they exploded. I tried to get them a recording contract here with Decca at that time, but the company wasn't interested. I thought, "God, these boys are really something." So I went to Decca and said, "There is this group of boys in England who are really great, called the Beatles. You should give them a listen." But they didn't care to. I knew the Beatles were gonna be big. Anyone who saw them knew that.'

As the sixties progressed, Lee wound up in unexpected company – cutting singles with future Led Zeppelin guitarist Jimmy Page in England ('I remember him. He was just a kid like me'), and tackling urban soul songs in New York. She even followed Dusty Springfield, Lulu and Cher to Memphis, to cut a downhome soul album. But in the early seventies, her records began to slip off the pop charts, and at that moment country radio was finally prepared to welcome her home. Lee is refreshingly clear-sighted about this shift in perception: 'It was them who changed, not me. We were still recording the way we had always done. But rock and pop – and country – were all going through these drastic changes. Country had become what pop used to be, and suddenly everyone decided I was a country singer after all. But I didn't change my style, not one bit.'

Wanda Jackson walked the same wire between country, pop and rock'n'roll. She was touring with western swing icon Hank Thompson in 1954 when her path collided with Elvis Presley's. He invited her home to inspect his blues collection – the boy was always a charmer – and when she signed to Capitol in 1956, at the age of 18, it was as a full-fledged rockabilly.

Capitol surrounded her with one of the richest back-up bands in history – future Bakersfield country legend Buck Owens was there, alongside the California guitar team of Speedy West and Joe Maphis, and veteran Skeets McDonald. 'Honey Bop' showed that she'd studied Elvis's records, while her musicians did their best to tame Jackson's teenage fire.

None of her accompanists had a more ambiguous relationship with rock'n'roll than Buck Owens. He found his fame in the sixties as a reliable purveyor of California honky-tonk music, a lean style that inspired everyone from Ringo Starr to Gram Parsons, not forgetting country stars like Merle Haggard and Dwight Yoakam, but never hinted at any loss of emotional control.

In the fifties, Owens switched back and forth from country to rockabilly, never quite certain which way to jump. He penned wild rock tunes like 'Flash, Crash And Thunder', cut with rural swagger by the evocatively named Farmer Boys. He was on hand when Gene Vincent or Wanda Jackson needed some rock'n'roll rhythm. But he was also alongside Stan Freberg when the humorist delivered his devastating satires on the teenage craze. Part booster, part subversive, Owens was not the ideal midwife for the birth of a rock'n'roll revolution. His fellow studio aces shared his apprehension.

Hank Williams and first wife Audrey.
Self-destructive and brilliant, Hank's
rowdy hillbilly music prepared the way for
rock'n'roll. *(Glenn A. Baker Archives/Redferns)*

Rockabilly pioneer Carl
Perkins, who was reared on
Hank's stark lyrical imagery
and rural Southern twang.
(Michael Ochs Archive/Redferns)

The Sun Studios on Union Avenue, Memphis: the birth-place of rockabilly. *(David Redfern and Ebet Roberts/Redferns)*

Sun Records boss Sam Phillips with Elvis, Scotty and Bill – the first of the country boys he transformed into rock'n'roll legends. *(Glenn A. Baker Archives/Redferns)*

December 1956: the one-off gathering of the Million Dollar Quartet at the Sun Studios. Left to right: Jerry Lee Lewis, Carl Perkins, Elvis Presley, Johnny Cash. *(Michael Ochs Archive/Redferns)*

Jerry Lee Lewis: the exuberance of 1958 had soured into sullen defiance a decade later. *(Michael Ochs Archive and Glen A. Baker/Redferns)*

Gram Parsons (second from left) infiltrates the Byrds.
(Michael Ochs Archive/Redferns)

Luxury and excess were the twin watchwords of Parsons' life.
(The Platt Collection/Archive Photos)

GP with Nudie suit — and Nudie.
(Glenn A. Baker Archives/Redferns)

Two approaches to country-rock iconography: the Band revisit the 1920s, the Eagles pose as jaded hippie troubadours. *(Elliot Landy and Gems/Redferns)*

Bob Dylan's early repertoire spanned Guthrie,
Leadbelly — and Hank Williams.
(Michael Ochs Archive/Redferns)

Ill at ease in his 'country suit' at the Isle of Wight
Festival, 1969. *(David Redfern/Redferns)*

Dylan with Johnny Cash, the man who
had salvaged his career three decades
earlier. *(Colorific)*

Discovered by Gram Parsons, Emmylou Harris blossomed during the eighties to become one of modern country's superstars. *(Ebet Roberts/Redferns)*

k.d. lang – a traditional outfit on a very modern performer. *(Ebet Roberts/Redferns)*

Neil Young, whose plaintive voice echoed the lonesome whine of a steel guitar. *(Michael Ochs Archive/Redferns)*

Young and Willie Nelson hold the fort at Farm Aid — an unashamedly American charity inspired by a chance remark from Bob Dylan. (*Ebet Roberts/Redferns*)

This lack of commitment was apparent on most of Jackson's rock records, so she simply screamed louder. Her first hit, 'I Gotta Know', was a schizophrenic effort, divided between a hillbilly lament and passages of frenzied rockabilly. On 'Long Tall Sally' and 'Mean Mean Man', she was Lolita, leading a band of hillbilly Humberts astray. But those sides paled alongside 'Fujiyama Mama', where the calming efforts of her support crew couldn't prevent Jackson unleashing a leonine roar. It was a demonstration of machismo – or should that be machisma? – unrivalled on a woman's country record until Tanya Tucker revived the rasp, and the *Lolita* imagery, in the seventies.

Finally, in 1960, Wanda Jackson landed another hit, with a scorching remake of the Elvis favourite, 'Let's Have A Party'. For a few glorious months, she ran two careers side by side, skipping from rock to country at a time when even Presley was fleeing the wreckage of rockabilly. As late as 1964, long after country had shed rock'n'roll from its collective memory, Jackson still slipped Carl Perkins tunes on to her albums. But her 1961 hit, 'Right Or Wrong', a textbook demonstration of the Nashville Sound, illustrated her dilemma. The former Fujiyama Mama was now typecast as a romantic slave, crooning pathetically: 'Won't you take me along to be with you, right or wrong.'

That was what the country audience – and, to be fair, the entire record industry – demanded from a woman in the early sixties. After a decade spent genuflecting to Nashville, Jackson bowed to an even more powerful force, jettisoning secular music to sing the praises of the Lord. When she allowed herself some dispensation in the eighties, it was rock'n'roll that called her back, not country ethics right or wrong.

On a rock'n'roll tour in the late fifties, country-pop star George Hamilton IV heard someone down the bus playing Hank Williams singles on a portable deck. He was startled to discover it was Chuck Berry – the premier black rock'n'roll star of the era, the genre's most brilliant lyricist and a man whose music was built around the blues templates of T-Bone Walker and Louis Jordan.

'I thought that was really strange,' Hamilton recalls, 'and I told him so. I said, "How come you're listening to country music?" He just looked at me and said, "Man, I don't understand what you're saying. I'm from the country, the same as you are. What do you think that 'little country boy' in 'Johnny B. Goode' was all about?"'

Berry told Bill Flanagan that there was another, more venial motive for that turn of phrase: 'It was originally "coloured". They told me that if I made it "country", I could get a national hit. It might even go country and western. If I could be introduced to the country market, I would. "Maybellene" got me into the country market.'

That was his first record, a car-chase song in the tradition of Johnny Bond's 'Hot Rod Lincoln' which borrowed from Bob Wills's thirties western swing tune 'Ida Red'. Berry cut 'Maybellene' in Chicago for R&B specialists Chess Records, whose country connections were minimal. But his song was picked up by Marty Robbins, even before Berry's original hit the national charts.

Berry lapped up hillbilly music as a kid. His trademark guitar riff may have come from Louis Jordan's guitarist, Carl Hogan, but licks from Chet Atkins, Merle Travis and Jimmie Rodgers can be identified in his solos. Many of his songs blended R&B and country influences: he built on Hank Williams' sardonic humour, while the storytelling tradition of hillbilly music freed Chuck to pursue 'Maybellene' or 'Nadine' down the road apiece. A rock'n'roll hit like 'Thirty Days' would be unthinkable without a grounding in country music.

George Hamilton IV confirms that Berry's affection for country music was real, albeit tinged with resentment: 'He told me that he used to go to hear the *Grand Ole Opry* whenever he could, but that as soon as he stepped into town, he had to watch his step. I wasn't aware of this at the time, but he said there was a colour bar back then at the *Opry*. "While you white folks was inside enjoying the music," he told me, "I was having to sneak around in the alley, trying to hear what was going on inside. If they caught me, they'd have thrown me in jail."'

Though the bluegrass brother duo Jim and Jesse cut an album of his songs, *Berry Pickin'*, in the mid-sixties, Nashville wasn't ready for Chuck Berry until the end of that decade. That was when Buck

Owens, who'd pledged to cut nothing but country music as long as he might live, took Berry's anthem 'Johnny B. Goode' to the top of the Nashville charts. Waylon Jennings revived 'Brown-Eyed Handsome Man', though – even after he'd cut 'Willie And Laura Mae Jones', about an inter-racial affair – he wasn't game enough to restore Chuck's original title: 'Brown-Skinned Handsome Man'. In the nineties, country acts regularly encored with Chuck Berry tunes, the way that rock bands did in the seventies. Blues singer Jimmy Witherspoon was once asked to describe what he heard in Chuck Berry's music. 'Chuck Berry is a country singer,' he replied starkly. 'People put everybody in categories – black, white. If he was white, he would be the top country star in the world.'

'I remember Gene Vincent and Eddie Cochran as very quiet, sensitive, Southern boys,' says George Hamilton IV. 'I related to them better than to guys like Paul Anka and Bobby Rydell, 'cos they were from the East Coast and were more into the Sinatra syndrome. The boys from the South grew up on the *Grand Ole Opry* and on country music like I did. We all started out wanting to be *Grand Ole Opry* stars, and ended up being called rockabillies, playing on rock'n'roll shows.'

Tied by friendship and by tragedy – Gene was seriously injured in the car crash which killed Eddie in 1960 – Vincent and Cochran are both revered by rock'n'roll fans. Each has been mythologized into a single, golden image: Vincent as a leather-clad, alcohol-wired wildman, Cochran as a slick, all-American stud. Eddie was the teen idol who could charm parents but offered the thrill of shame-free sex; Vincent the stuttering motorcycle hoodlum who lived out the screen roles of James Dean.

The truth was more complex. Vincent's reputation as an unfettered rocker is belied by the often timorous nature of his records, and it ignores the fact that his musical baptism was on *Country Time*, a radio show in his home town of Norfolk, Virginia. Capitol Records executive Ken Nelson signed Vincent as a potential country star, which is how he came to be in Owen Bradley's studio in 1956, cutting a monosyllabic anthem of teenage lust called 'Be-Bop-A-Lula' with a bunch of Nashville session aces. Such was the confusion amongst country programmers in the summer of '56 that 'Be-Bop-A-Lula' was not only playlisted across the South, but reached the Top 10 of the national country chart – where it slouched alongside equally delinquent offerings from the likes of Elvis Presley and Carl Perkins. Vincent never fooled the country stations again, and Eddie Cochran couldn't even slip one record on to their playlists. But few fifties rockers outside the Sun stable had a firmer grounding in country than the teenage prodigy from Oklahoma, who spent his adolescence in Los Angeles.

By his sixteenth birthday, in 1954, Cochran regularly guested with western bands like the Bell Gardens Ranch Gang and the Melodie Boys. 'He always loved the sound of the Gretsch guitar,' recalls Chuck Foreman, the first man to capture Cochran on tape, 'and he was comfortable with all sorts of music. He wanted to be able to play it all.' But commercial needs shaped his public performances: 'In the early fifties, western music was extremely big, particularly in this part of the country. They used to say in the mid-fifties that if you weren't playing in a western band, then you weren't playing! Virtually all of the clubs in town were decked out with western motifs.'

Foreman identifies two traditions sparring for space in mid-fifties Los Angeles: 'There were those taking it more towards the country, what we used to call the hillbilly side – people like Ernest Tubb, the Maddox Brothers & Rose, more to the Nashville Sound. And on the other side there was what was considered to be the more progressive organizations – Bob Wills, Hank Thompson, Tex Williams – that leaned the other way, more in the big band tradition. They had extensive arrangements and more instruments, more in the line of ballroom dance music.'

On his first recordings, guitar duets with Foreman, Cochran sounds like a cross between Chet Atkins and Les Paul, an adolescent whose technical dexterity has developed faster than his imagination. Within a few months, Eddie stumbled across a namesake, a Mississippi refugee named Hank Cochran. With their shared name offering an instant gimmick, they began trading as the Cochran Brothers, passing themselves off in the tradition of the fraternal duos who littered country music history from the thirties to the fifties.

'When rock'n'roll came along,' Chuck Foreman remembers,

'the slang for that was bubblegum music, because only the kids liked it. If you worked in nightclubs, you weren't playing for kids, so you steered clear of it.' Though Hank and Eddie were 20 and 17 respectively in 1955, not a hint of teenage attitude was apparent on the Cochran Brothers' first single, 'Mr Fiddle', a grating hillbilly duet that wouldn't have sounded anachronistic two decades earlier. The more senior Cochran took the lead, while Eddie supplied harmonies and restrained guitar licks.

By the following spring, Elvis Presley's revolution had registered across the San Andreas Fault, and the Cochrans added some gentle tremors of their own with a primitive rockabilly tune called 'Latch On'. They cut the song three times: Hank tackled it first, with the wariness of a middle-aged man. 'You are really gone,' he called out to Eddie as if he couldn't believe his ears, 'take off, cat, like a Rocket 88.'

A few weeks later, Hank reprised the song, and this time the youngster's guitar solo ripped like Scotty Moore's. But it was only when they recruited another would-be recording star, pop songwriter Jerry Capehart, that anyone would consider releasing 'Latch On', now smoothed into a Bill Haley pastiche.

Eddie Cochran wasn't averse to teen pop himself – his penchant for sentimental ballads scarred his brief career – and after the Cochran Brothers came close to mastering rockabilly on 'Tired And Sleepy', he set off for a solo career, hit records, and even movie roles. Only after his death did evidence emerge that he'd never abandoned the quest for a Sam Phillips-style blend of country and R&B. During the late fifties, when smashes like 'Summertime Blues' and 'C'mon Everybody' established him as a pop star, Cochran devoted much studio time to cutting savage guitar instrumentals that nailed both country and blues under a barrage of block chords. 'You are really gone,' Hank Cochran might have gasped, and in April 1960, Eddie was – killed during his only British tour. Meanwhile, his namesake moved to Nashville and began a career as a country songwriter, which soared when Patsy Cline took 'I Fall To Pieces' to the top of the charts. By 1980, Eddie Cochran had become an icon for punk bands like the Clash, while Hank Cochran was being treated to a career revival courtesy of his old friend, Willie Nelson.

*

Had he outlived Eddie Cochran, Buddy Holly might have shared Hank Cochran's fate – revered among his songwriting peers, then retrieved from obscurity by the newly empowered Willie Nelson in the late seventies. Instead, Holly remained unrecognized by the country industry until the mid-nineties, when Nashville's infatuation with all-star tribute albums finally led them to a fifties rocker who never enjoyed the hint of a country hit, but who served a three-year apprenticeship as a hillbilly before pop stardom transported him in 1957.

Nashville, in the person of producer Owen Bradley, felt little regard for Holly in the mid-fifties. 'That's the worst song I've ever heard,' he quipped when Buddy offered 'That'll Be The Day' at an early Decca session. Trade magazine *Billboard* were slightly more optimistic: 'Holly stands a good chance,' they remarked of his début single, 'Blue Days, Black Nights', 'if the public will take more than one Presley or Perkins, as it may.' Reflecting the confusion of the time, *Billboard* listed Holly's record under 'New Country & Western', then described it as 'rock and roll'. Either way, it flopped. Holly required an independent producer, Norman Petty – free from industry prejudices, out in Clovis, New Mexico – to mould him into an authentic rock'n'roll star.

Bradley's suspicions were partially correct: Buddy Holly wasn't a viable country star in 1956; nor did he share the visceral sexuality of a Presley or even a Perkins. The Decca producer didn't realize that Holly had been playing hillbilly music for almost a decade when he arrived in Nashville. 'When I first met him,' recalls his friend and bandmate Sonny Curtis, 'he was playing guitar and banjo. He wanted to be like Chet Atkins, but he seemed to have more of a bluegrass style. But he was a country musician. We all were, in Lubbock.'

Like Nashville, Lubbock is ambiguous about its musical heritage. Holly's example served to fuel a miniature boom in the West Texas city's creativity, with Joe Ely, Jimmie Dale Gilmore, Terry Allen and Butch Hancock the most obvious beneficiaries. But only in recent years have the city fathers deigned to acknowledge the man who carried Lubbock's name to the world.

The two towns share more than a snobbish attitude to hillbillies and rockers. Both have been tagged 'The City of Churches', both awarded the title of 'The Buckle of the Bible Belt'. And both did their best to smother the musical ambitions of Charles Hardin Holley (the 'e' vanished when he was signed to Decca).

When Holly was given his first guitar at the age of 12, he learned to play the Hank Williams and Bill Monroe tunes he'd heard over the *Opry* and the *Louisiana Hayride*. Hank was his idol – an adulation shared by his schoolfriend Bob Montgomery. To the amusement of their peers, who despised the rural whine of country music, the pair formed a duet partnership, Buddy & Bob, which survived until the mid-fifties.

In September 1953, KDAV radio began broadcasting from Lubbock – the nation's first station devoted solely to country music. Its managers were open to local talent, and Buddy & Bob guested on the regular *Sunday Party* show, graduating to their own weekly showcase by early 1955. They mixed country standards and acoustic blues with a handful of original tunes. Montgomery found it hard to escape 'heart' motifs – almost every song he penned in the mid-fifties carried that word in its title – but Holly chipped in some lyrics and chord changes as variety.

Through 1955, Buddy & Bob regularly taped their new compositions, either at KDAV or across the state in Wichita Falls. Their songs were derivative, and pure country, heightened by the extra instrumentation – fiddle, steel guitar and stand-up bass, the last provided by fellow songwriter Don Guess. But in October 1955, Buddy, Bob, Don and every other Lubbock teenager turned up at the Cotton Club, where Sun Records star Elvis Presley was due to perform. Buddy & Bob won a place on the bill – as they had the previous night, when Bill Haley and the Comets had been in town – and impressed Elvis enough for him to suggest that they should try out for the *Hayride*. Why, he'd even put in a word for them with the show's director, Horace Logan.

Such niceties were second nature to Presley, who'd probably promised the same to dozens of hopefuls across the South. The encounter had a more lasting impact on Holly, who prodded Montgomery into helping him write a rockabilly tune called 'Down The Line'. Montgomery slipped slowly out of the picture, as Holly assembled a rockabilly band and began to compile a set of Presley-style material. Over the next few weeks, he penned a succession of rockers in the Sun tradition – 'Baby Won't You Come Out Tonight' was the most blatant, blending the salient features of Elvis's 'That's All Right' and 'Baby Let's Play House' – and demoed them, first at Jim Beck's studio in town, and then at Norman Petty's base across the state line in Clovis.

By late January 1956, Holly, Curtis and Guess were in Nashville, auditioning for Decca. It took another year, but Buddy was on the path to rock stardom. Aware that his protégé would register beyond the South, Norman Petty disguised Holly's country roots, and there's little beyond the simplicity of his chord changes on his subsequent hits to suggest that the singer had ever modelled himself on Hank Williams or Ernest Tubb. It wasn't until 1965 that any of the Montgomery recordings surfaced in public, by which time Holly's cult status was assured. It took another two years for a country act to turn one of Buddy's compositions into a hit, when the Statler Brothers recorded the worst song Owen Bradley had ever heard, 'That'll Be The Day'.

Strangely, another sliver of Holly's influence had already slipped into the country mainstream – via Waylon Jennings, Buddy's bassist on his doomed final tour, a DJ at KDAV in Lubbock, and just about the only man in country music who was equally aware of the sparring traditions of Ernest Tubb, Buddy Holly and Bob Dylan. His success, and especially his declaration of independence from the Nashville industry in the early seventies, provided a tantalizing hint of what might have ensued had Holly made other travel arrangements in February 1959.

24 He'll Have to Go
Chet Atkins and the Nashville Sound, 1958–1963

After two years under siege from rockabilly, the country music establishment restored order in 1958. Even before the barrage of catastrophes that floored rock'n'roll – Jerry Lee Lewis's underage wife, Buddy Holly's plane crash, Chuck Berry's sexual misconduct rap, the payola scandal – the upstart's hold had begun to be loosened.

That year, country DJs dropped Lewis, Elvis Presley, Carl Perkins and Gene Vincent from their playlists. In their place were more sedate voices: Don Gibson, Jim Reeves, Stonewall Jackson and their like. Adult heartache, as opposed to teen romance, was restored as country's stock-in-trade. The reckless hedonism of Jerry Lee Lewis and the young Elvis Presley gave way to the historical story-songs of Johnny Horton.

The rebirth of the country industry was carefully planned. Broadcasters and music publishers formed the Country Music Association in 1958, superseding the ineffectual Country Music Disc Jockey Association. The CMA could assume automatic backing from local record labels, so their early efforts were concentrated on radio stations.

Their campaign was aided by an abrupt shift in the music being marketed as country. The sharp edges of 'traditional' hillbilly music had survived into rockabilly, albeit mutated into an explosion of energy and noise. As the rock elements were excised from country music, so were the hillbilly roots. What passed as country in 1959 bore little relation to its predecessor a decade earlier, though a good deal more to the mellifluous sound of pop stations before rock'n'roll. The architect of this transformation was Chester 'Chet' Atkins, a guitarist, producer, arranger, A&R man and ultimately label boss with the talent and determination to lead Nashville into a new era.

RCA signed Atkins in 1947 as a rival to Merle Travis, whose laconic vocals and hot guitar licks were captured on No. 1 hits like 'Divorce Me COD' and 'So Round, So Firm, So Fully Packed'. Atkins' virtuosity established him as one of Nashville's most respected guitarists. His roots were hillbilly – how else could he have worked with bands like the Georgia Clodhoppers? – but his guitarwork incorporated swing, melodic jazz and folk. He mastered the double-speed picking of Les Paul, not realizing at first that Paul had used studio trickery to achieve his effects, and his fluency assured him of plentiful session work. Atkins was unafraid of exploring other avenues: his début hit countrified the Chordettes' eerie pop tune, 'Mr Sandman'. He slipped easily into the session crew for Elvis Presley's RCA sessions, inducing nervous awe from Scotty Moore when he allowed Elvis's sidekick to take all the guitar solos.

In 1960, Atkins was named as RCA's regional A&R manager in Nashville, confirming a role he'd effectively adopted three years earlier, when he'd snatched songwriter Don Gibson from MGM. Gibson had penned the smash hit 'Sweet Dreams', after which his career had stalled. At RCA, Atkins recalled, 'We recorded him with fiddles and steel guitar, but nothing happened. So I said, "OK, now we'll do it my way." On the same session we recorded "Oh Lonesome Me" and "I Can't Stop Loving You". We put a heavy drumbeat on them, and I played an electric guitar solo through an echo device. "Oh Lonesome Me" was a really big hit. It was the first time we had ever used a bass drumbeat with a microphone on it, and the first time that type of guitar was on a record. But that's what people buy – they buy surprises.'

They also buy formulas, and Atkins' innovations were immediately copied. More importantly, 'Oh Lonesome Me' crossed high into the pop chart. It wasn't the first Nashville production to slip across the border: ostensibly country artists like Sonny James and Bobby Helms had reached the teenage pop market with ditties like 'Too Young' and 'Jingle Bell Rock'. Atkins' impact was more subtle, and enduring. He concocted a sound that would satisfy the country market without being rural enough to offend urban pop listeners.

'I was recording the Browns and Jim Reeves,' Atkins says,

'records that were country and crossed over to pop.' The sentimentality of the Browns' 'The Three Bells' proved irresistible, as did the smooth ambience of Reeves' 'Four Walls'. Shedding the whining fiddle of his early hits, Reeves oozed out of radio speakers like an anaesthetic. His progress charted the development of the Nashville Sound: first the hillbilly edges were smoothed away, then the warmth of his voice, closer to Bing Crosby than Jimmie Rodgers, was wrapped in soft strings and feather-light harmonies, courtesy of the Anita Kerr Singers. 'I didn't create the Nashville Sound,' Atkins insists. 'It was a whole bunch of musicians and A&R people. Because I had a name as a guitar player, people tended to give me credit for it.' But he was the genre's unchallenged master, who gathered together sympathetic musicians like pianist Floyd Cramer, guitarist Hank Garland and saxophonist Boots Randolph. 'We kept that smooth sound going because we didn't want to alienate the pop audience,' Atkins explains. 'We left off the fiddle and steel guitar and had a smooth sound with vibraharp and piano and electric guitar and bass. Sometimes we would use horns, sometimes strings.'

RCA's roster was unrivalled by the start of the sixties, when even Elvis Presley was cutting in Nashville with Atkins' session players. After years during which the country charts had been dominated by rock'n'roll, the pattern was reversed. The Browns, Jim Reeves, Hank Locklin, even Floyd Cramer himself, were established way beyond the South. The biggest hits from that era left their mark around the world – Marty Robbins' 'El Paso', Jimmy Dean's 'Big Bad John', Jim Reeves' 'He'll Have To Go', Patsy Cline's 'Crazy' and especially Leroy Van Dyke's 'Walk On By'. Never have country and pop been so closely in tune.

'Sometimes I got complaints,' Atkins admits. 'People like Hank Snow would say to me, "Chet, I think I should go back and record with a fiddle and a steel guitar like I used to do, because all my fans tell me that's what they want to hear." So we did, but they didn't sell.' There were murmurings that the music had lost its individuality. 'People ask me whether I'm sorry I moved the Nashville Sound so far uptown,' Atkins worried in the mid-seventies. 'Well, yes, in a way I am.' By 1980, he'd recanted: 'It's gone so far pop now, that anything I did was very minuscule. The way to sell records is to give people something different all the time. Maybe you put some strings on a record, and if that sells real well, then you do it again. Or you'll use horns in the background, and if that sells . . .'

George Jones, who followed the industry into the Nashville Sound in the early sixties, put it more starkly: 'I think it's only a very small corner that actually still likes honky-tonk music. Country music has fought for years to get out of being called hillbilly, away from mountaineers and uneducated people, or snuff-dipping, hellraising cowboys.' In the New Nashville of Chet Atkins, there was no snuff, no cows, and hell was discovering that the Anita Kerr Singers couldn't make it to your session.

25 Urge for Going

Country crosses into pop, 1957–1969: Johnny Cash; Ray Charles; Skeeter Davis; Roger Miller; Gene Pitney and George Jones; Waylon Jennings; Willie Nelson; Flatt & Scruggs; Buck Owens; Merle Haggard

The 'British invasion' sparked by the Beatles in January 1964 punctured the cosy superiority of American pop. In the wake of their first US chart-topper, 'I Want To Hold Your Hand', the Beatles visited the States for a promotional tour. Their first performance on the networked *Ed Sullivan Show* attracted the highest audience in US TV history. That year, British artists captured around 30 per cent of the American record market – and groups such as the Beatles, the Dave Clark Five and Herman's Hermits easily outsold their transatlantic rivals.

This influx of British talent has inspired its share of myths. The sales charts for 1964 and 1965 expose the fiction that American artists were sidelined after the Beatles arrived. Equally misleading is the belief that the British invasion rescued American pop from a creative slump. In fact, 1963 had starred the 'girl groups' produced by Phil Spector, surf acts from California such as the Beach Boys, production epics from Gene Pitney, Roy Orbison and Del Shannon, and a renaissance in the vocal group tradition spearheaded by the Four Seasons. It was also a golden era for Nashville, as an unprecedented number of country records crossed into the national – indeed, international – pop charts.

This was not the first time that country and pop had blurred into a commercial hybrid: a decade earlier, as Allen Churchill wrote in the *New York Times* in 1951, 'New York's writers of pop tunes look in envy and calculation at the "country" songsmiths now outsmarting the city slickers.'

Those songsmiths included Pee Wee King and Redd Stewart, who'd noted the success of Bill Monroe's 'Kentucky Waltz' in 1946, and penned 'The Tennessee Waltz', a sizeable country hit in

1948. But the song only escaped the hillbilly market when Patti
Page recorded it in 1950, on what proved to be the best-selling
single of the era.

Alerted to the potential of hillbilly songs, pop producers sized
up the latest hits by Hank Williams and Lefty Frizzell. Meanwhile,
Nashville publishers like Acuff-Rose – who handled 'The
Tennessee Waltz' – added some impetus from the South. Crooner
Tony Bennett took Hank's 'Cold, Cold Heart' to the top of the
Billboard pop chart; Jo Stafford borrowed Lefty's anthem, 'If
You've Got The Money, I've Got The Time', and Hank's
'Jambalaya'; and Guy Mitchell, Frankie Laine and Rosemary
Clooney also coated country hits with some pop gloss.

Hank Williams' death on New Year's Day 1953 robbed
Hollywood and New York of a vital source of material. Williams
was one of the few hillbilly singers whose own records regularly
appeared on the pop charts, an honour which evaded country
legends such as Webb Pierce, Ernest Tubb and Hank Thompson.
Tennessee Ernie Ford cornered the crossover market, with 1955
hits such as 'Sixteen Tons' and 'The Ballad Of Davy Crockett'.
The eruption of rockabilly, led by Carl Perkins and Elvis Presley,
created a new opening for country performers.

Rockabilly was a fading force by 1958; its backwoods rhythms
and sharp-edged vowels were drowned out by more sophisticated
offerings from New York labels. The so-called 'Nashville Sound',
masterminded by Chet Atkins, emulated this finesse with
technically immaculate productions which sanded down the
jagged surface of honky-tonk music. As early as 1957, when Marty
Robbins' 'The Story Of My Life' and Jim Reeves' 'Four Walls'
eased on to pop playlists, hillbilly purists voiced concern that the
essence of their music was being lost. These misgivings grew as
Reeves and Robbins were joined in the pop charts by Don Gibson
('I Can't Stop Loving You'), Ray Price ('City Lights') and even
Johnny Cash, whose 'Ballad Of A Teenage Queen' was a blatant
attempt to milk the pop cow.

Ironically, Cash's pop material was released by Sun Records, the
rockabilly home of Presley and Perkins. Transferred to Columbia
in 1958, Cash ventured out on a lengthy voyage of artistic
discovery, as he experimented with everything from folk-rock to

the tequila-drenched roar of mariachi bands – sometimes, as with Bob Dylan's 'Mama You've Been On My Mind', on the same song.

The best of Cash's Sun hits, songs such as 'I Walk The Line', 'Big River' and 'Folsom Prison Blues', carried a strong sense of the past. They were instant folksongs, excavated from a quarry of Americana already visited by John Steinbeck, John Ford and Jimmie Rodgers. 'I was deeply into folk music in the early sixties,' Cash has explained, 'both the authentic songs from various periods of American life and the new "folk revival" songs'. That impulse emerged through an ambitious, at times commercially suicidal, series of concept albums. Themed records weren't entirely new to country: *Opry* regular Jean Shepard had cut an equivalent to a Sinatra song cycle, *Songs Of A Love Affair*, as early as 1956. But Cash's projects stepped outside the domain of country songwriting.

'They brought out voices,' he explained, 'that weren't commonly heard at the time – voices that were ignored or even suppressed in the entertainment media, not to mention the political and educational establishments – and they addressed subjects I really cared about. I was trying to get at the reality behind some of our country's history.'

Blood, Sweat And Tears used worksongs to uncover the scuffed traces of the American working class. *Ballads Of The True West* unwrapped the mythology of cowboys and killers. Most controversially, *Bitter Tears* echoed the movement to ensure basic civic rights for Native Americans.

His enterprise had a precursor in Merle Travis, the Kentucky guitar-picker heard on many of the Californian country records which ushered hillbilly into rock'n'roll. When he arrived on the West Coast, Capitol Records greeted Travis as an authentic piece of Americana, and suggested that he document the songs from 'back home'. Instead, he recorded a collection of original tunes that were stained with history (gathered on the *Down Home* LP). They included 'I Am A Pilgrim' (later covered with affectionate humour by the Byrds); 'Sixteen Tons', a chart-topper for Tennessee Ernie Ford in 1955; and 'Dark As A Dungeon'. This eerie, claustrophobic tune escaped time, as if it had been carried through the American bloodstream since pre-history. Its mysterious imagery captivated Bob Dylan (much of whose *John Wesley Harding* album shares its ghostly ambience) and, inevitably, Johnny Cash, the only performer able to translate the song into a hit record. If 'Dark As A Dungeon' tinged Dylan's work in the late sixties, another skilfully constructed 'fakesong' intrigued his compadres, the Band. Their 1968 début album included a stark reading of 'Long Black Veil', a murder ballad that pulled the Appalachian pilgrims back to their English heritage. Its narrator was the spirit of an executed man who had accepted a wrongful murder charge rather than admit adultery with his best friend's wife; it emerged not from the shadows of the folk tradition, but from commercial songwriters Danny Dill and Marijohn Wilkin.

'Long Black Veil' was a 1959 hit for Lefty Frizzell, one of many historical narratives – authentic and invented – which filled the country charts at that time. Frizzell's effort failed to register in the pop market, because Columbia Records' promotion department concentrated on another story-song, also by Marijohn Wilkin: Stonewall Jackson's 'Waterloo'. Like Johnny Horton's 'Battle Of New Orleans' and 'North To Alaska', Marty Robbins' 'El Paso' and Jimmy Dean's 'Big Bad John', 'Waterloo' established Nashville as the source of narratives that could entrance a worldwide audience.

Though they emerged from the same studio system, these records were regarded as somehow more 'authentic' than Nashville's other commercial offerings. Indeed, as the Browns, Jim Reeves, Brenda Lee and Bob Luman carried the city's trademark sound into the pop Top 10, few listeners in London or Los Angeles registered any connection (however distant) to the music of Hank Williams or Ernest Tubb. 'It was a strange time,' recalls Brenda Lee. 'I thought we were cutting country records, but everyone assumed they were pop, so country stations wouldn't play them. Then, a few years later, the situation reversed. The records sounded the same, but everyone thought they were country, so pop stations dropped me.'

Her complaint could have been echoed by other artists cutting pop hits in Nashville – Elvis Presley, the Everly Brothers, Roy Orbison, or the unlikely figure of Ray Charles. Just as a generation of white country-rockers had tapped into the illicit pulse of rhythm and blues stations, so black soul singers tuned into the *Grand Ole Opry* and the *Louisiana Hayride*. The Southern soul tradition is hinged around that cultural embrace, from Solomon Burke's 'Just Out Of Reach' to the country albums cut by Joe Tex and Bobby Womack in the 1970s.

Already feted as the 'Genius of R&B', Ray Charles arrived in Nashville in 1962 to cut a full record of country standards. Three years earlier, he had transformed Hank Snow's proto-rocker 'I'm Movin' On' into a jet-powered slice of rhythm and blues. His *Modern Sounds In Country And Western Music* were more conventional. A sumptuous orchestra ushered him through 'I Can't Stop Loving You', 'Born To Lose' and 'You Don't Know Me', in a style too lush for even the mellowest practitioner of the Nashville Sound. Pop and R&B buyers were enticed by the collision of this orchestral elegance and the weatherbeaten growl of Ray Charles' voice. But country stations remained impervious, unwilling to accept Charles as one of their own for another two decades. Not that he was troubled: 'I wasn't trying to be the first black country singer,' he explained. 'I only wanted to take country songs, and sing them *my* way, not the country way.' Other black artists including Brook Benton followed suit.

The experiment continued through the sixties, as Charles created Southern soul out of Harlan Howard's song 'Busted' (Johnny Cash had the country original), and peppered his output with albums like *Crying Time* (named for a Buck Owens C&W hit), *C&W Meets R&B*, and *Love Country Style*. Heedless of musical and racial differences, Charles was laying down the path for Willie Nelson and Charlie Rich a decade later.

Bobby Darin didn't wait that long. A Ray Charles acolyte, Darin had even signed to the same label, Atlantic, in the hope of mirroring his success. He débuted with novelty rock hits like 'Splish Splash' (a bizarre crossover country hit in 1958), then became a Sinatra for teenage America, vamping his way through 'Mack The Knife'.

He'd already experimented with gospel, rock'n'roll, R&B, blues and jazz by the time he followed Ray Charles' trip into country in 1962. Country DJs defiantly ignored Nashville Sound hits like

'You're The Reason I'm Living', 'Things' and '18 Yellow Roses'. (So, for that matter, did Darin's publicists, who made no attempt to reach the country audience.) Maybe they sensed his conversion was only temporary: he was soon darting between folk-rock, R&B and even an album of songs from *Doctor Doolittle*.

Regional identity counted in country. Darin hailed from New York. But Skeeter Davis was a Kentucky girl. With her namesake Betty Jack Davis, killed in a 1953 car crash, she formed the Davis Sisters. Their solitary hit was 'I Forgot More Than You'll Ever Know', later recorded by Bob Dylan. They were also responsible for 'Rock-A-Bye Boogie', a hysterical rockabilly prototype that seemed to come from another dimension.

Skeeter Davis emerged as a solo artist in 1957. Her forte was answer songs – responses to hits from RCA labelmate Hank Locklin, for the most part. But her biggest hit was 1962's 'The End Of The World', a plaintive teen ballad sung by a woman who was already 31, which reached No. 2 on both pop and country charts. The country audience remained loyal even when she veered into girl group exercises like 'I Can't Stay Mad At You'. Davis's mercurial career saw her tackling an album of Buddy Holly songs nearly thirty years before the rest of Nashville recognized the Texan as a kindred spirit, cutting the hippie anthem 'Let's Get Together' with the genial but straitlaced George Hamilton IV, and receiving a lengthy ban from the *Opry* stage when she accused Nashville's police of brutality. Eventually she settled down with the hirsute drummer of rock band NRBQ, nearly twenty years her junior. Country fans, inured to their stars' eccentric marriages, didn't bat an eyelid.

With its heightened awareness of temptation, sin and remorse, country music has always embraced the backslider and the prodigal. Jerry Lee Lewis took both tendencies to extremes, but, on a smaller scale, other sixties country stars arrived 'home' from unlikely destinations. Johnny Tillotson was a child prodigy on a mid-fifties TV country show in Jacksonville, but 'Poetry In Motion' set him up as the next Neil Sedaka. He crossed back into country with 'It Keeps Right On A-Hurtin'' in 1962, and elected to stay there, extending his chart career for another two decades.

Dallas Frazier's flirtation with pop was more abrupt. He was a child of the Bakersfield country scene in California, whose breakthrough came when he wrote the endearingly infantile 'Alley Oop' for the pop vocal group the Hollywood Argyles. His recording of the near-identical 'Elvira' made him a star: his record label classed him as an R&B act. After that, uncategorizable songs such as 'Mohair Sam' and 'She's A Yum Yum' attracted covers from country stars such as Charlie Rich, and by 1966 he had won over George Jones, who recorded Frazier's typically off-beat 'I'm A People'. None of this prepared Nashville for 'There Goes My Everything', a lachrymose ballad which topped the country charts for Jack Greene. After that, anything was acceptable, whether it was O. C. Smith's soul hit 'Son Of Hickory Holler's Tramp' or Frazier's renditions of left-field songs like 'The Birthmark Henry Thompson Talks About'.

None of the returnees made a more lasting impact than Harold Jenkins – alias Conway Twitty. He auditioned for Sun, like dozens of rockabilly hopefuls, and wound up at MGM cutting Elvis-style hits such as 'It's Only Make Believe'. While Presley was on army service, Twitty made a convincing stand-in, starring in exploitation movies such as *Sexpot Goes To College*.

Like most fifties rockers, his career drifted in the early sixties, and Twitty itched for his roots. 'I wanted to do country so bad,' he recalled, 'that I told MGM I would change my name back to Harold Jenkins if they would sign me as a country artist.' The label relented, on the understanding that Twitty would turn-in equal numbers of country and rock songs. 'After I cut my first country record,' he explained, 'the rock stuff was never mentioned again.' Over the next three decades, Twitty achieved more No. 1 country singles than any other artist.

The months before the British invasion saw a rare synchronicity between country and pop tastes. A succession of hits bridged the divide without apparent strain – Ned Miller's 'From A Jack To A King', Bill Anderson's 'Still', Bobby Bare's 'Detroit City', George Hamilton IV's 'Abilene'. The border became more difficult to cross when Top 40 radio playlists were stuffed with British beat groups. For the next two years, only one country performer pierced the Beatles' armour: Roger Miller.

An eccentric, whimsical songwriter, Miller matched the

perceptive eye for detail of Chuck Berry. While Berry crammed hits like 'You Never Can Tell' with images of teen America, Miller responded with the country/pop chart-topper 'King Of The Road' – a tale of trailer life which doubled as comedy skit and social satire. Another songwriter with Miller's comic appeal, John D. Loudermilk, racked up pop hits via the Nashville Teens ('Tobacco Road') and Marianne Faithfull ('This Little Bird').

Miller captured the pop audience in his own right, aided by guest spots on TV variety shows hosted by Steve Allen, Johnny Carson and Merv Griffin. His lugubrious presence even graced *The TAMI Show*, the legendary concert movie which starred James Brown and the Rolling Stones. The six Grammy Awards he won for 'King Of The Road' included both Best Country Song and Best Contemporary (Rock'n'Roll) Single. But his tumultuous success took its toll: 'Suddenly I was Elvis,' he explained shortly before his death in 1992, 'and I didn't have any very good role models.' Or, as he quipped on another occasion: 'I used to be a one-man band, but I couldn't keep it together.'

Few American pop stars survived the British invasion with Miller's finesse. But Gene Pitney's melodramatic ballads of urban paranoia couldn't be imitated by the beat bands. They also made him an unlikely candidate for the country market, let alone for duets with one of Nashville's least compromising singers. 'They were looking for more product,' Pitney recalls. 'The record company came up with the idea.' One of those executives was George Jones' longtime manager, 'Pappy' Dailey, who noted the failure of his man's country hits to make more than a fleeting impression on the pop charts.

Jones was an accomplished duet singer, with a sheaf of collaborations to his credit. His 1963 smash with Melba Montgomery, 'We Must Have Been Out Of Our Minds', neatly conveyed Pitney's initial reaction to the experiment of teaming him with Jones: 'It was a good thing that I'd already recorded in foreign languages, because that's how I was able to tune in with the way George was singing. He had his own kind of phrasing.'

So did Pitney, whose forte was passion verging on hysteria. Fascinating though it might have been to capture that turmoil on a country record, or to hear Jones grappling with the urban neuroses of Pitney classics like 'Backstage' or 'Last Chance To Turn Around', their partnership was located strictly in Jones' territory. The material never wavered from a typical Nashville engagement, as the two singers gingerly approached vintage Jones hits like 'Why Baby Why' and 'That's All It Took'.

'George told me later that he was terrified,' Pitney reveals, which is no doubt why his voice was uncharacteristically bland on these duets. Pitney himself subjugated his piercing falsetto and long, quavering crescendos: 'I made myself country. I learned exactly where he was going to bend the notes.' Filling the 'female' role, Pitney's voice soared around Jones' unique phrasing with some dexterity. Only when he taped some solo sides did he apply his 'natural' voice to Nashville material. Intriguing though that was, it wasn't a commercial proposition for country or pop. The duets were, but only for specialist country stations. With neither artist having broadened his appeal, their collaboration was quietly abandoned.

Like Pitney and Jones, Johnny Cash and Bob Dylan failed to fulfil their apparent potential when they collaborated on an unreleased album in 1969. More intriguing is the fantasy of a much earlier liaison. 'I took note of Bob Dylan as soon as his album came out in early '62,' Cash writes in his autobiography, 'and listened almost continuously to *The Freewheelin' Bob Dylan* in '63. I'd put on *Freewheelin'* backstage, go out and do my show, then listen again as soon as I came off. After a while, I wrote Bob a letter telling him how much of a fan I was. He wrote back almost immediately, saying he'd been following my music since "I Walk The Line".'

Cash was recording tales of social outcasts and political oppression; so too, in increasingly oblique fashion, was Dylan. Unbeknown to Cash, one of the songs Dylan had attempted during the *Freewheelin'* sessions was written by Cash's hero, Hank Williams.

The two musicians shared more than mutual admiration for Hank. Each was caught up in the tangle of enthusiasms which came to be known as the Folk Revival. Heterogeneous to the point of incoherence, the Revival spanned a multitude of streams, which crossed and ran into each other at events such as the annual Newport Folk Festival.

Central to the Folk Revival was the intuition that commercial music was inferior to the 'natural', unfettered sound of the people – as personified by the blues, folk, gospel, hillbilly and bluegrass performers whose careers were awakened during the Revival's decade-long lifetime.

The movement (though it was never that precise) was sparked to life by the Kingston Trio's 1958 hit 'Tom Dooley' – itself an artificial piece of history marketed with enormous success. Despite its blandness, 'Tom Dooley' caught the moment, as student idealism, gently simmering in Eisenhower's America, coalesced with the left-wing activism that had been liberated from a decade of McCarthyite intolerance.

So it was that a fistful of different audiences – students, folklorists, scholars, socialists and disenfranchised radio listeners – gathered under a single banner to acclaim anyone who could pass as a folksinger. The Folk Revivalists maintained stricter principles than their heroes, many of whom were baffled by the limits imposed on their creativity. Bluesman Muddy Waters was advised to drop the electric R&B he'd been playing for a decade, and revive his 'authentic' acoustic blues style. Guitar wizard Doc Watson came under similar pressure to abandon rockabilly and retrace his acoustic roots. This intolerance climaxed when Bob Dylan caused outrage at the 1965 Newport Folk Festival, by daring to reveal his passion for electric rock'n'roll.

Johnny Cash's interest in American folklore, twinned with his rugged realism, ensured support from the Revivalists. Caught in the same wave of approval were bluegrass musicians such as Bill Monroe and Flatt & Scruggs, plus acoustic stylists from the string-band tradition, who filled the spectrum between country and folk.

Folk festivals and recitals in prestigious concert halls rescued many ailing strands of American music – and mummified them. A battle raged between the traditionalists, who rejected all contemporary sounds and lyrical references, and the polemicists, who saw the Folk Revival as a vehicle for political ideology.

Newport's annual Folk Festival marked the gathering of the tribes – and, in 1965, the arena in which the thinly masked chasms within the folk 'movement' were irretrievably exposed. But a year earlier, Newport had been wide enough to welcome Bob Dylan, John Lee Hooker and, introduced not as a Nashville star but as 'a songwriter . . . and a singer', Johnny Cash.

Cash's most successful record of the era was 'Ring Of Fire', a 1963 crossover hit. Simplistic to the point of hilarity – one lyrical image, and a melody so minimal that it scarcely changed note – 'Ring Of Fire' was ignited by the mariachi band that producer Don Law hired for the session.

In the weeks leading up to Newport, another, almost unrecognizable, Cash had been heard on the radio. Repeated exposure to *The Freewheelin' Bob Dylan* had inspired him to echo Dylan's penchant for borrowing a tune. The template was 'Don't Think Twice, It's Alright', which Cash mutated into 'Understand Your Man'. Rhythmically, the two songs were identical; lyrically, it was only a skip from Dylan's 'Don't look out your window baby, I'll be gone' to Cash's 'Don't call my name out your window, I'm leaving.' From an admirer, it was a heartfelt tribute, albeit one which escaped most country fans, for whom Dylan was still an unknown quantity.

At Newport, Cash was the outsider, but the vast audience splayed across the festival grounds responded to his tales of haunted men and primeval forces of nature. Sensibly, perhaps, Cash chose not to perform 'Understand Your Man'. Instead, he paid tribute to someone in the crowd: 'We think he's the best songwriter of the age,' Cash effused, 'since Pete Seeger.' He repaid his melodic debt with a sterling rendition of 'Don't Think Twice, It's Alright'. Walking off stage, he presented Dylan with his guitar.

The next day, Cash returned to Nashville, and a pre-arranged recording session. The mariachi band appeared in expectation of another 'Ring Of Fire', but Cash insisted on recording a song Dylan had performed at Newport: 'Mama You've Been On My Mind'. Once again, the borders of ownership were blurred: 'It's an old tune, based on another old tune by Bill Monroe,' Dylan explained once. The mariachi horns extinguished the spirits of Monroe and Dylan, so Cash set the track aside, and returned a month later with June Carter to cut another Dylan song: 'It Ain't Me Babe'. Charlie McCoy, who himself later recorded with Dylan, offered some melodic harmonica in honour of the song's author. Like the Turtles, who covered 'It Ain't Me Babe' the following year, Cash recognized the commercial hook: the descending chorus of 'no, no, no', which he emphasized as a parody of the Beatles' trademark 'yeah, yeah, yeah' from 'She Loves You'.

Cash and Carter's rendition reached No. 4 on the country chart, exposing Dylan to that market for the first time. While the record was still climbing, Cash returned to the Dylan songbook. This time he cut 'Mama You've Been On My Mind' without the mariachis, but with saxman Boots Randolph (a veteran of Elvis Presley sessions) contributing a rowdy solo. It wasn't country, it certainly wasn't folk, and it didn't begin to capture the emotional nuances of Dylan's lyric. So Cash returned to the simplicity of his Tennessee Three, taping 'Don't Think Twice, It's Alright' as if he was back at Sun, searching for a successor to 'I Walk The Line'.

Cash and Dylan remained in indirect contact via producer/ guitarist Bob Johnston. He took over Dylan's sessions for *Highway 61 Revisited* and *Blonde On Blonde*, while remaining Cash's rhythm guitarist on record. In the summer of 1967, he became Cash's producer as well, and began to fantasize about teaming the two talents in the studio.

By then, both Dylan and Cash had walked the line, peered into the abyss, and been hauled back from the edge. Paired in the public imagination as champions of the oppressed, they stumbled through the mid-sixties as slaves to amphetamine addiction. Dylan channelled his adrenalin into the exaggerated imagery of his songs. Cash giggled away his talent on material like 'Everybody Loves A Nut' and 'Boa Constrictor', while betraying his compulsive energy on stage. 'I hadn't seem him play before,' recalled Mervyn Conn, who promoted his 1966 UK tour, 'and it surprised me that he had so much rock sound. It wasn't pure country and nobody had ever seen anything like that here. He was such a fiery performer. The place just erupted.'

Cash painted the same picture from the inside: 'I'd slur the words or I'd miss a word. I'd try to smile, but the nervous twitch in my face kept the smile from coming. Sweat would be pouring out of me just after ten minutes. As soon as the show was over, I'd burst into the dressing-room in a rage, stomp my guitar or smash a hole in a door with my fist, striking out at something – anything. Then alone in my room with the beer and the amphetamines, I'd pace the floor all night, trying to outwalk and outlast whatever demon was snapping at my heels.'

Dylan spilled off his motorbike near his Woodstock home in 1966; Cash admitted that, 'I wrecked my car numerous times speeding away from somone who wasn't following me in the first place. I became paranoid. I carried a gun, and I thought everyone was plotting against me. I trusted no one.'

Dylan escaped the chain of 'protest singer' through songs such as 'My Back Pages' ('I was so much older then, I'm younger than that now'); Cash relied on Jack Clement's satirical commentary on the folk generation, 'The One On The Left Is On The Right'. While Dylan retained artistic focus throughout his drug dependency, Cash's creativity was sapped by his chemical abuse, marital problems, and skirmishes with the law and the Ku Klux Klan. In Nashville, Cash shared an apartment with fellow singer-songwriter Waylon Jennings. They shuffled around their tiny quarters, each popping pills to define their day, each convinced that his habit was a secret from the other. On the road, Cash had now recruited Carl Perkins, a comrade since the Sun days, who was battling through the fog of alcoholism. Small wonder that 1966, when he might have capitalized on his patronage of Dylan in the country market, was the least productive year of his career.

'Drugs felt good,' Cash admitted at the end of the sixties. 'I liked them, so I just kept on taking them. But the line between ecstasy and terror is so thin that I didn't realize when I crossed over. It was hard to get back.' He was rescued by June Carter, who stimulated his choice of sobriety in 1967. The couple were married the following year, and acted as angels of mercy to Carl Perkins, helping him to conquer his drinking habit.

The Cash ensemble began to visit jails in the late sixties, cutting explosive live albums at Folsom and San Quentin. During the latter, he recited a Shel Silverstein comedy skit called 'A Boy Named Sue' over a guitar riff improvised by Perkins. The resulting single was a hit, and ABC-TV offered Cash a weekly primetime show. For his first guest, he chose Bob Dylan: white-suited, shy, a country crooner ready to repay his host for his artistic and moral support earlier in the decade.

Dylan never achieved the same rapport with Cash's mid-sixties room-mate, Waylon Jennings. 'Personally, we haven't really gotten along,' Jennings admits. 'We've had a couple of run-ins. We've never actually fought, we're just kinda like two roosters, circling one another and watching. It was something in our personalities that clashed, immediately.'

Charismatic and unrestrained, Jennings is openly conservative: 'I'm Southern, and I'm a country boy, and we are slow to change, and suspicious of change. I was raised that way. But I'm the first one to say that you should try what you feel in music. Music is freedom. I may not like something, but I think people have a right to try it.'

Personalities aside, Jennings wasn't slow to recognize Bob Dylan's talent: 'I always liked his songs. I was one of the first people in country music to really like Bob Dylan. That kinda blew people's minds, when I started singing his songs.'

In the late fifties, Jennings was a DJ in Lubbock, Texas, where he met hometown boy Buddy Holly. The rock'n'roll star produced Jennings' first record, a hilariously inept version of 'Jole Blon'. No one could find a lyric sheet, so Jennings had to mimic Moon Mullican's eccentric translation of the Louisiana French dialect.

In January 1959, Holly persuaded Jennings to join his road band for a remorseless concert trek dubbed the Winter Dance Party. Two weeks later, Waylon arrived in Moorhead, Minnesota, to discover that his friend had been killed in a plane crash: 'It seemed like the end of the world. We were so shocked we didn't know what to do. So we did what we were told. They said we had to play the show without him, so we did. They wouldn't even let us go to the funeral.'

The tragedy unravelled Jennings' fantasies of rock'n'roll stardom, and he returned to Lubbock. His recording career resumed in 1963, when A&M boss Herb Alpert signed him as the label's first country artist. 'Herb had ideas that I would be a pop singer one day,' Jennings considered. 'I think he heard me as Al

Martino, and I was wanting to sound like Hank Williams. But he and the Tijuana Brass played on "Four Strong Winds", and it ended up sounding kinda country.'

More adventurous was Jennings' final A&M session, which yielded tentative versions of two Bob Dylan songs – 'Don't Think Twice, It's Alright' and 'I Don't Believe You'. It was October 1964, and Johnny Cash had yet to release his first Dylan cover. 'I thought they were two of the most wonderful songs in the world,' Jennings says today, 'but nobody knew what to do with them.'

After the A&M deal collapsed, Jennings could be found at JD's, a Phoenix dancehall, offering a blend of country and pop. 'The cross-section that we drew was unbelievable,' Jennings recalled. 'That was when the first long-hair people came in – the college students, plus the doctors, lawyers, and all the cowboys. We were predominantly country, and yet I started taking pop tunes, or tunes that I felt I could relate to as a country person. We did them in our own way.'

RCA country star Bobby Bare caught Jennings at JD's, and recommended that A&R supremo Chet Atkins sign him. Atkins agreed when Bare borrowed Jennings' arrangement of 'Four Strong Winds' and achieved his biggest hit of the sixties. The song had been written by Canadian folkies Ian & Sylvia, and its success persuaded Atkins that he should tailor RCA's output towards a hybrid of folk and country.

Ushered under this miniature umbrella was another Canadian, George Hamilton IV, who smuggled writing talent from his homeland into the country mainstream. He scored a Top 10 hit with Gordon Lightfoot's 'Early Morning Rain' in 1966, prompting Lightfoot to record in Nashville with sessionmen such as Charlie McCoy and Kenny Buttrey. Their precise, sparse sound inspired Bob Dylan to seek out the same musicians for *John Wesley Harding* in 1967.

Hamilton had another Canadian ace up his sleeve: folksinger Joni Mitchell. At the end of 1966, he recorded her 'Urge For Going', and was rewarded with another Top 10 country hit. 'I think that Tom Rush and myself were the first people to record Joni Mitchell's songs,' he explains. 'Tom Rush recorded "Urge For Going" for Columbia. But I was probably the first country singer to do it. I first heard "Urge For Going" on WBC in Boston. The DJ said, "Here's a tape we recorded in a coffee-house here in Boston. A fellow named Tom Rush is singing a song by a new young writer called Joni Mitchell." Gordon Lightfoot put me in touch with Joni. She sent me a demo tape, and we recorded it here in Nashville. It was a little radical in country music, to do something that metaphorical.'

Equally oblique was John Lennon's 'Norwegian Wood', another Chet Atkins production in 1966. The singer was Waylon Jennings, who explained at the time: 'The other side of my new record is a song from England, by the Beatles. Chet was playing it on the guitar one day, and asked me had I heard it, and I told him, "You bet. I bought their album just to hear that one song." "Do you like it?" Chester asked. "Yes," I told him. "Why don't you record it?" he asked, and we both laughed. Well, I said I would, and I did it – did it country, too. There are some Rolling Stones, Beatles and Donovan songs that can be done country, and I figure that turnabout is fair play. If they can do "Act Naturally", then we can do some of theirs, country.'

Nashville had regarded the British invasion with suspicion, bordering on distaste. (The exception was the Browns, who promoted their cosy harmony records in 1964 by claiming to be 'the Beatles' favourite singing group'. No evidence was offered to support this boast.) During the Beatles' initial American visit, *Country Song Roundup* magazine polled the city's luminaries about the recent arrivals. The responses were polite, at least in public, but often eloquent in their omissions. Singer Bill Anderson quipped cynically: 'They got what it takes – money.' 'Some of their material is fine,' opined 'Six Days On The Road' hitmaker Dave Dudley. Del Reeves forced himself to admit the Liverpudlians were 'smart dressers'.

Cajun star Jimmy Newman raised a common fear among country singers: 'They won't affect country music one way or another, but Capitol has been so busy pressing Beatle records that they might hold back on country releases.' Five years later, Faron Young echoed his complaint: 'Capitol got into the rock-roll thing pretty heavy. The Beatles came along, and Capitol were ignoring country music, so I quit them.'

Rod McKuen reasoned that the Beatles were the saviours of folk, because their success diverted those who weren't sincere away from imitating Bob Dylan or Joan Baez. Country could see no such benefits from the British influx. As Waylon Jennings reflects, 'They raised their eyebrows in Nashville when I decided to cut a Beatles tune. "Norwegian Wood" is nowhere near country. It's just a wonderful piece of work. That melody is a killer.'

Jennings' friend and RCA labelmate Willie Nelson escaped Chet Atkins' folk-country hybrid. He also missed Beatlemania. 'I'd heard of the Beatles,' he says today. 'I knew that they were out there. But I'd never listened to them. I was pretty much isolated in the country field. I was based in Nashville, I'd just signed a deal with a publishing company, and I was trying to get a lot of stuff recorded. So the Beatles, and all of that group stuff, went right behind me, without me realizing what was going on. I just tuned them out. They didn't seem to have anything to do with me.'

In late 1965, around the time Waylon Jennings was investigating the Beatles' *Rubber Soul* album, Nelson heard a ballad on the radio: 'This song started to haunt me. I asked what it was, and someone told me it was the Beatles, and it was called "Yesterday". And I said, "Wait a minute, I better go back and check this stuff out!"'

In his dress and repertoire, the mid-sixties Willie Nelson was far from being a rebel. He'd fashioned his image as, in his own words, 'Your old cotton pickin', snuff dippin', tobaccer chewin', stump jumpin', gravy soppin', coffee pot dodgin', dumplin' eatin', frog giggin' hillbilly from Hill County.' A staple on the Texas club circuit, his canny, jazz-tinged vocal phrasing made him difficult to market on record. His early studio productions were wrapped in the mist of the Nashville Sound, his individuality swamped beneath strings and choruses. But on a 1966 live album, cut in Fort Worth, Texas, the real Willie Nelson emerged.

So did his affection for the melody that had caught his attention the previous year. In front of a sign that read 'Cowtown Jamboree', Nelson announced 'a song recorded by a pretty fair little country group called the Beatles. I know you're familiar with them – you've heard 'em many times on the *Grand Ole Opry*.' Having carefully distanced himself from the long-haired

Liverpudlians, he could say what he really felt: 'This is a song which, as a songwriter myself, I appreciate very much.' Nelson delivered 'Yesterday' straight off the record, while his band staggered through the unfamiliar changes as if they were learning a new language. Emboldened by the audience response, Nelson delved further into pop, cutting a Sinatra-style arrangement of the Anthony Newley song 'What Now My Love'. There was no indication that the Rolling Stones or, heaven forbid, Bob Dylan had ever entered his consciousness.

That was a state of innocence Lester Flatt might have envied. The mandolin- and guitar-player was a veteran of Bill Monroe's Blue Grass Boys, who teamed up with bandmate and banjoist Earl Scruggs in 1948. Flatt & Scruggs imprinted themselves on the folk, bluegrass and country scenes as the premier interpreters of Bill Monroe's style, marked out by their dramatic stage presence and Scruggs' frenetic banjo playing. What exposed their skill to a much wider audience was 'The Ballad Of Jed Clampett', the theme song for the TV series *The Beverly Hillbillies*.

One of the most popular comedies of the 1960s, the show pitched an oil-rich family of Southern rubes into the urban sophistication of California. The Clampetts, all tobaccer-chewin' and sawdust, were set up as the fall-guys, but the humour cut both ways, satirizing both the pretensions of the middle-class and the backwoods naïvety of the newcomers.

'The Ballad Of Jed Clampett' topped the country charts early in 1963, becoming the best-selling bluegrass single of all time. Five years later, Flatt & Scruggs once again sprang out of their habitat, when their 1949 signature tune 'Foggy Mountain Breakdown' was used as the theme to the *Bonnie & Clyde* movie. This gave them an entrée to New York and Hollywood concert halls – and, by 1967, into the sickly-sweet air of the Avalon, the psychedelic San Francisco ballroom where they headlined over acid-rockers like the Sons Of Champlin.

Even the staunchly traditionalist Bill Monroe was now accepting pickers who were as familiar with the Beatles as with 'Blue Moon Of Kentucky', so Flatt & Scruggs merely seemed to be drifting with the flow. But while Flatt was searching for calmer waters, Scruggs had invested in an outboard motor. Columbia producer Don Law sided with Scruggs, encouraging the duo to record Chuck Berry's 'Memphis', and suggesting that, like Johnny Cash, they should tackle Bob Dylan's 'Mama You've Been On My Mind'. The intervention of producer Bob Johnston in 1967 increased the pace of reform. That November, Flatt & Scruggs became the first artists to cover Dylan's 'Down In The Flood', one of his newly minted 'Basement Tapes'. Thereafter, they were typecast as Dylan interpreters, when they weren't attempting material by Johnny Cash or Leonard Cohen (both of whom, not at all coincidentally, were also produced by Johnston). It was hard to imagine what appalled Lester Flatt most: being asked to perform Buffy Sainte-Marie's anti-war anthem 'The Universal Soldier', or grappling with the surreal wordplay of Dylan's imagist masterpiece 'Like A Rolling Stone', while a harpsichord and electric 12-string guitars battled the string band for space.

'We would record what Johnston came up with,' Flatt complained in 1971, 'regardless of whether I liked it or not. I can't sing Bob Dylan stuff. Columbia has already got Bob Dylan, why would they want me?' Scruggs responded that the market for bluegrass had dissipated by the late sixties, and that change and survival were inevitable partners. By then, Flatt had quit the band, vowing only to record 'pure' bluegrass music in future. Scruggs recruited his long-haired sons, and devoted the early seventies to exploring the potential of bluegrass rock. While he reached out to a new audience, his partner's name only surfaced when he was described as 'the late Lester Flatt' in a 1974 article in *Esquire*. He sued for damages, but in truth, his career had expired before him.

Other Nashville pickers were readier to adjust to what a 1967 album by Flatt & Scruggs called *Changing Times*. Chet Atkins was one of the first to recognize that the Beatles had inhaled some country air from their exposure to Carl Perkins and Jerry Lee Lewis. He cut an instrumental album called *Chet Atkins Picks On The Beatles* – and solicited a sleeve-note from someone happy to acknowledge Atkins' influence, George Harrison. 'For me,' the Beatles' guitarist wrote, 'the great thing about Mr Atkins is not the fact that he is capable of playing almost every type of music, but the conviction in the way he does it. Whilst listening to [this album], I got the feeling that these songs had been written specifically with Chet in mind. "I'll Cry Instead", "She's A Woman" and "Can't Buy Me Love", having a country feeling about them, lend themselves perfectly to Chet's own style of picking.'

On *Rubber Soul*, the album which introduced Waylon Jennings to 'Norwegian Wood', bluegrass musicians found a tune tailor-made for a lightning-fast string band. 'I've Just Seen A Face' had been written by Paul McCartney for acoustic guitar, but its tempo and changes cried out for a banjo and a mandolin – duly supplied on *Beatle Country*, a 1967 album by the Charles River Valley Boys. The Dillards also covered the tune, on their route from West Coast bluegrass to country-rock.

Where the Beatles and Bob Dylan left no mark was on the Nashville Sound. Johnny Cash, Waylon Jennings, Flatt & Scruggs and the bluegrass experimentalists were mavericks, already beyond the cloying embrace of strings and choirs. In the seventies, Beatles standards such as 'Michelle', 'Yesterday' and 'Hey Jude' were more likely to figure on country (or jazz, or reggae) albums than in the rock market, which was attempting to move beyond the Fab Four's legacy. But in the sixties, there was barely a hint of recognition from Nashville's country aristocracy that a revolution had transformed the musical landscape.

Neither did rock impinge on Nashville West – or Bakersfield, as it was marked on the map, the featureless Californian town stranded between the Sierra Nevada and the Coastal Ranges. Bakersfield required no education in rock etiquette, as its stripped-down brand of country was the missing link between fifties rockabilly and late-sixties country-rock. (The city's authorities weren't quite so tolerant: Bakersfield was the scene of a legendary confrontation between the members of Jefferson Airplane and local police, who tried to throw the band off stage during a 1968 concert because of their political rhetoric. The Airplane led the crowd in a hearty chant of 'Fat pig, fat pig'.)

Buck Owens was the resident monarch, the boss of a band (the Buckaroos) who exemplified the hard-edged precision of the Bakersfield Sound. When the Beatles recorded a faithful rendition of his hit 'Act Naturally' in 1965, they seemed to be crowning him the prime mover in American country music.

Owens had a pedigree in Los Angeles studio work which had required him to switch seamlessly from honky-tonk to rock'n'roll, and he strolled through the sixties immune to outside forces. In 1965 he pledged that he would never record any music but pure country: his subsequent hits included Chuck Berry's 'Johnny B. Goode' and Simon & Garfunkel's 'Bridge Over Troubled Water'. He shrugged off accusations of hypocrisy, calling these aliens 'country songs in disguise'.

Merle Haggard, who gradually supplanted Owens as Bakersfield's leading export, started out mixing rock and country tunes in the clubs. He claimed that the Bakersfield Sound 'has always been rockabilly – listen to Elvis and then to my records, it's the same kind of thing'. But he wasn't about to record Beatles or Dylan songs: he was too busy paying his dues to Bob Wills and Jimmie Rodgers, and recording an epic series of hit singles which confirmed him as America's poet of the working man. An ex-convict, he sang prison laments such as 'Sing Me Back Home' and 'Life In Prison' with unfeigned sincerity. On 'I'm A Lonesome Fugitive', 'Mama Tried' and 'Branded Man', the despair of his lyrics was held in check by the stoic precision of his band, the Strangers. Haggard wore an air of weariness and hunger, but never descended into cheap emotion. He was the Robert Mitchum of country, a doomed hero who carried his cross with dignity. It was an image which touched a generation of singers, among them a rich Georgia kid who was destined to pull Haggard's sound and quiet fury into the mainstream of rock: Gram Parsons.

26 A Star Is Born
Kris Kristofferson, 1965–1978

The sound of country music was subtly modified throughout the sixties, as stylists from Chet Atkins to the Beatles left their mark on the genre. Lyrically, Nashville was more impervious to change. 'Everyone had been so conditioned to countrified, Hank Williams-styled singers,' recalled singer-songwriter Chris Gantry. 'It was real tough for an out-and-out singer-songwriter to break in. The whole thing was like Paris in the late 1800s, like the Impressionists. There were all these writers around like Eddie Rabbitt, Kris Kristofferson, Mickey Newbury, Roger Miller and myself. It took us quite a long time to be accepted to the point where somebody would even consider recording one of our songs.'

Roger Miller, as Gantry explains, 'was really the one to break out of Nashville with his type of songs and get them worldwide. His thing was poetic. It was a whole new language style. He was a sort of country boy who made it.' And then, as an aside: 'Of course, he was an old pill freak.'

That titbit evaded the worldwide pop audience who lapped up Miller's wry tales of life in the rural South. Like a Broadway adaptor, he smoothed the texture of Southern life into songs like 'King Of The Road'.

'Hillbilly-intellectual', the writer Douglas B. Green tagged Miller, but his best songs were short stories that widened the fictional palette of country. While the folk tradition was located in the territory of the past, country was rooted in the immediacy of live emotion. When Hank Williams sang 'I'm So Lonesome I Could Cry', or Johnny Cash brooded over 'I Walk The Line', there was no gap between narrator and story. Country's very appeal was its authenticity; its heroes lived out the everyday dreams and nightmares of their audience.

Before Roger Miller, only two types of tale had dared to step beyond that brief – historical story-songs such as 'El Paso', 'Battle Of New Orleans' and 'Long Black Veil', which took their vocabulary from folk music; and comedy tunes, which were Nashville's equivalent to *The Beverly Hillbillies*, affectionately mocking the people at whom they were aimed.

Miller's success allowed country writers to conjure up a world in a handful of lines. Through the mid-to-late sixties, the country charts registered crossover hits like Jeannie C. Riley's 'Harper Valley PTA', a sharp-edged satire on small-town values penned by Tom T. Hall; Bobbie Gentry's 'Ode To Billie Joe', a mysterious tale of adolescent repression that was as dense as any Child Ballad (and which sparked an equally enigmatic parody from Bob Dylan, in 'Clothes Line Saga'); and from outside the country industry, Glen Campbell hits including 'Wichita Lineman' and 'Galveston', both written by teenage prodigy Jimmy Webb. 'Which country is that?' Webb quips when reminded of his success in Nashville, but his skeleton portraits of American originals – sung by a pop singer, whose roots were deep in country – worked at either end of the radio dial.

Of all those writers, Tom T. Hall was the archetype: the author of incisive, stark narratives such as 'The Year That Clayton Delaney Died' and 'A Week In A Country Jail'. 'I thought, "Well, if people are interested in that sort of thing, I've led an interesting and varied life,"' he explained later. 'So I started writing about places I'd been and things I've done.' Like a miniaturist, Hall could evoke complex characters with a few delicate brushstrokes.

Rock had no place for such nicety in the late sixties. Once it had outgrown the clichés of teen romance, the genre evolved its own standards of authenticity and meaning. The Beatles epitomized the shifting lyrical perspectives of the decade, from the fictional adolescent dramas of 'She Loves You' and 'I Want To Hold Your Hand', through tentative explorations of personal experience like 'I'm A Loser' and 'Help!', to full-blown epics of subjective psychological discovery ('Strawberry Fields Forever', 'I Am The Walrus'). In psychedelia, or acid-rock, the domain of rock's most adventurous players in 1967–8, lyrical obscurity was valued as proof of the intensity of the 'trip'.

This unprecedented freedom of expression was mirrored by a

new emotional and (to the outrage of many observers) sexual explicitness. In April 1968, Georgia state representative Edwin Mullinax launched a campaign to make it a felony for albums not to include printed lyrics, so parents could decide which records were unsuitable for their children.

Such controversy wasn't unknown in late-sixties country. Henson Cargill's 1968 No.1 'Skip A Rope' infuriated some listeners by suggesting that racism might be passed from parent to child. Waylon Jennings aroused opposition when he cut Tony Joe White's 'Willie And Laura Mae Jones', about an inter-racial love affair.

Mullinax's crusade was not directed against Nashville, however, and the Country Music Association was happy to support his aims. They issued a manifesto claiming that American schoolchildren were being 'subjected to a constant barrage of record music with lyrics dealing in sex, liquor, narcotics and profane and disrespectful language' – none of which accusations rock's ambassadors would have disowned. Where the two camps differed was in their interpretation. While rock icons such as John Lennon, Mick Jagger and Jim Morrison raised the banner of artistic freedom, the CMA complained: 'The effect of such music, along with the effect of other media of communications, on the rapidly deteriorating moral climate of the rest of the nation are to be seen in almost every daily newspaper.' They called not just for immorality to be identified, but for its expulsion from America's homes, with the aid of a review board – consisting of churchmen, politicians and parents – which would judge each record for moral failings before it was released.

'Almost every daily newspaper . . . the rest of the nation': the CMA carefully distanced itself from the evil seeping into American culture. Cowboy singer and *Opry* veteran Tex Ritter noted that 'The rock'n'roll kids, the folk-rockers, they're taking care of all the protest stuff. I don't want country music to fall into all of that. I don't mind singing about mother and home and flag all of the time.' One of the biggest country hits of 1968 was Tammy Wynette's 'Stand By Your Man', pegged by its producer and co-writer Billy Sherrill as 'a song for the truly liberated woman, one who is secure enough in her identity to enjoy it', but pilloried by rock critics and the emerging women's liberation movement as a call for female subservience.

Not that country was exiled from the shifting moral landscape. Sexual attraction had long been an acceptable topic in song, though outside marriage it was lashed with the sting of guilt. But in the late sixties, Kris Kristofferson began to circulate country songs that toyed with the concept of sexual healing – songs such as 'Help Me Make It Through The Night' and 'For The Good Times'.

'Now we got our own pet hippie,' Nashville insiders sneered as Kristofferson emerged as the city's most prolific and performed composer at the start of the seventies. His appearance alone would have touched off a scandal: he let his hair drift over his collar, sported a scraggly beard, and exposed his working-man's muscles through a leather vest.

Kristofferson had heavy backers. He'd been introduced to Nashville by Marijohn Wilkin, the composer of 'Waterloo' and 'Long Black Veil'. She introduced him to other writers, including Bobby Bare, who immediately recognized his talent: 'His songs are basic country, but the way he puts them across, the way he puts his words together, is much deeper than the average song.' Another Wilkin protégé, Chris Gantry, noted: 'His whole thing was that he specialized in one type of thing. Every song had a little bit of a tinge of another song, like they were all kinda interwoven. That's what this town likes, someone who specializes. That's how he got off so phenomenally.' That, plus the support of artists who recorded his songs, such as Ray Price ('For The Good Times'), Johnny Cash ('Sunday Morning Coming Down'), Roger Miller ('Me And Bobby McGee') and Jerry Lee Lewis ('Once More With Feeling').

With Hank Williams, Johnny Cash was an early hero for Kristofferson. But between late 1965, when Dave Dudley cut his unashamedly patriotic 'Viet Nam Blues', and 1967, when he began to circulate the songs that secured his legend, Kristofferson fell under the spell of another Nashville import: Bob Dylan.

He studied Dylan at close quarters in 1966. 'I was working at Columbia Studios in Nashville when Dylan was recording *Blonde On Blonde*,' says Kristofferson's longtime friend and touring partner, Billy Swan. 'I was cleaning up between sessions, emptying the ashtrays, keeping tapes supplied to the studio, getting food for the engineers. When I quit, it was midway through the two weeks of sessions. They said, "If you can find anyone who's looking for a job, send them in." I said, "Fine," walked out the studio door – and there was Kris Kristofferson coming in, saying, "Does anybody know where I can get a job?" So he took over from me, acting as a go-fer.'

Dylan was the most influential rock lyricist of the sixties, shifting terrain with almost every album. His rock contemporaries latched on to two of his personae, the impassioned protest singer of *The Times They Are A-Changin'*, and the free-flow beat poet of *Highway 61 Revisited*. It was another Dylan who marked Kristofferson and his successors: the cynical, unashamedly clear-eyed chronicler of romantic limitations who recorded *Another Side Of Bob Dylan* in 1964. While rock writers sought to match the oblique imagery of 'Tombstone Blues' or 'Sad-Eyed Lady Of The Lowlands' ('The kings of Tyrus with their convict lists, Are waiting in line for their geranium kiss'), Kristofferson's imagination was triggered by the emotional clarity of 'All I Really Want To Do' ('I ain't lookin' for you to feel like me, See like me or be like me') or the stark eroticism of 'I Don't Believe You' ('Her skirt it swayed as a guitar played, Her mouth was watery and wet'). It was a short step from 'It Ain't Me Babe' ('You say you're looking for someone, Who will promise never to part . . . It ain't me you're looking for') to Kristofferson's affecting admission that sexual bliss might mean nothing more than the night ('Let the devil take tomorrow, Cos tonight I need a friend').

Kristofferson's unashamed sexuality was accompanied by a doomed idealism which extended the thread of singer-songwriters such as Tim Hardin. In 'Reason To Believe' and 'How Can We Hang On To A Dream', Hardin had conjured up a vision of romance as impossible to grasp, yet endlessly beguiling. Not for him the all too believable crises portrayed by country singers such as Loretta Lynn and Tammy Wynette; his romance was racked by the elusive concept of 'freedom'. That word resounded through sixties struggles for national liberation, feminism and civil rights. It entered rock consciousness as a peculiarly male, and privileged, ideal: the search for an unfettered wholeness of being that required complete indulgence from the outside world.

Kristofferson wrestled with the concept in songs like 'Me And Bobby McGee': 'Freedom's just another word for nothing left to lose . . . feeling good was good enough for me.' Into country music he brought the first stirrings of self-consciousness. Despair had traditionally been a consequence of circumstance: 'I'm so lonesome I could cry,' as Hank Williams sang. After Kristofferson, it was possible for a country singer to feel pain because an existential crisis was looming over mankind.

Much was made in the country media of Kristofferson's unorthodox route to stardom. He'd been born in Brownsville, Texas, played football at college, joined the cadet corps, and boxed up to Golden Gloves level. He also won an award from the *Atlantic Monthly* for his short stories, gained a Rhodes Scholarship to Oxford University, and wrote a novel, when he wasn't auditioning as a rock'n'roller for British record companies. Hank Williams made it to Oxford, Mississippi, but he never wanted to be F. Scott Fitzgerald.

Rock'n'roll and the novel both escaped Kristofferson's grasp, so, when he returned to the States at the end of the fifties, he joined the US Army. 'My father was a two-star general,' he explained, 'and he tried to programme me for an army career. I don't think he really thought he could, because all that ever interested me was Hank Williams records. Nobody else in the house ever listened to country music. In those days, kids listened to nothing but Johnnie Ray and Patti Page. I was a total weirdo.'

His background ensured that he became an officer. Stationed briefly in Germany, he served as a helicopter pilot, apparently en route to high rank and a distinguished military career. 'Kris was in Germany with a second cousin of mine,' recalled songwriter Marijohn Wilkin. 'So even before he came back to Nashville, I'd heard about this guy. He was a sort of renegade already, because he was a Captain, and yet he played in a club band with non-commissioned officers. That scene was really looked down upon by his fellow officers.'

When he quit the army in 1965, Kristofferson vacationed in Nashville. 'He had a short haircut, and was very military,' recalls

Bobby Bare. But Marijohn Wilkin saw beneath his tightly disciplined surface. He played her songs he'd written, and she signed him to her Buckhorn Music company. He worked at Columbia Studios, then as a bartender, a labourer, even a helicopter pilot ferrying oilmen out to the Gulf of Mexico. 'I don't know if I'll ever be as prolific as I was when I worked in the Gulf,' he reflected afterwards. 'I turned out three songs a day then, because I had a bigger need to communicate with the outside world. I was more isolated then.'

Slowly, and not without opposition, Kristofferson wrote his way into the hearts of the Nashville community. Dottie West, who'd scored hits with such maudlin tunes as 'Getting Married Has Made Us Strangers' and 'Mommy, Can I Still Call Him Daddy' (the latter featuring her four-year-old son, Dale), refused to record 'Help Me Make It Through The Night' because it had immoral connotations. Kris's friend and fellow writer, Vince Matthews, advised him to lose the 'freedom' line from 'Me And Bobby McGee'. When Roger Miller finally cut that tune, chorus intact, Kristofferson was about to quit songwriting to work in construction. A year later, he won a Country Music Association award, when 'Sunday Morning Coming Down' (which he'd pitched to Johnny Cash by landing a helicopter in the star's backyard) was voted Song of the Year. At the glitzy awards ceremony, Kristofferson's refusal to don a conservative suit and tie outraged those already offended by his apparent lack of morals.

Kristofferson's reputation in Nashville wasn't boosted by his easy acceptance in the rock community. Few rock performers covered his tunes – it's ironic that this renegade figure launched his recording career with an album that contained two future easy-listening standards, 'Help Me Make It Through The Night' and 'For The Good Times'. But rock musicians quickly recognized that Kristofferson's worldview was closer to the hippies' than the rednecks'.

'Kris changed country music the way that Bob Dylan changed rock'n'roll,' says Bob Neuwirth, who'd been Dylan's sidekick on his mid-sixties tours, then essayed his own career as a country writer. 'He brought a new element that just shattered it. He led the pack. He had a nerve, he was young and good-looking, and he just kicked the shit out of anybody that gave him too much trouble.'

Janis Joplin, the Texan bluegrass singer who'd become an acid-rock icon with Big Brother and the Holding Company, also recognized a kindred spirit. In her troubled final months, she established a close relationship with Kristofferson; one of the last songs she recorded was 'Me And Bobby McGee'. 'I'd sung it to Janis,' recalls Neuwirth, the man with the most impressive address-book in rock history. 'She sang it when she came to Nashville, and it got into all the local papers – "rock star sings country song". So she cut the tune. Meanwhile Kris had taken me down to Nashville for the first time. The writers owned the town back then: we drove straight from the airport to Johnny Cash's house, where Kris pitched a couple of songs, then on to the *Grand Ole Opry*, where Kris took me backstage and I met everybody I'd ever wanted to meet in my whole life – Hank Cochran, Porter Wagoner, all those guys. It was bizarre.'

Neuwirth stayed with Norman Blake, a guitarist who'd played sessions with Kristofferson, Cash and Dylan: 'One morning Norman's wife came in and woke me. She said, "Bobby, I don't want you to hear this on the radio, but Janis died last night." It was in the days of the *Johnny Cash Show* on TV, and Norman had to go to a rehearsal. So we went down, and June Carter Cash came over to me and said, "We're so sorry about Janis. Come in here and we'll sing about it." So that was how we processed the news. By the time I got back to Los Angeles and had to deal with the aftermath of her death, I felt as if we'd already had the exorcism.'

Janis Joplin's cover of 'Me And Bobby McGee' became a sizeable rock hit; it inspired Jerry Lee Lewis to record the tune for the country market, where it reached the top of the charts. Kristofferson's stature was now acknowledged in both communities. His rugged good looks won him acting roles as early as 1970, when he appeared alongside Mick Jagger in *Ned Kelly* and cameoed in Dennis Hopper's extravagant piece of cinematic psychoanalysis, *The Last Movie*. In reply, Kristofferson dedicated a song to him: 'The Pilgrim (Chapter 33)'.

His first steps as a touring musician were less assured. 'I played my second gig at the Troubadour in San Francisco,' he recalled. 'My third was at the Bitter End in New York, where all these heroes of mine had started out. The fourth was at the Isle of Wight rock festival in England, in front of half a million people, who all hated me.'

Guitarist Billy Swan accompanied Kristofferson at this landmark event in summer 1970: 'The sound was bad, so what happened was partly misinterpretation, I think. Maybe the kids couldn't fully hear what Kris was singing. He had this song called "Blame It On The Stones", and I think some people took it wrong.'

The opening track of Kristofferson's début album, 'Blame It On The Stones' was a clumsy piece of cross-generational satire – country's equivalent to the Monkees' 'Pleasant Valley Sunday' or, more pertinently, the Rolling Stones' 'Mother's Little Helper'. That Jagger/Richard tune had poked fun at middle-class housewives needing chemical assistance to maintain the outward stability of their lives. It anticipated the moral crisis over teenage drug use, drawing a comparison between tranquillizer addiction and dope-smoking which the medical establishment took another decade to understand.

Kristofferson's satire was not so effective. Like the Flying Burrito Brothers' 'Hippie Boy', it parodied the backwoods country gospel tradition, as a brass band, a bass drum and a Salvation Army choir chorused their disapproval of the single most destructive force in modern society: the Rolling Stones. 'You'll feel so much better knowing that you won't stand alone,' trumpeted the chorus in its call to unite 'Mr Modern Middle-Class' with his equally threatened countrymen. A rowdy fuzz guitar, dipping in and out of the riff to the Stones' hit 'Paint It Black', made the irony even more obvious.

At the Isle of Wight, 'Blame It On The Stones' was stripped of these signposts, down to the bare bones of two acoustic guitars. Sprawled across the fields were several hundred thousand hippies, prepared for the youth icons of the counter-culture to entertain and reassure them.

The festival offered few easy solutions. At his last major UK concert, Jimi Hendrix tried to shake off the preconceptions of his audience. They wanted the theatrics of old – the guitar-burning, crotch-pumping display they'd witnessed at Monterey in 1967.

Hendrix was searching for an escape from his media image. In the event, neither party was satisfied. Other performers also suffered: Joni Mitchell's gentle set was interrupted by political activists, who reduced her to tears; Jim Morrison of the Doors, facing a similar crisis to Hendrix, stumbled through a parodic routine that suggested another sixties prophet was casting off his mantle.

The acts who captured the Isle of Wight crowd were heavy rock bands – the Who, Ten Years After, Emerson, Lake and Palmer. Into this unlikely arena stepped the newly acclaimed poet of country music. Kristofferson might have liberated Nashville songwriting, but the English audience wasn't prepared to search for hidden meanings. All that boomed out across the fields was a single refrain: 'Blame it on the Stones . . . blame it on the Stones'. Who did this Kristofferson guy think he was, bitching about Mick Jagger? 'People took it serious,' Billy Swan recalls. 'They missed the tongue-in-cheek side of it.' 'They thought I was putting the Stones down,' Kris confirmed. 'I mean, anybody that thinks that has got to really not be listening to the words. And if you don't listen to the words, what's my music at?'

A low hum of disapproval came out of the crowd, swelling slowly into a roar. 'I remember Kris turned to me at one point, with a quizzical look in his eyes,' Swan says, 'and I said, "Man, they love you." Finally, he looked out at the crowd, and said, "I came here to do forty-five minutes, goddammit, and I'm gonna do it." And he did.'

Even after 'Me And Bobby McGee' and 'Help Me Make It Through The Night', the Isle of Wight crowd couldn't see Kristofferson as anything more than a redneck intruder. Neither, it seems, could his fellow musicians: 'Before we went on, there was all this hustle and bustle backstage,' Swan explains. 'After we came off, nobody was there! I had to break a window in our trailer to get my guitar case so we could get out of there. No one would give us a hand. Everyone was spooked by what we'd done.' Kristofferson put it more succinctly: 'The devil won out. The audience didn't give a damn.'

In October 1971, showing off the kind of cultural reference that had already made Nashville suspicious, Kristofferson compared himself to 'The Outsider'. Critic Colin Wilson identified this archetypal figure in his book of that name: a man who functions as a commentator on a group or community but, appearances to the contrary, exists outside it. It was a canny piece of self-analysis for Kristofferson, who was distanced from both the rock and country mainstreams by his subtle intelligence. Nashville was suspicious of his rebelliousness and unconventional demeanour – not to mention the cracked rasp of his voice ('I sing like a frog,' he once admitted). Rock would have welcomed the rebel, but was less respectful of the poet. 'I don't get into rock much,' he explained in the seventies, 'because I don't dance and I'm more into lyrics. To me, country is just like R&B or soul. It's a lot more honest and emotionally moving than any other kind of pop music.'

So Kristofferson inhabited a strangely successful limbo for most of the seventies. Country welcomed his songs, but maintained its aloofness from the man. So did rock critics, who grew to despise his lifestyle, especially when his relationship with fellow singer Rita Coolidge spilled over into duet albums. 'They're the country Paul and Linda McCartney,' one writer quipped in the mid-seventies, and it wasn't intended as a compliment. Kristofferson's writing also suffered increasing abuse. In a memorable review of the *Border Lord* album, *Rolling Stone* reviewer Ben Gerson decried 'the kind of pseudo-poeticizing that should have gone out with Bob Lind and the Electric Prunes'. Gerson also attacked Kristofferson's 'inanity', 'obtuseness', 'egocentricity' and 'one-dimensional braggadocio', and dubbed him 'a country and western Jim Morrison'. That wasn't a compliment, either.

So it was to Hollywood that Kris Kristofferson fled. His early cameos led him to a starring role in *Cisco Pike*, then equally commended performances in *Pat Garrett And Billy The Kid*, *Alice Doesn't Live Here Anymore* and *The Sailor Who Fell From Grace With The Sea*.

When Elvis Presley and Mick Jagger declined the male lead alongside Barbra Streisand in a 1976 remake of *A Star Is Born*, Kristofferson won the part of the doomed, tempestuous rock star. Like his earlier movies, the project (with its million-selling soundtrack album) overshadowed his continuing career as a singer. 'If I had to make a choice between the two,' he explained in

1978, 'music's the most important, because it's my creation. I made up the songs. When you're acting, it's just like singing somebody else's stuff. But,' he added patiently, 'it doesn't make any difference what I think.' Right again: rock and country audiences now regarded Kristofferson as a movie star. Gradually history was rewritten, and his albums were reviewed as if they were the idle playthings of a Hollywood dilettante – equivalent to Cybill Shepherd's showtunes or Richard Harris's strained attempt to become a romantic balladeer. 'If You Don't Like Hank Williams (You Can Kiss My Ass)', wrote Kristofferson on his overlooked 1977 LP *Surreal Thing*. But then Hank never went to Hollywood.

27 Middle Age Crazy
Jerry Lee Lewis, 1963–1977

The scandal of his underage bride punctured Jerry Lee Lewis's career in the late fifties. Exiled to the roadhouse circuit, his record sales decimated, he leaped at the promise of a five-year deal with Mercury in 1963. The label attracted an array of fifties rockers – Chuck Berry, Fats Domino, Charlie Rich – with the promise of more lucrative contracts than they'd enjoyed in the past. But Mercury couldn't assemble a strategy to rebuild Lewis's career. Like Berry and Domino, he was left to recut his fifties hits – gaining a veneer of sophistication, but losing the spontaneity which had been his trademark at Sun.

Lewis now led a dual existence. In Europe, he was revered as the last of the unchained rock'n'rollers; in America, he was at best a regional attraction, with no key into the national market. In July 1964, as the Beatles filled stadiums across North America, Lewis was at the Municipal Auditorium, Birmingham, Alabama, cutting an album modestly entitled *The Greatest Live Show On Earth*. Rock'n'roll dominated the show, but Jerry hadn't forgotten his roots. 'I know we've got some people here who love good country,' he drawled. 'You're looking at the cat right here. I might do a blues tune and then turn around and do a good country record.' He proved it by combining the two genres on Charlie Rich's soul ballad, 'Who Will The Next Fool Be'.

The Greatest Live Show On Earth was his highest-grossing album of the decade. But that was preaching to the converted. What Mercury needed was regular hits. Producers Shelby Singleton, Jerry Kennedy and another Sun refugee, Jack Clement, sent out flares in all directions, distracting both the artist and his audience.

An increasingly desperate series of singles failed to sell, portraying Lewis as a soul man, a blues balladeer, a rocker, or even a country cat. George Jones' 'Seasons Of My Heart' was the first song he'd auditioned for Jack Clement in 1956, but Singleton suggested Jerry abandon his piano for a harpsichord, which might have fitted grand opera, but not the *Grand Ole Opry*.

Singleton was on safer ground with an album called *Country Songs For City Folks*. Jerry Lee tackled standards like 'Crazy Arms' and 'Funny How Time Slips Away' as if he was in a Louisiana bar with a crowd of restless truckers. He eased back only once, slipping into the persona of a death-row penitent for the Porter Wagoner hit 'Green Green Grass Of Home'. Four thousand miles away, Tom Jones borrowed his arrangement and wound up with a million-seller. Jerry's album didn't chart.

The Sun studio had moved round the block in the early sixties, but it still must have felt like a homecoming when Jerry walked through the door in January 1966, to be greeted by his old comrade in excess, Jack Clement. Maybe Jack was the only producer who would have let him record 'Lincoln Limousine'. The assassination of President Kennedy in 1963 aroused worldwide mourning, but in the Deep South, the scene of his shooting, there was some satisfaction that this suspect liberal had been removed from office – especially when he was succeeded by one of their own, Lyndon Johnson.

Jerry Lee never testified either way, but 'Lincoln Limousine' – on which he claimed the composer credit – was Exhibit A for the prosecution. Over a jaunty rock beat, he paid unusual 'tribute' to the martyred President, reserving his best attention for the car in which he died. 'They shot him in the back seat of a Lincoln limousine,' Jerry crowed, as if he was being sponsored. By the end, the commercial had become a travelogue. 'They shot him out in Texas,' he whooped, hitting the name like a cheerleader, 'where the longhorn cattle roam. It would have been better if he had stayed at home.' No doubt the President's ghost felt the same way.

'Lincoln Limousine' turned up on *Memphis Beat*, which briefly followed the parade of Kennedy tribute albums into the charts. But toying with the extremes of Southern politics wasn't a way back for Jerry Lee Lewis. In three years, Mercury had only struck one profitable idea, so they repeated it. The venue for *More Of The Greatest Show On Earth* was Fort Worth, Texas, thirty miles west of Kennedy's assassination site. Lewis felt right at home, calling the crowd 'neighbours' and offering some friendly advice: 'If I tell ya it's gonna rain, you'd better bring your umbrella.' Filling his set with country tunes. Lewis claimed allegiance with 'one of my favourite artists, Moon Mullican'. Who else remembered the King of the Hillbilly Piano-Players in 1966?

It was just another Southern night for Lewis, but it didn't ease Mercury's concerns. As the Beatles finished *Sgt Pepper*, Jerry Kennedy pulled Lewis into American Studios in Memphis. It was an idea before its time – Chips Moman revitalized Elvis Presley's career eighteen months later in the same location – but Kennedy's flaw was his conviction that Lewis could be a contemporary pop artist. Nothing in Jerry Lee's unruly career was as alien as the session's attempt at psychedelia, 'Just Dropped In (To See What Condition My Condition Was In)'.

The song had been written by Nashville staff writer Mickey Newbury as a parody of rock's flirtation with mind-expanding chemicals, and then recorded by future country star Kenny Rogers. Lewis was spared the Beatlesque backwards guitars that punctuated Rogers' single, but found it difficult to connect with such lyrics as 'I tore my mind on a jagged sky.' Even in this bizarre landscape, there were moments when acid-rock and Louisiana country collided. 'Got up so high I couldn't unwind,' Lewis sang wearily, the memory of a thousand honky-tonks, and cocktails of pills and whiskey, flashing across his brain. Soul, acid-rock, harpsichords – there was nothing left to keep Lewis from pure country when he arrived at Columbia's Nashville complex in January 1968. The most tolerant man in showbusiness, Jerry's new bandleader Kenneth Lovelace, was alongside him, beginning his three-decade trek with the Killer. But the essential ingredients were the songs, and a man steeped in pure country music.

'Mercury were getting ready to drop his contract,' recalls Jerry's sister, Linda Gail Lewis, 'and he wanted them to do that, because nothing was happening. So producer Eddie Kilroy went to Mercury and said, "Let me do Jerry with a traditional Nashville country sound with a new country song." Jerry said, "Hey, man, I don't know whether I want to do that," but Eddie talked him into it and found "Another Place, Another Time". And as soon as Eddie cut it on Jerry and it was a hit, Mercury fired him.'

It was only a three-song try-out, but Jerry delivered 'Another Place, Another Time' as if he'd stayed faithful to the honky-tonks since 1956. His spirit wasn't dulled: he cut Ernest Tubb's anthem, 'Walkin' The Floor Over You', at rock'n'roll pace, ending with a piano flourish that promised more mayhem to come. In these country tunes, he found an emotional core that was both personal and universal. Lewis sounded as if he'd been born to make this music, and the country audience responded. 'Another Place, Another Time' was his biggest hit since 'Breathless' a decade earlier, and it set up Jerry Lee for five years in which every single made the Top 20 country chart.

'That material suited me at the time,' he claimed years later. 'It was a way to get the disc jockeys to play my records again. I went through the country field, though I was still a rock'n'roller.' Linda Gail Lewis is even less circumspect: 'Jerry loves rock'n'roll. He only sings country music to make money.' Or, as Lewis told a BBC interviewer, 'You may come crawling in here like a hillbilly on your ass, but I ain't.'

As ever with Lewis, the truth is contradictory. The man who boasted that he fooled the country audience into financing his career revival took delight in frustrating audiences who'd come to see him rock'n'roll. He'd rouse a crowd to the point of hysteria, then reel off a succession of country ballads. If his fans were too narrow-minded to know that his taste was as broad as his ego, then they deserved a little provocation.

More honest was his admission that 'I lived a lot of those songs. As the years go by, you get into it. You've lived it.' That was how it sounded, as Jerry immersed himself in the self-pity of 'What's Made Milwaukee Famous (Has Made A Loser Out Of Me)' and 'She Still Comes Around (To Love What's Left Of Me)'. 'I know I'm not a model husband,' he lamented in the latter, 'although I'd like to be'; and while the record turned, it was impossible not to believe him.

A decade after being unofficially banned by American radio, Jerry Lee Lewis was the most-played country artist in 1968 and 1969. His past failings were forgiven, even secretly relished, by his audience. Like Johnny Cash's drugs and Merle Haggard's prison record, Jerry's apostasy in the evil world of rock'n'roll was viewed as a wrong turning on the road to salvation. And there is more joy in a sinner repenting in country music than anywhere else on the radio dial.

Sin and repentance were rarely far from his mind. 'He's had those hang-ups ever since he first went to the Assembly of God church,' says his sister. During the recording of 'Great Balls Of Fire' in 1957, Lewis delayed proceedings for a theological battle with Sam Phillips. While the Sun producer extolled his liberal beliefs, Jerry fell back on the unalterable word of scripture. The song's apocalyptic imagery stirred memories of hellfire preachers in Ferriday.

'You're a sinner,' Lewis cried to himself and his mentor, 'and unless you be saved and borned again and be made as a little child and walk before God and be holy – and, brother,' he said, an invisible congregation before him as if he'd never quit Bible College, 'I mean you got to be so pure. No sin shall enter there. NO SIN! For it says, no sin. It don't say just a little bit. It says NO SIN SHALL ENTER THERE. You got to WALK and TALK with God to go to heaven. You got to be so good.'

Phillips tried rational argument: 'Jerry, religious conviction doesn't mean anything resembling extremism. Do you mean to tell me that you're gonna take the Bible, that you're gonna take God's word, and that you're gonna revolutionize the whole universe?' But what did words count against the fear of God? 'Jerry,' Phillips continued, 'if you think you can't do good if you're a rock'n'roll exponent . . .' but Lewis cut him down. Sam tried again: 'You can save souls.' Lewis erupted, as if he could see the hand of God descending to smite this sinner from the face of the earth: 'NO! NO! NO! NO!' 'YES!' screamed Phillips.

Jerry's spirit was in revolt: 'How can the Devil save souls?' he cried. 'What are you talking about? JESUS! Heal this man!' And from his mouth poured Biblical phrases about demons and swine, his armour in the battle for his soul. 'It ain't what you believe,' he concluded triumphantly, 'it's what's written in the Bible!'

The weight of that faith never lifted from his mind. When his mother was stricken with cancer in October 1970, Mercury's hottest country artist announced that he was renouncing secular music, and would only record gospel. With Linda Gail, he cut an album of religious songs, *In Loving Memory*. And that Christmas, the Greatest Live Show on Earth reconvened at a fundamentalist church in the Memphis suburbs, as Jerry decided to chronicle the rebirth of his soul on a live album.

Though his heart was set on Jesus, the serpent toyed with his tongue, making this performance a surreal mixture of the sacred and profane. His repertoire was entirely religious. His congregation were ready to welcome back a lost soul to the paradise road. They whooped as Jerry declared: 'I'm sanctified and full of grace'. But their approval triggered an instinctive response, and he reeled off one of his bar-room lines: 'Never fear, Lewis is here.' Then he and his road band stomped into the gospel tune, 'Looking For A City'. The evening swayed back and forth between commerce and conviction. Jerry plugged his new album, on sale in the foyer 'after the show, er, service, is over'; then he pleaded, 'The money won't go to me, it'll pay for the boys in the band.' Sensing that he was losing his audience, he reverted to evangelism: 'Without a shadow of a doubt, I'm ready to go. I got saved, and I'm gonna stay saved. I'm more determined than ever.' His voice burst into a howl of joy: 'I'M GOING TO HEAVEN!' 'Blessed Saviour, Thou Wilt Guide Us', he sang as proof.

But Jerry could never experience religion without wanting to explain it. As if his argument with Sam Phillips were still raging, he told the congregation: 'I've been singing "Great Balls Of Fire" for so long, I got tired. There won't be any of that here. We might get the fire of glory, we could use some of that.'

Jerry eased into 'Peace In The Valley', which Elvis Presley had recorded a decade earlier, as proof that he was a God-fearing Southern boy at heart. With a sense of awed conviction, Lewis unfolded the good news. 'I'll be changed from this creature that I am,' he intoned, adding 'think about it now' as if he was speaking in tongues.

He turned to face the congregation. 'I've been saved now for two weeks and five days,' he gloried, lending the numbers a biblical significance. 'And I wouldn't trade what I've got now for all the nightclubs in Las Vegas.'

Las Vegas, where, earlier that year, he'd played the International hotel, an oasis of roulette and blackjack in the Nevada desert. The city was a beacon of American commercialism. Sinatra and Sammy Davis Jr, Dean Martin and Streisand: the icons of showbiz had filled its hotel lounges for years. The previous summer, the hotel had been the venue for Elvis Presley's triumphant return to live performance.

That rankled with Lewis, who was booked into a smaller lounge than Elvis. Presley wasn't in town when Jerry Lee opened, but the Killer talked as if his rival were trapped in the front row. 'Elvis,' he called out during one show, 'you have got more money, but I've got *more*. I've got talent, anyway. Elvis and Tom Jones couldn't shine my shoes.'

Any song could provoke another sideswipe. He borrowed one of Elvis's hits, 'Blue Suede Shoes', and turned it back at the King: 'Elvis recorded it when Carl [Perkins] was in the hospital after a car wreck. I think he mighta stole it.' He looked sheepish for a second: 'I'm just telling you what Carl told me.'

Through it all, Jerry behaved as if he were talking to a Louisiana bar crowd. When he launched into a country tune in the wrong key, he quipped: 'If I'd have kept going, you're talking about haemorrhoid trouble'. He introduced 'Whole Lotta Shakin' Goin' On', by bragging that 'this was the first record to sell 12 million copies with a curse word in it'. In 'Great Balls Of Fire', he crowed: 'Too much love drives a stud insane.' He all but reached for his wallet: 'I made a million dollars,' he claimed, 'but I spent two.' Then he laughed. 'If you don't get it with this song, then you'll never get it at all.' He wasn't talking about dollar bills.

'If you can't get a blessing for this,' Jerry announced in church, 'you better stay in your seat.' Well, at least he hadn't cursed. He'd tripped his way through the entire show, er, service, with nothing worse than a cryptic comment. 'For a long time,' he told the congregation, 'I had the right string but the wrong yo-yo.' There was a baffled silence. He was more eloquent in song, climaxing with a righteous rendition of the Southern spiritual, 'I'll Fly Away'. 'Money don't make you happy,' he said proudly, 'Jesus makes you happy.' With a clip of his toe on the piano – old habits die hard – and a reminder about the album on sale outside, he was gone. Three months later, his mother Mamie Lewis died. A few days after that, Jerry was back in the studio. When he cut Kris Kristofferson's 'Help Me Make It Through The Night', he was no longer addressing his music to Jesus. In future, he would let women and whiskey reclaim his soul, while all the time his mind reeled at the blasphemy and the judgement to come.

The weeks that Jerry Lee dedicated to Christ marked the apogee of his career in country music. The twelve months before had been the most successful of his career. He'd spent two years wooing the country audience, making all the expected career moves. But the straitjacket soon began to loosen. Even his calmest performances offered clues that the real Jerry Lee – a hellraising, ego-charged son of a gun – hadn't been subdued. In the middle of a honky-tonk lament, he'd sweep his hand up and down the piano, showering the song in sparks. He'd always been liable to self-mythology, and now he began to intrude in the most unlikely places. References to 'ol' Jerry Lee' littered songs that demanded humility.

Gradually, his antics marked out a distance between the man and his music. He stopped living his songs, and began to provide a commentary on them. When he tackled Merle Haggard's 'Workin' Man Blues', the lyrics seemed less important than the chance to explain what he was up to in the piano solo. 'Fade it out,' he called, as the performance drifted into chaos.

A decade earlier, he'd scandalized the industry by marrying his 13-year-old cousin. Now he cut an incendiary duet album with his kid sister, Linda Gail Lewis, who was a couple of years younger than his wife. 'We got married in a fever,' they sang, and every one of their duets sizzled with barely controlled passion. There was no hint of incest in real life – Linda was too busy marrying members of Jerry's band – but the implication added to the unease that cloaked his reputation.

'I've had over thirty country hits,' Jerry boasted in the early seventies, 'but I'd rather do rock'n'roll. Country music is just pretty songs. A lot of people can sing pretty songs, but only one man can rock his life away, and I'm the only one that's worth a damn.'

Rock songs crept back into his repertoire – at first with country trimmings, as when he tackled Chuck Berry's 'Brown Eyed Handsome Man' with steel guitar and chorus, but later without any apologies. In concert, he still opted for ambiguity. 'This was No. 1 for us in the country and western field of music,' he'd say after Kris Kristofferson's 'Once More With Feeling', 'and I regard that as the main field of music right now.' Then, he'd announce: 'This is the only rock'n'roll, rhythm and blues, country and western *Grand Ole Opry* in existence. That's the way I do it – all wrapped up in one.' Or he'd tell the audience: 'A lot of people say, "Jerry Lee, what made you go country?" Well, the flipside of my first record was "You Win Again", and I think that was country. When I was a kid, I was pickin' corn. I drank a little of it, too.'

'I'm just a hillbilly singer,' he explained, 'and I play hillbilly speeded up.' But slowly the hillbilly inside him died, to be replaced by a wilier version of the man-child who'd cut 'Great Balls Of Fire'. Throughout the 1970s, country music dominated his schedule, but he reserved his passion for rock'n'roll.

Mercury couldn't fight it, so they decided to hype it. *The Killer Rocks On*, was the boast of a 1972 album, on which Jerry delivered a version of 'Chantilly Lace' even more flamboyant than the Big Bopper's original. 'Pick you up at eight?' he sneered. 'Well, honey, I thought you might pick *me* up at eight.'

By now, even the country tunes were exercises in ego. 'Who's gonna play this old piano, after I'm not here?' he asked on a 1972 single. George Jones expounded the same sentiment on 'Who's Gonna Fill Their Shoes', though he sounded genuinely humble. Lewis knew that when it was time for him to burn, they might as well add the piano to the pyre.

In January 1973, he travelled to London. The arrival of an authentic giant of rock'n'roll attracted many British musicians to take part. Jerry both feared and despised his young rivals, and *The Session* was a disappointment. Only when he was on such secure ground as 'Drinkin' Wine Spo-Dee-O-Dee', did his swaggering arrogance translate into music.

A second experiment, teaming Jerry with fellow Louisiana

madcap Huey Meaux, proved more satisfying. But *Southern Roots* actually harmed Lewis's status as a chart contender. The visceral 'Meat Man' was a feast of innuendo and aggression, but it could hardly make country radio. Even rock DJs baulked at its cunnilingual metaphors and defiant ending: 'Meat man, you mother!'

Country stations picked up on Jerry when they could: the deliciously titled 'I Can Still Hear The Music In The Restroom' made the playlists in 1975, no doubt helped by the decision to send out promotional toilet seats. The semi-autobiographical 'Middle Age Crazy' in 1977 not only inspired a film, but racked up Jerry's biggest hit in five years. The proof that country could no longer hold Jerry Lee Lewis had already come in 1975, when he released Donnie Fritts' brutally honest ('My Life Would Make) A Damn Good Country Song': 'I've had my share of women, but they always seem to leave . . . I took enough pills for ol' Memphis town, I'm drinkin' enough whiskey to lift any ship off the ground.' It was everything the title promised, and more, but it was too real for an industry struggling to accept Conway Twitty's '(I Can Tell) You've Never Been This Far Before'. Ahead lay shootings, arrests, life-threatening illness, the mysterious deaths of two wives, a parade of accidents and intentions that matched his nickname of Killer. Even Hank couldn't do it that way.

28 Thank God I'm a Country Boy

Country crosses into pop, 1967–1975: Ray Price; Glen Campbell; John Denver; Anne Murray; Olivia Newton-John

In September 1970, veteran Ray Price topped the *Billboard* country chart for the first time in eleven years. The king of the honky-tonk shuffle, Price had nudged hillbilly music into a new era in the mid-fifties with records such as 'Crazy Arms' and 'My Shoes Keep Walking Back To You'. A decade later, he had initiated a new tradition, hiding his bar-room swagger beneath a lush canopy of strings. His 1967 hit 'Danny Boy' epitomized this approach – and brought him unaccustomed airplay on pop radio. Three years later, an equally sumptuous orchestra shimmered as Price crooned 'For The Good Times'.

Besides reaching No. 1 on the country chart, 'For The Good Times' entered the pop Top 10. 'I was fighting with the so-called establishment over that new sound,' Price admitted. 'They all said I'd gone pop but that wasn't true at all.'

A chain of ironies surrounded Price's crossover success. Not only was this staunch traditionalist abandoning the aural trademarks of country, but his vehicle was supplied by a composer regarded by Nashville stalwarts as an immoral hippie – Kris Kristofferson. Price was criticized for being too adventurous in his choice of material, and too conservative in his arrangements. Purists complained that his records were no longer country, but country pop. Meanwhile, a generation of rock bands was assimilating country influences – not from Price and his fellow country pop 'sell-outs', but from such loyalists as Merle Haggard and Buck Owens who refused to flirt with the devil and his orchestras.

Country-rock left no mark on Price or Haggard; likewise Price's Nashville schmaltz touched no one in the pop mainstream. As ever, the two genres were at odds, only this time from deep within each other's territory.

While performers such as Johnny Cash and Waylon Jennings were able to step back and forth between the two camps, the 'so-called establishment' of country was racked by internal warfare, which erupted into skirmishes and battles over the next decade. 'Sure, the country singers want to be pop,' reasoned former Country Music Association president Bill Williams in 1969. 'It's the difference between selling 70,000 and 500,000 singles. Money does it every time.'

Ray Price and another like-minded veteran, Eddy Arnold, championed the crossover cause from within. Hollywood added the support of Glen Campbell, a transplanted Southerner who had played bluegrass before joining the 'Wrecking Crew' of sessionmen who dominated the LA studio scene through the sixties. Campbell was briefly a member of the Beach Boys, and then a guitar-picker available for hire to any rock band or Vegas lounge legend in town.

In 1967 he began cutting country-flavoured tunes with pop orchestrations – none more successful than 'By The Time I Get To Phoenix', 'Galveston' and 'Wichita Lineman', all written by Jimmy Webb, and equally welcomed by pop and country audiences. Even rock'n'roll icons recognized his talent. 'Country phrasing is so soulful to me,' Little Richard beamed in 1969. 'When Glen Campbell says that one word, "Galveston", that shakes me up. That music is as real as the blues.'

Campbell's manifesto was simple: 'I don't care if it's country, pop or whatever. I just want a good song.' His vast international audience concurred. Listeners who'd escaped rural poverty for the comparative sophistication of urban life felt comfortable with the plush exterior of Campbell's music. The hint of hillbilly tradition which remained wasn't enough to repel those pop fans who were suspicious of anything 'country'.

Worse was to follow for those who abhorred the idea of country without a steel guitar or a cracker's whine. In Campbell's footsteps followed Freddy Weller, who scored in 1969 with mellifluous arrangements of swamp-rock tunes first recorded by Joe South and Billy Joe Royal. Where Campbell was manicured and conservatively attired, Weller let his hair slip onto his shoulder-blades. Worse still, his 'country' career wasn't his sole preoccupation: between hits, he played lead guitar with garage-rockers Paul Revere and the Raiders. Publisher Wesley Rose, who ran Acuff-Rose Music in Nashville and whose father had guided the career of Hank Williams, dripped scorn on the new style: 'You go to the Opry for country music, not for this rock'n'roll or rhythm and blues stuff they're having now. You can't be fish and fowl. You can't be country and be on the pop charts at the same time.' His exclusion zone would have robbed Nashville of Campbell, Johnny Cash, Sonny James, Tammy Wynette, Roy Clark and Bobby Gentry, all of whom stepped between the country and pop charts at the start of the seventies.

Rose's suspicion was echoed by the ambivalent figure of Chet Atkins, who had triggered a similar identity crisis at the start of the sixties by bathing country in the 'Nashville Sound'. 'I'm afraid that it's almost inevitable that we may get swallowed up by the pop market,' he lamented in spring 1970. 'That's something I personally would regret very much. I love country music, and want to keep it pure, but there is a danger.' His counterpart at Columbia Records, Billy Sherrill, scoffed at Atkins' misgivings: 'To think we can't broaden our appeal is ludicrous. I don't think we'll lose our identity. I think our identity will grow, with people who can do something with a wider range of lyrics, melodies and instruments. It doesn't necessarily have to be two guitars and a banjo. I don't think you're losing anything. I think you're gaining something.' Like an improved market share, as Sherrill noted when he softened the instrumentation on country releases by Tammy Wynette and David Houston, with enormous commercial success.

The convoluted logic of this argument, with its shifting allegiances of traditionalists and modernizers, was epitomized by Canadian singer George Hamilton IV. 'I think we've gone as far as we can with string orchestras and trumpets and the like,' he announced in 1970. 'I think Eddy Arnold was the last straw. This is as far uptown as we can go – I hope so, anyway, because I don't want to see us lose our identity. Country music is like the Mississippi River. It's a mighty river until it flows into the Gulf of

Mexico of pop music, and then it just becomes a ripple.' But Hamilton was also the man who had brought folk-rock songwriters such as Joni Mitchell and Gordon Lightfoot into country music; and in 1970 he was the first country performer to recognize the crossover potential of James Taylor. Royalties, rather than family tradition, might have earned Taylor his 'homestead on the farm', but his early albums evoked a far closer identification with the land and its values than Ray Price or Eddy Arnold were offering at the start of the decade.

Buck Owens, who'd already pledged his lifelong allegiance to country songs in the mid-sixties, extended his definition to include Chuck Berry, Bob Dylan and Simon & Garfunkel by the early seventies. His ambivalent attitude to the new order was reflected in his music: in 1970, he followed the strident 'I Wouldn't Live In New York City (If They Gave Me The Whole Dang Town)' with a mild country arrangement of 'Bridge Over Troubled Water', penned by that child of New York, Paul Simon. That same year, he announced his intention to cut two different versions of his singles, individually tailored for the pop and country markets. Sadly, his single-handed invention of the remix industry proved to be wishful thinking.

There was no more potent symbol of the rural tradition in country music than the *Grand Ole Opry*. On Friday and Saturday night, *Opry* listeners could pretend that the fiddle tunes and gentle sentimentality of Roy Acuff, Grandpa Jones and Bashful Brother Oswald were still the common language of the white South.

Acuff and his colleagues were present in the summer of 1970, when the ground was officially broken on a 369-acre site near Pennington Bend, a few miles outside Nashville alongside the Cumberland River. Fields and woods that were once the domain of the water-moccasin were now tamed to hold Opryland USA – a themed amusement park which included a new, enlarged and (most importantly) air-conditioned Opry House. The $25 million development was the clearest sign yet that Nashville's business community would not allow the trappings of tradition to baulk progress or profit.

The park would offer a sanitized version of the South, all

rippling clear-water creeks and backwoods wisdom, without a hint of the back-breaking cotton harvests, the poverty, the cultural isolation, let alone the twin layers of prejudice, that had pitched the South against the rest of the American nation and black Southerners against white.

This impulse to escape the stereotypes of the past affected the very language of country. In July 1971, *Look* magazine in New York ran a cover story on Kris Kristofferson headlined: 'Country Music – Hillbilly No More'. 'These days,' Ray Price complained, 'hillbilly connotes ignorance, and it's not true.' Country stations reacted angrily when Skeeter Davis revived unpleasant memories with a single entitled 'The Hillbilly Singer', which was banished from radio playlists.

More complex was the debate over 'Dueling Banjos', the bluegrass instrumental by Eric Weissberg and Steve Mandell which was used as the theme to the movie *Deliverance*. The film, based on James Dickey's more sensitive novel, portrayed the inhabitants of the Appalachians (the bedrock of the bluegrass tradition) as animalistic throwbacks to a more violent age, in-bred to the point of insanity, violent by instinct and fuelled by a noxious blend of moonshine whiskey and innate hostility to 'outsiders' (i.e., anyone not raised on the side of a mountain). 'Dueling Banjos' briefly catapulted bluegrass, that least violent of genres, into the commercial mainstream; a soundtrack album filled with decade-old banjo and guitar features sold to thousands who'd never heard of Bill Monroe. Country DJs had to go with the flow, playlisting the single but steering clear of the movie from which it came.

With radio stations prepared to air anything from Weissberg's banjo picking to the so-called 'countrypolitan' sounds of Ray Price, via Anne Murray's Canadian country-pop and Jerry Lee Lewis's romps through fifties rock hits, the early seventies was something of a golden age for country music – at least commercially. But few industry insiders could shake off the suspicion that they were in danger of betraying their own cause. 'You can't fake country people out,' insisted Harlan Howard, one of Nashville's leading songwriters since the mid-fifties. 'Country people are down to earth people. If you say something they won't understand, they won't listen again. That's the beauty of country songs, they don't mystify you.' And he had a warning: 'If you are a rock'n'roll idol doing country because you have run on lean times, man, they know it.'

Suddenly, though, Nashville was full of faded rock'n'roll idols – all selling more records as country stars than they had for a decade. Besides Jerry Lee Lewis, reinvented as a honky-tonker in 1968, there was Conway Twitty, who escaped the memory of 'It's Only Make Believe' to become the most successful Nashville performer of the seventies and eighties. Charlie Rich surfaced from years of commercial neglect to become an unlikely countrypolitan icon, his bluesy voice and jazz piano stylings subdued by Billy Sherrill's strings. Brenda Lee had dropped off the pop charts by the late sixties, but she extended her commercial life by concentrating on country. The irony, as she explains, was that she achieved this career transformation without altering a thing: 'It was the same music we'd always been making, but now they called it country. I would have been crazy not to go with the flow.' No wonder that Ray Price, of all people, was expressing alarm: 'The lines are getting awful thin. What is a pop song and what is a country song? What I think we are going to see now is a revolution within the industry. I think there will be no segregating lines.'

Crossover was the key word of 1973. Sociologist Paul Hemphill had anticipated the phenomenon at the start of the decade, when he identified the one-time good ol' boys from the rural South, who were now 'out in the suburbs, living in identical houses and shopping at the K-Mart and listening to Glen Campbell (Roy Acuff and Ernest Tubb are too tacky now) and hiding their racism behind code words. They have forfeited their style and spirit, traded it all in on a color TV and Styrofoam beams for the den.' Hemphill's account of this upward mobility betrayed more than a little snobbery, but he caught the prevailing feeling that the drift from country to town required a smoother soundtrack.

The shift in public mood was echoed within the pop and rock industry. After the turbulent experimentation of the late sixties, rock's unified front fragmented in the early seventies. With few exceptions, the radicals of the sixties slipped into self-parody, retaining the rhetoric of revolution while winding their artistic orbit into ever-decreasing circles. Over the course of the new decade, the ageing rock audience who had witnessed the frantic metamorphoses of the sixties began to insist on safety and stability. Artists such as Jefferson Airplane and Crosby, Stills and Nash, who had been standard-bearers of political activism at the time of Woodstock and Kent State, gradually shed their collective radicalism in favour of a purely individual search for 'freedom' and 'personal expression'.

Behind them rose a flurry of competing rock styles, from the hard rock and heavy metal of Led Zeppelin and Aerosmith to the glam theatrics of Alice Cooper and Kiss, who were the natural icons for the new decade's mid-point. This was unashamedly music for teenage boys, whose kid sisters were being targeted by unthreatening idols like David Cassidy and Donny Osmond. Once, their parents would once have settled back with Frank Sinatra or Bing Crosby; now they had to search elsewhere for melodic consolation.

One option was 'countrypolitan', a term coined by Columbia's Billy Sherrill in the late sixties to describe his blend of strings and steel guitar. Ray Price was countrypolitan; so was Eddy Arnold. Easy listening pop, mellow music, soft-rock: the solution came under many different names. Few record-buyers bought the whole ticket, which stretched from James Taylor or Joni Mitchell at one end of the spectrum to Perry Como singing Kris Kristofferson's 'For The Good Times' at the other. Occupying the central ground were a group of singers who effortlessly straddled the country/pop border – John Denver, Olivia Newton-John, Anne Murray and Charlie Rich.

From 1973 to 1975, this quartet dominated Top 40 country and pop stations. John Denver offered the acoustic whimsy of James Taylor without the veneer of angst, or the sly humour, that tinged Taylor's work. Anne Murray had lucked into a crossover hit with 'Snowbird' in 1970 – even Elvis thought that was country, as he immediately covered it on an album of Nashville favourites – and then concentrated on melodic pop, only to discover that she was still being playlisted on country stations. Charlie Rich forgot his fifteen-year career as a critic's favourite, delivering a stirring blend of blues, soul, rock and jazz, to achieve country stardom with a series of bland but immaculately performed ballads. Olivia Newton-John stumbled from teen pop success in Britain to unlikely acclaim in Nashville, thanks to some well-crafted songs by John Rostill – an Australian-born member of an English instrumental group, the Shadows.

None of these would have seemed a credible country star at the start of the decade. All were ambivalent about being tagged as country. John Denver revealed many years later that his record label, RCA, had begged him to target Nashville with his self-composed material, but he'd refused. Country radio still latched onto 'Rocky Mountain High' and 'Annie's Song'.

When John Rostill's 'Let Me Be There' ushered Newton-John across the border on to country radio, the singer appeared to be baffled by her new audience. 'Country music is all over the world,' she reasoned. 'Basically, it all means the same thing: it's about people and their lives. I don't know why this song broke in the country market. We just recorded it as a pop tune, but maybe with some country overtones.'

Anne Murray, who enjoyed three separate waves of country chart success in the seventies, remained the most outspoken about her crossover appeal: 'I don't play for country audiences. I think I've played maybe three specifically country events in my life, and I found them awful. They kind of set up gallows, they have thirty performers, and it's like a cattle call. I just found it distasteful. I don't really know what country music is anymore.' Regardless of her distaste, Murray was skilfully marketed to appeal simultaneously to both cultures. A sequence of events in 1974 was typical: Capitol issued a single which backed a slick remake of a country standard, 'He Thinks I Still Care', with an equally perky update of an obscure Beatles tune, 'You Won't See Me'. Then Murray's managers, Shep Gordon and Allan Strale, who'd masterminded Alice Cooper's invention as a media magnet, offered her services to the top country TV shows, while also arranging a prestigious PR event at the Troubadour in Hollywood. John Lennon, Harry Nilsson, Micky Dolenz and, of course, Alice Cooper turned up for the free drinks; *Rolling Stone* printed the resulting pics; and Murray's rock credibility stepped up a notch. So did her profile in the country market: neither audience noticed the strenuous efforts being made to attract the other.

Some country pop artists required no such scheming. Charlie Rich singles such as 'Behind Closed Doors' and 'The Most Beautiful Girl' slipped effortlessly across the dial from country to pop stations. These hits earned Rich three Country Music Association awards in 1973; a year later, the members of the CMA voted him Entertainer of the Year. Joining him at the victors' party in October 1974 was the newly crowned Best Female Vocalist – the British-born, Australia-raised Olivia Newton-John, whose most recent release, 'I Honestly Love You', had won more support from pop DJs than from their country counterparts. Newton-John's recognition by the CMA – and her pointed absence from the awards ceremony – outraged the traditional contenders for her crown, and none more so than Tammy Wynette. She and her husband, George Jones, gathered fifty like-minded performers to their Nashville mansion a few weeks after the awards ceremony. The embattled singers emerged with the skeleton of a new organization which was intended both to rival the CMA and to 'preserve the identity of country music' from the 'uptown 5th Avenue attitude' that was infecting the industry.

The Association of Country Entertainers (ACE) was doomed from the start: it wasn't an auspicious omen when Wynette and Jones separated a few days after its formation was announced. ACE's aims weren't entirely ideological; as singer and spokesman Billy Walker admitted, the stars were also 'trying to protect our business' from the financial deprivations that might be triggered by these 'outside influences'. Like most organizations built on negative rather than positive ideals, ACE foundered as soon as it attempted to switch from complaints to action.

By February 1975, Tammy Wynette was admitting that the founding of ACE had been premature: 'It got completely out of proportion. It made a mountain out of a molehill, and we're not fighting a lot of the things they said we were fighting. We were just trying to have a better relationship with country music.' Three years later, she preferred not to mention ACE in her autobiography.

Her personal crises aside, Wynette had little reason to rebel in the mid-seventies: her singles continued to top the country charts both before and after Olivia Newton-John won her CMA award. But the veteran Canadian star Hank Snow had been fighting a rearguard battle against modernization for more than a decade. He'd been one of the last to submit to Chet Atkins' Nashville Sound; now, apart from a freak 1974 hit with 'Hello Love', he had to watch while countrypolitan artists chipped away at his audience.

Of all the ACE founders, Snow most regarded the organization as a crusade. After the initial flurry of resignations early in 1975, he was elected ACE's president. Eighteen months later, however, even he was ready to admit defeat: 'I've been with the organization since its birth, and I've gone along with its goal of preserving the identity of country music. I've also said that I'd never change the style of recording I've had for forty years. Well, I've changed my mind after a complete study of the matter. I can truthfully say I was wrong. People would ask me to record with more fiddles and old country steel – but those same people do not buy Hank Snow records. Judging from my sales in the past three years, I've been doing something wrong. If you can't beat them, join them.'

Country fans were entranced by more sophisticated fare in the mid-seventies. The biggest selling American artist of 1975, in any genre, was John Henry Deutschendorf – alias John Denver. A folksinger through the sixties, he'd broken into public view when Peter, Paul and Mary recorded his song 'Leaving On A Jet Plane' in 1968. His breezy and sentimental acoustic style brought him a string of pop hits in the early seventies; clever marketing ensured that songs like 'Thank God I'm A Country Boy' would usher him over the border into another market by the middle of the decade. That song hymned the simple pleasures of outdoor life and traditional American values, using a country fiddle (rarely heard on countrypolitan records) and a sly reference to the string-band standard 'Sally Goodin' as trademarks of rural authenticity. Only Denver's earlier hit, 'Back Home Again', prevented 'Thank God I'm A Country Boy' from being acclaimed as the CMA's Song of the Year. As the reigning CMA Entertainer of the Year, Charlie Rich was asked to present the 1975 award to his successor. Smashed but definitely not high on booze, Rich slurred his way through the preliminaries, then tore open the envelope which held the winner's name. 'John Denver', he muttered in disgust, then pulled a lighter from his pocket and let the slip of paper burn in his hand. He was quickly ushered off stage. The incident was written off as an unforeseen side-effect of Rich's prescription medicine. Only later did Rich admit that he too had voted for Denver.

Charlie Rich's tortured ambivalence towards his newly acquired fame was one response to the country-pop explosion. Another came from a motley collection of musicians who had, like Rich, been recording since the late fifties. Their power base was not in Nashville, where the Country Music Association held sway, but several hundred miles west in Texas. Their stance was rebellious, but not revolutionary. They were ready to transport country music into a new era. Their vehicle was a marketing campaign as slick, and contrived, as anything conceived by the handlers of John Denver or Anne Murray. They were billed by a Nashville PR genius as the Outlaws – and within two years, they had become the new establishment of country music, arousing distrust bordering on hostility from countrypolitans and traditionalists alike.

29 Life's Little Ups and Downs
Charlie Rich, 1957–1993

'I never considered myself to sing country songs, but the public did.' In a line, Charlie Rich laid out the dilemma of his career. 'Charlie had more talent than anyone I ever worked with,' reckons Sam Phillips, the Sun Records boss who discovered Elvis Presley, Jerry Lee Lewis, Carl Perkins and Johnny Cash. But the qualities that impressed him – the mesh of black and white blues styles, the pained dignity with which he met the world – were also the barriers between Rich and public acceptance.

In 1973, at the age of 41, Charlie Rich became a country superstar and, for a year, the best-selling singer in America. 'It's the broadening of country music that has helped us,' he admitted. 'The things we are doing fell into the crossover section. Though they were basically country, they went middle of the road and pop.'

For Rich's loyal cult following, there was irony in the taste of success. After recording everything from late-night jazz to Southern soul, he achieved his breakthrough with a series of mellow, 'countrypolitan' records that reeked of middle-aged cosiness. Not that his hits entirely sold him short. There was compromise: on 'Behind Closed Doors', his first No. 1, his edgy, blue-note piano style was replaced by the smooth lyricism of sessionman 'Pig' Robbins. But the sonorous warmth of Rich's baritone added unexpected depth to the record.

Even the theme of 'Behind Closed Doors' suited the enigma of Charlie Rich. The title suggested illicit encounters at the dark end of the street, adultery and guilt; but the actual scenario was more subversive – a married couple with a conventional façade, behind which burned undimmed sensuality. Likewise, beneath Rich's calm exterior lurked a man ill at ease with stardom, who wanted nothing more than the freedom to play his music.

The gulf between Charlie Rich and commerce was apparent when he arrived at Sun Studios around 1957. 'He was a jazz pianist, who'd been playing with a small group in the air force,' recalled Sun A&R man and saxophonist Bill Justis. 'One night he came in as a substitute for my piano player. Somebody said he could sing, and after some persuasion he did a song. The crowd liked it, and he did another. I told him to come over to the studios and maybe we could cut something.

'I didn't hear anything until a month later when his wife came in with some tapes. Another month later he came in and sang. But he was too jazzy, all thirteenths. I gave him a bunch of Jerry Lee Lewis records and told him to come back when he could get that bad.'

Elvis Presley had auditioned for Sam Phillips as a second Dean Martin; Jerry Lee Lewis and Carl Perkins wanted to be honky-tonk country stars; Johnny Cash arrived at Sun as a gospel crooner. But none of these rockabillies required greater realignment than Charlie Rich, who sacrificed his diminished chords and subtle voicings to the demand of rock'n'roll. The real Charlie Rich only appeared after-hours. That was when he'd drift into Stephen Foster ballads, jazz improvisations, mournful tunes that pitched the blues against uncanny chord changes.

Some of those songs survived to become the currency of his career. 'Lonely Weekends' was his solitary Sun hit; like 'Break Up', it echoed the Jerry Lee Lewis style, and Lewis duly covered both tunes. Twenty years later, he also tackled Rich's majestic blues ballad, 'Who Will The Next Fool Be' – an early-sixties soul standard first heard in Sun's Memphis studio. Equally compelling was 'Stay', built around a shifting chord sequence that chipped away at the romantic certainties of the lyric.

Sun Records could find no home in 1958 for 'Don't Put No Headstone On My Grave', a grim piece of blues naturalism that might have come from Howlin' Wolf. Country DJs failed to respond to 'Sittin' And Thinkin'', a honky-tonk song which laid bare its landscape from the first line: 'I got loaded last night on a bottle of gin.' Rich's attempts at rock'n'roll novelty hits didn't satisfy himself or his audience.

So Rich drifted away from Sun in the early Sixties, winding up at

RCA, where Chet Atkins recognized his potential. 'We were trying then for something we've got going now,' Rich reflected in 1974, 'a smooth-type country sound.' Atkins encouraged Rich to record mellow ballads, from Lonnie Johnson's forties blues hit 'Tomorrow Night' to the Sinatra showcase 'Nice 'N' Easy', and teased the singer's own material into the same shape. At Sun, Rich had rasped through the melancholy changes of 'There Won't Be Anymore' like a wronged lover in the electric chair; at RCA, it was polished into something Bing Crosby could have handled.

Even at the height of the Nashville Sound, when audiences lapped up Atkins' productions like cats with cream, Charlie Rich was too eerie for mass consumption. In the mid-sixties, he moved to the Mercury subsidiary Smash, where he cut some of the finest music of his life. But when he followed his Top 20 smash 'Mohair Sam' with 'I Can't Go On', three minutes of sublime melancholy, his momentum was stalled.

His natural home might have been a blues label, such as Atlantic or Stax. A deal with Memphis R&B specialists Hi Records in 1966 ought to have salvaged his career, but Hi had no more idea than anyone else how to market Charlie Rich. They produced a puzzling series of records that veered from classic Southern soul (Rich cut 'When Something Is Wrong With My Baby' before Sam & Dave taped their hit version at Stax) to lush interpretations of Hank Williams songs. The combination oozed potential: one of the South's premier interpreters faced with country's most evocative lyrics. But Rich had never sounded so bored as when he tried to slice through the slush that coated 'Cold, Cold Heart' and 'I'm So Lonesome I Could Cry'.

At the end of 1967, Rich fell into the hands of Billy Sherrill – then producing two of Columbia Records' hottest acts, Tammy Wynette and David Houston. Sherrill had engineered some of Rich's sessions at Sun, so he was prepared for eclecticism. Their first Columbia session spawned a minor hit, 'Set Me Free': enough to maintain Rich on the roster, but not to distract Sherrill from more lucrative assignments.

Through 1968, Rich edged his way through a range of styles barely acceptable to Columbia's country division – Jimmy Reed blues tunes like 'Big Boss Man', Sinatra revivals (another shot at

'Nice 'N' Easy'), swamp-rock ('Down On The River') and contemporary country-pop hits ('By The Time I Get To Phoenix'). Sherrill even hit on the blueprint for 'Behind Closed Doors', offering Rich his own tune, 'I Do My Swingin' At Home'.

Elvis Presley returned home to Memphis in February 1969 to cut his most personal music in a decade. Rich caught the same spirit a few weeks later. 'Life's Little Ups And Downs', written by his wife, Margaret Ann, summed up her husband's ten-year devil-dance with the music industry, in its portrayal of a working man carrying home the weight of his failure to his wife: 'I don't know how to tell her I didn't get that raise in pay today.' But, as so often in Charlie's music, the bond of marriage conquered human weakness: 'She knows that life has its little ups and downs . . . She wears a gold ring on her finger, and it's mine.'

The poignancy of Rich's wife penning this message of support was reinforced by his performance. He delivered the lyrics like a man who'd already imagined every scenario – drunken excess, despair, divorce – but was still clinging to the fantasy of survival. After two short verses, the picture faded, a repeated guitar lick tolling the inevitability that the next day would bring another test of nerve.

Even for a genre built on the working-man's blues, 'Life's Little Ups And Downs' was not exactly easy listening. It lingered on the charts for several months in the summer of 1969, a dark counterpoint to the celebration of Woodstock and the moon landing.

Over the next few years, Rich haunted the margins of country music with tales of regret and desolation. 'July 12 1939' opened a murky window on the past, revealing a mystery as deep as Bobby Gentry's 'Ode To Billie Joe'. With 'A Woman Left Lonely', he retrieved a superb soul tune from Janis Joplin's posthumous *Pearl* album. But even after the country hit 'I Take It On Home' (another ode to marital fidelity), Rich's contract with Columbia seemed unlikely to be renewed. 'If I were you,' his manager Seymour Rosenberg told Billy Sherrill, 'I'd get Charlie in the studio and cut a hit with him.' At the next session, Rich taped 'Behind Closed Doors'.

The single transformed Rich's career. Eight more No. 1s

followed over the next five years. At one point, he held the three best-selling albums in the country market. His previous labels, Sun, Mercury and RCA among them, brushed down vintage masters – some cut almost a decade earlier – which charted with ease.

The flow of rewards was never-ending. The CMA voted him Entertainer of the Year; Rich even lent his name to Silver Fox jeans. In the most astute investment of his career, he funnelled his new-found wealth into the Wendy's hamburger chain before it became a multi-million-dollar enterprise.

Like the uneasy heroes of his songs, Rich was unable to relax into his success. For years, he'd bummed around clubs and bar-rooms, playing country, blues, jazz and rock, slipping some Ray Charles or Sinatra tunes in among his own singles. The clubs ballooned into concert halls, filled with punters who only knew Charlie from 'Behind Closed Doors'. Once he'd sat alone on stage with his piano, and eased every drinker in the place into a private world of small triumphs and deep disappointments. Now the spontaneity and intimacy were gone.

A more cynical spirit would have rolled with the flow, but nothing in Charlie Rich's life was that simple. Inured to failure, he found success impossible to control. His casual drinking swelled into addiction; his marriage rocked between chaos and tense stability. Rich chose to self-destruct in style, his drunken antics at the 1975 CMA Awards terminating his unbroken run of hits. Ironically, his next single was entitled 'Now Everybody Knows'. In a comeback worthy of Jerry Lee Lewis, Rich posted a surprise No. 1 in 1977 with 'Rollin' With The Flow': 'While folks my age are raisin' kids, I'm raisin' hell just like I did,' he crooned self-deprecatingly. By the end of the decade he'd figured that the only route out of the fast lane was on to the hard shoulder. He retired from the music business in 1981 and returned to Margaret Ann, and weekly jam sessions with musicians he trusted. Few exits from showbusiness have been handled with such grace.

Except that there was a renaissance – not a tawdry rekindling of old glories, but a return worthy of the man. Rock historian Peter Guralnick had championed Charlie's music since the early seventies. He'd even named his first book after what might be

Rich's finest song, 'Feel Like Going Home'. In 1993, not long before Charlie died in his early sixties, Guralnick captured Rich and his backroom buddies on tape, performing the way they did in private. *Pictures And Paintings* was the first Charlie Rich album on which compromise wasn't an issue; not surprisingly, it was the best of his career. Equally inevitable was its stylistic sweep, from a touching interpretation of Duke Ellington's 'Mood Indigo' to a revival of the lost Sun classic, 'Don't Put No Headstone On My Grave'. The album gathered together fifties rock'n'roll, gospel, cool jazz and big-band R&B – but not a trace of the music which was supposed to be Rich's home, country. Even when he returned to his 1975 Nashville hit, 'Every Time You Touch Me', it came out as syncopated jazz. For a country star who'd always claimed Ellington and Stan Kenton as his heroes, it was a fitting conclusion.

30 Wanted: The Outlaws

The country counter-culture, 1971–1977: Willie Nelson; Waylon Jennings; the Armadillo World Headquarters; Doug Sahm; Austin, Texas; Jerry Jeff Walker; the Cosmic Cowboys; David Allan Coe

Three desperate men stared out from the poster, coarse hair and ragged beards wrapping their faces. With them was a woman, unashamedly meeting the observer's gaze. 'Wanted!', ran the headline above their portraits: 'The Outlaws'.

It was the most shameless marketing exercise that country music had ever known. The beneficiaries were Waylon Jennings, Willie Nelson, Jessi Colter and Tompall Glaser. In 1976, RCA Records combined their rock and country divisions to push this album into uncharted territory for a country release. *Rolling Stone* associate editor Chet Flippo was recruited to ease its acceptance by the rock audience. To his credit, he didn't oversell the hype: 'There was effected a major shift in country music. "Progressive country" was on the map. And these are the people responsible for that. Call them outlaws, call them innovators, call them revolutionaries, call them what you will, they're just some damned fine people who are also some of the most gifted songwriters and singers anywhere.'

Thanks to a publicity campaign far in excess of Nashville's usual budgets, *Wanted! The Outlaws* became the first platinum country album. 'There had never been a country record that did that,' Waylon Jennings admitted later. 'I had to have someone tell me what platinum was.'

Three of the so-called Outlaws had at least earned their reputation. Tompall Glaser was the first country star to realize that by forming his own management, production and publishing companies, he could wrest creative approval – and more lucrative deals – from Nashville's power brokers. 'I talked to people,' he explained, 'then went home, formed a production company, incorporated it, called myself president and went back and talked to the same motherfucker and got another $100,000. I thought, "So that's what we've been missing." '

Glaser's businesses were housed in a studio complex nicknamed Hillbilly Central. In 1972, he convinced his tenant Waylon Jennings to strike a similar blow for independence. After almost a decade of answering to his producers' instructions, Jennings was finally able to call the shots on 1973's *Honky Tonk Heroes* album. He duly became the architect of Outlaw philosophy – before puncturing the hype with a song pointedly entitled 'Don't You Think This Outlaw Bit's Done Got Out Of Hand'.

A third Outlaw, Jessi Colter, won her status as Jennings' wife, though she'd already laid claim to rebel colours by taking her stage name from an authentic nineteenth-century outlaw, her distant relative Jesse Colter of the James Gang.

The final member was perhaps the least likely Outlaw of them all. Until the late sixties, Texan singer-songwriter Willie Nelson had been a local cult hero, acclaimed as the composer of country standards, but distrusted for his jazz timing and eclectic repertoire. Plump then, and unfashionably square, he was not ideal hippie material. But by (the cynic's view) astute marketing or (the idealist's choice) letting his true spirit run free, the straitlaced conformist of 1968 became a cosmic cowboy in the seventies, a weed-smoking, biker-friendly, bandanna-wearing son of a gun. 'It's hard for me to identify with those old photos, with the short hair,' Nelson admits today. 'It wasn't the same guy.'

That evolution was harder to chart through his music, but in 1975 Nelson signed to Columbia, to whom he delivered his third concept album in four years. Even that inveterate dreamer of rock operas, Pete Townshend, wouldn't have been so bold. Nelson's *Red Headed Stranger* was a quasi-religious, quasi-mythical piece, linking vintage country hits and original compositions with music so ethereal it might have been scored in gossamer. This sparse offering rivalled *Wanted! The Outlaws* as the best-selling country album to date – once, that is, Columbia's executives had rescinded their decision to veto the release of this 'commercially suicidal' product.

*

Here were musicians ripe for mythology, and *Wanted! The Outlaws* provided it. The smokescreen of publicity obscured the fact that this was not a coherent revolutionary statement, but a random selection of material to which RCA had easy access, almost all of it previously released.

'RCA producer Jerry Bradley called me in 1975 to ask me to write liner notes,' wrote Chet Flippo a decade later. ' "I'll send you tapes on it," he told me, "but I'll bet you heard most of it before. What I'm doing is I'm putting Willie and Waylon and Tompall together as the Outlaws, because that's the way they are regarded here in town. This is a total package that I'm looking to break outside the country market." '

Another myth contends that the Outlaws were unknown in rock circles before 1976. Not so: *Village Voice* critic Robert Christgau might memorably have complained in 1972 that 'Waylon lets you know he has balls by singing as if someone is twisting them,' but Flippo told *Rolling Stone* readers that year that Jennings 'has more than once been called the best country singer in the world and at times he lives up to that impossible title', while dubbing Nelson 'the most underrated writer in America today'.

The very nature of the Outlaws' rebellion was undermined by their album. 'I produced that record,' Waylon boasted. 'I was the one who put it all together.' 'Waylon is a very smart cookie,' countered RCA A&R supremo Chet Atkins, who, as his former producer, found himself in the enemy camp. 'He knows the value of publicity, of getting his name in the paper because he's fighting the establishment. He told me one day, "Willie thinks fighting the establishment is double-parking on Music Row." No, that was a PR thing. On that album, I produced several sides, as did other producers in Nashville, but the producers weren't listed. It was like they had gone in and made those sides against the wishes of the Nashville establishment, which was not true at all.'

In Atkins' eyes, the rebellion was purely cosmetic: 'The only thing that's different about those guys is that they had beards. Waylon doesn't wash his hair all that often, and he wears a lot of leather. He's real macho. Willie wears that headband and looks pretty funky. That's the way they fight the establishment. The kids who buy the records think that they're their kind of guys, that they're against adults and everything.' Or, as Brenda Lee put it: 'The younger crowd can identity with a guy singing country if he's got blue jeans on and an Indian headband. It's not the music that's influenced them at all.'

Like the album which sold it to the world, the outlaw movement wasn't exactly what it seemed. The trigger was songwriter Lee Clayton, who penned 'Ladies Love Outlaws' in 1972 as a sly comment on the romantic kudos of acting the outsider: 'Ladies love outlaws like babies love stray dogs,' ran the chorus, 'Outlaws touch ladies somewhere deep down in their souls.' One verse even told the tale of Jessi and 'Waymore', who 'had a reputation as a ladies' man'.

Jennings duly cut the song, which lent its name to an album – completed by RCA studio personnel while Waylon was in the hospital with hepatitis. 'The only good thing about that album is the cover,' Jennings says today.

A few months later, a North Carolina DJ was talking to Hazel Smith – the publicity director for the cabal of country singers who hung out at Hillbilly Central. When he asked if Glaser's friends had a name for their style, she thought back to Waylon's record and suggested Outlaw Music.

'I looked it up in the encyclopaedia,' she explained to Outlaw chronicler Michael Bane, 'and found that it meant someone who lived on the outside of the law. And I knew people like Willie and Waylon and Tompall, David Allan Coe, Jimmy Buffett, Kristofferson, who were not going along with the Music Row establishment. So I figured they could be living on the outside of the law.' Her description stuck.

Even without 'Ladies Love Outlaws', Jennings was an obvious recipient of the outlaw tag. Ever since he'd been trapped into Chet Atkins' Folk-Country scheme, he'd been chipping away at the boundaries of legitimate behaviour in Nashville. His pill-popping antics were just about acceptable: Hank Williams himself had ingested his calories in liquid or capsule form. But confronting the industry was more dangerous.

'They wouldn't let you do anything,' Jennings recalls. 'You had to dress a certain way: you had to do everything a certain way.

They wanted me to look like an alien. They kept trying to destroy me, but they destroyed themselves, and their whole system. I just went about my business, and did things my way.'

In the early seventies, Nashville exerted strict control over the music-making process. In the studio, the label executives ruled. They vetoed the material, selected the musicians, OK'd the mixes, and conceived the artwork. The same constraints had been banished from rock in the mid-sixties by the artistic and financial strength of the Beatles, Bob Dylan and Brian Wilson, but throughout the country industry, the pyramid of rule from above prevailed into the early seventies.

Waylon Jennings knew that his albums were a pale shadow of what he delivered on the road. In 1972, he confronted Chet Atkins: either he was freed from the studio system, or he'd ride out the last year of his deal without promoting his new releases. Pointing to a photo on Chet's wall of Willie Nelson, who'd recently escaped the label, Jennings snapped: 'You screwed up with that guy. Don't lose out on me.'

Atkins had to give way. That December, Waylon took his road band into the studio – and the difference was audible on every track. The productions were tighter and more imposing. The pulse that drove his live shows – the metronomic beat of Richie Albright's bass drum, against the jew's-harp drone of Waylon's lead guitar – now filled his records. RCA even repackaged his back catalogue with artwork befitting an outlaw. Although he hadn't yet won the degree of artistic freedom that most rock acts assumed by right in the late sixties, Jennings was now the most liberated artist signed to one of the old-school Nashville offices.

Atlantic Records didn't play by the Nashville rulebook. New York's premier R&B label had championed artistic innovation since the early fifties. Their output was a testament to benevolent dictatorship, the ethos which spawned the most enduring American music of the pre-Beatles era. Like Sam Phillips at Sun, Atlantic bosses Ahmet and Nesuhi Ertegun, and later Jerry Wexler, married quality control to a spirit of artistic licence which positively rewarded innovation. During the late sixties, the label that had already propelled Ray Charles, Wilson Pickett and Aretha

Frankin to stardom began to invest in underground rock. Soon the R&B stalwart was also home to Crosby, Stills, Nash and Young, Led Zeppelin and Yes.

In 1971, Wexler visited Nashville, eager to extend Atlantic's reach into another market. His goal was crossover – not to Top 40 pop, but to the rock audience whose contempt for the traditions of the white South contrasted with their respect for the pioneers of blues and soul.

An early signing to Atlantic's Nashville division was Doug Sahm, the San Francisco-based Texan who'd brought his passion for blues and country into the arena of psychedelic rock. In Sahm, Wexler recognized a kindred spirit, a man who knew the value of both Bob Wills and T-Bone Walker.

At a party in songwriter Harlan Howard's Nashville home, in October 1971, Wexler found the other pivot of his country roster. He watched a singer glide through a subtle song-suite about the break-up of a marriage – phrasing like a jazzman, slipping around the beat with uncanny precision, and echoing his unique timing on the nylon strings of a customized Martin guitar.

The singer was Willie Nelson, who recounted the scene in his autobiography: 'When I finished, a stranger came up and said, "I'm Jerry Wexler. We're starting a country division at Atlantic, and I run it. I'd love to have the album you just sang." I said, "I have been looking for you for a long time."'

Nelson empathized with Wexler's eclectic tastes. 'I've always thought, instinctively, that there are no differences between people as far as music is concerned,' he says today. 'Before anyone had thought up rock'n'roll, I'd listen to boogie-woogie, blues, jazz. I loved Hank Williams, Ernest Tubb, Bob Wills, of course. But I also listened to Bing Crosby – and Sinatra. The older I get, the more I realize that Sinatra was my favourite singer of them all.'

'[Nelson's] a jazz singer,' says Don Was, who produced him in the nineties. 'He's got more in common with Little Jimmy Scott, or Sinatra, than with Hank Williams or Lefty Frizzell, in his phrasing. And he improvises every night. I don't know if that's conscious or subconscious, but that's his genius.' Nelson doesn't even want to consider the question: 'I really don't think about it. I just do it. I respond to the way the music sounds. It's easier to do that than to try and remember how I sang it last time.'

With his band, the Family, Nelson delivered shows that were spontaneous but tightly disciplined. 'We know the songs and the chord progressions,' he explains, 'and we've got some head arrangements going. But as far as who's gonna do what, and what notes we're gonna play, we really don't know.'

That approach didn't translate easily into the Nashville studio system. 'Nobody would record him because they thought he sung funny,' recalled Joe Allison, who produced Nelson in the early sixties. 'We decided that the best approach would be just to play rhythm behind him, and stay the hell out of his way.'

His début album, *And Then I Wrote*, emphasized his talent: by 1963, Nelson had penned standards for Ray Price ('Night Life'), Patsy Cline ('Crazy'), Billy Walker ('Funny How Time Slips Away') and Faron Young ('Hello Walls'). The record was cut partly in Nashville and partly in Los Angeles, where Nelson worked with sessionmen such as Glen Campbell and Leon Russell.

Signed to RCA in late 1964, Nelson entered the fortress of the Nashville Sound, where he struggled to preserve the skeleton of his identity: 'I knew those records didn't sound the way I wanted them to. But there was nothing I could do about it.'

The road offered a sense of liberation. Nelson left the sixties as a slightly ill-at-ease figure in roll-necks and shades, like a salesman who'd once seen a TV show about flower-power. But his band members were stretching the dress-codes of country. Guitarist Jimmy Day laid down the manifesto in 1969: 'The old image of the haystacks and the hound dog chewing on the bone is gone. Uniforms are for the military. We dress and wear our hair like we want to. There's more people nowadays with long hair than without, and if they don't have long hair it's because they don't have enough.'

Nelson grew out his hair in the early seventies, toying with a mid-sixties Beatle cut. But his music was several steps ahead: 1971's *Yesterday's Wine* album opened with a conversation between Willie and God, the singer doing most of the talking. 'Do you know why you're here?' quizzed the Creator. 'Yes,' Nelson replied with the certainty of a missionary. 'There is great confusion here on earth, and the power that is has concluded the following. Perfect man has visited earth already, and his voice is heard. The voice of imperfect man must now be made manifest. And I have been selected as the most likely candidate' – chosen, as God went on to explain, because he was a double Taurus.

The 'great confusion' was also felt in RCA's marketing department, which had to promote a record that zigzagged from spirituality to the sins of the flesh. In 'Me And Paul', a nod to his veteran drummer Paul English, Nelson evoked the outlaw spirit two years early: 'Nashville was the roughest . . . I guess Nashville wasn't right for me and Paul.' The song contained country's first oblique reference to the marijuana that had been Nelson's regular consolation since the mid-fifties: 'Almost busted in Laredo, but for reasons that I'd rather not disclose.'

Two days before Christmas 1970, Nelson's Nashville home burned to the ground. The news interrupted a writing session on a tune called 'What Can You Do To Me Now'. The local press recounted how Nelson dived into the burning building for his guitar case, but not that he was retrieving the marijuana stash he'd hidden there. He interpreted the fire as a sign, and quit Nashville, taking over the aptly named Happy Valley Dude Ranch in Bandera, Texas.

Every time he slipped into the state capital, Austin, for a date, he noticed the changes: 'We used to play these real redneck joints. There'd be all these mean-looking guys there, throwing back shots of whiskey. But every now and then you'd see a long-haired guy come in, with hippie-style clothes, and smoking a joint. First there'd just be one or two, but gradually, over a few months, more and more started to appear.'

Nelson conceived a grand design: 'I knew it would be difficult to get the hippies and the rednecks, together. But I knew they all loved country music. The rednecks might want to kill the hippies, while the hippies might hate everything the rednecks stood for, but they both loved Hank Williams and Bob Wills.'

'He was our link,' admits Ray Benson, long-haired leader of the western swing band Asleep At The Wheel. 'Everyone liked to get high, and liked to have a beer. We loved country music, but we were also counter-culture. Willie got turned on with the rest of us. He got psychedelicized.'

The crime scene was a vacant National Armory building, situated opposite the Cactus Club – an Austin honky-tonk that opened its doors to local acid-rockers like Shiva's Head Band. The focal point of the city's psychedelic rock scene was the Vulcan Gas Co., which inspired freak-form poster art, in the vein of Rick Griffin's designs for Bill Graham's halls in San Francisco.

Shiva's agent Eddie Wilson viewed the empty building as a possible community arts centre, doubling as a rehearsal studio, concert hall and haven for the Austin underground. In July 1970, Shiva's 'company', Armadillo Productions, unveiled the Armadillo World Headquarters with a gig by Tracy Nelson and Mother Earth, who were about to augment their psychedelic blues-rock with some Texas country.

Though artist Jim Shelton designed the venue's posters, it was his underground namesake Gilbert Shelton who drew the first drug-crazed Austin 'dillo. The armour-plated mammal had become an unofficial student motif in the mid-sixties; in 1971, the armadillo was adopted as the official University of Texas mascot. Slow and lazy, it was a natural source of amused admiration for students permanently high on Mexican grass and peyote.

Financial need forced the Armadillo to broaden its scope in the early seventies. With visits from top California acid-rock bands a rarity, the venue opened its doors to musicians beyond the ambit of underground rock. Some bills mixed classical and rock performers; others incorporated dance or film. But the promoters couldn't afford to ignore anyone with commercial appeal, no matter how remote they seemed from the ambience of the venue.

On 12 August 1972, Willie Nelson visited the Armadillo World Headquarters for the first time. 'When I played in Austin,' he recalls, 'I used to play places like the Broken Spoke, a honky-tonk club. Then I realized I could play there and at the Armadillo as well, but to different crowds. And then the two crowds started to become one.'

As Nelson explains, 'Young people were picking up on country music – not so much country singers, but musicians like Gram Parsons and Commander Cody. The first time I played the

Armadillo, I knew that there was a future in this for me. I knew I could reach the kids who were listening to those country-rock performers, as well as the traditional ones who'd always been listening to my music.'

Nelson fell in with Mad Dog Inc., a hippie collective intent on performing 'indefinable services for mankind'. This unlikely teaming was mirrored a few weeks later, when another country star graced the venue: 'I called up Waylon Jennings, and said, "Listen, you have to come and see what's happening down here. There's hippie kids listening to country music!"' Jennings takes up the story: 'So I went down there innocently, and looked out at the crowd. Everyone in the hall seemed to have long hair, except me and the band. I dragged Willie out and said, "What the hell have you gotten me into?" He smiled at me and said, "Don't worry about a thing, hoss. Trust me." And I'll be damned if he wasn't right.' After an opening set from Commander Cody, who delivered truckers' anthems with a hippie sensibility, Jennings performed his traditional repertoire of hard-edged Texas country. As Ray Benson recalls, 'He and Willie were accepted by both camps. The country fans still loved them, but so did the counter-culture.'

This was the Willie Nelson whom Jerry Wexler signed as his flagship for Atlantic's country division. His first album was *Shotgun Willie*, a wonderfully ramshackle collection that reeked the sweet scent of marijuana. Wexler encouraged him to think beyond the trusted coterie of Nashville sessionmen. 'We had people like David Bromberg, Doug Sahm and Leon Russell come and play on that record,' Nelson remembers. 'Leon had been this quiet, clean-cut kid at my early sixties sessions. Then my daughter told me I had to listen to a record by a guy called Joe Cocker. I hadn't heard of him, so I didn't get around to it. She sat me down and made me listen to *Mad Dogs And Englishmen*.'

The live double-album documented a 1970 tour which was almost the breaking-point of Cocker's career. The idol of Woodstock had booked one US concert jaunt too many, with no financial support, and no band. His friend Leon Russell intervened, throwing together an instant supergroup, then sketching a thrilling set of horn arrangements unmatched since Ray Charles was in his prime.

'When I listened to that record,' Willie continues, 'I was amazed by the arrangements. I realized it was Leon, so I made a point of checking him out when he was playing. I thought it was the most incredible show I'd ever seen – not just the visual impact, with the top hat and the long hair and beard and all of that theatrical stuff he did, but the music, and the way it ranged from solo ballads through to out-and-out rock'n'roll. The first time after that I could meet him, I took the chance.'

Shotgun Willie sounded nothing like *Mad Dogs And Englishmen*, but neither did it connect with anything ever recorded in Nashville. When the sessions stalled, Willie retired to his hotel and penned some self-deprecating autobiography. Country had never been this laid-back: 'Shotgun Willie sits around in his underwear, biting on a bullet, pulling out all of his hair.' 'Kris Kristofferson told me later the song was "mind farts",' Willie wrote in his autobiography. 'Maybe so, but I thought of it more as clearing my mind.' And clearing his career of the past.

Doug Sahm's blend of black and white, hippie and redneck, beer and marijuana, exemplified the Armadillo spirit. But as that venue opened, Sahm was in Nashville, coaxing country picking out of session pros who'd never met anyone so disconnected from music-industry convention. As ever, he had a surprise in store. He might have followed his fellow Texan, Michael Nesmith, into playing psychedelic country-rock. Instead, he conjured up one of his many spirit guides, Hank Williams, for a session which revealed Sahm to be as natural a country singer as he was an acid-rocker or a Texas bluesman.

So convincing was his immersion in the Nashville experience that Mercury issued a sparkling honky-tonk two-step called 'Be Real' as a single, by the pseudonymous Wayne Douglas. Several country stations duly took the bait. Equally 'authentic' was a tune he'd written for Tracy Nelson. At a time when the sight of David Bowie wearing a 'man's dress' could outrage rock fans, Sahm crooning 'I Wanna Be Your Mama Again' over a crisp Nashville track was deemed too subversive to release.

There was nothing that strange on *Doug Sahm And Friends*, another of Atlantic's baptismal country releases – except maybe his raucous duet with Bob Dylan on a Charley Pride hit, 'Is Anybody Going To San Antone'; or their collaboration on the Delmore Brothers' country-blues anthem, 'Blues Stay Away From Me'. It was an almost schizophrenic record, with no middle ground between these sprawling, hillbilly romps and some streamlined T-Bone Walker blues.

Sahm fathered a more coherent hybrid on two 1974 records, *Texas Tornado* (which later christened his country/Tex-Mex band) and *Groover's Paradise*, which placed him against the Creedence Clearwater Revival rhythm section. By then, the great Atlantic country experiment was over. The imprint survived long enough to release Nelson's *Phases And Stages* – the study of marital failure which had originally enticed Wexler. A few months later, New York executives examined the accounts, and abruptly closed the Nashville office down. Wexler and the Atlantic board realized the kudos of keeping Nelson on the roster, but were generous enough to release him when he complained about dealing long-distance with the hierarchy in New York.

Atlantic weren't the only label burned in Nashville. In 1973, Southern rock specialists Capricorn, home of the Allman Brothers, amazed Music City by signing Kitty Wells – the 54-year-old Queen of Country Music, the first woman to tackle such 'unseemly' subjects as adultery and drunkenness in a country song. Though it had been seven years since her last hit, label boss Phil Walden promised that Wells would receive as much promotion as the Allmans.

Instead, Capricorn struggled for material to suit the demands of seventies country and Wells' own taste. A stray single struggled to No. 94 on the charts, but otherwise the liaison proved barren. Wells was elected to the Country Music Hall of Fame in 1976, prompting Ringo Starr to boast that she was his favourite singer. Three months later, she filed a lawsuit against Capricorn, alleging that they had refused to release any of her product. 'We've been unable to turn her career around,' Walden admitted. 'It's a classic example of when the expectations of neither party are realized.' The experiences of Atlantic and Capricorn helped to dissuade other outsiders from venturing into Nashville.

*

Austin was a different matter. KOKE-FM (rarely has a radio station been so aptly titled) developed a playlist based on 'progressive country'. This rainbow coalition stretched from such outlaw pioneers as Nelson and Jennings to the unashamedly hippie hillbilly of Commander Cody and the New Riders Of The Purple Sage.

It also showcased Texas writers who slotted between the outlaws and the singer-songwriters who populated Los Angeles. The most mercurial was Willis Alan Ramsey, who surfaced in 1972 with a remarkable album that married the acoustic styles of Crosby, Stills and Nash, James Taylor, Neil Young and English rocker Terry Reid. He recorded one tune with the musicians who'd worked on Young's *Harvest* LP; another with Leon Russell adding delicate touches on vibes and electric piano; and more with rock session aces such as Jim Keltner, Leland Sklar and Russ Kunkel. Few talents have emerged so fully formed, making it all the more mysterious that Ramsey hasn't recorded since.

Stephen Fromholz survived longer, though never assuming more than cult status. He'd briefly toured with Stephen Stills, but rapidly became disillusioned and disgusted by the rapacious milieu of the rock'n'roll star. His showpiece was 'Texas Trilogy', a song-suite which came close to capturing the small-town insights of Sherwood Anderson's story sequence, *Winesburg, Ohio*. He also wrote 'I'd Have To Be Crazy', which came to life in the hands of Willie Nelson: 'I'd have to be weird to grow me a beard, just to see what the rednecks would do.'

Like Fromholz, Townes Van Zandt inhabited the fringes of country music. In another era and town, he'd have been a Greenwich Village folkie, a rival to Tim Hardin, Fred Neil and Phil Ochs. His writing was intelligent and novelistic – and his most famous song, 'Pancho And Lefty', was translated seamlessly into country both by Emmylou Harris, and by Merle Haggard and Willie Nelson. He was a staple of the Austin scene, hymned by Steve Earle and Emmylou Harris as 'the greatest songwriter in the world', who veered no closer to rock than the arty orchestrations of his early albums. The flatness of his voice mirrored the bleak landscape of West Texas, but he carefully avoided the country

signifiers – fiddle, pedal steel, hillbilly imagery – adopted by most
of his contemporaries.

In the voice of his close friend Guy Clark, you could catch the
authentic note of Texas. Though he's admired as a writer in
Nashville, not least for penning one of the era's most enduring
songs, 'Desperadoes Waiting For A Train', Clark has enjoyed only
the mildest of flirtations with the mainstream country audience.
He's the archetypal Texan singer-songwriter, reaching back into
the rural past to fill songs such as 'Desperadoes' and 'Texas 1947'
with piquant images of local smells, sounds and tastes. (An early
album was called *Texas Cookin'*: something in the cuisine of the
Lone Star State encourages its inhabitants to sing about food.)

In 1975 Clark joined RCA, only to be faced with the same
battles as Waylon Jennings: 'They couldn't understand why I just
couldn't go into the studio with six sessionmen I'd never met and
make a nice comfortable country album. But I wanted people
who'd commit themselves musically to my work. *Old No. 1* ended
up as a mixture of demo tapes and things we'd done at odd times.'
But it evoked Texas as skilfully as any record of its era.

The man who popularized Clark's work was Jerry Jeff Walker,
the uncrowned king of Austin's 'progressive country'. He was
born Ron Crosby, deep in New York State, closer to Canada than
to Manhattan. In the mid-sixties he changed his name to play
psychedelic rock with Circus Maximus before drifting into the
Greenwich Village folk scene. Emmylou Harris was on the same
circuit, and she borrowed some of his songs as early as 1967. The
next year he wrote 'Mr Bojangles' – a tearjerker that became a pop
hit, and Richard Nixon's favourite song.

Neither accolade suited Walker's taste, and in 1971 he moved
south-west to Austin. There he fell in with some country-rock
corruptibles called the Austin Interchangeable Band. They
mutated into the Lost Gonzo Band, and for a few glorious years in
the mid-seventies, Walker and the Gonzos presented the ultimate
Austin experience. Walker never let his Texas mask slip for a
second, while the Gonzos played with an exuberance that rivalled
Bob Dylan's Rolling Thunder Revue.

For his 1973 album, *Viva Terlingua!*, Walker took over a ghost
town called Luckenbach, Texas, doubling its population when he

imported his band. There he cut tunes that have filled his repertoire ever since, from 'Gettin' By' ('Hello again, buckaroos') to Ray Wiley Hubbard's satirical sequel to Merle Haggard's 'Okie From Muskogee', 'Up Against The Wall, Redneck Mother'. The music roared like a long night in a cheap bar, but the evening ended in sentimentality, as Lost Gonzo guitarist Gary P. Nunn crooned 'London Homesick Blues'.

That song's chorus was purloined as the theme to a long-running PBS concert show, *Austin City Limits*. 'I want to go home to the Armadillo,' Nunn sang plaintively, as the credits rolled images that made Austin look like a cross between Harvard and Woodstock. *Austin City Limits* showcased the city's vibrant music scene from 1976, attracting performers as diverse as Ray Charles and Tammy Wynette, Neil Young and Bob Wills' Original Texas Playboys. Meanwhile, bands like the Cowboy Twinkies filled the city's bars, mixing Hendrix and Led Zeppelin tunes with their Texas country. It all added to the mystique of 'the Anti-Nashville'.

For some Austinites, mystique was the last thing they needed. 'This has always been an anti-commercial scene,' artist Jim Franklin complained in 1974. 'That's why most people moved here. The musicians are content to play the same clubs and smoke their dope and drink their beer. How do you take an atmosphere that's suspicious of capitalism and heavily anti-commercial, and market it?'

When executives like Atlantic's Jerry Wexler arrived in town, the locals did their best to play down the hype. 'I keep hearing about this great Austin scene,' Wexler griped to *Rolling Stone* in 1973, 'but whenever I ask who I should sign, nobody seems to know. Is it a mirage down there?'

The question vexed Michael Martin Murphey, a Texas songwriter who'd once written tunes for his pal Mike Nesmith in the Monkees. He'd since penned a country-rock concept album, *Calico Silver*, for Kenny Rogers, before launching a solo career. His first album, 1972's *Geronimo's Cadillac*, was an underground country classic. But it was '(I Want To Be A) Cosmic Cowboy' which really caught people's attention. 'I meant it as satire,' Murphey explained, 'but people here took it seriously, and now we've got a bunch of long-haired rednecks running around. I get calls every day from hucksters.' In the same breath, he was calling Doug Sahm 'the original cosmic cowboy'. Sahm was no more restrained, billing himself as the Texas Tornado and recording songs like 'You Can't Hide A Redneck (Under That Hippy Hair)'.

Once *Rolling Stone*'s reporters gave way to *Time* and *Newsweek*, and 'Austin' became shorthand for anyone in country music with long hair, the city's isolation was ended. *Austin City Limits* remained America's most eclectic TV music show; but the cosmic cowboy grew ever closer to Michael Martin Murphey's pastiche. Financial problems drained the joy from the Armadillo, which closed at the end of 1980, and was demolished to make way for a hotel. Another bastion of progressive country, the Soap Creek Saloon, followed it into liquidation. Doug Sahm, the last remaining Austin icon, opined that the city 'had gone down the tubes', and declared that he'd found a new artistic utopia in Amsterdam. Willie Nelson still came to town, but he played the salubrious Texas Opry House. 'If musicians stop in Nashville, they're not gonna sound any different than if they stop in Austin,' he announced in 1982. 'It just doesn't make any sense.'

In the spring of 1972, a field outside Austin housed the First Annual Dripping Springs Reunion. Staged by entrepreneurs from Dallas, the festival was hyped as a country Woodstock. The promoters explored traditional and progressive strands of country, booking veterans like Tex Ritter and Roy Acuff alongside Waylon Jennings, Willie Nelson and Kris Kristofferson. Leon Russell was recruited to drag in stray rock fans. The venue lived up to its name (and the memory of Woodstock) by enduring a torrential downpour. The Dallas promoters duly took a bath.

A year later, Willie Nelson turned promoter for the first of his Annual Picnics. These exposed anything from 20,000 to 150,000 fans to the scorching Texas heat of Independence Day weekend, where they were stripped of refreshments as they entered the site, and left to fend off heatstroke, exhaustion and an occasional assault from rattlesnakes as they watched Nelson jam with country and rock guests. 'Suddenly the Woodstock kids became the Austin kids,' explained promoter Tom Gresham. 'Willie came out of the Picnic a charismatic figure with an enormous audience.'

The new Nelson was unrecognizable as the man who'd played Texas dancehalls in a suit and tie. The hair that once fringed his collar now cascaded down his back. A straggling beard shadowed his face. His smart casual clothes were replaced with a T-shirt and blue jeans. Across his head he casually placed a red bandanna. The hip salesman of the late sixties had taken on the aura of a native savant, whose wisdom – fuelled by his copious intake of sacred weed – passed all understanding.

Billy Sherrill at Columbia Records was the man who inherited the services of this guru. The champion of crossover, who'd turned the reluctant Charlie Rich into an international star, he seemed ideally placed to craft a Willie Nelson record that could stretch across the radio dial.

Nelson chose to keep his distance from Sherrill's domain on Nashville's Music Row. Instead, he spent three days, and no more than $20,000, in Garland, Texas, recording a cowboy opera, a tale of violent death and the cleansing power of love called *Red Headed Stranger*. 'We'd go in the studio about dark and stay until three or four in the morning,' he explained in his autobiography. 'The first night we laid all the tracks. The second night we overdubbed and fixed the parts where I blew a line. The third day we mixed it. And not long afterward we had a gorilla of a hit and we became famous and lived happily ever after.'

It wasn't quite that simple. When Nelson delivered the tapes, Sherrill assumed he'd been sent a collection of demos for an album, and rang the singer to schedule some orchestrations. But Nelson's deal allowed him unprecedented artistic freedom, leaving Columbia's executives powerless to halt the album's release.

Sherrill's doubts were easy to comprehend. *Red Headed Stranger* was a complex weave of themes and motifs, with nothing to clothe the skeleton of Nelson's voice and guitar. Worse still, it held no trace of Austin rhetoric – no cosmic cowboys, no hippies, not a hint of the cross-generational appeal which had persuaded Sherrill to offer Nelson a deal.

Equally troubling was the song selection, which hinged around country tunes that pre-dated rock'n'roll. Why was Nelson reviving Eddy Arnold flipsides from the early forties? Was there even a nostalgic market for 'Blue Eyes Crying In The Rain', written by Fred Rose in the final weeks of the Second World War?

Columbia executives feared not. The album 'didn't follow the formula, the fashionable mix of the day', reflected the label's marketing head, Rick Blackburn: 'There were a thousand reasons why that record should not be a hit. But the *Red Headed Stranger* project took on Willie's personality and became a hit for all the right reasons – because it was Willie Nelson.'

Red Headed Stranger and *Wanted! The Outlaws* competed at the top of the country charts in early 1976. 'Blue Eyes Crying In The Rain' became the most-played song on country radio, then crossed into pop, exactly the way Billy Sherrill would have wanted.

While Nelson was bridging one ideological divide, Waylon Jennings was exploring the precarious territory between country and rock. In 1973, his New York-based manager Neil Reshen booked him into the city's most notorious venue, Max's Kansas City. The site of Lou Reed's last stand with the Velvet Underground in 1970 was the clubhouse for the Andy Warhol clique, who lapped up the theatrical androgyny of bands like the New York Dolls. But the jukebox at Max's had always been filled with country records.

RCA packed the club with press on opening night, but thereafter, Waylon was on his own. He arrived for the first show in combative mood: 'I hope you all like what we do,' he snapped, 'because if you don't, don't ever come to Nashville. We'll kick the hell out of you!' The New York Dolls couldn't have said it better.

That year, Jennings also shared a San Francisco stadium bill with the Grateful Dead. The Dead's spin-off band, the New Riders Of The Purple Sage, courted the vast crowd with tales of hippies, cowboys and dope scams, before Jennings delivered an earthier version of the same music.

'That was not an idea that worked,' he admits today. 'The Grateful Dead have such dyed-in-the-wool, fanatical fans that nobody can open for them. They wanted me to do it again, but I said no. And I didn't feel any musical bond with the Dead. I'm not a Dead fan. I love the guitar, but that's about it. I don't like their harmonies, or anything like that. It's all a little further out than I am used to.'

That was exactly how Nashville regarded Waylon Jennings. Having ignored him for years, the Country Music Association had to acknowledge his commercial success in 1974, when he'd scored back-to-back No. 1 singles. Not that their tribute was exactly effusive: 'They wanted me to come out during their awards show and sing one verse, less than a minute, of "Ramblin' Man",' Waylon snarls, still riled by the incident twenty-five years later. 'I said, "Why don't I just hang a sign round my neck that says 'Ramblin' Man' and dance across the stage?" I was only trying to be funny, but they said, "Why don't you leave, we don't need you here anyway." Actually, they had one too many artists and they were trying to get rid of one. And I said, "Well, you know what, you're right. You don't need me. But you might have to eat your words one day." And sure enough, a year or two later they had to give me a bunch of awards one night, and I wouldn't show up. That made them look kinda silly.' A diehard fan writing to *Country Music* magazine around this time aimed the same accusation at Jennings: 'I can't believe Waylon Jennings. What has happened to this man? He looked like a pig (and I don't mean policeman) and sounded worse. Can it be that pot has crept into country music?'

Cocaine and pills were Jennings' drugs of choice in this era; like Nelson, his appearance suggested that he was more hippie than redneck. But until 1975, his shift in attitude wasn't flagged by his music. After the CMA Awards débâcle, Jennings began to compose a tune called 'Music City Blues', which emerged as 'Are You Sure Hank Done It This Way'. The message was impossible to miss: 'Lord, it's the same old tune, fiddle and guitar, where do we take it from here? Rhinestone suits and big shiny cars, Lord, it's been the same way for years . . . We need a change.'

'I just wanted to play my music my way,' he reflects today. 'They wanted me to dress a certain way and kowtow to the CMA. And I remembered that Hank Williams had the same problem with WSM, the station that runs the *Opry*. They had such control over everything that they sent him down the road of no return. He was just a raw talent, and he didn't know what he was getting into.'

Jennings wasn't about to make the same mistake. His first album after the outlaw hype took its title from a song by Neil Young. Jennings relished the sturdy structure and steam-hammer rhythm of 'Are You Ready For The Country', but didn't care for Young's lyrics. 'I couldn't make sense of 'em', he says, 'so I changed them.'

The Outlaws' flirtation with rock continued when Nelson and Jennings were invited aboard Bob Dylan's Rolling Thunder Revue. Dylan's travelling circus had raged down the East Coast in the final weeks of 1975. With a mighty band to translate blues, folk, country and rock'n'roll into a giant American jubilee, Dylan breathed fire into songs new and old. Enticed aboard were musicians such as Joan Baez, Roger McGuinn, Joni Mitchell – and left-field Texan Kinky Friedman, another graduate of Tompall Glaser's Hillbilly Central. Friedman's confrontational lyrics and wicked humour scandalized Nashville, but fitted easily into a package that also held beat poet Allen Ginsberg and British glam-rocker Mick Ronson. The Rolling Thunder Revue regrouped in spring 1976 for a raid across the South, but the deeper Dylan ventured, the less enthusiastic the response. When there were shows scheduled in huge Texas amphitheatres, Dylan was forced to call on Willie Nelson to attract a crowd. The embarrassment punctured Dylan's enthusiasm, and Mid-Western dates were cancelled – robbing audiences of a bill which would have matched Dylan and Baez against Waylon Jennings, Leon Russell and the Marshall Tucker Band.

Most opposition to the Outlaws came from within the country industry – from the same veterans, in fact, who were appalled by the public's penchant for country pop. Cavorting with rock stars was no more acceptable than aiming at Hollywood. Outflanked on both sides, the traditionalists relied on moral certainty to pull them through. 'Willie Nelson will never replace Hank Snow,' reckoned Faron Young as he surveyed a chart now dominated by Willie and his friends. But Snow was facing commercial annihilation. 'I predicted that rock'n'roll wouldn't last more than five years,' he admitted, 'but I was very wrong. It took a great hold on the younger generation on account of the beat. It's just a bunch of noise, which covers up the singer.'

One country singer dared to criticize the Outlaws for being too conservative. David Allan Coe hailed from Akron, Ohio, which has no country heritage. But in 1967, he drove into Nashville with a stash of songs and a trailer on which was painted: 'Mysterious Rhinestone Cowboy'. Stories about this tattooed figure began to circulate through Music City – how he'd journeyed to Tennessee from Ohio State Prison, where he'd served time on death row after beating to death a fellow prisoner. He dressed like a biker, could handle a Harley-Davidson, and wore his long hair greased over his leather jacket – none of which annulled the fact that he was also a skilled songwriter.

The song which convinced Nashville he was more than a self-publicist was 'Tell Me Baby Can You Pray'. Billy Sherrill procured it for his teenage star, Tanya Tucker, and titled it after its most striking line: 'Would you lay with me in a field of stone'. It was an image of marital fidelity, which took on different connotations when sung by the 15-year-old Tucker. Though her career was strictly controlled by ambitious but ultra-respectable parents, Tucker was seized by the rock media as a trailer-trash Marie Osmond, country jail-bait. She later proved capable of attracting scandal on her own account, but the obscenity of 'Would You Lay With Me' was in the minds of the impure – including the country DJs who blacklisted the record until it was headed for No. 1.

David Allan Coe's career blossomed, and Nashville drew a frisson of excitement from its association with this particular Outlaw. Coe claimed that tag with pride: narrating his history in the third-person, like a self-obsessed sportsman, he boasted that 'The reason the term Outlaws came about was because David Allan Coe was a member of the Outlaws Motorcycle Club, and he got up on stage at a Waylon Jennings concert with his Outlaws colours on. His picture was taken, and the story said, "The Outlaws come to town".'

Not only did he christen the clan, he invented it: 'When I went to Nashville, I had long hair, I was wearing earrings, I had a beard – I was everything they were against. And I could sing better than any one of them.' And again: 'I was the first one to go in and use my band in the studio. But when Waylon became famous, someone said he was the first one to do that. It took me six months to talk Waylon into doing it.'

Coe named a 1975 album *Longhaired Redneck*, and reinforced his myth: 'Country DJs all think I'm an outlaw, They'd never come to see me in this dive, Where bikers stare at cowboys that are laughing at the hippies, Who are praying they'll get out of here alive.' To prove he knew the rock charts, he namechecked the Burritos and the Byrds as he staked his allegiance with 'Willie, Waylon And Me'.

Coe's rock credibility crumbled when *Rolling Stone* investigated his criminal past, and were unable to confirm that he'd ever done more than walk past death row. They declared him a 'rhinestone ripoff', and thereafter his crossover appeal was nil. The country market was more tolerant, shrugging off the exposé as long as he kept writing such classics as 'Take This Job And Shove It'. But Coe's involvement in a series of X-rated albums, and his delight in the Mormon custom of taking multiple wives, ensured that he would never win a CMA award.

He was certainly no match for Nelson and Jennings, who reinforced their market domination in 1977 by collaborating on a hit single, 'Luckenbach, Texas'. Journalists flocked to the Texas town, to discover a bar-owner, a domino board and a ready supply of beer. Anyone expecting to find Waylon Jennings was set for disappointment, however. He told audiences that he hated the song, and admitted: 'The guys that wrote the thing have never been to Luckenbach. Neither have I.' At the height of the Outlaw hype, that simply didn't matter. Country was now being marketed with the same manipulative skill as rock.

Dixie: A Diversion

In 1859, a theatre on Broadway in New York welcomed the
all-black Bryant's Minstrel Troupe. Their repertoire included a
routine entitled 'Plantation Song And Dance', and sub-titled
'Dixie's Land'. Six verses by Ohio composer Daniel D. Emmett
allowed the Troupe's leader to express his comic, yet wistful, wish
to be back on the plantation which had once been his home.
'Dixie's Land' imagined a world in which enslavement wasn't a
burden, but a reason to be alive. 'I wish I was in Dixie,' the Troupe
chimed, 'Hooray! Hooray!'

There was no historical Dixie, or Dixieland, and as Emmett's
song spread south, so it changed shape and meaning. In 1862,
when the Civil War erupted, 'Dixie's Land' became an anthem for
the Confederate Army – retaining the theme of the original, now
spiced with regional pride and military fervour. That 'Dixie' forms
the heart of Mickey Newbury's 'An American Trilogy', poised
uneasily between 'The Battle Hymn Of The Republic' (a Union
hymn from the same conflict, set to a tune written by a native
Southerner) and the slave lament turned folksong, 'All My
Trials'.

Thereafter, Dixie became a synonym for the South, especially
when identity was at stake. When Carl Perkins got 'Dixie Fried', it
wasn't on Californian wine or German beer, but liquor from
Tennessee. 'If Heaven ain't a lot like Dixie,' sang Hank Williams
Jr, 'I don't want to go.' The Band – four Canadians and one
genuine Southerner – lamented 'The Night They Drove Old Dixie
Down'.

And Emmett's melody never died. In 1992, John Anderson cut
Bobby Braddock's song 'Look Away'. 'The New South, thank
God, is still the same,' Hank Williams Jr had rejoiced, but
Braddock didn't see it that way. 'Dixie's had a facelift,' he wrote to
the familiar tune, 'I've heard she's lookin' better, but I kinda liked

the old one, I never will forget her' – and he spelled out what had been lost. As the Southernness of country music ebbed away in the mid-nineties, Braddock's words seemed strangely prophetic.

PART III
PARALLEL LINES

31 Hotel California

Country-rock, 1975–1999: the Eagles; Poco; Pure Prairie League; Chris Hillman; the Charlie Daniels Band; Alabama; the Dirt Band; the Desert Rose Band; Restless Heart; Diamond Rio; Great Plains; the Kentucky Headhunters; the Eagles reunion; the Mavericks

Little of the idealism of sixties country-rock survived beyond the mid-seventies. Under the twin pressures of cocaine and disco, the Los Angeles élite drifted into inertia, their artistic integrity buried beneath a slick layer of cynicism. More clear-sighted than their peers, the Eagles were able to maintain their momentum, but only at the expense of the country trimmings that had originally been their trademark.

'Society and music were becoming more urbanized and hard-edged,' theorized Eagles drummer Don Henley, 'and we changed with the times. Around 1976, when we made *Hotel California*, most traces of country had gone. With the addition of Joe Walsh and Don Felder to the group, we pretty much left the country influence behind. Disco and punk had come, and we wanted to rock.'

Not just rock: *Hotel California* reflected the widening world of rock culture, incorporating elements of blues, reggae and Latin music. There was suspicion about its pretensions – 'Don blew his literary nut on that album,' quipped Glenn Frey – but *Hotel California* set the tone for adult California rock over the next two decades. 'It's a song about loss of innocence,' Henley said of the title track, 'I was trying to use California as the microcosm for the rest of the nation.' He extended his theme of 'fading glory and decadence' on his solo albums, no doubt inspired by the self-indulgence that fuelled the Eagles' demise. As Frey recalled, they barely made it through their final shows in 1980: 'We were on stage in Long Beach, and Don Felder looks back at me and says, "Only three more songs until I kick your ass, pal." We were out there singing "Best Of My Love", but inside both of us were thinking, "As soon as this is over, I'm gonna kill him."'

By then, only journalistic laziness connected the Eagles with country-rock. There was no vestige of Gram Parsons and Chris Hillman's dream on *Hotel California* or its successor, *The Long Run* – or, indeed, Hillman's own albums from that period, or the equally vapid work produced by other Byrds/Burritos survivors.

Amid the debris, one strand of the scattered Los Angeles country-rock family remained true to the faith. After losing Richie Furay to David Geffen's grandiose scheming, Poco regrouped under the leadership of Paul Cotton, Rusty Young and Timothy Schmit. Albums such as *Seven*, *Cantamos* and *Head Over Heels* mixed smooth adult rock with eccentric country instrumentation. Given his head on 'Rocky Mountain Breakdown' and 'Sagebrush Serenade', Young evoked memories of old-time fiddling contests and banjo breakdowns, while the band's pristine vocal harmonies soared as clean as the Colorado mountain air. By 1976, Paul Cotton was voicing vague ambitions to emulate Aaron Copland's 'horse operas', *Rodeo* and *Billy The Kid*. 'It would be orchestrated,' he promised. 'Not so much country-rock, or whatever they call it, as western, which is what I think we really represent.'

Three months later, Poco released *Rose Of Cimarron*, with a title track that caught that epic quality. 'It filled my need to do some authentic country music,' Cotton explained later, as if bar-rooms always kept a string section in reserve. 'I wanted to get on the country charts, but not like the Eagles did, with a crossover.' But country radio, which had welcomed the Eagles' 'Lyin' Eyes' in 1975, chose to ignore 'Rose Of Cimarron'. 'What they say and what they sell are two very different things,' Cotton muttered darkly.

While country-rock tumbled into commercial insignificance by the late seventies, stymied as much by the failings of its protagonists as by a shift in public taste, Poco bucked the trend. In 1979, after Timothy Schmit and original drummer George Grantham had quit the band, they released the biggest-selling album of their entire career, *Legend*. It allowed them to cruise into the early eighties with albums that were little more than a pastiche of their early glories. Their 1981 Civil War concept record, *Blue And Gray*, and 1982's *Cowboys And Englishmen* signalled that their well was draining fast, and after the aptly named *Ghost Town* in 1983, Poco drifted quietly into retirement until the end of the decade.

Among those who retained their faith in country-rock, Poco's belated success was taken as some kind of validation. In 1975, British journalist Steve Burgess complained that 'The whole damn world's turned to Styrofoam, and the Eagles are the prestige band, even though they were musically bankrupt by the end of *Desperado*.' Burgess and his ilk clutched at even the faintest hope of relief – not just Poco's renaissance, but the birth of Firefall, who included original Byrds drummer Michael Clarke, Gram Parsons' replacement in the Burritos, Rick Roberts, and Gram's sidekick in his 1973 tour band, Jock Bartley. Their début album was billed as country-rock, though with no aural evidence; subsequent records failed even to match its low-grade competence.

Six months before Waylon Jennings, Willie Nelson and friends were rebranded as 'the Outlaws', five long-haired, moustachioed country-rockers were launched under the same name. They were hyped as 'the first full tilt rock'n'roll band to be signed to Arista', but it was an insidiously sleepy kind of rock'n'roll, and on stage these Outlaws spent more time raising their hats than raising hell.

The Amazing Rhythm Aces were another great white hope in 1975. 'Third Rate Romance' on their *Stacked Deck* album became a cult classic; as late as 1978, *Burning The Ballroom Down* showed off a canny command of styles from swamp-rock to Latin, via some country finesse. Their range was matched by the Ozark Mountain Daredevils, six multi-instrumentalists from Springfield, Missouri, whose influences stretched from Chuck Berry to Roscoe Holcomb, via Poco and the Burritos. Glyn Johns produced their first album in London, repeating the formula which had worked for the Eagles. Like the Eagles, they began to shed members after their fourth album, gradually losing the experimental edge which had been their chief appeal.

The most consistent of these second-line country-rock outfits were Pure Prairie League. Formed in Cincinnati in 1971, they at least had a sense of mythology: their album covers borrowed a

Norman Rockwell painting of an ageing cowboy, and set it in a variety of symbolic situations, reflecting the dislocation between the heritage of the Wild West and modern American society.

Nothing on their records was quite that incisive, although their 1972 efforts *Pure Prairie League* and *Bustin' Out* offered a distinctive take on the country-rock approach – particularly the latter, with string arrangements written by David Bowie's guitarist Mick Ronson. Personnel crises stalled the band's progress for almost three years, and it was almost a different group who recorded 1975's *Two Lane Highway*. Chet Atkins and Emmylou Harris supplied some country authenticity to this album, though Pure Prairie League retained their rock ethos: 'It's better to get stoned with a joint than a drink,' they sang on the pointedly titled 'I'll Change Your Flat Tyre, Merle'.

Thereafter, they slipped gently away from their country-rock roots. In 1979, bluegrass picker Vince Gill accompanied a friend to an audition, only to be selected as the band's new lead vocalist. 'I wasn't expecting it or looking for it,' says Gill of this unlikely detour on his route to country superstardom. 'I discovered that they were not nearly as country-rock as everyone thought they were. I was probably the most country guy that had ever been in the band, which made it kinda awkward.' The new line-up scored an immediate hit – in the pop, not country, charts – with 'Let Me Love You Tonight'. Gill rode out that success until 1983, when he signed a deal with RCA as a quasi-rockabilly singer, and Pure Prairie League disbanded.

Some apologetic honesty surfaced on some of the more desperate country-rock ventures of the late Seventies. The New Riders Of The Purple Sage marked their countless series of line-up changes, and subsequent loss of identity, with an album entitled *Who Are Those Guys?*. Country Gazette, the Flying Burrito Brothers spin-off band who'd now spun off all their Burritos, countered with *What A Way To Make A Living*. The Nitty Gritty Dirt Band cast off most of their founding members, much of their country-rock tradition, and half of their name, to re-emerge as the Dirt Band, and enter a new phase as a soft-rock group. By 1980, the lineage that ran from Gram Parsons and Chris Hillman through Poco and the Eagles to Pure Prairie League and the Ozark

Mountain Daredevils seemed to have died out. That was the year when the Eagles disintegrated, when the attempt to relaunch the Byrds as McGuinn, Clark and Hillman collapsed under the weight of public indifference, and when the estranged Austin branch of the country-rock family also exhausted its gene pool.

For the survivors, there was only one viable option: to scale down their ambitions. From being the dominant American music of the early seventies, country-rock became little more than a cottage industry. Some musicians fitted easily into this new landscape. Former Byrd and Burrito Gene Parsons belatedly followed up his remarkable 1973 album, *Kindling*, with *Melodies*, which began with a poignant tribute to his lost comrade Clarence White. But for Chris Hillman, who had once regarded the Beatles and Bob Dylan as his equals, the downsizing was more dramatic.

'It probably saved my life,' he says today. 'It was an escape from the madness of touring with a rock band. It enabled me to ground myself in the music again.'

Hillman cut the *Morning Sky* album for the tiny Sugar Hill label in 1982, cloaking songs by Dylan, the Grateful Dead and even Gram Parsons in simple, bluegrass-tinged arrangements. With old friends including former Eagles/Burritos guitarist Bernie Leadon and Burritos/Manassas steel player Al Perkins, he even collaborated on a bluegrass gospel album, *Ever Call Ready*. 'The name came from an old Monroe Brothers song,' Perkins explains. 'We thought, well, everyone has had an experience with God. It was almost like an offering.' Hillman prefers to maintain some distance from the evangelical flavour of the project: 'We were all swept up into that. I don't consider myself born-again anymore. I got into great areas of frustration with that particular look at Christianity.' As Perkins notes, however, *Ever Call Ready* had a musical as well as spiritual influence: 'We were country and rock musicians, not bluegrass musicians, but we came up with our own take on bluegrass – the same way that the English bands in the sixties took American R&B and rock'n'roll and threw it back at us. And it had a lasting effect. Lots of people asked me if I could produce something similar for them.'

Perkins also produced Hillman's second Sugar Hill album, *Desert Rose*. 'I envisaged that as a continuation of *Sweetheart Of*

The Rodeo,' Perkins explains. 'I used steel player J. D. Maness, who'd played on the original album, and drummer Ronnie Tutt, who'd worked with Gram. But Chris didn't want to go on the road with an electric band. We kept saying to him, if you're gonna make any money, you've got to do electric country music.' The veteran of the Monterey Pop Festival and Altamont was now reluctant to leave the gentility of the acoustic scene.

While the former aristocrats of LA country-rock adjusted to their straitened circumstances, the tradition passed into unexpected hands, as the country market welcomed a sound it had once regarded as alien. 'I don't consider the Charlie Daniels Band as being strictly country,' admitted its leader, but their ornate brand of Southern rock, augmented by Daniels' aggressive fiddle-playing, found a strong country audience in the late seventies. The trigger was their 1979 hit 'The Devil Went Down To Georgia', which transplanted the Faust legend into the Appalachian Mountains. Musically, too, it was a hybrid, linking bluegrass breakdowns to the rock theatrics of urban America. The single topped the country charts, and came close to matching that achievement in the pop market. But any unsuspecting country fans who bought the accompanying album, *Million Mile Reflections*, found music that owed more to the progressive rock of Yes or Kansas than to Bill Monroe or even the Allman Brothers.

For the next few years, the Charlie Daniels Band succeeded in satisfying two discrete audiences. Rock fans welcomed their allegiance to the sound of the seventies, while country radio empathized with their growing political engagement. Daniels was no Reaganite, but his songs about the suffering of 'The American Farmer' or the Vietnam vets 'Still In Saigon' chimed with the populist mood of the early eighties.

So too did the band Alabama, who inherited the imagery of the Southern rock tradition, though little of its rock'n'roll heritage. They had formed as early as 1969, under the name Wildcountry, but only escaped the club circuit in the late seventies, when they adopted the name of their home state. 'I think we're a country band that approaches our show with rock,' declared bassist Teddy Gentry. 'We're a high-energy band with backdrops and lights like you'd see at a rock concert, but our music stems from country roots.' They acknowledged the Marshall Tucker Band and Charlie Daniels as their forefathers, and proclaimed themselves to be 'progressive country' or, in a tautological moment, 'Southern country'. Little beyond their name and their stagecraft linked them with the seventies country-rock tradition.

Alabama's music, created in the studio by session players, was carefully drained of any edginess or sense of danger. Their safety-first attitude was exemplified in 1984 when their management blocked their videoclip for 'Fire In The Night' because it featured an actress playing a witch. 'There was a little bit of sexual explicitness,' explained director David Hogan. 'Even though there wasn't anything satanic about it, I know the group was concerned about the witch and her tattoos. I saw it as a fairytale for adults, but you have to remember I'm dealing with a Bible Belt audience.'

This risk-free approach to rock brought Alabama a remarkable run of success, including a run of twenty-four No. 1 singles, broken only once between 1980 and 1989. It prompted a flurry of imitators, including Atlanta and Savanna – who changed their name to Sawyer Brown, and survived their initial media branding as 'bubblegum country' to emerge as one of the most consistent country acts of the eighties and nineties. The 'bubblegum' dart was also aimed at Exile in the late seventies, when they registered an international pop hit with 'Kiss You All Over'. Reoriented towards country, they became Alabama's chief rivals by 1985.

The rock market ignored these lightweight country-rockers, just as country audiences didn't register the existence of guitar bands such as the Long Ryders, Green On Red, Giant Sand and Lone Justice, who were viewing the Byrds' and Burritos' legacy through the prism of punk. Connecting these two extremes were some veterans of late-sixties country-rock, who were able to appeal to mid-eighties country radio without betraying their heritage.

In the case of the Nitty Gritty Dirt Band, that allegiance was demonstrated by the retrieval of key personnel. Just as his recruitment in 1969 had signalled their shift away from good-time folk-rock into a more countrified sound, so Jimmy Ibbotson's return after an eight-year absence in 1983 helped to refocus the group. Manager Chuck Morris suggested that they reclaim the missing 'Nitty Gritty' in their title, and abandon their attempts to win back a rock audience. They set out to conquer country radio, eliciting a Rodney Crowell song and a Ricky Skaggs fiddle cameo for their 1984 chart-topper, 'Long Hard Road'. The departure of acoustic ace John McKuen in 1986 threatened their composure, but ex-Burrito and Eagle Bernie Leadon proved an ideal replacement, as the Dirt Band echoed the smooth harmonies and crisp instrumentation which had been those groups' hallmark.

In December 1988, the Dirt Band gathered at Randy Scruggs' Sound Studio in Nashville. Fifteen years after they'd bridged the ravine between traditional country and country-rock with *Will The Circle Be Unbroken*, they crafted a sequel – another conscious attempt to capture a dying generation for posterity, and channel their legacy into the contemporary flow. Many of the original participants had died, among them Mother Maybelle Carter and Merle Travis, but Roy Acuff, Earl Scruggs and Carter's children provided continuity. The Dirt Band themselves were no longer the hippie upstarts who'd shocked Nashville traditionalists. There was no hint of the culture clash which had sparked the early-seventies sessions, but the enlistment of Ricky Skaggs, Emmylou Harris, Levon Helm and Bruce Hornsby ensured that album was in many ways stronger than its predecessor.

Scarcely noted in the credits was another reunion: the first collaboration in almost a decade of Byrds founders Roger McGuinn and Chris Hillman. Fittingly, they returned to their own country-rock landmark, *Sweetheart Of The Rodeo*, for a revival of Bob Dylan's 'You Ain't Goin' Nowhere'. While McGuinn had been content to play the acoustic circuit as a soloist since the collapse of McGuinn, Clark and Hillman, his colleague had followed the Dirt Band in attracting a new audience.

'We had put together an experimental group in the mid-eighties,' Al Perkins recalls, 'with Chris, Bernie, myself, Jerry Scheff, and Cactus Moser. Bernie left to join the Dirt Band, so we got John Jorgenson to fill in. It was finally turning into an electric band, but I had an opportunity to go with Dolly Parton, and I chose to follow the money.'

With J. D. Maness as Perkins' replacement, and ex-Dillard Herb

Pedersen as second vocalist, Hillman's ensemble mutated into the Desert Rose Band. 'Out of every group I've played with,' he says, 'that was the best. I was out front, but with these incredible pickers and singers. I knew we had enormous potential, but I felt our age was against us. J. D., Herb Pedersen and I were in our forties, and we didn't think we'd be able to get a deal with a major.'

To Hillman's amazement, the Desert Rose Band were not only signed by Curb/MCA, but proceeded to score a series of No. 1 singles on the country charts. Their music harked back to the Flying Burrito Brothers, with an energy and focus that had been missing since *The Gilded Palace Of Sin*. If the Burritos' old spontaneity was missing, so too was their erraticism.

After playing variations on country music for almost thirty years, Chris Hillman was now exposed to the Nashville industry for the first time. 'It was a completely different world,' he says. 'What's interesting about Nashville is that if you don't live there, you're an outsider. There is a good ol' boy clique, and we weren't part of it. I got some bad press, because we'd do a ninety-minute show out in the sun at some state fair, and then when I didn't go back and sign autographs for two hours, they reckoned I was the worst villain in the music business!'

Within the Nashville industry, there was suspicion about the Desert Rose Band's country credentials. 'They used to call us carpet-baggers because we came from rock'n'roll,' Hillman laughs. 'Herb and I would say, "Excuse me, but we grew up playing bluegrass."' Beyond Music Row, however, Hillman's past counted for little: 'We reached really hard-core country people who had no idea who the Byrds were. There was no rock'n'roll hype as far as they were concerned: they just liked the way we played country music.'

The Nitty Gritty Dirt Band and the Desert Rose Band heralded a renaissance of the Poco/Eagles tradition at the end of the eighties. Southern Pacific were in the first wave, building on the experience of such rock veterans as John McFee and Keith Knudsen of the Doobie Brothers, and Creedence Clearwater Revival bassist Stu Cook. Their breakthrough hit was a Tom Petty tune, 'Thing About You', and their later repertoire would have fitted comfortably on to Los Angeles rock radio in the mid-seventies. Likewise Highway 101: with Paulette Carlson as the kind of charismatic frontwoman previously unknown in country-rock, they sounded like the original Lone Justice, whose new wave edge had excited roots-rock fans earlier in the decade.

The most pervasive and, ultimately, influential of the new Nashville bands were Restless Heart – former sessionmen whose energetic but unchallenging records sounded as if a bunch of teenage evangelists had been locked in a room with no sustenance but early Poco albums. As Restless Heart and their dozens of envious rivals soon discovered, seventies country-rock was the template for country bands in the nineties. The most successful groups of the era shamelessly plundered the soft-rock and AOR tradition. Diamond Rio matched Crosby, Stills and Nash harmonies with Eagles instrumentation; the Remingtons (featuring ex-Bread singer Jimmy Griffin) stopped at Crosby, Stills and Nash; Great Plains imitated the Eagles, right down to the jaded melancholy that was Don Henley's vocal signature. 'I don't listen to country radio because it's horrible,' Chris Hillman complains. 'There's nothing but these bad, generic Eagles bands. I listen to them and think, "We did that already, thank you." We didn't have to wear hats, either.'

Restless Heart and Diamond Rio had longevity; the Remingtons and Great Plains slipped away after a couple of albums. Great Plains enjoyed the least commercial success, and showed most understanding of the landscape from which they'd emerged. Singer-songwriter Jack Sundrud had been a professional musician for twenty years when the group was signed at the start of the nineties, and he had witnessed at close quarters the problems experienced by the veterans of sixties country-rock. 'I was a member of Poco in the late eighties,' he recalled, 'at the time when they finally gave up on the pop market. So we moved down to Nashville and tried to make it as a country act. But we could never figure out what the labels wanted to hear. Eventually, we had to admit defeat, and Rusty Young pulled the original line-up of the band together for a reunion album, which got them back on the rock charts.'

Sundrud was forthright about the reason that he stayed in

Nashville: 'It's the only place today that is interested in songs. I never had any ambitions to play country, though I loved country-rock in the sixties and seventies, but my tastes and needs brought me to Tennessee. Pop has got so narrow, that the whole baby-boomer generation has no music to listen to now than country.' Great Plains bucked the trend by insisting on playing their own instruments – still rare for a country band in the early nineties – and keeping post-production sweetening to a minimum. But even sharing management with Nashville's biggest star of the nineties, Garth Brooks, couldn't guarantee them success. 'That's opened doors for us,' said Sundrud in 1992, 'but if we can't take advantage, then the doors will close again.' And so they did.

For Diamond Rio, the decision to play country rather than rock was less opportunistic. 'My uncles were the Osborne Brothers bluegrass group,' says Dana Williams, 'and so that was pretty much all I heard as a kid. I missed out on the Beatles and the Stones; I didn't hear them until sometime in the seventies.' But, as Brian Crouch realizes, their fans came from both quarters: 'Rock music pretty much turned to trash. It got to where rock equalled metal, and nothing else.' And then there was rap, described as 'the best thing that ever happened to country' by former Bread leader David Gates, who began his own assault on Nashville.

For all the country bands' contempt for 'metal', the two genres shared a penchant for long, tightly permed hair and AOR theatrics. Visually, there was little to distinguish country acts like Little Texas from their hard rock adversaries. Stranger still was the emergence in 1992 of Confederate Railroad. With their chains and biker jackets, beards and tattoos, they strode into Nashville as if they were preparing to handle the security at Altamont. The Hell's Angel pose survived until they began to play, whereupon they were revealed as another slick Eagles tribute band.

The Kentucky Headhunters sent a similar frisson of menace through the country industry in the early nineties. They looked like extras from *Deliverance*, fuelled for fun and violence on moonshine. 'That was hard for us at first,' admits Greg Phelps, 'but then the record company realized that because we looked different to everyone else, they could market that as a style.' The Headhunters staked their claim to the Southern rock tradition of

Lynyrd Skynyrd, and the British reinvention of the blues via Cream and the Faces; and they repaid another debt by cutting an album with Chuck Berry's old piano-player, Johnny Johnson. But their rock edge was all too easily smoothed away on their own records.

It was inevitable that when Nashville realized the commercial potential of cutting multi-artist tribute records, the Eagles and Lynyrd Skynyrd should have been early beneficiaries. *Common Ground: The Songs Of The Eagles* was released in 1993, *Skynyrd Friends* a year later; both offered note-for-note imitations of the original arrangements from artists such as Travis Tritt, Clint Black and Alabama. Little Texas covered the Eagles' 'Peaceful Easy Feeling'; lead guitarist Porter Howell noted, 'We're pretty much the kind of rock that should never have died in the first place – country-rock crossover, smooth country, cool country, new country, call it what you will.' Meanwhile, George Jones soundalike Sammy Kershaw pushed for Skynyrd (who'd reformed in the nineties, having split after a 1977 air crash) to appear on the TV showcase *Nashville Now*. 'Skynyrd is country music with an edge,' Kershaw claimed.

In that climate, it was no surprise that the Eagles themselves should choose to reform in 1994. 'Don Henley must die,' satirist Mojo Nixon had sung in 1990, 'don't let him get back together with Glenn Frey.' But reunite they did – the late-seventies line-up, significantly, rather than the original unit with country picker Bernie Leadon. They staged one of the greediest tours in rock history, demanding up to $125 a ticket. Don Henley mused that 'There's a great silent majority that lives out there in the heartland, that had been forgotten by the record industry . . . Country is the resting-place of melody and lyric.' But his band made no attempt to reach the low-earning Eagles loyalists who inhabited that heartland. They returned in the same cynical spirit with which they had departed fourteen years earlier.

While the musicians he'd inspired secured their pensions, former Byrd Chris Hillman was forced to abandon his career as a country star with the Desert Rose Band. 'We'd started to scare country radio,' he explains. 'Plus we could never get clear signals from the record company. We did everything right, but our records were never in the stores. I made the decision to stop touring because I could see the writing on the wall.' Instead, he teamed up with bluegrass specialists the Rice brothers, and his longtime sidekick Herb Pedersen, to cut mellow acoustic records which paid tribute to the California country tradition (*Bakersfield Bound*) and his LA bluegrass roots (*Out Of The Woodwork*). Both records exuded a dignity entirely lacking from the Eagles' reunion.

At the end of a decade dominated by the joint legacies of the Eagles and Lynyrd Skynyrd, it's ironic that the only country-rock band based in Nashville to make any impact beyond America owed little to either act. The Mavericks surfaced in 1990 on a tiny Florida indie label, and began their unlikely journey to worldwide acclaim. Like Southern Pacific and Highway 101, they were promoted as a country band because there was nowhere else for them to go. But their music was defined by influences like the Tex-Mex R&B band, Los Lobos, the Roy Orbison-styled rock crooner, Chris Isaak, and British post-punk traditionalists such as Nick Lowe and Clive Gregson. Individually, the group had strong country backgrounds; one of them even married Nashville diva Trisha Yearwood. But in another age, the Mavericks could have been billed as power-pop, folk-rock, AOR or retro rock. Their acceptance in Nashville suggested that the industry was no longer concerned about maintaining even the faintest of links with the traditional sound to which it has always pledged its allegiance.

32 Urban Cowboy

Country crosses into pop (again), 1974–1984: Robert Altman; Dolly Parton; Kenny Rogers; John Travolta; Willie Nelson; Lionel Richie

In 1974, veteran Hollywood film director Robert Altman arrived in Nashville to shoot a movie around the country music industry. 'When a movie producer comes to town,' commented country star Tom T. Hall after the première of *Nashville* the following year, 'everybody just falls down. They flip. They want to be in the movies.' The country community prepared a traditional Southern welcome for Altman and his crew, but their expectations of a positive PR exercise were punctured by the movie's satirical edge.

As a social commentator himself, via such finely sketched vignettes as 'Ballad Of Forty Dollars' and 'The Year That Clayton Delaney Died', Hall could admire the breadth and intelligence of *Nashville*: 'It's probably one of the best movies ever made. But I was embarrassed. It was a little like getting back your wedding pictures and discovering you had your fly open during the ceremony.'

Exposing the country industry was only a minor priority for Altman, who was attracted to Nashville by the tension between the demands of a multi-million-dollar enterprise and traditional small-town values. But country insiders were taken aback by Altman's portrayal of their industry's greed and naïvety. British critic Bob Powel complained that, 'The whole film puts the country music industry in a bad light. I would be a liar if I didn't admit to recognizing some of the bad things depicted, but it is certainly a gross and unfair exaggeration of the way Nashville is run.'

Veteran singer Hank Snow, widely believed to have been one of Altman's main satirical targets, was equally outraged: 'I think the *Grand Ole Opry* should put out a real genuine country movie and tell it like it is, show people how wrong the picture was, how misleading it was.' Something like *Nashville Rebel*, perhaps, a cheapskate 1966 vehicle for Waylon Jennings; or *Cotton Chicken Pickers*, which allowed George Jones a rare appearance on celluloid; or *Las Vegas Hillbillies*, an anodyne showcase for the likes of Ferlin Husky; or *Your Cheatin' Heart*, a 1964 biopic of Hank Williams which featured his teenage son Hank Jr, singing on behalf of Hollywood star George Hamilton, after Elvis turned the role down.

These movies and their peers – *Gentleman Jim* with Jim Reeves, *A Time To Sing* with Hank Jr, or *The Fastest Guitar Alive* with Roy Orbison – coupled the dramatic tension of a Presley romp with the cultural insight of *The Beverly Hillbillies*. Even *Nashville Rebel* belied its title by including every imaginable teen cliché: the misunderstood hero, his jilted but still loyal belle, the suave, evil-hearted villain who attempts to sabotage his career, and the narrative acrobatics that provide an improbable happy ending – not to mention an array of cameos by famous stars, who conveniently burst into song.

Like the Presley movies, these country exploitations echoed the film-makers' contempt for their audience. By making hatred and disgust the predominant emotions of his movie, Robert Altman was at least playing an open hand.

Bob Powel and Hank Snow would probably have preferred another 1975 release, *W.W. And The Dixie Dance Kings*, one of a sequence of seventies caper movies which capitalized on the Southern chic that accompanied Jimmy Carter's rise to the White House. They were more sophisticated and knowing than their sixties counterparts, made with the same finesse Hollywood brought to its mainstream product – and, like TV's *The Dukes Of Hazzard*, they were aimed at an audience far beyond the country belt. But no stereotypes were challenged when stars like Burt Reynolds or Clint Eastwood (*Every Which Way But Loose, Any Which Way You Can*) set out on road trips across the South, meeting rural colour at every turn. Nevertheless, country stars such as Don Williams and Charlie Rich won cameo roles as their real-life selves, while guitar-picker and songwriter Jerry Reed launched a second career as a comic actor.

The success of these movies did not mean that the American

public and press were prepared to welcome hardcore Southern music. 'Country was not readily accepted by the New York media,' recalled Columbia Records executive Mary Ann McCready. 'Asking them to review a country artist was virtually impossible.' Faced with the problem of selling George Jones to the national media, McCready booked him into the prestigious Greenwich Village bar, the Bottom Line, and invited scenesters like Andy Warhol and Bianca Jagger to attend the show. She hadn't counted on Jones refusing to fly to the East Coast because he was convinced that he wouldn't be accepted by New York. Deep into the cocaine addiction that blighted his career, Jones let paranoia stall any attempt at widening his audience. By the end of the seventies, he was so deeply affected by his drug use that he devoted another showcase gig, at the Exit Inn in Nashville, to performing his classic hits in a Donald Duck voice. This tragic stunt finally won him some space in the rock press.

Other country artists used less extreme methods to reach a new audience. They noted the crossover success of country/pop singers such as Glen Campbell and the Bellamy Brothers, and followed suit. 'I'm not leaving the country, I'm taking the country with me,' declared Dolly Parton as she added R&B tunes such as 'My Girl' and 'Higher And Higher' to her repertoire. Her first major pop hit was 'Here You Come Again' in 1977, promoted via coast-to-coast TV talk shows. The song was written by pop veterans Barry Mann and Cynthia Weil, and when Parton heard the final mix she begged producer Gary Klein to add a steel guitar. 'She wanted people to be able to hear it,' Klein explained, 'so if someone said it isn't country, she could say it was and prove it. She was so relieved. It was like her life sentence was reprieved.'

After 'Here You Come Again' registered on both the pop and country charts, Parton grew more confident. 'I don't think there's a definition for country anymore,' she claimed. 'You wouldn't call my music country, you wouldn't call it pop. Why should it carry any label apart from the name of the artist?'

Kenny Rogers would have agreed. He became one of the best-selling artists of the late seventies by applying slick Hollywood production to songs that were rooted in traditional country scenarios. By the early eighties, he could call on Lionel

Richie or the Bee Gees to produce his records without endangering his airplay on country stations.

Not that this unashamed crossover passed entirely without criticism. Diehards voiced their disapproval as Parton and Rogers searched for an audience beyond their country following. It was the same complaint heard during the rockabilly explosion of the mid-fifties, again when Chet Atkins launched the Nashville Sound at the end of that decade, when Glen Campbell and Ray Price took country uptown in the late sixties, and when John Denver and Olivia Newton-John infiltrated Nashville in the mid-seventies. Publisher Wesley Rose muttered grimly about those who 'have failed in other spheres . . . country pseuds, latching on to some of the Nashville action'. Jean Shepard, whose twenty-five-year run of hits was petering out, mixed her metaphors but not her message: 'Country music is going down the drain. If you kill the roots, the tree will die.' And honky-tonk stalwart Hank Thompson, a star since the late forties, noted sourly that, 'The only thing I resent today is hearing rock music and they're calling it country.'

Not only rock music: Bill Anderson, a smooth, sophisticated writer and singer since the late fifties, and a bastion of the country establishment, introduced disco to Nashville in 1978, when 'I Can't Wait Any Longer' spawned country's first 12-inch dance mix. The Bee Gees, whose soundtrack for the John Travolta movie *Saturday Night Fever* epitomized the cream of late-seventies disco-pop, entered the fray by penning material for Tex-Mex country star Johnny Rodriguez. Inevitably, Dolly Parton wasn't shy of adding some disco fever to her music: she achieved a No. 1 country hit in spring 1980 with a Donna Summer song, 'Starting Over Again'.

A few weeks earlier, Chet Atkins might have had Parton in mind when he commented mournfully that 'Country music may be a dying art. The country people have moved to the city, had kids, and those kids love the Beatles or other rock bands. Maybe they don't like country anymore.'

Or maybe the transplanted Country Kid had become an Urban Cowboy – the title of the film which revolutionized the country industry in the summer of 1980. Based on an Aaron Latham short story, it was a clichéd and rather protracted tale of romantic misunderstanding, centred around the suitably exotic location of Gilley's Club in Houston, Texas. The urban cowboys still roped steers, but only at rodeos; in keeping with America's top-rated TV show, *Dallas*, they earned their living in the oilfields. At night, they drained bottles of Lone Star beer, and competed to impress their ladies on a mechanical 'bull' – an evocative metaphor for what had happened to country traditions over the past two decades. *Urban Cowboy* was billed as 'the movie that'll do for country music what *Saturday Night Fever* did for disco'. The comparison wasn't accidental: both films starred that New Jersey cowpoke, John Travolta. Initial box-office receipts were disappointing, so Paramount repromoted the film as a Travolta dance vehicle, with enormous success.

Its commercial impact reverberated across the industry. Mickey Gilley, the cousin of the piano-pumping Jerry Lee Lewis, had been recording since the early fifties, as a more sedate alternative to his hellraising relative. His cameo appearance in the movie paled alongside the publicity value of his name being mentioned in almost every flurry of dialogue. In the three years after *Urban Cowboy* was released, Gilley racked up nine No. 1 singles on the country chart. His real-life club became a prime Texas tourist attraction, and mechanical bulls were acquired by dancehalls across the land.

The reflected glory of the film extended way beyond Gilley's home turf. The soundtrack album – a carefully concocted mix of rock (the Eagles, Joe Walsh, Bonnie Raitt, Boz Scaggs) and urban country (Gilley, Kenny Rogers, Johnny Lee and Charlie Daniels, the last two heavily featured in the movie) – sold more than 500,000 copies in its week of release. It topped the country chart for most of the year, beating off the challenge of other crossover soundtracks such as *The Electric Horseman*, *Bronco Billy* and the Loretta Lynn biopic, *Coal Miner's Daughter*. (Ironically, the last of these movies also contained the least amount of country music: Hollywood preferred the romantic poverty of Lynn's early life to her hillbilly voice.)

Even without a Southern president – the Iran hostage affair ensured victory at the polls for California's Republican contender Ronald Reagan that November – the popularity of *Urban Cowboy* sparked another outburst of country chic. 'I'm not into urban cowboys much,' sneered Hank Williams Jr. 'I'm into Idaho and Montana cowboys.' It was a minority view.

Larry Gatlin, another of the beneficiaries of *Urban Cowboy*, expressed the majority verdict: 'The controversy over what is and what isn't country was first brought up by some of the traditional artists. They were big stars at one time and then all of a sudden their records weren't being played anymore. A lot of this talk is sour grapes and bitterness.'

There was no denying that country music had changed. Kenny Rogers was the best-selling country act of 1980, ending the year with 'Lady', a hit single written and produced by Lionel Richie – the leader of Motown R&B band the Commodores. Anne Murray scaled the charts with covers of Monkees and Beatles tunes, admitted defiantly 'I'm not country', and emerged as the best-selling female artist in country music. And then there was Willie Nelson, whose 1978 album *Stardust* had outsold even the *Urban Cowboy* soundtrack. Nelson wasn't the first country artist to record an album of standards; Marty Robbins had done the same thing in 1961. But Nelson's album expunged all the trademark instrumentation of country records in favour of some subtle orchestrations by Memphis rhythm and blues stalwart Booker T. Jones. 'Country music appears to be going off in all directions,' Nelson noted. 'There are no boundaries anymore.'

Stardust confirmed the point, reaching listeners who had never bought a country album before – or, in the case of Willie's hippie audience, had assumed that standards were only for the middle-aged. Having confounded the demographic theorists once, Nelson did it again by recording a double-album of duets with Leon Russell. 'We spent a week at his studio in California,' Nelson recalls, 'and we cut more than a hundred songs, most of them in one take. We sang every song we knew, plus plenty more that we didn't. We ended up one night around his piano, running through these pop and jazz standards like "Stormy Weather" and "Tenderly". Then Leon took the tapes away and overdubbed himself several times over as the band.' Their mellow romp through Elvis Presley's first major hit, 'Heartbreak Hotel', topped the country charts in 1979. By then, Nelson was a national celebrity, who could be heard right across the radio dial. There were branded Willie Jeans in the stores, Willie Nelson earrings, even Willie Nelson cologne for that funky night out in a Texas bar-room.

Merchandising was only the beginning. Nelson treated fame like open house at the candy store, inviting all his friends inside for a taste. 'Suddenly I could do anything I wanted,' he explains, 'so I was able to repay some old dues.' He cut duet albums with artists who'd inspired him, such as Hank Snow, Webb Pierce, Ray Price and Roger Miller; he dabbled with jazz, blues and gospel; and he opened his ears to songs that no other country act would have dared to cover. 'Chips Moman persuaded me to cut "A Whiter Shade Of Pale",' he recalls. 'I listened to the original version by Procol Harum, and I thought it had a pretty tune. I had no idea what the song was meant to be about, but I cut it anyway.'

With Waylon Jennings spurring him on, Nelson experimented with all kinds of pop tunes in the early eighties: Paul Simon, Jimmy Webb, the Beatles, even Otis Redding material. By 1982, he was so secure in his universal acceptance that he could list his ambitions for the years ahead without mentioning country: 'I would like to work with Miles Davis. I'd also like to do an album with Ray Charles, and maybe Bob Dylan and B. B. King.' His admiration for Miles Davis was mutual: the jazz trumpeter named a tune for Nelson in the early seventies, and a decade later the pair briefly collaborated as songwriters. Willie gradually collected the rest of his hit-list, snagging Ray Charles for a duet on 'Seven Spanish Angels', B. B. King for some live shows, and Bob Dylan at the 'We Are The World' session for a vague promise to collaborate which finally came to fruition in 1992. Only Frank Sinatra escaped him: a plan for Ol' Blue Eyes to tape an album of Nelson's songs was abandoned when Sinatra found himself billed as Willie's support act at some early eighties lounge shows. None of Nelson's collaborations aroused such contempt from the Nashville traditionalists as his duet with the Spanish crooner Julio Iglesias. 'That's a great one for country,' sneered veteran hitmaker Mel Tillis. 'Radio plays that, then they play Lionel Richie, and then they play Olivia Newton-John, who hates country music.'

Meanwhile, Tillis and his contemporaries found airplay ever more elusive.

With Lionel Richie recording country singles, and the Bee Gees producing Kenny Rogers, you could flip the American radio dial in the mid-eighties and no longer identify the station. The market for what had once been called country-pop had never been larger; but the urge towards crossover had severe repercussions for the rest of the industry. Although Rogers, Nelson, Dolly Parton and Anne Murray were flourishing at that time, country's overall share of the market declined sharply from its post-*Urban Cowboy* peak. The second rank of stars – reliable hitmakers such as Moe Bandy, Joe Stampley and Ronnie McDowell – were fortunate to sell more than 50,000 copies of their albums; to survive on a major label, pop acts were expected to rack up a minimum of 100,000 sales. Concert revenues were no more healthy. 'I have never seen it as bad as it is now,' clubowner Jerry Garrens told the International Country Music Buyers Association conference in 1985. 'Eight years ago, I could put anybody in my club and make money. But today I don't know of two country acts that cost under $7,000 [i.e., anyone below the status of a Willie Nelson or Kenny Rogers] that I can make a dime on.'

'You want to know why that happened?' asks John Mellencamp. 'People turned to country music 'cos of dance music. On the coasts, in New York and Los Angeles, people like to dance in clubs. The rest of the country doesn't do that. So when Donna Summer was making all these great dance records, the rest of the nation went, "Fuck You", and started listening to country music. That's why there was this great surge. Then disco went bang! Gone! And so did country, because people went back to rock'n'roll. That's what they want to listen to.' That's a simplification, with an element of truth: why else would the pop audience have responded so lavishly to the country artists who sounded least country? When that infatuation ended, Nashville was left with a cast of leading characters who had distanced themselves from their home audience, and who no longer appealed outside country's hinterland. The only option was to return to country music that country fans would recognize as their own.

Even as the crossover acts were reaching their commercial peak, the country industry began to distance itself from their tactics. 'It was fairly clear,' wrote *Billboard* columnist Kip Kirby at the end of 1984, 'that programmers would snap up almost any new release that sounded traditional with unfeigned eagerness, holding back on records with obvious crossover influences. The word went out in Nashville: cool it on crossover. Downplay the contemporary pop-sounding country.'

The chief beneficiaries of the new order were Reba McEntire and George Strait, whose music harked back to the more distinctive country sound of the late sixties. They were simply reaping the rewards of an earlier revolt against country-pop. While Nashville was acclaiming the crossover potential of Kenny Rogers and Dolly Parton, many of its consumers were opting for the purer, less commercialized sound of Emmylou Harris, Ricky Skaggs and John Anderson – retrospectively dubbed the New Traditionalists. They were too hillbilly for the pop charts, but their adherence to old-school values – plus, in Harris's case, her unusual pedigree – ensured that their music registered with rock listeners. This unusual alliance of old-timers who clung to the fiddles and steel guitars of fifties country, and post-punk rockers entranced by the 'authenticity' of the New Traditionalists, helped to topple a ruling order which had come close to robbing country music of its identity.

33 Elite Hotel

Country's New Traditionalists, 1973–1983: Emmylou Harris; Ricky Skaggs; John Anderson

She was an unlikely saviour of country music: the sidekick of a rock star who'd overdosed on heroin in a motel bathtub; a Greenwich Village folkie groomed by a Hollywood management team; a single mother whose roadie was a former cell-mate of Charles Manson. If Emmylou Harris maintained any tradition, it was the decadent country-rock of her soulmate and one-time duet partner, Gram Parsons. After his death in 1973, Harris inherited his 'road mangler', Phil Kaufman; his manager, Ed Tickner; and the collective sympathy of that small audience who'd mourned Parsons' demise. 'I was trying to keep that momentum I'd had with Gram going,' she explains today, 'but with a very important wheel missing. I don't know how I did it.'

'When Emmylou first came to England in 1975, it seemed as if everyone who had a copy of *Grievous Angel* was in the audience,' recalls critic Tom Richardson, a longtime observer of Harris's career. 'There was a real feeling of a shared discovery, as if we had access to this secret that nobody else knew about.'

Rolling Stone greeted Harris's major-label début, *Pieces Of The Sky*, as 'more of a country album than just about anything to come out of Nashville for years'. But Warner Brothers' Los Angeles office held few expectations that Emmylou would reach a mainstream rock or country audience. The singer agreed: 'I figured it would be ignored, because it wasn't a commercial pop record and it wasn't basic country, and it definitely wasn't rock'n'roll.' *Pieces Of The Sky* was built for cult appeal – the Parsons connection, the use of musicians who'd supported Elvis Presley in Las Vegas, guest appearances by Linda Ronstadt and Bernie Leadon. There was even 'a surrogate Parsons', as one critic put it, in Rodney Crowell, Emmylou's duet singer, guitarist and songwriter.

'I wasn't influenced by Nashville at all,' Harris admits. 'I was operating in a kind of sealed beam.' Nashville hadn't recognized Gram Parsons, or his country-rock endeavours. But against all odds, country radio seized on Harris's 1975 revival of the Louvin Brothers' 'If I Could Only Win Your Love'. Identical in style to Parsons' *GP* album, it reached No. 4 on the country chart.

For all its traditional values – she also tackled songs by Dolly Parton, Merle Haggard and Tammy Wynette – *Pieces Of The Sky* sounded nothing like the year's other country hits. Neither did it entirely convince as country or country-rock. There was an emotional distance between Harris and her material: like a true folkie, she only committed when she sang the self-consciously 'poetic' lyrics of Paul McCartney's 'For No One'. Faced with the honky-tonk profanity of Haggard's 'The Bottle Let Me Down', she sounded as if she'd downed one too many cappuccinos, then belched politely into a handkerchief.

'I was in awe of my band,' Harris confessed, and too often that uncertainty was apparent in the music. But on 1976's *Elite Hotel*, her Hot Band was looser – never more so than on Buck Owens' 'Together Again', with pianist Glen Hardin tumbling around the keyboard as if caught between despair and reckless humour. Emmylou tapped into the same spirit, and was rewarded with her first No. 1 country hit. The country audience had the best of her: the other side of the single, aimed at the pop market, was a florid, utterly fake reading of the Beatles' 'Here, There And Everywhere'. Gram Parsons would have headed back to the bathtub.

Parsons was an inescapable presence, not least because she featured his songs on almost every album. Reviving 'She' (one of the few *GP* tracks on which she hadn't duetted), Harris couldn't match his romantic intoxication, but nostalgic melancholy was an effective substitute. Elsewhere, on tunes such as 'Hot Burrito #2', she seemed to be reading the words, not living them.

Other avenues were equally uncertain. Those who'd marvelled at the resonance of her duet work with Parsons, Bob Dylan (on 1975's *Desire*) and Neil Young ('Star Of Bethlehem' that same year) winced as she rasped over the Cajun rhythms of 'C'est La

Vie' – alias Chuck Berry's decade-old rock hit, 'You Never Can Tell'. 'I'm not a rock'n'roll singer,' she had the grace to concede. 'It's great to play, but it doesn't come natural to me to sing. I hurt my voice when I consistently try to hit it really hard.'

On 1978's *Quarter Moon In A Ten Cent Town*, her first record not to carry any open references to Parsons, Harris finally unlocked the door to her heart. Her rowdy take on 'Two More Bottles Of Wine' brought her another country No. 1; a duet with Willie Nelson on 'One Paper Kid' suggested that she'd realized that country and soul were kindred spirits, not competing radio formats.

Three years into her Warners deal, she'd reached deeper into the country audience than any rock-based performer since Jerry Lee Lewis, without sacrificing an ounce of her country-rock credibility. When she suggested a collaboration with Dolly Parton and Linda Ronstadt, the trio's record labels recognized a rare marketing opportunity, one that could introduce Parton to the rock audience, take Ronstadt back to country, and widen Harris's appeal in both sectors.

'We all came in with different ideas,' Harris reminisces, 'whether it would be pop or country or bluegrass or acoustic. We tried to do a little bit of everything, and there wasn't enough focus. Then we ran out of time, and we were afraid to come back together, because we respected and liked each other too much to risk making something below par. We started out thinking that it was the event of the century, and we became overawed.' Remnants emerged on albums by all three participants, but the trio project was quietly abandoned. So Warners altered their line of persuasion. 'They kept pushing me to cross over into pop,' she recalls, 'but I was having too much fun playing country. So I made *Blue Kentucky Girl*, showing them that you could make a record that was nothing but country, and still be successful.'

Among the musicians on that album was the bluegrass multi-instrumentalist from Kentucky, Ricky Skaggs. In 1980, as the *Urban Cowboy* phenomenon sent Nashville scurrying in search of country-pop, Skaggs encouraged Emmylou Harris to immerse herself in the purism of bluegrass. 'There was a desire inside of me to keep music more traditional,' Skaggs says. 'I didn't have to sit and study and get a game-plan together: it was natural for me. I wanted to bring bluegrass and country together in a way that hadn't been done for years. In the forties and fifties, there wasn't any segregation between hillbilly music, Appalachian, bluegrass, country, call them what you will. There wasn't a bluegrass Top 40, a hillbilly Top 40 and a country Top 40 – it was all meshed into one. Bill Monroe was as hot as Ernest Tubb. People just said, 'Well, that's Bill's style of music.' They didn't say, "Well, that's bluegrass, we'll have to play that on Saturdays between four and six in the morning, when no one's awake."'

Roses In The Snow was the result of Skaggs' intervention; as he noted at the time, 'I don't think Emmy had ever had anyone in her band that was as much of an authority on old-time mountain music as I was.' Harris recalled that 'the record company were nervous, to say the least', but they were partly assuaged when her album of Louvins and Stanley Brothers songs also included the Simon & Garfunkel hit 'The Boxer', delivered with a reverence usually reserved for holy texts. It took its place on country radio alongside Mickey Gilley's versions of old Ben E. King and Buddy Holly hits, and smooth ballads by Anne Murray and Crystal Gayle.

Harris remains unimpressed by the impact of *Urban Cowboy*. 'I didn't understand how people could get so excited over music so watered-down, when you had all these rich traditions you could steal from and extend,' she says. 'Music had to change, but I felt it could be done in an organic way, so you don't forget about harmonies and mandolins – and, my God, the songs. Also, at that point I was trying to shine a light on country music as a valid American art form, which was still looked down upon by my peer group. No one took it seriously. It was considered politically incorrect, because it came from the white South.'

In 1981, she made the unpredictable decision to follow her bluegrass record with *Evangeline*, which she describes as 'not a country record – on purpose'. Ricky Skaggs left for a solo career, removing some of her artistic certainty. The following year found her covering Poco's 'Rose Of Cimarron', a slick pastiche of the Eagles' country-rock sound which Gram Parsons had rejected nearly a decade earlier. The live *Last Date* was even more disorienting: between Bruce Springsteen and Neil Young songs were revivals of old Parsons/Harris duets, with the duo's early-seventies collaborator Barry Tashian her new vocal partner.

Harris seemed compelled to re-examine the formative musical relationship of her life. The result was *The Ballad Of Sally Rose*, a romanticized concept album assembled with the British songwriter she later married, Paul Kennerley. The storyline concerns an icon called simply The Singer, who is entranced by Sally Rose: 'She was the prettiest thing that he had ever heard, playin' rhythm guitar and singin' the third.' The couple share a brief but overpowering partnership, before The Singer dies and Sally Rose is left to carry on his name. The narrative has the unreal glow of a fairytale, but there are clues a-plenty for those seeking autobiography: one song is named 'Sweetheart Of The Rodeo', after Gram's album with the Byrds; another mentions his death-site, Joshua Tree.

The story ends with Sally Rose abandoning her own music, so she can broadcast The Singer's gospel via radio station KSOS. Having distanced herself from the narrative when the album was released, Harris now admits that, 'Emotionally, it's very autobiographical. There's a great deal of me there. That was the whole reason for doing it. I wouldn't have put myself through the anguish of writing an entire album unless it was something extremely important to me.'

The Ballad Of Sally Rose may have provided emotional closure for its creator, but it also fractured her relationship with the country industry. Aside from her overdue collaboration with Linda Ronstadt and Dolly Parton (finally delivered in 1987), she was never again a major presence on country radio.

The career of her one-time collaborator Ricky Skaggs stalled at the same moment. He signed to Epic in 1981, and achieved five years of almost unbroken No. 1 hits by applying bluegrass principles to country songs – exactly as he'd done with Emmylou. The Country Music Association voted him Entertainer of the Year in 1985, the same year he transformed 'Country Boy', by sometime Hot Band member Albert Lee, into a dazzling display of instrumental and vocal dexterity. His revival of Bill Monroe's 'Uncle Pen' was the first pure bluegrass song to top the country charts in two decades. Elvis Costello joined him for a London concert; and the rock audience which had responded to Parsons and Harris now welcomed Skaggs as a guardian of country tradition amidst the glossiness of country-pop.

Another New Traditionalist proved too country for the rock market. During the early eighties, John Anderson rivalled Ricky Skaggs as the most convincing keeper of country's flame. After years of Nashville artists softening their vowels and smoothing out their productions, Anderson's records were a throwback to the rough-edged fifties honky-tonk of Lefty Frizzell. 'When I had a high school band,' Anderson says of his upbringing in Florida, 'I learned to play the Beatles and Stones, plus stuff like Creedence's "Proud Mary". But when I was 13 or 14, the country bug bit me pretty good. By 16, around 1970, I wasn't playing any rock'n'roll. I guess I've always been an extremist, and when I did go into country, I went into hard country. I started working in the Nashville clubs when I was 18: you had to be pretty much honky-tonk or they'd get somebody else.'

Nothing on Nashville radio in 1981 sounded as honky-tonk, or as ancient, as Anderson's 'I'm Just An Old Chunk Of Coal'. This revival of a Billy Joe Shaver song recalled the dawn of rockabilly, when musicians learned that you could spark a crowd into life with an electric guitar. Subsequent hits kept faith with this tradition, even when Anderson added female crooners for his closest shot at a crossover hit, 1983's 'Swingin''.

In other ways, he was a modernist: 'I tried to persuade the record company to let me make videos, when no one else in country was doing it. Then I brought in a harder rock sound, more like the Creedence records I loved as a kid. I insisted on using my road band in the studio, which wasn't really done in Nashville at that time.' Rowdy hits like 'Black Sheep Of The Family' and 'Let Somebody Else Drive' were still immediately recognizable as country, but delivered with an edge only Hank Williams Jr could match. 'That was pretty left-field for the time,' Anderson says, 'but it cut its way through. I think it opened a door for other people to follow.'

In different ways, Emmylou Harris, Ricky Skaggs and John Anderson all paraded the flag of traditional country at a time when crossover was king. Their success in the era of *Urban Cowboy* made it all the more surprising that their careers should flounder in the mid-eighties, when the Nashville labels realized that country-pop had soured. What halted the New Traditionalists was not a more blatant appeal for the pop audience, but a roots-based sound which was soon dubbed New Country. Ahead lay another cycle of rejections and flirtations between country, pop and rock, as if nothing had been learned or remembered from the kisses and collisions of the previous three decades.

34 The New South
Hank Williams Jr and the Southern rock tradition, 1966–1999

On 8 August 1975, Randall Hank Williams tumbled five hundred feet down a Montana mountainside. When his companions reached his body, they assumed he was dead. His skull was split, his face ripped back to the bone, his features scarcely recognizable as human. Somehow Williams survived, to endure months of reconstructive surgery. As the surgeons rebuilt his face, he had time to focus on his legacy, as the son of the most famous father in country music.

Randall Williams was 8 years old when he was sent out on stage by his mother Audrey, the ex-wife of Hank Williams, who had died five years earlier. At 13, Hank Jr – or Bocephus, as his father had dubbed him, this being his variation on the name of Alexander the Great's faithful steed, Bucephalus – began his career as, in his own words, 'the reincarnation of the famous Hank Williams'. 'Everybody wanted him to sing his daddy's songs,' recalls Waylon Jennings, who befriended the teenage Hank Jr. 'They didn't want anything else from him.' 'I would do old Chuck Berry and Jerry Lee Lewis songs and play all the instruments,' Hank Jr remembered. 'The audiences would get off on it, but backstage, people would tell me not to do that rock'n'roll crap. Just go out and sing like your dad.'

Hank Jr complied for a decade – dubbing George Hamilton's singing voice in the biopic of his father, cutting staid duets with Connie Francis, playing Texas dancehalls and Vegas ballrooms. His voice was fuller than his father's, but none the less evocative, and only Jerry Lee Lewis could match the ease with which he switched between hillbilly laments and barnstorming rock'n'roll. But as early as 1966, the 17-year-old Bocephus admitted that he was 'Standing In The Shadows'. MGM Records accentuated the comparison by prodding the boy to overdub his daddy's old records, or set unfinished Hank lyrics to music.

The year before the accident, Hank Jr made a stand for independence. 'I could take it easy with a cheque every six months,' he explained later, 'or make the music I wanted. It was time to sweep out the closet.' To MGM's horror, he began recording in Muscle Shoals and Macon, and cutting songs by rock group the Marshall Tucker Band. Worse still, two other Southern rockers, Charlie Daniels and Chuck Leavell, were invited to play on the sessions.

The *Hank Williams Jr & Friends* LP was only a tentative step out of line. Its packaging, which emphasized the contributors from the world of rock, was more revolutionary than its contents. The accident rendered it irrelevant: imprisoned in hospitals for months, Williams escaped physical destruction only to slip into depression. Instinct kept him alive; Southern rock bands like the Allman Brothers and Lynyrd Skynyrd refuelled his enthusiasm for creating music.

'I would listen to Doc Watson, then Skynyrd, then Jerry Lee, then the Allman Brothers, then Jimmie Rodgers,' Hank Jr told Jimmy Guterman years later. 'Phil Walden [the Allmans' manager] had the best line about all these guys. They're not country singers. They're not hillbillies. They're white blues singers. That's what my daddy was, and that's what I am.'

White blues was the source of the Southern rock tradition. Like dozens of American outfits in the late sixties, the Allman Brothers Band were obsessed with Chicago R&B, Robert Johnson's country blues, and the reinvention of both traditions by rock groups such as Cream and the Butterfield Blues Band. Duane Allman was an idiosyncratic blues guitarist; his brother Gregg had the voice of a Southern soulman and the keyboard verve of Ray Charles. Underpinning them was a propulsive rhythm section – and the country-tinged licks of guitarist Dickie Betts. After Duane Allman was killed in a 1971 bike crash, Betts steered the Allmans into a glorious country/rock/blues union on *Brothers And Sisters*, where 'Jessica' and the anthemic 'Ramblin' Man' added a hillbilly dimension to their trademark blues sound.

The Allmans were the exemplars of Southern rock, and manager Phil Walden built a business empire in their hometown of Macon, Georgia. Their chief rivals were Lynyrd Skynyrd, discovered in Atlanta, Georgia by ex-Dylan cohort Al Kooper, who signed them to his Sounds of the South production company. Skynyrd were less blues-based, owing more to the sleazy raunch of the Rolling Stones. Like Walden's charges, they caught the imagination of Southern teenagers with music that wasn't country, but carried an unmistakable badge of regional pride.

'I'm proud of being a Southerner,' boasted Charlie Daniels. 'I used to work at a marine base in North Carolina, where guys came from all over. It was the first time I'd run into that anti-South mentality: everyone down South is shufflin', incestuous . . . good ol' people with nothing on the ball. That used to make me mad. There are still things wrong with the South, but it's better than it used to be.'

Only two years younger than Elvis Presley, Charlie Daniels was the elder statesman of Southern rock. He recorded with Bob Dylan, Ringo Starr and Flatt & Scruggs, before launching a solo career in 1971 with an album that featured country sessionmen alongside ex-Jimi Hendrix bassist Billy Cox and Neil Young's Stray Gators.

His music was equally eccentric, ranging from pure honky-tonk to satires such as 'The Pope And The Dope', as if Frank Zappa had been translated to the Tennessee backwoods. But he was swept into a media-invented movement. 'Southern rock wasn't a genre at all,' he reflects today. 'All those bands were different. The Allmans were a blues band, Marshall Tucker were more country, Skynyrd were the best rock'n'roll band since the Stones, and our band was in the middle. What we shared was a blue-collar background, so we saw the world the same way.'

Hippie cowboys, the Southern rockers expressed their pride through such anthems as Lynyrd Skynyrd's 'Sweet Home Alabama' and Charlie Daniels' 'The South's Gonna Do It Again'. Their simplistic tributes to the eternal righteousness of the South seemed to conflict with their passion for roots music, black and white.

That ambiguity haunted the annual Volunteer Jam concerts that Daniels staged from 1974. A rowdier version of Willie Nelson's Fourth of July Picnics, they were jamborees of rock and Southern pride. The Confederate flags beloved of Lynyrd Skynyrd hung over the stage, as Daniels played host to boogie bands and country-rockers – Black Oak Arkansas, Wet Willie, the Outlaws, the Marshall Tucker Band and, in time, Hank Williams Jr. Soaking up Skynyrd and Merle Haggard, the Allmans and George Jones, Hank Jr re-emerged in 1976 with his traumatized features hidden behind a beard and shades. His first album after the fall, *One Night Stands*, was a reminder that he was still alive; but Williams had a more substantial statement on his mind.

He turned for help to one of the most powerful men in country music: Waylon Jennings. 'After he fell off the mountain, nobody wanted him,' Jennings explains. 'They thought he was over with. But I took him out on the road with me, 'cos I knew he had something else to give. Everyone had been trying to hold him back, but I told him, "Do what you want to do, and I'll sing harmony with you." *The New South* album was a stepping stone to bring him back into the fold. Plus it gave him a chance to sing what he was thinking about.' Hank Jr laid out his manifesto on the opening cut, 'Feelin' Better'. 'I had to get out of Music City and I had to get off the road,' he sang, 'the people wouldn't let me sing nothing but them sad old songs.' He recruited Southern rock luminaries such as Dickie Betts to flesh out the Muscle Shoals rhythm section.

With the title track, Hank Jr claimed allegiance to more than a rock style: he slipped into line with a mythic view of the South which had enticed intellectuals and politicians since the Civil War. As early as 1865, the deeds of surrender barely dry, the defeated Southerners consoled themselves with the phoenix of a New South, economically regenerated, spiritually cleansed, but retaining the pride which the recent conflict had failed to extinguish.

By 1880, the dream had become a political goal, which mirrored the South's unstable economy over the next century. The prosperity of the sixties revitalized the crusade, and the election to the White House of Jimmy Carter from Plains, Georgia, in

November 1976 prompted a rash of editorials boasting that the ideal was within reach.

Hank Jr heard the buzz of expectation: 'Last year we elected the man from Plains,' 'The New South' began, 'and there was lots of talk about a great big change.' But why change what was already fixed? There was football, girls with all-over tans and a side of grits on every table, 'and the New South, thank God, is still the same'. The same couldn't be said for Hank's records: Dickie Betts and Charlie Daniels duelled guitar and violin in a lengthy break that would never have been countenanced in Nashville.

Until excessive self-confidence fuelled an artistic and eventually commercial decline in the early nineties, Hank Williams Jr was the most adventurous, rowdy, ridiculous, vain, thrilling and uncompromising figure in country. He hunted wild animals and *Playboy* models, staged rampaging arena gigs in front of crowds of beer-stoked rednecks, and made albums which ran endless variations on his obsessions – the superiority of the South, the inescapable legacy of his father, and the emotional power of Southern rock. Hank Jr was a party animal, addicted to beer, babes and loud rock'n'roll, with the instincts of a survivalist. 'A Country Boy Will Survive' was his anthem, boasting his ability to thrive after apocalypse or urban upheaval with a shotgun in his hand; but inside his isolationist shack, the TV was tuned to *Monday Night Football*.

His 1979 *Family Traditions* formalized that contradiction, dividing into a side of country-pop (he covered 'To Love Somebody', then complained, 'I always knew these goddamn Bee Gees songs was never gonna work') and another of good-time honky-tonk. Two years earlier he'd written despairingly in 'Feelin' Better': 'Could they ever forget my name?' Now almost every song contained a gratuitous reference to 'ol' Hank' or 'daddy' – and 'Family Tradition' (not to mention 'If You Don't Like Hank Williams' and 'Are You Sure Hank Done It This Way') turned his parentage into a battlecry. After years of escaping his daddy's repertoire, he began to celebrate it, tying hard rock riffs to 'Kaw-Liga' and 'Mind Your Own Business'.

Few songwriters have ever been so self-referential. Even Jerry Lee Lewis, who couldn't get through a chorus of 'The

Star-Spangled Banner' without dropping his own name, might have baulked at Hank's ongoing conversation with his audience, each arrogant declaration spawning a response on his next album. Having carved his father's legend in 'The Conversation', Hank Jr drafted his own in 'My Name Is Bocephus', 'Born To Boogie' and Muddy Waters' 'Mannish Boy', rewritten to reflect his own glory.

Along the way, he signalled his latest musical passions – not just via metallic renditions of Aerosmith, ZZ Top and Lynyrd Skynyrd songs, but by slipping in the names of his heroes. 'I love all those Allman Brothers, Merle Haggard and George Jones,' he sang in 1980, and his cavalier blend of hard rock guitar and honky-tonk song structures made Southern rock sound as country as Hank Williams Sr.

His example wasn't lost on Travis Tritt, as distinctive a vocal stylist as anyone in 1990s 'New Country'. 'I was influenced by Merle Haggard and George Jones when I was a kid,' Tritt says, 'but when I turned 13, I started listening to the Allmans, Lynyrd Skynyrd, Marshall Tucker and Bob Seger. My father loved country, and hated me listening to rock'n'roll. That was one of the reasons I enjoyed it, that rebellious quality. Hank Jr showed me that it was OK to listen to both kinds of music, and to put them in the same song.' Briefly groomed as a country traditionalist, Tritt emerged on his early albums as a Hank Jr disciple. His voice pulled at a tangle of Southern roots, Otis Redding, George Jones and Ronnie Van Zant among them. Like his hero, he was eventually sidetracked into repetition, but in the early nineties Tritt briefly promised to inaugurate a new era of Southern country-rock. His explosive cover of the Atlanta Rhythm Section's 'Homeless' broke him on to rock radio – rekindling memories of Bocephus a decade earlier, screaming ZZ Top's 'La Grange' from atop a piano on the hallowed stage of the *Opry*.

Southern rock wasn't all that Travis Tritt learned from Hank Jr. On the same album as 'Homeless' was a song called 'The New South'. 'I love Hank's album,' he explains, 'but there was no relationship between that and my song. I wanted to say, "Look, the South is not what it was a hundred years ago. We're not into slavery. And we want you to recognize that."' The homogenized country stars of the nineties rarely allude to political conflict. Tritt is more open: 'Sometimes it seems like the Civil War never really ended. People from the North talk about us as if we're backward, barefoot, uneducated, deprived. Some of the smartest people and greatest inventions this country ever had came out of the South. I'm not ashamed to stand up and say, I'm from the South, and I'm proud of it, and here's a song about it.'

Bocephus must have cheered. But by the mid-nineties, both Tritt and Hank Jr were marginalized. Tritt survived by softening his music, and excising the traces of Lynyrd Skynyrd and the Allmans; Hank Jr was less repentant, and was exiled by the country stations he'd dominated a decade earlier. By 1996, he was rewriting his own past on 'Let's Keep The Heart In Country': 'I don't care if it's Old Country gold or New Country soul, I've had enough of this rock'n'roll.' His concerts were still the rowdiest events on the country calendar, but his reign as the genre's most compelling voice was over.

35 Interiors

Singer-songwriters in country music, 1975–1999: Rosanne Cash; Rodney Crowell; John Hiatt; Mary Chapin Carpenter

Country music was inevitably altered by the first generation of performers who were young enough to have been rock'n'roll fans. The country stars of the sixties could choose to ignore the Beatles, the Rolling Stones and Bob Dylan. For those who arrived in Nashville in the late seventies – Rosanne Cash, Rodney Crowell and their like – Dylan and the Beatles weren't alien invaders, but part of their collective past.

Cash and Crowell were married in 1979, adding to a tangled dynasty that stretched back to the earliest stirrings of commercial hillbilly music. Rosanne's father was Johnny Cash; her step-sister, Carlene Carter, was the heir to the Carter Family tradition. Unrelated by blood, Cash and Carter were pinned to a family tree that now extended into rock, via Cash and Crowell, and Carter's marriage to British singer Nick Lowe.

Brought up on the West Coast by her mother, Vivian Libero, Rosanne Cash slipped easily into the hedonism of late-sixties California. 'I started taking drugs when I was 14,' she confessed. 'You do it off and on for several years recreationally, and then one day you wake up and it's not recreational anymore.' Her father, addicted to amphetamines and painkillers for much of his adult life, had already made the same discovery. Both Rosanne and Carlene Carter were incorporated into the dynasty led by Johnny Cash and June Carter Cash. As teenagers, they featured on Johnny's 1974 album *The Junkie, The Juicehead Minus Me* (not, sadly, the narcotic confession that its title suggests). He also recorded his daughters' songs: 'That doesn't count,' Rosanne scowled later. In 1976, she was sent to CBS Records' London office to study the music industry, in time to witness the first wave of punk rock. Thereafter, she flitted between excuses for avoiding a career, studying in Nashville, then at the Lee Strasberg acting school in Hollywood. During a weekend return to Tennessee, she was invited to a party at Waylon Jennings' house, where she met Rodney Crowell, a songwriter and guitarist for Emmylou Harris since 1975.

Before they were married, Rosanne Cash had a record contract – not in Nashville, Hollywood or London, but in Germany, where she and her fiancé constructed her début album. It was an ungainly mix of original songs and covers, including (at her label's insistence) a revival of her father's mid-sixties hit, 'Understand Your Man'.

Back in Tennessee, a more orthodox career began with *Right Or Wrong* in 1980. Emmylou Harris and Ricky Skaggs were among the guests; her husband produced; and country veteran Bobby Bare joined her for a hit duet. But immediately she began to buck the system. With 1981's *Seven Year Ache*, she fashioned a smooth sound on which only a steel guitar hinted at her background. 'You could call it a concept album,' she explained. 'It's about a woman whose man isn't treating her right, but she's trying not to be a victim.' Though country had accepted Loretta Lynn's declarations of female pride, such as 'Your Squaw Is On The Warpath', this was its first exposure to overt feminism. The industry didn't know how to react, so they accused Cash of being 'new wave'. 'I do listen to it,' she admitted, 'but I'm not a new wave singer. This is a country record.' The single topped the charts to prove it.

Crowell's progress had been less swift, though he'd already left his mark as a songwriter with Waylon Jennings' ode to excess, 'I Ain't Living Long Like This', plus the poignant 'Till I Gain Control Again', recorded by Emmylou Harris and Willie Nelson. 'He was a Texas boy,' Emmylou explains, 'who had played in his dad's band, and could play whatever instrument was required. But also he had this great gift as a writer, because like Gram Parsons he was my age but had come to country from his roots, not as a sort of intellectual exercise.' Harris's support was vital: until then, Crowell admitted, 'I was writing songs that no one wanted to record. Everyone thought they were too progressive and lyrical for mainstream country.'

Like his wife's, Crowell's albums would have fitted easily on to rock radio. But two songs he gave to Harris in 1983 exposed his distance from the rock industry. 'It's Only Rock And Roll' used the genre as a cynical euphemism for hypocrisy, while 'Baby, Better Start Turning 'Em Down' seemed to blame rock for teenage promiscuity: 'It's a brave new wave we're roaring in, hanging out on the rock'n'roll fringe, speaking of running around, all over town.'

His loyalty was ill-rewarded. When he delivered his fourth album to Warner Brothers' Nashville office in 1984, they complained that it was neither country nor rock. Revamped and re-recorded, it emerged in 1986 as *Street Language*, occupying the same ambiguous ground. 'I thought Rodney was going to be the one to carry the torch forward,' Emmylou Harris sighs. 'I thought he would be this enormous superstar. But he was cursed with wearing too many hats, almost being too talented. Sometimes it's easier for a more one-dimensional person to make it.'

Crowell wasn't alone in his dilemma. A single from *Street Language* was 'She Loves The Jerk', penned by another early-seventies arrival in Nashville, John Hiatt. 'I like showing up where I'm least expected,' Hiatt says, to explain how his career began as an 18-year-old staff writer in Music City. 'Anyway, for a kid from an Indiana cornfield, it was the nearest place to go. New York and California were too terrifying and strange. I loved the feel of Nashville. It seemed small and accessible – and it *was* in those days.'

Three years as a staff writer at Tree Publishing produced two recordings of his songs, and one hit – not by a country artist, but by pop band Three Dog Night. 'I was looking for a style,' Hiatt admits, and his quest led him to sign with Epic's New York office as a solo artist in 1974. Financial pressures drove him out of Nashville and on to the road. His career only began to take shape when he heard the first new wave records by Nick Lowe and Elvis Costello that were coming out of London. 'I remember thinking, "I understand this stuff,"' he says. 'It was a bloated period in American music, and these English guys were tongue-in-cheek and edgy at the same time. It was the pinprick we'd been waiting for.' Costello's influence on his work proved so strong that comparisons between the two artists became a critical commonplace. Like Crowell, Hiatt won more approval as a songwriter than as a performer. Ry Cooder scored a hit with 'The Way We Make A Broken Heart', while Rosanne Cash recorded his 'It Hasn't Happened Yet'.

Through the early eighties, Hiatt's dependence on alcohol and drugs ate into his creativity, and his career options. Close to bankruptcy, he was offered a lifeline by Andrew Lauder, who ran the British label Demon Records in association with Elvis Costello and his management. 'Andrew said he'd put out any record I made,' Hiatt recalls, 'and my agent asked me who I'd ideally like to work with. I came up with this fantasy line-up of Ry Cooder, Jim Keltner and Nick Lowe, never believing for a second it would happen. But they all said yes.' The budget only ran to four days in the studio, which was long enough for Hiatt to cut the finest album of his career, *Bring The Family*. Like Elvis Costello's *King Of America*, it was an adventure in Americana, which stripped back his music to its roots in country, blues and gospel. 'I don't think [country star] Ronnie Milsap is ever gonna cut this song,' Hiatt sang defiantly on the opening 'Memphis In The Meantime'. But his revitalization was recognized by Nashville's left-field – and nowhere more so than in the Crowell/Cash household.

That establishment held mixed emotions in 1986. While Rodney Crowell complained that 'I don't seem to have a country base anymore', Rosanne Cash scored enormous success with music only tenuously connected with country.

She had followed *Seven Year Ache* with *Somewhere In The Stars*, before taking a leave of absence that threatened her career. At first, she claimed that she had begun to question the validity of her artistic voice. Later, she revealed that she had been battling against cocaine addiction.

Country fans have always rewarded repentance, but they take less kindly to pretension. Cash promoted her 1985 comeback record, *Rhythm And Romance*, as being 'about the process of what Jung called "individuation" '. She strayed again by issuing a single with the line 'I can't live like a whore', which was banned by many country stations. And she incited the Nashville industry by insisting that her album was marketed out of Columbia's pop division in New York.

'They said they were going to help me,' Cash complained, 'but they didn't. It's gotten to the top of the country charts, but in the pop charts? Zero.' Steve Earle saw her lack of acceptance by the pop market as prejudice: 'MTV won't play her videos, even though Rose is essentially a pop artist. They penalize her just because she records in Nashville.' It was an exact reversal of the situation two decades earlier, when the country industry refused to accept records made by Brenda Lee and Roy Orbison in Nashville with country musicians because they were 'pop'.

Rejected by the rock industry, Rosanne Cash retained the loyalty of country fans. In 1987 she scored a No. 1 with John Hiatt's 'The Way We Make A Broken Heart', maintaining the strange logic whereby Hiatt can register multiple hits as a writer (Suzy Bogguss's 'Drive South' and the Desert Rose Band's 'She Don't Love Nobody' are other examples) without being accepted as a country performer himself.

The market was full of such contradictions by the late eighties. Perhaps the most unlikely country star of the era was East Coast folkie Mary Chapin Carpenter. She was a natural successor to the singer-songwriters of the seventies: twenty years earlier, she'd have been welcomed into the soft-rock aristocracy alongside Joni Mitchell and James Taylor. Working Washington bars and folk clubs for food money in the mid-eighties, she mixed Townes Van Zandt material with her Eagles and Dan Fogelberg covers. 'I didn't know who I wanted to be,' she confesses. 'I was all over the house. I think I still am.'

In 1986 she financed the recording of her début album *Hometown Girl*, an indie deal being the height of her ambition. Instead, she was signed by the Nashville office of Columbia Records, who had just lost Rosanne Cash to New York. Carpenter is clear-eyed about their motives: 'The only reason I got signed there was because there was no market in the mid-eighties for singer-songwriters in New York or California. Otherwise, that's where I would have gone.' Within two years, she'd quit her job fundraising for a Washington arts organization – another first for country – to concentrate on her transformation into a Nashville star.

Carpenter maintained her distance from the industry by keeping her East Coast home. Musically, she made equally few concessions. Instead, the audience – or, rather, two audiences – came to her. In 1989 she began to pick up substantial country airplay for *State Of The Heart*, her first professionally recorded album, while her music was also reaching rock fans alienated by the decay of the singer-songwriter tradition.

Her self-mocking performance of 'Opening Act' at the 1990 CMA Awards widened her appeal; the following year, her Cajun-rock single 'Down At The Twist And Shout' became a sizeable hit, the first time in years that an accordion had been heard on country radio. In June 1992 she released her richest album to date, *Come On, Come On*, as the annual Fan Fair celebration was staged in Nashville. With misgivings, she agreed to appear during Columbia's portion of the show. 'I didn't want to do that,' she told me that summer. 'I didn't feel like I belong there. It proved to me that it wasn't my audience.' A few weeks later, she was voted the CMA's Female Vocalist of the Year, after which her suspicions of the country audience seemed to vanish.

Her unease with country radio remained, despite their acceptance of 'Down At The Twist And Shout' and 'I Feel Lucky'. 'I've been told there might be some trepidation about releasing "He Thinks He'll Keep Her" as a single,' she told me in 1992, 'because radio will think it's a man-bashing song. I'm not surprised, because I've met radio programmers who think they can dictate the way people live their lives. It's crazy.' Once again, she under-estimated country's ability to bend; 'He Thinks He'll Keep Her' proved to be a major hit single, while an all-star rendition formed the centrepiece of a *Women In Country* TV spectacular.

Rosanne Cash was a conspicuous absentee from that show. Her 1987 revival of her father's 'Tennessee Flat Top Box' maintained her run of country hits, and her follow-up, a duet with Rodney Crowell, finally assured him of star status. There seemed no limits to her country stardom: she remodelled herself with a punk hairstyle (a decade late), campaigned against nuclear power, and maintained her feminist principles on record and in print.

Still she felt confined by Nashville – the vacuity of the media, the annual chore of Fan Fair, the constant reminders of her family heritage. In 1990, she finally made a record country radio wouldn't play: the stark and anguished *Interiors*. 'I'm going to take you into a long, dark tunnel,' she told her audiences, as she examined the disintegration of a female psyche and its reliance on a romantic façade. She was still promising an album of duets with Crowell, to be entitled *Twin Flames*, but instead the couple separated amicably, and Cash moved to New York. There she crafted *The Wheel*, a psychologically intense work rooted in Buddhist philosophy, and began to share writers' showcases with Lou Reed. Another long silence was broken by 1996's *10-Song Demo*, a fragile song cycle closer to Joni Mitchell's *For The Roses* than anything in country. Finally, she had escaped from Nashville, and the audience with whom she felt only the most tenuous of connections.

Mary Chapin Carpenter assumed her role as a bewildered outsider in the heart of the country industry. Meanwhile, John Hiatt lives in Nashville, without any recognition from the audience which welcomes his songs from other voices. With Ry Cooder and Jim Dickinson, Hiatt penned one of the most resonant country songs of all time, 'Across The Borderline', but most country fans have never heard it. As Rosanne Cash could tell him, identity is less a matter of what you are than what you are perceived to be.

36 Misfits
Neil Young, Live Aid and Farm Aid, 1969—1986

July 13, 1985: concerts in London and Philadelphia draw the biggest worldwide television audience in history. The occasion is Live Aid, the culmination of a year-long effort by Irish singer Bob Geldof to alleviate the crippling famine in Ethiopia.

It is a day for humility, and for self-congratulation. Geldof has already assembled a galaxy of British pop stars to record a charity single, 'Do They Know It's Christmas'. Around the world, other nations have responded in kind – not least in America, where USA For Africa, masterminded by Lionel Richie, Michael Jackson and producer Quincy Jones, persuaded stars from every quarter of popular music to 'check their egos at the door' and contribute to a song called, modestly, 'We Are The World'.

Those gestures pale alongside Live Aid, which is broadcast live around the globe. Led Zeppelin, the Who and Crosby, Stills, Nash and Young reform for the day; the Beach Boys, Elton John, U2, Madonna, Queen and dozens more provide their services for free. Teams of aides accept credit card donations. In London, the exhausted Geldof finally loses control: 'Just send us the fucking money,' he screams into a live camera. Another bank of phones immediately lights up.

Late at night in Philadelphia, the final performer reaches the stage. Bob Dylan is flanked by two of the Rolling Stones, and their ramshackle set is a disaster. But this is Dylan, doyen of the sixties protest movement, the single most influential figure in rock history. He can be forgiven anything. Almost anything.

Between songs, Dylan shakes his fingers through his tangled hair, as if that might free him from his inertia. Then he ventures to speak: 'I'd just like to say,' he mumbles, his face a bleary mask, 'that I hope that some of the money that's raised for the people in Africa, maybe they could take just a little bit of it – maybe one or

two million, maybe – and use it, say,' – his voice starts to stumble –
'to pay the, er, pay the mortgages on some of the farms, that the
farmers owe to the banks.' There's a smattering of applause, but
mostly a shocked silence, as the Philadelphia crowd tries to grasp
what he's said. Mercifully, his performance soon ends, and Dylan
makes a drifter's escape.

In the afterglow, Dylan's contribution arouses derision. Musical
incoherence is all part of the legend, but what was that stuff about
farmers? Trust the Americans to think of themselves first, Europe
complains. And even the US rock community distances itself from
its mentor. Farmers are losing their homes; but children in Africa
are starving to death. What was Dylan thinking?

Except: ten weeks later, another stadium fills in Champaign,
Illinois – a town Dylan once celebrated in song – as rock and
country performers share a benefit concert. The occasion? Farm
Aid, the first in an annual series of televised shows to raise money
for America's farming community. Many Live Aid stars are on
hand, among them Bob Dylan, who delivers a set which banishes
the memory of Philadelphia. This time he speaks not a word.

Dylan's comments at Live Aid didn't come out of a void. In April
1985, as 'We Are The World' began to pick up airplay on
America's country stations, singer Ronnie McDowell tried to
involve the Nashville music industry in Ethiopian famine relief.
His crusade attracted few supporters. Poverty in Africa was
regrettable, but closer to home, financial ruin was threatening a
way of life.

President Ronald Reagan launched his re-election campaign in
January 1984 by declaring that 'America is back, standing tall,
looking to the eighties with courage, confidence and hope.' That
confidence was threadbare in the agricultural community, as
economic depression forced down the value of farm goods, and
farmers defaulted on their loan payments. To avoid bankruptcy,
banks foreclosed on the loans – effectively stripping the farmers of
their land.

High interest rates and low farm prices threatened to annihilate
the farming community of the Mid-West and central South, and
1985 brought regular demonstrations, as natural Reagan

supporters were racked by unemployment and poverty. 'When people made fifteen or twenty dollars a week, beef was thirty-seven cents a pound,' Willie Nelson wrote in his autobiography. 'Now it's still thirty-seven cents a pound, and people are making five hundred dollars a week. It's not right.'

At the 'We Are The World' session in January 1985, Nelson raised the issue with Ray Charles. Three months later, Ronnie McDowell agreed to add his name to the cause, as long as Nashville pledged to back the Ethiopian relief effort. (The Nashville labels promised to release a charity single called 'From Nashville To The World With Love', but the record was never made.)

Nashville wasn't represented at Live Aid: the only country music heard on the Philadelphia stage came from veteran rocker Neil Young. Willie Nelson heard Dylan's comments, and flashed upon the idea of a second benefit concert, targeted at both rock and country audiences: 'I talked to John Mellencamp, Neil Young, Waylon Jennings. We had a nucleus already. Neil's agent, Elliott Roberts, called Bob Dylan. I talked to Kris Kristofferson and Alabama and Kenny Rogers. The next thing you know, we had a show going. We did it in six weeks. So it had to be a popular idea.'

As the bill suggested, this was an entirely American concept. But not an orthodox one: only at Willie Nelson's Fourth of July Picnics had rock and country performers mingled so easily, and Nelson had never dared to present punk rockers such as X alongside country icons such as Loretta Lynn and George Jones.

For those artists already trying to span the country/rock divide, Farm Aid was a golden moment. 'We really thought we could cross country over into punk rock,' recalled Maria McKee of Lone Justice. 'We wanted to open for Willie Nelson one night and the Clash the next. Farm Aid was the closest I ever saw to that. It was what we'd dreamed of. You had Merle Haggard, Lou Reed, X, us, Los Lobos, the Blasters, Steve Earle, Loretta Lynn, Bob Dylan, Neil Young, Dwight Yoakam, Joni Mitchell – all on the same stage.' The Farm Aid experiment has been regularly repeated since 1985, with varying degrees of financial success.

The first Farm Aid was Neil Young's last show with the International Harvesters, the country band with whom he'd toured since the previous year. Young zigzagged through the eighties like a lab rat in a fiendish experiment on the side-effects of constant change. At times, his progress seemed baffling, as he jerked from techno-pop to rockabilly, country to heavy metal. It was easier to dismiss his work – an album where his voice became a computerized whine, another filled with two-minute rock'n'roll novelties – as wilful evasion of his responsibilities, rather than face the possibility that each side-turn was an honest attempt to find a comfort zone.

None of his eighties personae survived so long, or was pursued with such vigour, as his transformation into a country singer. Though the results weren't made public at the time, Young began work on an album in Nashville in January 1983; three years later, he attempted to release a benefit record for Farm Aid. Between those dates, he performed around a hundred gigs with a country band, cut duets with Waylon Jennings and Willie Nelson, and threatened to turn his back on rock for ever. 'I love this music,' he explained in 1984, 'and I could play it for the rest of my life.'

When he began his thirty-year collaboration with Crazy Horse in 1969, bar-room country was assimilated into their sparse, ramshackle sound. From 'The Losing End' on *Everybody Knows This Is Nowhere* to 'Country Home' on 1990's *Ragged Glory*, via 'Powderfinger', 'Lookin' For A Love', 'Southern Pacific' and a dozen more, Young and Crazy Horse regularly played country material with a rock'n'roll attitude. In 1970, they came close to documenting this hybrid on record, with an album of nonchalant country-rock'n'roll performances that was aborted when guitarist Danny Whitten's heroin addiction began to sap the energy of the sessions.

Even without Crazy Horse, Young maintained his enthusiasm for country music. In 1971, he recorded *Harvest*, the biggest-selling album of his solo career, dividing the sessions between London, Nashville and his barn in California. 'I was in Nashville to do the *Johnny Cash Show*,' he recalled, 'and James Taylor and Linda Ronstadt were there. We figured we could cut some things and have them sing on them. It was just a total accident.' Those brief Nashville encounters provided *Harvest*'s hit singles, 'Heart Of Gold' and 'Old Man' – sensitive songs which matched the public demand for acoustic troubadours, played as if they were Nashville laments from the age of Ernest Tubb and Faron Young.

In his California barn, Young strapped on an electric guitar. While tracks such as 'Alabama' and 'Words' seemed to anticipate the Southern rock explosion, another song posed a question that would trouble Young and his audience for the next two decades: 'Are You Ready For The Country'. Country music? A trip into the country? The lyrics didn't explain, though they hinted at the haphazard journey ahead: 'Lefting and then righting is not a crime, you know.'

Harvest offered more surface than depth, but it defined a moment in rock culture. From its textured sleeve to its child-like scrawl of lyrics, it promised grass-roots authenticity, offering rural values as a touchstone amid the urban madness. It also offered Young a template of how to make a hit record, which he studiously avoided for the next few years. Instead, he devoted albums to testing his own emotional strength – records such as *Tonight's The Night*, which became (alongside the Rolling Stones' *Exile On Main Street*) a major influence on alternative country performers in the eighties and nineties; and the unreleased *Homegrown*, on which Young teamed up with Emmylou Harris to cut fragile songs of romantic despair.

Reunited with Crazy Horse in 1975, he recut the title track of *Homegrown* as a western stomp, hymning the joys of cultivating your own weed. Two years later, he invited Linda Ronstadt and Nicolette Larson to a rehearsal, then released the results on the *American Stars'n'Bars* album. The songs were sensuous, drunken and loud, as if a Texas country band had stumbled into a tequila factory.

Larson was retained when Young assembled a long-overdue successor to *Harvest*. In November 1977, he interrupted the sessions so that his Gone With The Wind Orchestra could play a one-night stand in Miami Beach. Topping and tailing their set with 'Are You Ready For The Country', they delivered a playful but heartfelt collection of left-field country tunes. Two days later, they were back in the studio, taping material as unlikely as Hank Locklin's 1960 Nashville hit, 'Please Help Me, I'm Falling'. That didn't make the *Comes A Time* album, but some equally mellow material did – undercut by the sweet cynicism of a new song, 'Field Of Opportunity'. 'It's plowing time again,' he sang shamelessly. Young promoted *Comes A Time* by ignoring it in favour of the material which comprised 1979's *Rust Never Sleeps*. But his rampant creativity was abruptly fractured by personal traumas. His toddler son, Ben, was discovered to be suffering from cerebral palsy, and Young abandoned his touring schedule to steer the boy through experimental therapy. Then in spring 1980, his wife Pegi was diagnosed as suffering from a brain tumour. Her condition was severe enough to require immediate surgery, but she gradually recovered – as Young celebrated on 'Staying Power', one of the downhome country tunes which filled half of the opaque *Hawks And Doves* album.

'That was just a funky little record that represented where I was at and what I was doing at the time,' Young commented later, without explaining either the dense poetic metaphors that constituted the other side of the album, or the significance of the title. Hawks and doves had been recurring political images since the Vietnam War had polarized the hawks of the military establishment and the peace-seeking doves of radical youth. Did his acoustic self-analysis represent the voice of that hippie tradition, and the country suite the redneck mentality? And if so, where did Neil Young belong – subjecting his relationship with Crosby, Stills and Nash to complex lyrical scrutiny on 'The Old Homestead', or deploring the cracks in the American fabric on 'Comin' Apart At Every Nail'? The title track was equally elusive: Young spotted 'Hawks and doves hovering overhead,' but was his declaration that he was 'Proud to be living in the USA, ready to stay and pay' meant to be satirical?

At the end of 1981, Neil Young ended his thirteen-year liaison with Reprise Records to join Geffen, the label run by CSNY's former manager. Young had effectively enjoyed creative freedom at Reprise, and can hardly have expected his old friend to challenge his call. But Geffen rejected *Island In The Sun*, the country-rock album which Young delivered as his label début. The problem recurred in 1983, after another sequence of Nashville sessions (scheduled, so Young claimed, 'whenever there's a full moon'). The album he submitted was called *Old Ways*. 'Geffen rejected it,' he recounted. 'They said, "Frankly, Neil, this record scares us a lot. We don't think this is the right direction for you to be going in." It was like *Harvest II*, a combination of the musicians from *Harvest* and *Comes A Time*. It was much more of a Neil Young record than *Old Ways II*.'

Geffen's tactics are hard to comprehend. In place of *Island In The Sun*, they released *Trans*, a wilfully uncommercial investigation of computer technology. Now they turned down the very saleable *Old Ways*, but allowed Young to release a disposable set of rockabilly pastiches, *Everybody's Rockin'*. 'They said they wanted more rock'n'roll,' Young explained, 'so I said, "OK, fine, I'll give you some rock'n'roll." I was almost vindictive about it.'

Geffen followed tack, initiating a lawsuit which accused Young of deliberately delivering 'unrepresentative' material. He was in no mood to compromise. He abandoned plans for a rock album with Crazy Horse, and in May 1984, formed a fully fledged country band – the International Harvesters.

With the exception of Nashville sessionman Anthony Crawford, all the Harvesters had previous experience of Young's flirtations with country. Steel guitarist Ben Keith and bassist Tim Drummond had worked with him on *Harvest* in 1971. A less regular cohort was Louisiana fiddle ace, Rufus Thibodeaux, who remains utterly convinced of Young's fidelity to country: 'He really loved that music. He was a joy to work with. In fact, he told me that country was really his favourite kind of music.'

The International Harvesters had the pick of Young's country material, back to the inevitable 'Are You Ready For The Country'. At their first show, they also débuted songs such as 'Amber Jean' (penned for Neil's baby daughter) and 'Get Back To The Country'. This was nothing less than a hillbilly rewrite of his epic 'Don't Be Denied', with Young relishing the chance to get 'back in the barn again' – which was where he'd cut much of *Harvest* in 1971.

Over the next few months, he eschewed familiar rock venues in favour of country haunts – the Opry House in Austin, the *Nashville Now* TV studios, Gilley's Rodeo Arena in Pasadena, even the *Grand Ole Opry* stage itself. In September 1984, the Harvesters visited the studios of *Austin City Limits*, the TV showcase which had become a beacon for those alienated by the increasing sterility of Nashville. Their two-hour performance climaxed with a rare Harvesters rendition of Young's anthemic rock tune, 'Down By The River'. Rufus Thibodeaux sat the song out, but Ben Keith's steel whistled through this tale of murder and psychological dissipation as a reminder of who Neil Young was claiming to be.

Identity was a complex issue in 1984, as Young slipped deeper into his persona. That July, he cancelled a European tour – for commercial reasons, his manager claimed, though other sources suggested he was fearful of a possible terrorist attack on his aircraft. Such isolationism sat uneasily on a man who'd adopted risk and uncertainty as the watchwords of his career.

Instead, Young scheduled another American tour, sharing the bill with country icon Waylon Jennings and his wife Jessi Colter. With a presidential election looming, Young began to echo Jennings' innate conservatism. 'So what if Reagan's a trigger-happy cowboy?' he told reporters in Louisiana. 'He hasn't pulled the trigger. I'm tired of listening to people say that America is bad everywhere, that our involvement in Central America is wrong, that we're a bunch of aggressive animals and don't have any cool.' Rock columnist Dave Marsh viewed Young's 'rightward shift' as 'part of the transformation to country singer he's undertaken in the latest attempt to revive a flagging career'.

It was inevitable that Waylon Jennings would contribute to the sessions for Young's country album, which he stubbornly delivered to Geffen in spring 1985 under a title they had already rejected, *Old Ways*. 'That was the most fun I've had in a hundred years,' Jennings beams. 'One time he had an orchestra, a rhythm section and me singing harmony – all live!' That was on the aptly titled 'Misfits', a surreal account of paranoia and displacement set to a typical Phil Spector rhythm, which was closer to earlier Young material such as 'Broken Arrow' and 'Last Trip To Tulsa' than anything else from the sessions.

Not that any of *Old Ways* conformed to Waylon Jennings' expectations: 'There's a funny thing about his songs. He would come in with something and start singing it. Now, I'm a songwriter too, and I reckon I can judge a tune. I'd listen, and I'd be thinking, "That ain't gonna make it, hoss! That's not that good." But then in the studio he'd get a groove with it, and it would turn out wonderful, just because it was so different. Sometimes, I'd turn out to be right after all. But 80 per cent of the time he managed to prove me wrong.'

Geffen's reaction to a record even less 'representative' of Young's career than *Island In The Sun* or the original *Old Ways* is easy to imagine. Young had softened his customary bar-room country sound in favour of arrangements closer to Chet Atkins' mid-sixties Nashville Sound. If the title track offered a clue to his thinking – 'Old ways,' he sang, 'can be a ball and chain' – much of the record seemed to be deliberately confrontational, albeit in the politest possible way. Why else would Young revive the western standard, 'The Wayward Wind', or place the twang of a jew's harp at the heart of 'Get Back To The Country'?

Waylon Jennings failed to detect any hidden agenda: 'Neil's a real country fan, pure and simple. We went out and did shows together for a while. You don't do that unless you mean it. He didn't have to do that. Besides, anybody that can run round with Rufus Thibodeaux has gotta be country!'

Artistic pleasure aside, Young had a specific target in mind as he completed *Old Ways*, and then headed into the studio to cut a follow-up. Between April and July 1985, the International Harvesters – now including Nashville piano veteran Pig Robbins, plus songwriter Matraca Berg and Mother Earth country-rocker Tracy Nelson – taped a dozen songs in various Nashville studios. 'Amber Jean', 'Hillbilly Band' and 'Leavin' The Top 40 Behind' explained themselves; 'Silver And Gold' and 'One More Sign' were destined to resurface later in his career.

Some material felt forced: the extended metaphor of 'Let Your Fingers Do The Walking' would never have survived a Nashville writers' workshop. But another song, débuted at Live Aid, hinted that Young was finding an authentic country voice. Like 'This Old House', written around the same time, 'Nothing Is Perfect' humanized the financial ruin of America's agricultural economy. The extent of Young's immersion in Nashville imagery was apparent when he acknowledged one of the city's all-time standards: 'I've got a woman who's standing beside me, She really knows how to stand by her man.'

That week, Young and Willie Nelson shot a video for their *Old Ways* duet, 'Are There Any More Real Cowboys'. Proceeds from a single were diverted to the Farm Aid cause. (If Geffen had sanctioned its release, so would have the royalties from a five-track EP featuring 'Nothing Is Perfect', but it was rejected by the label.)

By 1986, country music no longer played a useful role in Young's career, as Geffen had withdrawn their legal action. 'They dropped that lawsuit after a year-and-a-half of harrassing me,' Young explained, 'because I told them, "The longer you sue me for playing country music, the longer I'm going to play country music. Either you back off or I'm going to play country music forever. And then you won't be able to sue me because country music will be what I always do, so it won't be uncharacteristic anymore." ' The successor to *Old Ways* was quietly forgotten; the International Harvesters were disbanded; and when Young was quizzed in 1988 about his volte-face, he offered a convenient soundbite: 'One morning I woke up and all I could hear was this massive fucking beat. And my guitar was just rising out of it. I just heard rock'n'roll in my head so fucking loud that I couldn't ignore it.'

Rock'n'roll led him back to Crazy Horse, whose bassist, Billy Talbot, shifts uneasily when asked about Young's allegiance to country music: 'I'm sure that when he's doing it, it's very important to him. When he gets involved in any phase of his career, he's sincere.' 'You have to be, don't you?' adds drummer Ralph Molina. 'You couldn't do a country thing just for the sake of doing it. Could you?'

37 Rednecks

Satire and suspicion between country and rock, 1969–1992: Merle Haggard; Frank Zappa; Neil Young; Lynyrd Skynyrd; Randy Newman; Eugene Chadbourne; Mojo Nixon and Jello Biafra; k.d. lang

When Culture Club's success in the mid-eighties created a media personality out of their flamboyant lead singer, Boy George, country stars Moe Bandy and Joe Stampley saw the opportunity for some harmless fun. They donned women's clothes and tied braids in their hair to promote their hit single 'Where's The Dress?', which imagined a world in which honky-tonk cowboys would have to become transvestites to make it on to the radio.

Hillbilly entertainers could always laugh at their prejudices. In the mid-nineties, comedian Jeff Foxworthy built a career on his 'You might be a redneck' routine. But 'Where's The Dress?' was something new – a parody of the pop charts which assumed that its audience would recognize the target. No country singer lampooned the Beatles or the Stones in the sixties; it was easier to pretend that they didn't exist. By 1984, in the world of cable TV and pop videos, that degree of isolation was no longer possible. When country tiptoed into the video age, it wasn't unusual for rock icons to become the subject of gentle abuse – like the Rolling Stones lookalikes who were thrown off-camera in the clip for Alan Jackson's 1991 hit, 'Don't Rock The Jukebox'.

What was missing from 'Where's The Dress?' and 'Don't Rock The Jukebox' was contempt. Moe 'n' Joe didn't want to lynch Boy George, they were just enjoying a cheap laugh at his expense. Hank Williams Jr was more acerbic, but between his lyrical barbs at tight-assed New Yorkers and Saddam Hussein, he proclaimed his right to listen to the Allman Brothers Band and Hank Williams – and if you didn't like it, you could kiss his ass. Country hadn't always been so tolerant. The best-selling country single of 1969, the year of Woodstock and Altamont, was Merle Haggard's 'Okie

From Muskogee'. Haggard was inspired to write the song when his tour bus was headed into Tulsa, past a sign that read 'Muskogee – 19 miles'. 'Hell,' quipped one of his band, 'I'll bet they don't smoke marijuana in Muskogee,' and twenty minutes later a redneck anthem was complete.

Haggard intended his song as a piece of playful name-calling, but he hadn't reckoned on the public reaction. From President Richard Nixon down, 'Okie' was adopted by American conservatives as a rallying-call against dope-smoking, bearded hippies. Haggard had no quarrel with hippies ('I didn't give a shit how long their hair was'), but he drew the line at abusing the American flag: 'It wasn't popular to be patriotic then. I had a brother who was a Marine, and I grew up saluting the flag. I believed in it, I really did. The thing that bothered me was that some of the people known as long-hairs were burning the flag. I didn't like that. I still don't.'

Haggard followed 'Okie' with 'The Fightin' Side Of Me', another patriotic blast widely interpreted as an assault on underground culture. He admitted later that, 'Those songs actually hurt me. They alienated me from a lot of people who might otherwise have been fans of mine.' Rock groups such as the Grateful Dead and the Beach Boys defused 'Okie From Muskogee' by turning it into a satirical singalong. But Haggard's defiance, at the height of the conflict in Vietnam, polarized the rock and country audiences. By the end of the sixties, rock itself had divided between those who revered country as a cornerstone of American music, and those who viewed it as a symbol of racism, bigotry and mindless support for US imperialism.

That paragon of rock satire, Frank Zappa, whose boundless musical eclecticism wasn't matched by his worldview, used country as a euphemism for idiocy in his 1971 movie *200 Motels*. Lonesome Cowboy Burt is the stupidest man in Centerville, the mindless small town which plays reluctant host to Zappa's travelling freakshow. Burt (real name Burtram Redneck) hates Commies, loves beer, and hasn't washed in weeks. Zappa lets Burt betray his prejudices via a clichéd country hoedown; the Mothers Of Invention, Zappa's band, throw themselves into a parody of Texas banality. The irony is that Zappa, with his endless jabs at feminism, proved himself every bit as bigoted as the Lonesome Cowboy. Another Lonesome Cowboy – Bill, this time – was spotlighted by Lou Reed on the Velvet Underground's 1970 album *Loaded*. But Reed skipped the opportunity for some regional rhetoric; his cowboy was a clubland clone, a refugee from Andy Warhol's movie *Lonesome Cowboy*.

Even as country-rock swept through underground culture at the end of the sixties, some of its luminaries maintained an emotional distance. There was affectionate parody in the way Roger McGuinn sang '(I Like) The Christian Life' on the Byrds' *Sweetheart Of The Rodeo*; while Gram Parsons wasn't unaware of the comic potential in cloaking the Flying Burrito Brothers in Nudie suits. The New Riders Of The Purple Sage demonstrated their love of hillbilly music, and pastiched it, on their doper's concept album *The Adventures Of Panama Red*. Dan Hicks and his Hot Licks crooned western swing favourites such as 'I'm An Old Cowhand (From The Rio Grande)' with the same amused devotion. Both Asleep At The Wheel and Commander Cody and his Lost Planet Airmen created careers out of the cultural mismatch between hippie values and their love of fifties country music.

That kind of role-playing left the country industry uncertain how they should react to Leon Russell when he reinvented himself as country singer Hank Wilson. Texas Jewboy and comic novelist Kinky Friedman brought a cynical rock sensibility to his redneck persona on albums such as *Sold American* and *Lasso From El Paso*. But Friedman was being marketed as a country singer; so too was Jerry Jeff Walker, a transplanted New Yorker who cut Ray Wylie Hubbard's 'Up Against The Wall Redneck Mother' as a satirical anthem for the Texas honky-tonks.

Walker, Friedman and Zappa were playing cultural stereotypes for laughs. Neil Young eventually reached the same accommodation with redneck traditions, romping through outlaw cowboy anthems like 'Saddle Up The Palomino' and 'Bite The Bullet'. But fifteen years earlier, the performer who in the mid-eighties would (briefly) pledge the rest of his career to country music had delivered the most outspoken assault on the territory which was its home.

'Southern Man', the key track on his 1970 album *After The*

Gold Rush, was delivered with a passion never heard in Young's music before. It evoked visions of the flaming crosses of the Ku Klux Klan, of the nightmarish 'screaming and bullwhips crashing' of institutional slavery. But the same lines which were widely interpreted as a cry against bigotry ('Southern change gonna come at last . . . how long? How long?') echoed the South's quest for justice after the torching of their cities in the Civil War. To muddy the currents still further, Young delivered his final verse in character, as a frenzied Southerner driven to murder by the sight of his woman in a black man's arms. 'Swear by God I'm gonna cut him down,' he wailed, his voice cracking into a scream of anguish.

Young obviously regarded the song as an anthem of freedom; when he was told of a ceasefire in Vietnam during a New York show in 1973, he played 'Southern Man' to celebrate the moment. By then, he had telegraphed other confused messages about the mind of the South. In 1971, he recorded 'Alabama', a lukewarm attempt to match the fire of 'Southern Man'. The state which regularly re-elected George Wallace as its governor was widely regarded as the most racist part of the country, and 'Alabama' was hailed as another liberal crusade. Yet Young was in conciliatory mood: 'Can I see you and shake your hand, Make friends down in Alabama.' A year later, Wallace was running for president (with the open support of country stars like Tammy Wynette and George Jones) when he was shot and paralysed. Young responded with a campaign song for anti-Vietnam War candidate Eugene McCarthy, which seemed to doubt his ability to deliver on his central promise. 'There's a man who says he can put an end to war,' he sang uncertainly, saving his sympathy for another candidate: 'They shot George Wallace down, he'll never walk again.' It was hardly a cry of jubilation.

In 1974, boogie band Lynyrd Skynyrd made a belated response to Young's rhetoric. Pointedly, their song was called 'Sweet Home Alabama': 'We've heard Mr Young sing about us . . . I hope Neil Young will remember, A Southern man don't want him around.' An unambiguous message from a group signed to Al Kooper's Sounds of the South production company – except that Skynyrd's sweet home wasn't Alabama but Florida, a thousand miles to the east. Neil Young closed the circle by performing their attack as a medley with 'Southern Man', a few weeks after several members of Skynyrd had died in an air crash. His band that night was dubbed the Gone With The Wind Orchestra, a reminder of the South's most tragic role in Hollywood history.

Randy Newman condensed the entire confused debate into a single album, 1974's *Good Old Boys*. The tattooed hands of love and hate were clenched in every song. 'Rednecks' stacked up the layers of irony, as Newman ridiculed his Southern targets ('we don't know our ass from a hole in a ground') with a chorus that sounded like a celebration. 'He may be a fool but he's our fool,' his redneck narrator sang of Louisiana governor Lester Maddox; but the jester could speak wisdom forbidden to the other courtiers: 'The North has set the nigger free . . . Yes, he's free to be put in a cage in Harlem in New York City.' As the Mississippi floods rise in 'Louisiana 1927', Newman sings, 'They're trying to wash us away.' Like Neil Young watching Governor Wallace condemned to a wheelchair, Randy Newman found compassion in his heart for the tragic racism of the Old South. 'Southern Man', 'Sweet Home Alabama' and 'Rednecks' were products of a unique era of cultural uncertainty that fell between the civil rights battles of the sixties and the Southern chic inspired by Jimmy Carter's presidential victory in 1976. The blurring of mainstream country, rock and pop styles in the late seventies and early eighties pushed these investigations of identity out to the margins.

Only there could Eugene Chadbourne maintain a decade-long marriage between honky-tonk and the avant-garde, performing what he called 'free improvised country and western bebop . . . insane, foolish, craved and depraved'. On 1981's *There'll Be No Tears Tonight*, he deconstructed such country hits as Merle Haggard's 'Swinging Doors' and Johnny Paycheck's 'Take This Job And Shove It'; later festivities included *LSD C&W* (the avant-garde plays Roger Miller and the Beatles) and *Country Music In The World Of Islam* (Christian and Muslim fundamentalisms collide).

Like the cowpunks who filled Blood On The Saddle, Tex and the Horseheads and the Screaming Sirens, Chadbourne approached country as a fan. The putative Frank Zappas of the eighties and nineties no longer treated the hillbilly tradition with scorn. Instead, they used its very 'authenticity', and its façade of morality, as a weapon against hypocrisy and good taste. The Hickoids from Austin delivered satirical country-rock records filled with songs about bestiality (with Texas cows, of course) and transvestites. One of their albums was named *Waltz A Crossdress Texas*. Ween indulged their adolescent humour with *12 Golden Country Greats*, a record inflated with fart jokes and gratuitous expletives.

Then there were the cultural terrorists, for whom country was a signifier of the impending collapse of American civilization. Caroliner made albums of 'industrial bluegrass', crushing rural imagery, acoustic instruments and random explosions of factory noise into a surreal critique of late-twentieth-century capitalism. The Residents, the pseudonymous creators of a twenty-five-year tradition of cut-and-paste musical adventures, rounded up Hank Williams, John Philip Sousa, George Gershwin and James Brown into their *American Composer Series* albums, and emerged with music that sounded like none of them.

At the heart of all these raids on country music was a philosophy that the avant-gardists shared with the hillbilly traditionalists: things were better in the old days. 'Garth Brooks is the anti-Hank Williams,' declares Kinky Friedman. 'Country singers today seem devoid of emotional heritage. I miss the undecaffeinated sound of the fifties and sixties.'

His nostalgia was echoed by two unlikely country fans, incendiary rock satirist Mojo Nixon and punk icon turned campaigner for freedom-of-speech Jello Biafra of the Dead Kennedys. They combined for a glorious 1994 album, *Prairie Home Invasion*, on which Nixon proclaimed, 'Let's Go Burn Ole Nashville Down': 'Burn burn Nash Vegas, char its rancid soul . . . Let's go burn ole Nashville down, save the country soul.'

At its least restrained, *Prairie Home Invasion* sounded like a duet between Jerry Lee Lewis and Johnny Rotten, two performers who might have been ready to take Nixon's instruction seriously. But what would Lewis, the breakneck Baptist, or Rotten, author of the anti-abortion rant 'Bodies', have made of 'Will The Fetus Be Aborted'? What seemed at first like naked iconoclasm, perverting the country gospel standard 'Will The Circle Be Unbroken', proved to be a scabrous protest against the professed Christians who'd bombed abortion clinics in the South: 'Kathy had two kids already, And an abortion is what she chose, Christian showed her a bloody fetus, She said, "That's fine, I'll have one of those."' 'Mojo Nixon, Andrew Dice Clay, those kind of guys, they're sort of Kinky Friedman godchildren,' Friedman says. 'Lenny Bruce was doing it before me.' As Bob Dylan wrote, 'Lenny Bruce is dead . . . He was an outlaw, that's for sure.' And the arch satirist of the fifties and sixties would have taken his pleasure in Jello Biafra, Randy Newman and probably Merle Haggard as well.

Not even Lenny Bruce dared to immerse himself so fully in his satire that humour became confused with adoration. But k.d. lang, the creation of Canadian performance artist Kathy Lang, slipped almost effortlessly across the line between caricature and reality. For almost a decade, lang masqueraded as a new traditionalist, a keeper of Patsy Cline's flame, convincing enough for veteran producer Owen Bradley and singers Loretta Lynn, Brenda Lee and Kitty Wells to aid her career. So fully did she inhabit her new personality that she herself seemed uncertain where satire and sincerity divided.

Raised in the tiny farming community of Consort, Alberta, Lang escaped to Edmonton at the end of the seventies, involving herself in avant-garde art groups and musical theatre. One of her earliest stage roles was in a 1981 musical called *Country Chorale*. Lyricist Ray Storey suggested that Lang should model herself on Nashville's leading balladeer of the early sixties, Patsy Cline. 'Who's Patsy Cline?' Lang retorted. Two years later, the renamed k.d. lang was leading a country band called the Reclines, and claiming herself as Patsy's reincarnation. 'Somehow I've inherited her emotions, her soul,' she told a reporter in 1984. 'I know that sounds weird, but I do believe it.' 'If some idiotic interviewer asks me if I'm really the reincarnation of Patsy Cline, of course I'm going to say yes,' she admitted to another journalist.

lang documented her infatuation with a suitably exuberant album, *A Truly Western Experience* – part rockabilly, part torch ballad, yet climaxing with a non-country tribute to a fellow satirist, 'Hooked On Junk'. Nobody who heard that track, or who witnessed lang's stage attire – the cropped punk hair, winged spectacles with the lenses removed, cut-off cowboy boots and mock Nudie jacket – could have mistaken her for a country girl. But her rhetoric and her voice, which soared from a whisper to a bluesy cry, somehow persuaded the Canadian country establishment that lang was nothing more than mildly eccentric. Sire Records boss Seymour Stein, who had already signed the Ramones and Madonna, was less fazed by lang's eccentricity. 'You are what country music would have been if Nashville hadn't screwed it up,' he told her. Stein could already imagine how lang might win over Nashville with her voice and New York with her image. The joke was lost on Dave Edmunds, who produced her major label début *Angel With A Lariat* as if lang were another Emmylou Harris. Stein's prediction was only confirmed when Owen Bradley, who'd produced Patsy Cline's biggest hits, rose from the bed where he was recovering from a severe heart attack and demanded the chance to produce this exuberant revivalist of the music he'd helped to create.

The result was *Shadowland*, a stunning recreation of the torch-ballad tradition which disappointed none of the interested observers of lang's career. lang now felt bold enough to admit that she was after 'people who are too artsy to like country and people who are too country to like art'. When *Shadowland* picked up both country and pop airplay, she noted that 'I've gotten the first taste of acceptance, but the game's not over.'

In Europe, lang had already attracted a loyal lesbian following, who'd quickly recognized a role model – even if lang was not yet prepared to admit her own sexual orientation. Reaction in Nashville was far more suspicious. An industry which regarded the mildly suggestive antics of Tanya Tucker as risqué was not yet ready for a woman who moved like the teenage Elvis and dressed like Gertrude Stein. 'I don't eat meat, I'm not a Christian and I don't have big fluffy hair,' lang told *Spin* magazine in 1988. Eighteen months later, she took part in the 'Meat Stinks' campaign organized by PETA (People for the Ethical Treatment of Animals). Her hometown disowned her, and so did Nashville. She countered with 1992's *Ingénue* album, a delicious, sensuous collection of orchestral pop. Finally relaxing into her status as a gay icon, lang bid her old flame goodbye: 'I don't want to be bitter about the country music scene. I did it with respect and with humour. But it's like a love affair. It's over.' The country industry breathed a sigh of relief.

38 Stranger in the House

Country-punk, cowpunk and the Paisley Underground, 1977–1987: Elvis Costello; Joe Ely and the Clash; Jason and the Nashville Scorchers; the Long Ryders; Green On Red; Giant Sand and the Band Of Blacky Ranchette; Lone Justice; Rank & File

The British punk explosion fractured the narrative of rock history, its rhetoric demanding a scorched-earth policy towards the past. Before 1976, critical consensus had viewed rock's progress as a great tradition – a seamless path from Elvis Presley and Chuck Berry through the Beatles, Stones and Bob Dylan to Bruce Springsteen, Van Morrison and Joni Mitchell. Now this comfortable road was replaced by a tangle of shortcuts and dead-ends.

Not only the past was open to claims. In the battle for the future, ideological fences were immediately erected between 'punk' (three-chord barrages of anarchy, aggression and angst) and 'new wave' (punk imagery applied to more melodic material which betrayed the heritage of sixties beat). The more artificial the divide, the more vehemently it was applied. Meanwhile, the British rock press delighted in unearthing long-haired skeletons. The Stranglers were revealed as Doors-obsessed glam-rockers, the Clash as diehard disciples of the Rolling Stones. Even such uncompromising figures as Johnny Rotten or Captain Sensible were unmasked as shameless champions of progressive rock.

Most of the British punk vanguard came out of an even less glamorous tradition: 'pub-rock'. By the mid-seventies, bar-room venues in and around London were playing host to bands who felt distanced from the arrogance of rock's decadent aristocrats. They mourned the lost simplicity of Merseybeat, fifties rock'n'roll and Chicago R&B, and self-consciously reversed the clock to 1963, hoping to recreate the passion that had driven the Beatles and the Rolling Stones to forge new music out of American archetypes.

Brinsley Schwarz typified the pub-rock ideology. Their repertoire was filled with fifties rock, sixties beat and soul, and cunning pastiches penned by bassist Nick Lowe. While rivals such as Dr Feelgood restricted themselves to rhythm and blues, Lowe was open to the honky-tonk laments of George Jones and the Bakersfield rhythms of Buck Owens and Merle Haggard. Other musicians who shared Lowe's tastes were fired by his example. Among them was Declan McManus, the Liverpudlian son of a big-band vocalist who had been exposed to everything from Ella Fitzgerald to Chuck Berry. His band Flip City joined the pub-rock circuit, playing the usual round of covers plus original songs that were heavily influenced by the Band, the Beatles – and Gram Parsons.

In 1977, McManus rechristened himself Elvis Costello, signed to the innovative Stiff label in London, and issued a début single, 'Less Than Zero', that was raw, radical and not remotely like a punk record. But his image – his eyes bulging behind Buddy Holly glasses, his voice howling two-minute rants of self-hatred and revenge – ensured that he was greeted as a kindred spirit to Johnny Rotten, Joe Strummer and Rat Scabies.

As 'Radio Sweetheart', the flipside of his first record, revealed, Costello was soaked in influences that punk preferred to forget. Not only was it overtly American in style, at a time when the Clash were ranting 'I'm So Bored With The USA'; it betrayed comfortable familiarity with the two-step rhythms of honky-tonkers such as Ray Price and Ernest Tubb.

'I started listening to country music seriously when I heard the Byrds,' Costello says. 'Around 1970, I was interested in this strand of Americana, groups like the Band and the Grateful Dead – and that's when I heard the Byrds' *Sweetheart Of The Rodeo*. I got curious to hear the people they were covering, George Jones and Merle Haggard. It was the same process people went through in the early sixties, of discovering Howlin' Wolf through the Rolling Stones. I'd been exposed to R&B at home, but country had never really got into our household, so I had to find it by myself. It was quite hard, because although you could hear people like Johnny Cash on the radio, you couldn't come across Jones or Haggard unless you were a specialist country fan. I liked the plainness of the chords, the churchy harmony. It was a natural step to try and write something in that style.'

The first song Costello recorded for his début album was 'Stranger In The House', an unashamed homage to George Jones. 'We had to leave that off the record,' he explains, 'because the country element would have put me back on the other side of these style wars that were going on. At that stage, I could have been killed by that sort of thing.'

Costello owned up to his passion for Jones and Gram Parsons in early interviews, but his comments were lost in the swamp of controversy about his name, his supposed misogyny, and his more obvious misanthropy. By the end of 1977 he'd formed a band, the Attractions, and thrown himself into a hyped-up pastiche of sixties Swinging London that came to epitomize 'new wave'.

Touring America in 1978 to promote *This Year's Model*, Costello arrived in Nashville: 'The kids there didn't want us to be country. They wanted us to be even more punk than we were perceived to be elsewhere in America. We were accepted wholesale as the real thing, because for many people in America, we were the first group that was anything like a punk band.'

The gesture of opening their Nashville show with a suite of Hank Williams songs backfired; and the culture clash continued as the Attractions walked the streets of Music City: 'These kids started giving us a hard time because we had short hair. A few years earlier we'd have been beaten up there for having long hair. Which just goes to show how silly all this style stuff is. But we did have to be careful when we went down South. Some towns were hipper than others. We never went to Memphis early on, for obvious reasons.'

That US tour coincided with a bizarre attempt to widen George Jones' appeal by teaming him with performers outside his own sphere. 'He was doing this duets album,' Costello explains, 'and they figured they ought to cover all the markets. Somebody in New York had played somebody in Nashville "Stranger In The House", and they got the idea I should record with George. So I went down there – and George didn't show. There was a warrant out for his arrest for non-payment of alimony, or something like that. They were hounding him at the time.' The 'Stranger In The House' duet was eventually completed the following year. While the media hyped the story of a stolid country star daring to meet England's rowdy punk rocker, it was not Costello but George Jones who was the drink- and drug-racked outlaw flirting with self-destruction.

Another country/punk liaison in the late seventies aroused equal confusion. Unaware of the Clash's roots in the pub-rock scene – singer Joe Strummer had led the American-inspired 101ers – Lubbock country star Joe Ely was surprised to be courted by a British punk band: 'They came to a show in London. I'd never heard of them, but they seemed to know the songs from my early albums. They said, "We're in a band. C'mon, we'll show you the town." They showed me all these places I never knew existed, a whole different world of London to what I'd seen before.'

Ely and the Clash made a drunken pledge to connect when the punk rockers toured America in 1979. 'They'd heard Marty Robbins and they liked the old rockabilly stuff from West Texas,' Ely explained, 'so I invited them down to play in some out-of-the-way places that would not normally be on a rock band's agenda – San Antonio, Lubbock, Laredo. They reminded me of the fifties James Dean thing, and they thought us Texas guys were kinda outlaws in our own right. So we hit it off pretty well.'

In February 1980, the Clash toured Britain to promote *London Calling*, their classic amalgam of punk energy and traditional rock mythology. It was a pivotal moment in their career, as they attempted to encompass the American influences they'd disavowed so vocally three years earlier. Outside the venues, skinheads and punks erupted in violent skirmishes, each eager to claim the Clash as their own. Inside, the atmosphere was equally uncertain. Reggae toaster Mikey Dread performed a rambling set of ganja-dulled dub; the Clash dampened any potential violence by playing at a volume so extreme that hardened punks reeled away from the stage, hands clasped to their ears. Completing a bizarre evening, the Joe Ely Band thundered through their Texas rock'n'roll, all country subtlety lost in the assault of noise and tension. 'We didn't get kicked off anywhere,' Ely noted after the tour was over. 'The people we were playing for had never heard our songs, and didn't know where in the hell we came from, or why we were on the bill. Considering all that, it went pretty good.'

The Clash/Ely liaison was never documented in the studio, but in 1981, Elvis Costello returned to Nashville to record an album of country songs with veteran producer Billy Sherrill. 'It wasn't so much what went on in the studio that coloured *Almost Blue*,' Costello claims, 'it was more what didn't go on, or what I got up to the rest of the time.' Hints of his extra-curricular adventures surfaced when he jerked the Attractions through a rocket-fuelled trashing of Hank Williams' 'Why Don't You Love Me'. But most of the album was devoted to respectful renditions of country standards. 'More than anything,' he recalls, 'Billy Sherrill was bemused about us wanting to cut what were to him worn-out songs. But they weren't worn out to our audience, and those that didn't freak out at the mere thought of us doing a country record bought it.' Costello labelled the record with a mock warning sticker, to guard 'narrow-minded' listeners from disappointment. The album sold to British fans who would never have bought the original versions of the same songs, despite the fact that George Jones sang 'A Good Year For The Roses' 'better' (that is, with less apparent strain) than his devoted disciple. But, as Elvis explains, 'The album sold nothing in America because they didn't know how to market it.'

Costello and George Jones, Ely and the Clash – these collaborations were too isolated to arouse more than idle curiosity in Britain. But in America, it was easier for the adrenalin rush of punk to drag country – or, to be more precise, rockabilly – in its wake. 'We take earlier forms, rub them together and create little explosions,' explained Tav Falco, whose rockabilly punk band Panther Burns were active in both Memphis and New York during the late seventies. 'It started as a real garage phenomenon. We played alongside all these No Wave bands in New York, like DNA and James White. Then in Memphis, a lot of young kids came to listen to us – punk rockers, new wave kids, hillbilly kids, black kids. Down South they were not really separated the way they were in New York.' From Tav Falco's Panther Burns evolved an entire tradition of punkabilly or, as it came to be known, psychobilly, which pumped the basic structure of Sun rockabilly full of punk aggression – and ignored or expelled the country roots.

On the West Coast, country and punk co-existed more easily. In the music of bands such as X and Social Distortion, traces of Bakersfield icons such as Buck Owens could be discerned amid the chaotic barrage of Clash-style rhetoric. That same eclecticism was apparent in the San Francisco and Los Angeles clubs, where punk bands such as Black Flag would regularly share bills with such diverse acts as roots rockers the Blasters and honky-tonk revivalist Dwight Yoakam.

These collaborations baffled the small community of Nashville punks who survived in the heart of the country industry. Among them was Jason Ringenberg, who'd been raised among Illinois farmers but had moved to Tennessee in time to hear the delayed echo of the Sex Pistols' revolution. 'We got everything so late,' he recalls. 'You wouldn't believe how long it took that stuff to reach Nashville. But when we heard it, it hit us so hard.'

In his childhood, Ringenberg explains, 'country was everywhere. All the farm people listened to it. It was on all the truck radios. The country stations were playing at the corn markets and hog markets. I loved it when I was a young kid, but then I rejected it in my teens. When punk hit Nashville, I plugged right into that scene, because country had nothing to do with me. There were these clubs in town like Frankenstein's and Cantrell's, and that's where we gathered – and where we played, when we started the band.'

The band was Jason and the Nashville Scorchers, who built their shows around incendiary punk tunes and iconoclastic arrangements of Hank Williams songs. They shed the punk ideology by the early eighties, but retained the raucous rock'n'roll energy. Warner Hodges thrashed sheets of noise out of his guitar; Jason careered around the stage like Jerry Lee Lewis let loose in an amphetamine factory. Their 1982 EP *Reckless Country Soul* captured their almost incoherent power; 1983's *Fervor* refined it.

EMI America then offered the band a deal, on one condition: that the Nashville Scorchers become the Scorchers. 'That was a piece of marketing genius,' says Ringenberg sarcastically. 'The record company said it made us sound too country. We were just a bunch of kids, and to us it didn't seem too big a deal. We thought, "It's only a name." But right after we'd done it, I knew we'd made a big mistake. It was so stupid, because the original name was much cooler. For five years, I was too embarrassed to tell anyone the real reason why we changed it.'

The renamed Jason and the Scorchers added a rousing cover of Bob Dylan's 'Absolutely Sweet Marie' to the *Fervor* EP, and visited Europe for the first time. Their arrival coincided with a wave of British enthusiasm for American 'guitar bands', which fused dozens of isolated units and scenes into something that looked like a movement.

Early-eighties Britain was dominated by the New Romantics, whose synthesizer-based pop tunes and dandyish imagery repelled those who'd looked to 'classic rock' – or, indeed, punk – for some kind of emotional authenticity. The American bands were greeted as flag-bearers for rock's traditional values, lauded as much for their influences (always the Stones, the Velvet Underground and the Byrds) as for any originality.

In the mid-eighties, these bands – among them Green On Red, the Dream Syndicate, the Long Ryders, Giant Sand, the Bangles and REM – occupied a far more central place in British rock culture than they did at home. Bands who were unknown outside their hometown were suddenly offered UK deals. 'Whether we liked each other's music or not, we respected the fact that all of us came out of the clubs,' reckons Jason Ringenberg. 'These bands weren't record company creations: we all came out of old-school American bars. Even if you didn't know them, you felt like they were friends.'

The British media struggled to find a title for this American invasion. The garage-punk and psychedelic influences on bands such as Green On Red and Plasticland led some journalists to dub them 'the Paisley Underground'. Less sympathetic commentators dismissed the movement as sixties revivalism – a perception heightened by the open affection that these musicians showed for the past.

None of these bands paid deeper homage to the sixties country-rock tradition than the Long Ryders. Stephen McCarthy came from Virginia, loved country music and psychedelia, and recognized a way of combining the two genres when he heard the Misunderstood's steel guitarist, Glenn Campbell, using the instrument for psychedelic ends. Sid Griffin grew up in the bluegrass state of Kentucky: 'I hated country music. I never listened to it until my sister told my uncle to buy me *Sweetheart Of The Rodeo*, not suspecting that it wouldn't sound like *Mr Tambourine Man*, because she knew that I loved the Byrds. I was stunned when I heard it. Later I listened to the Burritos, and finally I caught up with Gram Parsons again around the time he issued his *GP* album. Then I was a goner, and realized this was the guy.'

During the mid-seventies, the teenage Griffin played garage-rock in a band called the Frosties, covering tunes by the Kinks and the Byrds. In 1977, he moved to California, joining the punk group Death Wish, and then another garage outfit, the Unclaimed. The Long Ryders were a way of connecting all his enthusiasms. Inadvertently, they performed the same role for the Southern California rock audience.

'There were older people on the scene who were really thrilled that somebody was playing that sixties-influenced music again,' Griffin recalls. 'That was the first time that anyone had done Buffalo Springfield- and Byrds-oriented music with punk attitude and energy. So we got these weird crowds – Black Flag and Circle Jerks fans, who liked the fact that we played fast, hard and heavy; and an older crowd who hadn't heard this kind of music in fifteen years, and who liked the 12-strings, and the Clarence White-styled lead guitar.

'When we went to middle America and to England, it became more or less just young people. But in Southern California we had this real cross-pollination, with hippies and people from communes standing next to people with purple hair or shaven heads. It was a beautiful thing to see.'

Their 1984 album *Native Sons* captured the Long Ryders at their peak. As a private joke for sixties aficionados, the cover artwork mirrored the design of an unissued Buffalo Springfield album, *Stampede*. There was more revivalism when the band borrowed Gram Parsons' arrangement of an old Waylon Jennings hit, 'Mental Revenge'. But the rest of the album was a more cunning blend of old and new, evoking memories of the past without repeating it. Griffin even produced a tribute to Jerry Lee Lewis on 'Final Wild Son', a bar-room rocker that captured the Killer's enigma: 'He's possessed by something which never comes quite clear.'

Native Sons had a confidence which suggested the Long Ryders might grow to outlive the nostalgic comparisons. But the cultural experiment of recording 1985's *State Of Our Union* in England with an English producer (pub-rocker Will Birch) backfired. Griffin is adamant that 'The guitar doesn't know if you're from England, or from Gambia, or from California. Musical notes do not respect international borders.' But *State Of Our Union* stripped the Long Ryders of their national dress, and left them sounding like an imitation of a British pub-rock band. 'We were a fish out of water,' Griffin concedes. 'It would have been smarter to have someone like Jim Dickinson recording us in Mississippi, rather than Will Birch in Chipping Norton.' Though subsequent Long Ryders records redeemed much of their lost ground, their moment had passed, and the band dissolved before the end of the eighties – dogged to the last by the British media's embarrassment at having promoted them so heavily in 1984.

With the perennial exception of REM – and the Bangles, who made territorial arguments irrelevant by scoring Top 40 singles – most of the Paisley Underground bands careered from premature adulation at the hands of the press to premature dismissal. Their treatment masked their eclectic approaches to the puzzle of how to play sixties-inspired music in the 1980s.

One solution was to view the sixties through the distorted prism of the Rolling Stones' 1972 album *Exile On Main Street* – a Gothic adventure in which the Southern breezes of country, soul, blues and gospel were soured by urban paranoia and decay. No American band lived out that scenario more blatantly than Green On Red, whose sixties punk roots were soon swamped by leader Dan Stuart's penchant for living out his worst nightmares. With guitarist and sidekick Chuck Prophet, Stuart allowed producer Jim Dickinson (who'd contributed to the sessions for the Stones' equally dark 1969 album *Let It Bleed*) to guide him through 1987's *The Killer Inside Me* – as black a vision of humanity as rock has ever produced. 'That's music to hang your wife by,' Stuart admits. 'I can't even listen to it. After that, I had a big nervous breakdown and went to live in a shack in the desert.'

The hiatus allowed him to rethink his musical direction. 'I'd always thought country was too square,' he explains. 'As a kid, I had to share a room with my brother, and he wanted to go to sleep every night listening to this hard country station out of Tucson, Arizona. He loved that hardcore shit, and some of it I liked, but I couldn't admit it, because I wanted to listen to the Stones and Lynyrd Skynyrd on FM. It was only when I was out on the road with Green On Red that it started to make sense. When you're a middle-class kid, and you hear these guys on the radio, whining that they've lost their girl and they're stuck out on the road, you just think, "Who are these losers?" But when you're out on the road yourself, and your life's on the line, you start to feel, "Hey, he's singing about me."'

Through a series of albums, cut with producers including Jim Dickinson, Glyn Johns and Al Kooper, Stuart investigated different aspects of his mental landscape. The Kooper collaboration was *Scapegoats*, the closest Green On Red ever came to making a straight country record. On stage, they'd long been prone to delivering outlaw standards like 'Are You Sure Hank Done It This Way' as if they were bulletins from the frontline of psychic distress. On *Scapegoats*, recorded in Nashville, Stuart immersed himself in the craft of country writing, under the tutelage of veterans such as Dickinson and country/soul maestro Dan Penn. 'I really respect the Nashville songwriting formula,' he concedes. 'It's got to make literal sense, and it has to have a beginning, a middle and an end. What's great about Dan is that he doesn't get distracted, no matter what madness is going down.' When Penn had to leave the sessions, Stuart and Prophet attempted to work without him: 'We finished up this song called "You're The Sweetest Thing This Side Of Heaven", which could be country or Aretha Franklin soul. We got to this point in the bridge where I came up with these lines: "The little things you whisper into my ear, Honey it soothes my very soul". Chuck kept saying, "We've got to keep it sugary, like cotton-candy," so I said, "OK, we'll have, 'Just like cotton-candy you're crystal clear, You'll stay with me as I grow old.'" We thought that was great.

'Any time a producer came into the session, we'd grab him, play him the song and beg him to find someone to cut it – we had Don

Williams in mind. One producer came in, and he loved it. Then it got to the bridge, and he said, "Hey, wait a minute, man. What the hell are you doing there? That was a good song until then. There's nothing crystal clear about cotton-candy!" And he said, "Never forget that in Nashville you're writing for that guy who has a six-pack of beer, watching TV. It's gotta make sense, and it's gotta rhyme." In rock'n'roll, free verse rules!'

For Stuart's friend and occasional collaborator, Howie Gelb, the rock/country border has been the guiding line for his entire career – based for the last fifteen years in Arizona, on the fringes of the Mojave Desert. Stuart is affectionately sarcastic about Gelb's credentials: 'Howie's from Scranton, Pennsylvania. He didn't move to Tucson until he was 22, and that was a studied thing. He spent a lot of time developing that persona. Hell, the guy even lives in Joshua Tree, where Gram Parsons died!'

Gelb's catalogue is split between two groups, Giant Sand and the Band Of Blacky Ranchette, who co-exist with similar but not identical philosophies and line-ups. As Giant Sand, Gelb channels the influence of his desert location ('It's almost like being underwater. In the desert, everything you know is wrong') into music that conveys an inverted sense of psychedelia. As Blacky Ranchette, he creates a mythic western landscape, and then peoples it with ghosts from the Charles Manson school of acting.

'I've always written country stuff,' Gelb explained, 'but I never put it out. Danny Stuart's girlfriend, Suzie Wrenn, was the one who first got the ball rolling. We used to do country stuff in town as *The Good, The Bad And The Ugly*. At the same time, I made up a little cassette. Suzie heard it and said, "I'm putting together a country record, not a country punk record, and 'Spinning Room Waltz' sounds just like the kind of thing I'm doing." She brought me out to Los Angeles, and all these other people like John Doe were supposed to be involved in this project.'

Over six months in early 1984, Wrenn compiled a collection of unorthodox country material from LA punk rockers – John Doe from X, Stephen McCarthy from the Long Ryders, Chris D and Julie Christensen from the Divine Horsemen, and now Gelb, under the guise of Blacky Ranchette. Gelb's efforts mutated into an album of his own, headed by 'Code Of The Road', a desert howl of joy which caught the raucous energy of punk without sounding remotely like the Sex Pistols. Connecting his desert myth with the dark angel of sixties rock, Charles Manson, Gelb revived 'Revolution Blues', Neil Young's ambivalent tale of dune-buggy outlaws sweeping down from the mountains to squeeze the lifeblood out of the Los Angeles élite. Gelb recited the lyrics like a drunken actor while steel guitars buzzed around the corpses like flies.

In the early nineties, Howie Gelb was still using Blacky Ranchette as a vehicle of loving subversion – writing an entire album, *Sage Advice*, during an eight-hour drive into the desert, then filling it out with a chaotic cover of Waylon Jennings' 'Trouble Man' which sounded like three movie soundtracks running over the same flickering cowboy picture. 'They're playing new fashion western with that old fashion hardcore,' Gelb sang elsewhere on the album, neatly paraphrasing Blacky Ranchette's career.

There was a conceptual intelligence to Gelb and Stuart's work which marked them out from the rest of the West Coast punk scene. Most of the new wave bands who displayed blatant country influences were dubbed 'cowpunks'. Rosie Flores of the Screaming Sirens, who became a doyenne of New Traditionalism in the late eighties, laid out the blueprint: 'Our music was a mix of aggressive country and rockabilly with a punk-looking style. We all had different-coloured hair, and wore big buckles and spiky belts. There were other notable bands like Blood On The Saddle and the True Believers doing the same thing.'

'People were looking for a new hybrid,' noted Maria McKee, lead vocalist of another California band, Lone Justice, 'and they decided it would be cowpunk. It was a hat I wore very comfortably and very well. I didn't have country roots – I come from Hollywood, and my family were artists and bohemians – but I loved country music.'

The band's début album showcased a band who matched new wave energy to the roots rock of Tom Petty and the Heartbreakers. The teenage McKee performed with a rare blend of aggression, passion and vulnerability that brought comparisons with Janis Joplin. Then Lone Justice were matched with top-flight rock producer Jimmy Iovine. 'He wanted me to be the new Linda Ronstadt or Stevie Nicks,' McKee explained. 'I love them, but my own style of music has always been very raw and urgent – until those qualities got sublimated by people who thought they would impede the commercial process. The minute the record business got involved, I was fodder to those satin-jacketed men. Lone Justice was one of the big sell-outs of the eighties.' The original line-up disbanded and the band became nothing more than a brand-name for McKee's remarketing as a younger Fleetwood Mac.

Brothers Chip and Tony Kinman were the most promising of the cowpunk bands. As the Dils, they had brought their Everly Brothers harmonies to San Francisco's punk scene. In the early eighties, they relocated to Austin and reinvented themselves as a country-punk band. For once, the concept was fully realized: the renamed Rank & File performed original material that harked back to fifties country and bluegrass and beyond, with a ferocious energy that matched the Clash. *Sundown*, their 1982 début, emphasized their songcraft rather than their aural assault; a second album, *Long Gone Dead*, pitched the Kinmans against sessionmen, internal problems having robbed them of guitarist Alejandro Escovedo (who soon formed the True Believers, and maintained a precarious if critically admired career as a purveyor of Americana into the late nineties). But any fantasy that Rank & File might steer country-rock into a new era were demolished when the Kinmans abruptly changed direction, first into hard rock and then avant-garde industrial pop. In 1996, they regrouped as Cowboy Nation, acting out a role that had once been their life.

The cowpunk tag rounded up a host of other contenders. There was Blood On The Saddle, whose firecracker hillbilly was memorably described by one critic as 'a rodeo where even the horses are doing speed'. Tex and the Horseheads played it strictly for laughs, befitting a band whose members claimed to have been christened Texacala Jones, Rock Vodka and Smog Vomit. The Meat Puppets toyed with a marriage between Hank Williams and Joe Strummer, before perfecting the slacker's grunge which was a major influence on Nirvana's Kurt Cobain. Rubber Rodeo (from that least country of states, Rhode Island) scrawled 'It don't mean a thang if it ain't got that twang' in the run-off grooves of their records, and covered Dolly Parton's 'Jolene'. John Trubee sacrificed the punk sound but retained the attitude for his traditionally played, sacrilegiously penned single, 'A Blind Man's Penis'. Nouveau rockabilly outfit Charlie Burton and the Cutouts punctured another taboo by recording a tune called 'Breathe For Me, Presley'.

Jason and the Scorchers were never so irreverent. Even when they were subjecting Leon Payne's 'Lost Highway' and Don Robertson's 'I Really Don't Want To Know' to full-fisted hard rock treatments on their *Lost And Found* album, Jason Ringenberg's band managed to preserve a modicum of respect for country traditions. But as the eighties progressed, the Scorchers' sound began to take on a metallic polish.

'The creative partnership between me and guitarist Warner Hodges was doomed,' Ringenberg explains. 'He was getting more and more into metal, and I was getting more and more into country. It was inevitable. We started out from more or less the same place, and then you can hear on the records how it changed. There was no way it was gonna last.'

The band's realignment also undermined their position at their new label, A&M: 'We scared away a lot of people. People could maybe get into the idea of cowpunk, but when we started to get into country metal, they couldn't understand that concept. I couldn't understand it myself! We were way off, trying to do two different things at the same time.' Ringenberg also reckons that the band suffered from the cultural stereotypes associated with country music: 'Where I was from originally, the Mid-West, we never really thought about racism. And in the South, I've never met a musician who was proud of that sort of thing. Most people from the South are ashamed of that connection. But in Europe, that image is still alive, that anyone who plays country – even rock'n'roll country, like we were doing – must be a racist. Plus, when all of those bands came out, it was at the height of the Reagan era, when he was trying to place all these American missiles in Europe. So there was a sudden backlash against anything American – particularly when Neil Young came out and said he supported Reagan.'

Completing the circle, Elvis Costello chose this moment to free himself from his band, the Attractions, and record an album entitled *King Of America* – using an almost entirely American cast, and shedding his sixties and seventies British influences in favour of US folk, blues and country. The new album was self-consciously soaked in Americana, as if Costello had returned to his Band albums to discover exactly what happened when outsiders infiltrated United States culture. That it was an ambiguous pledge of allegiance was apparent from his lyrics: much of the album was devoted to exploring the cultural chasm between Britain and the colony it had lost two hundred years earlier. By returning the debate to its roots, Costello echoed the equally difficult relationship between punk and country.

39 Born in the USA

The Woody Guthrie tradition, 1975–1999: Bruce Springsteen; Steve Earle; John Mellencamp

'Woody Guthrie was my last idol', wrote Bob Dylan in 1963. Arriving in Greenwich Village three years earlier, Dylan had orphaned himself from his past. To replace Bobby Zimmerman, the Little Richard fan from Hibbing who became a Minneapolis college kid, he created a teenage hobo, who had run away from home, hopped railroad trucks to the South, and learned his music from itinerant bluesmen.

His model was Woody Guthrie's *Bound For Glory*, a road map for the wandering spirit. What Dylan didn't know was that Guthrie had also rewritten his own history. Nearly a decade of his life was condensed into a sentence: 'An uncle of mine taught me to play the guitar and I got to going out a couple of nights a week to the cow ranches around to play for the square dances.'

That was in Pampa, Texas, where around 1930 Uncle Jeff and Nephew Woody ran a hillbilly band who leaned on Carter Family and Jimmie Rodgers material. Guthrie dismissed the hillbilly tradition as 'songs about the cow trails or the moon skipping through the sky', but when he joined his cousin Jack Guthrie in Los Angeles in 1937, he was still in the Carters' shadow. 'I got a little braver,' he wrote, 'and made up songs telling what I thought was wrong and how to make it right, songs that said what everybody in that country was thinking. And this has held me ever since' – and since his death in 1967, via his songs of freedom and injustice such as 'This Land Is Your Land', set to the tune of Carter Family favourite 'Little Darling, Pal Of Mine'.

'Woody Guthrie occupies an unusual position in American country and folk music,' wrote scholar Bill C. Malone in his epic *Country Music USA*, 'and is admittedly difficult to categorize.' So is his heritage, a mix of liberal ideology and overt populism claimed by every breed of post-war politician. 'Pastures Of Plenty', 'I Ain't Got No Home In This World Anymore', 'Do-Re-Mi' – the so-called protest songs that were his trademark – captured the resentment of the rural poor who endured the Great Depression of the 1930s. Like John Steinbeck's *The Grapes Of Wrath*, they voiced the agony of displaced Southerners who trudged west towards the chimera of a promised land.

Devouring *Bound For Glory*, the young Bobby Zimmerman found more romance than despair in Guthrie's tales. When he wrote 'Song To Woody' in 1961, his final lines echoed his debt: 'The very last thing that I'd want to do, is to say I've been hitting some hard travelling too.'

Having won the approval of 'his last idol' at Guthrie's hospital bed, where the troubadour lay stricken by the family curse of Huntington's chorea, Dylan quickly outgrew him. But he retained enough of Guthrie's spirit to persuade other musicians to investigate the source. Bruce Springsteen, Steve Earle and John Mellencamp drew lifelong inspiration from Dylan's role model. Like Guthrie's and Dylan's, their music drifted beyond categorization into a semi-fictional America peopled from the mythic past.

Springsteen fell deepest under Guthrie's spell. He came out of the New Jersey bars, raised on fifties rockabilly, sixties R&B and the garage-rock trinity of the Stones, the Yardbirds and the Animals. The decadent imagery of Dylan's mid-sixties work infected his songwriting, and when poverty forced him to scale down his ambitions in the early seventies, he was signed to Columbia as an acoustic bard, openly inspired by Dylan's *Bringing It All Back Home* and *Highway 61 Revisited*.

On his second album, *The Wild, The Innocent & The E Street Shuffle*, his recruitment of the E Street Band expanded his musical vocabulary. Now his songs were sketched in epic proportions, and Springsteen filled them with teen rebels and angels, as if Martin Scorsese were directing *West Side Story*.

Prolonged legal battles after his third album, *Born To Run*, capped Springsteen's naïve exuberance. During the three-year hiatus, his work darkened and matured – partly in response to his discovery of Woody Guthrie and, in 1978, Hank Williams.

Their influence transformed his music. *Darkness At The Edge Of Town* (1978) eschewed adolescent liberation in favour of a brooding melancholy. Once his characters had driven the streets as a cry of freedom; now they ran in circles, fleeing their relentless destiny. As the walls closed in, so did his music: increasingly, Springsteen narrowed his vision to the three chords that had sufficed for Woody and Hank.

On *The River* (1980), Springsteen's macho rock'n'roll was outclassed by dark, introspective songs about life without the possibility of escape. He then stripped down to an acoustic guitar, and shed his music of melodic flourish, for *Nebraska* (1982), a bleak album peopled by condemned men and sons racked by their fathers' expectations. It was no coincidence that one of the darkest songs, 'Mansion On The Hill', borrowed its title from Hank Williams.

The tumultuous reception of his next album, *Born In The USA*, allowed observers to dismiss *Nebraska* as an aberration. By the mid-eighties, Springsteen was the king of stadium rock, a blue-collar hero leading the ultimate garage band. That wasn't the man who intrigued country singers such as Emmylou Harris and Johnny Cash, both of whom covered songs from *The River* and *Nebraska*. For Cash, who himself rarely extended beyond three chords, Springsteen's landscapes merged into his own. 'Johnny 99', which Cash covered in 1983, might have been a cry of defiance from the narrator of his own 'Folsom Prison Blues'. But the melodic simplicity of 'The Price You Pay' proved less suitable for Harris's fragile voice, despite her belief that 'The way we did it, it's a country song.' She continued to record his songs thereafter, proving how much she could forgive for a compelling narrative.

Springsteen took the same decision. When his first marriage faltered, he composed *Tunnel Of Love* – and turned first to seasoned Nashville sessionmen (though this experiment foundered). His subsequent work rarely wavered from the three-chord prison of *Nebraska*. With *The Ghost Of Tom Joad* in 1995, he moved closer to the Guthrie and Steinbeck tradition, scripting despairing narratives that were echoed by the monotony of his music. His long journey towards lyrical integrity had driven him into a desert, where no one – not even Johnny Cash or Emmylou Harris – was prepared to follow.

Springsteen has always been classified as a rock artist, while Steve Earle is called country, but the two men might have been cousins. The link annoys Earle, whose career has been dogged by comparisons with Springsteen and John Mellencamp. 'I understand it,' Earle has said, 'but I think it's irrelevant.' When a writer noted similarities between the covers of Mellencamp's *Scarecrow* and Earle's breakthrough album, *Guitar Town*, Earle responded: 'I never thought about it.'

Guitar Town was a dot on the map of Springsteen's *Nebraska*. The title track was a Top 10 country hit, but it shared more with Mellencamp's 'Small Town' than with the best-selling country artists of 1986. Where a Merle Haggard would have painted his landscape in fine detail, Earle – like Springsteen before him – opted for images like 'the lost highway', which suggested a filmic romance, not a documentary.

Both Haggard and Earle recognized that one of the purposes of country music was to tell stories, and Earle's tales had a political edge. 'Nobody liked me using the word "hillbilly",' he says, 'because they were embarrassed about it still being used. But I wasn't afraid of the word. I looked up "hillbilly" in a dictionary, and you know what it said? "A Michigan farmer." It was a term of abuse, directed at these guys who'd come off the farms during the Depression and were looking for jobs in the city. I was happy to be identified with them.'

Indiana-born John Mellencamp experienced the same mistrust of his farming background: 'The first time I went to New York, I remember a guy asking me if we had radio yet. People in New York talk about people from the South or the Mid-West being bigoted, but they're more prejudiced than anyone. There's one reason why New York people shouldn't look down their nose at people from the South. Hey, fucker, they're the ones that brought you the blues, they're the ones that invented rock'n'roll and country music. And you have stolen it and made it into a business. Shut the fuck up!'

Mellencamp's aggression and studied naïvety ('My music isn't about words, it's about getting on stage and having a good time') made him an ideal subject for crass PR hype. Billed in the seventies as 'John Cougar' ('they figured I couldn't be a rock star called Mellencamp'), he was promoted as a James Dean rebel with a stack of Bruce Springsteen albums. On 1983's *Uh-Huh*, he matched Springsteen's social commentary; 1985's *Scarecrow*, which included the illuminating hit single 'Small Town', plugged Mellencamp into the Woody Guthrie tradition; while 1987's *The Lonesome Jubilee* nudged country influences into the foreground.

Turning film director in 1992 with *Falling Into Grace*, Mellencamp enlisted Dwight Yoakam and Joe Ely for the soundtrack, but kept country at arm's length: 'To me, guys like Dwight Yoakam are like Bob Dylan or the Stones – they write songs and they sing them.' He's ferocious in his desire to avoid identification with his most emblematic songs: 'I wrote a song called "Small Town". All of a sudden, I'm the keeper of the small town. I wrote a song about farmers called "Rain On The Scarecrow", one fucking song. Then I couldn't pick up a paper that didn't say Woody Guthrie was my dad. I mean, I like Woody Guthrie, but I'm not the keeper of the common man.'

Steve Earle was less shy about connecting with his audience. In the early eighties, he'd cut a bunch of surprisingly convincing rockabilly records, 'Back when Nashville was looking for another Stray Cats. It wasn't until much later that I realized that there wasn't any room for me as a writer in that format.'

His hold-out against the push to brand him as another Elvis was 'The Devil's Right Hand', a four-minute *noir* movie. On the sequence of albums that began with *Guitar Town*, he created characters who could have been on the run from Springsteen's *Nebraska* – outlaws, hoodlums, Vietnam vets, downtrodden hillbillies – and fired them into melodramatic life. Gradually, the country rock'n'roll of *Guitar Town* expanded into the metallic roar of *Copperhead Road* – and then, as Earle's own life distorted under the weight of his crack cocaine habit, into the faux metal of *The Hard Way*, all bombast and blast. On *Copperhead Road*, he'd merged the Irish folk-punk of the Pogues with his own hard country to create a compelling backdrop for his veteran's tragedy, 'Johnny Come Lately'. Now every moment of music was strained, from his drug-diluted voice to the introspective clichés of his songs.

Earle made it back from drug addiction, via imprisonment and public humiliation, and emerged in the mid-nineties with the semi-acoustic *The Train Kept A-Comin'*, as stark and deliberate as anything he'd ever recorded. Thereafter he dabbled with Seattle grunge, bluegrass and reggae, without ever shedding his debt to the tradition that Woody Guthrie invented sixty years earlier.

40 Million Dollar Quartet
The country lives of Johnny Cash, Carl Perkins, Elvis Presley and Jerry Lee Lewis

706 Union Avenue, Memphis: 4 December 1956

The piano player wasn't fazed for a second. Yes, that was Carl Perkins at the microphone, the 'Blue Suede Shoes' man. He was Sun's biggest star now that Sam Phillips had sold Elvis to keep his business alive. But Jerry Lee Lewis was no respecter of reputations. He had a talent, and by God he was going to show it off. So when Perkins called another take, Lewis hustled him for every inch of tape. As the band spun out of the chorus, the two men stared right ahead, each determined it was his solo. The guitarist won out, striking shards of noise from his ramshackle amplifier. But Lewis kept pummelling that piano, treating the record as an exhibition hall for his ego.

There was a flurry of excitement at the door. Into the cramped Sun studio strolled Elvis Presley, a nightclub dancer on his arm. The session broke up right there. Elvis was only a year out of Sun himself, but he'd become arguably the most popular entertainer in America. Even Jerry Lee Lewis was impressed by that.

Not that he'd admit it. When Presley tinkled the studio piano, Lewis took his chance. 'So you're Elvis Presley, huh?' he drawled nonchalantly. 'Well, I'm Jerry Lee Lewis.' And he bragged about the record he'd just cut, the way he could play a piano, the fact that Mr Phillips wouldn't make a record on anyone these days without calling Jerry Lee for the session. He rolled a few boogie-woogie chords to prove the point. 'You sure can play great,' Presley mumbled politely. 'You reckon so?' Lewis snapped back. 'Well, you ain't heard anything yet.'

More at ease with music, the Sun stars gathered at the piano and swapped parts round gospel and country tunes. Johnny Cash, recently knocked off the top of the country charts by Elvis, wandered in and out of the studio. He told Phillips he'd love to stay, but he had to meet his wife downtown. 'Stick around and have your picture made with the boys,' Phillips told him, and a few minutes later a photographer arrived with a reporter, who began to compose a story about the million dollar quartet Mr Phillips had assembled. Cash dutifully posed, then headed for the door. 'Where are you going, man?' asked Presley. 'Shopping with my wife,' Cash replied, and the rest of the guys cracked up at the thought of the country star trawling down to Lansky's with his wallet stuffed deep into his pocket.

Johnny Cash slipped out of the Million Dollar Quartet session, the same way he escaped the Sun rockabilly sound. He became a country icon, a TV star, an evangelist for America, Jesus and the hillbilly spirit. In the way of icons, his fame outlived his success. Hungry for a hit, he began to reacquaint himself with what he called 'the sound of youth' in the late seventies. He teamed up with former Sun engineer Jack Clement, who helped him steer the Rolling Stones' 'No Expectations' into a roadhouse stomp.

The more Cash experimented, the less his public seemed to care. He cut tunes by Nick Lowe, Bruce Springsteen and Elvis Costello, duetted with Paul McCartney, and on 1990's 'Goin' By The Book' conjured up the kind of apocalyptic imagery favoured by heavy metal bands. Columbia Records sacked him after thirty years; Mercury posed as saviours, but had to admit that Cash's legend didn't shift units.

In 1993 he met Rick Rubin, the entrepreneur who'd masterminded the union between rap and hard rock. He was setting up a label called American Recordings, and who was more American than Johnny Cash? 'His dark side was what interested me,' Rubin explained. 'I just did whatever I could to get that point across.'

Cash had long fantasized about cutting an album with just his acoustic guitar, and Rubin set up a mike in his living-room so that Cash could demonstrate what he meant. After a week, there were dozens of tunes on tape. Both men assumed these were demos, and rock musicians from Tom Petty's Heartbreakers and the Red Hot Chili Peppers were enlisted to cut some tracks. But Cash and

Rubin preferred the starkness of the demos, which were culled for the *American Recordings* album.

There was no place to hide on this record, in the music or the savagery of songs like 'Delia's Gone', a murder ballad narrated by an unrepentant criminal, or 'The Beast In Me', in which his former son-in-law Nick Lowe laid bare Cash's blackest demons. Country radio had no appetite for a man in his sixties, least of all one serviced by a rap producer. But *American Recordings* brought Cash to listeners who saw him as the archetypal outlaw hero, from Hollywood rock clubs to a triumphant appearance at the Glastonbury Festival, where a crowd of 60,000 experienced the mythic scale of his music.

Rick Rubin still wasn't satisfied. 'It would be interesting to hear a really good rock'n'roll Johnny Cash,' he noted in 1994. Two years later, Cash released *Unchained*, easing songs by Beck, Soundgarden and Tom Petty into his own vocabulary. For the first time in his life, his voice was framed by ramshackle electric guitars – a bar-room sound that connected the alternative country of the nineties to its roots in Sun rockabilly. 'A Country Boy has alert senses,' wrote Sam Phillips on the back of a Sun record in 1956. Forty years on, as Cash reprised 'Country Boy' with a raucous rock'n'roll band, he completed the unbroken circle that he and his in-laws, the Carter Family, had described so often in song.

706 Union Avenue, Memphis: 4 December 1956

In the control room, Sam Phillips nudged engineer Jack Clement towards the 'record' button: 'You may never have these people together again.' Presley and Lewis were whooping it up with Perkins and his band. Their shared heritage kicked into gear as they fell into a gospel anthem.

'I'm gonna walk that lonesome valley,' Elvis began. Behind him, Lewis wailed like a Pentecostal preacher when it was time to start passing the rattlesnakes: 'Weeeeeell, you gotta gotta gotta go, go by yourself.' Carl picked up on the frenzy, stuttering into an over-excited solo, then Jerry Lee stole the song, testifying to God's greatness and his own as if they were one and the same.

The gospel glory washed away the liquor which muddied Carl Perkins' fingers. Spiritual and secular were intertwined, as the trio drifted from Bill Monroe bluegrass to country hymns, and then into the stately crawl of Wynn Stewart's 'Keeper Of The Key'. Carl Perkins sang the mournful lyric as if it were the story of his life. 'Boy, that's a beautiful song,' he whispered reverently. 'I'm gonna cut that record.'

Carl Perkins was already a fading star that December afternoon. He wasted the rest of the fifties looking for another 'Blue Suede Shoes', and drowned the sixties in liquor. By 1980, he was reduced to cutting anodyne country-pop tunes for his own Suede label. He could still bring audiences to their feet with 'Blue Suede Shoes', but that was less a career than a circus act.

In the mid-sixties, the Beatles kept Perkins alive by recording his songs; in 1985, they did it again. To mark the thirtieth anniversary of his biggest hit, Carl headlined a TV special, for which George Harrison and Ringo Starr crawled out of semi-retirement. Perkins might have been a one-trick pony decades past his prime, but the ex-Beatles regarded him as a god; and that night Carl believed them.

Carl Perkins – A Rockabilly Session raised the stakes of his career, and earned him a series of lucrative record deals. More significant was his patronage by a new generation of country stars – including the Judds, who invited him to play at their farewell show, George Strait, and the New Nashville Cats. This one-off assembly of guitarists and singers Vince Gill, Steve Wariner and Ricky Skaggs, convened by fiddle virtuoso Mark O'Connor, chose one of Carl's less familiar gems, 'Restless', as the vehicle for an explosive demonstration of rockabilly licks which won them a CMA Award.

Their respect was flattering, but Perkins hadn't abandoned hope of rekindling his own career. Gradually he assembled the pieces for an album that would draw together the music he'd made and inspired over the last forty years. The result was *Go, Cat, Go* (1996), his most convincing release since the Sun *Dance Album* that had bewitched the 13-year-old George Harrison. It was awash with guest stars, including all four Beatles (John Lennon, like Jimi Hendrix, represented by a vintage rendition of 'Blue Suede Shoes'), Tom Petty, John Fogerty, Johnny Cash and Willie Nelson. As at his TV showcase in 1985, Perkins effortlessly dominated the proceedings. Classics from his catalogue were updated with affection and humour; collaborations with Paul McCartney and George Harrison reflected the sentimentality that had always balanced his honky-tonk menace.

It was an unlikely teaming with Paul Simon that provided the album's manifesto. 'Rockabilly Music' hung around a simple guitar lick, until Simon's characteristic intervention pulled out chord patterns never attempted on a country record. 'Rockabilly music, there ain't nothing to it,' chorused the Tennessee sharecropper's son and the Brooklyn intellectual. 'It's just a hopped-up country song.' And in that phrase Perkins encapsulated his whole career.

Little over a year later, he succumbed to the lung and throat cancer he'd been battling since the start of the decade. Country and rock stars mingled at the graveside. Wynonna Judd delivered a tribute; Bob Dylan sent condolences; George Harrison and Jerry Lee Lewis grasped each other for support, aware that with the death of Carl Perkins, the spirit of fifties rock'n'roll, which had infused their own lives, was slipping closer to extinction.

706 Union Avenue, Memphis: 4 December 1956

'That song I was talkin' about, it's called "That's When Your Heartaches Begin",' Elvis Presley stuttered as Jerry Lee paused momentarily at the piano. Presley ushered him aside: 'When I first started out, I came in here and made a little record of it.' He began to croon the Inkspots' ballad, which he'd last sung in this room three years earlier, when there was no rockabilly or rock'n'roll, and none of them, not even Jerry Lee, dreamed that one of their songs might end up on a jukebox.

Country was the identity that Elvis Presley sacrificed for international stardom. Tom Parker smoothed out the hillbilly crack of his voice; New York songwriters did the rest. As late as 1960, after he'd returned from the army stint which, according to legend, smothered his rock'n'roll instincts, Elvis could still breeze his way through a gutbucket blues like 'Reconsider Baby'. But there'd been not a hint of rockabilly in his music since he'd left the Million Dollar Quartet session in 1956.

During the sixties, Elvis split his time between crass Hollywood musicals, and studio sessions where his exquisite balladeer's voice was cloaked in the Nashville Sound. These mellifluous productions were as gorgeous as anything to come out of Music City in that era, but they had none of the man's original daring. That surfaced only when he toyed with a stray Bob Dylan tune or some Stax soul grit.

The *Elvis!* TV special filmed in June 1968 is often regarded as his moment of liberation, but the escape route from Hollywood was visible nine months earlier, when he cut a song which had been a hit for Alabama singer-songwriter Jerry Reed. The hero of 'Guitar Man' was spat out of Memphis, and found his home in Mobile, Alabama, 'leading the hottest little five-piece band up and down the Gulf of Mexico'. Elvis recognized himself in the song, and invited Reed down to re-create his guitar licks.

'That session was a big turning point for Elvis,' recalls Charlie McCoy, a regular Presley sideman. 'He got a real affection for Jerry Reed. The Colonel went to Jerry's publisher and tried to get the publishing transferred to Elvis. They wouldn't do it, so the Colonel wanted to throw the song away. But Elvis insisted, and the Colonel had to back down.' It was a rare show of independence, echoed by the 1968 TV special (which used 'Guitar Man' as one of its themes). Elvis recorded another Reed song, 'US Male', his first country hit since 1960. Sadly, he never got around to 'Tupelo Mississippi Flash', Reed's fictionalized account of Presley's rise to fame.

Such material would have been too lightweight for the sessions which returned Elvis to Memphis in 1969. Like the TV special, these dates with producer Chips Moman have assumed landmark status. Southern soul, gospel, country: every track came from a space where genre distinctions no longer mattered. Jody Miller had just slipped off the country charts with 'Long Black Limousine', the first number Elvis cut, but he lived out her maudlin tale of a Southern singer returning home in a hearse as if it had been tailored for him. That realization of his mortality was present in every song, pushing him to celebrate the moment – whether with the burlesque eroticism of 'Power Of My Love' or the adult emotion of 'True Love Travels On A Gravel Road'.

The Memphis sessions coloured his work for the next five years, until ill-health and drug addiction robbed him of his judgement. Nothing after 1969 quite recaptured that blend of soul and country, but the homecoming reconnected Presley with his roots, and his identity. Now he could be himself, a mature man with a failing marriage, nagged by a vague memory of unrealized dreams.

That was the very stuff of country music, and when he wasn't cutting orchestral pop songs to fill his Vegas act, Presley called on country as his native language. There was even an album titled *Elvis Country* – territory wide enough to span Anne Murray's pop hit 'Snowbird' and Jerry Lee Lewis's 'Whole Lotta Shakin' Goin' On'.

As his impending divorce and separation from his daughter began to encroach on his health, so Elvis sank into sentimental melancholy. Country had an endless repertoire of songs about lost love, and he seemed prepared to record them all. In 1973, he ventured across Memphis to Stax, where Southern R&B classics had been taped in the sixties. There was no blues on the menu; instead, Elvis treated himself to the finest songs that country could supply – Billy Joe Shaver's 'You Asked Me To', Tom Jans' 'Lovin' Arms', Danny O'Keeffe's 'Good Time Charlie's Got The Blues', every one of them steeped in regret. The eternal child in Elvis Presley – the kid who'd still take over amusement parks with his friends – was finally being crushed by the weight of adult life.

'You Asked Me To' was Waylon Jennings' most recent hit. 'He told me he imitated me on that song,' Jennings says today. 'We were friends, and the people at RCA talked to me about going over and seeing if I could get him interested in music again. But I didn't know what I could say, and I have a strange feeling that if I'd found out back then that he was a drug addict, me and him might just have got more interested in drugs together! Music was something else. He'd lost interest in that along the way, but he got it back on that album. If they'd have just got him a country band and let him loose, he'd have been happy.'

Not that Elvis Presley had much connection with happiness in the seventies. There were moments on stage when he'd lose himself in the theatrics of 'Polk Salad Annie', or the spiritual excess of 'How Great Thou Art'. But his final years were an exercise in self-parody. As the TV special filmed a few weeks before his death revealed, the real Elvis Presley was trapped inside that bloated body and equally obese career.

706 Union Avenue, Memphis: 4 December 1956
Jerry Lee Lewis regained the piano when Perkins and Presley were called aside by Sam Phillips, and there was no way he'd relinquish his place. He ran through 'Crazy Arms', the Ray Price country hit he'd covered that week as his first record. Presley watched from the door of the control-room, then prepared to leave. 'Good luck, boy,' he said, and stepped out into the street. Lewis turned back to the piano, and began to bend another tune to his own design.

Jerry Lee Lewis had already destroyed one career as a rock'n'roll star. In the late seventies, he lit the fuse on his reincarnation as a country singer, and watched it burn. 'Jerry Lee is the most self-destructive person I've seen in my life,' says Waylon Jennings. By the time he'd shot his bass-player, been arrested outside Elvis Presley's home with a loaded gun, seen two wives die in mysterious circumstances, shed several yards of intestines, and skipped out on dozens of commitments and contracts, Lewis had sabotaged any chance of making it through the eighties with a career to match his talent.

That talent was undiminished, and in 1979 Jerry Lee cut some of the most compelling music of his career. His country audience were so loyal that they bought records as weird as the apocalyptic, virtually incoherent 'Rockin' My Life Away', and 'Over The Rainbow' – yes, the Judy Garland theme from *The Wizard Of Oz* – redesigned as a drunkard's lament. Lewis even managed a traditional honky-tonk hit, 'Thirty Nine And Holding', a belated successor to his all too apt 'Middle Age Crazy'.

Eventually Jerry Lee grew too crazy for anyone to handle. There were a succession of deals through the eighties, each promising a return to former glories, each dissolving into chaos. Between the lawsuits, the IRS witch hunts, the *National Enquirer* scandals and the emergency-room dramas, Lewis stayed out on the road. He inhabited a private world where Moon Mullican, Hank Williams, Chuck Berry and the Killer – always the Killer – were the rulers. His live shows were a spontaneous combustion of half-remembered country hits from the forties and rock'n'roll classics performed with reckless contempt.

Meanwhile, Lewis kept up a scabrous public dialogue with his evangelist cousin, Jimmy Swaggert, who opined that 'Any Christian who would allow any type of rock or country recording in his home is inviting in the powers of darkness . . . All of the rock music (and probably all, or at least most, of the country music) being aired today is demonically inspired.' When Swaggert was later caught *in flagrante* with a prostitute, Jerry Lee reacted as if the Lord had settled the argument in his favour.

Occasionally, an entrepreneur would ignore reality and book Lewis for an event that might revitalize his commercial standing. In 1989, the Killer came to London to film a TV special with a host of minor rock stars. He cancelled the first date, as usual, then arrived late for the second, stumbled out on stage, hollered at the cameramen to move aside, and tore up the carefully choreographed set-list. When his impromptu repertoire briefly coincided with the cue sheet, a crocodile of second-division guitar heroes trooped on to the stage ready for an ensemble finale of 'Great Balls Of Fire'. Lewis glared over his piano and launched into a slow Kris Kristofferson tune, as the sheepish guitarists shuffled backwards into the wings.

And so Lewis continued, defying the doctors and lawyers by remaining so unpredictable that he himself had no idea what he was about to do. Into the nineties, the comebacks grew less frequent, the offers less inviting, and as the Killer eased into his sixties, he took on the appearance of a myopic hellraiser in grandpa's clothing. But the old fury still burned: promoting his first new album in a decade, Lewis threatened to kill an Irish journalist who'd dared to tell him how much he liked it. It was a stunt worthy of Hank Williams; indeed, Jerry Lee is the one man in rock history whom Hank might have wanted to be.

*

706 Union Avenue, Memphis: 1985

They were the *Class Of '55* – survivors from Sam Phillips' rock'n'roll academy who'd returned to make an album. Three of the Million Dollar Quartet were there, with Roy Orbison – the Sun cast-off who'd created fabulous pop melodramas out of the tragedy that filled his own life – taking the place of Elvis Presley, lost in action almost a decade earlier. It wasn't an easy reunion, as Carl Perkins told his biographer, David McGee: 'I could have killed Jerry Lee Lewis . . . One time he stood on his hands and was gonna walk across the studio floor and ten thousand pills fell out of his pocket in front of the damn *Rolling Stone* camerawoman . . . John (Cash) said, "Oh boy, here we go. There's enough pills on that floor to get us all arrested and sent away for life."'

Future country star Marty Stuart joined the sessions: 'That was one of the highlights of my life. Not that the album was that great; it was a little uninspired and clinical, but that room had a magic about it, and the sound came back. The best stuff never made the album. Jerry Lee did a triple X-rated version of "16 Candles" that was pretty cool.'

To close up the record, the *Class Of '55* rounded up everyone from Sam Phillips and John Fogerty to the Judds and Rick Nelson, to breeze through Fogerty's 'Big Train From Memphis', a faux-rockabilly tribute to the absent Elvis Presley.

But the real conclusion to both the reunion and the whole Sun saga came from Carl Perkins. He slipped back into the man who'd penned those rockabilly classics thirty years before. 'I was here when it happened,' he sang, his voice skipping arrogantly across the rhythm, 'don't y'all think I oughta know. I was here when it happened, I watched Memphis give birth to rock'n'roll.'

41 Lone Star State of Mind

The Texas tradition, 1970–1999: Joe Ely; Jimmie Dale Gilmore; Butch Hancock; Terry Allen; Lyle Lovett; Nanci Griffith

It took the civic authorities in Lubbock, Texas more than twenty years to commemorate their most famous son. After Buddy Holly's death in 1959, the city fathers ignored countless pleas by his friends and fans for his legacy to be marked by a statue or a plaque. 'Buddy was almost a kind of underground thing in Lubbock,' recalled Joe Ely, who moved there in 1958. 'He wasn't really an accepted part of the music scene there.' Holly had to flee his hometown to prosper: almost all of his records were cut across the state border in Clovis, New Mexico. 'Lubbock certainly isn't a music centre,' Ely confirmed, 'but it is a musically creative area. I don't know why.' Sonny Curtis, the songwriter and sometime Cricket who first collaborated with Buddy Holly in 1956, has an explanation for Lubbock's cluster of talent: 'Most musicians there do it because there's nothing else to do. Nothing ever happens in Lubbock, unless you make it happen.'

While the state capital Austin became the capital of progressive country in the early seventies, Lubbock let its talent slip away. 'A lot of musicians and artists passed through there,' Joe Ely contends, 'but they never stayed.' In 1971, the city spawned a shortlived country rock'n'roll band which contained three of the most distinctive songwriters ever to emerge from Texas. Typically, they had to move to Nashville to make a record, and to Austin to rekindle the dying country-rock tradition at the end of the seventies.

Joe Ely's early career is as far-fetched as the fake biography concocted by the young Bob Dylan. Entranced, like Dylan, by Jack Kerouac's *On The Road*, Ely lived out the beatnik manifesto by riding boxcars to the end of the line, which turned out to be Venice, California. Instead of settling on the West Coast, alongside other Texans such as Doug Sahm and Janis Joplin, Ely rode back across America to New York, where he ran into 'some strange kind of rock, lights, multi-media thing out of Austin, called Stomp. I played with them for a couple of months in New York, and some girl from Paris brought the whole troupe over for six months in Europe.'

In his absence, Austin developed as a haven for the counter-culture and country-rock. When Ely returned, he overlooked the changing scene in the state capital and chose to live in Lubbock, where the few non-conformists in town naturally drifted together. Among them was Jimmie Dale Gilmore, named after the Singing Brakeman, Jimmie Rodgers. 'When my friends and I drove around, we played rock'n'roll stations on the radio, and I loved that music,' Gilmore says. 'But I also loved it when I drove around alone, and I could put on the country stations without everyone else laughing at me.'

Ely and Gilmore cut some demos at a studio run by Buddy Holly's father, before forming a band whose name matched the Lubbock landscape – Jimmie Dale and the Flatlanders. 'We put that group together out of delight at having found others like ourselves who had a genuine interest in traditional music,' Ely recalled. 'But we couldn't go into places where they played country music. We were too weird. We had long hair and we wore funny clothes. So we went to the rock clubs instead, which was fine with me, because I also loved that music. At that time, the two worlds just didn't mingle.'

'Both sides thought we were pretty strange,' adds Butch Hancock, another songwriter who was recruited into the group by Gilmore. 'The country music we were writing didn't sound anything like what was on the radio, but neither did we sound like a rock band. Nobody knew what to make of us. We had a better reception when we went to Austin and played places like the Armadillo.'

In February 1972, the Flatlanders were invited to Nashville, to cut an album for Plantation Records – a subsidiary of the seminal rockabilly label Sun which had been sold by Sam Phillips to the country producer and entrepreneur, Shelby Singleton. Plantation released Gilmore's melancholy 'Dallas' as a single, though the album was cancelled when Ely refused to sign what he considered to be 'a shady deal'. Country radio ignored their idiosyncratic throwback of a record, which featured fiddle, mandolin, acoustic guitars – and Steve Wesson evoking the eerie sound of the wind rustling through the tumbleweeds by vibrating a saw. 'The saw-player was also a carpenter,' Ely claimed, 'and he couldn't decide which union to join, the carpenters' or the musicians'!'

The Flatlanders disbanded soon afterwards, leaving Gilmore and Hancock to haunt the Texas bars for work. Their companion was more fortunate. In 1974 he formed the Joe Ely Band, and in 1977 he unleashed his début album, a rowdy collection of honky-tonk tunes underpinned by an ironic worldview provided by Butch Hancock, who composed most of *Joe Ely* and 1978's equally impressive *Honky Tonk Masquerade*. (The latter was the only country-related album listed among *Rolling Stone* magazine's '50 Essential Albums of the Seventies' in 1990.)

The critical acclaim prompted Hancock to launch a solo career and record label. *West Texas Waltzes* was recorded in Ely's back room. 'He was really trying to get the feel of the plains,' Ely considered, and Hancock's nasal, keening voice certainly evoked the unyielding landscape of West Texas. The album was merely the first in a succession of entirely independent efforts over the next decade – sometimes cut solo, sometimes with a band who caught the manic energy of Bob Dylan's Rolling Thunder Revue. A man who has heard the Dylan comparison once too often, Hancock will only admit that 'I wasn't trying to sound like anyone. When you have a voice like mine, you don't have any choice but to sing the way you sing.' He is a major talent, with a verbal dexterity worthy of any comparison, and potentially a commercial one, as other singers have proved with such covers as 'She Never Spoke Spanish To Me' and 'Fools Fall In Love'. But Hancock is also a polymath, distracted from music by his work as an artist and an architect, and no major label has ever dared to take him on.

His former comrades did succeed in infiltrating the mainstream. Ely cut a series of albums for MCA, fashioned a country/hard rock hybrid years before Jason and the Scorchers, and was even taken under the wing of the Clash. After years hanging out at Austin clubs such as the Alamo Hotel and Emmajoe's, Gilmore finally won a shot at the major leagues in the early nineties. Not that this dampened his sense of adventure: in 1994, he collaborated with Mudhoney on a single for Sub Pop, the label that pioneered the Seattle grunge sound. While Gilmore tackled the bluesy cowboy ballad 'Blinding Sun', Mudhoney repaid the compliment on Gilmore's most-recorded song, 'Tonight I Think I'm Gonna Go Downtown'. Two years later, Gilmore stepped even further out of line, effectively dooming his Warner Brothers contract with *Braver Newer World*. He described the record as 'West Texas psychedelic blues-rockabilly', which allowed him to add almost baroque textures to his familiar sound – aptly described by one reviewer as 'the most lonesome voice in the world'.

Any state that is home to towns called Dickens and Bronte is likely to encourage storytellers, and there's a distinctive strain of Texas songwriters which leads from Guy Clark and Townes Van Zandt, through Ely, Hancock and Gilmore, to dozens of performers who command tiny but fanatical cult followings. As Terry Allen has proved, it is possible to extend a Texas career for more than three decades without ever flirting with the mainstream.

Allen's connection to the Texas country-rock tradition began when he was 12 years old, and his father promoted the gig which brought together Elvis Presley and Buddy Holly in Lubbock. A decade later, Allen briefly tried out as a psychedelic protest rocker, winning a spot on TV's *Shindig*. But it wasn't until 1974 that he released his first album, *Juarez*, a sparse piece of musical theatre that overturned the clichés of the outlaw tradition. 'My cousin was the Jefferson Airplane's road manager, and he got me studio time at 3 a.m.,' Allen recalled, explaining why an album soaked in south-western mythology should have been recorded in San Francisco.

In 1978, Allen recorded the double-album widely regarded as his masterpiece: *Lubbock (On Everything)*. Bobby Bare and Little Feat both sampled its material, which opened in familiar Texas territory ('I don't wear a stetson, But I'm willin' to bet, son, That I'm as big a Texan as you are'), and turned sharply left to encompass songs about the philosophy of art, and the nature of existence. 'I did not transcend,' the final song ended, 'No, I just walked out on me again.' Allen's willingness to subvert his genre was equally apparent on the albums *Smokin' The Dummy*, *Bloodlines* and *Ourland*, which utilized violent imagery to assault the complacency of American capitalism. David Byrne of Talking Heads recognized a kindred spirit, recruiting him as a co-writer on his *True Stories* movie and album project in the mid-eighties, and renewing the collaboration a decade later by adapting *Juarez* for the theatre.

Another Texas ironist, Lyle Lovett, won the international acclaim that Allen deserved. His ill-fated marriage to actress Julia Roberts sparked 'beauty and the beast' headlines in the American tabloids, but threatened to overshadow his musical career. Emerging somewhat shaken from the media feeding-frenzy, Lovett grounded himself with 1998's *Step Inside This House*, a tribute to the Texas songwriters who had inspired him as a teenager. In the mid-seventies, Lovett arrived at the home of Eric Taylor and his then wife, Nanci Griffith, eager to pay homage to the man he had adopted as a role model. As Griffith recalls, 'He knocked on the door one night to interview Eric for a college newspaper, and ended up staying for weeks!' Ironically, Taylor's career floundered after their marriage collapsed, while both Lovett and Griffith emerged as major talents in the eighties, winning cult adulation in the USA and a much broader following in Britain and Europe.

A born teacher, earnestly determined to share her enthusiasms with her audience, Nanci Griffith has kept alive the spirit of the early-sixties folk revival. Her two *Other Voices, Other Rooms* albums reunited many of the liberal voices who were swept aside by Bob Dylan's acerbic cynicism. 'Lyrically, folk is where I always wanted to be,' she admits. But as the intelligence of her songwriting on eighties albums such as *Last Of The True Believers* and *Lone Star State Of Mind* revealed, Griffith is a broader talent than her gushing stage demeanour might suggest.

She's also anything but a folk purist. 'My older sister was into sixties punk bands like the Thirteenth Floor Elevators,' she says of her Texas upbringing, 'so that was the music I listened to in my teens. Our parents were beatniks, but they couldn't understand why we liked that music at all. They didn't exactly share my passion for punk rock in the seventies, either, but I adored the Clash and all of that. That's just not the kind of music I can sing, or write.'

While the rest of the country underground flocked to her hometown of Austin, Griffith escaped to Nashville from her marriage. 'It was a hard adjustment living there for me,' she confesses, 'because Nashville really is the South. In Texas and New Mexico, we feel we're from the South-West, not the South. Texas is more rebellious and renegade.' Those were qualities which marked Griffith out from the Nashville mainstream, and stalled her acceptance as an artist by major country labels. From the mid-eighties onwards, singers such as Kathy Mattea began to score regular hits with Griffith's songs, while country radio proved resistant to Nanci's own recordings. 'She is so talented that I cannot understand why Nashville won't accept her,' Mattea said in 1991. 'Maybe it's because she doesn't conform.' Griffith doesn't shy away from this analysis: 'MCA wanted me to call in at all these country radio stations, but I told them I wasn't prepared to do that. I don't do call-ins, I don't do lunch, I don't play those games. I'm not cut out for the Nashville mainstream, anyway. They just want all these Barbie Dolls and hat acts, which I find extraordinarily boring.'

Instead, Griffith preferred life on the margins, promoting her heroes and heroines – Dave Van Ronk, Carolyn Hester, Odetta – and collaborating with such unlikely country performers as Hootie and the Blowfish frontman Darius Rucker. 'Hootie used to come and hear us play in South Carolina,' she explains. 'Darius told me that he used to have this fantasy, that I'd call him up on stage to sing the duet on "Gulf Coast Highway". So when I wanted to recut the song, he was the first person I thought of.' Griffith also joined Hootie and the Blowfish for their MTV *Unplugged* performance, around the same time that Alison Krauss – another maverick acoustic performer refusing to toe the Nashville line – worked with Hootie's arena-rock contemporaries Phish.

Griffith's one-time house guest Lyle Lovett has endured a similarly troubled encounter with the Nashville record industry.

His angular face and almost comically sculpted hair immediately cast him as an outsider, an impression supported by the acute sense of irony that was the backbone of his 1986 début album.

'When my tape was making the rounds in Nashville, it was a really experimental time in country music,' he recalled. 'The door was wide open, and Nashville was looking for the next thing.' The industry was briefly prepared to welcome non-conformists such as k.d. lang, Dwight Yoakam and Nanci Griffith into their midst, though Lovett's reputation as the country Randy Newman ensured that he was never entirely trusted in Music City. After he delivered an album of big-band jazz (including a straight-faced cover of 'Stand By Your Man'), MCA shifted his account from Nashville to Los Angeles, where his knowing intelligence would be less of a threat.

In Europe, Lovett and Griffith appealed to left-field rock fans who welcomed their distance from Nashville. In 1992, the year that Lovett released the wry, exquisitely crafted *Joshua Judges Ruth*, he was chosen as a fashion model for a *Rolling Stone* pictorial, donning Italian suits which smart New York executives could aspire to. 'I dabbled briefly in country clothing because I felt obligated to for professional reasons,' Lovett told the rock magazine, 'but I never did feel particularly comfortable with it. I'm just not a big-hat kind of guy. I want to wear something that makes me look like a generic man who might, say, have a job.'

When the director of *Nashville*, Robert Altman, turned his attention to the movie industry with *The Player*, Lovett won a suitably surreal cameo role. The shoot also introduced him to Julia Roberts, a Hollywood starlet who – to the astonishment of the American popular press – became his wife a few months later. Their brief relationship, lived out almost entirely in public, made him a household name across America, for reasons which had nothing to do with his work. Lovett was suddenly stereotyped as 'Julia Roberts' country singer husband', as if he were a rural hick who'd struck it lucky with a misguided belle. As he noted, 'People who don't listen to country music still have very little idea about it.'

While Nashville struggled to swallow the spirit of Texas, recognition came from other sources. U2 signed Guy Clark to their record label in the late eighties, prior to borrowing Johnny Cash's iconic power for their *Zooropa* album. Though alcoholism sapped his creative energies, Townes Van Zandt's song catalogue continued to attract covers from artists as diverse as Bob Dylan and British art-rockers Tindersticks. And Dylan was also a participant in a project that revived the recording career of the original Texas outlaw: Willie Nelson.

42 Across the Borderline

The Don Was productions, 1992–1997: Willie Nelson; the Highwaymen; *Rhythm Country* and Blues; Kelly Willis; Kris Kristofferson; Orqestra Was

Barefoot, dreadlocked, dishevelled, a dazed ancestor of grunge's Generation X: few musicians have been less likely champions of country than Don Was. The Detroit-born bassist and songwriter was one of the linchpins of Was (Not Was), an eighties rock-funk outfit known as much for their sly humour as for their slick R&B grooves. In the late eighties, Was became a freelance producer, handling projects by the Rolling Stones and Bob Dylan. His 1992 collaboration with Willie Nelson on *Across The Borderline* proved to be a landmark in both men's careers – expanding the singer's audience via duets with Bob Dylan, Paul Simon and Sinéad O'Connor, and launching Was on a sequence of left-field country projects which occupied a unique place in the nineties rock mainstream.

'Willie Nelson had become the butt of late-night comedians' jokes about his problems with the IRS,' Was recalls. 'He had ceased to be a vital artist. Yet vocally, in his phrasing and interpretative powers, he was still a creative guy. I was introduced to Willie's manager, Mark Rothbaum, who said, "Would you be interested in working with him?" I said sure, so he suggested it to Willie.' Nelson continues the story: 'Mark called up and said, "What do you think of Don Was?" And I said, "As a what?"'

Informed that Was had worked with his friend Bonnie Raitt, Nelson placed a call. 'He asked Bonnie if I was any good,' Was smiles. 'Bonnie said, "Not only will you like him, but I'll come in and sing a duet." She inspired the idea that the album should have all these collaborations.'

Anxious to widen Nelson's traditional repertoire and audience, Was compiled a tape of material by such artists as Peter Gabriel, Paul Simon and Bob Dylan, and sent it for the singer's approval. 'I would never have picked a lot of those songs, because I would never have found them,' Nelson admits. 'But when I heard "Graceland", I remembered Paul Simon asking me to do it before he released it himself. I thought it was a great song, but I just couldn't hear me singing it.'

Stripping away the South African township jive of Simon's original recording, Was relocated 'Graceland' in its lyrical milieu of the American South. His weary voice soaked in experience, Nelson delivered Simon's lyric like a pilgrim's confession. Equally affecting was his interpretation of another of Simon's explorations of national identity, 'American Tune'.

As Don Was reveals, Simon's studio technique clashed violently with his own: 'I knew it was a risk involving Paul in the record, because our working methods are so different. He can spend a year on a record. But when it came to "American Tune", I thought, "It's his song, so he'll know how to play it!" Paul came in to play the guitar at noon. At eight I sent the band home, because we weren't even close. Paul was being really fussy. At nine, I walked out of the room. I said, "This guy should be committed. This is the most insane, frustrating thing I've ever seen in my life." But I swear to God, at three in the morning, what he came up with – I could have sat behind that machine for two thousand years and I wouldn't have thought of it. It was fucking beautiful. I felt foolish for doubting Paul Simon for a second.'

Don Was's pedigree as a producer triggered another meeting of country and rock icons. Nelson and Bob Dylan had first met during the troubled shooting of Sam Peckinpah's *Pat Garrett And Billy The Kid* in 1973, and had remained respectful acquaintances ever since. Strangely, Nelson had never cut any Dylan material, though he had delved into the song catalogues of contemporaries like Neil Young, Joni Mitchell, James Taylor, the Rolling Stones and even Procol Harum. 'Years before, Bob and I had talked about writing something together,' he explains. 'My idea was for one of us to write a song and send it to the other, and then the other write something to go with it. Eventually, Bob went into the studio with his band, and just recorded this melody.'

As Don Was notes, Dylan's gift wasn't purpose-built: 'When I was making *Under The Red Sky* with him, we'd cut another song, and the band came in for the playback. Bob stayed out, and the assistant engineer was smart enough to turn the recorder on. It was a very cool track, but he never wrote the lyrics. So I asked him if he would mind if Willie finished it.'

'When I heard the tape,' Nelson says, 'Bob had the tune, but he sort of hummed it (*sings*): "Nah nah nah nah nah nah, Heartland". That was all I had to work with! So I wrote the rest of the lyrics. Bob never heard the rest of the words until the day we recorded the song.'

The session took place the day after Columbia Records' extravagant thirtieth-anniversary celebration of Dylan's career in New York – at which the controversial Irish singer Sinéad O'Connor had been barracked off the stage. A few hours later, she was in the studio with Nelson, duplicating Peter Gabriel and Kate Bush's duet on 'Don't Give Up' with an emotional resonance that outstripped the original. 'Willie totally related to her,' Was concludes, 'especially after she got booed off.'

That same afternoon, Bob Dylan arrived at Columbia's New York studio to record 'Heartland'. 'It was really strange,' Was remembers. 'Bob came in and Willie was already seated in the vocal booth, and they just nodded hello to each other. I thought the mike was off. I said to the engineer, "Are you sure that's working?" He said, "Yeah, they didn't say a word to each other." I thought, "God, that's peculiar." And then I realized, these two guys are so deep, they don't need to engage in small talk. You know, maybe I haven't seen you in five years, but we're friends and I know we're cool, we don't have to trivialize the moment. It was a great lesson to me. There was no bullshit. They sat there and were perfectly comfortable not saying a word. It was the weirdest thing I ever saw. Then they sang live together.'

'Heartland' proved to be a highlight on an album which fulfilled all of its producer's intentions except one – a hit record. Artistically, *Across The Borderline* began a renaissance in Nelson's career which lasted for the rest of the decade, through projects like the sparse, haunting acoustic album *Spirit*; a murky and enigmatic collaboration with Daniel Lanois and Emmylou Harris called *Teatro*; and another Don Was liaison which treated some of Nelson's earliest material to reggae arrangements.

Nelson's approval enabled Was to produce an album by his country supergroup, the Highwaymen, plus projects by two other members of the quartet, Waylon Jennings (*Right For The Time*) and Kris Kristofferson (*A Moment Of Forever*). 'Kris's record might be the favourite record I've ever worked on,' Was concedes. 'But hardly anyone noticed it was out there.'

The producer won more commercial recognition for *Rhythm Country And Blues*, an unlikely 1994 collection of duets between contemporary Nashville stars and soul performers from the sixties, tackling equally aged R&B hits. 'That was Al Teller's idea, the president of MCA,' Was explains. 'He realized he had a strong R&B roster, and the most commercial country roster. He wanted to cross into both markets. But his R&B department didn't want anything to do with the idea. Street credibility is so important in young black music, that singing an old song with some cracker was not of interest to anybody. So the idea had to come down a notch – which increased it in value to me, because suddenly you could go to Al Green and Gladys Knight, who don't sell millions of records anymore, but who are still wonderful singers.'

The first pairing were country star Vince Gill and Motown veteran Gladys Knight, who cut a conservative arrangement of the Marvin Gaye/Tammi Terrell hit 'Ain't Nothing Like The Real Thing'. Gradually, Was and his artists began to twist the formula, in terms both of material (Marty Stuart and the Staple Singers combining on the Band's late-sixties rock anthem 'The Weight') and of style. The eccentric team of Al Green and Lyle Lovett bent Willie Nelson's 'Funny How Time Slips Away' into a playful slice of Memphis soul; Conway Twitty (in his last ever studio recording) and Sam & Dave survivor Sam Moore rekindled the Southern soul tradition with 'Rainy Night In Georgia'. Though *Rhythm Country And Blues* made only a minimal impact on the R&B marketplace, it was a substantial hit on the rock charts – and also topped the country listing, despite making few concessions to the sound of Nashville in 1994.

'When the album was finished,' Don Was recalls, 'Bob Dylan called me up and told me he loved it. I told him, "A lot of the inspiration for this record comes from you." What I'd been attempting to do, in a heavy-handed way, was what Dylan had done really elegantly years before – to wed blues and country music. He was like a musicology instructor, the way he took Woody Guthrie folk music and blended it with Robert Johnson and Muddy Waters and Allen Ginsberg's beat poetry. I learned more about music from his stuff than anything, so I told him, "You're the living embodiment of this project."'

Rhythm Country And Blues barely approached the sonic potential of that concept. A year later, British art-rocker Matt Johnson performed a more adventurous chemical experiment, by subjecting many of Hank Williams' most famous songs to the ambient dance-pop treatment he usually reserved for his own material. Yet *Hanky Panky*, issued under Johnson's pseudonym of The The, paled alongside Don Was's rejoinder. In 1997, the newly dubbed 'Orqestra Was' issued *Forever's A Long Long Time*, a daring adventure which not only erased all the conventional boundaries between genres, but created new R&B-rooted melodies for a set of obscure Hank Williams lyrics. Hank's homely *aperçus* were now adrift on a turbulent sea of Miles Davis jazz, Detroit garage-rock and uptown R&B – before the album ended with Merle Haggard and a piece of traditional country that seemed like a prophet's commentary on the aftermath of an apocalypse.

'The first thing I had was the musical texture of the record,' Was explains. 'No matter how good a communicator Willie Nelson is, the Stooges didn't play at his high school, like they did at mine. I grew up with this incredible mixture of sound in Detroit – the MC5, Monk and Coltrane, George Clinton, Motown, a lot of country music. The atmosphere in sixties Detroit was one of cross-pollination, all about breaking down barriers. I wanted to reflect those textures and unify them.' The album was perhaps doomed to commercial failure; its stylistic courage was no more viable in the late nineties than the political radicalism of sixties Detroit. But *Forever's A Long Long Time* remains a defiant statement of idealism from one of the few musicians for whom the clash of cultures between country, rock, R&B and jazz was simply an irrelevance.

43 Gone Country

The rise and fall of New Country, 1986–1999: Randy Travis; Dwight Yoakam; Marty Stuart; Garth Brooks; Billy Ray Cyrus; Shania Twain; the Dixie Chicks; Alison Krauss

The birth of cable TV channels devoted entirely to rock videos altered the landscape of the music industry in the early eighties. By 1982, MTV was already recognized as the single most powerful force in selling rock music to the American audience. Alternative/ underground artists could try to subvert the visual clichés of the age, but they couldn't escape MTV's influence.

The country market was unsurprisingly suspicious of this innovation, but even traditionalists realized that if country wasn't to be sidelined as the music of the middle-aged, then the industry had to compete with the slick visuals and glamorous presentation of MTV.

The Nashville Network (TNN) cable TV group was launched in 1983, with an unappetizing schedule of variety shows and old movies. Only the *Nashville Now* talk show, hosted by Ralph Emery, suggested that the network understood the demands of specialist programming.

Slowly, TNN modernized its presentation. The *Country Clips* show was devoted to the first tentative promo videos, made on a fraction of the budget allotted to rock clips. While MTV assumed that its audience could cope with irony, pastiche and simplistic visual metaphors, early country videos fell into two categories: performance clips, and naïve storylines. This approach had its benefits; for years, country viewers were spared the slow-motion shots of breaking glass or spilled water that were an MTV cliché, while the overall lack of pretension helped to persuade traditionalists that video wasn't perverting the nature of country music. But this low-budget philosophy was doomed, and the birth of a full-scale country-video channel, Country Music Television

(CMT), ensured that the medium became an increasingly high priority for artists and record labels alike.

The birth of country video coincided with the mid-eighties slump in record sales. Desperate to expand its market, the Country Music Association looked to Europe. The country-pop phenomenon triggered by *Urban Cowboy* had made little impact outside the USA, so the CMA's challenge was fundamental: selling modern country music to audiences who equated the genre with Tammy Wynette, Jim Reeves, cowboy boots and spurs.

So was born New Country – a European marketing campaign which reached back across the Atlantic and eventually christened an era. The initial campaign, in 1986, proved to be premature. The CMA's slogan was 'Discover New Country: Leave The Wagon Wheels Behind', but the artists they highlighted – including Don Williams, Exile, the Oak Ridge Boys, Alabama and Gary Morris – weren't likely to appeal to pop, rock or even country fans in Britain, where the effort was centred.

A year later, the 'New Country '87' campaign reflected the changing face of Nashville. Since 1985, a new generation had infiltrated the industry, declaring their contempt for country-pop and their loyalty to vintage stars such as Merle Haggard, Buck Owens, Lefty Frizzell and Hank Williams. Their traditional stance was all the more powerful because it came from singers young enough to have been enticed by the sounds of the rock revolution.

'New Country '87' introduced Europe to Steve Earle, whose music owed as much to the Rolling Stones as to Merle Haggard; the O'Kanes, a singer-songwriter duo whose harmonies harked back to the Everlys and the Beatles; former soul singer T. Graham Brown; and the Judds, a mother/daughter partnership who backed their big-hair glamour with vocal nuances that came straight from the Appalachian string-band tradition. Wynonna Judd also boasted a voice to rival Aretha Franklin, one of her earliest influences.

Not everyone in New Country was raised on rock. Randy Travis was dubbed the 'King of the New Traditionalists' for his honky-tonk arrangements and a voice that echoed the phrasing of George Jones and the timbre of Lefty Frizzell. A teenage hellraiser, prone to careering through the backroads of North Carolina in stolen cars while stoked on a cocktail of illegal drugs, Travis was in theory the prototypical rock rebel. 'That stuff never interested me,' he insists. 'Even when I was speeding down the road in someone else's Cadillac, I always punched in a country station.'

Travis was the exception. Dwight Yoakam, another significant newcomer to mid-eighties country, is unashamed of his mixed roots: 'I listened to country and to rock, everything from Haggard to the Grateful Dead. I was interested in country-rock, because it suggested there might be a place I could go. I knew from the start that I sounded more country than anything else.'

Yoakam was rejected by Nashville in 1977, and ended up in Los Angeles, playing stripped-down honky-tonk on the same bills as punk bands such as X and the Blasters. Signed to Warner Brothers in 1985, he was initially viewed as a rockabilly singer, and he was the only country artist of the era to feature on MTV: 'They don't like to mention it, because they ostracized me as soon as I had a country hit, but they interviewed me. I appeared on this show called *The Cutting Edge*.'

When Warners launched him in Nashville, Yoakam was told he was 'too country to make it. That was hard for me to take. I got to where I am because someone crawled down a mine everyday, and I don't intend to forget that.' His response was brusque: 'Much of what is being marketed from Nashville today as country music isn't country at all,' he complained in 1986. 'It's much too smooth. It's sterile. We have the chance to re-educate young people, put the record straight.'

Yoakam's success with revivals of Johnny Horton, Lefty Frizzell and Buck Owens hits proved he knew more about the country audience than the record companies who'd been scurrying after the pop audience. Moreover, his image – leather-clad legs, cowboy hat, infinitely cool demeanour, and offstage friendships with the stars of *Easy Rider* – attracted listeners back across the dial from rock stations.

Among them was Pam Tillis, daughter of country star Mel Tillis: 'Dwight showed me that somebody else had finally caught the Emmylou Harris drift – that you can have an edge and be cool but also be in touch with your roots.' Tillis dabbled in new wave, jazz-rock and blues, but returned to her roots in the late eighties, when 'Country suddenly started getting interesting again. Dwight, Steve Earle, Foster & Lloyd – it had a sort of twang to it, and I really related to that.'

The CMA's third European invasion was titled 'Route '88', boosting artists such as Lyle Lovett, Nanci Griffith and k.d. lang – all of whom achieved an impact in Britain not matched by their outsider status in their homeland. 'If you don't fit the main flow of vanilla ice-cream cones they crank off the conveyor-belt round here, they don't know what to do with you,' says Marty Stuart, who struggled for acceptance in mid-eighties Nashville, despite his heritage as a teenage bluegrass/rockabilly prodigy who'd worked with Johnny Cash, Bob Dylan and Neil Young.

Even rockabilly was acceptable in the new Nashville. Ricky Van Shelton's tastes ran from Elvis Presley to Lawrence Welk, but he hit the charts in 1987 with the updated Carl Perkins sound of 'Crime Of Passion'. Marty Stuart broke through by the end of the decade, after British-born writer Paul Kennerley crafted him songs which softened his Perkins licks into uptempo country. Mark Collie – proud to admit that 'Sun Records blew my mind. That's the most exciting music in the world' – achieved a short spasm of fame with singles like 'Hardin County Line', which sounded as if it had come from an undocumented jam session between Elvis Presley and John Fogerty.

By the end of the eighties, industry pundits were predicting another boom era for country – this time without compromise. CMT was now programming such artists as Clint Black and Alan Jackson, who might once have channelled their talent into the singer-songwriter genre. They sold intelligent, well-crafted honky-tonk music, rooted in the past but recorded with remarkable clarity on modern digital equipment. The inevitable cowboy hats on their heads, Black, Jackson, Randy Travis and Dwight Yoakam were marketed as sex symbols to teenage fans and as saviours of vintage country to their parents. In the pre-Nirvana era when America seemed to offer nothing but metal, hip-hop and fabricated soul, their three-minute gems harked back to the golden age of sixties pop.

There were limits, of course. 'We can't stretch the lyrics as far as a rock band in terms of being real sexual,' admitted Alan Jackson. 'In country, we're a little more subtle.' But Ricky Skaggs spoke for many when he asked, 'Who wants to hear the messages that come out of rap and metal? I don't want my kids to listen to that, or Madonna, that's for sure.' Lyrically safe but not banal, musically predictable but not tired, country music in 1990 seemed to be on the verge of infinite expansion. It was strong enough to welcome the Kentucky Headhunters' revision of the Southern rock tradition, K. T. Oslin's poignant songs about the dilemmas facing women in middle-age, the Desert Rose Band's return to the sound of the Byrds and the Burritos, and left-field, sometimes satirical offerings from Lyle Lovett and k.d. lang.

Country even had its own superstar in the unlikely figure of Garth Brooks. Overweight and balding, a college graduate and a stadium-rock fan, Brooks became the best-selling American artist of the 1990s – in any genre. His forte was honky-tonk music, recognizable to veterans such as George Jones, and anguished ballads closer to the acoustic folk-rock of James Taylor and Dan Fogelberg than anyone who'd come out of Nashville. Brooks sold both his styles like a rock star.

He had never forgotten how he'd felt as a teenager when he saw Queen perform in Oklahoma City: 'I was standing on my seat when Brian May started playing this guitar solo. Then this light moves in on him, and suddenly this fan kicks on and his hair's blowing everywhere and he's leaning into the wind and the light is burning into him and he's burning in the light. And I stood up, with my fist high in the air, and I screamed so loud I could feel the veins in my neck. I was feeling, "Bring me anything in the world that hasn't been done by mankind, I want to take a crack at it right this second."' As his audience expanded, so did his stage theatrics, until his stadium shows rivalled Michael Jackson's for visual and sensory impact.

The full impact of Garth Brooks wasn't registered nationally until May 1991. That was when *Billboard* adopted a more accurate system of logging record sales across America. Overnight, the US album chart was transformed. Now the public could see what the accountants already knew: country was outselling rock, and Garth Brooks was the most popular artist in the nation. Country sales increased by 47 per cent in 1991, and by a further 52 per cent the following year.

The most remarkable aspect of Brooks' crossover success was that it wasn't fuelled by pop radio. Though he released some of the best-selling singles of the early nineties, none of them reached *Billboard*'s Hot 100 chart – because they weren't serviced to pop and rock stations. 'Capitol said, "Do you wanna go pop?" and I said no,' Brooks explained in 1992. 'If you hear Garth Brooks on the radio, it's either a country station, or else the pop people went out and bought it, and there's nothing I can do about that. I am not pop. I'm flattered with the pop success we've had, but I'm damn proud to say I'm country.'

His current hit single then was 'Shameless', an explosive cover of a Billy Joel song. 'That scared people,' Brooks admitted, 'and everybody took a pretty safe position by saying, "I'm not sure about that." But I could only go by my crowd, and they went nuts for "Shameless" when we started playing it. They're the ones who told me to cut it.' 'Shameless' was duly ignored by pop radio. 'I couldn't care less about pop music,' Brooks told me, before boasting that his favourite record of recent years was Michael Bolton's ersatz rock'n'soul album *Soul Provider*.

Brooks' success inevitably triggered resentment. 'I thought it was some kind of white supremacist plot when Garth Brooks first hit,' complained ex-Lone Justice singer Maria McKee. 'I thought they saw rap music getting bigger and bigger, and concocted this plot to bring people back. I just wish they wouldn't use the medium of country music.' Kinky Friedman, who dubbed Brooks 'the anti-Hank', relies on pure sarcasm: 'Kansas and Styx are his favourite bands. He majored in marketing. That's an exciting man.' Waylon Jennings opts for cynicism: 'I think his hero was Elton John. That's who he tries to sound like. The little yodel in his voice is for country. He is so smart, to do that.'

His co-manager Pam Lewis was aware that Brooks was a soft target: 'Everybody says he's going to be the next Elvis. Great. Look what happened to Elvis.' But she had reckoned without the strength of her client. Calculating he might be, but he demonstrated an uncanny self-possession in the face of his celebrity status. He showed unprecedented loyalty and generosity to his staff and band, and applied the same rigorous standards to his personal and creative life. Brooks might have worshipped Billy Joel as much as he did Hank Williams, but he never disguised his taste, contributing to a Kiss tribute album and using a massive Central Park concert to invite mellow seventies folkie Don McLean on stage. He even ignored the seemingly irresistible rise of country video, rarely shooting clips after CMT banned one of his early offerings.

Like his musical blend, Brooks' success proved impossible to emulate. His secret was his honesty: he never claimed to be anything more than an outspoken patriot with an innate feel for free speech who was passionate about country and album-oriented rock.

Nashville interpreted his sales figures another way. They saw a young guy in a hat with a voice pitched somewhere between Billy Joel and Merle Haggard, who'd brought the industry unimagined wealth. So they set out to clone the maverick. Label rosters were filled with 'hat acts' – cute guys with bland voices playing soft country and never removing their stetsons. The result was homogeneous and lukewarm. 'On the old records, you'd hear one bar and say, "Oh yeah, that's Jerry Lee Lewis,"' Marty Stuart notes. 'Now you have to ask. There's great singers now, but I'm not sure how many stars there are.' Veterans like Waylon Jennings were equally disgusted: 'John Cash called me not long ago and said, "Waylon, aren't you glad that you don't wake up every morning and sound like twenty-five other singers?"'

In the quest for success, Nashville squeezed everyone it signed into the same straitjacket. When country-rock'n'rollers Jason and the Scorchers split, lead singer Jason – a punk Jerry Lee Lewis – was enlisted as a potential country star. Signed by Capitol in 1992, he fingered Bob Dylan as the genius behind his move: 'Bob could see the Scorchers were breaking up, and he said, "Why don't you try more of a Nashville approach?" He was saying, "You'd stand out more in the country world than the rock'n'roll world, because what you do is more exciting and more visual." That really made sense to me.' Although his solo album sounded, as one critic noted, like two different records being played at once, Jason was insistent that 'The country world's opened up and created the space where I can move in.'

The strategy proved disastrous. The album flopped, CMT ignored his videos, and no country fan was tricked into mistaking him for the next Garth Brooks. 'The whole country star thing just didn't work out,' he admitted in 1996. 'Looking back, I can't even imagine what I was thinking. It was absolutely absurd. I'm way too raw to ever work in that world. I pretty much hate everything on country radio.'

Dire Straits guitarist Mark Knopfler echoes his distaste. 'You can't find a song there that's worth hearing again,' he says, throwing an imaginary Frisbee across the room. 'They're so disposable.' Knopfler was another outsider in early-nineties Nashville, cutting an album with guitar veteran Chet Atkins and trying to persuade Vince Gill to abandon his career as country's leading balladeer to join Dire Straits as a backing vocalist. 'I was flattered,' Gill says politely, 'but I couldn't afford to put my career on hold like that.'

Another beneficiary of Knopfler's attentions was John Anderson, whose career had slipped since his pioneering days as a New Traditionalist in the early eighties. The English guitarist contributed to his 1992 comeback album, *Seminole Wind* – the title track of which rekindled the spirit of the Band's finest work. Anderson recognized that his commercial renaissance went against the trend: 'When they start worrying about image, and they bring through all these guys with nice trim figures, no pot bellies, and they've got perfect teeth – Jesus Christ, I hope they don't forget the music.'

The teeth, the physique, not to mention the stadium-rocker's hair: Billy Ray Cyrus, the biggest country star of 1993, had it all. He also had an annoying bubblegum rock song called 'Achy Breaky Heart' which became the biggest crossover country hit in years. Travis Tritt lampooned it in an interview, and was forced by his record label to apologize. That summer, Cyrus's rivals competed to sneer at his success in private, while expressing nothing but polite praise for his rapid rise to prominence as soon as a microphone appeared.

Desert Rose Band leader and former Byrd Chris Hillman had

less to protect. 'That has nothing to do with country,' he said. 'It's a line-dancing song. It's like disco in the seventies. Country has become the background Muzak to a mating ritual.'

A highly profitable mating ritual: in 1993, country secured its highest ever percentage of the American radio audience. More people from San Francisco to New York, Minneapolis to New Orleans, now tuned in to country than to the Top 40 pop stations. But what they heard was less recognizable than ever as the product of the white South. 'There's always a danger in hillbillies trying to be pop stars,' Marty Stuart notes dryly. Waylon Jennings is more direct: 'When I hear a song, the first thing I say is, "Is it any good? Can people relate to it?" Now they say, "Is it a good video? Can they dance to it?" That's the suffering country music is going through.'

The wheel had turned full circle – back to 1958, to 1963, to 1968, to 1975, to 1980, to 1985, to every era when pursuit of the pop market had drained the country out of country music. What was different was the hypocrisy that ran through the Nashville industry. In private, it was almost impossible to find anyone, from session musicians to industry heads, who had a positive word to say about the direction the music had taken. Yet in public the Nashville hierarchy pretended that their product was the artistic pinnacle of country music history.

The air was sour with compromise. One of the most eclectic and independent of the New Country stars, Pam Tillis, recruited honky-tonk singer Dale Watson to appear in a 1993 video. 'She asked me to comb down my quiff,' he reported drolly. 'She don't want Nashville to think she's got a rockabilly band.' He wrote up the incident as 'Nashville Rash', a sweeping indictment of the New Country ethos, and watched his career disappear into the ghetto of indie labels and cult appeal. Dwight Yoakam, keeper of the honky-tonk spirit, allowed himself to be talked into covering sixties pop hits in a misguided attempt to break into the British market. He toured the UK as the album was released, and didn't play a single track from it. 'That wasn't an album to us,' he apologized, 'that was just a marketing strategy.' Either way, it tainted his reputation.

At least Yoakam was willing to experiment. Most of the stars who'd enlivened country music in 1990 became too comfortable in their stardom to mess with their formula. There were rare moments when Clint Black seemed anxious to break out – his chart-topping 1993 hit 'No Time To Kill' drifted into an extended instrumental jam, which was almost revolutionary on Nashville radio – but it was easier to flow with the current rather than disrupt it.

The current could also sweep him away. The cliché about country audiences was that one hit record would win you their loyalty for life. By the mid-nineties, country had become as ephemeral as pop. There was a shared, though unspoken, belief that the New Country audience attracted by Billy Ray Cyrus and Garth Brooks had no patience with veterans, a category which now included Randy Travis – purely on the basis that he'd been recording for almost a decade. Just as 40-year-old rock performers found airplay elusive, programmers in Nashville began to reject George Jones and Willie Nelson, regardless of what they produced.

Demographics now ruled the industry, allowing young artists such as Faith Hill and Shania Twain to aim unashamedly at a teenage audience. Twain's career was skilfully directed by her husband and record producer, the British hard-rock specialist Mutt Lange. The pair met at a 1993 country festival, and Lange crafted her phenomenally successful album, *The Woman In Me*, which pitched country trademarks – fiddle, steel guitar, and the joyous twang of Twain's voice – against rock rhythm tracks. 'Country audiences are capable of stretching, and we can take them with us,' Twain reckoned, and their strategy also opened up the pop charts to teenybop country. In a masterstroke that appalled many in Nashville, Twain and Lange prepared two different versions of her 1997 album, *Come On Over*, subtly tailored for the country and rock audiences. Discovering that British audiences were resistant to anything marketed as 'country', Lange's publicists barred her from speaking to the local country media, and successfully sold her as a mainstream rock act. Equally successful beyond the US country charts were the Dixie Chicks, whose blend of sleek pop material and country instrumentation achieved similar crossover appeal around the world to those exponents of Irish folk/AOR, the Corrs.

The comedy duo, the Geezinslaw Brothers, captured the mood of old Nashville in a song title: 'You Call It Country, We Call It Bad Rock'n'Roll'. In the words of a masterful Alan Jackson hit, written by Bob McDill, the whole world had 'Gone Country'. The song painted acidic portraits of Vegas lounge acts, Greenwich Village folksingers, LA pop stars, all drawn to Nashville in search of opportunistic country gold.

Jackson's single seemed to stir a response from Nashville's corporate memory. So did hints that, a decade after the last sales slump, country's commercial expansion had peaked. Video budgets were slashed, record company rosters trimmed. The voters at the 1995 Country Music Association Awards delivered a calculated snub to the ruling order. Bluegrass prodigy Alison Krauss, who was signed to an East Coast acoustic label, was unexpectedly voted Female Vocalist of the Year. Krauss was scarcely a purist: her favourite bands included Def Leppard and AC/DC, and she'd recently covered sixties hits by the Beatles and the Foundations. But she steadfastly refused to abandon her bluegrass band, Union Station, or her label, Rounder. 'If we'd wanted to sell out,' she says, 'we could have done it years ago.' Other awards for the Tractors and the Mavericks, both rock-rooted country bands, represented a shift away from the 'hat acts' who had dominated the industry in recent years.

Even Garth Brooks caught the new mood, dubbing his *Fresh Horses* album 'garage country, extremely loose, extremely free'. So was his definition of country, which included a rewrite of an Aerosmith song, 'The Fever'. By 1998, Brooks had even succeeded in bringing Bob Dylan his first No. 1 country hit, when he covered Dylan's 'To Make You Feel My Love'. A year later, he indulged his fantasies of rock stardom by releasing a country-free album in the image of his heroes, under the pseudonym of Chris Gaines.

'I don't even think Hank Williams could get on country radio right now,' Merle Haggard noted in 1996. There was no 'even' about it. Hank was too thin, his teeth were suspect, he drank too much, and he sounded like a hillbilly. By then, the 'even' applied to Hank Williams Jr, still one of the biggest concert draws in American music, who was no longer heard on country radio except during the Sunday morning oldies hour. The man who'd introduced country to the delights of the Allman Brothers, ZZ Top and the Rolling Stones was now whining, 'I don't care if it's Old Country gold or New Country soul, I've had enough of this rock'n'roll'.

As the 1990s neared their end, the dominant style in country, as in pop, was the power ballad. In a farcical 'battle', Trisha Yearwood and the 13-year-old Lee Ann Rimes released virtually identical arrangements of 'How Will I Live', a torch ballad of no great emotional resonance. Yearwood's was proclaimed 'country', Rimes' pop – and the latter duly became the longest-charting single in American history. You could have switched the labels on the two records and no one would have noticed. Nor was it easy to distinguish the melodramatic style of these country performers from their pop and soul rivals such as Celine Dion or Mariah Carey.

It was as if all the signs had been switched to confuse an invading army. The country charts welcomed bland voices and equally insipid songs, suggesting that the most influential figures in Nashville history were James Taylor, Tina Turner and Elton John. The real country singers were sidelined on the handful of radio stations who'd adopted the 'Americana' format, a last refuge for Texas mavericks, honky-tonkers, folkies and other endangered species. Or else, like Johnny Cash and Willie Nelson, they led a dual existence – performing in concert for the country loyalists who'd helped them become stars, but marketing their new albums to the alternative rock audience.

Absent from country, mainstream rock and Top 40 stations alike were an assembly of groups who offered another perspective on country tradition. Loyal to the spirit of Gram Parsons, they were gathered under the vague disguise of 'alt.country' – lending honky-tonk and hillbilly an underground glamour that had been missing since Gram Parsons left the Flying Burrito Brothers in 1970.

44 Country Feedback

Alternative country, 1987–1999: Uncle Tupelo; Souled American; the Cowboy Junkies; Son Volt; Wilco; the Jayhawks; Golden Smog; the Mekons; Will Oldham; Beck; Freakwater; Hazeldine; the Gourds; Lambchop

'It was never a movement. We were just different bands playing different music from different parts of America. All we had in common was guitars, and our nationality. The rest of it was hype, just media bullshit.'

Green On Red's Dan Stuart is talking about 1985, when the British rock press welcomed a 'new wave of American guitar bands', connecting dozens of outfits from across the fifty states under headings as diverse and vague as 'roots rock', 'new country rock', 'desert rock', 'cowpunk', 'country punk' and 'the Paisley Underground'.

A decade later, another equally eclectic array of American bands was swept into a wave of 'alternative country', 'alt.country', 'No Depression music', 'rebel country', 'insurgent country', 'country grunge' or 'underground country'. The editors of *No Depression*, the in-house magazine of this spurious movement, had the grace to call their subject 'alternative country (whatever that is)'.

No Depression was launched as a fanzine in the summer of 1995. It took its title from the début album by the Illinois band Uncle Tupelo; in turn, their source was a 1930s hillbilly gospel tune by the Carter Family. The magazine was intended as a celebration of 'alternative country', a tag which the editors applied with 'gentle sarcasm'. With the retrospective logic of history, the arrival of the magazine convinced the rest of the media that there was a movement, which they defined from the pages of *No Depression*. No wonder that Grant Alden and Peter Blackstock, who published two thousand copies of their first issue with a picture of Uncle Tupelo spin-off band Son Volt on the cover, noted wryly that 'the phrase "No Depression" is now tossed around by many of the same hands that dealt "grunge" when we started the magazine . . . the magazine is as much definition as we're prepared to offer.' The christening of 'alternative country' focused media attention on dozens of American, and some British, rock bands who were exploring aspects of country's heritage. To their bewilderment, the members of Uncle Tupelo – who split just before the 'movement' was identified – found themselves acclaimed as its inventors. But like many of the bands with whom they were categorized, Uncle Tupelo's music was less a revolution than a continuation of the spirit of 1985.

In the spirit of Green On Red, the Long Ryders, Jason and the Scorchers, Giant Sand and the other stalwarts of the original country-punk crossover, Uncle Tupelo founders Jeff Tweedy and Jay Farrar began the 1980s as diehard punk fans. 'We used to go and see the Minutemen, Black Flag, all these bands when they played in St Louis,' Tweedy recalled. 'Me and Jay weren't even friends with anyone who wasn't into Black Flag.'

The same fanatical spirit had caught Dan Stuart, Sid Griffin of the Long Ryders and Howie Gelb of Giant Sand. While those bands began their recording careers in the early eighties, combining their country roots, teenage passion for classic sixties rock and punk sensibility, Uncle Tupelo weren't formed until 1987, by which time the two musicians had outgrown their punk apprenticeship and discovered a shared fascination with country music. 'Country was always around when we were growing up,' Farrar explained. 'We'd hear it through our parents.' 'What we used to hear sounded like George Jones or Hank Williams,' Tweedy added. 'The stuff going on now doesn't have much to do with that anymore. There's something wrong when Garth Brooks lists one of his main inspirations as Journey.'

The year 1987 witnessed the death of the media hype surrounding the original American guitar groups. The Long Ryders split that Christmas, with Sid Griffin promising that in his next band, 'the country element will definitely be downplayed'. Green On Red released *The Killer Inside Me*, an album so oppressive that it effectively suffocated their deal with Mercury. Jason and the Scorchers tumbled into hard rock; the Beat Farmers lost their way with *The Pursuit Of Happiness* (and MCA's big bucks); the Rave-Ups became enmired in a legal swamp; Maria McKee abandoned her efforts to keep Lone Justice alive.

The only means of survival for the Class of '85 was success – either by luck, as when Los Lobos scored a Top 10 hit with the theme to the Ritchie Valens biopic, *La Bamba*, or by design, as REM applied AOR production ethics to their major label début, *Document*.

Like the Beatles and Merseybeat, the Eagles and LA country-rock, REM's leap to arena status wiped the rest of their generation off the map. But the spirit of '85 lingered defiantly on – not just via the maverick spirits of Stuart and Gelb, who were too driven to be pushed aside by anything as transient as failure, but by new bands such as the Jayhawks and Souled American.

The Jayhawks emerged out of the Minneapolis scene which had spawned the Replacements and Hüsker Dü – both of whom channelled their punk aggression into deceptively melodic songs. To this strange but influential hybrid, the Jayhawks brought leader Mark Olson's passion for Gram Parsons. On 1989's *Blue Earth*, Olson tapped into the spirit that had fled the Burritos after Gram became distracted in 1970, while 1995's *Tomorrow The Green Grass* was a sequel to the ill-fated liaison between Parsons and the Rolling Stones.

Joe Adducci and Chris Grigoroff, the pivots of Souled American, came from Chicago, but they sang with a hillbilly drawl not heard on country radio since the 1950s. They painted a rowdy, drunken landscape of the Deep South, peopled with characters who might have walked out of the pages of Harry Crews' Southern Gothic novels. When they collided their roadhouse country with dub reggae on 'Marleyphine Hank', from their 1989 album *Flubber*, two outlaw cultures were telescoped into one three-dimensional cartoon.

Other acts opted to revive the more sedate heritage of the Band. Blue Rodeo shared their Canadian background, and their musical textures, but their uneventful style suggested they had never been exposed to anything as uncouth as rock'n'roll. The Cowboy Junkies, also from Toronto, shared this emotional frigidity, but in singer Margo Timmins, they had a genuinely unsettling figurehead, her voice as barren and cold as the wastes of Northern

Canada. Performing Hank Williams' 'I'm So Lonesome I Could Cry' and Patsy Cline's 'Walking After Midnight' on 1988's *The Trinity Session*, she seemed to be reporting from the scene of some vast desolation, as if the nightmares of the Confederate Army had been entombed in ice.

The enigma of the American South continued to spark unexpected reactions. From the vantage point of Australia, Nick Cave saw it as the home of Gothic terror and perversity. He personified his obsession in the empty vessel of Elvis Presley's stillborn twin, Jesse Garon Presley, on 'Tupelo', the key moment of 1985's *The Firstborn Is Dead*. While Cave immersed himself in Southern myth, REM's Michael Stipe skimmed teasingly over the surface. The title of their *Fables Of The Reconstruction/Reconstruction Of The Fables* album hinted at a take on the New South which wasn't matched by the contents; likewise 'Country Feedback', on *Out Of Time*, didn't fulfil either of the criteria in its title. For real engagement with the South, REM guitarist Peter Buck chose to jam with the country-rock band, the Normaltown Flyers; while Stipe produced Vic Chestnutt, of whom Buck raved that 'His songs smack of such authenticity that you don't have to be from the South to know what he's singing about.' Emotionally raw, Chestnutt's music owed as much to Captain Beefheart as to Hank Williams.

Uncle Tupelo, who issued their début album *No Depression* in 1990, could afford a more considered approach. There was a delicious melancholy to their sound, and that of their spin-off bands, Son Volt and Wilco, which immediately removed them from the country tradition. Twenty years earlier, Neil Young had sulked like an adolescent through Don Gibson's country hit 'Oh Lonesome Me', glorying in every second of self-pity. Don Henley and Jackson Browne perfected what Elvis Costello called the 'fuck me, I'm sensitive' school of songwriting, and Uncle Tupelo's Jay Farrar relied on the same romantic despair.

'It wasn't like we were ever intentionally trying to merge punk and country,' Farrar's partner Jeff Tweedy reflected. 'That's just what came out.' *No Depression* mixed the sonic propulsion of Hüsker Dü with some rockabilly recklessness, never more effectively than on 'Whiskey Bottle', where Farrar used hard-rock guitar riffs to drive home his desolation, then a gentle pedal steel to breathe in some humanity.

With *Anodyne*, cut in two weeks of sessions in Austin during 1993, Uncle Tupelo laid their claim to continuity with the country-rock tradition. Farrar duetted with the revitalized Doug Sahm on one tune, and laced the album with guitar licks that could have been pulled from Neil Young's 'Powderfinger'. Michelle Shocked's brother Max Johnston sketched delicate brushstrokes of fiddle, lap steel and banjo, accentuating the thoughtful atmosphere of the record.

Farrar reserved his most enigmatic writing for the title track. 'Threw out the past, threw out what was mine,' he sang, 'threw out the years, it was hard to make it last.' The payoff line sounded like self-accusation: 'Anodyne, the sound of reconciliation . . . without a word you're out the door.' A few months later, Farrar quit the band, leaving no explanation beyond the timeless cliché about 'musical differences'.

Those were apparent as Farrar formed Son Volt with former Uncle Tupelo drummer Mike Heidorn, and issued *Trace*, the first in a series of albums situated in the heart of that gentle despondency which was his trademark. In his hands, country became a vehicle for exploring the nature of depression, a cerebral response to a genre rooted in physicality. Even as Son Volt began to shed their emblematic sound on 1998's *Wide Swing Tremolo*, 'Hanging Blue Side' remained as a sign of Farrar's conviction of the link between country and emotional barrenness.

Meanwhile, the rest of Uncle Tupelo recruited Jay Bennett and renamed themselves Wilco, for *A.M.* and *Being There*. The latter was ecstatically reviewed – one critique called it 'the best double-album since *Exile On Main Street*' – but its raucous rock energy could be traced directly back to the Replacements' *Let It Be*. Divided by unspoken differences, neither Farrar nor Tweedy was able to revisit that meeting place of country, punk and classic rock, and by 1999's *Summerteeth*, Wilco too had cast off the overt country influences on their work.

While Uncle Tupelo inadvertently provided a name for that territory, they were hardly its only residents. The Jayhawks continued to provide a Minneapolis slant on the Southern rock tradition on *Hollywood Town Hall* and *Tomorrow The Green Grass*, until Olson left to collaborate with his wife, maverick songwriter Victoria Williams. By the late nineties, the Uncle Tupelo camp followers began to turn into a crowd, as bands such as Wagon, the Schramms, the Blood Oranges, the Pinetop 7 and the Bottle Rockets messed with the same ingredients. Whiskeytown's Ryan Adams caught their spirit in 'Faithless Street': 'I started this damn country band 'cause punk rock was too hard to sing.'

Like Uncle Tupelo, the Bottle Rockets came out of Missouri, churning together the familiar influences of REM, Neil Young and Steve Earle. Not for these boys any hip rock credentials: on 'Idiot's Revenge' they lambasted the kind of woman who 'likes Dinosaur Jr, though she can't tell you why, She says, you like country music, then you deserve to die.' The culmination of this activity was, as in the mid-eighties, an impromptu supergroup. The Long Ryders and Green On Red had conspired to produce Danny & Dusty; now members of the Jayhawks, the Replacements and, later, Wilco's Jeff Tweedy became Golden Smog. Their amusing 1992 début EP covered tunes by the Rolling Stones, Bad Company and Thin Lizzy, but when they regrouped with Tweedy in 1996 for *Down By The Old Mainstream*, there was an inevitability about the results.

More adventurous behaviour was taking place around the margins of alternative country, from musicians whose ambitions extended beyond replacing the Long Ryders. Austin, the capital of Texas eccentricity, spawned the Bad Livers, a bluegrass and gospel group who started out by covering Iggy Pop's 'Lust For Life', turned over the production of their 1992 début CD to Paul Leary of the hardcore punk experimentalists the Butthole Surfers, and then gradually refined the avant-gardisms out of their music to the point where they were accepted by bluegrass traditionalists.

An equally strange journey was made by the Geraldine Fibbers. Nothing in the history of their parent group, hip-hop terrorists Ethyl Meatplow, prepared the way for their aggressive blend of hillbilly and hardcore. German guitarist Alexander Hacke underwent a similar transition, interrupting his work with the avant-garde white noise specialists, Einstürzende Neubaten, to form a country band called the Jever Mountain Boys – named after a town on the coastal flatlands of northern Germany.

No venture into country-rock was more surreal than that of Jon Langford. At the end of the seventies he was the leader of the Mekons, a politically committed English punk band from Leeds, who merged rigorous anarchism, determined amateurism and rampant paranoia. Fading from view in the early eighties, they resurfaced in 1985 with *Fear And Whiskey*, on which the British punks reimagined themselves as fear- and beer-soaked American troops in the Second World War.

Thereafter, the Mekons shifted closer to the sound of the American heartland with every release, while maintaining a strictly anti-American, anti-imperialist worldview. They covered tunes by Merle Haggard and Gram Parsons, and named an album of ramshackle political folk *Honky Tonkin'* after a Hank Williams song. In 1988, they masterminded *'Til Things Are Brighter*, a Johnny Cash tribute album which beat Nashville to this particular punch by a decade, and assembled such unlikely vocalists as Marc Almond, Pete Shelley of the Buzzcocks and Stephen Mallinder of Cabaret Voltaire.

Now relocated in Chicago, Jon Langford divided his time in the nineties between episodic Mekons projects and a series of increasingly surreal country-rock projects – such as the Pine Valley Cosmonauts, the Waco Brothers, or Jon Langford's Hillbilly Wagon. 'Langford is the perfect example of insurgent country, rebel country, whatever term they're using to market it this week,' says critic Greil Marcus, a longtime champion of the Mekons. 'If these people are linked by anything, it's that they were raised on rock and roll, and that's what they really play, but they are fascinated by old country music – from the fifties, the forties, the thirties. They haven't really got to the twenties yet, but they will. There's a tone in their music that's really different. Lots of it, like the Waco Brothers, Langford's band, isn't even American. It's a genre, in a way, but it's more idiosyncratic than the Hollywood country-rock stuff ever was – and that's partly because it comes from all over the place, not one area.'

Will Oldham was so passionate about the Mekons that he wrote them a song: 'For The Mekons, et al.'. It was the first recording issued under the pseudonym which he adopted for most of the nineties – Palace (or the Palace Brothers, Palace Songs or Palace Music). Working solo or with minimal accompaniment, usually with alternative rock 'recordist' Steve Albini at the controls, Oldham is responsible for one of the least accessible catalogues of the last decade. His music has the strangeness of a serial killer, secluded in rural desolation on the verge of madness. Though it's often marketed as 'alternative country', it's no closer to the tradition of Hank Williams and Gram Parsons – let alone Uncle Tupelo and the Bottle Rockets – than to that of Neil Young or Charles Manson. But all of those figures might recognize Oldham as one of their own.

Mark Linkous, the Virginian linchpin of Sparklehorse, occupies a similarly oblique role in this landscape. 'I'm quite inspired by bluegrass and George Jones,' he has said of his sparse, compulsive music, exemplified by *Vivadixiesubmarinetransmissionplot*, the band's 1997 début album.

Connecting Oldham and Linkous is an approach to American roots music which bypasses the previous three decades of country-rock. For Palace, Sparklehorse, Beck, Lambchop, the Gourds, Freakwater – a whole generation of musical explorers who have wandered off the main highways and deep into the backwoods – the road from the Byrds through LA country-rock to the Long Ryders doesn't show up on their maps. Only the maverick figure of Gram Parsons survives, resting alongside Robert Johnson, Hank Williams and Jimmie Rodgers as a signpost along the path.

These adventurers not only escaped the country-rock tradition; they also tore down the fences that separated country from soul, blues from folk, and all those 'pure' styles from the distorted beast that is rock'n'roll. This psychological freedom allowed Beck to slip from backroom hip-hop to country-tinged acoustic blues on 1998's *Mutations*, continuing the pick'n'mix approach of his earlier major-label albums *Mellow Gold* and *Odelay*. With music this eclectic, calculating the precise amount of 'country' or 'blues' became a self-defeating exercise. *Mutations* wasn't a country album, or even a country-rock album, but it was fused with an affection for the hillbilly tradition. In 1999, no one was surprised when Beck contributed to a Gram Parsons tribute record assembled by Emmylou Harris. 'I knew he was a real Gram fan,' she says, 'but it was ironic that he came up with one of the more traditional tracks on the record. His music is so innovative, and yet he went back full circle and became even more traditional than Gram had been – which was his way of still being innovative.'

There was a sense of liberation from the baggage of rock history about many roots-rock projects in the nineties. Janet Bean, drummer with Chicago post-punk band Eleventh Dream Day, had to shed her cultural preconceptions: 'I was embarrassed by country, and didn't want any part of it. I wanted to be in a punk band, which was sort of the antithesis of country. It wasn't until I was exposed to it on an underground level that I started to like it.' Her entrée was provided by Catherine Irwin, a fellow punk who introduced Bean to the music of the Carter Family and Buck Owens. At the end of the eighties, the pair formed Freakwater – a side-project which eventually upstaged Eleventh Dream Day in time and attention.

The clash and clang of Irwin and Bean's hillbilly harmonies, which climaxed on their fourth album, 1995's *Old Paint*, was a throwback to an age when a stylist such as Ernest Tubb could become a superstar without being able to hit a single line on-key. Freakwater initially operated with a self-conscious layer of irony, subjecting alien material such as Black Sabbath's 'War Pigs' to bluegrass treatment, but on *Old Paint* they located an emotional core beneath the kitsch. While their music seemed to belong to the distant past, their words were anything but traditional. 'There's nothing so pure as the kindness of an atheist,' Bean sang on 'Gone To Stay', subverting the entire bluegrass gospel tradition at a stroke.

The male domination of country-rock, which had been evident from the beginning, was finally weakened in the nineties, allowing acts such as Gillian Welch, Victoria Williams, Janet Bean and Catherine Irwin to be recognized as distinctive voices, rather than as sex symbols fronting male bands. Hazeldine also benefited from this shedding of prehistoric prejudices, which mirrored the changing face of US alternative rock through the 1990s. 'Gram and Emmylou built the house of Hazeldine,' says Shawn Barton of their delicate acoustic hillbilly music, but their 1998 covers album, *Orphans*, showcased some less obvious influences, from Genesis and Thin Lizzy to Radiohead. As a neat illustration of the way that tradition is handed down, Hazeldine covered 'Wild And Blue' believing it to be a Mekons song, not knowing it had already been a substantial hit for New Traditionalist icon John Anderson in the early eighties.

No band captured the mix of post-grunge intelligence and pre-Second World War naïvety better than the Gourds, fronted by Texas songwriters Kevin Russell and Jimmy Smith. On *Dem's Good Beeble* and the more aggressive *Stadium Blitzer*, they sounded like survivors from a twenties string band who'd been left by the roadside for half a century with nothing but bourbon for company. As they romped through 'Piss & Moan Blues' or 'Magnolia', it was as if decades of history had been erased, and a bunch of Southern boys with energy to burn and Bill Monroe records in their pockets had arrived on Sam Phillips' doorstep.

There was a surreal beauty in the fact that the least conventional 'country' band of the nineties should emerge from Music City itself, Nashville. Lambchop was a loose assembly of as many as fourteen musicians playing in combinations unimaginable in any era of country – mandolin juxtaposed with clarinet, for instance, or trombone and cello – and working to the equally individual vision of Kurt Wagner. They débuted in 1994 with *I Hope You're Sitting Down*, an eerie, textured record of almost pastoral music which borrowed from seventies Dylan, Neil Young, thirties hillbilly, cool jazz and ambient atmospherics.

This was country as mood music, carrying Wagner's precise, strangely affecting tales of emotional miscues and missed connections. 'Visit the Country Music Hall of Fame in Nashville,' Wagner insists on every album, but nothing there explains his haunting juxtaposition of easy listening and the avant-garde. After the mesmeric *How I Quit Smoking* in 1995, Wagner crafted the more varied *Thriller* in 1997, which introduced elements of punk and R&B. Neither impulse confined 'Gloria Leonard', a compelling conversation piece set against steel guitar and white noise. The following year's *What Another Man Spills* exposed another influence, the sweet soul of Curtis Mayfield, and also contained 'Magnificent Obsession' – not just the most overtly country tune in the Lambchop catalogue, but also a rationale for a band as inexplicable as anything in nineties rock.

Epilogue

In 1993, Evan Dando, leader of the grunge/pop band the
Lemonheads, was holed up in Hollywood at the Château
Marmont, rewiring his system on coke and speed. 'When I got
famous, I had this real Gram Parsons obsession,' he explained
later, and the Marmont had been Parsons' favourite West Coast
haunt. 'I started to think I *was* Gram.'

More than twenty-five years after his death, Gram Parsons'
mercurial career has assumed the proportions of myth. Why else
would disciples like U2 and Giant Sand congregate around the
surreal rock formations and heat-cracked cacti of the Mojave
Desert, turning his Joshua Tree death site into a place of
pilgrimage? Like Hank Williams, Parsons exists beyond music:
he's become a role model for mavericks and outsiders, a paragon
of excess whose lifestyle has proved as influential as his art. As
Emmylou Harris concedes, 'he has entered the mythic
consciousness'. The irony is that none of his disciples and
imitators has ever built upon Gram Parsons' music – for the simple
reason that his unwavering traditionalism always pointed to the
past, and not the future. Death saved him from his ambivalent
destiny as a pioneer who wanted only to stay safe at home in the
bosom of country music.

A poignant moment in 1992 caught the barbed nature of
Parsons' inheritance. In a Nashville cellar bar, Gram's daughter
Polly Parsons and her band She – named for one of his finest songs
– rekindled his memory while trying to ignite their own careers.
Polly's role was purely visual: her boyfriend carried the show,
strutting through a succession of her father's standards with a
Jaggeresque swagger he'd borrowed from a promo film clip of the
Flying Burrito Brothers. The young couple's mutual affection, for
each other and for Parsons' memory, was touching; but the GP

they were celebrating was a myth, not the troubled, tempestuous Southern gentleman who'd always denied that he was Polly's father.

Watching from the floor were Barry and Holly Tashian, who'd agreed to support She as a gesture to the daughter of their old friend. They applauded Polly politely, but appeared bemused by the chasm between the man they'd known in the sixties and seventies and the cartoon Parsons being celebrated on stage.

Earlier, they'd performed their own set of stark, unadorned bluegrass tunes. 'I spent years on the road in rock bands,' Barry Tashian explained after the show. 'I don't find that music satisfying anymore. Bluegrass is a lot more real. It's simple, but it has a spiritual core. You can live your life by this music.' Parsons would have echoed their respect for the tradition that he adored. Meanwhile, every summer brings another Gram Parsons tribute concert, and a new band of devotees soaks up the legend.

'We who must remain go on singing just the same,' sang the Eagles in their tribute to Parsons, and for many of the inheritors of his tradition, the road goes on for ever. Chris Hillman can still gain international exposure for his gentle explorations of country-rock history, but his less fortunate peers – Rick Roberts, Gene Parsons, Sneaky Pete Kleinow, the Dillards, and many more besides – are still trading on their lineage to increasingly smaller audiences. Unwavering in their devotion to the music, they play on as if it is 1971. 'It used to be that if you had one hit, country fans would stick with you for ever,' says Chris Hillman. 'That was true in the fifties, sixties and seventies, but now your shelf-life expires as soon as your record falls off the charts.' As the country audience has grown more restless and fickle, its role as the keeper of the flame has passed to the survivors of the counter-culture. In the nineties, there was the Eagles reunion, a Poco revival, the reappearance of Commander Cody, the tenth or twentieth relaunch of the Flying Burrito Brothers and New Riders Of The Purple Sage. The country-rock musicians once worshipped for their innovation are now rewarded for their fidelity to the past. Forget perpetual revolution: this is revolution in aspic.

Gram Parsons' method of escaping this fate was effective, but not perhaps to everyone's taste. His fellow pioneers had to adopt more subtle tactics. Michael Nesmith evaded the responsibility of reinventing country-rock by switching into video production, before emerging as a writer of magical realist fiction. Neil Young paused briefly to reap *Harvest Moon* in 1992, reviving the musical relationships (if not the impact) of 1972's *Harvest*. It proved to be nothing more than a social call on an old flame, and he soon lurched off in other directions.

Emmylou Harris outgrew her branding as Gram Parsons' soulmate by sheer persistence, emerging as one of the formative influences on eighties country, and then – when age exiled her from the Nashville mainstream – staking a proud claim to a place in left-field. There she could stroll through the sonic debris of Daniel Lanois' production on *Wrecking Ball*, or glide between the edgy guitars of her band Spyboy.

And it was with Daniel Lanois that Bob Dylan recorded 1997's *Time Out Of Mind*, his first album of original material in seven years. Its mere existence bluffed many critics into proclaiming it a work of genius, which was over-generous. But *Time Out Of Mind* did re-establish Dylan as a remarkable white bluesman. Like the other great vocal stylists of the country/rock collision – Willie Nelson, Jerry Lee Lewis, Hank Williams Jr – Dylan was incapable of being confined by mere description. As his age-stained voice echoed across the clattering guitars of 'Old Dirt Road', it was as if Jimmie Rodgers and Robert Johnson had met at some Mississippi crossroads in 1933 and decided to create rockabilly twenty years too soon.

For Dylan, the connections with Rodgers, Johnson and a pantheon of pioneers – Bill Monroe, the Carter Family, John Lee Hooker, Woody Guthrie, Carl Perkins and Blind Willie McTell – had become interwoven with his own heritage. With each year, he seemed to sink his roots deeper into the past. Once he'd pledged himself 'to join Little Richard'; now he soaked himself in twenties bluesmen and thirties string bands, forties R&B and fifties bluegrass. In his rare interviews, he celebrated the Delmore Brothers and Hank Williams, dipping his head in awe before the mysterious power of their music.

Dylan's restless touring schedule in the nineties allowed him to acknowledge his debts. Audiences in New Mexico or Budapest would be puzzled when he dropped a Marty Robbins or Dolly Parton tune into his repertoire. But these unrepeated covers – and there were countless more, as Dylan exhumed country songs by Gordon Lightfoot, Johnny Cash, Merle Kilgore, Don Gibson, Hank Snow – splashed colour on to the epic canvas of his music.

'The fallout of artwork is always revolutionary,' wrote Allen Ginsberg of Dylan in 1970. The Dylan of the late nineties – often clad in a cowboy hat and suit that would have fitted a honky-tonk hero such as Ernest Tubb – shaped that revolution as the full turning of a wheel, back to the whine and scurry of fiddle and banjo that filled the American landscape before he was born. In this vision, echoed by younger musicians such as Beck, Lambchop and the Gourds, country and rock were no longer rivals on a collision course, but twin responses to a single impulse: the desire to restore the tradition of the past at the instant that they replace it.

Acknowledgements

Many thanks to the following musicians, producers and observers of the events in this book, not all of whom are quoted in the final text, but who all contributed priceless memories and analysis: Jerry Allison, Dave Alvin, John Anderson, Joan Baez, Garth Brooks, Jackson Browne, Denny Bruce, Sonny Burgess, Mary Chapin Carpenter, Carlene Carter, Jack Clement, B. J. Cole, Mark Collie, Elvis Costello, Sonny Curtis, Charlie Daniels, Ray Davies, Micky Dolenz, Holly Dunn, Steve Earle, John Fogerty, Kinky Friedman, David Gates, Vince Gill, Jimmie Dale Gilmore, Jenny Grech, Jimmy Griffin, Sid Griffin, Nanci Griffith, George Hamilton IV, Butch Hancock, Jeff Hanna, Glen D. Hardin, Emmylou Harris, Levon Helm, John Hiatt, Chris Hillman, Bruce Hornsby, Waylon Jennings, Matt Johnson, Wynonna Judd, Phil Kaufman, Merle Kilgore, Mark Knopfler, Al Kooper, Bernie Leadon, Brenda Lee, Linda Gail Lewis, Greil Marcus, Kathy Mattea, Joe B. Mauldin, Charlie McCoy, John McKuen, John Mellencamp, Augie Meyers, Ralph Molina, the late Bill Monroe, Anne Murray, Graham Nash, Willie Nelson, Michael Nesmith, Bob Neuwirth, Barbara Orbison, Van Dyke Parks, Gene Parsons, Herb Pedersen, Al Perkins, the late Carl Perkins, Greg Phelps, Jason Ringenberg, Robbie Robertson, Kenny Rogers, the late Doug Sahm, Ricky Van Shelton, Ricky Skaggs, the late Hank Snow, Stephen Stills, Dan Stuart, Marty Stuart, Jack Sundrud, Billy Swan, Billy Talbot, Barry Tashian, Holly Tashian, Rufus Thibodeaux, Pam Tillis, Randy Travis, Travis Tritt, Don Was, Jimmy Webb, Roland White, Dana Williams, Bill Wyman and Dwight Yoakam.

Thanks also to Trevor Cajiao, editor of the world's best rock'n'roll magazine, *Now Dig This*, for the Sam Phillips quotes.

Thanks for advice and music business contacts to Janet Aspley,

Craig Baguley, Stuart Batsford, Bobbi Boyce, Trevor Cajaio, Chris Carr, Chris Charlesworth, Jim Della Croce, Claire Horton, Spike Hyde, Colin Larkin, Pam Lewis, Erin Morris, Geoff Mullen, Lee Ellen Newman, Jon Philibert, Sally Reeves, Alan Robinson, Tony Rounce, Nanci Russell, Bob Saporiti, Evelyn Shriver, John Tobler, Wyndham Wallace, Duncan Warwick, Sarah Wells, the late Wally Whyton, Richard Wootton, the Country Music Association, and dozens of helpful PR agents and record company personnel in Nashville, London, New York and Los Angeles. Thanks also to Sean O'Mahony, for first allowing me to write in public.

Special thanks for the American connection to Rhondda Scott, Ronna Rubin, Kathy Chiavola, the late Randy Howard and (down the wire) Lou Ann Bardash and Tom Ovans.

This book could not have been written without the inspiration, encouragement and selfless co-operation of Mike Grant, Clinton Heylin, Brian Hogg, Tony Lacey, Spencer Leigh, Mark Paytress and Johnny Rogan.

Much-needed and much-valued personal support for my work was provided, whether they realized it or not, by Georgia Ansell, Helen Bailey, Sean Body, Debbie Cassell, Alan Clayson, Louise Cripps, Kitty Crosby, Dave Dingle, Clare Dobson, Rebecca Gibbs, Ian Gray, Sarah Hodgson, Patrick Humphries, Krystyna Jezewska, Linda Laban, Nikki Lloyd, Nicci Pritchard, Caroline Singer, Elizabeth Stroebel, Kieron Tyler, Carey Wallace, Ian and Janet Woodward, and my mother and late father.

ARE YOU READY FOR THE COUNTRY: THE SOUNDTRACK
100 Recommended Albums

PART I: COUNTRY-ROCK

Area Code 615: *Area Code 615*

The Band: *The Band*

The Beau Brummels: *Bradley's Barn*

The Byrds: *Sweetheart Of The Rodeo*

The Byrds: *The Ballad Of Easy Rider*

Gene Clark: *Gene Clark & The Gosdin Brothers*

Gene Clark: *No Other*

Creedence Clearwater Revival: *Willie & The Poor Boys*

Dillard & Clark: *The Fantastic Expedition Of Dillard & Clark*

The Dillards: *Wheatstraw Suite*

Bob Dylan: *John Wesley Harding*

Bob Dylan: *Nashville Skyline*

Bob Dylan and the Band: *The Genuine Basement Tapes (5-CD bootleg collection)*

The Eagles: *Desperado*

The Everly Brothers: *Roots*

The Flying Burrito Brothers: *The Gilded Palace Of Sin*

The Flying Burrito Brothers: *The Flying Burrito Brothers*

The Grateful Dead: *Workingman's Dead*

International Submarine Band: *Safe At Home*

Michael Nesmith and the First National Band: *Magnetic South*

Michael Nesmith and the First National Band: *Loose Salute*

Michael Nesmith and the Second National Band: *Tantamount To Treason*

Nitty Gritty Dirt Band: *Will The Circle Be Unbroken*

Phil Ochs: *Greatest Hits*

Old And In The Way: *Old And In The Way*

Gene Parsons: *Kindling*

Gram Parsons: *GP*

Gram Parsons: *Grievous Angel*

Poco: *Pickin' Up The Pieces*

Linda Ronstadt: *Linda Ronstadt*

Sir Douglas Quintet: *Mendocino*

John Stewart: *California Bloodlines*

Stephen Stills and Manassas: *Manassas*

PART II: COUNTRY INTO ROCK

Johnny Cash: *Man In Black: 1954–1958*
Guy Clark: *Old No. 1*
Merle Haggard: *Swinging Doors*
Bill Haley and the Comets: *Rock This Joint*
Buddy Holly: *Holly In The Hills*
Wanda Jackson: *Rockin' In The Country*
Waylon Jennings: *Honky Tonk Heroes*
Waylon Jennings: *Dreaming My Dreams*
Kris Kristofferson: *Help Me Make It Through The Night*
Jerry Lee Lewis: *Classic: The Sun Years*
Willie Nelson: *Shotgun Willie*
Willie Nelson: *Red Headed Stranger*
Buck Owens: *The Buck Owens Collection*
Carl Perkins: *Classic: The Sun Years*
Elvis Presley: *The Sun Sessions*
Willis Alan Ramsey: *Willis Alan Ramsey*
Charlie Rich: *The Original Smash Sessions*
Charlie Rich: *The Fabulous Charlie Rich*
Jerry Jeff Walker: *Great Gonzos*
Hank Williams: *40 Greatest Hits*

Pre-1970 country and rock'n'roll is best sampled via compilations rather than the (notoriously short) original LPs. There are numerous budget CDs documenting (for example) the Sun Records rockabilly archive, the Everly Brothers' Cadence recordings, and Brenda Lee's early Decca sides. Also highly recommended are the That'll Flat Git It series of CDs issued by the German label Bear Family, which collect together dozens of fifties rockabilly and rock'n'roll sides.

PART III: PARALLEL LINES

Terry Allen: *Lubbock (On Everything)*
John Anderson: *Seminole Wind*
The Band of Blacky Ranchette: *The Band Of Blacky Ranchette*
Mary Chapin Carpenter: *Come On, Come On*
Johnny Cash: *Unchained*
The Costello Show: *King Of America*
The Desert Rose Band: *The Desert Rose Band*
Steve Earle: *Guitar Town*
Joe Ely: *Honky Tonk Masquerade*
Freakwater: *Old Paint*
Jimmie Dale Gilmore: *Braver Newer World*
The Gourds: *Dem's Good Beeble*

Green on Red: *The Killer Inside Me*

Nanci Griffith: *Last Of The True Believers*

Butch Hancock: *Firewater Seeks Its Own Level*

Emmylou Harris: *Quarter Moon In A Ten Cent Town*

Emmylou Harris: *Blue Kentucky Girl*

Emmylou Harris: *Wrecking Ball*

John Hiatt: *Bring The Family*

Alan Jackson: *Greatest Hits Collection*

Jason and the Scorchers: *Reckless Country Soul*

The Jayhawks: *Blue Earth*

Kris Kristofferson: *A Moment Of Forever*

Lambchop: *Thriller*

k.d. lang: *Shadowland*

Jerry Lee Lewis: *Jerry Lee Lewis*

The Long Ryders: *Native Sons*

Lyle Lovett: *Joshua Judges Ruth*

Randy Newman: *Good Old Boys*

Willie Nelson: *Stardust*

Willie Nelson: *Across The Borderline*

Willie Nelson: *Spirit*

Nitty Gritty Dirt Band: *Will The Circle Be Unbroken Vol. 2*

Carl Perkins: *Go, Cat, Go*

Elvis Presley: *From Elvis In Memphis*

Rank & File: *Sundown*

Ricky Skaggs: *Waitin' For The Sun To Shine*

Son Volt: *Trace*

Sparklehorse: *Vivadixiesubmarine-transmissionplot*

Travis Tritt: *It's All About To Change*

Uncle Tupelo: *No Depression*

Uncle Tupelo: *Anodyne*

Hank Williams Jr: *The New South*

Hank Williams Jr: *Whiskey Bent And Hell Bound*

Dwight Yoakam: *This Time*

Neil Young: *Comes A Time*

Bibliography

Allen, Bob: *George Jones* (Dolphin Books, 1984)

Baez, Joan: *And A Voice To Sing With* (Summit, 1987)

Bane, Michael: *The Outlaws: Revolution In Country Music* (Doubleday, 1978)

Bangs, Lester: *Psychotic Reactions and Carburetor Dung* (Mandarin, 1991)

Berry, Chuck: *The Autobiography* (Harmony Books, 1990)

Cantwell, Robert: *When We Were Good: The Folk Revival* (Harvard University Press, 1996)

Cash, Johnny: *Man In Black* (Zondervan Publishing, 1975)

—— *The Autobiography* (HarperCollins, 1997)

Charles, Ray and Ritz, David: *Brother Ray* (Macdonald, 1978)

Christgau, Robert: *Any Old Way You Choose It: Rock And Other Pop Music, 1967–1973* (Penguin, 1973)

—— *Rock Albums Of The 70s* (Vermilion, 1982)

—— *Christgau's Record Guide: The 80s* (Pantheon, 1990)

Cross, Charles R. (ed.): *Backstreets: Springsteen – The Man And His Music* (Sidgwick & Jackson, 1990)

Davies, Hunter: *The Beatles* (Heinemann, 1968)

Davis, Clive: *Clive: Inside The Record Business* (Ballantine, 1974)

Dellar, Fred and Wootton, Richard: *The Country Music Book Of Lists* (Thames & Hudson, 1984)

Eisen, Jonathan (ed.): *The Age Of Rock* (Random House, 1969)

—— *The Age Of Rock 2* (Random House, 1970)

Endres, Clifford: *Austin City Limits* (University of Texas Press, 1987)

Escott, Colin: *Good Rockin' Tonight* (St Martin's Press, 1991)

—— *Hank Williams: The Biography* (Little, Brown, 1994)

Escott, Colin and Hawkins, Martin: *Sun Records: The Discography* (Bear Family, 1987)

Escott, Paul D. and Goldfield, David R. (eds.): *The South For New Southerners* (University of North Carolina Press, 1991)

Flanagan, Bill: *Written In My Soul* (Contemporary, 1987)

Flippo, Chet: *Your Cheating Heart: A Biography Of Hank Williams* (Simon & Schuster, 1981)

Fong-Torres, Ben: *Hickory Wind: The Life And Times Of Gram Parsons* (Pocket Books, 1991)

Fong-Torres, Ben (ed.): *The Rolling Stone Rock'n'Roll Reader* (Bantam Books, 1974)

Friedman, Myra: *Janis Joplin: Buried Alive* (Bantan Books, 1974)

Goldrosen, John and Beecher, John: *Remembering Buddy* (Pavilion, 1987)

Greenfield, Robert: *Dark Star: An Oral Biography Of Jerry Garcia* (Plexus, 1996)

Griffin, Sid: *Gram Parsons* (Sierra, 1985)

Grissim, John: *Country Music: White Man's Blues* (Paperback Library, 1970)

Guralnick, Peter: *Feel Like Going Home* (Omnibus, 1978)

——*Last Train To Memphis: The Rise Of Elvis Presley* (HarperCollins, 1994)

Guthrie, Woody: *Bound For Glory* (New American Library, 1970)

Haggard, Merle: *Sing Me Back Home* (Times Books, 1982)

Haley, John W. and Hoelle, John: *Bill Haley: Sound & Glory* (Dyne-American, 1990)

Hemphill, Paul: *The Nashville Sound* (Simon & Schuster, 1970)

Heylin, Clinton: *Bob Dylan: Behind The Shades* (Viking, 1991)

——*Bob Dylan: The Recording Sessions* (Penguin, 1995)

——*Bob Dylan: A Life In Stolen Moments* (Heylin, 1996)

Hoskyns, Barney: *Say It One More Time For The Broken Hearted* (Fontana, 1991)

——*Across The Great Divide* (Viking, 1993)

Hunter, Robert: *A Box Of Rain* (Viking, 1992)

Kingsbury, Paul, Axelrod, Alan and Costello, Susan (eds.): *Country: The Music And The Musicians* (Abbeville, 1994)

Kirby, Jack: *Media-Made Dixie: The South In The American Imagination* (University of Georgia Press, 1986)

Lewis, Jerry Lee and White, Charles: *Killer!* (Random House, 1995)

Lewisohn, Mark: *The Complete Beatles Recording Sessions* (Hamlyn, 1990)

Mairowitz, David Zane: *The Radical Soap Opera* (Wildwood House, 1974)

Malone, Bill C.: *Southern Music, American Music* (University of Kentucky Press, 1979)

——*Country Music USA* (Equation, 1987)

Marcus, Greil: *Dead Elvis* (Viking, 1992)

——*Mystery Train* (Dutton, 1975; revised edn., Plume, 1997)

Martin, Linda and Segrave, Kerry: *Anti-Rock* (Archon Books, 1988)

McGregor, Craig: *Bob Dylan: A Retrospective* (Morrow, 1972)

Morthland, John: *The Best Of Country Music* (Dolphin Books, 1984)

Nash, Alanna: *Behind Closed Doors* (Knopf, 1988)

Nelson, Willie and Shrake, Bud: *Willie, An Autobiography* (Simon & Schuster, 1988)

Palmer, Robert: *Jerry Lee Lewis* (Omnibus, 1981)

Perkins, Carl: *Disciple In Blue Suede Shoes* (Zondervan Publishing, 1978)

Perkins, Carl and McGee, David: *Go, Cat, Go!* (Hyperion, 1996)

Perry, Charles: *The Haight-Ashbury: A History* (Random House, 1984)

Pickering, Stephen: *Dylan: A Commemoration* (privately published, 1971)

Reed, John Shelton: *Whistling Dixie* (University of Missouri Press, 1990)

——*My Tears Spoiled My Aim, & Other Reflections On Southern Culture* (University of Missouri Press, 1993)

Robbins, Ira A. (ed.): *The Trouser Press Record Guide* (Collier Books, various years)

Rogan, Johnny: *Timeless Flight Revisited* (Rogan House, 1997)

Roland, Tom: *The Billboard Book Of Number One Country Hits* (Billboard, 1991)

The Rolling Stone Record Review (Straight Arrow, 1971)

The Rolling Stone Record Review Volume II (Straight Arrow, 1974)

Roxon, Lillian: *Lillian Roxon's Rock Encyclopaedia* (Grosset & Dunlap, 1969)

Rubin, Louis D. Jr (ed.): *The American South* (Louisiana State University Press, 1980)

Scaduto, Anthony: *Bob Dylan: An Intimate Biography* (Abacus, 1973)

Scoppa, Bud: *The Byrds* (Scholastic Book Services, 1971)

Shelton, Robert: *No Direction Home: The Life And Music Of Bob Dylan* (Beech Tree, 1986)

Tosches, Nick: *Country* (Scarborough House, 1977)

——*Hellfire: The Jerry Lee Lewis Story* (Plexus, 1983)

Turner, Steve: *Conversations With Eric Clapton* (Abacus, 1976)

White, Roger: *The Everly Brothers: Walk Right Back* (Plexus, 1985)

Williams, Paul: *Outlaw Blues* (Dutton, 1969)

——*Performing Artist: The Music Of Bob Dylan Vol. 1* (Xanadu, 1991)

Wren, Christopher S.: *Johnny Cash: Winners Got Scars Too* (Dial Press, 1971)

Wyman, Bill and Coleman, Ray: *Stone Alone* (Viking, 1990)

Magazines, newspapers and periodicals consulted: *Bam Balam*, *Billboard*, the *BOB*, *Broadside*, *Broken Arrow*, *Bucketfull Of Brains*, *Close-Up*, *Comstock Lode*, *Country Guitar*, *Country Music*, *Country Music International*, *Country Music People*, *Country Song Roundup*, *Crawdaddy*, *Dark Star*, *Details*, *Fusion*, *Goldmine*, the *Guardian*, *Guitar Player*, *Isis*, *Journal of Country Music*, the *LA Free Press*, *Let It Rock*, *Melody Maker*, *Mojo*, *Musician*, the *Nashville Banner*, *New Musical Express*, *Newsweek*, *No Depression*, *Now Dig This*, *Omaha Rainbow*, *Opry*, *Playboy*, *Q*, *Record Collector*, *Rolling Stone*, *Sing Out!*, *Songtalk*, *Sounds*, *Spin*, the *Telegraph*, the *Tennessean*, *Time*, *The Times*, the *Village Voice*, *Vox*.

Index

Brown, T. Graham, 480
Brown County Jamboree, 39
'Brown-Eyed Handsome Man', 277, 328
Browne, Jackson, 159, 167, 168, 169, 195, 494
Browns, the, 284, 285, 290, 302
Bruce, Denny, 101
Bruce, Lenny, 432
Brumley, Tom, 72
Bryant, Felice, 269
Bryant, Jimmy, 234–5
Bryant's Minstrel Troupe, 369
Buchanan, Bob, 52
Buck, Peter, 494
Buckhorn Music, 314
Buddy & Bob, 281
Buffalo Springfield, 33, 42–3, 62–3, 64, 73, 106, 108, 109, 139, 142, 159, 189, 190, 192, 442
Buffett, Jimmy, 350
Bulger, Ray, 215
Burgess, Sonny, 219, 238, 252, 254–5
Burgess, Steve, 126, 375
Burke, Solomon, 291
Burlison, Paul, 253
Burnette, Johnny, 219, 253
Burning The Ballroom Down, 375
Burns, Freddie, 235
Burrito Deluxe, 78, 79, 82, 146
Burritos *see* Flying Burrito Brothers
Burton, Charlie, 448
Burton, Gary, 93
Burton, James, 45, 46, 135, 144, 152, 159, 187, 235
Bush, Kate, 476
Bush, Roger, 147
'Busted', 291
Bustin' Out, 376
'Butchie's Tune', 41
Butterfield Blues Band, 403
Butthole Surfers, the, 496

Buttrey, Kenny, 8, 22, 25, 30, 32, 47, 93, 95, 97, 111, 301
'By The Time I Get To Phoenix', 331, 344
'Bye Bye Love', 242, 269
Byrds, the, xiii, 10, 11, 28, 29, 30, 31, 33, 39, 48, 49, 52, 73, 78, 84, 86, 93, 105, 107, 108, 127, 129–30, 140, 145, 150, 154, 166, 171, 190, 271, 441, 442, 483
    history of, 35–6, 37–8, 53–61, 62, 63, 64, 65, 67–8, 139, 169–70, 172, 181–2, 192
    see also Sweetheart Of The Rodeo; names of band members; titles of songs
Byrds, The, 181–2, 194
Byrne, David, 470

C&W Meets R&B, 291
Cadence, 268, 271
Cale, J. J., 69
Cale, John, 129
Calico Silver, 361
California
    1960s, 34, 35, 36, 40–1, 73, 93, 101, 111
    1968–72: country rock reaches California mainstream, 139–55
    and the Eagles, 156, 159, 161, 373
    shift in radicalism 1968–1975, 164–5
    see also Bakersfield; Los Angeles; San Francisco
California Bloodlines, 111
Campbell, Glen, 46, 63, 309, 331, 332, 353, 388, 389, 441–2
'Can't Buy Me Love', 306
Cantamos, 374
Capehart, Jerry, 279
Capitol Records, 274, 277, 289, 302, 337, 484, 485

'Help', 309
'Help Me Make It Through The
    Night', 311, 314, 317, 327
Hemphill, Paul, 335
Hendrix, Jimi, 157–8, 171, 316–17,
    361, 459
Henley, Don, 38, 140, 142, 159, 494
    in the Corvettes, 158
    in the Eagles, 161, 165, 168, 169,
        188, 189, 373, 382, 384
Henry, John, 17
Henson, Curlcy, 225
'Here, There And Everywhere', 396
'Here You Come Again', 388
Herman's Hermits, 287
Hester, Carolyn, 471
'Hey, Good Lookin'', 229
'Hey Jude', 96, 306
'Hey Mister, That's Me Up On The
    Jukebox', 161
'Hey Porter', 255
Heylin, Clinton, 16–17
Hi Records, 343
Hiatt, John, 411–12, 413, 415
Hickoids, the, 431
'Hickory Wind', 53, 57, 59, 60, 71,
    75, 181
Hicks, Dan, 428
'High And Dry', 126
'High Fashion Queen', 78
'High School Confidential', 264
'High Time', 116
'Higher And Higher', 388
Highway 61 Revisited, 13, 20, 24,
    298, 312, 451
'Highway 99 With Mélange', 136
Highway 101, 382
Highwaymen, the, 477
Hill, Faith, 488
'Hillbilly Band', 424
'Hillbilly Boogie', 233
Hillbilly Central, 348, 350, 366

'Hillbilly Heaven', 74
'Hillbilly Singer, The', 334
Hillman, Chris, 29, 66, 150, 166, 190,
    191, 196, 376, 486–7
    1962–67, 35, 36, 37–8, 54, 55,
        56–7, 58, 59, 60
    1968–70, 63, 64, 68, 69, 70, 71, 72,
        73, 74, 75, 76, 77–8, 79–80, 82,
        83
    1971–2, 146, 147, 148–9
    1973–5, 181, 186, 192–3, 195
    1975–99, 374, 377–8, 380, 381,
        382, 384–5, 503
Hillmen, the, 36, 37, 78
Hillsiders, the, 125, 130
Hinton, Bruce, 140
'Hippie Boy', 74, 316
Hodges, Warner, 440, 448
Hogan, Carl, 276
Hogan, David, 379
Hoh, Eddie, 71
Holcomb, Roscoe, 375
Holiday (record label), 231
Holiday, Billie, 273
Holly, Buddy, 239, 251, 283, 292,
    298, 469
    career, 280–2
    commemoration in Lubbock, 469
    death, 300
    influence on other artists, 16, 120,
        241
Hollywood, 44, 51, 58, 106, 144, 152,
    166, 167, 271, 288, 304, 318,
    331, 337, 386, 387, 461, 472,
    502
Hollywood Argyles, 293
Hollywood Town Hall, 496
'Home Of The Blues', 257
Homegrown, 420
'Homeless', 407
Hometown Girl, 413
'Honey Bop', 274

Maphis, Joe, 249, 274
Marcus, Greil, xii–xiii, 33, 86, 87,
    145, 157, 497
Mardi Gras, 104
'Marines Hymn, The', 262
'Marleyphine Hank', 493
'Marrakesh Express' 4
Marsh, Dave, 423
Marshall Tucker Band, 366, 379,
    403, 404, 405, 407
Martin, Dean, 204, 206, 209, 326
Martin, Grady, 95, 247
Martin, Moon, 84
Martindale, Wink, 74
'Mary Don't You Weep', 50
'Matchbox', 11, 121, 123, 223
Mattea, Kathy, 471
Matthews, Bob, 117
Matthews, Ian, 128, 137
Matthews, Vince, 314
Matthews Southern Comfort, 128,
    131
Mavericks, the, 385, 489
Maxine, Brian, 130
May, Brian, 483
'Maybelline', 239, 276
Mayfield, Curtis, 158, 500
Mazer, Elliot, 96
MCA, 140, 468, 471, 472, 477
McCarthy, Eugene, 429
McCarthy, Stephen, 441, 445
McCartney, Paul, 44, 74, 120, 122,
    124, 269, 306, 396, 457, 460
McCoy, Charlie
  and Area Code 615, 95, 96, 97
  and Bob Dylan, 19–20, 21, 22, 23,
    25, 30, 32, 93, 301
  and Elvis Presley, 461
  and Gordon Lightfoot, 301
  and John Stewart, 111
  and Johnny Cash, 298
McCready, Mary Ann, 388

McDill, Bob, 489
McDonald, Country Joe, 94–5
McDonald, Skeets, 242–3, 274
McDowell, Ronnie, 393, 417,
    418
McEntire, Reba, 394
McFee, John, 98, 381
McGee, David, 465
McGuinn, Jim, 35–6, 37
McGuinn, Roger, 66, 141–2, 182,
    366, 380
  in the Byrds, 54, 55–6, 57, 58, 59,
    60, 61, 63, 67, 68, 170, 172, 181,
    428
  on country music, 69
  and *Easy Rider*, 171, 172
  and *Gene Tryp*, 169–70
  and Gram Parsons, 55–6, 58, 59,
    82
McGuinn, Clark and Hillman, 377,
    380
McGuire, Barry, 73
McKee, Maria, 418, 446–7, 484, 493
McKenzie, Scott, 102
McKernan, Ron 'Pigpen', 113, 115
McKuen, John, 173, 380
McKuen, Rod, 303
McKuen, William, 174
McLean, Don, 485
McTell, Blind Willie, 504
'Me And Bobby McGee', 4, 100, 311,
    313, 314, 315, 317
'Me And Paul', 354
Meal Ticket, 130
'Mean-Eyed Cat', 255
'Mean Mean Man', 275
'Meat Man', 329
Meat Puppets, 447
Meaux, Huey, 329
Medicine Ball Caravan, 175
'Medley From Northern Quebec',
    180–1

209, 214, 238–9, 240, 248, 276, 285, 288, 290, 391, 438, 505

Robbins, 'Pig', 21, 341, 424

Roberts, Elliott, 6, 418

Roberts, Julia, 470, 472

Roberts, Rick, 145–6, 147, 195, 375, 503

Robertson, Don, 448

Robertson, Robbie, 21, 22, 27, 88, 89, 90, 91, 92, 131

Rock, Salt And Nails, 76

'Rock-A-Bye Boogie', 292

'Rock A Chicka', 243–4

Rock and Roll Hall of Fame, 226

'Rock Around The Clock', 227, 231, 235, 236

'Rock It', 244–5

Rock'n'Roll Circus, 73

'Rock'n'Roll Ruby', 255

'Rock'n'Roll Time', 183

'Rock The Bop', 272

'Rock This Joint', 235

'Rockabilly Music', 460

'Rocket 88', 218, 233, 235

'Rockin' Daddy', 245

'Rockin' Chair Daddy', 219

'Rockin' In The Congo', 243

'Rockin' My Life Away', 463

Rockin' Rollin' Robbins, 239

'Rocking Chair', 91

'Rocky Mountain Breakdown', 374

'Rocky Mountain High', 337

Rodgers, Jimmie, 17, 45, 103, 108, 111, 121, 134, 135, 162, 182, 205, 226, 227, 258, 259, 263, 276, 307, 403, 450, 498, 504

Rodriguez, Johnny, 389

Rogers, Kenny, 140, 146, 322, 361, 388–9, 390, 391, 393, 394, 418

Rogers, Rock (pseudonym of Leon Payne), 244, 245

'Rollin' With The Flow', 345

Rolling Stones, 28, 33, 86, 105, 106, 121, 144, 179, 197, 294, 302, 316, 317, 400, 404, 409, 435, 436, 441, 443, 444, 451, 457, 474, 475, 480, 490, 496

and Gram Parsons, 49, 58, 71, 73, 79, 81, 82, 85

impact of country music on, 80–2, 85, 125–6

Rolling Thunder Revue, 366

Rompin' and Stompin', 217

Ronk, Dave Van, 471

Ronson, Mick, 366, 376

Ronstadt, Linda, 96, 97, 133, 139, 140, 141–2, 147, 156, 157, 158, 159, 190, 192, 195, 395, 397, 399, 419, 420

Roots, 108

Rose, Fred, 364

Rose, Wesley, 122, 268, 271, 332, 389

Rose Of Cimarron, 374

'Rose Of Cimarron', 374, 398

Rosenberg, Seymour, 344

Roses In The Snow, 398

Ross, Lee, 243

Ross, Nancy, 75

Rostill, John, 337

Rothbaum, Mark, 474

Rothman, Sandy, 39

Rotten, Johnny, 431, 435

Rounder, 489

Rowan, Peter, 38, 39, 98–9, 118, 165, 182

Royal, Billy Joe, 332

Rubber Rodeo, 447–8

Rubber Soul, 126, 303, 306

Rubin, Rick, 457, 458

Rucker, Darius, 471

'Run For Your Life', 126

Ruppenthal, Sara, 33

Rush, Tom, 147, 301, 302

Russell, Kevin, 500

FOR THE BEST IN PAPERBACKS, LOOK FOR THE

In every corner of the world, on every subject under the sun, Penguin represents quality and variety—the very best in publishing today.

For complete information about books available from Penguin—including Puffins, Penguin Classics, and Compass—and how to order them, write to us at the appropriate address below. Please note that for copyright reasons the selection of books varies from country to country.

In the United Kingdom: Please write to *Dept. EP, Penguin Books Ltd, Bath Road, Harmondsworth, West Drayton, Middlesex UB7 0DA.*

In the United States: Please write to *Penguin Putnam Inc., P.O. Box 12289 Dept. B, Newark, New Jersey 07101-5289* or call 1-800-788-6262.

In Canada: Please write to *Penguin Books Canada Ltd, 10 Alcorn Avenue, Suite 300, Toronto, Ontario M4V 3B2.*

In Australia: Please write to *Penguin Books Australia Ltd, P.O. Box 257, Ringwood, Victoria 3134.*

In New Zealand: Please write to *Penguin Books (NZ) Ltd, Private Bag 102902, North Shore Mail Centre, Auckland 10.*

In India: Please write to *Penguin Books India Pvt Ltd, 11 Panchsheel Shopping Centre, Panchsheel Park, New Delhi 110 017.*

In the Netherlands: Please write to *Penguin Books Netherlands bv, Postbus 3507, NL-1001 AH Amsterdam.*

In Germany: Please write to *Penguin Books Deutschland GmbH, Metzlerstrasse 26, 60594 Frankfurt am Main.*

In Spain: Please write to *Penguin Books S. A., Bravo Murillo 19, 1° B, 28015 Madrid.*

In Italy: Please write to *Penguin Italia s.r.l., Via Benedetto Croce 2, 20094 Corsico, Milano.*

In France: Please write to *Penguin France, Le Carré Wilson, 62 rue Benjamin Baillaud, 31500 Toulouse.*

In Japan: Please write to *Penguin Books Japan Ltd, Kaneko Building, 2-3-25 Koraku, Bunkyo-Ku, Tokyo 112.*

In South Africa: Please write to *Penguin Books South Africa (Pty) Ltd, Private Bag X14, Parkview, 2122 Johannesburg.*